NEW YORK REVIEW BOOKS
CLASSICS

THE NEW YORK STORIES
OF HENRY JAMES

HENRY JAMES (1843–1916), the younger brother of
the psychologist William James and one of the greatest of
American writers, was born in New York but lived for most
of his life in England. Among the best known of his many
stories and novels are *The Portrait of a Lady*, *The Turn of the
Screw*, and *The Wings of the Dove*. In addition to *The New
York Stories of Henry James*, New York Review Classics has
published several long-unavailable James novels: *The Other
House*, *The Outcry*, and *The Ivory Tower*.

COLM TÓIBÍN is the author of five novels, including
The Story of the Night, *The Blackwater Lightship*, and
The Heather Blazing. *The Master*, a novel based on the
life of Henry James, was published in 2004 and shortlisted
for the Man Booker Prize. Among his nonfiction works
are *Bad Blood: A Walk Along the Irish Border*, *Homage to
Barcelona*, *The Sign of the Cross: Travels in Catholic Europe*,
and, most recently, *Love in a Dark Time*. In 2004, his first
play, *Beauty in a Broken Place*, was produced in Dublin,
where Tóibín currently lives.

THE NEW YORK STORIES OF HENRY JAMES

Selected and with an introduction by
COLM TÓIBÍN

NEW YORK REVIEW BOOKS

New York

THIS IS A NEW YORK REVIEW BOOK
PUBLISHED BY THE NEW YORK REVIEW OF BOOKS
1755 Broadway, New York, NY 10019
www.nyrb.com

Library of Congress Cataloging-in-Publication Data
James, Henry, 1843–1916.
  The New York stories of Henry James / by Henry James; selected and with an
introduction by Colm Tóibín.
    p. cm. — (New York Review Books classics)
  ISBN 1-59017-162-4 (alk. paper)
  1. New York (N.Y.)—Social life and customs—Fiction. I. Tóibín, Colm,
1955–
II. Title. III. Series.

  PS2112.T65 2005
  813'.4—dc22

                                    2005013331

ISBN-13: 978-1-59017-162-2
ISBN-10: 1-59017-162-4

Printed in the United States of America on acid-free paper.
10 9 8 7 6 5 4 3 2

CONTENTS

INTRODUCTION

Henry James's New York

VERY EARLY in his career as a writer Henry James made his position clear. He would not be a public novelist or a social commentator but would instead deal with the reverse of the picture; the intricacies and vagaries of feeling in the relations between people, and mainly between men and women, would be his subject. Duplicity and greed, disappointment and renunciation, which became his most pressing themes, occurred for James the novelist in the private realm. It was his genius to make this realm seem more dramatic and ample than any space inhabited by government or business.

James himself was a figure of complexity and ambiguity and secrecy; a number of matters in his life seemed greatly unresolved. His personality, like his later prose style, was one in which things could not be easily named, in which nuance was more substantial than fact and the flickering of consciousness more interesting than knowledge. James was, above all, guarded. He was the supreme artist concerned with the architecture and tone of fiction; he specialized in the deliberate, the considered, and the exertion of control; he did not seek to bare his soul for the reader.

Nonetheless, it is possible to read between the lines of James's work, searching for clues, seeking moments in which the author came close to unmasking himself. Many of his stories, written quickly and for money, give more away perhaps than he intended. Here, more than in the novels, he comes closer to opening a chink, for example, in the grand armor of his own sexuality, allowing us to catch a brief glimpse of his deepest and darkest concerns. These stories include "The Pupil," "The Master of Beltraffio," and "The Beast in the Jungle." The stories are careful and restrained, but it is clear from them that the subject of illicit love or misguided loyalty interested him deeply, as did the subject of sexual coldness.

Thus it is possible to trace James's sometimes unwitting, unconscious, and often quite deliberate efforts to mask and explore matters which concerned him deeply and uneasily. It would be possible to trace, for example, in his copious writings, all references to Ireland or England, or to his brother William, or to the novelist George Eliot, and find areas of ambiguity and uncertainty as well as strange contradictions, underlining the fact that these things mattered very deeply to James, so deeply indeed that they appear in many layers and guises.

Perhaps of all the provinces in his realm whose contours remain shadowy and whose topography is unresolved, the city of New York is a prime example. James's writings about New York disclose, more than anything, an anger, quite unlike any other anger in James, at what has been lost to him, what has been done, in the name of commerce and material progress, to a place he once knew. It is not an ordinary anger at the destruction of beauty and familiarity; it is much stranger and complex than that, and it deserves a great deal of attention.

There is a peculiar intensity in the tone of Henry James's memoir of his first fourteen years, *A Small Boy and Others*, written in 1911, when James was sixty-eight, one year after the death of his brother William. Much of the memory evoked and most of the scenes conjured up in the book took place in New York between 1848, when the Jameses moved to the city, and 1855, when they left for Europe. Since he had no notes or letters or diaries to work from, it is astonishing how fresh and detailed his memory is, how many names he can remember, including those of teachers and actors, how sharply he can evoke places and their atmospheres, precise smells and sights and locations, including many shows and plays in the New York theaters of the time. "I have lost nothing of what I saw," he wrote, "and that though I can't now quite divide the total into separate occasions the various items surprisingly swarm for me."

It was as though old New York, as he saw it between the ages of five and twelve, had remained still and frozen and perfect in his memory. He had not watched it change, or participated in its growth. It was the ground which formed him; he was never to have a place again which would belong to him so fundamentally. He would not possess another territory until 1897 when he signed the lease on Lamb House in Rye in England. The fact that his New York had been taken from him and not replaced, save by hotel rooms and temporary abodes, may explain the sheer driven enthusiasm with which he pursued Lamb House and his sense of relief when he had made it his. Indeed, the year before he purchased the lease he wrote his novel *The Spoils of Poynton*, a drama about owning and losing a treasured house. Having signed the lease, he wrote "The Turn of the Screw," about a lone figure attempting to make a home in a house already possessed.

New York after 1855 was lost to him, not merely, he realized as the years went on, by his father's removing the family from there, but by changes in the city which would be absolute and overwhelming. A new world was being built on the site of his dreams. This site's most hallowed quarter was 58 West Fourteenth Street, first seen during "an afternoon call with my father at a house there situated, one of an already fairly mature row on the south side and quite near Sixth Avenue. It was 'our' house, just acquired by us ... the place was to become to me for ever so long afterwards a sort of anchorage of the spirit."

Henry James's New York, the city of his childhood, "the small warm dusky homogeneous New York world of the mid-century," was situated between Fifth and Sixth Avenues down to Washington Square, where his maternal grandmother lived, and up eastwards to Union Square, which was, in his day, surrounded by a high railing. Close by were members of James's extended family, including his mother's cousin Helen. "I see in her strong simplicity," he wrote, "that of an earlier, quieter world, a New York of better manners and better morals and homelier beliefs." James saw that "her goodness somehow testifies for the whole tone of a society, a remarkable cluster of private decencies." Thus his book became an elegy not only to a lost childhood, but a set of values which began to erode as soon as the village James could wander in freely was replaced by a great city. "Character," he wrote about the changing city, "is so lost in quantity."

As James grew older he was allowed to wander farther. He remembered

> hard by the Fourteenth Street home...the poplars, the pigs, the poultry, and the "Irish houses," two or three in number, exclusive of a very fine Dutch one, seated then, this last, almost as among gardens and groves—a breadth of territory still apparent, on the spot, in that marginal ease, that spread of occupation, to the nearly complete absence of which New York aspects owe their general failure of "style."

He and his brother wandered up and down Broadway "like perfect little men of the world; we must have been let loose there to stretch our legs and fill our lungs, without prejudice either to our earlier and later freedoms of going and coming... Broadway must have been then as one of the alleys of Eden."

In this city which was a mixture of a remembered Eden and a failed style, James set eight stories and one novel; he also devoted considerable space to New York in his book *The American Scene*, written several years before his autobiography. In his fiction, he did not set out to chart the history of the city or the emotion surrounding its growth. What he disclosed about his attitude towards the city he did in passing. In the foreground were his characters, more real and more pressing in their needs than mere bricks and mortar.

As his own scope as a writer widened and his ambition hard-ened Henry James became, at times, acutely alert to the thin-ness of the American experience. In his book on Hawthorne, written in 1879, he famously listed what was absent in Amer-ican life:

> No sovereign, no court, no personal loyalty, no aristoc-racy, no church, no clergy, no army, no diplomatic service, no country gentlemen, no palaces, no castles, nor manors, nor old country-houses, nor parsonages, nor thatched cottages, nor ivied ruins; no cathedrals, nor abbeys, nor little Norman churches; no great Universities, nor public schools—no Oxford, nor Eton, nor Harrow; no litera-ture, no novels, no museums, no pictures, no political so-ciety, no sporting class.

Eight years earlier, however, in a letter to Charles Norton Eliot, he had written: "It's a complex fate, being an American, and one of the responsibilities it entails is fighting against a su-perstitious valuation of Europe."

He worked then in the interstices between American as a wasteland, untouched by tradition, and America as a golden opportunity for a novelist interested in complexity. Thus in his first New York story, "The Story of a Masterpiece," published in the magazine *Galaxy* in 1868, when James was twenty-five, his hero can be a man of taste and the city a place where such a man will rub shoulders with artists, one of whom will paint "the best portrait that has yet been painted in America." He will also begin to display in some of his stories a view of women as somehow untrustworthy and of love as a loss of balance. In this story, the painter manages to catch the true nature of Marian Everett and it for this reason that John Lennox, her suitor, must destroy the painting. This story was welcomed by *The Nation*, who wrote, "within the narrow limits to which he confines himself Mr James is . . . the best writer of short stories in America."

By this time James had only written six short stories. The two most substantial of these, "The Story of a Year" and "Poor Richard," concerned the aftermath of the Civil War, more precisely the relationship between the men who had fought in the war and the women who stayed at home. James's ninth story, "A Most Extraordinary Case," published in *The Atlantic Monthly* in April 1868, dramatized that same subject.

The story opens in "one of the uppermost chambers of one of the great New York hotels." Mason, whose injuries in the war, while grave, remain unspecified, is living in an "ugly little hotel chamber." This is one of James's New York stories in which it is imperative for the protagonist to leave the city, which is too lonely or unhealthy, or just too hot. It would be impossible for James to imagine anyone recovering from anything in the city he had lost; thus he moves Mason to a house on the Hudson River. Miss Hofmann, his hostess's niece, someone remarks, "looks as if she had come out of an American novel, I don't know that that's great praise," to which Mason replies: "You are bound in honor, then...to put her into another." The heroine in question is notable because she inspired the most un-American sentence in James's career thus far: "She was now twenty-six years of age, beautiful, accomplished, and *au mieux* with her bankers."

James, as he developed as a novelist, became seriously *au mieux* with the recognition scene, in which a character watches a scene between two people from a distance and, by their gestures and movements and silences, realizes what is between them. This offers us the central drama of both *The Portrait of a Lady* and *The Ambassadors*. In "A Most Extraordinary Case," written when he was twenty-five, he tries it out for the first time. Mason, now recovering with the help of a talented young doctor, notices, on entering the room as Miss Hofmann sits at the piano, "A gentleman was leaning on the instrument with his back toward the window, intercepting her face...The silence was unnatural, or, at the least, disagreeable." It is the doctor who will eventually win Miss Hofmann's hand. Later, towards the end of the story, Mason will catch a "glance of intelligence" between the two, and the knowledge of their deep bond will hasten his decline.

In this story, as in "The Story of a Year," the business of injury and illness interests James. It will surface in a great deal of his work, in the cases of Ralph Touchett in *The Portrait of a Lady* and Milly Theale in *The Wings of the Dove*. Although Mason's wounds were caused by the Civil War, and resemble those of Oliver Wendell Holmes to some extent, his recovery depends on his happiness and his decline will be caused by unrequited love. In James's early world, it was still possible to die of a broken heart. "A Most Extraordinary Case" won the approval of James's harshest critic throughout his career, his brother William. "Your style grows easier, firmer," he wrote, "and more concise as you go on writing...the face of the whole story is bright and sparkling."

"Crawford's Consistency," James's next New York story, was published in *Scribner's Monthly* in August 1876, a few months before he moved from Paris to London. For that and the story "The Ghostly Rental" he was paid three hundred dollars. "I have lately sent two short tales to Scribner," he wrote to his father in April 1876 from his address at the rue du Luxembourg, "which you will see when they are printed, and I trust judge according to their pretensions, which are very small." James did not include the story in any single volume in his lifetime. In this story, as in his memoir, he plays the elegiac note, making it clear that the story is set in the 1840s. When Crawford and the narrator take a walk into the countryside, the narrator remarks, for example, "for in those days New Yorkers could walk out into the country."

In those days Crawford was a man with a fortune about to marry the beautiful but penniless Miss Ingram, who has always inspired the narrator "with a vague mistrust." Miss Ingram finally jilts him and then comes down with smallpox whereupon James allows his narrator one of his most distasteful observations. "Several months afterward," he wrote, "I saw the young girl, shrouded in a thick veil, beneath which I could just distinguish her absolutely blasted face. On either side of her walked her father and mother, each of them showing a visage almost as blighted as her own."

Crawford, instead, marries unsuitably, and, having lost his fortune, becomes prey to his wife, who pushes him down a set of steps, thus breaking his leg. The narrator believes that he can never go back to her, but, like Isabel Archer in *The Portrait of a Lady*, which James began a few years after the composition of "Crawford's Consistency," he returns to his spouse, renouncing the possibility of easy freedom.

———

"An International Episode," a sort of companion piece to *Daisy Miller*, which had appeared six months earlier, was first published in the *Cornhill Magazine* in December 1878 and January 1879. Two young Englishmen, one the heir to a title and a fortune, come to New York; they experience the city in the stifling heat of summer. They are great blank creations, almost stupid at times, alert only to their own station and the newness and strangeness of the New World. The hot summer allows James to follow the routine he had already developed in "A Most Extraordinary Case" and make the city a site to begin the story but not a place where a story could unfold. Their contact in New York, J. L. Westgate, is one of James's few creations who actually has a job, who puts in a full day at the office. Westgate's wife and sister-in-law are at Newport, and the reader can feel James itching to remove his two young men from the "sinister hum of mosquitoes" in the sinister and inhospitable city, to Newport, away from the world of J. L. Westgate and his money-making activities to the world of leisure and American women, led by Westgate's sister-in-law Miss Alden. These women are forward, intelligent, charming, curious and opinionated, ripe for a young English lord, who is used to more stuffy company, to fall in love with.

Miss Alden is Daisy Miller's opposite. She is too intelligent to be doomed; if she breaks the rules, it is due to her genuine lack of respect for them rather than any weakness. The English are seen in the story as snobbish, thoughtless, bad-mannered, a race on whom everything is lost. The Americans are democratic and hospitable. When the story appeared, it was roundly attacked by Mrs. F. H. Hill, the wife of the editor of the *Daily News*, whom James knew socially in London. "Mrs. Hill," Leon Edel writes, "accused James of caricaturing the British nobility, and of putting language into its mouth which it would never utter. Henry on this occasion replied, since he knew the lady, the letter is a magisterial defense of his work and his art. It is the only letter extant that he ever wrote to a reviewer."

"A man in my position," James wrote to Mrs. Hill,

and writing the sort of things I do, feels the need of protesting against this extension of his idea in which, in many cases, many readers are certain to indulge. One may make figures and figures without intending generalizations—generalizations of which I have a horror. I make a couple of English ladies do a disagreeable thing—*cela c'est vu*: excuse me!—and forthwith I find myself responsible for a representation of English manners! Nothing is my *last* word about anything—I am interminably supersubtle and analytic and with the blessing of heaven, I shall live to make all sorts of representations of all sorts of things. It will take a much cleverer person than myself to discover my last impression—among all these things—of anything. And then, in such a matter, the bother of being an American! Trollope, Thackeray, Dickens, even with their authoritative talents, were free to draw all sorts of unflattering English pictures, by the thousand. But if I make a single one, I am forthwith in danger of being confronted with a criminal conclusion—and sinister rumours reach me as to what I think of English society. I think more things than I can undertake to tell in

40 pages of the Cornhill. Perhaps some day I shall take more pages, and attempt to tell some of these things; in that case, I hope, there will be a little, of every sort, for every one! Meanwhile I shall draw plenty of pictures of disagreeable Americans, as I have done already and the friendly Briton will see no harm in that!—it will seem to him part of the natural fitness."

On January 4, 1879, James wrote about the matter to his friend Grace Norton in Boston: "You may be interested to know that I hear my little 'International Episode' has given offence to various people of my acquaintance here. Don't you wonder at it? So long as one serves up Americans for their entertainment it is all right—but hands off the sacred natives. They are really I think, thinner-skinned than we!" Two weeks later, James wrote to his mother: "It seems to me myself that I have been very delicate; but I shall keep off dangerous ground in the future."

Later that year, when he published his book on Hawthorne, James discovered that Americans could also be thin-skinned. He was attacked by critics in both New York and Boston ("the clucking of a brood of prairie hens," he called them), including his friend William Dean Howells, whose tone was milder but whose opinion was pointed. Howells wrote: "We foresee, without any powerful prophetic lens, that Mr. James will be in some quarters promptly attainted of high treason." On the accusation that Hawthorne was provincial, Howells wrote: "If it is not provincial for an Englishman to be English, or a Frenchman French, then it is not so for an American to be American; and if Hawthorne was 'exquisitely provincial' one had better take one's chances of universality with him than with any Londoner or Parisian of his time." He sent James his review.

James was unrepentant. He replied:

I think it is extremely provincial for a Russian to be very Russian, a Portuguese very Portuguese; for the simple reason that certain national types are essentially and intrinsically provincial. I sympathise even less with your protest against the idea that it takes an old civilization to set a novelist in motion—a proposition that seems to me to be so true as to be a truism.

In that same letter James mentioned a forthcoming serialization in the *Cornhill Magazine* of "a poorish story in three numbers—a tale purely American, the writing of which made me feel acutely the want of the 'paraphernalia.'"

The paraphernalia in question were, James had written earlier in the letter, the "manners, customs, usages, habits, forms, upon all these things matured and established that a novelist lives—they are the very stuff his work is made of." The "poorish story" was "Washington Square." While it is clear that he was being modest when he mentioned the book to Howells (and his general tendency in referring to his own work was to be self-deprecating), it still must seem that he underestimated the book. It is certainly his best short novel, and remains one of his best books. It was the first of his books to be serialized simultaneously on both sides of the Atlantic, thus offering him the freedom to devote a great deal of time to *The Portrait of a Lady*, his next project.

"Washington Square" tells the story or Dr. Sloper and his only daughter, Catherine, whom he considers dull. When Catherine falls in love with a penniless young man, her father becomes determined, in ways which are cold and cruel, that his daughter must not marry the interloper. James's portrait of the vulnerable and sensitive and unassertive daughter is one of the most sustained and convincing of his career. The value of "Washington Square" also lies in the lack of "paraphernalia," thus forcing James to intensify the psychology, to draw the father and daughter with greater subtlety and care because he, at the apex of his social power in London, did not know enough about the city and the society in which he had set the novel. He knew about the interior of the houses where he had been a small boy; he could write about familiar rooms; but he had not grown up in that world enough to know its wider personality.

He placed the events of "Washington Square" in the very years when he and his family were living in the city; he made his grandmother's house become the house of Dr. Sloper, as a year later he would make his other grandmother's house become Isabel Archer's house in Albany. The original story was told to him by Fanny Kemble, whose brother had jilted an heiress when he discovered that her father intended to disinherit her. James moved this story to his own lost territory, to the site which belonged now merely to his dreams, to the old New York, whose contours he had barely made out before he was removed from it. In chapter two of the book he inserted a passage about Washington Square and its environs which strikes the reader as strange, almost clumsy, and unthinkable for a novelist who is about to write *The Portrait of a Lady*.

"I know not," he wrote of the area around the square,

whether it is owing to the tenderness of early associations, but this portion of New York appears to many persons the most delectable. It has a kind of established repose which is not of frequent occurrence in other quarters of the long, shrill city; it has a riper, richer, more honourable look than any of the upper ramifications of the great longitudinal thoroughfare—the look of having had something of a social history... It was here that your grandmother lived, in venerable solitude, and dispensed a hospitality which commended itself alike to the infant imagination and the infant palate; it was here that you took your first walks abroad, following the nursery-maid with unequal step... It was here, finally, that your first school, kept by a broad-bosomed, broad-based old lady with a ferule, who was always having tea in a blue cup, with a saucer that didn't match, enlarged the circle both of your observations and your sensations. It was here, at any rate, that my heroine spent many years of her life; which is my excuse for this topographical parenthesis.

This may well be the excuse, but it is hardly the reason. The reason is that, a quarter of a century after it had been lost to him, James was prepared to disrupt the sacred seamlessness of his fiction to evoke this square as belonging to his memory, his primary sense of himself which could be brought back now only in words. The need was so pressing and urgent that he would allow such a paragraph to remain; had it been about another place, he would surely have removed it. He was claiming Washington Square for himself. It was here also, soon afterwards, that he began to evoke the next generation, who were too ready to eschew social history for the blight, as James saw it, of newness.

Dr. Sloper's niece, for example, is about to marry Arthur Townsend, who speaks about his new house:

It's only for three or four years. At the end of three or four years we'll move. That's the way to live in New York—to move every three or four years. Then you always get the last thing. It's because the city's growing so quick—you've got to keep up with it. It's going straight up town—that's where New York's going...I guess we'll move up little by little; when we get tired of one street we'll go higher. So you see we'll always have a new house; it's a great advantage to have a new house; you get all the latest improvements. They invent everything all over again about every five years, and it's a great thing to keep up with the new things.

It is easy to feel James's rage and exasperation at the new ethos of easy and quick change which has eaten up his city of old values, destroyed the few buildings and streets with many rich old associations for him. Like the passage quoted above about Washington Square itself, however, this long speech by the young man seems forced and makes its point rather too heavily. These two passages stand out in a novel which is otherwise compact and tightly constructed. They are part of James's deeply irrational response to the New York he had known and what had replaced it; his emotions about the city, as about no other place, moved at times slowly and strangely out of his control.

Three years later, after the death of his parents and a return to the United States, James wrote another story set in New York, "The Impressions of a Cousin," one of his slackest and weakest stories but interesting nonetheless for the further light it shines on his attitude to New York. The story opens as the narrator wonders how she can inhabit Fifty-third Street:

> When I turn into it from Fifth Avenue the vista seems too hideous: the narrow, impersonal houses, with the dry, hard tone of their brown-stone, a surface as uninteresting as that of sandpaper; their steep stiff stoops, giving you such a climb to the door; their lumpish balustrades, porticoes, and cornices, turned out by the hundred and adorned with heavy excrescences—such an eruption of ornament and such a poverty of effect!

The narrator is a painter, returned from Italy, who remarks in the early pages that there is nothing to sketch in the city, not even the people. "What people? the people in the Fifth Avenue? They are even less pictorial than their houses. I don't perceive that those in the Sixth are any better, or those in the Fourth and Third, or in the Seventh and Eighth. Good heavens! What a nomenclature! The city of New York is like a tall sum in addition, and the streets are like columns of figures."

Later, she will see the stoops "as ugly as a bad dream," as earlier she has seen the sky over New York as seeming "part of the world at large; in Europe it's part of the particular place." This echoes James's assertion in his Hawthorne book of four years earlier that in the United States, in Hawthorne's day, "there were no great things to look at (save forests and rivers)."

For the next twenty years and more, as he wrote increasingly about England and the English, James remained silent on the subject of New York. His bad dreams of the city seemed to be over. He had other places, such as Paris and Rome and Florence, to remember and note as they changed. But nothing in James's most complex personality was ever that simple. The city of New York, in all its unresolved power, remained like an undertow in his consciousness for all the years. In 1906, in his book *The American Scene,* he devoted three chapters to the city, having kept in reserve, during his long exile, a body of adjectives which he now heaped down on the teeming metropolis like a plague of locusts.

James began by disliking New York Harbor: "The shores are low and for the most part depressingly furnished and prosaically peopled; the islands, though numerous, have not a grace to exhibit." He admits to "the beauty of light and air," which is like admitting that the United States has forests and rivers to look at. Soon, however, James, using a peculiarly fervid tone, was writing about power, about which he was both uneasy and oddly thrilled:

> The aspect of power...is indescribable; it is the power of the most extravagant of cities, rejoicing as with the voice of the morning, in its might, its fortune, its unsurpassable conditions, and imparting to every object and element, to the motion and expression of every floating, hurrying, panting thing, to the throb of ferries and tugs...something of its sharp free accent.

He writes about "the bigness and bravery and insolence, especially, of everything that rushed and shrieked."

The city's skyscrapers struck him as

> impudently new and still more impudently "novel"—this in common with so many other terrible things in America —and they are triumphant payers of dividends...Crowned

not only with no history, but with no credible possibility of time for history, and consecrated by no uses save the commercial at any cost, they are simply the most piercing notes in the concert of the expensively provisional into which your supreme sense of New York resolves itself.

It gets worse, as James, visiting the business quarter, notes "the consummate monotonous commonness...of the pushing male crowd, moving in its dense mass." He is appalled by the disappearance of buildings and the dwarfing of others. He is, he admits, "haunted" by a "sense of dispossession." He revisits his old city: "The precious stretch of space between Washington Square and Fourteenth Street had a value, had even a charm, for the revisiting spirit—a mild and melancholy glamour which I am conscious of the difficulty of 'rendering' for new and heedless generations." The demolition of his birthplace at Washington Place had the effect, James wrote, "of having amputated of half my history." He realizes that the building which could have sported a tablet announcing the author's very birthplace had been destroyed.

As he rails against the city, James finds astonishing images for the levels of distress he detects in the natives:

Free existence and good manners, in New York, are too much brought down to a bare rigour of marginal relations to the endless electric coil, the monstrous chain that winds around the general neck and body, the general middle and legs, very much as the boa-constrictor winds around the group of the Laocoon. It struck me that when these folds are tightened in the terrible stricture of the snow-smothered months of the year, the New York predicament leaves far behind the anguish represented in the Vatican figures."

Nothing pleases him. "This original sin," he writes,

of the longitudinal avenues perpetually, yet meanly inter-
sected, and of the organised sacrifice of the indicated alternative, the great perspectives from East to West, might
still have earned forgiveness by some occasional departure from its pettifogging consistency. But, thank to this
consistency, the city is, of all great cities, the least endowed
with any blest item of stately square or goodly garden,
with any happy accident or surprise, any fortunate nook
or casual corner, any deviation, in fine, into the liberal or
the charming.

Even the city's energy appalls him: "The very sign of its energy
is that it doesn't believe in itself; it fails to succeed, even at a
cost of millions, in persuading you that it does."

James's horror of the new arrivals in the city and his use
of animal imagery to evoke them make for some of the most
uncomfortable reading in his entire opus. The immigrant in
New York "resembles for the time the dog who sniffs round
the freshly-acquired bone, giving it a push and a lick, betraying
a sense of its possibilities, but not—and quite as from a positive
deep tremor of consciousness—directly attacking it." Of the
Jewish population, he wrote: "There are small strange animals,
known to natural history, snakes or worms I believe, who,
when cut into pieces, wriggle away contentedly and live in the
snippet as completely as in the whole. So the denizens of
the New York Ghetto, heaped as thick as the splinters on the
table of a glass-blower, had each, like the fine glass particle, his
or her individual share of the whole hard glitter or Israel." The
fire escapes, "omnipresent in the 'poor' regions" of the city,
remind James "of the speciously organised cage for the nimbler
class of animals in some great zoological garden. This general
analogy is irresistible—it seems to offer, in each district, a little
world of bars and perches and swings for human squirrels and
monkeys." He watched, from a window in the Ghetto, on "a
swarming little square in which an ant-like population darted
to and fro."

It is hard to be precise about what exactly is biting Henry James as he wanders the streets of New York, "this terrible town," as he puts it, hating the voices and the accents he heard in the cafés, "the torture rooms of the living idiom," disliking even Central Park, comparing it "to an actress in a company destitute, through an epidemic or some other stress, of all feminine talent; so that she assumes on successive nights the most dissimilar parts and ranges in the course of a week from the tragedy queen to the singing chambermaid."

It is as though something has been stolen from James, as indeed it has, and it is not something ordinary. For certain writers, both places long abandoned and experiences that might just as well have been forgotten continue to exist in the present tense. They can be conjured up at will, and sometimes they come unwilled. They live lives of their own in the mind. They are like rooms whose electric lights cannot be dimmed or switched off. For James, the New York of 1848 to 1855 was such a place and his experiences there, so happy with the innocence of prepuberty and full of ease, did not fade in his memory, as they must have done in his brother's memory. They remained living presences. He was moving now fifty years later in a city which tried, in name of novelty, to prevent him reinhabiting his lighted rooms. He was not simply in the new city while remembering the old. The old city had never ended for him; it lived as an aspect of the imperative of his genius. Now the lights in his rooms were flickering madly, almost blinding him. To protect himself, he heaped insult upon insult on New York.

For a writer, the blurring of time present and time past is a way of freeing the imagination but it has also a way of making the personality both troubled and willful. What he saw in 1905 in New York caused James to use imagery wildly disproportionate to his experience, but apt for the battle going on within him between a past which clung to him and the terrible novelty of modernity. Writers die when they grow up; New York that year was asking James for too much.

It should be possible, also, to argue that the case was much simpler, that James found more decent, human, and civilized values in the city of his childhood and genuinely disliked the city he found in 1905, and expressed himself robustly on the matter, having done so in a number of stories also. But one of the last stories he set in New York, and one of his last pieces of fiction, tends to favor the opposite argument, that there was something unresolved and haunting in James's dislike of New York and in his fear of it. This story is called "The Jolly Corner."

James, like many of his contemporaries in London, was interested in doubles. His story "The Private Life," published in 1892, mirrored the world of Dorian Gray and Dr. Jekyll. In it, James dramatized his own life in society and company and his own vocation as a solitary man, a writer. In the story he manages to place his writer in two places at exactly the same moment; he is both in company and alone at his desk. Now in early August 1906, James wrote to his agent, "I have an excellent little idea through not having slept a wink last night *all* for thinking of it, and must therefore at least get the advantage while the iron is hot." In "The Jolly Corner," written after his American sojourn of 1905, James found a new doubled self to dramatize, the man who had left New York and lived in England, and his double, still haunting him, who had never left, who still wandered in those same rooms which would fill James's autobiography and had filled his novel "Washington Square."

Brydon in the story has been thirty-three years away from New York. He shares James's view of it. The city now seems to him reduced "to some vast ledger-page, overgrown, fantastic, of ruled and criss-crossed lines and figures." He sees his old friend Alice Staverton and muses on what a great man of business he might have become had he stayed in New York. He has kept his old house downtown empty all the years, having it cleaned and cared for every day. He now goes there to be haunted by a figure moving in its dark rooms, the figure who has never left them, just as James himself in part of his mind has never left them.

Both men then engage in a tussle throughout a long night, a battle to turn off the light in these rooms. "Rigid and conscious, spectral yet human, a man of his own substance and stature waited there to measure himself with his power to dismay." Two fingers on his right hand which cover his face have been shot away. "The hands, as he looked, began to move, to open; then, as if deciding in a flash, dropped from the face and left it uncovered and presented. Horror, with the sight, had leaped into Brydon's throat, gasping there in a sound he couldn't utter." "It is," Leon Edel has written, "a profoundly autobiographical tale." It is a reenactment of the battle which had taken place within James's own self as he returned to New York and set out to describe the world he saw, seeking in his descriptions to destroy it, seeking to puncture its great power with the steel point of his great paragraphs. He wanted to restore life to the world that lingered within him, the old New York, which he had experienced before the complications of puberty and unsettlement, which he had left when he was twelve. It is significant that at the end of "The Jolly Corner," Brydon, who has come unscathed through his dark night with his double, is rescued by his old friend called Alice—James's sister and sister-in-law and the wife of his nephew were all called Alice. In the last sentence of "The Jolly Corner," he draws her to his breast. His reward for turning off the light has been a hint of love, the possibility of an uncomplicated sexuality as enjoyed by his brother William. "The Jolly Corner" leaves its protagonist stranded between a presexual past and an implausible present.

Two of the last stories James wrote were also set in the New York he had explored and deplored for *The American Scene*. The city as viewed in both "Crapy Cornelia" and "A Round of Visits" is almost sinister, quite vulgar, and deeply unsettled. Theodora Bosanquet, James's typist, to whom he dictated his fiction, noted on December 17, 1908: "Mr James going on with 'short' story for Harpers which extends mightily—& is, I think, dull." Once more in "Crapy Cornelia" James is working with an idea of a returned exile, a man who dislikes the new city and remembers, with great nostalgia, the old. His protagonist notes the house of Mrs. Worthingham in which "every particular expensive object shriek[ed] at him in its artless pride." He also makes what is James's most eloquent attack on the lack of social cohesion in the city: "This was clearly going to be the music of the future—that if people were but rich enough and furnished enough and fed enough, exercised and sanitated and manicured . . . all they had to do for civility was to take the amused ironic view of those who might be less initiated." He railed against the lack of modesty in New Yorkers' display of their advantages: "In *his* time . . . the best manners had been the best kindness, and the best kindness had mostly been some art of not insisting on one's luxurious differences, of concealing rather, for common humanity, if not for common decency, a part at least of the intensity or the ferocity with which one might be 'in the know.'"

The city in "A Round of Visits," which was the last short story James wrote, is even more inhospitable than usual as Mark Monteith, another exile, returns to New York, where he has been swindled by a New Yorker. As in "A Most Extraordinary Case," written forty years earlier, the protagonist is ill in a New York hotel. As in "An International Episode," written thirty years earlier, the weather is impossible, this time "a blinding New York blizzard," a "great white savage storm." As in "Crapy Cornelia," the hero goes to visit a number of old friends, deploring once more the interiors of their houses with their "rather glaringly false accents." What is notable about these two stories is the deeply unsympathetic way in which the New York women are presented. Leon Edel has commented: "The women particularly in these tales are devoid of all sympathy, fat and fatuous, ugly, rich, cruel, they seem to have lost the meaning of kindness." It is perhaps not surprising that the last moment of James's last New York story involves a New Yorker blowing his brains out with a revolver.

"The Jolly Corner" was the single American tale that James allowed into his twenty-three-volume New York Edition, from which he excluded *The Europeans*, "Washington Square," and *The Bostonians*. He worked on the edition in the years between writing *The American Scene* and writing his autobiography. In case there was any doubt that he meant business in his battle to make his personal New York stand up to the Goliath daily rising on the island of Manhattan, he wrote to his publishers, Scribners, on July 30, 1905: "If a *name* be wanted for the edition, for convenience and distinction, I should particularly like to call it the New York Edition if that may pass for a general title of sufficient dignity and distinctness. My feeling about the matter is that it refers the whole enterprise explicitly to my native city—to which I have had no great opportunity of rendering that sort of homage." James's work would show to a world, much hardened against the idea, that the reverse of the picture, the soft side as he would call it, could endure and matter, could have a fame beyond money. The great house of fiction would stand as tall as any skyscraper, its rooms would remain well lit even as the world outside darkened.

—Colm Tóibín

THE NEW YORK STORIES
OF HENRY JAMES

THE STORY OF A MASTERPIECE

I

NO LONGER ago than last summer, during a six weeks' stay at Newport, John Lennox became engaged to Miss Marian Everett of New York. Mr. Lennox was a widower, of large estate, and without children. He was thirty-five years old, of a sufficiently distinguished appearance, of excellent manners, of an unusual share of sound information, of irreproachable habits and of a temper which was understood to have suffered a trying and salutary probation during the short term of his wedded life. Miss Everett was, therefore, all things considered, believed to be making a very good match and to be having by no means the worst of the bargain.

And yet Miss Everett, too, was a very marriageable young lady—the pretty Miss Everett, as she was called, to distinguish her from certain plain cousins, with whom, owing to her having no mother and no sisters, she was constrained, for decency's sake, to spend a great deal of her time—rather to her own satisfaction, it may be conjectured, than to that of these excellent young women.

Marian Everett was penniless, indeed; but she was richly endowed with all the gifts which make a woman charming. She was, without dispute, the most charming girl in the circle in which she lived and moved. Even certain of her elders, women of a larger experience, of a heavier calibre, as it were, and, thanks to their being married ladies, of greater freedom of action, were practically not so charming as she. And yet, in her emulation of the social graces of these, her more fully licensed sisters, Miss Everett was quite guiltless of any aberration from the strict line of maidenly dignity. She professed an almost religious devotion to good taste, and she looked with horror upon the boisterous graces of many of her companions. Beside being the most entertaining girl in New York, she was, therefore, also the most irreproachable. Her beauty was, perhaps, contestable, but it was certainly uncontested. She was the least bit below middle height, and her person was marked by a great fulness and roundness of outline; and yet, in spite of this comely ponderosity, her movements were perfectly light and elastic. In complexion, she was a genuine blonde—a warm blonde; with a midsummer bloom upon her cheek, and the light of a midsummer sun wrought into her auburn hair. Her features were not cast upon a classical model, but their expression was in the highest degree pleasing. Her forehead was low and broad, her nose small, and her mouth—well, by the envious her mouth was called *enormous*. It is certain that it had an immense capacity for smiles, and that when she opened it to sing (which she did with infinite sweetness) it emitted a copious flood of sound. Her face was, perhaps, a trifle too circular, and her shoulders a trifle too high; but, as I say, the general effect left nothing to be desired. I might point out a dozen discords in the character of her face and figure, and yet utterly fail to invalidate the impression they produced. There is something essentially uncivil, and, indeed, unphilosophical, in the attempt to verify or to disprove a woman's beauty in detail, and a man gets no more than he deserves when he finds that, in strictness, the aggregation of the different features fails to make up the total. Stand off, gentlemen, and let *her* make the addition. Beside her beauty, Miss Everett shone by her good nature and her lively perceptions. She neither made harsh speeches nor resented them; and, on the other hand, she keenly enjoyed intellectual cleverness, and even cultivated it. Her great merit was that she made no claims or pretensions. Just as there was nothing artificial in her beauty, so there was nothing pedantic in her acuteness and nothing sentimental in her amiability. The one was all freshness and the others all *bonhomie*.

John Lennox saw her, then loved her and offered her his hand. In accepting it Miss Everett acquired, in the world's eye, the one advantage which she lacked—a complete stability and regularity of position. Her friends took no small satisfaction in contrasting her brilliant and comfortable future with her somewhat precarious past. Lennox, nevertheless, was congratulated on the right hand and on the left; but none too often for his faith. That of Miss Everett was not put to so severe a test, although she was frequently reminded by acquaintances of a moralizing turn that she had reason to be very thankful for Mr. Lennox's choice. To these assurances Marian listened with a look of patient humility, which was extremely becoming. It was as if for *his* sake she could consent even to be bored.

Within a fortnight after their engagement had been made known, both parties returned to New York. Lennox lived in a house of his own, which he now busied himself with repairing and refurnishing; for the wedding had been fixed for the end of October. Miss Everett lived in lodgings with her father, a decayed old gentleman, who rubbed his idle hands from morning till night over the prospect of his daughter's marriage.

John Lennox, habitually a man of numerous resources, fond of reading, fond of music, fond of society and not averse to politics, passed the first weeks of the Autumn in a restless, fidgety manner. When a man approaches middle age he finds it difficult to wear gracefully the distinction of being engaged. He finds it difficult to discharge with becoming alacrity the various *petits soins* incidental to the position. There was a certain pathetic gravity, to those who knew him well, in Lennox's attentions. One-third of his time he spent in foraging in Broadway, whence he returned half-a-dozen times a week, laden with trinkets and gimcracks, which he always finished by thinking it puerile and brutal to offer his mistress. Another third he passed in Mrs. Everett's drawing-room, during which period Marian was denied to visitors. The rest of the time he spent, as he told a friend, God knows how. This was stronger language than his friend expected to hear, for Lennox was neither a man of precipitate utterance, nor, in his friend's belief, of a strongly passionate nature. But it was evident that he was very much in love; or at least very much off his balance.

"When I'm with her it's all very well," he pursued, "but when I'm away from her I feel as if I were thrust out of the ranks of the living."

"Well, you must be patient," said his friend; "you're destined to live hard, yet."

Lennox was silent, and his face remained rather more sombre than the other liked to see it.

"I hope there's no particular difficulty," the latter resumed; hoping to induce him to relieve himself of whatever weighed upon his consciousness.

"I'm afraid sometimes I—afraid sometimes she doesn't really love me."

"Well, a little doubt does no harm. It's better than to be too sure of it, and to sink into fatuity. Only be sure you love her."

"Yes," said Lennox, solemnly, "that's the great point."

One morning, unable to fix his attention on books and papers, he bethought himself of an expedient for passing an hour.

He had made, at Newport, the acquaintance of a young artist named Gilbert, for whose talent and conversation he had conceived a strong relish. The painter, on leaving Newport, was to go to the Adirondacks, and to be back in New York on the first of October, after which time he begged his friend to come and see him.

It occurred to Lennox on the morning I speak of that Gilbert must already have returned to town, and would be looking for his visit. So he forthwith repaired to his studio.

Gilbert's card was on the door, but, on entering the room, Lennox found it occupied by a stranger—a young man in painter's garb, at work before a large panel. He learned from this gentleman that he was a temporary sharer of Mr. Gilbert's studio, and that the latter had stepped out for a few moments.

Lennox accordingly prepared to await his return. He entered into conversation with the young man, and, finding him very intelligent, as well as, apparently, a great friend of Gilbert, he looked at him with some interest. He was of something less than thirty, tall and robust, with a strong, joyous, sensitive face, and a thick auburn beard. Lennox was struck with his face, which seemed both to express a great deal of human sagacity and to indicate the essential temperament of a painter.

"A man with that face," he said to himself, "does work at least worth looking at."

He accordingly asked his companion if he might come and look at his picture. The latter readily assented, and Lennox placed himself before the canvas.

It bore a representation of a half-length female figure, in a costume and with an expression so ambiguous that Lennox remained uncertain whether it was a portrait or a work of fancy: a fair-haired young woman, clad in a rich mediæval dress, and looking like a countess of the Renaissance. Her figure was relieved against a sombre tapestry, her arms loosely folded, her head erect and her eyes on the spectator, toward whom she seemed to move—*"Dans un flot de velours traînant ses petits pieds."*

As Lennox inspected her face it seemed to reveal a hidden likeness to a face he well knew—the face of Marian Everett. He was of course anxious to know whether the likeness was accidental or designed.

"I take this to be a portrait," he said to the artist, "a portrait 'in character.'"

"No," said the latter, "it's a mere composition: a little from here and a little from there. The picture has been hanging about me for the last two or three years, as a sort of receptacle of waste ideas. It has been the victim of innumerable theories and experiments. But it seems to have survived them all. I suppose it possesses a certain amount of vitality."

"Do you call it anything?"

"I called it originally after something I'd read—Browning's poem, 'My Last Duchess.' Do you know it?"

"Perfectly."

"I am ignorant of whether it's an attempt to embody the poet's impression of a portrait actually existing. But why should I care? This is simply an attempt to embody my own private impression of the poem, which has always had a strong hold on my fancy. I don't know whether it agrees with your own impression and that of most readers. But I don't insist upon the name. The possessor of the picture is free to baptize it afresh."

The longer Lennox looked at the picture the more he liked it, and the deeper seemed to be the correspondence between the lady's expression and that with which he had invested the heroine of Browning's lines. The less accidental, too, seemed that element which Marian's face and the face on the canvas possessed in common. He thought of the great poet's noble lyric and of its exquisite significance, and of the physiognomy of the woman he loved having been chosen as the fittest exponent of that significance.

He turned away his head; his eyes filled with tears. "If I were possessor of the picture," he said, finally, answering the artist's last words, "I should feel tempted to call it by the name of a person of whom it very much reminds me."

"Ah?" said Baxter; and then, after a pause—"a person in New York?"

It had happened, a week before, that, at her lover's request, Miss Everett had gone in his company to a photographer's and had been photographed in a dozen different attitudes. The proofs of these photographs had been sent home for Marian to choose from. She had made a choice of half a dozen—or rather Lennox had made it—and the latter had put them in his pocket, with the intention of stopping at the establishment and giving his orders. He now took out of his pocket-book and showed the painter one of the cards.

"I find a great resemblance," said he, "between your Duchess and that young lady."

The artist looked at the photograph. "If I am not mistaken," he said, after a pause, "the young lady is Miss Everett."

Lennox nodded assent.

His companion remained silent a few moments, examining the photograph with considerable interest; but, as Lennox observed, without comparing it with his picture.

"My Duchess very probably bears a certain resemblance to Miss Everett, but a not exactly intentional one," he said, at last. "The picture was begun before I ever saw Miss Everett. Miss Everett, as you see—or as you know—has a very charming face, and, during the few weeks in which I saw her, I continued to work upon it. You know how a painter works—how artists of all kinds work: they claim their property wherever they find it. What I found to my purpose in Miss Everett's appearance I didn't hesitate to adopt; especially as I had been feeling about in the dark for a type of countenance which her face effectually realized. The Duchess was an Italian, I take it; and I had made up my mind that she was to be a blonde. Now, there is a decidedly southern depth and warmth of tone in Miss Everett's complexion, as well as that breadth and thickness of feature which is common in Italian women. You see the resemblance is much more a matter of type than of expression. Nevertheless, I'm sorry if the copy betrays the original."

"I doubt," said Lennox, "whether it would betray it to any other perception than mine. I have the honor," he added, after a pause, "to be engaged to Miss Everett. You will, therefore, excuse me if I ask whether you mean to sell your picture?"

"It's already sold—to a lady," rejoined the artist, with a smile; "a maiden lady, who is a great admirer of Browning."

At this moment Gilbert returned. The two friends exchanged greetings, and their companion withdrew to a neighboring studio. After they had talked a while of what had happened to each since they parted, Lennox spoke of the painter of the Duchess and of his remarkable talent, expressing surprise that he shouldn't have heard of him before, and that Gilbert should never have spoken of him.

"His name is Baxter—Stephen Baxter," said Gilbert, "and until his return from Europe, a fortnight ago, I knew little more about him than you. He's a case of improvement. I met him in Paris in '62; at that time he was doing absolutely nothing. He has learned what you see in the interval. On arriving in New York he found it impossible to get a studio big enough to hold him. As, with my little sketches, I need only occupy one corner of mine, I offered him the use of the other three, until he should be able to bestow himself to his satisfaction. When he began to unpack his canvases I found I had been entertaining an angel unawares."

Gilbert then proceeded to uncover, for Lennox's inspection, several of Baxter's portraits, both of men and women. Each of these works confirmed Lennox's impression of the painter's power. He returned to the picture on the easel. Marian Everett reappeared at his silent call, and looked out of the eyes with a most penetrating tenderness and melancholy.

"He may say what he pleases," thought Lennox, "the resemblance *is*, in some degree, also a matter of expression. Gilbert," he added, wishing to measure the force of the likeness, "whom does it remind you of?"

"I know," said Gilbert, "of whom it reminds *you*."

"And do you see it yourself?"

"They are both handsome, and both have auburn hair. That's all I can see."

Lennox was somewhat relieved. It was not without a feeling of discomfort—a feeling by no means inconsistent with his first moment of pride and satisfaction—that he thought of Marian's peculiar and individual charms having been subjected to the keen appreciation of another than himself. He was glad to be able to conclude that the painter had merely been struck with what was most superficial in her appearance, and that his own imagination supplied the rest. It occurred to him, as he walked home, that it would be a not unbecoming tribute to the young girl's loveliness on his own part, to cause her portrait to be painted by this clever young man. Their engagement had as yet been an affair of pure sentiment, and he had taken an almost fastidious care not to give himself the vulgar appearance of a mere purveyor of luxuries and pleasures. Practically, he had been as yet for his future wife a poor man—or rather a man, pure and simple, and not a millionaire. He had ridden with her, he had sent her flowers, and he had gone with her to the opera. But he had neither sent her sugar-plums, nor made bets with her, nor made her presents of jewelry. Miss Everett's female friends had remarked that he hadn't as yet given her the least little betrothal ring, either of pearls or of diamonds. Marian, however, was quite content. She was, by nature, a great artist in the *mise en scène* of emotions, and she felt instinctively that this classical moderation was but the converse presentment of an immense matrimonial abundance. In his attempt to make it impossible that his relations with Miss Everett should be tinged in any degree with the accidental condition of the fortunes of either party, Lennox had thoroughly understood his own instinct. He knew that he should some day feel a strong and irresistible impulse to offer his mistress some visible and artistic token of his affection, and that his gift would convey a greater satisfaction from being sole of its kind. It seemed to him now that his chance had come. What gift could be more delicate than the gift of an opportunity to contribute by her patience and good-will to her husband's possession of a perfect likeness of her face?

On that same evening Lennox dined with his future father-in-law, as it was his habit to do once a week.

"Marian," he said, in the course of the dinner, "I saw, this morning, an old friend of yours."

"Ah," said Marian, "who was that?"

"Mr. Baxter, the painter."

Marian changed color—ever so little; no more, indeed, than was natural to an honest surprise.

Her surprise, however, could not have been great, inasmuch as she now said that she had seen his return to America mentioned in a newspaper, and as she knew that Lennox frequented the society of artists. "He was well, I hope," she added, "and prosperous."

"Where did you know this gentleman, my dear?" asked Mr. Everett.

"I knew him in Europe two years ago—first in the Summer in Switzerland, and afterwards in Paris. He is a sort of cousin of Mrs. Denbigh." Mrs. Denbigh was a lady in whose company Marian had recently spent a year in Europe—a widow, rich, childless, an invalid, and an old friend of her mother. "Is he always painting?"

"Apparently, and extremely well. He has two or three as good portraits there as one may reasonably expect to see. And he has, moreover, a certain picture which reminded me of you."

"His 'Last Duchess'?" asked Marian with some curiosity. "I should like to see it. If you think it's like me, John, you ought to buy it up."

"I wanted to buy it, but it's sold. You know it then?"

"Yes, through Mr. Baxter himself. I saw it in its rudimentary state, when it looked like nothing that I should care to look like. I shocked Mrs. Denbigh very much by telling him I was glad it was his 'last.' The picture, indeed, led to our acquaintance."

"And not *vice versa*," said Mr. Everett, facetiously.

"How *vice versa*?" asked Marian, innocently. "I met Mr. Baxter for the first time at a party in Rome."

"I thought you said you met him in Switzerland," said Lennox.

"No, in Rome. It was only two days before we left. He was introduced to me without knowing I was with Mrs. Denbigh, and indeed without knowing that she had been in the city. He was very shy of Americans. The first thing he said to me was that I looked very much like a picture he had been painting."

"That you realized his ideal, etc."

"Exactly, but not at all in that sentimental tone. I took him to Mrs. Denbigh; they found they were sixth cousins by marriage; he came to see us the next day, and insisted upon our going to his studio. It was a miserable place. I believe he was very poor. At least Mrs. Denbigh offered him some money, and he frankly accepted it. She attempted to spare his sensibilities by telling him that, if he liked, he could paint her a picture in return. He said he would if he had time. Later, he came up into Switzerland, and the following Winter we met him in Paris."

If Lennox had had any mistrust of Miss Everett's relations with the painter, the manner in which she told her little story would have effectually blighted it. He forthwith proposed that, in consideration not only of the young man's great talent, but of his actual knowledge of her face, he should be invited to paint her portrait.

Marian assented without reluctance and without alacrity, and Lennox laid his proposition before the artist. The latter requested a day or two to consider, and then replied (by note) that he would be happy to undertake the task.

Miss Everett expected that, in view of the projected renewal of their old acquaintance, Stephen Baxter would call upon her, under the auspices of her lover. He called in effect, alone, but Marian was not at home, and he failed to repeat the visit. The day for the first sitting was therefore appointed through Lennox. The artist had not as yet obtained a studio of his own, and the latter cordially offered him the momentary use of a spacious and well-lighted apartment in his house, which had been intended as a billiard room, but was not yet fitted up. Lennox expressed no wishes with regard to the portrait, being content to leave the choice of position and costume to the parties immediately interested. He found the painter perfectly well acquainted with Marian's "points," and he had an implicit confidence in her own good taste.

Miss Everett arrived on the morning appointed, under her father's escort, Mr. Everett, who prided himself largely upon doing things in proper form, having caused himself to be introduced beforehand to the painter. Between the latter and Marian there was a brief exchange of civilities, after which they addressed themselves to business. Miss Everett professed the most cheerful deference to Baxter's wishes and fancies, at the same time that she made no secret of possessing a number of strong convictions as to what should be attempted and what should be avoided.

It was no surprise to the young man to find her convictions sound and her wishes thoroughly sympathetic. He found himself called upon to make no compromise with stubborn and unnatural prejudices, nor to sacrifice his best intentions to a short-sighted vanity.

Whether Miss Everett was vain or not need not here be declared. She had at least the wit to perceive that the interests of an enlightened sagacity would best be served by a painting which should be good from the painter's point of view, inasmuch as these are the painting's chief end. I may add, moreover, to her very great credit, that she thoroughly understood how great an artistic merit should properly attach to a picture executed at the behest of a passion, in order that it should be anything more than a mockery—a parody—of the duration of that passion; and that she knew instinctively that there is nothing so chilling to an artist's heat as the interference of illogical self-interest, either on his own behalf or that of another.

Baxter worked firmly and rapidly, and at the end of a couple of hours he felt that he had begun his picture. Mr. Everett, as he sat by, threatened to be a bore; laboring apparently under the impression that it was his duty to beguile the session with cheap aesthetic small talk. But Marian good-humoredly took the painter's share of the dialogue, and he was not diverted from his work.

The next sitting was fixed for the morrow. Marian wore the dress which she had agreed upon with the painter, and in which, as in her position, the "picturesque" element had been religiously suppressed. She read in Baxter's eyes that she looked supremely beautiful, and she saw that his fingers tingled to attack his subject. But she caused Lennox to be sent for, under the pretense of obtaining his adhesion to her dress. It was black, and he might object to black. He came, and she read in his kindly eyes an augmented edition of the assurance conveyed in Baxter's. He was enthusiastic for the black dress, which, in truth, seemed only to confirm and enrich, like a grave maternal protest, the young girl's look of undiminished youth.

"I expect you," he said to Baxter, "to make a masterpiece."

"Never fear," said the painter, tapping his forehead. "It's made."

On this second occasion, Mr. Everett, exhausted by the intellectual strain of the preceding day, and encouraged by his luxurious chair, sank into a tranquil sleep. His companions remained for some time, listening to his regular breathing; Marian with her eyes patiently fixed on the opposite wall, and the young man with his glance mechanically travelling between his figure and the canvas. At last he fell back several paces to survey his work. Marian moved her eyes, and they met his own.

"Well, Miss Everett," said the painter, in accents which might have been tremulous if he had not exerted a strong effort to make them firm.

"Well, Mr. Baxter," said the young girl.

And the two exchanged a long, firm glance, which at last ended in a smile—a smile which belonged decidedly to the family of the famous laugh of the two angels behind the altar in the temple.

"Well, Miss Everett," said Baxter, going back to his work; "such is life!"

"So it appears," rejoined Marian. And then, after a pause of some moments: "Why didn't you come and see me?" she added.

"I came and you weren't at home."

"Why didn't you come again?"

"What was the use, Miss Everett?"

"It would simply have been more decent. We might have become reconciled."

"We seem to have done that as it is."

"I mean 'in form.'"

"That would have been absurd. Don't you see how true an instinct I had? What could have been easier than our meeting? I assure you that I should have found any talk about the past, and mutual assurances or apologies extremely disagreeable."

Miss Everett raised her eyes from the floor and fixed them on her companion with a deep, half-reproachful glance, "Is the past, then," she asked, "so utterly disagreeable?"

Baxter stared, half amazed. "Good heavens!" he cried, "of course it is."

Miss Everett dropped her eyes and remained silent.

I may as well take advantage of the moment, rapidly to make plain to the reader the events to which the above conversation refers.

Miss Everett had found it expedient, all things considered, not to tell her intended husband the whole story of her acquaintance with Stephen Baxter; and when I have repaired her omissions, the reader will probably justify her discretion.

She had, as she said, met this young man for the first time at Rome, and there in the course of two interviews had made a deep impression upon his heart. He had felt that he would give a great deal to meet Miss Everett again. Their reunion in Switzerland was therefore not entirely fortuitous; and it had been the more easy for Baxter to make it possible, for the reason that he was able to claim a kind of roundabout relationship with Mrs. Denbigh, Marian's companion. With this lady's permission he had attached himself to their party. He had made their route of travel his own, he had stopped when they stopped and been prodigal of attentions and civilities. Before a week was over, Mrs. Denbigh, who was the soul of confiding good nature, exulted in the discovery of an invaluable kinsman. Thanks not only to her naturally unexacting disposition, but to the apathetic and inactive habits induced by constant physical suffering, she proved a very insignificant third in her companions' spending of the hours. How delightfully these hours were spent, it requires no great effort to imagine. A suit conducted in the midst of the most romantic scenery in Europe is already half won. Marian's social graces were largely enhanced by the satisfaction which her innate intelligence of natural beauty enabled her to take in the magnificent scenery of the Alps. She had never appeared to such advantage; she had never known such perfect freedom and frankness and gayety. For the first time in her life she had made a captive without suspecting it. She had surrendered her heart to the mountains and the lakes, the eternal snows and the pastoral valleys, and Baxter, standing by, had intercepted it. He felt his long-projected Swiss tour vastly magnified and beautified by Miss Everett's part in it—by the constant feminine sympathy which gushed within earshot, with the coolness and clearness of a mountain spring. Oh! if only it too had not been fed by the eternal snows! And then her beauty—her indefatigable beauty—was a continual enchantment. Miss Everett looked so thoroughly in her place in a drawing-room that it was almost logical to suppose that she looked well nowhere else. But in fact, as Baxter learned, she looked quite well enough in the character of what ladies call a "fright"—that is, sunburnt, travel-stained, overheated, exhilarated and hungry—to elude all invidious comparisons.

At the end of three weeks, one morning as they stood together on the edge of a falling torrent, high above the green concavities of the hills, Baxter felt himself irresistibly urged to make a declaration. The thunderous noise of the cataract covered all vocal utterance; so, taking out his sketch-book, he wrote three short words on a blank leaf. He handed her the book. She read the message with a beautiful change of color and a single rapid glance at his face. She then tore out the leaf.

"Don't tear it up!" cried the young man.

She understood him by the movement of his lips and shook her head with a smile. But she stooped, picked up a little stone, and wrapping it in the bit of paper, prepared to toss it into the torrent.

Baxter, uncertain, put out his hand to take it from her. She passed it into the other hand and gave him the one he had attempted to take.

She threw away the paper, but she let him keep her hand.

Baxter still had a week at his disposal, and Marian made it a very happy one. Mrs. Denbigh was tired; they had come to a halt, and there was no interruption to their being together.

They talked a great deal of the long future, which, on getting beyond the sound of the cataract, they had expeditiously agreed to pursue in common.

It was their misfortune both to be poor. They determined, in view of this circumstance, to say nothing of their engagement until Baxter, by dint of hard work, should have at least quadrupled his income. This was cruel, but it was imperative, and Marian made no complaint. Her residence in Europe had enlarged her conception of the material needs of a pretty woman, and it was quite natural that she should not, close upon the heels of this experience, desire to rush into marriage with a poor artist. At the end of some days Baxter started for Germany and Holland, portions of which he wished to visit for purposes of study. Mrs. Denbigh and her young friend repaired to Paris for the Winter. Here, in the middle of February, they were rejoined by Baxter, who had achieved his German tour. He had received, while absent, five little letters from Marian, full of affection. The number was small, but the young man detected in the very temperance of his mistress a certain delicious flavor of implicit constancy. She received him with all the frankness and sweetness that he had a right to expect, and listened with great interest of his account of the improvement in his prospects. He had sold three of his Italian pictures and had made an invaluable collection of sketches. He was on the high road to wealth and fame, and there was no reason their engagement should not be announced. But to this latter proposition Marian demurred—demurred so strongly, and yet on grounds so arbitrary, that a somewhat painful scene ensued. Stephen left her, irritated and perplexed. The next day, when he called, she was unwell and unable to see him; and the next—and the next. On the evening of the day that he had made his third fruitless call at Mrs. Denbigh's, he overheard Marian's name mentioned at a large party. The interlocutors were two elderly women. On giving his attention to their talk, which they were taking no pains to keep private, he found that his mistress was under accusal of having trifled with the affections of an unhappy young

man, the only son of one of the ladies. There was apparently no
lack of evidence or of facts which might be construed as evidence. Baxter went home, *la mort dans l'âme*, and on the following day called again on Mrs. Denbigh. Marian was still in
her room, but the former lady received him. Stephen was in
great trouble, but his mind was lucid, and he addressed himself
to the task of interrogating his hostess. Mrs. Denbigh, with her
habitual indolence, had remained unsuspicious of the terms on
which the young people stood.

"I'm sorry to say," Baxter began, "that I heard Miss Everett
accused last evening of very sad conduct."

"Ah, for heaven's sake, Stephen," returned his kinswoman,
"don't go back to that. I've done nothing all Winter but defend
and palliate her conduct. It's hard work. Don't make me do it
for you. You know her as well as I do. She was indiscreet, but I
know she is penitent, and for that matter she's well out of it. He
was by no means a desirable young man."

"The lady whom I heard talking about the matter," said
Stephen, "spoke of him in the highest terms. To be sure, as it
turned out, she was his mother."

"His mother? You're mistaken. His mother died ten years
ago."

Baxter folded his arms with a feeling that he needed to sit
firm. "*Allons,*" said he, "of whom do you speak?"

"Of young Mr. King."

"Good heavens," cried Stephen. "So there are two of them?"

"Pray, of whom do *you* speak?"

"Of a certain Mr. Young. The mother is a handsome old
woman with white curls."

"You don't mean to say there has been anything between
Marian and Frederic Young?"

"*Voilà!* I only repeat what I hear. It seems to me, my dear
Mrs. Denbigh, that you ought to know."

Mrs. Denbigh shook her head with a melancholy movement. "I'm sure I don't," she said, "I give it up. I don't pretend
to judge. The manners of young people to each other are very

different from what they were in my day. One doesn't know whether they mean nothing or everything."

"You know, at least, whether Mr. Young has been in your drawing-room?"

"Oh, yes, frequently. I'm very sorry that Marian is talked about. It's very unpleasant for me. But what can a sick woman do?"

"Well," said Stephen, "so much for Mr. Young. And now for Mr. King."

"Mr. King is gone home. It's a pity he ever came away."

"In what sense?"

"Oh, he's a silly fellow. He doesn't understand young girls."

"Upon my word," said Stephen, "with expression," as the music sheets say, "he might be very wise and not do that."

"Not but that Marian was injudicious. She meant only to be amiable, but she went too far. She became adorable. The first thing she knew he was holding her to an account."

"Is he good-looking?"

"Well enough."

"And rich?"

"Very rich, I believe."

"And the other?"

"What other—Marian?"

"No, no; your friend Young."

"Yes, he's quite handsome."

"And rich, too?"

"Yes, I believe he's also rich."

Baxter was silent a moment. "And there's no doubt," he resumed, "that they were both far gone?"

"I can only answer for Mr. King."

"Well, I'll answer for Mr. Young. His mother wouldn't have talked as she did unless she'd seen her son suffer. After all, then, it's perhaps not so much to Marian's discredit. Here are two handsome young millionaires, madly smitten. She refuses them both. She doesn't care for good looks and money."

"I don't say that," said Mrs. Denbigh, sagaciously. "She doesn't care for those things alone. She wants talent, and all the rest of it. Now, if you were only rich, Stephen——" added the good lady, innocently.

Baxter took up his hat. "When you wish to marry Miss Everett," he said, "you must take good care not to say too much about Mr. King and Mr. Young."

Two days after this interview, he had a conversation with the young girl in person. The reader may like him less for his easily-shaken confidence, but it is a fact that he had been unable to make light of these lightly-made revelations. For him his love had been a passion; for *her*, he was compelled to believe, it had been a vulgar pastime. He was a man of a violent temper; he went straight to the point.

"Marian," he said, "you've been deceiving me."

Marian knew very well what he meant; she knew very well that she had grown weary of her engagement and that, however little of a fault her conduct had been to Messrs. Young and King, it had been an act of grave disloyalty to Baxter. She felt that the blow was struck and that their engagement was clean broken. She knew that Stephen would be satisfied with no half-excuses or half-denials; and she had none others to give. A hundred such would not make a perfect confession. Making no attempt, therefore, to save her "prospects," for which she had ceased to care, she merely attempted to save her dignity. Her dignity for the moment was well enough secured by her natural half-cynical coolness of temper. But this same vulgar placidity left in Stephen's memory an impression of heartlessness and shallowness, which in that particular quarter, at least, was destined to be forever fatal to her claims to real weight and worth. She denied the young man's right to call her to account and to interfere with her conduct; and she almost anticipated his proposal that they should consider their engagement at an end. She even declined the use of the simple logic of tears. Under these circumstances, of course, the interview was not of long duration.

"I regard you," said Baxter, as he stood on the threshold, "as the most superficial, most heartless of women."

He immediately left Paris and went down into Spain, where he remained till the opening of the Summer. In the month of May Mrs. Denbigh and her *protégée* went to England, where the former, through her husband, possessed a number of connections, and where Marian's thoroughly un-English beauty was vastly admired. In September they sailed for America. About a year and a half, therefore, had elapsed between Baxter's separation from Miss Everett and their meeting in New York.

During this interval the young man's wounds had had time to heal. His sorrow, although violent, had been short-lived, and when he finally recovered his habitual equanimity, he was very glad to have purchased exemption at the price of a simple heart-ache. Reviewing his impressions of Miss Everett in a calmer mood, he made up his mind that she was very far from being the woman of his desire, and that she had not really been the woman of his choice. "Thank God," he said to himself, "it's over. She's irreclaimably light. She's hollow, trivial, vulgar." There had been in his addresses something hasty and feverish, something factitious and unreal in his fancied passion. Half of it had been the work of the scenery, of the weather, of mere juxtaposition, and, above all, of the young girl's picturesque beauty; to say nothing of the almost suggestive tolerance and indolence of poor Mrs. Denbigh. And finding himself very much interested in Velasquez, at Madrid, he dismissed Miss Everett from his thoughts. I do not mean to offer his judgment of Miss Everett as final; but it was at least conscientious. The ample justice, moreover, which, under the illusion of sentiment, he had rendered to her charms and graces, gave him a right, when free from that illusion, to register his estimate of the arid spaces of her nature. Miss Everett might easily have accused him of injustice and brutality; but this fact would still stand to plead in his favor, that he cared with all his strength for truth. Marian, on the contrary, was quite indifferent to it. Stephen's angry sentence on her conduct had awakened no echo in her contracted soul.

The reader has now an adequate conception of the feelings

with which these two old friends found themselves face to face. It is needful to add, however, that the lapse of time had very much diminished the force of those feelings. A woman, it seems to me, ought to desire no easier company, none less embarrassed or embarrassing, than a disenchanted lover; premising, of course, that the process of disenchantment is thoroughly complete, and that some time has elapsed since its completion.

Marian herself was perfectly at her ease. She had not retained her equanimity—her philosophy, one might almost call it—during that painful last interview, to go and lose it now. She had no ill feeling toward her old lover. His last words had been—like all words in Marian's estimation— a mere *façon de parler*. Miss Everett was in so perfect a good humor during these last days of her maidenhood that there was nothing in the past that she could not have forgiven.

She blushed a little at the emphasis of her companion's remark; but she was not discountenanced. She summoned up her good humor. "The truth is, Mr. Baxter," she said, "I feel at the present moment on perfect good terms with the world; I see everything *en rose*; the past as well as the future."

"I, too, am on very good terms with the world," said Mr. Baxter, "and my heart is quite reconciled to what you call the past. But, nevertheless, it's very disagreeable to me to think about it."

"Ah then," said Miss Everett, with great sweetness, "I'm afraid you're not reconciled."

Baxter laughed—so loud that Miss Everett looked about at her father. But Mr. Everett still slept the sleep of gentility. "I've no doubt," said the painter, "that I'm far from being so good a Christian as you. But I assure you I'm very glad to see you again."

"You've but to say the word and we're friends," said Marian.

"We were very foolish to have attempted to be anything else."

" 'Foolish,' yes. But it was pretty folly."

"Ah no, Miss Everett. I'm an artist, and I claim a right of

property in the word 'pretty.' You musn't stick it in there. Nothing could be pretty which had such an ugly termination. It was all false."

"Well—as you will. What have you been doing since we parted?"

"Travelling and working. I've made great progress in my trade. Shortly before I came home I became engaged."

"Engaged?—*à la bonne heure*. Is she good?—is she pretty?"

"She's not nearly so pretty as you."

"In other words, she's infinitely more good. I'm sure I hope she is. But why did you leave her behind you?"

"She's with a sister, a sad invalid, who is drinking mineral waters on the Rhine. They wished to remain there to the cold weather. They're to be home in a couple of weeks, and we are straightway to be married."

"I congratulate you, with all my heart," said Marian.

"Allow me to do as much, sir," said Mr. Everett, waking up; which he did by instinct whenever the conversation took a ceremonious turn.

Miss Everett gave her companion but three more sittings, a large part of his work being executed with the assistance of photographs. At these interviews also, Mr. Everett was present, and still delicately sensitive to the soporific influences of his position. But both parties had the good taste to abstain from further reference to their old relations, and to confine their talk to less personal themes.

II

ONE AFTERNOON, when the picture was nearly finished, John Lennox went into the empty painting-room to ascertain the degree of its progress. Both Baxter and Marian had expressed a wish that he should not see it in its early stages, and this, accordingly, was his first view. Half an hour after he had entered the room, Baxter came in, unannounced, and found him sitting before the canvas, deep in thought. Baxter had been furnished with a house-key, so that he might have immediate and easy access to his work whenever the humor came upon him.

"I was passing," he said, "and I couldn't resist the impulse to come in and correct an error which I made this morning, now that a sense of its enormity is fresh in my mind." He sat down to work, and the other stood watching him.

"Well," said the painter, finally, "how does it satisfy you?"

"Not altogether."

"Pray develop your objections. It's in your power materially to assist me."

"I hardly know how to formulate my objections. Let me, at all events, in the first place, say that I admire your work immensely. I'm sure it's the best picture you've painted."

"I honestly believe it is. Some parts of it," said Baxter, frankly, "are excellent."

"It's obvious. But either those very parts or others are singularly disagreeable. That word isn't criticism, I know; but I pay you for the right to be arbitrary. They are too hard, too strong, of too frank a reality. In a word, your picture frightens me, and if I were Marian I should feel as if you'd done me a certain violence."

"I'm sorry for what's disagreeable; but I meant it all to be real. I go in for reality; you must have seen that."

"I approve you; I can't too much admire the broad and firm methods you've taken for reaching this same reality. But you can be real without being brutal—without attempting, as one may say, to be *actual.*"

"I deny that I'm brutal. I'm afraid, Mr. Lennox, I haven't taken quite the right road to please you. I've taken the picture too much *au sérieux.* I've striven too much for completeness. But if it doesn't please you it will please others."

"I've no doubt of it. But that isn't the question. The picture is good enough to be a thousand times better."

"That the picture leaves room for infinite improvement, I, of course, don't deny; and, in several particulars, I see my way to make it better. But, substantially, the portrait is there. I'll tell you what you miss. My work isn't 'classical'; in fine, I'm not a man of genius."

"No; I rather suspect you are. But, as you say, your work isn't classical. I adhere to my term *brutal*. Shall I tell you? It's too much of a study. You've given poor Miss Everett the look of a professional model."

"If that's the case, I've done very wrong. There never was an easier, a less conscious sitter. It's delightful to look at her."

"Confound it, you've given all her ease, too. Well, I don't know what's the matter. I give up."

"I think," said Baxter, "you had better hold your verdict in abeyance until the picture is finished. The classical element is there, I'm sure; but I've not brought it out. Wait a few days, and it will rise to the surface."

Lennox left the artist alone; and the latter took up his brushes and painted hard till nightfall. He laid them down only when it was too dark to see. As he was going out, Lennox met him in the hall.

"*Exegi monumentum*," said Baxter; "it's finished. Go and look at your ease. I'll come to-morrow and hear your impressions."

The master of the house, when the other had gone, lit half-a-dozen lights and returned to the study of the picture. It had grown prodigiously under the painter's recent handling, and whether it was that, as Baxter had said, the classical element had disengaged itself, or that Lennox was in a more sympathetic mood, it now impressed him as an original and powerful work, a genuine portrait, the deliberate image of a human face and figure. It was Marian, in very truth, and Marian most patiently measured and observed. Her beauty was there, her sweetness, and her young loveliness and her aerial grace, imprisoned forever, made inviolable and perpetual. Nothing could be more simple than the conception and composition of the picture. The figure sat peacefully, looking slightly to the right, with the head erect and the hands—the virginal hands, without rings or bracelets—lying idle on its knees. The blonde hair was gathered into a little knot of braids on the top of the head (in the fashion of the moment), and left free the almost childish contour of the ears and cheeks. The eyes were full of color, contentment and light; the lips were faintly parted. Of color in the picture, there was, in strictness, very little; but the dark draperies told of reflected sunshine, and the flesh-spaces of human blushes and pallors, of throbbing life and health. The work was strong and simple, the figure was thoroughly void of affectation and stiffness, and yet supremely elegant.

"That's what it is to be an artist," thought Lennox. "All this has been done in the past two hours."

It was his Marian, assuredly, with all that had charmed him—with all that still charmed him when he saw her: her appealing confidence, her exquisite lightness, her feminine enchantments. And yet, as he looked, an expression of pain came into his eyes, and lingered there, and grew into a mortal heaviness.

Lennox had been as truly a lover as a man may be; but he loved with the discretion of fifteen years' experience of human affairs. He had a penetrating glance, and he liked to use it. Many a time when Marian, with eloquent lips and eyes, had poured out the treasures of her nature into his bosom, and he had taken them in his hands and covered them with kisses and passionate vows, he had dropped them all with a sudden shudder and cried out in silence, "But ah! where is the heart?" One day he had said to her (irrelevantly enough, doubtless), "Marian, where *is* your heart?"

"*Where*—what do you mean?" Miss Everett had said.

"I think of you from morning till night. I put you together and take you apart, as people do in that game where they make words out of a parcel of given letters. But there's always one letter wanting. I can't put my hand on your heart."

"My heart, John," said Marian, ingeniously, "is the whole word. My heart's everywhere."

This may have been true enough. Miss Everett had distributed her heart impartially throughout her whole organism, so that, as a natural consequence, its native seat was somewhat scantily occupied. As Lennox sat and looked at Baxter's consummate handiwork, the same question rose again to his lips; and if Marian's portrait suggested it, Marian's portrait failed to answer it. It took Marian to do that. It seemed to Lennox that some strangely potent agency had won from his mistress the confession of her inmost soul, and had written it there upon the canvas in firm yet passionate lines. Marian's person was lightness—her charm was lightness; could it be that her soul was levity too? Was she a creature without faith and without conscience? What else was the meaning of that horrible blankness and deadness that quenched the light in her eyes and stole away the smile from her lips? These things were the less to be eluded because in so many respects the painter had been profoundly just. He had been as loyal and sympathetic as he had been intelligent. Not a point in the young girl's appearance had been slighted; not a feature but had been forcibly and delicately rendered. Had Baxter been a man of marvellous insight—an unparalleled observer; or had he been a mere patient and unflinching painter, building infinitely better than he knew? Would not a mere painter have been content to paint Miss Everett in the strong, rich, objective manner of which the work was so good an example, and to do nothing more? For it was evident that Baxter had done more. He had painted with something more than knowledge—with imagination, with feeling. He had almost *composed*; and his composition had embraced the truth. Lennox was unable to satisfy his doubts. He would have been glad to believe that there was no imagination in the picture but what his own mind supplied; and that the unsubstantial sweetness on the eyes and lips of the image was but the smile of youth and innocence. He was in a muddle—he was absurdly suspicious and capricious; he put out the lights and left the portrait in kindly darkness. Then, half as a reparation to his mistress, and half as a satisfaction to himself, he went up to spend an hour with Marian. She, at least, as he found, had no scruples. She thought the portrait altogether a success, and she was very willing to be handed down in that form to posterity. Nevertheless, when Lennox came in, he went back into the painting-room to take another glance. This time he lit but a single light. Faugh! it was worse than with a dozen. He hastily turned out the gas.

Baxter came the next day, as he had promised. Meanwhile poor Lennox had had twelve hours of uninterrupted reflection, and the expression of distress in his eyes had acquired an intensity which, the painter saw, proved it to be of far other import than a mere tribute to his power.

"Can the man be jealous?" thought Baxter. Stephen had been so innocent of any other design than that of painting a good portrait, that his conscience failed to reveal to him the source of his companion's trouble. Nevertheless he began to pity him. He had felt tempted, indeed, to pity him from the first. He had liked him and esteemed him; he had taken him for a man of sense and of feeling, and he had thought it a matter of regret that such a man—a creature of strong spiritual needs—should link his destiny with that of Marian Everett. But he had very soon made up his mind that Lennox knew very well what he was about, and that he needed no enlightenment. He was marrying with his eyes open, and had weighed the risks against the profits. Everyone had his particular taste, and at thirty-five years of age John Lennox had no need to be told that Miss Everett was not quite all that she might be. Baxter had thus taken for granted that his friend had designedly selected as his second wife a mere pretty woman—a woman with a genius for receiving company, and who would make a picturesque use of his money. He knew nothing of the serious character of the poor man's passion, nor of the extent to which his happiness was bound up in what the painter would have called his delusion. His only concern had been to do his work well; and he had done it the better because of his old interest in Marian's bewitching face. It is very certain that he had actually infused into his picture that force of characterization and that depth of reality which had arrested his friend's attention; but he had done so wholly without effort and without malice. The artistic half of Baxter's nature exerted a lusty dominion over the human half— fed upon its disappointments and grew fat upon its joys and tribulations. This, indeed, is simply saying that the young man was a true artist. Deep, then, in the unfathomed recesses of his strong and sensitive nature, his genius had held communion with his heart and had transferred to canvas the burden of its disenchantment and its resignation. Since his little affair with Marian, Baxter had made the acquaintance of a young girl whom he felt that he could love and trust forever; and, sobered and strengthened by this new emotion, he had been able to re-sume with more distinctness the shortcomings of his earlier love. He had, therefore, painted with feeling. Miss Everett could not have expected him to do otherwise. He had done his honest best, and conviction had come in unbidden and made it better.

Lennox had begun to feel very curious about the history of his companion's acquaintance with his destined bride; but he was far from feeling jealous. Somehow he felt that he could never again be jealous. But in ascertaining the terms of their former intercourse, it was of importance that he should not al-low the young man to suspect that he discovered in the portrait any radical defect.

"Your old acquaintance with Miss Everett," he said, frankly, "has evidently been of great use to you."

"I suppose it has," said Baxter. "Indeed, as soon as I began to paint, I found her face coming back to me like a half-remembered tune. She was wonderfully pretty at that time."

"She was two years younger."

"Yes, and I was two years younger. Decidedly, you are right. I *have* made use of my old impressions."

Baxter was willing to confess to so much; but he was re-solved not to betray anything that Marian had herself kept se-cret. He was not surprised that she had not told her lover of her former engagement; he expected as much. But he would have held it inexcusable to attempt to repair her omission.

Lennox's faculties were acutely sharpened by pain and suspicion, and he could not help detecting in his companion's eyes an intention of reticence. He resolved to baffle it.

"I am curious to know," he said, "whether you were ever in love with Miss Everett?"

"I have no hesitation in saying Yes," rejoined Baxter; fancying that a general confession would help him more than a particular denial. "I'm one of a thousand, I fancy. Or one, perhaps, of only a hundred. For you see I've got over it. I'm engaged to be married."

Lennox's countenance brightened. "That's it," said he. "Now I know what I didn't like in your picture—the point of view. I'm not jealous," he added. "I should like the picture better if I were. You evidently care nothing for the poor girl. You have got over your love rather too well. You loved her, she was indifferent to you, and now you take your revenge." Distracted with grief, Lennox was taking refuge in irrational anger.

Baxter was puzzled. "You'll admit," said he, with a smile, "that it's a very handsome revenge." And all his professional self-esteem rose to his assistance. "I've painted for Miss Everett the best portrait that has yet been painted in America. She herself is quite satisfied."

"Ah!" said Lennox, with magnificent dissimulation; "Marian is generous."

"Come, then," said Baxter; "what do you complain of? You accuse me of scandalous conduct, and I'm bound to hold you to an account." Baxter's own temper was rising, and with it his sense of his picture's merits. "How have I perverted Miss Everett's expression? How have I misrepresented her? What does the portrait lack? Is it ill-drawn? Is it vulgar? Is it ambiguous? Is it immodest?" Baxter's patience gave out as he recited these various charges. "Fiddlesticks!" he cried; "you know as well as I do that the picture is excellent."

"I don't pretend to deny it. Only I wonder that Marian was willing to come to you."

It is very much to Baxter's credit that he still adhered to his resolution not to betray the young girl, and that rather than do so he was willing to let Lennox suppose that he had been a rejected adorer.

"Ah, as you say," he exclaimed, "Miss Everett is so generous!"

Lennox was foolish enough to take this as an admission. "When I say, Mr. Baxter," he said, "that you have taken your revenge, I don't mean that you've done so wantonly or consciously. My dear fellow, how could you help it? The disappointment was proportionate to the loss and the reaction to the disappointment."

"Yes, that's all very well; but, meanwhile, I wait in vain to learn wherein I've done wrong."

Lennox looked from Baxter to the picture, and from the picture back to Baxter.

"I defy you to tell me," said Baxter. "I've simply kept Miss Everett as charming as she is in life."

"Oh, damn her charms!" cried Lennox.

"If you were not the gentleman, Mr. Lennox," continued the young man, "which, in spite of your high temper, I believe you to be, I should believe you—"

"Well, you should believe me?"

"I should believe you simply bent on cheapening the portrait."

Lennox made a gesture of vehement impatience. The other burst out laughing and the discussion closed. Baxter instinctively took up his brushes and approached his canvas with a vague desire to detect latent errors, while Lennox prepared to take his departure.

"Stay!" said the painter, as he was leaving the room; "if the picture really offends you, I'll rub it out. Say the word," and he took up a heavy brush, covered with black paint.

But Lennox shook his head with decision and went out. The next moment, however, he reappeared. "You *may* rub it out," he said. "The picture is, of course, already mine."

But now Baxter shook his head. "Ah! now it's too late," he answered. "Your chance is gone."

Lennox repaired directly to Mr. Everett's apartments. Marian was in the drawing-room with some morning callers, and her lover sat by until she had got rid of them. When they were alone together, Marian began to laugh at her visitors and to parody certain of their affectations, which she did with infinite grace and spirit. But Lennox cut her short and returned to the portrait. He had thought better of his objections of the preceding evening; he liked it.

"But I wonder, Marian," he said, "that you were willing to go to Mr. Baxter."

"Why so?" asked Marian, on her guard. She saw that her lover knew something, and she intended not to commit herself until she knew how much he knew.

"An old lover is always dangerous."

"An old lover?" and Marian blushed a good honest blush. But she rapidly recovered herself. "Pray where did you get that charming news?"

"Oh, it slipped out," said Lennox.

Marian hesitated a moment. Then with a smile: "Well, I was brave," she said. "I went."

"How came it," pursued Lennox, "that you didn't tell me?"

"Tell you what, my dear John?"

"Why, about Baxter's little passion. Come, don't be modest."

Modest! Marian breathed freely. "What do you mean, my dear, by telling your wife not to be modest? Pray don't ask me about Mr. Baxter's passions. What do I know about them?"

"Did you know nothing of this one?"

"Ah, my dear, I know a great deal too much for my comfort. But he's got bravely over it. He's engaged."

"Engaged, but not quite disengaged. He's an honest fellow, but he remembers his *penchant*. It was as much as he could do to keep his picture from turning to the sentimental. He saw you as he fancied you—as he wished you; and he has given you a little look of what he imagines moral loveliness, which comes within an ace of spoiling the picture. Baxter's imagination isn't very strong, and this same look expresses, in point of fact, nothing but inanity. Fortunately he's a man of extraordinary talent, and a real painter, and he has made a good portrait in spite of himself."

To such arguments as these was John Lennox reduced, to stifle the evidence of his senses. But when once a lover begins to doubt, he cannot cease at will. In spite of his earnest efforts to believe in Marian as before, to accept her without scruple and without second thought, he was quite unable to repress an impulse of constant mistrust and aversion. The charm was broken, and there is no mending a charm. Lennox stood half-aloof, watching the poor girl's countenance, weighing her words, analyzing her thoughts, guessing at her motives.

Marian's conduct under this trying ordeal was truly heroic. She felt that some subtle change had taken place in her future husband's feelings, a change which, although she was powerless to discover its cause, yet obviously imperilled her prospects. Something had snapped between them; she had lost half of her power. She was horribly distressed, and the more so because that superior depth of character which she had all along gladly conceded to Lennox, might now, as she conjectured, cover some bold and portentous design. Could he meditate a direct rupture? Could it be his intention to dash from her lips the sweet, the spiced and odorous cup of being the wife of a good-natured millionaire? Marian turned a tremulous glance upon her past, and wondered if he had discovered any dark spot. Indeed, for that matter, might she not defy him to do so? She had done nothing really amiss. There was no visible blot in her history. It was faintly discolored, indeed, by a certain vague moral dinginess; but it compared well enough with that of other girls. She had cared for nothing but pleasure; but to what else were girls brought up? On the whole, might she not feel at ease? She assured herself that she might; but she nevertheless felt that if John wished to break off his engagement, he would do it on high abstract grounds, and not because she had committed a naughtiness the more or the less. It would be simply because he had ceased to love her. It would avail her but little to assure him that she would kindly overlook this circumstance and remit the obligations of the heart. But, in spite of her hideous apprehensions, she continued to smile and smile.

The days passed by, and John consented to be still engaged. Their marriage was only a week off—six days, five days, four. Miss Everett's smile became less mechanical. John had apparently been passing through a crisis—a moral and intellectual crisis, inevitable in a man of his constitution, and with which she had nothing to do. On the eve of marriage he had questioned his heart; he had found that it was no longer young and capable of the vagaries of passion, and he had made up his mind to call things by their proper names, and to admit to himself that he was marrying not for love, but for friendship, and a little, perhaps, for prudence. It was only out of regard for what he supposed Marian's own more exalted theory of the matter, that he abstained from revealing to her this common-sense view of it. Such was Marian's hypothesis.

Lennox had fixed his wedding-day for the last Thursday in October. On the preceding Friday, as he was passing up Broadway, he stopped at Goupil's to see if his order for the framing of the portrait had been fulfilled. The picture had been transferred to the shop, and, when duly framed, had been, at Baxter's request and with Lennox's consent, placed for a few days in the exhibition room. Lennox went up to look at it.

The portrait stood on an easel at the end of the hall, with three spectators before it—a gentleman and two ladies. The room was otherwise empty. As Lennox went toward the picture, the gentleman turned out to be Baxter. He proceeded to introduce his friend to his two companions, the younger of whom Lennox recognized as the artist's betrothed. The other, her sister, was a plain, pale woman, with the look of ill health, who had been provided with a seat and made no attempt to talk. Baxter explained that these ladies had arrived from Europe but the day before, and that his first care had been to show them his masterpiece.

"Sarah," said he, "has been praising the model very much to the prejudice of the copy."

Sarah was a tall, black-haired girl of twenty, with irregular features, a pair of luminous dark eyes, and a smile radiant of white teeth—evidently an excellent person. She turned to Lennox with a look of frank sympathy, and said in a deep, rich voice:

"She must be very beautiful."

"Yes, she's very beautiful," said Lennox, with his eyes lingering on her own pleasant face. "You must know her—she must know you."

"I'm sure I should like very much to see her," said Sarah.

"This is very nearly as good," said Lennox. "Mr. Baxter is a great genius."

"I know Mr. Baxter is a genius. But what is a picture, at the best? I've seen nothing but pictures for the last two years, and I haven't seen a single pretty girl."

The young girl stood looking at the portrait in very evident admiration, and, while Baxter talked to the elder lady, Lennox bestowed a long, covert glance upon his *fiancée*. She had brought her head into almost immediate juxtaposition with that of Marian's image, and, for a moment, the freshness and the strong animation which bloomed upon her features seemed to obliterate the lines and colors on the canvas. But the next moment, as Lennox looked, the roseate circle of Marian's face blazed into remorseless distinctness, and her careless blue eyes looked with cynical familiarity into his own.

He bade an abrupt good morning to his companions, and went toward the door. But beside it he stopped. Suspended on the wall was Baxter's picture, *My Last Duchess*. He stood amazed. Was *this* the face and figure that, a month ago, had reminded him of his mistress? Where was the likeness now? It was as utterly absent as if it had never existed. The picture, moreover, was a very inferior work to the new portrait. He looked back at Baxter, half tempted to demand an explanation, or at least to express his perplexity. But Baxter and his sweetheart had stooped down to examine a minute sketch near the floor, with their heads in delicious contiguity.

How the week elapsed, it was hard to say. There were moments when Lennox felt as if death were preferable to the heartless union which now stared him in the face, and as if the only possible course was to transfer his property to Marian and to put an end to his existence. There were others, again, when he was fairly reconciled to his fate. He had but to gather his old dreams and fancies into a faggot and break them across his knee, and the thing were done. Could he not collect in their stead a comely cluster of moderate and rational expectations, and bind them about with a wedding favor? His love was dead, his youth was dead; that was all. There was no need of making a tragedy of it. His love's vitality had been but small, and since it was to be short-lived it was better that it should expire before marriage than after. As for marriage, that should stand, for that was not of necessity a matter of love. He lacked the brutal consistency necessary for taking away Marian's future. If he had mistaken her and overrated her, the fault was his own, and it was a hard thing that she should pay the penalty. Whatever were her failings, they were profoundly involuntary, and it was plain that with regard to himself her intentions were good. She would be no companion, but she would be at least a faithful wife.

With the help of this grim logic, Lennox reached the eve of his wedding day. His manner toward Miss Everett during the preceding week had been inveterately tender and kind. He felt that in losing his love she had lost a heavy treasure, and he offered her instead the most unfailing devotion. Marian had questioned him about his lassitude and his preoccupied air, and he had replied that he was not very well. On the Wednesday afternoon, he mounted his horse and took a long ride. He came home toward sunset, and was met in the hall by his old housekeeper.

"Miss Everett's portrait, sir," she said, "has just been sent home, in the most beautiful frame. You gave no directions, and I took the liberty of having it carried into the library. I thought," and the old woman smiled deferentially, "you'd like best to have it in your own room."

Lennox went into the library. The picture was standing on the floor, back to back with a high arm-chair, and catching, through the window, the last horizontal rays of the sun. He stood before it a moment, gazing at it with a haggard face.

"Come!" said he, at last, "Marian may be what God has made her; but *this* detestable creature I can neither love nor respect!"

He looked about him with an angry despair, and his eye fell on a long, keen poinard, given him by a friend who had bought it in the East, and which lay as an ornament on his mantel-shelf. He seized it and thrust it, with barbarous glee, straight into the lovely face of the image. He dragged it downward, and made a long fissure in the living canvas. Then, with half a dozen strokes, he wantonly hacked it across. The act afforded him an immense relief.

I need hardly add that on the following day Lennox was married. He had locked the library door on coming out the evening before, and he had the key in his waistcoat pocket as he stood at the altar. As he left town, therefore, immediately after the ceremony, it was not until his return, a fortnight later, that the fate of the picture became known. It is not necessary to relate how he explained his exploit to Marian and how he disclosed it to Baxter. He at least put on a brave face. There is a rumor current of his having paid the painter an enormous sum of money. The amount is probably exaggerated, but there can be no doubt that the sum was very large. How he has fared—how he is destined to fare—in matrimony, it is rather too early to determine. He has been married scarcely three months.

1868

A MOST EXTRAORDINARY CASE

LATE IN the spring of the year 1865, just as the war had come to a close, a young invalid officer lay in bed in one of the uppermost chambers of one of the great New York hotels. His meditations were interrupted by the entrance of a waiter, who handed him a card superscribed *Mrs. Samuel Mason*, and bearing on its reverse the following words in pencil: "Dear Colonel Mason—I have only just heard of your being here, ill and alone. It's too dreadful. Do you remember me? Will you see me? If you do, I think you *will* remember me. I insist on coming up. M. M."

Mason was undressed, unshaven, weak, and feverish. His ugly little hotel chamber was in a state of confusion which had not even the merit of being picturesque. Mrs. Mason's card was at once a puzzle and a heavenly intimation of comfort. But all that it represented was so dim to the young man's enfeebled perception that it took him some moments to collect his thoughts.

"It's a lady, sir," said the waiter, by way of assisting him.

"Is she young or old?" asked Mason.

"Well, sir, she's a little of both."

"I can't ask a lady to come up here," groaned the invalid.

"Upon my word, sir, you look beautiful," said the waiter. "They like a sick man. And I see she's of your own name," continued Michael, in whom constant service had bred great frankness of speech; "the more shame to her for not coming before."

Colonel Mason concluded that, as the visit had been of Mrs. Mason's own seeking, he would receive her without more ado.

"If she doesn't mind it, I am sure I needn't," said the poor fellow, who hadn't the strength to be over-punctilious. So in a very few moments his visitor was ushered up to his bedside. He saw before him a handsome, middle-aged blond woman, stout of figure, and dressed in the height of the fashion, who displayed no other embarrassment than such as was easily explained by the loss of breath consequent on the ascent of six flights of stairs.

"Do you remember me?" she asked, taking the young man's hand.

He lay back on his pillow and looked at her. "You used to be my aunt,—my aunt Maria," he said.

"I'm your Aunt Maria, still," she answered. "It's very good of you not to have forgotten me."

"It's very good of you not to have forgotten *me*," said Mason, in a tone which betrayed a deeper feeling than the simple wish to return a civil speech.

"Dear me, you've had the war and a hundred dreadful things. I've been living in Europe, you know. Since my return I've been living in the country, in your uncle's old house on the river, of which the lease had just expired when I came home. I came to town yesterday on business, and accidentally heard of your condition and your whereabouts. I knew you'd gone into the army, and I had been wondering a dozen times what had become of you, and whether you wouldn't turn up now that the war's at last over. Of course I didn't lose a moment in coming to you. I'm *so* sorry for you." Mrs. Mason looked about her for a seat. The chairs were encumbered with odds and ends belonging to her nephew's wardrobe and to his equipment, and with the remnants of his last repast. The good lady surveyed the scene with the beautiful mute irony of compassion.

The young man lay watching her comely face in delicious submission to whatever form of utterance this feeling might take. "You're the first woman—to call a woman—I've seen in I don't know how many months," he said, contrasting her appearance with that of his room, and reading her thoughts.

"I should suppose so. I mean to be as good as a dozen." She disembarrassed one of the chairs, and brought it to the bed. Then, seating herself, she ungloved one of her hands, and laid it softly on the young man's wrist. "What a great full-grown young fellow you've become!" she pursued. "Now, tell me, are you very ill?"

"You must ask the doctor," said Mason. "I actually don't know. I'm extremely uncomfortable, but I suppose it's partly my circumstances."

"I've no doubt it's more than half your circumstances. I've seen the doctor. Mrs. Van Zandt is an old friend of mine; and when I come to town, I always go to see her. It was from her I learned this morning that you were here in this state. We had begun by rejoicing over the new prospects of peace; and from that, of course, we had got to lamenting the numbers of young men who are to enter upon it with lost limbs and shattered health. It happened that Mrs. Van Zandt mentioned several of her husband's patients as examples, and yourself among the number. You were an excellent young man, miserably sick, without family or friends, and with no asylum but a suffocating little closet in a noisy hotel. You may imagine that I pricked up my ears, and asked your baptismal name. Dr. Van Zandt came in, and told me. Your name is luckily an uncommon one: it's absurd to suppose that there could be two Ferdinand Masons. In short, I felt that you were my husband's brother's child, and that at last I too might have my little turn at hero-nursing. The little that the Doctor knew of your history agreed with the little that I knew, though I confess I was sorry to hear that you had never spoken of our relationship. But why should you? At all events you have got to acknowledge it now. I regret your not having said something about it before, only because the Doctor might have brought us together a month ago, and you would now have been well."

"It will take more than a month to get well," said Mason, feeling that, if Mrs. Mason was meaning to exert herself on his behalf, she should know the real state of the case. "I never spoke of you, because I had quite lost sight of you. I fancied you were still in Europe; and indeed," he added, after a moment's hesitation, "I heard that you had married again."

"Of course you did," said Mrs. Mason, placidly. "I used to hear it once a month myself. But I had a much better right to fancy you married. Thank Heaven, however, there's nothing of that sort between us. We can each do as we please. I promise to cure you in a month, in spite of yourself."

"What's your remedy?" asked the young man, with a smile very courteous, considering how sceptical it was.

"My first remedy is to take you out of this horrible hole. I talked it all over with Dr. Van Zandt. He says you must get into the country. Why, my dear boy, this is enough to kill you outright,—one Broadway outside of your window and another outside of your door! Listen to me. My house is directly on the river, and only two hours' journey by rail. You know I've no children. My only companion is my niece, Caroline Hofmann. You shall come and stay with us until you are as strong as you need be,—if it takes a dozen years. You shall have sweet, cool air, and proper food, and decent attendance, and the devotion of a sensible woman. I shall not listen to a word of objection. You shall do as you please, get up when you please, dine when you please, go to bed when you please, and say what you please. I shall ask nothing of you but to let yourself be very dearly cared for. Do you remember how, when you were a boy at school, after your father's death, you were taken with measles, and your uncle had you brought to our own house? I helped to nurse you myself, and I remember what nice manners you had in the very midst of your measles. Your uncle was very fond of you; and if he had had any considerable property of his own, I know he would have remembered you in his will. But of course he couldn't leave away his wife's money. What I wish to do for you is a very small part of what he would have done, if he had only lived, and heard of your gallantry and your sufferings. So it's settled. I shall go home this afternoon. To-morrow morning I shall despatch my man-servant to you with instructions. He's an Englishman. He thoroughly knows his business, and he will put up your things, and save you every particle of trouble. You've only to let yourself be dressed, and driven to the train. I shall, of course, meet you at your journey's end. Now don't tell me you're not strong enough."

"I feel stronger at this moment than I've felt in a dozen weeks," said Mason. "It's useless for me to attempt to thank you."

"Quite useless. I shouldn't listen to you. And I suppose," added Mrs. Mason, looking over the bare walls and scanty furniture of the room, "you pay a fabulous price for this bower of bliss. Do you need money?"

The young man shook his head.

"Very well then," resumed Mrs. Mason, conclusively, "from this moment you're in my hands."

The young man lay speechless from the very fulness of his heart; but he strove by the pressure of his fingers to give her some assurance of his gratitude. His companion rose, and lingered beside him, drawing on her glove, and smiling quietly with the look of a long-baffled philanthropist who has at last discovered a subject of infinite capacity. Poor Ferdinand's weary visage reflected her smile. Finally, after the lapse of years, he too was being cared for. He let his head sink into the pillow, and silently inhaled the perfume of her sober elegance and her cordial good-nature. He felt like taking her dress in his hand, and asking her not to leave him,—now that solitude would be bitter. His eyes, I suppose, betrayed this touching apprehension,—doubly touching in a war-wasted young officer. As she prepared to bid him farewell, Mrs. Mason stooped, and kissed his forehead. He listened to the rustle of her dress across the carpet, to the gentle closing of the door, and to her retreating footsteps. And then, giving way to his weakness, he put his hands to his face, and cried like a homesick school-boy. He had been reminded of the exquisite side of life.

Matters went forward as Mrs. Mason had arranged them. At six o'clock on the following evening Ferdinand found himself deposited at one of the way stations of the Hudson River

Railroad, exhausted by his journey, and yet excited at the prospect of its drawing to a close. Mrs. Mason was in waiting in a low basket-phaeton, with a magazine of cushions and wrappings. Ferdinand transferred himself to her side, and they drove rapidly homeward. Mrs. Mason's house was a cottage of liberal make, with a circular lawn, a sinuous avenue, and a well-grown plantation of shrubbery. As the phaeton drew up before the porch, a young lady appeared in the doorway. Mason will be forgiven if he considered himself presented *ex officio*, as I may say, to this young lady. Before he really knew it, and in the absence of the servant, who, under Mrs. Mason's directions, was busy in the background with his trunk, he had availed himself of her proffered arm, and had allowed her to assist him through the porch, across the hall, and into the parlor, where she graciously consigned him to a sofa which, for his especial use, she had caused to be wheeled up before a fire kindled for his especial comfort. He was unable, however, to take advantage of her good offices. Prudence dictated that without further delay he should betake himself to his room.

On the morning after his arrival he got up early, and made an attempt to be present at breakfast; but his strength failed him, and he was obliged to dress at his leisure, and content himself with a simple transition from his bed to his arm-chair. The chamber assigned him was designedly on the ground-floor, so that he was spared the trouble of measuring his strength with the staircase,—a charming room, brightly carpeted and uphol-stered, and marked by a certain fastidious freshness which be-trayed the uncontested dominion of women. It had a broad high window, draped in chintz and crisp muslin and opening upon the greensward of the lawn. At this window, wrapped in his dressing-gown, and lost in the embrace of the most unre-sisting of arm-chairs, he slowly discussed his simple repast. Before long his hostess made her appearance on the lawn out-side the window. As this quarter of the house was covered with warm sunshine, Mason ventured to open the window and talk to her, while she stood out on the grass beneath her parasol.

"It's time to think of your physician," she said. "You shall choose for yourself. The great man here is Dr. Gregory, a gentleman of the old school. We have had him but once, for my niece and I have the health of dairy-maids. On that one occasion he—well, he made a fool of himself. His practice is among the 'old families,' and he only knows how to treat certain old-fashioned, obsolete complaints. Anything brought about by the war would be quite out of his range. And then he vacillates, and talks about his own maladies *à lui*. And, to tell the truth, we had a little repartee which makes our relations somewhat ambiguous."

"I see he would never do," said Mason, laughing. "But he's not your only physician?"

"No: there is a young man, a newcomer, a Dr. Knight, whom I don't know, but of whom I've heard very good things. I confess that I have a prejudice in favor of the young men. Dr. Knight has a position to establish, and I suppose he's likely to be especially attentive and careful. I believe, moreover, that he has been an army surgeon."

"I knew a man of his name," said Mason. "I wonder if this is he. His name was Horace Knight,—a light-haired, near-sighted man."

"I don't know," said Mrs. Mason; "perhaps Caroline knows." She retreated a few steps, and called to an upper window: "Caroline, what's Dr. Knight's first name?"

Mason listened to Miss Hofmann's answer,—"I haven't the least idea."

"Is it Horace?"

"I don't know."

"Is he light or dark?"

"I've never seen him."

"Is he near-sighted?"

"How in the world should I know?"

"I fancy he's as good as any one," said Ferdinand. "With you, my dear aunt, what does the doctor matter?"

Mrs. Mason accordingly sent for Dr. Knight, who, on

arrival, turned out to be her nephew's old acquaintance. Although the young men had been united by no greater intimacy than the superficial comradeship resulting from a winter in neighboring quarters, they were very well pleased to come together again. Horace Knight was a young man of good birth, good looks, good faculties, and good intentions, who, after a three years' practice of surgery in the army, had undertaken to push his fortune in Mrs. Mason's neighborhood. His mother, a widow with a small income, had recently removed to the country for economy, and her son had been unwilling to leave her to live alone. The adjacent country, moreover, offered a promising field for a man of energy,—a field well stocked with large families of easy income and of those conservative habits which lead people to make much of the cares of a physician. The local practitioner had survived the glory of his prime, and was not, perhaps, entirely guiltless of Mrs. Mason's charge, that he had not kept up with the progress of the "new diseases." The world, in fact, was getting too new for him, as well as for his old patients. He had had money invested in the South,— precious sources of revenue, which the war had swallowed up at a gulp; he had grown frightened and nervous and querulous; he had lost his presence of mind and his spectacles in several important conjectures; he had been repeatedly and distinctly fallible; a vague dissatisfaction pervaded the breasts of his patrons; he was without competitors: in short, fortune was propitious to Dr. Knight. Mason remembered the young surgeon only as a good-humored, intelligent companion; but he soon had reason to believe that his medical skill would leave nothing to be desired. He arrived rapidly at a clear understanding of Ferdinand's case; he asked intelligent questions, and gave simple and definite instructions. The disorder was deeply seated and virulent, but there was no apparent reason why unflinching care and prudence should not subdue it.

"Your strength is very much reduced," he said, as he took his hat and gloves to go; "but I should say you had an excellent constitution. It seems to me, however,—if you will pardon me for saying so,—to be partly your own fault that you have fallen so low. You have opposed no resistance; you haven't cared to get well."

"I confess I haven't,—particularly. But I don't see how you should know it."

"Why, it's obvious."

"Well, it was natural enough. Until Mrs. Mason discovered me, I hadn't a friend in the world. I had become demoralized by solitude. I had almost forgotten the difference between sickness and health. I had nothing before my eyes to remind me in tangible form of that great mass of common human interests for the sake of which—under whatever name he may disguise the impulse—a man continues in health and recovers from disease. I had forgotten that I ever cared for books or ideas, or anything but the preservation of my miserable carcass. My carcass had become quite too miserable to be an object worth living for. I was losing time and money at an appalling rate; I was getting worse rather than better; and I therefore gave up resistance. It seemed better to die easy than to die hard. I put it all in the past tense, because within these three days I've become quite another man."

"I wish to Heaven I could have heard of you," said Knight. "I would have made you come home with me, if I could have done nothing else. It was certainly not a rose-colored prospect; but what do you say now?" he continued, looking around the room. "I should say that at the present moment rose-color was the prevailing hue."

Mason assented with an eloquent smile.

"I congratulate you from my heart. Mrs. Mason—if you don't mind my speaking for her—is so thoroughly (and, I should suppose, incorrigibly) good-natured, that it's quite a surprise to find her extremely sensible."

"Yes; and so resolute and sensible in her better moments," said Ferdinand, "that it's quite a surprise to find her good-natured. She's a fine woman."

"But I should say that your especial blessing was your

servant. He looks as if he had come out of an English novel."

"My especial blessing! You haven't seen Miss Hofmann, then?"

"Yes: I met her in the hall. She looks as if she had come out of an American novel. I don't know that that's great praise; but, at all events, I make her come out of it."

"You are bound in honor, then," said Mason, laughing, "to put her into another."

Mason's conviction of his newly made happiness needed no enforcement at the Doctor's hands. He felt that it would be his own fault if these were not among the most delightful days of his life. He resolved to give himself up without stint to his impressions,—utterly to vegetate. His illness alone would have been a sufficient excuse for a long term of intellectual laxity; but Mason had other good reasons besides. For the past three years he had been stretched without intermission on the rack of duty. Although constantly exposed to hard service, it had been his fortune never to receive a serious wound; and, until his health broke down, he had taken fewer holidays than any officer I ever heard of. With an abundance of a certain kind of equanimity and self-control,—a faculty of ready self-adaptation to the accomplished fact, in any direction,—he was yet in his innermost soul a singularly nervous, over-scrupulous person. On the few occasions when he had been absent from the scene of his military duties, although duly authorized and warranted in the act, he had suffered so acutely from the apprehension that something was happening, or was about to happen, which not to have witnessed or to have had a hand in would be matter of eternal mortification, that he can be barely said to have enjoyed his recreation. The sense of lost time was, moreover, his perpetual bugbear,—the feeling that precious hours were now fleeting uncounted, which in more congenial labors would suffice almost for the building of a monument more lasting than brass. This feeling he strove to propitiate as much as possible by assiduous reading and study in the intervals of his actual occupations. I cite the fact merely as an evidence of the uninterrupted austerity of his life for a long time before he fell sick. I might triple this period, indeed, by a glance at his college years, and at certain busy months which intervened between this close of his youth and the opening of the war. Mason had always worked. He was fond of work to begin with; and, in addition, the complete absence of family ties had allowed him to follow his tastes without obstruction or diversion. This circumstance had been at once a great gain to him and a serious loss. He reached his twenty-seventh year a very accomplished scholar, as scholars go, but a great dunce in certain social matters. He was quite ignorant of all those lighter and more evanescent forms of conviviality attached to being somebody's son, brother, or cousin. At last, however, as he reminded himself, he was to discover what it was to be the nephew of somebody's husband. Mrs. Mason was to teach him the meaning of the adjective *domestic*. It would have been hard to learn it in a pleasanter way. Mason felt that he was to learn something from his very idleness, and would leave the house a wiser as well as a better man. It became probable, thanks to that quickening of the faculties which accompanies the dawning of a sincere and rational attachment, that in this last respect he would not be disappointed. Very few days sufficed to reveal to him the many excellent qualities of his hostess,—her warm capacious heart, her fairness of mind, her good temper, her good taste, her vast fund of experience and of reminiscence, and, indeed, more than all, a certain passionate devotedness, to which fortune, in leaving her a childless widow, had done but scant justice. The two accordingly established a friendship,—a friendship that promised as well for the happiness of each as any that ever undertook to meddle with happiness. If I were telling my story from Mrs. Mason's point of view, I take it that I might make a very good thing of the statement that this lady had deliberately and solemnly conferred her affection upon my hero; but I am compelled to let it stand in this simple shape. Excellent, charming person that she was, she had every right to the rich satisfaction which belonged to a liberal—yet not too liberal—estimate of her guest. She had di-vined him,—so much the better for her. That it was very much the better for him is obviously one of the elementary facts of my narrative; a fact of which Mason became so rapidly and profoundly sensible, that he was soon able to dismiss it from his thoughts to his life,—its proper sphere.

In the space of ten days, then, most of the nebulous impres-sions evoked by change of scene had gathered into substantial form. Others, however, were still in the nebulous state,—diffusing a gentle light upon Ferdinand's path. Chief among these was the mild radiance of which Miss Hofmann was the centre. For three days after his arrival Mason had been confined to his room by the aggravation of his condition consequent upon his journey. It was not till the fourth day, therefore, that he was able to renew the acquaintance so auspiciously com-menced. When at last, at dinner-time, he reappeared in the drawing-room, Miss Hofmann greeted him almost as an old friend. Mason had already discovered that she was young and gracious; he now rapidly advanced to the conclusion that she was uncommonly pretty. Before dinner was over, he had made up his mind that she was neither more nor less than beautiful. Mrs. Mason had found time to give him a full account of her life. She had lost her mother in infancy, and had been adopted by her aunt in the early years of this lady's widowhood. Her fa-ther was a man of evil habits,—a drunkard, a gambler, and a rake, outlawed from decent society. His only dealings with his daughter were to write her every month or two a begging letter, she being in possession of her mother's property. Mrs. Mason had taken her niece to Europe, and given her every advantage. She had had an expensive education; she had travelled; she had gone into the world; she had been presented, like a good repub-lican, to no less than three European sovereigns; she had been admired; she had had half a dozen offers of marriage to her aunt's knowledge, and others, perhaps, of which she was igno-rant, and had refused them all. She was now twenty-six years of age, beautiful, accomplished, and *au mieux* with her bankers.

She was an excellent girl, with a will of her own. "I'm very fond of her," Mrs. Mason declared, with her habitual frankness; "and I suppose she's equally fond of me; but we long ago gave up all idea of playing at mother and daughter. We have never had a disagreement since she was fifteen years old; but we have never had an agreement either. Caroline is no sentimentalist. She's honest, good-tempered, and perfectly discerning. She foresaw that we were still to spend a number of years together, and she wisely declined at the outset to affect a range of feelings that wouldn't stand the wear and tear of time. She knew that she would make a poor daughter, and she contented herself with being a good niece. A capital niece she is. In fact we're almost sisters. There are moments when I feel as if she were ten years older than I, and as if it were absurd in me to attempt to interfere with her life. I never do. She has it quite in her own hands. My attitude is little more than a state of affectionate curiosity as to what she will do with it. Of course she'll marry, sooner or later; but I'm curious to see the man of her choice. In Europe, you know, girls have no acquaintances but such as they share with their parents and guardians; and in that way I know most of the gentlemen who have tried to make themselves acceptable to my niece. There were some excellent young men in the number; but there was not one—or, rather, there was but one —for whom Caroline cared a straw. That one she loved, I believe; but they had a quarrel, and she lost him. She's very discreet and conciliating. I'm sure no girl ever before got rid of half a dozen suitors with so little offence. Ah, she's a dear, good girl!" Mrs. Mason pursued. "She's saved me a world of trouble in my day. And when I think what she might have been, with her beauty, and what not! She has kept all her suitors as friends. There are two of them who write to her still. She doesn't answer their letters; but once in a while she meets them, and thanks them for writing, and that contents them. The others are married, and Caroline remains single. I take for granted it won't last forever. Still, although she's *not* a sentimentalist, she'll not marry a man she doesn't care for, merely because she's growing old. Indeed, it's only the sentimental girls, to my belief, that do that. They covet a man for his money or his looks, and then give the feeling some fine name. But there's one thing, Mr. Ferdinand," added Mrs. Mason, at the close of these remarks, "you will be so good as not to fall in love with my niece. I can assure you that she'll not fall in love with you, and a hopeless passion will not hasten your recovery. Caroline is a charming girl. You can live with her very well without that. She's good for common daylight, and you'll have no need of wax-candles and ecstasies."

"Be reassured," said Ferdinand, laughing. "I'm quite too attentive to myself at present to think of any one else. Miss Hofmann might be dying for a glance of my eye, and I shouldn't hesitate to sacrifice her. It takes more than half a man to fall in love."

At the end of ten days summer had fairly set in; and Mason found it possible, and indeed profitable, to spend a large portion of his time in the open air. He was unable either to ride or to walk; and the only form of exercise which he found practicable was an occasional drive in Mrs. Mason's phaeton. On these occasions Mrs. Mason was his habitual companion. The neighborhood offered an interminable succession of beautiful drives; and poor Ferdinand took a truly exquisite pleasure in reclining idly upon a pile of cushions, warmly clad, empty-handed, silent, with only his eyes in motion, and rolling rapidly between fragrant hedges and springing crops, and beside the outskirts of woods, and along the heights which overlooked the river. Detested war was over, and all nature had ratified the peace. Mason used to gaze up into the cloudless sky until his eyes began to water, and you would have actually supposed he was shedding sentimental tears. Besides these comfortable drives with his hostess, Mason had adopted another method of inhaling the sunshine. He used frequently to spend several hours at a time on the veranda beside the house, sheltered from the observation of visitors. Here, with an arm-chair and a footstool, a cigar and half a dozen volumes of novels, to say nothing of the society of either of the ladies, and sometimes of both, he suffered the mornings to pass unmeasured and uncounted. The chief incident of these mornings was the Doctor's visit, in which, of course, there was a strong element of prose,—and very good prose, as I may add, for the Doctor was turning out an excellent fellow. But, for the rest, time unrolled itself like a gentle strain of music. Mason knew so little, from direct observation, of the *vie intime* of elegant, intelligent women, that their habits, their manners, their household motions, their principles, possessed in his view all the charm of a spectacle,—a spectacle which he contemplated with the indolence of an invalid, the sympathy of a man of taste, and a little of the awkwardness which women gladly allow, and indeed provoke, in a soldier, for the pleasure of forgiving it. It was a very simple matter to Miss Hofmann that she should be dressed in fresh crisp muslin, that her hands should be white and her attitudes felicitous; she had long since made her peace with these things. But to Mason, who was familiar only with books and men, they were objects of constant, half-dreamy contemplation. He would sit for half an hour at once, with a book on his knees and the pages unturned, scrutinizing with ingenious indirectness the simple mass of colors and contours which made up the physical personality of Miss Hofmann. There was no question as to her beauty, or as to its being a warm, sympathetic beauty, and not the cold perfection of poetry. She was the least bit taller than most women, and neither stout nor the reverse. Her hair was of a dark and lustrous brown, turning almost to black, and lending itself readily to those multitudinous ringlets which were then in fashion. Her forehead was broad, open, and serene; and her eyes of that deep and clear sea-green that you may observe of a summer's afternoon, when the declining sun shines through the rising of a wave. Her complexion was the color of perfect health. These, with her full, mild lips, her generous and flexible figure, her magnificent hands, were charms enough to occupy Mason's attention, and it was but seldom that he allowed it to be diverted. Mrs. Mason was frequently called away by her household cares, but Miss Hofmann's time was apparently quite her own. Nevertheless, it came into Ferdinand's head one day, that she gave him her company only from a sense of duty, and when, according to his wont, he had allowed this impression to ripen in his mind, he ventured to assure her that, much as he valued her society, he should be sorry to believe that her gracious bestowal of it interfered with more profitable occupations. "I'm no companion," he said. "I don't pretend to be one. I sit here deaf and dumb, and blind and halt, patiently waiting to be healed,—waiting till this vagabond Nature of ours strolls my way, and brushes me with the hem of her garment."

"I find you very good company," Miss Hofmann replied on this occasion. "What do you take me for? The hero of a hundred fights, a young man who has been reduced to a shadow in the service of his country,—I should be very fastidious if I asked for anything better."

"O, if it's on theory!" said Mason. And, in spite of Miss Hofmann's protest, he continued to assume that it *was* on theory that he was not intolerable. But she remained true to her post, and with a sort of placid inveteracy which seemed to the young man to betray either a great deal of indifference or a great deal of self-command. "She thinks I'm stupid," he said to himself. "Of course she thinks I'm stupid. How should she think otherwise? She and her aunt have talked me over. Mrs. Mason has enumerated my virtues, and Miss Hofmann has added them up: total, a well-meaning bore. She has armed herself with patience. I must say it becomes her very well." Nothing was more natural, however, than that Mason should exaggerate the effect of his social incapacity. His remarks were desultory, but not infrequent; often trivial, but always good-humored and informal. The intervals of silence, indeed, which enlivened his conversation with Miss Hofmann, might easily have been taken for the natural, confident pauses in the talk of old friends.

Once in a while Miss Hofmann would sit down at the piano and play to him. The veranda communicated with the little sitting-room by means of a long window, one side of which stood open. Mason would move his chair to this aperture, so that he might see the music as well as hear it. Seated at the instrument, at the farther end of the half-darkened room, with her figure in half-profile, and her features, her movements, the color of her dress, but half defined in the cool obscurity, Miss Hofmann would discourse infinite melody. Mason's eyes rested awhile on the vague white folds of her dress, on the heavy convolutions of her hair, and the gentle movement of her head in sympathy with the music. Then a single glance in the other direction revealed another picture,—the dazzling midday sky, the close-cropped lawn, lying almost black in its light, and the patient, round-backed gardener, in white shirtsleeves, clipping the hedge or rolling the gravel. One morning, what with the music, the light, the heat, and the fragrance of the flowers,—from the perfect equilibrium of his senses, as it were,—Mason manfully went to sleep. On waking he found that he had slept an hour, and that the sun had invaded the veranda. The music had ceased; but on looking into the parlor he saw Miss Hofmann still at the piano. A gentleman was leaning on the instrument with his back toward the window, intercepting her face. Mason sat for some moments, hardly sensible, at first, of his transition to consciousness, languidly guessing at her companion's identity. In a short time his observation was quickened by the fact that the picture before him was animated by no sound of voices. The silence was unnatural, or, at the least, disagreeable. Mason moved his chair, and the gentleman looked round. The gentleman was Horace Knight. The Doctor called out, "Good morning!" from his place, and finished his conversation with Miss Hofmann before coming out to his patient. When he moved away from the piano, Mason saw the reason of his friends' silence. Miss Hofmann had been trying to decipher a difficult piece of music, the Doctor had been trying to assist her, and they had both been brought to a stop.

"What a clever fellow he is!" thought Mason. "There he stands, rattling off musical terms as if he had never thought of anything else. And yet, when he talks medicine, it's impossible to talk more to the point." Mason continued to be very well satisfied with Knight's intelligence of his case, and with his treatment of it. He had been in the country now for three weeks, and he would hesitate indeed to affirm that he felt materially better; but he felt more comfortable. There were moments when he feared to push the inquiry as to his real improvement, because he had a sickening apprehension that he would discover that in one or two important particulars he was worse. In the course of time he imparted these fears to his physician. "But I may be mistaken," he added, "and for this reason. During the last fortnight I have become much more sensible of my condition than while I was in town. I then accepted each additional symptom as a matter of course. The more the better, I thought. But now I expect them to give an account of themselves. Now I have a positive wish to recover."

Dr. Knight looked at his patient for a moment curiously. "You are right," he said; "a little impatience is a very good thing."

"O, I'm not impatient. I'm patient to a most ridiculous extent. I allow myself a good six months, at the very least."

"That is certainly not unreasonable," said Knight. "And will you allow me a question? Do you intend to spend those six months in this place?"

"I'm unable to answer you. I suppose I shall finish the summer here, unless the summer finishes me. Mrs. Mason will hear of nothing else. In September I hope to be well enough to go back to town, even if I'm not well enough to think of work. What do you advise?"

"I advise you to put away all thoughts of work. That is imperative. Haven't you been at work all your life long? Can't you spare a pitiful little twelvemonth to health and idleness and pleasure?"

"Ah, pleasure, pleasure!" said Mason, ironically.

"Yes, pleasure," said the Doctor. "What has she done to you that you should speak of her in that manner?"

"O, she bothers me," said Mason.

"You are very fastidious. It's better to be bothered by plea-sure than by pain."

"I don't deny it. But there is a way of being indifferent to pain. I don't mean to say that I have found it out, but in the course of my illness I have caught a glimpse of it. But it's be-yond my strength to be indifferent to pleasure. In two words, I'm afraid of dying of kindness."

"O, nonsense!"

"Yes, it's nonsense; and yet it's not. There would be nothing miraculous in my not getting well."

"It will be your fault if you don't. It will prove that you're fonder of sickness than health, and that you're not fit company for sensible mortals. Shall I tell you?" continued the Doctor, af-ter a moment's hesitation. "When I knew you in the army, I al-ways found you a step beyond my comprehension. You took things too hard. You had scruples and doubts about everything. And on top of it all you were devoured with a mania of appear-ing to take things easily and to be perfectly indifferent. You played your part very well, but you must do me justice to con-fess that it *was* a part."

"I hardly know whether that's a compliment or an imperti-nence. I hope, at least, that you don't mean to accuse me of playing a part at the present moment."

"On the contrary. I'm your physician; you're frank."

"It's not because you're my physician that I'm frank," said Mason. "I shouldn't think of burdening you in that capacity with my miserable caprices and fancies"; and Ferdinand paused a moment. "You're a man!" he pursued, laying his hand on his companion's arm. "There's nothing here but women, Heaven reward them! I'm saturated with whispers and perfumes and smiles, and the rustling of dresses. It takes a man to understand a man."

"It takes more than a man to understand you, my dear Mason," said Knight, with a kindly smile. "But I listen."

Mason remained silent, leaning back in his chair, with his eyes wandering slowly over the wide patch of sky disclosed by the window, and his hands languidly folded on his knees. The Doctor examined him with a look half amused, half perplexed. But at last his face grew quite sober, and he contracted his brow. He placed his hand on Mason's arm and shook it gently, while Ferdinand met his gaze. The Doctor frowned, and, as he did so, his companion's mouth expanded into a placid smile. "If you don't get well," said Knight,—"if you don't get well—" and he paused.

"What will be the consequences?" asked Ferdinand, still smiling.

"I shall hate you," said Knight, half smiling too.

Mason broke into a laugh. "What shall I care for that?"

"I shall tell people that you were a poor, spiritless fellow,— that you are no loss."

"I give you leave," said Ferdinand.

The Doctor got up. "I don't like obstinate patients," he said.

Ferdinand burst into a long loud laugh, which ended in a fit of coughing.

"I'm getting too amusing," said Knight; "I must go."

"Nay, laugh and grow fat," cried Ferdinand. "I promise to get well." But that evening, at least, he was no better, as it turned out, for his momentary exhilaration. Before turning in for the night, he went into the drawing-room to spend half an hour with the ladies. The room was empty, but the lamp was lighted, and he sat down by the table and read a chapter in a novel. He felt excited, light-headed, light-hearted, half-intoxicated, as if he had been drinking strong coffee. He put down his book, and went over to the mantelpiece, above which hung a mirror, and looked at the reflection of his face. For almost the first time in his life he examined his features, and wondered if he were good-looking. He was able to conclude only that he looked very thin and pale, and utterly unfit for the business of life. At last he heard an opening of doors overhead, and a rustling of voluminous skirts on the stairs. Mrs. Mason came in, fresh from the hands of her maid, and dressed for a party.

And is Miss Hofmann going?" asked Mason. He felt that his

heart was beating, and that he hoped Mrs. Mason would say no. His momentary sense of strength, the mellow lamplight, the open piano, and the absence, of the excellent woman before him, struck him as so many reasons for her remaining at home. But the sound of the young lady's descent upon the stairs was an affirmative to his question. She forthwith appeared upon the threshold, dressed in crape of a kind of violent blue, with desultory clusters of white roses. For some ten minutes Mason had the pleasure of being witness to that series of pretty movements and preparations with which women in full dress beguile the interval before their carriage is announced; their glances at the mirror, their slow assumption of their gloves, their mutual revisions and felicitations.

"Isn't she lovely?" said Miss Hofmann to the young man, nodding at her aunt, who looked every inch the handsome woman that she was.

"Lovely, lovely, lovely!" said Ferdinand, so emphatically, that Miss Hofmann transferred her glance to him; while Mrs. Mason good-humoredly turned her back, and Caroline saw that Mason was engaged in a survey of her own person.

Miss Hofmann smiled discreetly. "I wish very much you might come," she said.

"I shall go to bed," answered Ferdinand, simply.

"Well, that's much better. We shall go to bed at two o'clock. Meanwhile I shall caper about the rooms to the sound of a piano and fiddle, and Aunt Maria will sit against the wall with her toes tucked under a chair. Such is life!"

"You'll dance then," said Mason.

"I shall dance. Dr. Knight has invited me."

"Does he dance well, Caroline?" asked Mrs. Mason.

"That remains to be seen. I have a strong suspicion that he does not."

"Why?" asked Ferdinand.

"He does so many other things well."

"That's no reason," said Mrs. Mason. "Do you dance, Ferdinand?"

Ferdinand shook his head.

"I like a man to dance," said Caroline, "and yet I like him not to dance."

"That's a very womanish speech, my dear," said Mrs. Mason.

"I suppose it is. It's inspired by my white gloves and my low dress, and my roses. When once a woman gets on such things, Colonel Mason, expect nothing but nonsense.—Aunt Maria," the young lady continued, "will you button my glove?"

"Let me do it," said Ferdinand. "Your aunt has her gloves on."

"Thank you." And Miss Hofmann extended a long white arm, and drew back with her other hand the bracelet from her wrist. Her glove had three buttons, and Mason performed the operation with great deliberation and neatness.

"And now," said he, gravely, "I hear the carriage. You want me to put on your shawl."

"If you please,"—Miss Hofmann passed her full white drapery into his hands, and then turned about her fair shoulders. Mason solemnly covered them, while the waiting-maid, who had come in, performed the same service for the elder lady.

"Good by," said the latter, giving him her hand. "You're not to come out into the air." And Mrs. Mason, attended by her maid, transferred herself to the carriage. Miss Hofmann gathered up her loveliness, and prepared to follow. Ferdinand stood leaning against the parlor door, watching her; and as she rustled past him she nodded farewell with a silent smile. A characteristic smile, Mason thought it,—a smile in which there was no expectation of triumph and no affectation of reluctance, but just the faintest suggestion of perfectly good-humored resignation. Mason went to the window and saw the carriage roll away with its lighted lamps, and then stood looking out into the darkness. The sky was cloudy. As he turned away the maidservant came in, and took from the table a pair of rejected gloves. "I hope you're feeling better, sir," she said, politely.

"Thank you, I think I am."

"It's a pity you couldn't have gone with the ladies."

"I'm not well enough yet to think of such things," said

Mason, trying to smile. But as he walked across the floor he felt himself attacked by a sudden sensation, which cannot be better described than as a general collapse. He felt dizzy, faint, and sick. His head swam and his knees trembled. "I'm ill," he said, sitting down on the sofa; "you must call William."

William speedily arrived, and conducted the young man to his room. "What on earth had you been doing, sir?" asked this most irreproachable of serving-men, as he helped him to undress.

Ferdinand was silent a moment. "I had been putting on Miss Hofmann's shawl," he said.

"Is that all, sir?"

"And I had been buttoning her glove."

"Well, sir, you must be very prudent."

"So it appears," said Ferdinand.

He slept soundly, however, and the next morning was the better for it. "I'm certainly better," he said to himself, as he slowly proceeded to his toilet. "A month ago such an attack as that of last evening would have effectually banished sleep. Courage, then. The Devil isn't dead, but he's dying."

In the afternoon he received a visit from Horace Knight. "So you danced last evening at Mrs. Bradshaw's," he said to his friend.

"Yes, I danced. It's a great piece of frivolity for a man in my position; but I thought there would be no harm in doing it just once, to show them I know how. My abstinence in future will tell the better. Your ladies were there. I danced with Miss Hofmann. She was dressed in blue, and she was the most beautiful woman in the room. Every one was talking about it."

"I saw her," said Mason, "before she went off."

"You should have seen her there," said Knight. "The music, the excitement, the spectators, and all that, bring out a woman's beauty."

"So I suppose," said Ferdinand.

"What strikes me," pursued the Doctor, "is her—what shall I call it?—her vitality, her quiet buoyancy. Of course, you didn't see her when she came home? If you had, you would have noticed, unless I'm very much mistaken, that she was as fresh and elastic at two o'clock as she had been at ten. While all the other women looked tired and jaded and used up, she alone showed no signs of exhaustion. She was neither pale nor flushed, but still light-footed, rosy, and erect. She's solid. You see I can't help looking at such things as a physician. She has a magnificent organization. Among all those other poor girls she seemed to have something of the inviolable strength of a goddess"; and Knight smiled frankly as he entered the region of eloquence. "She wears her artificial roses and dew-drops as if she had gathered them on the mountain-tops, instead of buying them in Broadway. She moves with long steps, her dress rustles, and to a man of fancy it's the sound of Diana on the forest-leaves."

Ferdinand nodded assent. "So you're a man of fancy," he said.

"Of course I am," said the Doctor.

Ferdinand was not inclined to question his friend's estimate of Miss Hofmann, nor to weigh his words. They only served to confirm an impression which was already strong in his own mind. Day by day he had felt the growth of this impression. "He must be a strong man who would approach her," he said to himself. "He must be as vigorous and elastic as she herself, or in the progress of courtship she will leave him far behind. He must be able to forget his lungs and his liver and his digestion. To have broken down in his country's defence, even, will avail him nothing. What is that to her? She needs a man who has defended his country without breaking down,—a being complete, intact, well seasoned, invulnerable. Then,—then," thought Ferdinand, "perhaps she will consider him. Perhaps it will be to refuse him. Perhaps, like Diana, to whom Knight compares her, she is meant to live alone. It's certain, at least, that she is able to wait. She will be young at forty-five. Women who are young at forty-five are perhaps not the most interesting women. They are likely to have felt for nobody and for nothing. But it's often less their own fault than that of the men and women about them. This one at least *can* feel; the thing is to move her. Her soul is an instrument of a hundred strings, only it takes a strong hand to draw sound. Once really touched, they will reverberate for ever and ever."

In fine, Mason was in love. It will be seen that his passion was not arrogant nor uncompromising; but, on the contrary, patient, discreet, and modest,—almost timid. For ten long days, the most memorable days of his life,—days which, if he had kept a journal, would have been left blank,—he held his tongue. He would have suffered anything rather than reveal his emotions, or allow them to come accidentally to Miss Hofmann's knowledge. He would cherish them in silence until he should feel in all his sinews that he was himself again, and then he would open his heart. Meanwhile he would be patient; he would be the most irreproachable, the most austere, the most insignificant of convalescents. He was as yet unfit to touch her, to look at her, to speak to her. A man was not to go a wooing in his dressing-gown and slippers.

There came a day, however, when, in spite of his high resolves, Ferdinand came near losing his balance. Mrs. Mason had arranged with him to drive in the phaeton after dinner. But it befell that, an hour before the appointed time, she was sent for by a neighbor who had been taken ill.

"But it's out of the question that you should lose your drive," said Miss Hofmann, who brought him her aunt's apologies. "If you are still disposed to go, I shall be happy to take the reins. I shall not be as good company as Aunt Maria, but perhaps I shall be as good company as Thomas." It was settled, accordingly, that Miss Hofmann should act as her aunt's substitute, and at five o'clock the phaeton left the door. The first half of their drive was passed in silence; and almost the first words they exchanged were as they finally drew near to a space of enclosed ground, beyond which, through the trees at its farther extremity, they caught a glimpse of a turn in the river. Miss Hofmann involuntarily pulled up. The sun had sunk low, and the cloudless western sky glowed with rosy yellow. The trees which concealed the view flung over the grass a great screen of shadow, which reached out into the road. Between their scattered stems gleamed the broad white current of the Hudson. Our friends both knew the spot. Mason had seen it from a boat, when one morning a gentleman in the neighborhood, thinking to do him a kindness, had invited him to take a short sail; and with Miss Hofmann it had long been a frequent resort.

"How beautiful!" she said, as the phaeton stopped.

"Yes, if it wasn't for those trees," said Ferdinand. "They conceal the best part of the view."

"I should rather say they indicate it," answered his companion. "From here they conceal it; but they suggest to you to make your way in, and lose yourself behind them, and enjoy the prospect in privacy."

"But you can't take a vehicle in."

"No: there is only a footpath, although I have ridden in. One of these days, when you're stronger, you must drive to this point, and get out, and walk over to the bank."

Mason was silent a moment—a moment during which he felt in his limbs the tremor of a bold resolution. "I noticed the place the day I went out on the water with Mr. McCarthy. I immediately marked it as my own. The bank is quite high, and the trees make a little amphitheatre on its summit. I think there's a bench."

"Yes, there are two benches," said Caroline.

"Suppose, then, we try it now," said Mason, with an effort.

"But you can never walk over that meadow. You see it's broken ground. And, at all events, I can't consent to your going alone."

"That, madam," said Ferdinand, rising to his feet in the phaeton, "is a piece of folly I should never think of proposing. Yonder is a house, and in it there are people. Can't we drive thither, and place the horse in their custody?"

"Nothing is more easy, if you insist upon it. The house is occupied by a German family with a couple of children, who are old friends of mine. When I come here on horseback they always clamor for 'coppers.' From their little garden the walk is shorter."

So Miss Hofmann turned the horse toward the cottage, which stood at the head of a lane, a few yards from the road. A little boy and girl, with bare heads and bare feet,—the former members very white and the latter very black,—came out to meet her. Caroline greeted them good-humoredly in German. The girl, who was the elder, consented to watch the horse, while the boy volunteered to show the visitors the shortest way to the river. Mason reached the point in question without great fatigue, and found a prospect which would have repaid even greater trouble. To the right and to the left, a hundred feet below them, stretched the broad channel of the seaward-shifting waters. In the distance rose the gentle masses of the Catskills with all the intervening region vague and neutral in the gathering twilight. A faint odor of coolness came up to their faces from the stream below.

"You can sit down," said the little boy, doing the honors.

"Yes, Colonel, sit down," said Caroline. "You've already been on your feet too much."

Ferdinand obediently seated himself, unable to deny that he was glad to do so. Miss Hofmann released from her grasp the skirts which she had gathered up in her passage from the phaeton, and strolled to the edge of the cliff, where she stood for some moments talking with her little guide. Mason could only hear that she was speaking German. After the lapse of a few moments Miss Hofmann turned back, still talking—or rather listening—to the child.

"He's very pretty," she said in French, as she stopped before Ferdinand.

Mason broke into a laugh. "To think," said he, "that that dirty little youngster should forbid us the use of two languages! Do you speak French, my child?"

"No," said the boy, sturdily, "I speak German."

"Ah, there I can't follow you!"

The child stared a moment, and then replied, with pardonable irrelevancy, "I'll show you the way down to the water."

"There I can't follow you either. I hope *you'll* not go, Miss Hofmann," added the young man, observing a movement on Caroline's part.

"Is it hard?" she asked of the child.

"No, it's easy."

"Will I tear my dress?"

The child shook his head; and Caroline descended the bank under his guidance.

As some moments elapsed before she reappeared, Ferdinand ventured to the edge of the cliff, and looked down. She was sitting on a rock on the narrow margin of sand, with her hat in her lap, twisting the feather in her fingers. In a few moments it seemed to Ferdinand that he caught the tones of her voice, wafted upward as if she were gently singing. He listened intently, and at last succeeded in distinguishing several words; they were German. "Confound her German!" thought the young man. Suddenly Miss Hofmann rose from her seat, and, after a short interval, reappeared on the platform. "What did you find down there?" asked Ferdinand, almost savagely.

"Nothing,—a little strip of a beach and a pile of stones."

"You *have* torn your dress," said Mason.

Miss Hofmann surveyed her drapery. "Where, if you please?"

"There, in front." And Mason extended his walking-stick, and inserted it into the injured fold of muslin. There was a certain graceless *brusquerie* in the movement which attracted Miss Hofmann's attention. She looked at her companion, and, seeing that his face was discomposed, fancied that he was annoyed at having been compelled to wait.

"Thank you," she said; "it's easily mended. And now suppose we go back."

"No, not yet," said Ferdinand. "We have plenty of time."

"Plenty of time to catch cold," said Miss Hofmann, kindly.

Mason had planted his stick where he had let it fall on withdrawing it from contact with his companion's skirts, and stood leaning against it, with his eyes on the girl's face. "What if I do catch cold?" he asked abruptly.

"Come, don't talk nonsense," said Miss Hofmann.

"I never was more serious in my life." And, pausing a moment, he drew a couple of steps nearer. She had gathered her shawl closely about her, and stood with her arms lost in it, holding her elbows. "I don't mean that quite literally," Mason continued. "I wish to get well, on the whole. But there are moments when this perpetual self-coddling seems beneath the dignity of man, and I'm tempted to purchase one short hour of enjoyment, of happiness, at the cost—well, at the cost of my life if necessary!"

This was a franker speech than Ferdinand had yet made; the reader may estimate his habitual reserve. Miss Hofmann must have been somewhat surprised, and even slightly puzzled. But it was plain that he expected a rejoinder.

"I don't know what temptations you may have had," she answered, smiling; "but I confess that I can think of none in your present circumstances likely to involve the great sacrifice you speak of. What you say, Colonel Mason, is half—"

"Half what?"

"Half ungrateful. Aunt Maria flatters herself that she has made existence as easy and as peaceful for you—as stupid, if you like—as it can possibly be for a—a clever man. And now, after all, to accuse her of introducing temptations."

"Your aunt Maria is the best of women, Miss Hofmann," said Mason. "But I'm not a clever man. I'm deplorably weak-minded. Very little things excite me. Very small pleasures are gigantic temptations. I would give a great deal, for instance, to stay here with you for half an hour."

It is a delicate question whether Miss Hofmann now ceased to be perplexed; whether she discerned in the young man's accents—it was his tone, his attitude, his eyes that were fully significant, rather than his words—an intimation of that sublime and simple truth in the presence of which a wise woman puts off coquetry and prudery, and stands invested with perfect charity. But charity is nothing if not discreet; and Miss Hofmann may very well have effected the little transaction I speak of, and yet have remained, as she did remain, gracefully wrapped in her shawl, with the same serious smile on her face. Ferdinand's heart was thumping under his waistcoat; the words in which he might tell her that he loved her were fluttering there like frightened birds in a storm-shaken cage. Whether his lips would form them or not depended on the next words she uttered. On the faintest sign of defiance or of impatience he would really give her something to coquet withal. I repeat that I do not undertake to follow Miss Hofmann's feelings; I only know that her words were those of a woman of great instincts. "My dear Colonel Mason," she said, "I wish we might remain here the whole evening. The moments are quite too pleasant to be wantonly sacrificed. I simply put you on your conscience. If you believe that you can safely do so,—that you'll not have some dreadful chill in consequence,—let us by all means stay awhile. If you do not so believe, let us go back to the carriage. There is no good reason, that I see, for our behaving like children."

If Miss Hofmann apprehended a scene,—I do not assert that she did,—she was saved. Mason extracted from her words a delicate assurance that he could afford to wait. "You're an angel, Miss Hofmann," he said, as a sign that this kindly assurance had been taken. "I think we had better go back."

Miss Hofmann accordingly led the way along the path, and Ferdinand slowly followed. A man who has submitted to a woman's wisdom generally feels bound to persuade himself that he has surrendered at discretion. I suppose it was in this spirit that Mason said to himself as he walked along, "Well, I got what I wanted."

The next morning he was again an invalid. He woke up with symptoms which as yet he had scarcely felt at all; and he was obliged to acknowledge the bitter truth that, small as it was, his adventure had exceeded his strength. The walk, the evening air, the dampness of the spot, had combined to produce a violent attack of fever. As soon as it became plain that, in vulgar terms, he was "in for it," he took his heart in his hands and succumbed. As his condition grew worse, he was fortunately relieved from the custody of this valuable organ, with all it contained of hopes delayed and broken projects, by several intervals of prolonged unconsciousness.

For three weeks he was a very sick man. For a couple of days his recovery was doubted of. Mrs. Mason attended him with inexhaustible patience and with the solicitude of real affection. She was resolved that greedy Death should not possess himself, through any fault of hers, of a career so full of bright possibilities and of that active gratitude which a good-natured elderly woman would relish, as she felt that of her *protégé* to be. Her vigils were finally rewarded. One fine morning poor long-silent Ferdinand found words to tell her that he was better. His recovery was very slow, however, and it ceased several degrees below the level from which he had originally fallen. He was thus twice a convalescent,—a sufficiently miserable fellow. He professed to be very much surprised to find himself still among the living. He remained silent and grave, with a newly contracted fold in his forehead, like a man honestly perplexed at the vagaries of destiny. "It must be," he said to Mrs. Mason,—"it must be that I am reserved for great things."

In order to insure absolute quiet in the house, Ferdinand learned Miss Hofmann had removed herself to the house of a friend, at a distance of some five miles. On the first day that the young man was well enough to sit in his arm-chair Mrs. Mason spoke of her niece's return, which was fixed for the morrow. "She will want very much to see you," she said. "When she comes, may I bring her into your room?"

"Good heavens, no!" said Ferdinand, to whom the idea was very disagreeable. He met her accordingly at dinner, three days later. He left his room at the dinner hour, in company with Dr. Knight, who was taking his departure. In the hall they encountered Mrs. Mason, who invited the Doctor to remain, in honor of his patient's reappearance in society. The Doctor hesitated a moment, and, as he did so, Ferdinand heard Miss Hofmann's step descending the stair. He turned towards her just in time to catch on her face the vanishing of a glance of intelligence. As Mrs. Mason's back was against the staircase, her glance was evidently meant for Knight. He excused himself on the plea of an engagement, to Mason's regret, while the latter greeted the younger lady. Mrs. Mason proposed another day,—the following Sunday; the Doctor assented, and it was not till some time later that Ferdinand found himself wondering why Miss Hofmann should have forbidden him to remain. He rapidly perceived that during the period of their separation this young lady had lost none of her charms; on the contrary, they were more irresistible than ever. It seemed to Mason, moreover, that they were bound together by a certain pensive gentleness, a tender, submissive look, which he had hitherto failed to observe. Mrs. Mason's own remarks assured him that he was not the victim of an illusion.

"I wonder what is the matter with Caroline," she said. "If it were not that she tells me that she never was better, I should believe she is feeling unwell. I've never seen her so simple and gentle. She looks like a person who has a great fright,—a fright not altogether unpleasant."

"She has been staying in a house full of people," said Mason. "She has been excited, and amused, and preoccupied; she returns to you and me (excuse the juxtaposition,—it exists)—a kind of reaction asserts itself." Ferdinand's explanation was ingenious rather than plausible.

Mrs. Mason had a better one. "I have an impression," she said, "George Stapleton, the second of the sons, is an old admirer of Caroline's. It's hard to believe that he could have been in the house with her for a fortnight without renewing his suit, in some form or other."

Ferdinand was not made uneasy, for he had seen and talked with Mr. George Stapleton,—a young man very good-looking, very good-natured, very clever, very rich, and very unworthy, as he conceived, of Miss Hofmann. "You don't mean to say that your niece has listened to him," he answered, calmly enough.

"Listened, yes. He has made himself agreeable, and he has succeeded in making an impression,—a temporary impression," added Mrs. Mason with a business-like air.

"I can't believe it," said Ferdinand.

"Why not? He's a very nice fellow."

"Yes,—yes," said Mason, "very nice indeed. He's very rich too." And here the talk was interrupted by Caroline's entrance.

On Sunday the two ladies went to church. It was not till after they had gone that Ferdinand left his room. He came into the little parlor, took up a book, and felt something of the stir of his old intellectual life. Would he ever again know what it was to work? In the course of an hour the ladies came in, radiant with devotional millinery. Mrs. Mason soon went out again, leaving the others together. Miss Hofmann asked Ferdinand what he had been reading; and he was thus led to declare that he really believed he should, after all, get the use of his head again. She listened with all the respect which an intelligent woman who leads an idle life necessarily feels for a clever man when he consents to make her in some degree the confidant of his intellectual purposes. Quickened by her delicious sympathy, her grave attention, and her intelligent questions, he was led to unbosom himself of several of his dearest convictions and projects. It was easy that from this point the conversation should advance to matters of belief and hope in general. Before he knew it, it had done so; and he had thus the great satisfaction of discussing with the woman on whom of all others his selfish and personal happiness was most dependent those great themes in whose expansive magnitude persons and pleasures and passions are absorbed and extinguished, and in whose austere effulgence the brightest divinities of earth remit their shining. Serious passions are a good preparation for the highest kinds of speculation. Although Ferdinand was urging no suit whatever upon his companion, and consciously, at least, making use in no degree of the emotion which accompanied her presence, it is certain that, as they formed themselves, his conceptions were the clearer for being the conceptions of a man in love. And, as for Miss Hofmann, her attention could not, to all appearances, have been more lively, nor her perception more delicate, if the atmosphere of her own intellect had been purified by the sacred fires of a responsive passion.

Knight duly made his appearance at dinner, and proved himself once more the entertaining gentleman whom our friends had long since learned to appreciate. But Mason, fresh from his contest with morals and metaphysics, was forcibly struck with the fact that he was one of those men from whom these sturdy beggars receive more kicks than halfpence. He was nevertheless obliged to admit, that, if he was not a man of principles, he was thoroughly a man of honor. After dinner the company adjourned to the piazza, where, in the course of half an hour, the Doctor proposed to Miss Hofmann to take a turn in the grounds. All around the lawn there wound a narrow footpath, concealed from view in spots by clusters of shrubbery. Ferdinand and his hostess sat watching their retreating figures as they slowly measured the sinuous strip of gravel; Miss Hofmann's light dress and the Doctor's white waistcoat gleaming at intervals through the dark verdure. At the end of twenty minutes they returned to the house. The Doctor came back only to make his bow and to take his departure; and, when he had gone, Miss Hofmann retired to her own room. The next morning she mounted her horse, and rode over to see the friend with whom she had stayed during Mason's fever. Ferdinand saw her pass his window, erect in the saddle, with her horse scattering the gravel with his nervous steps. Shortly afterwards Mrs. Mason came into the room, sat down by the young man, made her habitual inquiries as to his condition, and then paused in such a way that he instantly felt she had something to tell him. "You've something to tell me," he said; "what is it?"

Mrs. Mason blushed a little, and laughed. "I was first made to promise to keep it a secret," she said. "If I'm so transparent now that I have leave to tell it, what should I be if I hadn't? Guess."

Ferdinand shook his head peremptorily. "I give it up."

"Caroline is engaged."

"To whom?"

"Not to Mr. Stapleton,—to Dr. Knight."

Ferdinand was silent a moment; but he neither changed color nor dropped his eyes. Then, at last, "Did she wish you not to tell me?" he asked.

"She wished me to tell no one. But I prevailed upon her to let me tell *you*."

"Thank you," said Ferdinand, with a little bow—and an immense irony.

"It's a great surprise," continued Mrs. Mason. "I never suspected it. And there I was talking about Mr. Stapleton! I don't see how they have managed it. Well, I suppose it's for the best. But it seems odd that Caroline should have refused so many superior offers, to put up at last with Dr. Knight."

Ferdinand had felt for an instant as if the power of speech was deserting him; but volition nailed it down with a great muffled hammer-blow.

"She might do worse," he said mechanically.

Mrs. Mason glanced at him as if struck by the sound of his voice. "You're not surprised, then?"

"I hardly know. I never fancied there was anything between them, and yet, now that I look back, there has been nothing against it. They have talked of each other neither too much nor too little. Upon my soul, they're an accomplished couple!" Glancing back at his friend's constant reserve and self-possession, Ferdinand—strange as it may seem—could not repress a certain impulse of sympathetic admiration. He had had no vulgar rival. "Yes," he repeated gravely, "she might do worse."

"I suppose she might. He's poor, but he's clever; and I'm sure I hope to Heaven he loves her!"

Ferdinand said nothing.

"May I ask," he resumed at length, "whether they became engaged yesterday, on that walk around the lawn?"

"No; it would be fine if they had, under our very noses! It was all done while Caroline was at the Stapletons'. It was agreed between them yesterday that she should tell me at once."

"And when are they to be married?"

"In September, if possible. Caroline told me to tell you that she counts upon your staying for the wedding."

"Staying where?" asked Mason, with a little nervous laugh.

"Staying here, of course,—in the house."

Ferdinand looked his hostess full in the eyes, taking her hand as he did so. " 'The funeral baked meats did coldly furnish forth the marriage tables.' "

"Ah, hold your tongue!" cried Mrs. Mason, pressing his hand. "How can you be so horrible? When Caroline leaves me, Ferdinand, I shall be quite alone. The tie which binds us together will be very much slackened by her marriage. I can't help thinking that it was never very close, when I consider that I've had no part in the most important step of her life. I don't complain. I suppose it's natural enough. Perhaps it's the fashion,—come in with striped petticoats and pea-jackets. Only it makes me feel like an old woman. It removes me twenty years at a bound from my own engagement, and the day I burst out crying on my mother's neck because your uncle had told a young girl I knew, that he thought I had beautiful eyes. Now-a-days I suppose they tell the young ladies themselves, and have them cry on their own necks. It's a great saving of time. But I shall miss Caroline all the same; and then, Ferdinand, I shall make a great deal of you."

"The more the better," said Ferdinand, with the same laugh; and at this moment Mrs. Mason was called away.

Ferdinand had not been a soldier for nothing. He had received a heavy blow, and he resolved to bear it like a man. He refused to allow himself a single moment of self-compassion. On the contrary, he spared himself none of the hard names offered by his passionate vocabulary. For not guessing Caroline's secret, he was perhaps excusable. Women were all inscrutable, and this one especially so. But Knight was a man like himself,

—a man whom he esteemed, but whom he was loath to credit with a deeper and more noiseless current of feeling than his own, for his own was no babbling brook, betraying its course through green leaves. Knight had loved modestly and decently, but frankly and heartily, like a man who was not ashamed of what he was doing, and if he had not found it out it was his own fault. What else had he to do? He had been a besotted day-dreamer, while his friend had simply been a genuine lover. He deserved his injury, and he would bear it in silence. He had been unable to get well on an illusion; he would now try getting well on a truth. This was stern treatment, the reader will admit, likely to kill if it didn't cure.

Miss Hofmann was absent for several hours. At dinner-time she had not returned, and Mrs. Mason and the young man accordingly sat down without her. After dinner Ferdinand went into the little parlor, quite indifferent as to how soon he met her. Seeing or not seeing her, time hung equally heavy. Shortly after her companions had risen from table, she rode up to the door, dismounted, tired and hungry, passed directly into the dining-room, and sat down to eat in her habit. In half an hour she came out, and, crossing the hall on her way up stairs, saw Mason in the parlor. She turned round, and, gathering up her long skirts with one hand, while she held a little sweet-cake to her lips with the other, stopped at the door to bid him good day. He left his chair, and went towards her. Her face wore a somewhat weary smile.

"So you're going to be married," he began abruptly.

Miss Hofmann assented with a slight movement of her head.

"I congratulate you. Excuse me if I don't do it with the last grace. I feel all I dare to feel."

"Don't be afraid," said Caroline, smiling, and taking a bite from her cake.

"I'm not sure that it's not more unexpected than even such things have a right to be. There's no doubt about it?"

"None whatever."

"Well, Knight's a very good fellow. I haven't seen him yet," he pursued, as Caroline was silent. "I don't know that I'm in any hurry to see him. But I mean to talk to him. I mean to tell him that if he doesn't do his duty by you, I shall—"

"Well?"

"I shall remind him of it."

"O, I shall do that," said Miss Hofmann.

Ferdinand looked at her gravely. "By Heaven! you know," he cried with intensity, "it must be either one thing or the other."

"I don't understand you."

"O, I understand myself. You're not a woman to be thrown away, Miss Hofmann."

Caroline made a gesture of impatience. "I don't understand you," she repeated. "You must excuse me. I'm very tired." And she went rapidly up stairs.

On the following day Ferdinand had an opportunity to make his compliments to the Doctor. "I don't congratulate you on doing it," he said, "so much as on the way you've done it."

"What do you know about the way?" asked Knight.

"Nothing whatever. That's just it. You took good care of that. And you're to be married in the autumn?"

"I hope so. Very quietly, I suppose. The parson to do it, and Mrs. Mason and my mother and you to see it's done properly." And the Doctor put his hand on Ferdinand's shoulder.

"O, I'm the last person to choose," said Mason. "If he were to omit anything, I should take good care not to cry out." It is often said, that, next to great joy, no state of mind is so frolicsome as great distress. It was in virtue of this truth, I suppose, that Ferdinand was able to be facetious. He kept his spirits. He talked and smiled and lounged about with the same deferential languor as before. During the interval before the time appointed for the wedding it was agreed between the parties interested that Miss Hofmann should go over and spend a few days with her future mother-in-law, where she might partake more freely and privately than at home of the pleasure of her lover's company. She was absent a week; a week during which Ferdinand was thrown entirely upon his hostess for entertain-

ment and diversion,—things he had a very keen sense of needing. There were moments when it seemed to him that he was
living by mere force of will, and that, if he loosened the screws
for a single instant, he would sink back upon his bed again, and
never leave it. He had forbidden himself to think of Caroline,
and had prescribed a course of meditation upon that other mistress, his first love, with whom he had long since exchanged
pledges,—she of a hundred names,—work, letters, philosophy,
fame. But, after Caroline had gone, it was supremely difficult
not to think of her. Even in absence she was supremely conspicuous. The most that Ferdinand could do was to take refuge in
books,—an immense number of which he now read, fiercely,
passionately, voraciously,—in conversation with Mrs. Mason,
and in such society as he found in his path. Mrs. Mason was a
great gossip,—a gossip on a scale so magnificent as to trans-
form the foible into a virtue. A gossip, moreover, of imagination, dealing with the future as well as the present and the
past,—with a host of delightful half-possibilities, as well as
with stale hyper-verities. With her, then, Ferdinand talked of
his own future, into which she entered with the most outspo-
ken and intelligent sympathy. "A man," he declared, "couldn't
do better; and a man certainly would do worse." Mrs. Mason
arranged a European tour and a residence for her nephew, in
the manner of one who knew her ground. Caroline once married, she herself would go abroad, and fix herself in one of the
several capitals in which an American widow with an easy income may contrive to support existence. She would make her
dwelling a base of supplies—a *pied-à-terre*—for Ferdinand,
who should take his time to it, and visit every accessible spot in
Europe and the East. She would leave him free to go and come
as he pleased, and to live as he listed; and I may say that, thanks
to Mrs. Mason's observation of Continental manners, this
broad allowance covered in her view quite as much as it did in
poor Ferdinand's, who had never been out of his own country.
All that she would ask of him would be to show himself say
twice a year in her drawing-room, and to tell her stories of what

he had seen; that drawing-room which she already saw in her mind's eye,—a compact little *entresol* with tapestry hangings in the doorways and a coach-house in the court attached. Mrs. Mason was not a severe moralist; but she was quite too sensible a woman to wish to demoralize her nephew, and to persuade him to trifle with his future,—that future of which the war had already made light, in its own grim fashion. Nay, she loved him; she thought him the cleverest, the most promising, of young men. She looked to the day when his name would be on men's lips, and it would be a great piece of good fortune to have very innocently married his uncle. Herself a great observer of men and manners, she wished to give him advantages which had been sterile in her own case.

In the way of society, Ferdinand made calls with his hostess, went out twice to dine, and caused Mrs. Mason herself to entertain company at dinner. He presided on these occasions with distinguished good grace. It happened, moreover, that invitations had been out some days for a party at the Stapletons',—Miss Hofmann's friends,—and that, as there was to be no dancing, Ferdinand boldly announced his intention of going thither. "Who knows?" he said; "it may do me more good than harm. We can go late, and come away early." Mrs. Mason doubted of the wisdom of the act; but she finally assented, and prepared herself. It was late when they left home, and when they arrived the rooms—rooms of exceptional vastness—were at their fullest. Mason received on this his first appearance in society a most flattering welcome, and in a very few moments found himself in exclusive possession of Miss Edith Stapleton, Caroline's particular friend. This young lady has had no part in our story, because our story is perforce short, and condemned to pick and choose its constituent elements. With the least bit wider compass we might long since have whispered to the reader, that Miss Stapleton—who was a charming girl—had conceived a decided preference for our Ferdinand over all other men whomsoever. That Ferdinand was utterly ignorant of the circumstance is our excuse for passing it by; and we linger upon it, therefore, only long enough to suggest that the young girl must have been very happy at this particular moment.

"Is Miss Hofmann here?" Mason asked, as he accompanied her into an adjoining room.

"Do you call that being here?" said Miss Stapleton, looking across the apartment. Mason, too, looked across.

There he beheld Miss Hofmann, full-robed in white, standing fronted by a semicircle of no less than five gentlemen,—all good-looking and splendid. Her head and shoulders rose serene from the *bouillonnement* of her beautiful dress, and she looked and listened with that half-abstracted air which is pardonable in a woman beset by half a dozen admirers. When Caroline's eyes fell upon her friend, she stared a moment, surprised, and then made him the most gracious bow in the world,— a bow so gracious that her little circle half divided itself to let it pass, and looked around to see where the deuce it was going. Taking advantage of this circumstance, Miss Hofmann advanced several steps. Ferdinand went towards her, and there, in sight of a hundred men and as many women, she gave him her hand, and smiled upon him with extraordinary sweetness. They went back together to Miss Stapleton, and Caroline made him sit down, she and her friend placing themselves on either side. For half an hour Ferdinand had the honor of engrossing the attention of the two most charming girls present,—and, thanks to this distinction, indeed the attention of the whole company. After which the two young ladies had him introduced successively to every maiden and matron in the assembly in the least remarkable for loveliness or wit. Ferdinand rose to the level of the occasion, and conducted himself with unprecedented gallantry. Upon others he made, of course, the best impression, but to himself he was an object almost of awe. I am compelled to add, however, that he was obliged to fortify himself with repeated draughts of wine; and that even with the aid of this artificial stimulant he was unable to conceal from Mrs. Mason and his physician that he was looking far too much like an invalid to be properly where he was.

"Was there ever anything like the avidity of these dreadful girls?" said Mrs. Mason to the Doctor. "They'll let a man swoon at their feet sooner than abridge a *tête-à-tête* that amuses them. Then they'll have up another. Look at little Miss McCarthy, yonder, with Ferdinand and George Stapleton before her. She's got them contradicting each other, and she looks like a Roman fast lady at the circus. What does she care so long as she makes her evening? They like a man to look as if he were going to die,—it's interesting."

Knight went over to his friend, and told him sternly that it was high time he should be at home and in bed. "You're looking horribly," he added shrewdly, as Ferdinand resisted.

"You're *not* looking horribly, Colonel Mason," said Miss McCarthy, a very audacious little person, overhearing this speech.

"It isn't a matter of taste, madam," said the Doctor, angrily; "it's a fact." And he led away his patient.

Ferdinand insisted that he had not hurt himself, that, on the contrary, he was feeling uncommonly well; but his face contradicted him. He continued for two or three days more to play at "feeling well," with a courage worthy of a better cause. Then at last he let disease have its way. He settled himself on his pillows, and fingered his watch, and began to wonder how many revolutions he would still witness of those exquisite little needles. The Doctor came, and gave him a sound rating for what he called his imprudence. Ferdinand heard him out patiently; and then assured him that prudence or imprudence had nothing to do with it; that death had taken fast hold of him, and that now his only concern was to make easy terms with his captor. In the course of the same day he sent for a lawyer and altered his will. He had no known relatives, and his modest patrimony stood bequeathed to a gentleman of his acquaintance who had no real need of it. He now divided it into two unequal portions, the smaller of which he devised to William Bowles, Mrs. Mason's man-servant and his personal attendant; and the larger—which represented a considerable sum—to

Horace Knight. He informed Mrs. Mason of these arrangements, and was pleased to have her approval.

From this moment his strength began rapidly to ebb, and the shattered fragments of his long-resisting will floated down its shallow current into dissolution. It was useless to attempt to talk, to beguile the interval, to watch the signs, or to count the hours. A constant attendant was established at his side, and Mrs. Mason appeared only at infrequent moments. The poor woman felt that her heart was broken, and spent a great deal of time in weeping. Miss Hofmann remained, naturally, at Mrs. Knight's. "As far as I can judge," Horace had said, "it will be a matter of a week. But it's the most extraordinary case I ever heard of. The man was steadily getting well." On the fifth day he had driven Miss Hofmann home, at her suggestion that it was no more than decent that she should give the young man some sign of sympathy. Horace went up to Ferdinand's bedside, and found the poor fellow in the languid middle condition between sleeping and waking in which he had passed the last forty-eight hours. "Colonel," he asked gently, "do you think you could see Caroline?"

For all answer, Ferdinand opened his eyes. Horace went out, and led his companion back into the darkened room. She came softly up to the bedside, stood looking down for a moment at the sick man, and then stooped over him.

"I thought I'd come and make you a little visit," she said. "Does it disturb you?"

"Not in the least," said Mason, looking her steadily in the eyes. "Not half as much as it would have done a week ago. Sit down."

"Thank you. Horace won't let me. I'll come again."

"You'll not have another chance," said Ferdinand. "I'm not good for more than two days yet. Tell them to go out. I wish to see you alone. I wouldn't have sent for you, but, now that you're here, I might as well take advantage of it."

"Have you anything particular to say?" asked Knight, kindly.

"O, come," said Mason, with a smile which he meant to be good-natured, but which was only ghastly; "you're not going to be jealous of me at this time of day."

Knight looked at Miss Hofmann for permission, and then left the room with the nurse. But a minute had hardly elapsed before Miss Hofmann hurried into the adjoining apartment, with her face pale and discomposed.

"Go to him!" she exclaimed. "He's dying!"

When they reached him he was dead.

In the course of a few days his will was opened, and Knight came to the knowledge of his legacy. "He was a good, generous fellow," he said to Mrs. Mason and Miss Hofmann, "and I shall never be satisfied that he mightn't have recovered. It was a most extraordinary case." He was considerate enough of his audience to abstain from adding that he would give a great deal to have been able to make an autopsy. Miss Hofmann's wedding was, of course, not deferred. She was married in September, "very quietly." It seemed to her lover, in the interval, that she was very silent and thoughtful. But this was certainly natural under the circumstances.

1868

CRAWFORD'S CONSISTENCY

WE were great friends, and it was natural that he should have let me know with all the promptness of his ardor that his happiness was complete. Ardor is here, perhaps, a misleading word, for Crawford's passion burned with a still and hidden flame; if he had written sonnets to his mistress's eyebrow, he had never declaimed them in public. But he was deeply in love; he had been full of tremulous hopes and fears, and his happiness, for several weeks, had hung by a hair—the extremely fine line that appeared to divide the yea and nay of the young lady's parents. The scale descended at last with their heavily-weighted consent in it, and Crawford gave himself up to tranquil bliss. He came to see me at my office—my name, on the little tin placard beneath my window, was garnished with an M.D., as vivid as new gilding could make it—long before that period of the morning at which my irrepressible buoyancy had succumbed to the teachings of experience (as it usually did about twelve o'clock), and resigned itself to believe that the particular day was not to be distinguished by the advent of the female form that haunted my dreams—the confiding old lady, namely, with a large account at the bank, and a mild, but expensive chronic malady. On that day I quite forgot the paucity of my patients and the vanity of my hopes in my enjoyment of Crawford's contagious felicity. If we had been less united in friendship, I might have envied him; but as it was, with my extreme admiration and affection for him, I felt for half an hour as if I were going to marry the lovely Elizabeth myself. I reflected after he had left me that I was very glad I was not, for lovely as Miss Ingram was, she had always inspired me with a vague mistrust. There was no harm in her, certainly; but there was nothing else either. I don't know to what I compared her—to a blushing rose that had no odor, to a blooming peach that had no taste. All that nature had asked of her was to be the prettiest girl of her time, and this request she obeyed to the letter. But when, of a morning, she had opened wide her beautiful, candid eyes, and half parted her clear, pink lips, and gathered up her splendid golden tresses, her day, as far as her own opportunity was concerned, was at an end; she had put her house in order, and she could fold her arms. She did so invariably, and it was in this attitude that Crawford saw her and fell in love with her. I could heartily congratulate him, for the fact that a blooming statue would make no wife for me, did not in the least discredit his own choice. I was human and erratic; I had an uneven temper and a prosaic soul. I wished to get as much as I gave—to be the planet, in short, and not the satellite. But Crawford had really virtue enough for two—enough of vital fire, of intelligence and devotion. He could afford to marry an inanimate beauty, for he had the wisdom which would supply her shortcomings, and the generosity which would forgive them.

Crawford was a tall man, and not particularly well made. He had, however, what is called a gentlemanly figure, and he had a very fine head—the head of a man of books, a student, a philosopher, such as he really was. He had a dark coloring, thin, fine black hair, a very clear, lucid, dark gray eye, and features of a sort of softly-vigorous outline. It was as if his face had been cast first in a rather rugged and irregular mold, and the image had then been lightly retouched, here and there, by some gentler, more feminine hand. His expression was singular; it was a look which I can best describe as a sort of intelligent innocence—the look of an absent-minded seraph. He knew, if you insisted upon it, about the corruptions of this base world; but, left to himself, he never thought of them. What he did think of, I can hardly tell you: of a great many things, often, in which I was not needed. Of this, long and well as I had known him, I was perfectly conscious. I had never got behind him, as it were; I had never walked all round him. He was reserved, as I am inclined to think that all first-rate men are; not capriciously or consciously reserved, but reserved in spite of, and in the midst of, an extreme frankness. For most people he was a clear-visaged, scrupulously polite young man, who, in giving up business so suddenly, had done a thing which required a good deal of charitable explanation, and who was not expected to express any sentiments more personal than a literary opinion reinforced by the name of some authority, as to whose titles and attributes much vagueness of knowledge was excusable. For me, his literary opinions were the lightest of his sentiments; his good manners, too, I am sure, cost him nothing. Bad manners are the result of irritability, and as Crawford was not irritable he found civility very easy. But if his urbanity was not victory over a morose disposition, it was at least the expression of a very agreeable character. He talked a great deal, though not volubly, stammering a little, and casting about him for his words. When you suggested one, he always accepted it thankfully,—though he sometimes brought in a little later the expression he had been looking for and which had since occurred to him. He had a great deal of gayety, and made jokes and enjoyed them— laughing constantly, with a laugh that was not so much audible as visible. He was extremely deferential to old people, and among the fairer sex, his completest conquests, perhaps, were the ladies of sixty-five and seventy. He had also a great kindness for shabby people, if they were only shabby enough, and I remember seeing him, one summer afternoon, carrying a baby across a crowded part of Broadway, accompanied by its mother, —a bewildered pauper, lately arrived from Europe. Crawford's father had left him a very good property; his income, in New York, in those days, passed for a very easy one. Mr. Crawford was a cotton-broker, and on his son's leaving college, he took him into his business. But shortly after his father's death he sold out his interest in the firm—very quietly, and without asking any one's advice, because, as he told me, he hated buying and selling. There were other things, of course, in the world that he hated too, but this is the only thing of which I remember to have heard him say it. He had a large house, quite to himself (he had lost his mother early, and his brothers were dispersed); he filled it with books and scientific instruments, and passed most of his time in reading and in making awkward experiments. He had the tastes of a scholar, and he consumed a vast number of octavos; but in the way of the natural sciences, his curiosity was greater than his dexterity. I used to laugh at his experiments and, as a thrifty neophyte in medicine, to deprecate his lavish expenditure of precious drugs. Unburdened, independent, master of an all-sufficient fortune, and of the best education that the country could afford, good-looking, gallant, amiable, urbane—Crawford at seven and twenty might fairly be believed to have drawn the highest prizes in life. And, indeed, except that it was a pity he had not stuck to business, no man heard a word of disparagement either of his merit or of his felicity. On the other hand, too, he was not envied—envied at any rate with any degree of bitterness. We are told that though the world worships success, it hates successful people. Certainly it never hated Crawford. Perhaps he was not regarded in the light of a success, but rather of an ornament, of an agreeable gift to society. The world likes to be pleased, and there was something pleasing in Crawford's general physiognomy and position. They rested the eyes; they were a gratifying change. Perhaps we were even a little proud of having among us so harmonious an embodiment of the amenities of life.

In spite of his bookish tastes and habits, Crawford was not a recluse. I remember his once saying to me that there were some sacrifices that only a man of genius was justified in making to science, and he knew very well that he was not a man of genius. He was not, thank heaven; if he had been, he would have been a much more difficult companion. It was never apparent, indeed, that he was destined to make any great use of his acquisitions. Every one supposed, of course, that he would "write something"; but he never put pen to paper. He liked to bury his nose in books for the hour's pleasure; he had no dangerous *arrière pensée*, and he was simply a very perfect specimen of a class which has fortunately always been numerous—the class of men who contribute to the advancement of learning by zealously opening their ears and religiously closing their lips. He was fond of society, and went out, as the phrase is, a great deal,—the mammas in especial, making him extremely welcome. What the daughters, in general, thought of him, I hardly know; I suspect that the younger ones often preferred worse men. Crawford's merits were rather thrown away upon little girls. To a considerable number of wise virgins, however, he must have been an object of high admiration, and if a good observer had been asked to pick out in the whole town, the most propitious victim to matrimony, he would certainly have designated my friend. There was nothing to be said against him—there was not a shadow in the picture. He himself, indeed, pretended to be in no hurry to marry, and I heard him more than once declare, that he did not know what he should do with a wife, or what a wife would do with him. Of course we often talked of this matter, and I—upon whom the burden of bachelorhood sat heavy—used to say, that in his place, with money to keep a wife, I would change my condition on the morrow. Crawford gave a great many opposing reasons; of course the real one was that he was very happy as he was, and that the most circumspect marriage is always a risk.

"A man should only marry in self-defense," he said, "as Luther became Protestant. He should wait till he is driven to the wall."

Some time passed and our Luther stood firm. I began to despair of ever seeing a pretty Mrs. Crawford offer me a white hand from my friend's fireside, and I had to console myself with the reflection, that some of the finest persons of whom history makes mention, had been celibates, and that a desire to lead a single life is not necessarily a proof of a morose disposition.

"Oh, I give you up," I said at last. "I hoped that if you did not marry for your own sake, you would at least marry for mine. It would make your house so much pleasanter for me. But you have no heart! To avenge myself, I shall myself take a wife on the first opportunity. She shall be as pretty as a picture, and you shall never enter my doors."

"No man should be accounted single till he is dead," said Crawford. "I have been reading Stendhal lately, and learning the philosophy of the *coup de foudre*. It is not impossible that there is a *coup de foudre* waiting for me. All I can say is that it will be lightning from a clear sky."

The lightning fell, in fact, a short time afterward. Crawford saw Miss Ingram, admired her, observed her, and loved her. The impression she produced upon him was indeed a sort of summing up of the impression she produced upon society at large. The circumstances of her education and those under which she made her first appearance in the world, were such as to place her beauty in extraordinary relief. She had been brought up more in the manner of an Italian princess of the middle ages—sequestered from conflicting claims of ward-ship—than as the daughter of a plain American citizen. Up to her eighteenth year, it may be said, mortal eye had scarcely be-held her; she lived behind high walls and triple locks, through which an occasional rumor of her beauty made its way into the world. Mrs. Ingram was a second or third cousin of my mother, but the two ladies, between whom there reigned a scanty sym-pathy, had never made much of the kinship; I had inherited no claim to intimacy with the family, and Elizabeth was a perfect stranger to me. Her parents had, for economy, gone to live in the country—at Orange—and it was there, in a high-hedged old garden, that her childhood and youth were spent. The first definite mention of her loveliness came to me from old Dr. Beadle, who had been called to attend her in a slight illness. (The Ingrams were poor, but their daughter was their golden goose, and to secure the most expensive medical skill was but an act of common prudence.) Dr. Beadle had a high apprecia-tion of a pretty patient; he, of course, kept it within bounds on the field of action, but he enjoyed expressing it afterward with the freedom of a profound anatomist, to a younger colleague. Elizabeth Ingram, according to this report, was perfect in every particular, and she was being kept in cotton in preparation for her *début* in New York. He talked about her for a quarter of an hour, and concluded with an eloquent pinch of snuff; whereupon I remembered that she was, after a fashion, my cousin, and that pretty cousins are a source of felicity, in this hard world, which no man can afford to neglect. I took a holiday, jumped into the train, and arrived at Orange. There, in a pretty cottage, in a shaded parlor, I found a small, spare woman with a high forehead and a pointed chin, whom I immediately felt to be that Sabrina Ingram, in her occasional allusions to whom my poor mother had expended the very small supply of acerbity with which nature had intrusted her.

"I am told my cousin is extremely beautiful," I said. "I should like so much to see her."

The interview was not prolonged. Mrs. Ingram was frigidly polite; she answered that she was highly honored by my curiosity, but that her daughter had gone to spend the day with a friend ten miles way. On my departure, as I turned to latch the garden gate behind me, I saw dimly through an upper window, the gleam of a golden head, and the orbits of two gazing eyes. I kissed my hand to the apparition, and agreed with Dr. Beadle that my cousin was a beauty. But if her image had been dim, that of her mother had been distinct.

They came up to New York the next winter, took a house, gave a great party, and presented the young girl to an astonished world. I succeeded in making little of our cousinship, for Mrs. Ingram did not approve of me, and she gave Elizabeth instructions in consequence. Elizabeth obeyed them, gave me the tips of her fingers, and answered me in monosyllables. Indifference was never more neatly expressed, and I wondered whether this was mere passive compliance, or whether the girl had put a grain of her own intelligence into it. She appeared to have no more intelligence than a snowy-fleeced lamb, but I fancied that she was, by instinct, a shrewd little politician. Nevertheless, I forgave her, for my last feeling about her was one of compassion. She might be as soft as swan's-down, I said; it could not be a pleasant thing to be her mother's daughter, all the same. Mrs. Ingram had black bands of hair, without a white thread, which descended only to the tops of her ears, and were there spread out very wide, and polished like metallic plates. She had small, conscious eyes, and the tall white forehead I have mentioned, which resembled a high gable beneath a steep roof. Her chin looked like her forehead reversed, and her lips were perpetually graced with a thin, false smile. I had seen how little it cost them to tell a categorical fib. Poor Mr. Ingram was a helpless colossus; an immense man with a small plump face, a huge back to his neck, and a pair of sloping shoulders. In talking to you, he generally looked across at his wife, and it was easy to see that he was mortally afraid of her.

For this lady's hesitation to bestow her daughter's hand upon Crawford, there was a sufficiently good reason. He had money, but he had not money enough. It was a very comfortable match, but it was not a splendid one, and Mrs. Ingram, in putting the young girl forward, had primed herself with the highest expectations. The marriage was so good that it was a vast pity it was not a little better. If Crawford's income had only been twice as large again, Mrs. Ingram would have pushed Elizabeth into his arms, relaxed in some degree the consuming eagerness with which she viewed the social field, and settled down, possibly, to contentment and veracity. That was a bad year in the matrimonial market, for higher offers were not freely made. Elizabeth was greatly admired, but the ideal suitor did not present himself. I suspect that Mrs. Ingram's charms as a mother-in-law had been accurately gauged. Crawford pushed his suit, with low-toned devotion, and he was at last accepted with a good grace. There had been, I think, a certain amount of general indignation at his being kept waiting, and Mrs. Ingram was accused here and there, of not knowing a first-rate man when she saw one. "I never said she was honest," a trenchant critic was heard to observe, "but at least I supposed she was clever." Crawford was not afraid of her; he told me so distinctly. "I defy her to quarrel with me," he said, "and I don't despair of making her like me."

"Like you!" I answered. "That's easily done. The difficulty will be in your liking her."

"Oh, I do better—I admire her," he said. "She knows so perfectly what she wants. It's a rare quality. I shall have a very fine woman for my mother-in-law."

Elizabeth's own preference bore down the scale in Crawford's favor a little, I think; how much I hardly know. She liked him, and though her mother took little account of her likes (and the young girl was too well-behaved to expect it), Mrs. Ingram reflected probably that her pink and white complexion would last longer if she were married to a man she fancied. At any rate, as I have said, the engagement was at last announced, and Crawford came in person to tell me of it. I had never seen a happier-looking man; and his image, as I beheld it that morning, has lived in my memory all these years, as an embodiment of youthful confidence and deep security. He had said that the art of knowing what one wants was rare, but he apparently possessed it. He had got what he wanted, and the sense of possession was exquisite to him. I see again my shabby little consulting-room, with an oil-cloth on the floor, and a paper, representing seven hundred and forty times (I once counted them) a young woman with a pitcher on her head, on the walls; and in the midst of it I see Crawford standing upright, with his thumbs in the arm-holes of his waistcoat, his head thrown back, and his eyes as radiant as two planets.

"You are too odiously happy," I said. "I should like to give you a dose of something to tone you down."

"If you could give me a sleeping potion," he answered, "I should be greatly obliged to you. Being engaged is all very well, but I want to be married. I should like to sleep through my engagement—to wake up and find myself a husband."

"Is your wedding-day fixed?" I asked.

"The twenty-eighth of April—three months hence. I declined to leave the house last night before it was settled. I offered three weeks, but Elizabeth laughed me to scorn. She says it will take a month to make her wedding-dress. Mrs. Ingram has a list of reasons as long as your arm, and every one of them is excellent; that is the abomination of it. She has a genius for the practical. I mean to profit by it; I shall make her turn my mill-wheel for me. But meanwhile it's an eternity!"

"Don't complain of good things lasting long," said I. "Such eternities are always too short. I have always heard that the three months before marriage are the happiest time of life. I advise you to make the most of these."

"Oh, I am happy, I don't deny it," cried Crawford. "But I propose to be happier yet." And he marched away with the step of a sun-god beginning his daily circuit.

He was happier yet, in the sense that with each succeeding week he became more convinced of the charms of Elizabeth Ingram, and more profoundly attuned to the harmonies of prospective matrimony. I, of course, saw little of him, for he was always in attendance upon his betrothed, at the dwelling of whose parents I was a rare visitor. Whenever I did see him, he seemed to have sunk another six inches further into the mystic depths. He formally swallowed his words when I recalled to him his former brave speeches about the single life.

"All I can say is," he answered, "that I was an immeasurable donkey. Every argument that I formerly used in favor of not marrying, now seems to me to have an exactly opposite application. Every reason that used to seem to me so good for not taking a wife, now seems to me the best reason in the world for taking one. I not to marry, of all men on earth! Why, I am made on purpose for it, and if the thing did not exist, I should have invented it. In fact, I think I *have* invented some little improvements in the institution—of an extremely conservative kind—and when I put them into practice, you shall tell me what you think of them."

This lasted several weeks. The day after Crawford told me of his engagement, I had gone to pay my respects to the two ladies, but they were not at home, and I wrote my compliments on a card. I did not repeat my visit until the engagement had become an old story—some three weeks before the date appointed for the marriage—I had then not seen Crawford in several days. I called in the evening, and was ushered into a small parlor reserved by Mrs. Ingram for familiar visitors. Here I found Crawford's mother-in-law that was to be, seated, with an air of great dignity, on a low chair, with her hands folded rigidly in her lap, and her chin making an acuter angle than ever. Before the fire stood Peter Ingram, with his hands under his coat-tails; as soon as I came in, he fixed his eyes upon his wife. "She has either just been telling, or she is just about to tell, some particularly big fib," I said to myself. Then I expressed my regret at not having found my cousin at home upon my former visit, and hoped it was not too late to offer my felicitations upon Elizabeth's marriage.

For some moments, Mr. Ingram and his wife were silent; after which, Mrs. Ingram said with a little cough, "It *is* too late."

"Really?" said I. "What has happened?"

"Had we better tell him, my dear?" asked Mr. Ingram.

"I didn't mean to receive any one," said Mrs. Ingram. "It was a mistake your coming in."

"I don't offer to go," I answered, "because I suspect that you have some sorrow. I couldn't think of leaving you at such a moment."

Mr. Ingram looked at me with huge amazement. I don't think he detected my irony, but he had a vague impression that I was measuring my wits with his wife. His ponderous attention acted upon me as an incentive, and I continued.

"Crawford has been behaving badly, I suspect?—Oh, the shabby fellow!"

"Oh, not exactly behaving," said Mr. Ingram; "not exactly badly. We can't say that, my dear, eh?"

"It is proper the world should know it," said Mrs. Ingram, addressing herself to me; "and as I suspect you are a great gossip, the best way to diffuse the information will be to intrust it to you."

"Pray tell me," I said bravely, "and you may depend upon it the world shall have an account of it." By this time I knew what was coming. "Perhaps you hardly need tell me," I went on. "I have guessed your news; it is indeed most shocking. Crawford has broken his engagement!"

Mrs. Ingram started up, surprised into self-betrayal. "Oh, really?" she cried, with a momentary flash of elation. But in an instant she perceived that I had spoken fantastically, and her elation flickered down into keen annoyance. But she faced the situation with characteristic firmness. "We have broken the engagement," she said. "Elizabeth has broken it with our consent."

"You have turned Crawford away?" I cried.

"We have requested him to consider everything at an end."

"Poor Crawford!" I exclaimed with ardor.

At this moment the door was thrown open, and Crawford in person stood on the threshold. He paused an instant, like a falcon hovering; then he darted forward at Mr. Ingram.

"In heaven's name," he cried, "what is the meaning of your letter?"

Mr. Ingram looked frightened and backed majestically away. "Really, sir," he said; "I must beg you to desist from your threats."

Crawford turned to Mrs. Ingram; he was intensely pale and profoundly agitated. "Please tell me," he said, stepping toward her with clasped hands. "I don't understand—I can't take it this way. It's a thunderbolt!"

"We were in hopes you would have the kindness not to make a scene," said Mrs. Ingram. "It is very painful for us, too, but we cannot discuss the matter. I was afraid you would come."

"Afraid I would come!" cried Crawford. "Could you have believed I would not come? Where is Elizabeth?"

"You cannot see her!"

"I cannot see her?"

"It is impossible. It is her wish," said Mrs. Ingram.

Crawford stood staring, his eyes distended with grief, and rage, and helpless wonder. I have never seen a man so thoroughly agitated, but I have also never seen a man exert such an effort at self-control. He sat down; and then, after a moment— "What have I done?" he asked.

Mr. Ingram walked away to the window, and stood closely examining the texture of the drawn curtains. "You have done nothing, my dear Mr. Crawford," said Mrs. Ingram. "We accuse you of nothing. We are very reasonable; I'm sure you can't deny that, whatever you may say. Mr. Ingram explained everything in the letter. We have simply thought better of it. We have decided that we can't part with our child for the present. She is all we have, and she is so very young. We ought never to have consented. But you urged us so, and we were so good-natured. We must keep her with us."

"Is that all you have to say?" asked Crawford.

"It seems to me it is quite enough," said Mrs Ingram.

Crawford leaned his head on his hands. "I must have done something without knowing it," he said at last. "In heaven's name tell me what it is, and I will do penance and make reparation to the uttermost limit."

Mr. Ingram turned round, rolling his expressionless eyes in quest of virtuous inspiration. "We can't say that you have done anything; that would be going too far. But if you had, we would have forgiven you."

"Where is Elizabeth?" Crawford again demanded.

"In her own apartment," said Mrs. Ingram majestically.

"Will you please to send for her?"

"Really, sir, we must decline to expose our child to this painful scene."

"Your tenderness should have begun farther back. Do you expect me to go away without seeing her?"

"We request that you will."

Crawford turned to me. "Was such a request ever made before?" he asked, in a trembling voice.

"For your own sake," said Mrs. Ingram, "go away without seeing her."

"For my own sake? What do you mean?"

Mrs. Ingram, very pale, and with her thin lips looking like the blades of a pair of scissors, turned to her husband. "Mr. Ingram," she said, "rescue me from this violence. Speak out—do your duty."

Mr. Ingram advanced with the air and visage of the stage manager of a theater, when he steps forward to announce that the favorite of the public will not be able to play. "Since you drive us so hard, sir, we must tell the painful truth. My poor child would rather have had nothing said about it. The truth is that she has mistaken the character of her affection for you. She has a high esteem for you, but she does not love you."

Crawford stood silent, looking with formidable eyes from the father to the mother. "I must insist upon seeing Elizabeth," he said at last.

Mrs. Ingram gave a toss of her head. "Remember it was your own demand!" she cried, and rustled stiffly out of the room.

We remained silent; Mr. Ingram sat slowly rubbing his knees, and Crawford, pacing up and down, eyed him askance with an intensely troubled frown, as one might eye a person just ascertained to be liable to some repulsive form of dementia. At the end of five minutes, Mrs. Ingram returned, clutching the arm of her daughter, whom she pushed into the room. Then followed the most extraordinary scene of which I have ever been witness.

Crawford strode toward the young girl, and seized her by both hands; she let him take them, and stood looking at him. "Is this horrible news true?" he cried. "What infernal machination is at the bottom of it?"

Elizabeth Ingram appeared neither more nor less composed than on most occasions; the pink and white of her cheeks was as pure as usual, her golden tresses were as artistically braided, and her eyes showed no traces of weeping. Her face was never expressive, and at this moment it indicated neither mortification nor defiance. She met her lover's eyes with the exquisite blue of her own pupils, and she looked as beautiful as an angel. "I am very sorry that we must separate," she said. "But I have mistaken the nature of my affection for you. I have the highest esteem for you, but I do not love you."

I listened to this, and the clear, just faintly trembling, child-like tone in which it was uttered, with absorbing wonder. Was the girl the most consummate of actresses, or had she, literally, no more sensibility than an expensive wax doll? I never discovered, and she has remained to this day, one of the unsolved mysteries of my experience. I incline to believe that she was, morally, absolutely nothing but the hollow reed through which her mother spoke, and that she was really no more cruel now than she had been kind before. But there was something monstrous in her quiet, flute-like utterance of Crawford's damnation.

"Do you say this from your own heart, or have you been instructed to say it? You use the same words your father has just used."

"What can the poor child do better in her trouble than use her father's words?" cried Mrs. Ingram.

"Elizabeth," cried Crawford, "you don't love me?"

"No, Mr. Crawford."

"Why did you ever say so?"

"I never said so."

He stared at her in amazement, and then, after a little—"It is very true," he exclaimed. "You never said so. It was only I who said so."

"Good-bye!" said Elizabeth; and turning away, she glided out of the room.

"I hope you are satisfied, sir," said Mrs. Ingram. "The poor child is before all things sincere."

In calling this scene the most extraordinary that I ever beheld, I had particularly in mind the remarkable attitude of Crawford at this juncture. He effected a change of base, as it were, under the eyes of the enemy—he descended to the depths and rose to the surface again. Horrified, bewildered, outraged, fatally wounded at heart, he took the full measure of his loss, gauged its irreparableness, and, by an amazing effort of the will, while one could count fifty, superficially accepted the situation.

"I have understood nothing!" he said. "Good-night."

He went away, and of course I went with him. Outside the house, in the darkness, he paused and looked around at me.

"What were you doing there?" he asked.

"I had come—rather late in the day—to pay a visit of congratulation. I rather missed it."

"Do you understand—can you imagine?" He had taken his hat off, and he was pressing his hand to his head.

"They have backed out, simply!" I said. "The marriage had never satisfied their ambition—you were not rich enough. Perhaps they have heard of something better."

He stood gazing, lost in thought. "They," I had said; but he, of course, was thinking only of *her*; thinking with inexpressible bitterness. He made no allusion to her, and I never afterward heard him make one. I felt a great compassion for him, but knew not how to help him, nor hardly, even, what to say. It would have done me good to launch some objurgation against the precious little puppet, within doors, but this delicacy forbade. I felt that Crawford's silence covered a fathomless sense of injury; but the injury was terribly real, and I could think of no healing words. He was injured in his love and his pride, his hopes and his honor, his sense of justice and of decency.

"To treat *me* so!" he said at last, in a low tone. "Me! me!—are they blind—are they imbecile? Haven't they seen what I have been to them—what I was going to be?"

"Yes, they are blind brutes!" I cried. "Forget them—don't think of them again. They are not worth it."

He turned away and, in the dark empty street, he leaned his arm on the iron railing that guarded a flight of steps, and dropped his head upon it. I left him standing so a few moments—I could just hear his sobs. Then I passed my arm into his own and walked home with him. Before I left him, he had recovered his outward composure.

After this, so far as one could see, he kept it uninterruptedly. I saw him the next day, and for several days afterward. He looked like a man who had had a heavy blow, and who had yet not been absolutely stunned. He neither raved nor lamented, nor descanted upon his wrong. He seemed to be trying to shuffle it away, to resume his old occupations, and to appeal to the good offices of the arch-healer, Time. He looked very ill—pale, preoccupied, heavy-eyed, but this was an inevitable tribute to his deep disappointment. He gave me no particular opportunity to make consoling speeches, and not being eloquent, I was more inclined to take one by force. Moral and sentimental platitudes always seemed to me particularly flat upon my own lips, and, addressed to Crawford, they would have been fatally so. Nevertheless, I once told him with some warmth, that he was giving signal proof of being a philosopher. He knew that people always end by getting over things, and he was showing himself able to traverse with a stride a great moral waste. He made no rejoinder at the moment, but an hour later, as we were separating, he told me, with some formalism, that he could not take credit for virtues he had not.

"I am not a philosopher," he said; "on the contrary. And I am not getting over it."

His misfortune excited great compassion among all his friends, and I imagine that this sentiment was expressed, in some cases, with well-meaning but injudicious frankness. The Ingrams were universally denounced, and whenever they appeared in public, at this time, were greeted with significant frigidity. Nothing could have better proved the friendly feeling, the really quite tender regard and admiration that were felt for Crawford, than the manner in which every one took up his cause. He knew it, and I heard him exclaim more than once with intense bitterness that he was that abject thing, an "object of sympathy." Some people flattered themselves that they had made the town, socially speaking, too hot to hold Miss Elizabeth and her parents. The Ingrams anticipated by several weeks their projected departure for Newport—they had given out that they were to spend the summer there—and, quitting New York, quite left, like the gentleman in "The School for Scandal," their reputations behind them.

I continued to observe Crawford with interest and, although I did full justice to his wisdom and self-control, when the summer arrived I was ill at ease about him. He led exactly the life he had led before his engagement, and mingled with society neither more nor less. If he disliked to feel that pitying heads were being shaken over him, or voices lowered in tribute to his misadventure, he made at least no visible effort to ignore these manifestations, and he paid to the full the penalty of being "interesting." But, on the other hand, he showed no disposition to drown his sorrow in violent pleasure, to deafen himself to its echoes. He never alluded to his disappointment, he discharged all the duties of politeness, and questioned people about their own tribulations or satisfactions as deferentially as if he had had no weight upon his heart. Nevertheless, I knew that his wound was rankling—that he had received a dent, and that he would keep it. From this point onward, however, I do not pretend to understand his conduct. I only was witness of it, and I relate what I saw. I do not pretend to speak of his motives.

I had the prospect of leaving town for a couple of months—a friend and fellow-physician in the country having offered me his practice while he took a vacation. Before I went, I made a point of urging Crawford to seek a change of scene—to go abroad, to travel and distract himself.

"To distract myself from what?" he asked, with his usual clear smile.

"From the memory of the vile trick those people played you."

"Do I look, do I behave as if I remembered it?" he demanded with sudden gravity.

"You behave very well, but I suspect that it is at the cost of a greater effort than it is wholesome for a man—quite unassisted—to make."

"I shall stay where I am," said Crawford, "and I shall behave as I have behaved—to the end. I find the effort, so far as there is an effort, extremely wholesome."

"Well, then," said I, "I shall take great satisfaction in hearing that you have fallen in love again. I should be delighted to know that you were well married."

He was silent a while, and then—"It is not impossible," he said. But, before I left him, he laid his hand on my arm, and, after looking at me with great gravity for some time, declared that it would please him extremely that I should never again allude to his late engagement.

The night before I left town, I went to spend half an hour with him. It was the end of June, the weather was hot, and I proposed that instead of sitting indoors, we should take a stroll. In those days, there stood, in the center of the city, a concert-garden, of a somewhat primitive structure, into which a few of the more adventurous representatives of the best society were occasionally seen—under stress of hot weather—to penetrate. It had trees and arbors, and little fountains and small tables, at which ice-creams and juleps were, after hope deferred, dispensed. Its musical attractions fell much below the modern standard, and consisted of three old fiddlers playing stale waltzes, or an itinerant ballad-singer, vocalizing in a language perceived to be foreign, but not further identified, and accompanied by a young woman who performed upon the triangle, and collected tribute at the tables. Most of the frequenters of this establishment were people who wore their gentility lightly, or had none at all to wear; but in compensation (in the latter case), they were generally provided with a substantial sweetheart. We sat down among the rest, and had each a drink with a straw in it, while we listened to a cracked Italian tenor in a velvet jacket and ear-rings. At the end of half an hour, Crawford proposed we should withdraw, whereupon I busied myself with paying for our juleps. There was some delay in making change, during which, my attention wandered; it was some ten minutes before the waiter returned. When at last he restored me my dues, I said to Crawford that I was ready to depart. He was looking another way and did not hear me; I repeated my observation, and then he started a little, looked round, and said that he would like to remain longer. In a moment I perceived the apparent cause of his changing mind. I checked myself just in time from making a joke about it, and yet—as I did so—I said to myself that it was surely not a thing one could take seriously.

Two persons had within a few moments come to occupy a table near our own. One was a weak-eyed young man with a hat poised into artful crookedness upon a great deal of stiffly brushed and much-anointed straw-colored hair, and a harmless scowl of defiance at the world in general from under certain barely visible eyebrows. The defiance was probably prompted by the consciousness of the attractions of the person who accompanied him. This was a woman, still young, and to a certain extent pretty, dressed in a manner which showed that she regarded a visit to a concert-garden as a thing to be taken seriously. Her beauty was of the robust order, her coloring high, her glance unshrinking, and her hands large and red. These last were encased in black lace mittens. She had a small dark eye, of a peculiarly piercing quality, set in her head as flatly as a button-hole in a piece of cotton cloth, and a lower lip which protruded beyond the upper one. She carried her head like a person who pretended to have something in it, and she from time to time surveyed the ample expanse of her corsage with a complacent sense of there being something in that too. She was a large woman, and, when standing upright, must have been much taller than her companion. She had a certain conscious dignity of demeanor, turned out her little finger as she ate her pink ice-cream, and said very little to the young man, who was evidently only her opportunity, and not her ideal. She looked about her, while she consumed her refreshment, with a hard, flat, idle stare, which was not that of an adventuress, but that of a person pretentiously and vulgarly respectable. Crawford, I saw, was observing her narrowly, but his observation was earnestly exercised, and she was not—at first, at least,—aware of it. I wondered, nevertheless, why he was observing her. It was not his habit to stare at strange women, and the charms of this florid damsel were not such as to appeal to his fastidious taste.

"I see you are struck by our lovely neighbor," I said. "Have you ever seen her before?"

"Yes!" he presently answered. "In imagination!"

"One's imagination," I answered, "would seem to be the last place in which to look for such a figure as that. She belongs to the most sordid reality."

"She is very fine in her way," said Crawford. "My image of her was vague; she is far more perfect. It is always interesting to see a supreme representation of any type, whether or no the type be one that we admire. That is the merit of our neighbor. She resumes a certain civilization; she is the last word—the flower."

"The last word of coarseness, and the flower of commonness," I interrupted. "Yes, she certainly has the merit of being unsurpassable, in her own line."

"She is a very powerful specimen," he went on. "She is complete."

"What do you take her to be?"

Crawford did not answer for some time, and I suppose he was not heeding me. But at last he spoke. "She is the daughter of a woman who keeps a third-rate boarding-house in Lexington Avenue. She sits at the foot of the table and pours out bad coffee. She is considered a beauty, in the boarding-house. She makes out the bills—'for three weeks' board,' with *week* spelled *weak*. She has been engaged several times. That young man is one of the boarders, inclined to gallantry. He has invited her to come down here and have ice-cream, and she has consented, though she despises him. Her name is Matilda Jane. The height of her ambition is to be 'fashionable.'"

"Where the deuce did you learn all this?" I asked. "I shouldn't wonder if it were true."

"You may depend upon it that it is very near the truth. The boarding-house may be in the Eighth Avenue, and the lady's name may be Araminta; but the general outline that I have given is correct."

We sat awhile longer; Araminta—or Matilda Jane—finished her ice-cream, leaned back in her chair, and fanned herself with a newspaper, which her companion had drawn from his pocket, and she had folded for the purpose. She had by this time, I suppose, perceived Crawford's singular interest in her person, and she appeared inclined to allow him every facility for the gratification of it. She turned herself about, placed her head in attitudes, stroked her glossy tresses, crooked her large little finger more than ever, and gazed with sturdy coquetry at her incongruous admirer. I, who did not admire her, at last, for a second time, proposed an adjournment; but, to my surprise, Crawford simply put out his hand in farewell, and said that he himself would remain. I looked at him hard; it seemed to me that there was a spark of excitement in his eye which I had not seen for many weeks. I made some little joke which might have been taxed with coarseness; but he received it with perfect gravity, and dismissed me with an impatient gesture. I had not walked more than half a block away when I remembered some last word—it has now passed out of my mind—that I wished to say to my friend. It had, I suppose, some importance, for I walked back to repair my omission. I re-entered the garden and returned to the place where we had been sitting. It was vacant; Crawford had moved his chair, and was engaged in conversation with the young woman I have described. His back was turned to me and he was bending over, so that I could not see his face, and that I remained unseen by him. The lady herself was looking at him strangely; surprise, perplexity, pleasure, doubt as to whether "fashionable" manners required her to seem elated or offended at Crawford's overture, were mingled on her large, rosy face. Her companion appeared to have decided that his own dignity demanded of him grimly to ignore the intrusion; he had given his hat another cock, shouldered his stick like a musket, and fixed his eyes on the fiddlers. I stopped, embraced the group at a glance, and then quietly turned away and departed.

As a physician—as a physiologist—I had every excuse for taking what are called materialistic views of human conduct; but this little episode led me to make some reflections which, if they were not exactly melancholy, were at least tinged with the irony of the moralist. Men are all alike, I said, and the best is, at bottom, very little more delicate than the worst. If there was a man I should have called delicate, it had been Crawford; but he too was capable of seeking a vulgar compensation for an exquisite pain—he also was too weak to be faithful to a memory. Nevertheless I confess I was both amused and reassured; a limit seemed set to the inward working of his resentment—he was going to take his trouble more easily and naturally. For the next few weeks I heard nothing from him; good friends as we were, we were poor correspondents, and as Crawford, moreover, had said about himself—What in the world had he to write about? I came back to town early in September, and on the evening after my return, called upon my friend. The servant who opened the door, and who showed me a new face, told me that Mr. Crawford had gone out an hour before. As I turned away from the house it suddenly occurred to me—I am quite unable to say why—that I might find him at the concert-garden to which we had gone together on the eve of my departure. The night was mild and beautiful, and—though I had not supposed that he had been in the interval a regular *habitué* of those tawdry bowers—a certain association of ideas directed my steps. I reached the garden and passed beneath the arch of paper lanterns which formed its glittering portal. The tables were all occupied, and I scanned the company in vain for Crawford's familiar face. Suddenly I perceived a countenance which, if less familiar, was, at least, vividly impressed upon my memory. The lady whom Crawford had ingeniously characterized as the daughter of the proprietress of a third-rate boarding-house was in possession of one of the tables where she was enthroned in assured preeminence. With a garland of flowers upon her bonnet, an azure scarf about her shoulders, and her hands flashing with splendid rings, she seemed a substantial proof that the Eighth Avenue may, after all, be the road to fortune. As I stood observing her, her eyes met mine, and I saw that they were illumined with a sort of gross, good-humored felicity. I instinctively connected Crawford with her transfiguration, and concluded that he was effectually reconciled to worldly joys. In a moment I saw that she recognized me; after a very brief hesitation she gave me a familiar nod. Upon this hint I approached her.

"You have seen me before," she said. "You have not forgotten me."

"It's impossible to forget you," I answered, gallantly.

"It's a fact that no one ever does forget me?—I suppose I oughtn't to speak to you without being introduced. But wait a moment; there is a gentleman here who will introduce me. He has gone to get some cigars." And she pointed to a gayly bedizened stall on the other side of the garden, before which, in the act of quitting it, his purchase made, I saw Crawford.

Presently he came up to us—he had evidently recognized me from afar. This had given him a few moments. But what, in such a case, were a few moments? He smiled frankly and heartily, and gave my hand an affectionate grasp. I saw, however, that in spite of his smile he was a little pale. He glanced toward the woman at the table, and then, in a clear, serene voice: "You have made acquaintance?" he said.

"Oh, I know him," said the lady; "but I guess he don't know me! Introduce us."

He mentioned my name, ceremoniously, as if he had been presenting me to a duchess. The woman leaned forward and took my hand in her heavily begemmed fingers. "How d'ye do, Doctor?" she said.

Then Crawford paused a moment, looking at me. My eyes rested on his, which, for an instant, were strange and fixed; they seemed to defy me to see anything in them that he wished me not to see. "Allow me to present you," he said at last, in a tone I shall never forget—"allow me to present you to my wife."

I stood staring at him; the woman still grasped my hand. She gave it a violent shake and broke into a loud laugh. "He don't believe it! There's my wedding-ring!" And she thrust out the ample knuckles of her left hand.

A hundred thoughts passed in a flash through my mind, and a dozen exclamations—tragical, ironical, farcical—rose to my lips. But I happily suppressed them all; I simply remained portentously silent, and seated myself mechanically in the chair which Crawford pushed toward me. His face was inscrutable, but in its urbane blankness I found a reflection of the glaring hideousness of his situation. He had committed a monstrous folly. As I sat there, for the next half-hour—it seemed an eternity—I was able to take its full measure. But I was able also to resolve to accept it, to respect it, and to side with poor Crawford, so far as I might, against the consequences of his deed. I remember of that half-hour little beyond a general, rapidly deepening sense of horror. The woman was in a talkative mood; I was the first of her husband's friends upon whom she had as yet been able to lay hands. She gave me much information—as to when they had been married (it was three weeks before), what she had had on, what her husband (she called him "Mr. Crawford") had given her, what she meant to do during the coming winter. "We are going to give a great ball," she said, "the biggest ever seen in New York. It will open the winter, and I shall be introduced to all his friends. They will want to see me, dreadfully, and there will be sure to be a crowd. I don't know whether they will come twice, but they will come once, I'll engage."

She complained of her husband refusing to take her on a wedding-tour—was ever a woman married like that before? "I'm not sure it's a good marriage, without a wedding-tour," she said. "I always thought that to be really man and wife, you had to go to Niagara, or Saratoga, or some such place. But he insists on sticking here in New York; he says he has his reasons.

He gave me that to keep me here." And she made one of her rings twinkle.

Crawford listened to this, smiling, unflinching, unwinking. Before we separated—to say something—I asked Mrs. Crawford if she liked music? The fiddlers were scraping away. She turned her empty glass upside down, and with a thump on the table—"I like that!" she cried. It was most horrible. We rose, and Crawford tenderly offered her his arm; I looked at him with a kind of awe.

I went to see him repeatedly, during the ensuing weeks, and did my best to behave as if nothing was altered. In himself, in fact, nothing was altered, and the really masterly manner in which he tacitly assumed that the change in his situation had been in a high degree for the better, might have furnished inspiration to my more bungling efforts. Never had incurably wounded pride forged itself a more consummately impenetrable mask; never had bravado achieved so triumphant an imitation of sincerity. In his wife's absence, Crawford never alluded to her; but, in her presence, he was an embodiment of deference and attentive civility. His habits underwent little change, and he was punctiliously faithful to his former pursuits. He studied—or at least he passed hours in his library. What he did—what he was—in solitude, heaven only knows; nothing, I am happy to say, ever revealed it to me. I never asked him a question about his wife; to feign a respectful interest in her would have been too monstrous a comedy. She herself, however, more than satisfied my curiosity, and treated me to a bold sketch of her life and adventures. Crawford had hit the nail on the head; she was veritably, at the time he made her acquaintance, residing at a boarding-house, not in the capacity of a boarder. She even told me the terms in which he had made his proposal. There had been no love-making, no nonsense, no flummery. "I have seven thousand dollars a year," he had said—all of a sudden;—"will you please to become my wife? You shall have four thousand for your own use." I have no desire to paint the poor woman who imparted to me these facts in blacker colors than she deserves; she was to be pitied certainly, for she had been lifted into a position in which her defects acquired a glaring intensity. She had made no overtures to Crawford; he had come and dragged her out of her friendly obscurity, and placed her unloveliness aloft upon the pedestal of his contrasted good-manners. She had simply taken what was offered her. But for all one's logic, nevertheless, she was a terrible creature. I tried to like her, I tried to find out her points. The best one seemed to be that her jewels and new dresses— her clothes were in atrocious taste—kept her, for the time, in loud good-humor. Might they never be wanting? I shuddered to think of what Crawford would find himself face to face with in case of their failing;—coarseness, vulgarity, ignorance, vanity, and, beneath all, something as hard and arid as dusty bricks. When I had left them, their union always seemed to me a monstrous fable, an evil dream; each time I saw them the miracle was freshly repeated.

People were still in a great measure in the country, and though it had begun to be rumored about that Crawford had taken a very strange wife, there was for some weeks no adequate appreciation of her strangeness. This came, however, with the advance of the autumn and those beautiful October days when all the world was in the streets. Crawford came forth with his terrible bride upon his arm, took every day a long walk, and ran the gauntlet of society's surprise. On Sundays, he marched into church with his incongruous consort, led her up the long aisle to the accompaniment of the opening organ-peals, and handed her solemnly into her pew. Mrs. Crawford's idiosyncrasies were not of the latent and lurking order, and, in the view of her fellow-worshipers of her own sex, surveying her from a distance, were sufficiently summarized in the composition of her bonnets. Many persons probably remember with a good deal of vividness the great festival to which, early in the winter, Crawford convoked all his friends. Not a person invited was absent, for it was a case in which friendliness and curiosity went most comfortably, hand in hand. Every one wished well to Crawford and was anxious to show it, but when they said they wouldn't for the world seem to turn their backs upon the poor fellow, what people really meant was that they would not for the world miss seeing how Mrs. Crawford would behave. The party was very splendid and made an era in New York, in the art of entertainment. Mrs. Crawford behaved very well, and I think people were a good deal disappointed and scandalized at the decency of her demeanor. But she looked deplorably, it was universally agreed, and her native vulgarity came out in the strange bedizenment of her too exuberant person. By the time supper was served, moreover, every one had gleaned an anec-dote about her bad grammar, and the low level of her conversa-tion. On all sides, people were putting their heads together, in threes and fours, and tittering over each other's stories. There is nothing like the bad manners of good society, and I, myself, acutely sensitive on Crawford's behalf, found it impossible, by the end of the evening, to endure the growing exhilaration of the assembly. The company had rendered its verdict; namely, that there were the vulgar people one could, at a pinch accept, and the vulgar people one couldn't, and that Mrs. Crawford be-longed to the latter class. I was savage with every one who spoke to me. "Yes, she is as bad as you please," I said; "but you are worse!" But I might have spared my resentment, for Craw-ford, himself, in the midst of all this, was simply sublime. He was the genius of hospitality in person; no one had ever seen him so careless, so free, so charming. When I went to bid him good-night, as I took him by the hand—"You will carry it through!" I said. He looked at me, smiling vaguely, and not showing in the least that he understood me. Then I felt how deeply he was attached to the part he had undertaken to play; he had sacrificed our old good-fellowship to it. Even to me, his oldest friend, he would not raise a corner of the mask.

Mrs. Ingram and Elizabeth were, of course, not at the ball; but they had come back from Newport, bringing an ardent suitor in their train. The event had amply justified Mrs. Ingram's circumspection; she had captured a young Southern planter, whose estates were fabled to cover three-eighths of the State of Alabama. Elizabeth was more beautiful than ever, and the marriage was being hurried forward. Several times, in public, to my knowledge, Elizabeth and her mother, found themselves face to face with Crawford and his wife. What Crawford must have felt when he looked from the exquisite creature he had lost to the full-blown dowdy he had gained, is a matter it is well but to glance at and pass—the more so, as my story approaches its close. One morning, in my consulting-room, I had been giving some advice to a little old gentleman who was as sound as a winter-pippin, but, who used to come and see me once a month to tell me that he felt a hair on his tongue, or, that he had dreamed of a blue-dog, and to ask to be put upon a "diet" in consequence. The basis of a diet, in his view, was a daily pint of port wine. He had retired from business, he belonged to a club, and he used to go about peddling gossip. His wares, like those of most peddlers, were cheap, and usually, for my prescription, I could purchase the whole contents of his tray. On this occasion, as he was leaving me, he remarked that he supposed I had heard the news about our friend Crawford. I said that I had heard nothing. What was the news?

"He has lost every penny of his fortune," said my patient. "He is completely cleaned out." And, then, in answer to my exclamation of dismay, he proceeded to inform me that the New Amsterdam Bank had suspended payment, and would certainly never resume it. All the world knew that Crawford's funds were at the disposal of the bank, and that two or three months before, when things were looking squally, he had come most generously to the rescue. The squall had come, it had proved a hurricane, the bank had capsized, and Crawford's money had gone to the bottom. "It's not a surprise to me," said Mr. Niblett, "I suspected something a year ago. It's true, I am very sharp."

"Do you think any one else suspected anything?" I asked.

"I dare say not; people are so easily humbugged. And, then, what could have looked better, above board, than the New Amsterdam?"

"Nevertheless, here and there," I said, "an exceptionally sharp person may have been on the watch."

"Unquestionably—though I am told that they are going on to-day, down town, as if no bank had ever broken before."

"Do you know Mrs. Ingram?" I asked.

"Thoroughly! She is exceptionally sharp, if that is what you mean."

"Do you think it is possible that she foresaw this affair six months ago?"

"Very possible; she always has her nose in Wall street, and she knows more about stocks than the whole board of brokers."

"Well," said I, after a pause, "sharp as she is, I hope she will get nipped, yet!"

"Ah," said my old friend, "you allude to Crawford's affairs? But you shouldn't be a better royalist than the king. He has forgiven her—he has consoled himself. But what will console him now? Is it true his wife was a washerwoman? Perhaps she will not be sorry to know a trade."

I hoped with all my heart that Mr. Niblett's story was an exaggeration, and I repaired that evening to Crawford's house, to learn the real extent of his misfortune. He had seen me coming in, and he met me in the hall and drew me immediately into the library. He looked like a man who had been thrown by a vicious horse, but had picked himself up and resolved to go the rest of the way on foot.

"How bad is it?" I asked.

"I have about a thousand a year left. I shall get some work, and with careful economy we can live."

At this moment I heard a loud voice screaming from the top of the stairs. "Will *she* help you?" I asked.

He hesitated a moment, and then—"No!" he said simply. Immediately, as a commentary upon his answer, the door was thrown open and Mrs. Crawford swept in. I saw in an instant that her good-humor was in permanent eclipse; flushed, disheveled, inflamed, she was a perfect presentation of a vulgar fury. She advanced upon me with a truly formidable weight of wrath.

"Was it you that put him up to it?" she cried. "Was it you that put it into his head to marry me? I'm sure I never thought of him—he isn't the twentieth part of a man! I took him for his money—four thousand a year, clear; I never pretended it was for anything else. To-day, he comes and tells me that it was all a mistake—that we must get on as well as we can on twelve hundred. And he calls himself a gentleman—and so do you, I suppose! There are gentlemen in the State's prison for less. I have been cheated, insulted and ruined; but I'm not a woman you can play that sort of game upon. The money's mine, what is left of it, and he may go and get his fine friends to support him. There ain't a thing in the world he can do—except lie and cheat!"

Crawford, during this horrible explosion, stood with his eyes fixed upon the floor; and I felt that the peculiarly odious part of the scene was that his wife was literally in the right. She had been bitterly disappointed—she had been practically deceived. Crawford turned to me and put out his hand. "Good-bye," he said. "I must forego the pleasure of receiving you any more in my own house."

"I can't come again?" I exclaimed.

"I will take it as a favor that you should not."

I withdrew with an insupportable sense of helplessness. In the house he was then occupying, he, of course, very soon ceased to live; but for some time I was in ignorance of whither he had betaken himself. He had forbidden me to come and see him, and he was too much occupied in accommodating himself to his change of fortune to find time for making visits. At last I disinterred him in one of the upper streets, near the East River, in a small house of which he occupied but a single floor. I disobeyed him and went in, and as his wife was apparently absent, he allowed me to remain. He had kept his books, or most of them, and arranged a sort of library. He looked ten years older, but he neither made nor suffered me to make, an allusion to himself. He had obtained a place as clerk at a wholesale chemist's, and he received a salary of five hundred dollars. After this, I not infrequently saw him; we used often, on a Sunday, to take a long walk together. On our return we parted at his door; he never asked me to come in. He talked of his reading, of his scientific fancies, of public affairs, of our friends—of everything, except his own troubles. He suffered, of course, most of his purely formal social relations to die out; but if he appeared not to cling to his friends, neither did he seem to avoid them. I remember a clever old lady saying to me at this time, in allusion to her having met him somewhere—"I used always to think Mr. Crawford the most agreeable man in the world, but I think now he has even improved!" One day—we had walked out into the country, and were sitting on a felled log by the roadside, to rest (for in those days New Yorkers could walk out into the country),—I said to him that I had a piece of news to tell him. It was not pleasing, but it was interesting.

"I told you six weeks ago," I said, "that Elizabeth Ingram had been seized with small-pox. She has recovered, and two or three people have seen her. Every ray of her beauty is gone. They say she is hideous."

"I don't believe it!" he said, simply.

"The young man who was to marry her does," I answered. "He has backed out—he has given her up—he has posted back to Alabama."

Crawford looked at me a moment, and then—"The idiot!" he exclaimed.

For myself, I felt the full bitterness of poor Elizabeth's lot; Mrs. Ingram had been "nipped," as I had ventured to express it, in a grimmer fashion than I hoped. Several months afterward, I saw the young girl, shrouded in a thick veil, beneath which I could just distinguish her absolutely blasted face. On either side of her walked her father and mother, each of them showing a visage almost as blighted as her own.

I saw Crawford for a time, as I have said, with a certain frequency; but there began to occur long intervals, during which he plunged into inscrutable gloom. I supposed in a general way, that his wife's temper gave him plenty of occupation at home;

but a painful incident—which I need not repeat—at last informed me how much. Mrs. Crawford, it appeared, drank deep; she had resorted to liquor to console herself for her disappointments. During her periods of revelry, her husband was obliged to be in constant attendance upon her, to keep her from exposing herself. She had done so to me, hideously, and it was so that I learned the reason of her husband's fitful absences. After this, I expressed to Crawford my amazement that he should continue to live with her.

"It's very simple," he answered. "I have done her a great wrong, and I have forfeited the right to complain of any she may do to me."

"In heaven's name," I said, "make another fortune and pension her off."

He shook his head. "I shall never make a fortune. My working-power is not of a high value."

One day, not having seen him for several weeks, I went to his house. The door was opened by his wife, in curl-papers and a soiled dressing-gown. After what I can hardly call an exchange of greetings,—for she wasted no politeness upon me,—I asked for news of my friend.

"He's at the New York Hospital," she said.

"What in the world has happened to him?"

"He has broken his leg, and he went there to be taken care of—as if he hadn't a comfortable home of his own! But he's a deep one; that's a hit at me!"

I immediately announced my intention of going to see him, but as I was turning away she stopped me, laying her hand on my arm. She looked at me hard, almost menacingly. "If he tells you," she said, "that it was me that made him break his leg—that I came behind him, and pushed him down the steps of the back-yard, upon the flags, you needn't believe him. I could have done it; I'm strong enough"—and with a vigorous arm she gave a thump upon the door-post. "It would have served him right, too. But it's a lie!"

"He will not tell me," I said. "But you have done so!"

Crawford was in bed, in one of the great, dreary wards of the hospital, looking as a man looks who has been laid up for three weeks with a compound fracture of the knee. I had seen no small amount of physical misery, but I had never seen anything so poignant as the sight of my once brilliant friend in such a place, from such a cause. I told him I would not ask him how his misfortune occurred: I knew! We talked awhile and at last I said, "Of course you will not go back to her!"

He turned away his head, and at this moment, the nurse came and said that I had made the poor gentleman talk enough.

Of course he did go back to her—at the end of a very long convalescence. His leg was permanently injured; he was obliged to move about very slowly, and what he had called the value of his working-power was not thereby increased. This meant permanent poverty, and all the rest of it. It lasted ten years longer—until 185–, when Mrs. Crawford died of *delirium tremens*. I cannot say that this event restored his equanimity, for the excellent reason that to the eyes of the world—and my own most searching ones—he had never lost it.

1876

AN INTERNATIONAL EPISODE

I

FOUR years ago—in 1874—two young Englishmen had occasion to go to the United States. They crossed the ocean at midsummer, and, arriving in New York on the first day of August, were much struck with the fervid temperature of that city. Disembarking upon the wharf, they climbed into one of those huge high-hung coaches which convey passengers to the hotels, and with a great deal of bouncing and bumping, took their course through Broadway. The midsummer aspect of New York is not perhaps the most favourable one; still, it is not without its picturesque and even brilliant side. Nothing could well resemble less a typical English street than the interminable avenue, rich in incongruities, through which our two travellers advanced—looking out on each side of them at the comfortable animation of the sidewalks, the high-coloured, heterogeneous architecture, the huge white marble façades, glittering in the strong, crude light and bedizened with gilded lettering, the multifarious awnings, banners and streamers, the extraordinary number of omnibuses, horse-cars and other democratic vehicles, the vendors of cooling fluids, the white trousers and big straw-hats of the policemen, the tripping gait of the modish young persons on the pavement, the general brightness, newness, juvenility, both of people and things. The young men had exchanged few observations; but in crossing Union Square, in front of the monument to Washington—in the very shadow, indeed, projected by the image of the *pater patriæ*—one of them remarked to the other, "It seems a rum-looking place."

"Ah, very odd, very odd," said the other, who was the clever man of the two.

"Pity it's so beastly hot," resumed the first speaker, after a pause.

"You know we are in a low latitude," said his friend.

"I daresay," remarked the other.

"I wonder," said the second speaker, presently, "if they can give one a bath."

"I daresay not," rejoined the other.

"Oh, I say!" cried his comrade.

This animated discussion was checked by their arrival at the hotel, which had been recommended to them by an American gentleman whose acquaintance they made—with whom, indeed, they became very intimate—on the steamer, and who had proposed to accompany them to the inn and introduce them, in a friendly way, to the proprietor. This plan, however, had been defeated by their friend's finding that his "partner" was awaiting him on the wharf, and that his commercial associate desired him instantly to come and give his attention to certain telegrams received from St. Louis. But the two Englishmen, with nothing but their national prestige and personal graces to recommend them, were very well received at the hotel, which had an air of capacious hospitality. They found that a bath was not unattainable, and were indeed struck with the facilities for prolonged and reiterated immersion with which their apartment was supplied. After bathing a good deal—more indeed than they had ever done before on a single occasion—they made their way into the dining-room of the hotel, which was a spacious restaurant, with a fountain in the middle, a great many tall plants in ornamental tubs, and an array of French waiters. The first dinner on land, after a sea-voyage, is under any circumstances a delightful occasion, and there was something particularly agreeable in the circumstances in which our young Englishmen found themselves. They were extremely good-natured young men; they were more observant than they appeared; in a sort of inarticulate, accidentally dissimulative fashion, they were highly appreciative. This was perhaps especially the case with the elder, who was also, as I have said, the man of talent. They sat down at a little table which was a very different affair from the great clattering see-saw in the saloon of the steamer. The wide doors and windows of the restaurant stood open, beneath large awnings, to a wide pavement, where there were other plants in tubs, and rows of spreading trees, and beyond which there was a large shady square, without any palings and with marble-paved walks. And above the vivid verdure rose other façades of white marble and of pale chocolate-coloured stone, squaring themselves against the deep blue sky. Here, outside, in the light and the shade and the heat, there was a great tinkling of the bells of innumerable street-cars, and a constant strolling and shuffling and rustling of many pedestrians, a large proportion of whom were young women in Pompadour-looking dresses. Within, the place was cool and vaguely-lighted; with the plash of water, the odour of flowers and the flitting of French waiters, as I have said, upon soundless carpets.

"It's rather like Paris, you know," said the younger of our two travellers.

"It's like Paris—only more so," his companion rejoined.

"I suppose it's the French waiters," said the first speaker. "Why don't they have French waiters in London?"

"Fancy a French waiter at a club," said his friend.

The young Englishman stared a little, as if he could not fancy it. "In Paris I'm very apt to dine at a place where there's an English waiter. Don't you know, what's-his-name's, close to the thingumbob? They always set an English waiter at me. I suppose they think I can't speak French."

"No more you can." And the elder of the young Englishmen unfolded his napkin.

His companion took no notice whatever of this declaration. "I say," he resumed, in a moment, "I suppose we must learn to speak American. I suppose we must take lessons."

"I can't understand them," said the clever man.

"What the deuce is *he* saying?" asked his comrade, appealing from the French waiter.

"He is recommending some soft-shell crabs," said the clever man.

And so, in desultory observation of the idiosyncrasies of the new society in which they found themselves, the young Englishmen proceeded to dine—going in largely, as the phrase is, for cooling draughts and dishes, of which their attendant offered them a very long list. After dinner they went out and slowly walked about the neighbouring streets. The early dusk of waning summer was coming on, but the heat was still very great. The pavements were hot even to the stout boot-soles of the British travellers, and the trees along the kerb-stone emitted strange exotic odours. The young men wandered through the adjoining square—that queer place without palings, and with marble walks arranged in black and white lozenges. There were a great many benches, crowded with shabby-looking people, and the travellers remarked, very justly, that it was not much like Belgrave Square. On one side was an enormous hotel, lifting up into the hot darkness an immense array of open, brightly-lighted windows. At the base of this populous structure was an eternal jangle of horse-cars, and all round it, in the upper dusk, was a sinister hum of mosquitoes. The ground-floor of the hotel seemed to be a huge transparent cage, flinging a wide glare of gaslight into the street, of which it formed a sort of public adjunct, absorbing and emitting the passers-by promiscuously. The young Englishmen went in with every one else, from curiosity, and saw a couple of hundred men sitting on divans along a great marble-paved corridor, with their legs stretched out, together with several dozen more standing in a *queue*, as at the ticket-office of a railway station, before a brilliantly-illuminated counter, of vast extent. These latter persons, who carried portmanteaux in their hands, had a dejected, exhausted look; their garments were not very fresh, and they seemed to be rendering some mysterious tribute to a magnificent young man with a waxed moustache and a shirt front adorned with diamond buttons, who every now and then dropped an absent glance over their multitudinous patience. They were American citizens doing homage to an hotel-clerk.

"I'm glad he didn't tell us to go there," said one of our Englishmen, alluding to their friend on the steamer, who had told them so many things. They walked up the Fifth Avenue, where, for instance, he had told them that all the first families lived. But the first families were out of town, and our young travellers had only the satisfaction of seeing some of the second—or perhaps even the third—taking the evening air upon balconies and high flights of doorsteps, in the streets which radiate from the more ornamental thoroughfare. They went a little way down one of these side-streets, and they saw young ladies in white dresses—charming-looking persons—seated in graceful attitudes on the chocolate-coloured steps. In one or two places these young ladies were conversing across the street with other young ladies seated in similar postures and costumes in front of the opposite houses, and in the warm night air their colloquial tones sounded strange in the ears of the young Englishmen. One of our friends, nevertheless—the younger one—intimated that he felt a disposition to intercept a few of these soft familiarities; but his companion observed, pertinently enough, that he had better be careful. "We must not begin with making mistakes," said his companion.

"But he told us, you know—he told us," urged the young man, alluding again to the friend on the steamer.

"Never mind what he told us!" answered his comrade, who, if he had greater talents, was also apparently more of a moralist.

By bed-time—in their impatience to taste of a terrestrial couch again our seafarers went to bed early—it was still insufferably hot, and the buzz of the mosquitoes at the open windows might have passed for an audible crepitation of the temperature. "We can't stand this, you know," the young Englishmen said to each other; and they tossed about all night more boisterously than they had tossed upon the Atlantic billows.

On the morrow, their first thought was that they would re-embark that day for England; and then it occurred to them that they might find an asylum nearer at hand. The cave of Æolus became their ideal of comfort, and they wondered where the Americans went when they wished to cool off. They had not the least idea, and they determined to apply for information to Mr. J. L. Westgate. This was the name inscribed in a bold hand on the back of a letter carefully preserved in the pocket-book of our junior traveller. Beneath the address, in the left-hand corner of the envelope, were the words, "Introducing Lord Lambeth and Percy Beaumont, Esq." The letter had been given to the two Englishmen by a good friend of theirs in London, who had been in America two years previously and had singled out Mr. J. L. Westgate from the many friends he had left there as the consignee, as it were, of his compatriots. "He is a capital fellow," the Englishman in London had said, "and he has got an awfully pretty wife. He's tremendously hospitable—he will do everything in the world for you; and as he knows every one over there, it is quite needless I should give you any other introduction. He will make you see every one; trust to him for putting you into circulation. He has got a tremendously pretty wife." It was natural that in the hour of tribulation Lord Lambeth and Mr. Percy Beaumont should have bethought themselves of a gentleman whose attractions had been thus vividly depicted; all the more so that he lived in the Fifth Avenue and that the Fifth Avenue, as they had ascertained the night before, was contiguous to their hotel. "Ten to one he'll be out of town," said Percy Beaumont; "but we can at least find out where he has gone, and we can immediately start in pursuit. He can't possibly have gone to a hotter place, you know."

"Oh, there's only one hotter place," said Lord Lambeth, "and I hope he hasn't gone there."

They strolled along the shady side of the street to the number indicated upon the precious letter. The house presented an imposing chocolate-coloured expanse, relieved by facings and window-cornices of florid sculpture, and by a couple of dusty rose-trees, which clambered over the balconies and the portico. This last-mentioned feature was approached by a monumental flight of steps.

"Rather better than a London house," said Lord Lambeth, looking down from this altitude, after they had rung the bell.

"It depends upon what London house you mean," replied his companion. "You have a tremendous chance to get wet between the house-door and your carriage."

"Well," said Lord Lambeth, glancing at the burning heavens, "I 'guess' it doesn't rain so much here!"

The door was opened by a long negro in a white jacket, who grinned familiarly when Lord Lambeth asked for Mr. Westgate.

"He ain't at home, sir; he's down town at his o'fice."

"Oh, at his office?" said the visitors. "And when will he be at home?"

"Well, sir, when he goes out dis way in de mo'ning, he ain't liable to come home all day."

This was discouraging; but the address of Mr. Westgate's office was freely imparted by the intelligent black, and was taken down by Percy Beaumont in his pocket-book. The two gentlemen then returned, languidly, to their hotel, and sent for a hackney-coach; and in this commodious vehicle they rolled comfortably down town. They measured the whole length of Broadway again, and found it a path of fire; and then, deflecting to the left, they were deposited by their conductor before a fresh, light, ornamental structure, ten stories high, in a street crowded with keen-faced, light-limbed young men, who were running about very quickly and stopping each other eagerly at corners and in doorways. Passing into this brilliant building, they were introduced by one of the keen-faced young men—he was a charming fellow, in wonderful cream-coloured garments and a hat with a blue ribbon, who had evidently perceived them to be aliens and helpless—to a very snug hydraulic elevator, in which they took their place with many other persons, and which, shooting upward in its vertical socket, presently projected them into the seventh horizontal compartment of the edifice. Here, after brief delay, they found themselves face to face with the friend of their friend in London. His office was composed of several different rooms, and they waited very silently in one of these after they had sent in their letter and their cards. The letter was not one which it would take Mr. Westgate very long to read, but he came out to speak to them more instantly than they could have expected; he had evidently jumped up from his work. He was a tall, lean personage, and was dressed all in fresh white linen; he had a thin, sharp, familiar face, with an expression that was at one and the same time sociable and business-like, a quick, intelligent eye, and a large brown moustache, which concealed his mouth and made his chin, beneath it, look small. Lord Lambeth thought he looked tremendously clever.

"How do you do, Lord Lambeth—how do you do, sir?" he said, holding the open letter in his hand. "I'm very glad to see you—I hope you're very well. You had better come in here—I think it's cooler;" and he led the way into another room, where there were law-books and papers, and windows wide open beneath striped awnings. Just opposite one of the windows, on a line with his eyes, Lord Lambeth observed the weather-vane of a church steeple. The uproar of the street sounded infinitely far below, and Lord Lambeth felt very high in the air. "I say it's cooler," pursued their host, "but everything is relative. How do you stand the heat?"

"I can't say we like it," said Lord Lambeth; "but Beaumont likes it better than I."

"Well, it won't last," Mr. Westgate very cheerfully declared; "nothing unpleasant lasts over here. It was very hot when Captain Littledale was here; he did nothing but drink sherry-cobblers. He expresses some doubt in his letter whether I shall remember him—as if I didn't remember making six sherry-cobblers for him one day, in about twenty minutes. I hope you left him well; two years having elapsed since then."

"Oh, yes, he's all right," said Lord Lambeth.

"I am always very glad to see your countrymen," Mr. Westgate pursued. "I thought it would be time some of you should be coming along. A friend of mine was saying to me only a day or two ago, 'It's time for the water-melons and the Englishmen.'"

"The Englishmen and the water-melons just now are about the same thing," Percy Beaumont observed, wiping his dripping forehead.

"Ah, well, we'll put you on ice, as we do the melons. You must go down to Newport."

"We'll go anywhere!" said Lord Lambeth.

"Yes, you want to go to Newport—that's what you want to do," Mr. Westgate affirmed. "But let's see—when did you get here?"

"Only yesterday," said Percy Beaumont.

"Ah, yes, by the 'Russia.' Where are you staying?"

"At the 'Hanover,' I think they call it."

"Pretty comfortable?" inquired Mr. Westgate.

"It seems a capital place, but I can't say we like the gnats," said Lord Lambeth.

Mr. Westgate stared and laughed. "Oh, no, of course you don't like the gnats. We shall expect you to like a good many things over here, but we shan't insist upon your liking the gnats; though certainly you'll admit that, as gnats, they are fine, eh? But you oughtn't to remain in the city."

"So we think," said Lord Lambeth. "If you would kindly suggest something——"

"Suggest something, my dear sir?"—and Mr. Westgate looked at him, narrowing his eyelids. "Open your mouth and shut your eyes! Leave it to me, and I'll put you through. It's a matter of national pride with me that all Englishmen should have a good time; and, as I have had considerable practice, I have learned to minister to their wants. I find they generally want the right thing. So just please to consider yourselves my property; and if any one should try to appropriate you, please to say, 'Hands off; too late for the market.' But let's see," continued the American, in his slow, humorous voice, with a distinctness of utterance which appeared to his visitors to be part of a facetious intention—a strangely leisurely, speculative voice for a man evidently so busy and, as they felt, so professional—"let's see; are you going to make something of a stay, Lord Lambeth?"

"Oh dear no," said the young Englishman; "my cousin was coming over on some business, so I just came across, at an hour's notice, for the lark."

"Is it your first visit to the United States?"

"Oh dear, yes."

"I was obliged to come on some business," said Percy Beaumont, "and I brought Lambeth with me."

"And *you* have been here before, sir?"

"Never—never."

"I thought, from your referring to business——" said Mr. Westgate.

"Oh, you see I'm by way of being a barrister," Percy Beaumont answered. "I know some people that think of bringing a suit against one of your railways, and they asked me to come over and take measures accordingly."

Mr. Westgate gave one of his slow, keen looks again. "What's your railroad?" he asked.

"The Tennessee Central."

The American tilted back his chair a little, and poised it an instant. "Well, I'm sorry you want to attack one of our institutions," he said, smiling. "But I guess you had better enjoy yourself *first!*"

"I'm certainly rather afraid I can't work in this weather," the young barrister confessed.

"Leave that to the natives," said Mr. Westgate. "Leave the Tennessee Central to me, Mr. Beaumont. Some day we'll talk it over, and I guess I can make it square. But I didn't know you Englishmen ever did any work, in the upper classes."

"Oh, we do a lot of work; don't we, Lambeth?" asked Percy Beaumont.

"I must certainly be at home by the 19th of September," said the younger Englishman, irrelevantly, but gently.

"For the shooting, eh? or is it the hunting—or the fishing?" inquired his entertainer.

"Oh, I must be in Scotland," said Lord Lambeth, blushing a little.

"Well then," rejoined Mr. Westgate, "you had better amuse yourself first, also. You must go down and see Mrs. Westgate."

"We should be so happy—if you would kindly tell us the train," said Percy Beaumont.

"It isn't a train—it's a boat."

"Oh, I see. And what is the name of—a—the—a—town?"

"It isn't a town," said Mr. Westgate, laughing. "It's a—well, what shall I call it? It's a watering-place. In short, it's Newport. You'll see what it is. It's cool; that's the principal thing. You will greatly oblige me by going down there and putting yourself into the hands of Mrs. Westgate. It isn't perhaps for me to say it; but you couldn't be in better hands. Also in those of her sister, who is staying with her. She is very fond of Englishmen. She thinks there is nothing like them."

"Mrs. Westgate or—a—her sister?" asked Percy Beaumont, modestly, yet in the tone of an inquiring traveller.

"Oh, I mean my wife," said Mr. Westgate. "I don't suppose my sister-in-law knows much about them. She has always led a very quiet life; she has lived in Boston."

Percy Beaumont listened with interest. "That, I believe," he said, "is the most—a—intellectual town?"

"I believe it is very intellectual. I don't go there much," responded his host.

"I say, we ought to go there," said Lord Lambeth to his companion.

"Oh, Lord Lambeth, wait till the great heat is over!" Mr. Westgate interposed. "Boston in this weather would be very trying; it's not the temperature for intellectual exertion. At Boston, you know, you have to pass an examination at the city limits; and when you come away they give you a kind of degree."

Lord Lambeth stared, blushing a little; and Percy Beaumont stared a little also—but only with his fine natural complexion;

glancing aside after a moment to see that his companion was not looking too credulous, for he had heard a great deal about American humour. "I daresay it is very jolly," said the younger gentleman.

"I daresay it is," said Mr. Westgate. "Only I must impress upon you that at present—to-morrow morning, at an early hour—you will be expected at Newport. We have a house there; half the people in New York go there for the summer. I am not sure that at this very moment my wife can take you in; she has got a lot of people staying with her; I don't know who they all are; only she may have no room. But you can begin with the hotel, and meanwhile you can live at my house. In that way—simply sleeping at the hotel—you will find it tolerable. For the rest, you must make yourself at home at my place. You mustn't be shy, you know; if you are only here for a month that will be a great waste of time. Mrs. Westgate won't neglect you, and you had better not try to resist her. I know something about that. I expect you'll find some pretty girls on the premises. I shall write to my wife by this afternoon's mail, and to-morrow she and Miss Alden will look out for you. Just walk right in and make yourself comfortable. Your steamer leaves from this part of the city, and I will immediately send out and get you a cabin. Then, at half-past four o'clock, just call for me here, and I will go with you and put you on board. It's a big boat; you might get lost. A few days hence, at the end of the week, I will come down to Newport and see how you are getting on."

The two young Englishmen inaugurated the policy of not resisting Mrs. Westgate by submitting, with great docility and thankfulness, to her husband. He was evidently a very good fellow, and he made an impression upon his visitors; his hospitality seemed to recommend itself, consciously—with a friendly wink, as it were—as if it hinted, judicially, that you could not possibly make a better bargain. Lord Lambeth and his cousin left their entertainer to his labours and returned to their hotel, where they spent three or four hours in their respective showerbaths. Percy Beaumont had suggested that they ought to see something of the town; but "Oh, damn the town!" his noble kinsman had rejoined. They returned to Mr. Westgate's office in a carriage, with their luggage, very punctually; but it must be reluctantly recorded that, this time, he kept them waiting so long that they felt themselves missing the steamer and were deterred only by an amiable modesty from dispensing with his attendance and starting on a hasty scramble to the wharf. But when at last he appeared, and the carriage plunged into the purlieus of Broadway, they jolted and jostled to such good purpose that they reached the huge white vessel while the bell for departure was still ringing and the absorption of passengers still active. It was indeed, as Mr. Westgate had said, a big boat, and his leadership in the innumerable and interminable corridors and cabins, with which he seemed perfectly acquainted, and of which any one and every one appeared to have the *entrée*, was very grateful to the slightly bewildered voyagers. He showed them their state-room—a spacious apartment, embellished with gas-lamps, mirrors *en pied* and sculptured furniture—and then, long after they had been intimately convinced that the steamer was in motion and launched upon the unknown stream that they were about to navigate, he bade them a sociable farewell.

"Well, good-bye, Lord Lambeth," he said. "Good-bye, Mr. Percy Beaumont; I hope you'll have a good time. Just let them do what they want with you. I'll come down by-and-by and look after you."

II

THE young Englishmen emerged from their cabin and amused themselves with wandering about the immense labyrinthine steamer, which struck them as an extraordinary mixture of a ship and an hotel. It was densely crowded with passengers, the larger number of whom appeared to be ladies and very young children; and in the big saloons, ornamented in white and gold, which followed each other in surprising succession, beneath the swinging gas-lights and among the small side-passages where the negro domestics of both sexes assembled with an air of philosophic leisure, every one was moving to and fro and exchanging loud and familiar observations. Eventually, at the instance of a discriminating black, our young men went and had some "supper," in a wonderful place arranged like a theatre, where, in a gilded gallery upon which little boxes appeared to open, a large orchestra was playing operatic selections, and, below, people were handing about bills of fare, as if they had been programmes. All this was sufficiently curious; but the agreeable thing, later, was to sit out on one of the great white decks of the steamer, in the warm, breezy darkness, and, in the vague starlight, to make out the line of low, mysterious coast. The young Englishmen tried American cigars—those of Mr. Westgate—and talked together as they usually talked, with many odd silences, lapses of logic and incongruities of transition; like people who have grown old together and learned to supply each other's missing phrases; or, more especially, like people thoroughly conscious of a common point of view, so that a style of conversation superficially lacking in finish might suffice for a reference to a fund of associations in the light of which everything was all right.

We really seem to be going out to sea," Percy Beaumont observed. "Upon my word, we are going back to England. He has shipped us off again. I call that 'real mean.'"

"I suppose it's all right," said Lord Lambeth. "I want to see those pretty girls at Newport. You know he told us the place was an island; and aren't all islands in the sea?"

"Well," resumed the elder traveller after a while, "if his house is as good as his cigars, we shall do very well."

"He seems a very good fellow," said Lord Lambeth, as if this idea had just occurred to him.

"I say, we had better remain at the inn," rejoined his companion, presently. "I don't think I like the way he spoke of his house. I don't like stopping in the house with such a tremendous lot of women."

"Oh, I don't mind," said Lord Lambeth. And then they smoked awhile in silence. "Fancy his thinking we do no work in England!" the young man resumed.

"I daresay he didn't really think so," said Percy Beaumont.

"Well, I guess they don't know much about England over here!" declared Lord Lambeth, humorously. And then there was another long pause. "He was devilish civil," observed the young nobleman.

"Nothing, certainly, could have been more civil," rejoined his companion.

"Littledale said his wife was great fun," said Lord Lambeth.

"Whose wife—Littledale's?"

"This American's—Mrs. Westgate. What's his name? J.L."

Beaumont was silent a moment. "What was fun to Littledale," he said at last, rather sententiously, "may be death to us."

"What do you mean by that?" asked his kinsman. "I am as good a man as Littledale."

"My dear boy, I hope you won't begin to flirt," said Percy Beaumont.

"I don't care. I daresay I shan't begin."

"With a married woman, if she's bent upon it, it's all very well," Beaumont expounded. "But our friend mentioned a young lady—a sister, a sister-in-law. For God's sake, don't get entangled with her."

"How do you mean, entangled?"

"Depend upon it she will try to hook you."

"Oh, bother!" said Lord Lambeth.

"American girls are very clever," urged his companion.

"So much the better," the young man declared.

"I fancy they are always up to some game of that sort," Beaumont continued.

"They can't be worse than they are in England," said Lord Lambeth, judicially.

"Ah, but in England," replied Beaumont, "you have got your natural protectors. You have got your mother and sisters."

"My mother and sisters—" began the young nobleman, with a certain energy. But he stopped in time, puffing at his cigar.

"Your mother spoke to me about it, with tears in her eyes," said Percy Beaumont. "She said she felt very nervous. I promised to keep you out of mischief."

"You had better take care of yourself," said the object of maternal and ducal solicitude.

"Ah," rejoined the young barrister, "I haven't the expectation of a hundred thousand a year—not to mention other attractions."

"Well," said Lord Lambeth, "don't cry out before you're hurt!"

It was certainly very much cooler at Newport, where our travellers found themselves assigned to a couple of diminutive bed-rooms in a far-away angle of an immense hotel. They had gone ashore in the early summer twilight, and had very promptly put themselves to bed; thanks to which circumstance and to their having, during the previous hours, in their commodious cabin, slept the sleep of youth and health, they began to feel, towards eleven o'clock, very alert and inquisitive. They looked out of their windows across a row of small green fields, bordered with low stone dykes, of rude construction, and saw a deep blue ocean lying beneath a deep blue sky and flecked now and then with scintillating patches of foam. A strong, fresh breeze came in through the curtainless casements and prompted our young men to observe, generously, that it didn't seem half a bad climate. They made other observations after they had emerged from their rooms in pursuit of breakfast—a meal of which they partook in a huge bare hall, where a hundred negroes, in white jackets, were shuffling about upon an uncarpeted floor; where the flies were superabundant and the tables and dishes covered over with a strange, voluminous integument of coarse blue gauze; and where several little boys and girls, who had risen late, were seated in fastidious solitude at the morning repast. These young persons had not the morning paper before them, but they were engaged in languid perusal of the bill of fare.

This latter document was a great puzzle to our friends, who, on reflecting that its bewildering categories had relation to breakfast alone, had an uneasy prevision of an encyclopædic dinner-list. They found a great deal of entertainment at the hotel, an enormous wooden structure, for the erection of which it seemed to them that the virgin forests of the West must have been terribly deflowered. It was perforated from end to end with immense bare corridors, through which a strong draught was blowing—bearing along wonderful figures of ladies in white morning-dresses and clouds of Valenciennes lace, who seemed to float down the long vistas with expanded furbelows, like angels spreading their wings. In front was a gigantic verandah, upon which an army might have encamped—a vast wooden terrace, with a roof as lofty as the nave of a cathedral. Here our young Englishmen enjoyed, as they supposed, a glimpse of American society, which was distributed over the measureless expanse in a variety of sedentary attitudes, and appeared to consist largely of pretty young girls, dressed as if for a *fête champêtre*, swaying to and fro in rocking-chairs, fanning themselves with large straw fans, and enjoying an enviable exemption from social cares. Lord Lambeth had a theory, which it might be interesting to trace to its origin, that it would be not only agreeable, but easily possible, to enter into relations with one of these young ladies; and his companion found occasion to check the young nobleman's colloquial impulses.

"You had better take care," said Percy Beaumont, "or you will have an offended father or brother pulling out a bowie-knife."

"I assure you it is all right," Lord Lambeth replied. "You know the Americans come to these big hotels to make acquaintances."

"I know nothing about it, and neither do you," said his kinsman, who, like a clever man, had begun to perceive that the observation of American society demanded a readjustment of one's standard.

"Hang it, then, let's find out!" cried Lord Lambeth with some impatience. "You know, I don't want to miss anything."

"We will find out," said Percy Beaumont, very reasonably. "We will go and see Mrs. Westgate and make all the proper inquiries."

And so the two inquiring Englishmen, who had this lady's address inscribed in her husband's hand upon a card, descended from the verandah of the big hotel and took their way, according to direction, along a large straight road, past a series of fresh-looking villas, embosomed in shrubs and flowers and enclosed in an ingenious variety of wooden palings. The morning was brilliant and cool, the villas were smart and snug, and the walk of the young travellers was very entertaining. Everything looked as if it had received a coat of fresh paint the day before—the red roofs, the green shutters, the clean, bright browns and buffs of the house-fronts. The flower-beds on the little lawns seemed to sparkle in the radiant air, and the gravel in the short carriage-sweeps to flash and twinkle. Along the road came a hundred little basket-phaetons, in which, almost always, a couple of ladies were sitting—ladies in white dresses and long white gloves, holding the reins and looking at the two Englishmen, whose nationality was not elusive, through thick blue veils, tied tightly about their faces as if to guard their complexions. At last the young men came within sight of the sea again, and then, having interrogated a gardener over the paling of a villa, they turned into an open gate. Here they found themselves face to face with the ocean and with a very picturesque structure, resembling a magnified *chalet*, which was perched upon a green embankment just above it. The house had a verandah of extraordinary width all around it, and a great many doors and windows standing open to the verandah. These various apertures had, in common, such an accessible, hospitable air, such a breezy flutter, within, of light curtains, such expansive thresholds and reassuring interiors, that our friends hardly knew which was the regular entrance, and, after hesitating a moment, presented themselves at one of the windows. The room within was dark, but in a moment a graceful figure vaguely shaped itself in the rich-looking gloom, and a lady came to meet them. Then they saw that she had been seated at a table, writing, and that she had heard them and had got up. She stepped out into the light; she wore a frank, charming smile, with which she held out her hand to Percy Beaumont.

"Oh, you must be Lord Lambeth and Mr. Beaumont," she said. "I have heard from my husband that you would come. I am extremely glad to see you." And she shook hands with each of her visitors. Her visitors were a little shy, but they had very good manners; they responded with smiles and exclamations, and they apologised for not knowing the front door. The lady rejoined, with vivacity, that when she wanted to see people very much she did not insist upon those distinctions, and that Mr. Westgate had written to her of his English friends in terms that made her really anxious. "He said you were so terribly prostrated," said Mrs. Westgate.

"Oh, you mean by the heat?" replied Percy Beaumont. "We were rather knocked up, but we feel wonderfully better. We had such a jolly—a—voyage down here. It's so very good of you to mind."

"Yes, it's so very kind of you," murmured Lord Lambeth.

Mrs. Westgate stood smiling; she was extremely pretty. "Well, I did mind," she said; "and I thought of sending for you this morning, to the Ocean House. I am very glad you are better, and I am charmed you have arrived. You must come round to the other side of the piazza." And she led the way, with a light, smooth step, looking back at the young men and smiling.

The other side of the piazza was, as Lord Lambeth presently remarked, a very jolly place. It was of the most liberal proportions, and with its awnings, its fanciful chairs, its cushions and rugs, its view of the ocean, close at hand, tumbling along the base of the low cliffs whose level tops intervened in lawnlike smoothness, it formed a charming complement to the drawing-room. As such it was in course of use at the present moment; it was occupied by a social circle. There were several ladies and two or three gentlemen, to whom Mrs. Westgate proceeded to introduce the distinguished strangers. She mentioned a great many names, very freely and distinctly: the young Englishmen, shuffling about and bowing, were rather bewildered. But at last they were provided with chairs—low wicker chairs, gilded and tied with a great many ribbons—and one of the ladies (a very young person, with a little snub nose and several dimples) offered Percy Beaumont a fan. The fan was also adorned with pink love-knots; but Percy Beaumont declined it, although he was very hot. Presently, however, it became cooler; the breeze from the sea was delicious, the view was charming, and the people sitting there looked exceedingly fresh and comfortable. Several of the ladies seemed to be young girls, and the gentlemen were slim, fair youths, such as our friends had seen the day before in New York. The ladies were working upon bands of tapestry, and one of the young men had an open book in his lap. Beaumont afterwards learned from one of the ladies that this young man had been reading aloud—that he was from Boston and was very fond of reading aloud. Beaumont said it was a great pity that they had interrupted him; he should like so much (from all he had heard) to hear a Bostonian read. Couldn't the young man be induced to go on?

"Oh no," said his informant, very freely; "he wouldn't be able to get the young ladies to attend to him now."

There was something very friendly, Beaumont perceived, in the attitude of the company; they looked at the young Englishmen with an air of animated sympathy and interest; they smiled, brightly and unanimously, at everything either of the visitors said. Lord Lambeth and his companion felt that they were being made very welcome. Mrs. Westgate seated herself between them, and, talking a great deal to each, they had occasion to observe that she was as pretty as their friend Littledale had promised. She was thirty years old, with the eyes and the smile of a girl of seventeen, and she was extremely light and graceful, elegant, exquisite. Mrs. Westgate was extremely spontaneous. She was very frank and demonstrative, and appeared always—while she looked at you delightedly with her beautiful young eyes—to be making sudden confessions and concessions, after momentary hesitations.

"We shall expect to see a great deal of you," she said to Lord Lambeth, with a kind of joyous earnestness. "We are very fond of Englishmen here; that is, there are a great many we have been fond of. After a day or two you must come and stay with us; we hope you will stay a long time. Newport's a very nice place when you come really to know it, when you know plenty of people. Of course, you and Mr. Beaumont will have no difficulty about that. Englishmen are very well received here; there are almost always two or three of them about. I think they always like it, and I must say I should think they would. They receive ever so much attention. I must say I think they sometimes get spoiled; but I am sure you and Mr. Beaumont are proof against that. My husband tells me you are a friend of Captain Littledale; he was such a charming man. He made himself most agreeable here, and I am sure I wonder he didn't stay. It couldn't have been pleasanter for him in his own country. Though I suppose it is very pleasant in England, for English people. I don't know myself; I have been there very little. I have been a great deal abroad, but I am always on the Continent. I must say I'm extremely fond of Paris; you know we Americans always are; we go there when we die. Did you ever hear that before? that was said by a great wit. I mean the good Americans; but we are all good; you'll see that for yourself. All I know of England is London, and all I know of London is that place—on that little corner, you know, where you buy jackets—jackets with that coarse braid and those big buttons. They make very good jackets in London, I will do you the justice to say that. And some people like the hats; but about the hats I was always a heretic; I always got my hats in Paris. You can't wear an English hat—at least, I never could—unless you dress your hair à *l'Anglaise;* and I must say that is a talent I never possessed. In Paris they will make things to suit your peculiarities; but in England I think you like much more to have—how shall I say it?—one thing for everybody. I mean as regards dress. I don't know about other things; but I have always supposed that in other things everything was different. I mean according to the people—according to the classes, and all that. I am afraid you will think that I don't take a very favourable view; but you know you can't take a very favourable view in Dover Street, in the month of November. That has always been my fate. Do you know Jones's Hotel, in Dover Street? That's all I know of England. Of course, every one admits that the English hotels are your weak point. There was always the most frightful fog; I couldn't see to try my things on. When I got over to America—into the light—I usually found they were twice too big. The next time I mean to go in the season; I think I shall go next year. I want very much to take my sister; she has never been to England. I don't know whether you know what I mean by saying that the Englishmen who come here sometimes get spoiled. I mean that they take things as a matter of course—things that are done for them. Now, naturally, they are only a matter of course when the Englishmen are very nice. But, of course, they are almost always very nice. Of course, this isn't nearly such an interesting country as England; there are not nearly so many things to see, and we haven't your country life. I have never seen anything of your country life; when I am in Europe I am always on the Continent. But I have heard a great deal about it; I know that when you are among yourselves in the country you have the most beautiful time. Of course, we have nothing of that sort, we have nothing on that scale. I don't apologise, Lord Lambeth; some Americans are always apologising; you must have noticed that. We have the reputation of always boasting and bragging and waving the American flag; but I must say that what strikes me is that we are perpetually making excuses and trying to smooth things over. The American flag has quite gone out of fashion; it's very carefully folded up, like an old table-cloth. Why should we apologise? The English never apologise—do they? No, I must say I never apologise. You must take us as we come—with all our imperfections on our heads. Of course we haven't your country life, and your old ruins, and your great estates, and your leisure-class, and all that. But if we haven't, I should think you might find it a pleasant change—I think any country is pleasant where they have pleasant manners. Captain Littledale told me he had never seen such pleasant manners as at Newport; and he had been a great deal in European society. Hadn't he been in the diplomatic service? He told me the dream of his life was to get appointed to a diplomatic post in Washington. But he doesn't seem to have succeeded. I suppose that in England promotion—and all that sort of thing—is fearfully slow. With us, you know, it's a great deal too fast. You see I admit our drawbacks. But I must confess I think Newport is an ideal place. I don't know anything like it anywhere. Captain Littledale told me he didn't know anything like it anywhere. It's entirely different from most watering-places; it's a most charming life. I must say I think that when one goes to a foreign country, one ought to enjoy the differences. Of course there are differences; otherwise what did one come abroad for? Look for your pleasure in the differences, Lord Lambeth; that's the way to do it; and then I am sure you will find American society—at least Newport society—most charming and most interesting. I wish very much my husband were here; but he's dreadfully confined to New York. I suppose you think that's very strange—for a gentleman. Only you see we haven't any leisure-class."

Mrs. Westgate's discourse, delivered in a soft, sweet voice, flowed on like a miniature torrent and was interrupted by a hundred little smiles, glances and gestures, which might have figured the irregularities and obstructions of such a stream. Lord Lambeth listened to her with, it must be confessed, a rather ineffectual attention, although he indulged in a good many little murmurs and ejaculations of assent and deprecation. He had no great faculty for apprehending generalisations. There were some three or four indeed which, in the play of his own intelligence, he had originated, and which had seemed convenient at the moment; but at the present time he could hardly have been said to follow Mrs. Westgate as she darted gracefully about in the sea of speculation. Fortunately she asked for no especial rejoinder, for she looked about at the rest of the company as well, and smiled at Percy Beaumont, on the other side of her, as if he too must understand her and agree with her. He was rather more successful than his companion; for besides being, as we know, cleverer, his attention was not vaguely distracted by close vicinity to a remarkably interesting young girl, with dark hair and blue eyes. This was the case with Lord Lambeth, to whom it occurred after a while that the young girl with blue eyes and dark hair was the pretty sister of whom Mrs. Westgate had spoken. She presently turned to him with a remark which established her identity.

"It's a great pity you couldn't have brought my brother-in-law with you. It's a great shame he should be in New York in these days."

"Oh yes; it's so very hot," said Lord Lambeth.

"It must be dreadful," said the young girl.

"I daresay he is very busy," Lord Lambeth observed.

"The gentlemen in America work too much," the young girl went on.

"Oh, do they? I daresay they like it," said her interlocutor.

"I don't like it. One never sees them."

"Don't you, really?" asked Lord Lambeth. "I shouldn't have fancied that."

"Have you come to study American manners?" asked the young girl.

"Oh, I don't know. I just came over for a lark. I haven't got long." Here there was a pause, and Lord Lambeth began again. "But Mr. Westgate will come down here, will not he?"

"I certainly hope he will. He must help to entertain you and Mr. Beaumont."

Lord Lambeth looked at her a little with his handsome brown eyes. "Do you suppose he would have come down with us, if we had urged him?"

Mr. Westgate's sister-in-law was silent a moment, and then—"I daresay he would," she answered.

"Really!" said the young Englishman. "He was immensely civil to Beaumont and me," he added.

"He is a dear good fellow," the young lady rejoined. "And he is a perfect husband. But all Americans are that," she continued, smiling.

"Really!" Lord Lambeth exclaimed again; and wondered whether all American ladies had such a passion for generalising as these two.

III

HE sat there a good while: there was a great deal of talk; it was all very friendly and lively and jolly. Every one present, sooner or later, said something to him, and seemed to make a particular point of addressing him by name. Two or three other persons came in, and there was a shifting of seats and changing of places; the gentlemen all entered into intimate conversation with the two Englishmen, made them urgent offers of hospitality and hoped they might frequently be of service to them. They were afraid Lord Lambeth and Mr. Beaumont were not very comfortable at their hotel—that it was not, as one of them said, "so private as those dear little English inns of yours." This last gentleman went on to say that unfortunately, as yet, perhaps, privacy was not quite so easily obtained in America as might be desired; still, he continued, you could generally get it by paying for it; in fact you could get everything in America nowadays by paying for it. American life was certainly growing a great deal more private; it was growing very much like England. Everything at Newport, for instance, was thoroughly private; Lord Lambeth would probably be struck with that. It was also represented to the strangers that it mattered very little whether their hotel was agreeable, as every one would want them to make visits; they would stay with other people, and, in any case, they would be a great deal at Mrs. Westgate's. They would find that very charming; it was the pleasantest house in

Newport. It was a pity Mr. Westgate was always away; he was a man of the highest ability—very acute, very acute. He worked like a horse and he left his wife—well, to do about as she liked. He liked her to enjoy herself, and she seemed to know how. She was extremely brilliant, and a splendid talker. Some people preferred her sister; but Miss Alden was very different; she was in a different style altogether. Some people even thought her prettier, and, certainly, she was not so sharp. She was more in the Boston style; she had lived a great deal in Boston and she was very highly educated. Boston girls, it was intimated, were more like English young ladies.

Lord Lambeth had presently a chance to test the truth of this proposition; for on the company rising in compliance with a suggestion from their hostess that they should walk down to the rocks and look at the sea, the young Englishman again found himself, as they strolled across the grass, in proximity to Mrs. Westgate's sister. Though she was but a girl of twenty, she appeared to feel the obligation to exert an active hospitality; and this was perhaps the more to be noticed as she seemed by nature a reserved and retiring person, and had little of her sister's fraternising quality. She was perhaps rather too thin, and she was a little pale; but as she moved slowly over the grass, with her arms hanging at her sides, looking gravely for a moment at the sea and then brightly, for all her gravity, at him, Lord Lambeth thought her at least as pretty as Mrs. Westgate, and reflected that if this was the Boston style the Boston style was very charming. He thought she looked very clever; he could imagine that she was highly educated; but at the same time she seemed gentle and graceful. For all her cleverness, however, he felt that she had to think a little what to say; she didn't say the first thing that came into her head; he had come from a different part of the world and from a different society, and she was trying to adapt her conversation. The others were scattering themselves near the rocks; Mrs. Westgate had charge of Percy Beaumont.

"Very jolly place, isn't it?" said Lord Lambeth. "It's a very jolly place to sit."

"Very charming," said the young girl; "I often sit here; there are all kinds of cosy corners—as if they had been made on purpose."

"Ah! I suppose you have had some of them made," said the young man.

Miss Alden looked at him a moment. "Oh no, we have had nothing made. It's pure nature."

"I should think you would have a few little benches—rustic seats and that sort of thing. It might be so jolly to sit here, you know," Lord Lambeth went on.

"I am afraid we haven't so many of those things as you," said the young girl, thoughtfully.

"I daresay you go in for pure nature as you were saying. Nature, over here, must be so grand, you know." And Lord Lambeth looked about him.

The little coast-line hereabouts was very pretty, but it was not at all grand; and Miss Alden appeared to rise to a perception of this fact. "I am afraid it seems to you very rough," she said. "It's not like the coast scenery in Kingsley's novels."

"Ah, the novels always overdo it, you know," Lord Lambeth rejoined. "You must not go by the novels."

They were wandering about a little on the rocks, and they stopped and looked down into a narrow chasm where the rising tide made a curious bellowing sound. It was loud enough to prevent their hearing each other, and they stood there for some moments in silence. The young girl looked at her companion, observing him attentively but covertly, as women, even when very young, know how to do. Lord Lambeth repaid observation; tall, straight and strong, he was handsome as certain young Englishmen, and certain young Englishmen almost alone, are handsome; with a perfect finish of feature and a look of intellectual repose and gentle good temper which seemed somehow to be consequent upon his well-cut nose and chin. And to speak of Lord Lambeth's expression of intellectual repose is not simply a civil way of saying that he looked stupid. He was evidently not a young man of an irritable imagination;

he was not, as he would himself have said, tremendously clever; but, though there was a kind of appealing dulness in his eye, he looked thoroughly reasonable and competent, and his appearance proclaimed that to be a nobleman, an athlete, and an excellent fellow, was a sufficiently brilliant combination of qualities. The young girl beside him, it may be attested without farther delay, thought him the handsomest young man she had ever seen; and Bessie Alden's imagination, unlike that of her companion, was irritable. He, however, was also making up his mind that she was uncommonly pretty.

"I daresay it's very gay here—that you have lots of balls and parties," he said; for, if he was not tremendously clever, he rather prided himself on having, with women, a sufficiency of conversation.

"Oh yes, there is a great deal going on," Bessie Alden replied. "There are not so many balls, but there are a good many other things. You will see for yourself; we live rather in the midst of it."

"It's very kind of you to say that. But I thought you Americans were always dancing."

"I suppose we dance a good deal; but I have never seen much of it. We don't do it much, at any rate, in summer. And I am sure," said Bessie Alden, "that we don't have so many balls as you have in England."

"Really!" exclaimed Lord Lambeth. "Ah, in England it all depends, you know."

"You will not think much of our gaieties," said the young girl, looking at him with a little mixture of interrogation and decision which was peculiar to her. The interrogation seemed earnest and the decision seemed arch; but the mixture, at any rate, was charming. "Those things, with us, are much less splendid than in England."

"I fancy you don't mean that," said Lord Lambeth, laughing.

"I assure you I mean everything I say," the young girl declared. "Certainly, from what I have read about English society, it is very different."

"Ah, well, you know," said her companion, "those things are

often described by fellows who know nothing about them. You mustn't mind what you read."

"Oh, I *shall* mind what I read!" Bessie Alden rejoined. "When I read Thackeray and George Eliot, how can I help minding them?"

"Ah, well, Thackeray—and George Eliot," said the young nobleman; "I haven't read much of them."

"Don't you suppose they know about society?" asked Bessie Alden.

"Oh, I daresay they know; they were so very clever. But those fashionable novels," said Lord Lambeth, "they are awful rot, you know."

His companion looked at him a moment with her dark blue eyes, and then she looked down into the chasm where the water was tumbling about. "Do you mean Mrs. Gore, for instance?" she said presently, raising her eyes.

"I am afraid I haven't read that either," was the young man's rejoinder, laughing a little and blushing. "I am afraid you'll think I am not very intellectual."

"Reading Mrs. Gore is no proof of intellect. But I like reading everything about English life—even poor books. I am so curious about it."

"Aren't ladies always curious?" asked the young man, jestingly.

But Bessie Alden appeared to desire to answer his question seriously. "I don't think so—I don't think we are enough so—that we care about many things. So it's all the more of a compliment," she added, "that I should want to know so much about England."

The logic here seemed a little close; but Lord Lambeth, conscious of a compliment, found his natural modesty just at hand. "I am sure you know a great deal more than I do."

"I really think I know a great deal—for a person who has never been there."

"Have you really never been there?" cried Lord Lambeth. "Fancy!"

"Never—except in imagination," said the young girl.

"Fancy!" repeated her companion. "But I daresay you'll go soon, won't you?"

"It's the dream of my life!" declared Bessie Alden, smiling.

"But your sister seems to know a tremendous lot about London," Lord Lambeth went on.

The young girl was silent a moment. "My sister and I are two very different persons," she presently said. "She has been a great deal in Europe. She has been in England several times. She has known a great many English people."

"But you must have known some, too," said Lord Lambeth.

"I don't think that I have ever spoken to one before. You are the first Englishman that—to my knowledge—I have ever talked with."

Bessie Alden made this statement with a certain gravity—almost, as it seemed to Lord Lambeth, an impressiveness. Attempts at impressiveness always made him feel awkward, and he now began to laugh and swing his stick. "Ah, you would have been sure to know!" he said. And then he added, after an instant—"I'm sorry I am not a better specimen."

The young girl looked away; but she smiled, laying aside her impressiveness. "You must remember that you are only a beginning," she said. Then she retraced her steps, leading the way back to the lawn, where they saw Mrs. Westgate come towards them with Percy Beaumont still at her side. "Perhaps I shall go to England next year," Miss Alden continued; "I want to, immensely. My sister is going to Europe, and she has asked me to go with her. If we go, I shall make her stay as long as possible in London."

"Ah, you must come in July," said Lord Lambeth. "That's the time when there is most going on."

"I don't think I can wait till July," the young girl rejoined. "By the first of May I shall be very impatient." They had gone farther, and Mrs. Westgate and her companion were near them. "Kitty," said Miss Alden, "I have given out that we are going to London next May. So please to conduct yourself accordingly."

Percy Beaumont wore a somewhat animated—even a slightly irritated—air. He was by no means so handsome a man as his cousin, although in his cousin's absence he might have passed for a striking specimen of the tall, muscular, fair-bearded, clear-eyed Englishman. Just now Beaumont's clear eyes, which were small and of a pale grey colour, had a rather troubled light, and, after glancing at Bessie Alden while she spoke, he rested them upon his kinsman. Mrs. Westgate meanwhile, with her superfluously pretty gaze, looked at every one alike.

"You had better wait till the time comes," she said to her sister. "Perhaps next May you won't care so much about London. Mr. Beaumont and I," she went on smiling at her companion, "have had a tremendous discussion. We don't agree about anything. It's perfectly delightful."

"Oh, I say, Percy!" exclaimed Lord Lambeth.

"I disagree," said Beaumont, stroking down his black hair, "even to the point of not thinking it delightful."

"Oh, I say!" cried Lord Lambeth again.

"I don't see anything delightful in my disagreeing with Mrs. Westgate," said Percy Beaumont.

"Well, I do!" Mrs. Westgate declared; and she turned to her sister. "You know you have to go to town. The phaeton is there. You had better take Lord Lambeth."

At this point Percy Beaumont certainly looked straight at his kinsman; he tried to catch his eye. But Lord Lambeth would not look at him; his own eyes were better occupied. "I shall be very happy," cried Bessie Alden. "I am only going to some shops. But I will drive you about and show you the place."

"An American woman who respects herself," said Mrs. Westgate, turning to Beaumont with her bright expository air, "must buy something every day of her life. If she cannot do it herself, she must send out some member of her family for the purpose. So Bessie goes forth to fulfil my mission."

The young girl had walked away, with Lord Lambeth by her side, to whom she was talking still; and Percy Beaumont watched them as they passed towards the house. "She fulfils her own mission," he presently said; "that of being a very attractive young lady."

"I don't know that I should say very attractive," Mrs. Westgate rejoined. "She is not so much that as she is charming when you really know her. She is very shy."

"Oh indeed?" said Percy Beaumont.

"Extremely shy," Mrs. Westgate repeated. "But she is a dear good girl; she is a charming species of girl. She is not in the least a flirt; that isn't at all her line; she doesn't know the alphabet of that sort of thing. She is very simple—very serious. She has lived a great deal in Boston, with another sister of mine—the eldest of us—who married a Bostonian. She is very cultivated, not at all like me—I am not in the least cultivated. She has studied immensely and read everything; she is what they call in Boston 'thoughtful.'"

"A rum sort of girl for Lambeth to get hold of!" his lordship's kinsman privately reflected.

"I really believe," Mrs. Westgate continued, "that the most charming girl in the world is a Boston superstructure upon a New York *fonds;* or perhaps a New York superstructure upon a Boston *fonds*. At any rate it's the mixture," said Mrs. Westgate, who continued to give Percy Beaumont a great deal of information.

Lord Lambeth got into a little basket-phaeton with Bessie Alden, and she drove him down the long avenue, whose extent he had measured on foot a couple of hours before, into the ancient town, as it was called in that part of the world, of Newport. The ancient town was a curious affair—a collection of fresh-looking little wooden houses, painted white, scattered over a hill-side and clustered about a long, straight street, paved with enormous cobble-stones. There were plenty of shops—a large proportion of which appeared to be those of fruit-vendors, with piles of huge water-melons and pumpkins stacked in front of them; and, drawn up before the shops, or bumping about on the cobble-stones, were innumerable other basket-phaetons freighted with ladies of high fashion, who greeted each other from vehicle to vehicle and conversed on the edge of the pavement in a manner that struck Lord Lambeth as demonstrative —with a great many "Oh, my dears," and little quick exclamations and caresses. His companion went into seventeen shops —he amused himself with counting them—and accumulated, at the bottom of the phaeton, a pile of bundles that hardly left the young Englishman a place for his feet. As she had no groom nor footman, he sat in the phaeton to hold the ponies; where, although he was not a particularly acute observer, he saw much to entertain him—especially the ladies just mentioned, who wandered up and down with the appearance of a kind of aimless intentness, as if they were looking for something to buy, and who, tripping in and out of their vehicles, displayed remarkably pretty feet. It all seemed to Lord Lambeth very odd, and bright, and gay. Of course, before they got back to the villa, he had had a great deal of desultory conversation with Bessie Alden.

The young Englishmen spent the whole of that day and the whole of many successive days in what the French call the *intimité* of their new friends. They agreed that it was extremely jolly—that they had never known anything more agreeable. It is not proposed to narrate minutely the incidents of their sojourn on this charming shore; though if it were convenient I might present a record of impressions none the less delectable that they were not exhaustively analysed. Many of them still linger in the minds of our travellers, attended by a train of harmonious images—images of brilliant mornings on lawns and piazzas that overlooked the sea; of innumerable pretty girls; of infinite lounging and talking and laughing and flirting and lunching and dining; of universal friendliness and frankness; of occasions on which they knew every one and everything and had an extraordinary sense of ease; of drives and rides in the late afternoon, over gleaming beaches, on long sea-roads, beneath a sky lighted up by marvellous sunsets; of tea-tables, on the return, informal, irregular, agreeable; of evenings at open windows or on the perpetual verandahs, in the summer starlight, above the warm Atlantic. The young Englishmen were introduced to everybody, entertained by everybody, intimate with everybody. At the end of three days they had removed their luggage from the hotel, and had gone to stay with Mrs. Westgate—a step to which Percy Beaumont at first offered some conscientious opposition. I call his opposition conscientious because it was founded upon some talk that he had had, on the second day, with Bessie Alden. He had indeed had a good deal of talk with her, for she was not literally always in conversation with Lord Lambeth. He had meditated upon Mrs. Westgate's account of her sister and he discovered, for himself, that the young lady was clever and appeared to have read a great deal. She seemed very nice, though he could not make out that, as Mrs. Westgate had said, she was shy. If she was shy she carried it off very well.

"Mr. Beaumont," she had said, "please tell me something about Lord Lambeth's family. How would you say it in England?—his position."

"His position?" Percy Beaumont repeated.

"His rank—or whatever you call it. Unfortunately we haven't got a 'Peerage,' like the people in Thackeray."

"That's a great pity," said Beaumont. "You would find it all set forth there so much better than I can do it."

"He is a great noble, then?"

"Oh yes, he is a great noble."

"Is he a peer?"

"Almost."

"And has he any other title than Lord Lambeth?"

"His title is the Marquis of Lambeth," said Beaumont; and then he was silent; Bessie Alden appeared to be looking at him with interest. "He is the son of the Duke of Bayswater," he added, presently.

"The eldest son?"

"The only son."

"And are his parents living?"

"Oh yes; if his father were not living he would be a duke."

"So that when his father dies," pursued Bessie Alden, with more simplicity than might have been expected in a clever girl, "he will become Duke of Bayswater?"

"Of course," said Percy Beaumont. "But his father is in excellent health."

"And his mother?"

Beaumont smiled a little. "The Duchess is uncommonly robust."

"And has he any sisters?"

"Yes, there are two."

"And what are they called?"

"One of them is married. She is the Countess of Pimlico."

"And the other?"

"The other is unmarried; she is plain Lady Julia."

Bessie Alden looked at him a moment. "Is she very plain?"

Beaumont began to laugh again. "You would not find her so handsome as her brother," he said; and it was after this that he attempted to dissuade the heir of the Duke of Bayswater from accepting Mrs. Westgate's invitation. "Depend upon it," he said, "that girl means to try for you."

"It seems to me you are doing your best to make a fool of me," the modest young nobleman answered.

"She has been asking me," said Beaumont, "all about your people and your possessions."

"I am sure it is very good of her!" Lord Lambeth rejoined.

"Well, then," observed his companion, "if you go, you go with your eyes open."

"Damn my eyes!" exclaimed Lord Lambeth. "If one is to be a dozen times a day at the house, it is a great deal more convenient to sleep there. I am sick of travelling up and down this beastly Avenue."

Since he had determined to go, Percy Beaumont would of course have been very sorry to allow him to go alone; he was a man of conscience, and he remembered his promise to the Duchess. It was obviously the memory of this promise that made him say to his companion a couple of days later that he rather wondered he should be so fond of that girl.

"In the first place, how do you know how fond I am of her?" asked Lord Lambeth. "And in the second place, why shouldn't I be fond of her?"

"I shouldn't think she would be in your line."

"What do you call my 'line'? You don't set her down as 'fast'?"

"Exactly so. Mrs. Westgate tells me that there is no such thing as the 'fast girl' in America; that it's an English invention and that the term has no meaning here."

"All the better. It's an animal I detest."

"You prefer a blue-stocking."

"Is that what you call Miss Alden?"

"Her sister tells me," said Percy Beaumont, "that she is tremendously literary."

"I don't know anything about that. She is certainly very clever."

"Well," said Beaumont, "I should have supposed you would have found that sort of thing awfully slow."

"In point of fact," Lord Lambeth rejoined, "I find it uncommonly lively."

After this, Percy Beaumont held his tongue; but on August 10th he wrote to the Duchess of Bayswater. He was, as I have said, a man of conscience, and he had a strong, incorruptible sense of the proprieties of life. His kinsman, meanwhile, was having a great deal of talk with Bessie Alden—on the red sea-rocks beyond the lawn; in the course of long island rides, with a slow return in the glowing twilight; on the deep verandah, late in the evening. Lord Lambeth, who had stayed at many houses, had never stayed at a house in which it was possible for a young man to converse so frequently with a young lady. This young lady no longer applied to Percy Beaumont for information concerning his lordship. She addressed herself directly to the young nobleman. She asked him a great many questions, some of which bored him a little; for he took no pleasure in talking about himself.

"Lord Lambeth," said Bessie Alden, "are you an hereditary legislator?"

"Oh, I say," cried Lord Lambeth, "don't make me call myself such names as that."

"But you are a member of Parliament," said the young girl.

"I don't like the sound of that either."

"Doesn't your father sit in the House of Lords?" Bessie Alden went on.

"Very seldom," said Lord Lambeth.

"Is it an important position?" she asked.

"Oh dear no," said Lord Lambeth.

"I should think it would be very grand," said Bessie Alden, "to possess simply by an accident of birth the right to make laws for a great nation."

"Ah, but one doesn't make laws. It's a great humbug."

"I don't believe that," the young girl declared. "It must be a great privilege, and I should think that if one thought of it in the right way—from a high point of view—it would be very inspiring."

"The less one thinks of it the better," Lord Lambeth affirmed.

"I think it's tremendous," said Bessie Alden; and on another occasion she asked him if he had any tenantry. Hereupon it was that, as I have said, he was a little bored.

"Do you want to buy up their leases?" he asked.

"Well—have you got any livings?" she demanded.

"Oh, I say!" he cried. "Have you got a clergyman that is looking out?" But she made him tell her that he had a Castle; he confessed to but one. It was the place in which he had been born and brought up, and, as he had an old-time liking for it, he was beguiled into describing it a little and saying it was really very jolly. Bessie Alden listened with great interest, and declared that she would give the world to see such a place.

Whereupon—"It would be awfully kind of you to come and stay there," said Lord Lambeth. He took a vague satisfaction in the circumstance that Percy Beaumont had not heard him make the remark I have just recorded.

Mr. Westgate, all this time, had not, as they said at Newport, "come on." His wife more than once announced that she expected him on the morrow; but on the morrow she wandered about a little, with a telegram in her jewelled fingers, declaring it was very tiresome that his business detained him in New York; that he could only hope the Englishmen were having a good time. "I must say," said Mrs. Westgate, "that it is no thanks to him if you are!" And she went on to explain, while she continued that slow-paced promenade which enabled her well-adjusted skirts to display themselves so advantageously, that unfortunately in America there was no leisure-class. It was Lord Lambeth's theory, freely propounded when the young men were together, that Percy Beaumont was having a very good time with Mrs. Westgate, and that under the pretext of meeting for the purpose of animated discussion, they were indulging in practices that imparted a shade of hypocrisy to the lady's regret for her husband's absence.

"I assure you we are always discussing and differing," said Percy Beaumont. "She is awfully argumentative. American ladies certainly don't mind contradicting you. Upon my word I don't think I was ever treated so by a woman before. She's so devilish positive."

Mrs. Westgate's positive quality, however, evidently had its attractions; for Beaumont was constantly at his hostess's side. He detached himself one day to the extent of going to New York to talk over the Tennessee Central with Mr. Westgate; but he was absent only forty-eight hours, during which, with Mr. Westgate's assistance, he completely settled this piece of business. "They certainly do things quickly in New York," he observed to his cousin; and he added that Mr. Westgate had seemed very uneasy lest his wife should miss her visitor—he had been in such an awful hurry to send him back to her. "I'm afraid you'll never come up to an American husband—if that's what the wives expect," he said to Lord Lambeth.

Mrs. Westgate, however, was not to enjoy much longer the entertainment with which an indulgent husband had desired to keep her provided. On August 21st Lord Lambeth received a telegram from his mother, requesting him to return immediately to England; his father had been taken ill, and it was his filial duty to come to him.

The young Englishman was visibly annoyed. "What the deuce does it mean?" he asked of his kinsman. "What am I to do?"

Percy Beaumont was annoyed as well; he had deemed it his duty, as I have narrated, to write to the Duchess, but he had not expected that this distinguished woman would act so promptly upon his hint. "It means," he said, "that your father is laid up. I don't suppose it's anything serious; but you have no option. Take the first steamer; but don't be alarmed."

Lord Lambeth made his farewells; but the few last words that he exchanged with Bessie Alden are the only ones that have a place in our record. "Of course I needn't assure you," he said, "that if you should come to England next year, I expect to be the first person that you inform of it."

Bessie Alden looked at him a little and she smiled. "Oh, if we come to London," she answered, "I should think you would hear of it."

Percy Beaumont returned with his cousin, and his sense of duty compelled him, one windless afternoon, in mid-Atlantic, to say to Lord Lambeth that he suspected that the Duchess's telegram was in part the result of something he himself had written to her. "I wrote to her—as I explicitly notified you I had promised to do—that you were extremely interested in a little American girl."

Lord Lambeth was extremely angry, and he indulged for some moments in the simple language of resentment. But I have said that he was a reasonable young man, and I can give no better proof of it than the fact that he remarked to his companion at the end of half-an-hour—"You were quite right after all. I am very much interested in her. Only, to be fair," he added, "you should have told my mother also that she is not—seriously—interested in me."

Percy Beaumont gave a little laugh. "There is nothing so charming as modesty in a young man in your position. That speech is a capital proof that you are sweet on her."

"She is not interested—she is not!" Lord Lambeth repeated.

"My dear fellow," said his companion, "you are very far gone."

IV

IN point of fact, as Percy Beaumont would have said, Mrs. Westgate disembarked on the 18th of May on the British coast. She was accompanied by her sister, but she was not attended by any other member of her family. To the deprivation of her husband's society Mrs. Westgate was, however, habituated; she had made half-a-dozen journeys to Europe without him, and she now accounted for his absence, to interrogative friends on this side of the Atlantic, by allusion to the regrettable but conspicuous fact that in America there was no leisure-class. The two ladies came up to London and alighted at Jones's Hotel, where Mrs. Westgate, who had made on former occasions the most agreeable impression at this establishment, received an obsequious greeting. Bessie Alden had felt much excited about coming to England; she had expected the "associations" would be very charming, that it would be an infinite pleasure to rest her eyes upon the things she had read about in the poets and historians. She was very fond of the poets and historians, of the picturesque, of the past, of retrospect, of mementoes and reverberations of greatness; so that on coming into the great English world, where strangeness and familiarity would go hand in hand, she was prepared for a multitude of fresh emotions. They began very promptly—these tender, fluttering sensations; they began with the sight of the beautiful English landscape, whose dark richness was quickened and brightened by the season; with the carpeted fields and flowering hedge-rows, as she looked at them from the window of the train; with the spires of the rural churches, peeping above the rook-haunted tree-tops; with the oak-studded parks, the ancient homes, the cloudy light, the speech, the manners, the thousand differences. Mrs. Westgate's impressions had of course much less novelty and keenness, and she gave but a wandering attention to her sister's ejaculations and rhapsodies.

"You know my enjoyment of England is not so intellectual as Bessie's," she said to several of her friends in the course of her visit to this country. "And yet if it is not intellectual, I can't say it is physical. I don't think I can quite say what it is, my enjoyment of England." When once it was settled that the two ladies should come abroad and should spend a few weeks in England on their way to the Continent, they of course exchanged a good many allusions to their London acquaintance.

"It will certainly be much nicer having friends there," Bessie Alden had said one day, as she sat on the sunny deck of the steamer, at her sister's feet, on a large blue rug.

"Whom do you mean by friends?" Mrs. Westgate asked.

"All those English gentlemen whom you have known and entertained. Captain Littledale, for instance. And Lord Lambeth and Mr. Beaumont," added Bessie Alden.

"Do you expect them to give us a very grand reception?"

Bessie reflected a moment; she was addicted, as we know, to reflection. "Well, yes."

"My poor sweet child!" murmured her sister.

"What have I said that is so silly?" asked Bessie.

"You are a little too simple; just a little. It is very becoming, but it pleases people at your expense."

"I am certainly too simple to understand you," said Bessie.

"Shall I tell you a story?" asked her sister.

"If you would be so good. That is what they do to amuse simple people."

Mrs. Westgate consulted her memory, while her companion sat gazing at the shining sea. "Did you ever hear of the Duke of Green-Erin?"

"I think not," said Bessie.

"Well, it's no matter," her sister went on.

"It's a proof of my simplicity."

"My story is meant to illustrate that of some other people," said Mrs. Westgate. "The Duke of Green-Erin is what they call in England a great swell; and some five years ago he came to America. He spent most of his time in New York, and in New York he spent his days and his nights at the Butterworths'. You have heard at least of the Butterworths. *Bien.* They did everything in the world for him—they turned themselves inside out. They gave him a dozen dinner-parties and balls, and were the means of his being invited to fifty more. At first he used to come into Mrs. Butterworth's box at the opera in a tweed travelling-suit; but some one stopped that. At any rate, he had a beautiful time, and they parted the best friends in the world. Two years elapse, and the Butterworths come abroad and go to London. The first thing they see in all the papers—in England those things are in the most prominent place—is that the Duke of Green-Erin has arrived in town for the Season. They wait a little, and then Mr. Butterworth—as polite as ever—goes and leaves a card. They wait a little more; the visit is not returned; they wait three weeks—*silence de mort*—the Duke gives no sign. The Butterworths see a lot of other people, put down the Duke of Green-Erin as a rude, ungrateful man, and forget all about him. One fine day they go to Ascot Races, and there they meet him face to face. He stares a moment and then comes up to Mr. Butterworth, taking something from his pocket-book—something which proves to be a bank-note. 'I'm glad to see you, Mr. Butterworth,' he says, 'so that I can pay you that ten pounds I lost to you in New York. I saw the other day you remembered our bet; here are the ten pounds, Mr. Butterworth. Good-bye, Mr. Butterworth.' And off he goes, and that's the last they see of the Duke of Green-Erin."

"Is that your story?" asked Bessie Alden.

"Don't you think it's interesting?" her sister replied.

"I don't believe it," said the young girl.

"Ah!" cried Mrs. Westgate, "you are not so simple after all. Believe it or not as you please; there is no smoke without fire."

"Is that the way," asked Bessie after a moment, "that you expect your friends to treat you?"

"I defy them to treat me very ill, because I shall not give them the opportunity. With the best will in the world, in that case, they can't be very disobliging."

Bessie Alden was silent a moment. "I don't see what makes you talk that way," she said. "The English are a great people."

"Exactly; and that is just the way they have grown great—by dropping you when you have ceased to be useful. People say they are not clever; but I think they are very clever."

"You know you have liked them—all the Englishmen you have seen," said Bessie.

"They have liked me," her sister rejoined; "it would be more correct to say that. And of course one likes that."

Bessie Alden resumed for some moments her studies in sea-green. "Well," she said, "whether they like me or not, I mean to like them. And happily," she added, "Lord Lambeth does not owe me ten pounds."

During the first few days after their arrival at Jones's Hotel our charming Americans were much occupied with what they would have called looking about them. They found occasion to make a large number of purchases, and their opportunities for conversation were such only as were offered by the deferential London shopmen. Bessie Alden, even in driving from the station, took an immense fancy to the British metropolis, and, at the risk of exhibiting her as a young woman of vulgar tastes, it must be recorded that for a considerable period she desired no higher pleasure than to drive about the crowded streets in a Hansom cab. To her attentive eyes they were full of a strange picturesque life, and it is at least beneath the dignity of our historic muse to enumerate the trivial objects and incidents which this simple young lady from Boston found so entertaining. It may be freely mentioned, however, that whenever, after a round of visits in Bond Street and Regent Street, she was about to return with her sister to Jones's Hotel, she made an earnest request that they should be driven home by way of Westminster Abbey. She had begun by asking whether it would not be possible to take the Tower on the way to their lodgings; but it happened that at a more primitive stage of her culture Mrs. Westgate had paid a visit to this venerable monument, which she spoke of ever afterwards, vaguely, as a dreadful disappointment; so that she expressed the liveliest disapproval of any attempt to combine historical researches with the purchase of hair-brushes and note-paper. The most she would consent to do in this line was to spend half-an-hour at Madame Tussaud's, where she saw several dusty wax effigies of members of the Royal Family. She told Bessie that if she wished to go to the Tower she must get some one else to take her. Bessie expressed hereupon an earnest disposition to go alone; but upon this proposal as well Mrs. Westgate sprinkled cold water.

"Remember," she said, "that you are not in your innocent little Boston. It is not a question of walking up and down Beacon Street." Then she went on to explain that there were two classes of American girls in Europe—those that walked about alone and those that did not. "You happen to belong, my dear," she said to her sister, "to the class that does not."

"It is only," answered Bessie, laughing, "because you happen to prevent me." And she devoted much private meditation to this question of effecting a visit to the Tower of London.

Suddenly it seemed as if the problem might be solved; the two ladies at Jones's Hotel received a visit from Willie Woodley. Such was the social appellation of a young American who had sailed from New York a few days after their own departure, and who, having the privilege of intimacy with them in that city, had lost no time, on his arrival in London, in coming to pay them his respects. He had, in fact, gone to see them directly after going to see his tailor; than which there can be no greater exhibition of promptitude on the part of a young American who has just alighted at the Charing Cross Hotel. He was a slim, pale youth, of the most amiable disposition, famous for the skill with which he led the "German" in New York. Indeed, by the young ladies who habitually figured in this fashionable frolic he was believed to be "the best dancer in the world;" it was in these terms that he was always spoken of, and that his identity was indicated. He was the gentlest, softest young man it was possible to meet; he was beautifully dressed—"in the English style"—and he knew an immense deal about London. He had been at Newport during the previous summer, at the time of our young Englishmen's visit, and he took extreme pleasure in the society of Bessie Alden, whom he always ad-dressed as "Miss Bessie." She immediately arranged with him, in the presence of her sister, that he should conduct her to the scene of Lady Jane Grey's execution.

"You may do as you please," said Mrs. Westgate. "Only—if you desire the information—it is not the custom here for young ladies to knock about London with young men."

"Miss Bessie has waltzed with me so often," observed Willie Woodley; "she can surely go out with me in a Hansom."

"I consider waltzing," said Mrs. Westgate, "the most inno-cent pleasure of our time."

"It's a compliment to our time!" exclaimed the young man, with a little laugh, in spite of himself.

"I don't see why I should regard what is done here," said Bessie Alden. "Why should I suffer the restrictions of a society of which I enjoy none of the privileges?"

"That's very good—very good," murmured Willie Woodley.

"Oh, go to the Tower, and feel the axe, if you like!" said Mrs. Westgate. "I consent to your going with Mr. Woodley; but I should not let you go with an Englishman."

"Miss Bessie wouldn't care to go with an Englishman!" Mr. Woodley declared, with a faint asperity that was, perhaps, not unnatural in a young man who, dressing in the manner that I have indicated, and knowing a great deal, as I have said, about

London, saw no reason for drawing these sharp distinctions. He agreed upon a day with Miss Bessie—a day of that same week.

An ingenious mind might, perhaps, trace a connection between the young girl's allusion to her destitution of social privileges and a question she asked on the morrow as she sat with her sister at lunch.

"Don't you mean to write to—to any one?" said Bessie.

"I wrote this morning to Captain Littledale," Mrs. Westgate replied.

"But Mr. Woodley said that Captain Littledale had gone to India."

"He said he thought he had heard so; he knew nothing about it."

For a moment Bessie Alden said nothing more; then, at last, "And don't you intend to write to—to Mr. Beaumont?" she inquired.

"You mean to Lord Lambeth," said her sister.

"I said Mr. Beaumont because he was so good a friend of yours."

Mrs. Westgate looked at the young girl with sisterly candour. "I don't care two straws for Mr. Beaumont."

"You were certainly very nice to him."

"I am nice to every one," said Mrs. Westgate, simply.

"To every one but me," rejoined Bessie, smiling.

Her sister continued to look at her; then, at last, "Are you in love with Lord Lambeth?" she asked.

The young girl stared a moment, and the question was apparently too humorous even to make her blush. "Not that I know of," she answered.

"Because if you are," Mrs. Westgate went on, "I shall certainly not send for him."

"That proves what I said," declared Bessie, smiling—"that you are not nice to me."

"It would be a poor service, my dear child," said her sister.

"In what sense? There is nothing against Lord Lambeth, that I know of."

Mrs. Westgate was silent a moment. "You *are* in love with him, then?"

Bessie stared again; but this time she blushed a little. "Ah! if you won't be serious," she answered, "we will not mention him again."

For some moments Lord Lambeth was not mentioned again, and it was Mrs. Westgate who, at the end of this period, reverted to him. "Of course I will let him know we are here; because I think he would be hurt—justly enough—if we should go away without seeing him. It is fair to give him a chance to come and thank me for the kindness we showed him. But I don't want to seem eager."

"Neither do I," said Bessie, with a little laugh.

"Though I confess," added her sister, "that I am curious to see how he will behave."

"He behaved very well at Newport."

"Newport is not London. At Newport he could do as he liked; but here, it is another affair. He has to have an eye to consequences."

"If he had more freedom, then, at Newport," argued Bessie, "it is the more to his credit that he behaved well; and if he has to be so careful here, it is possible he will behave even better."

"Better—better," repeated her sister. "My dear child, what is your point of view?"

"How do you mean—my point of view?"

"Don't you care for Lord Lambeth—a little?"

This time Bessie Alden was displeased; she slowly got up from table, turning her face away from her sister. "You will oblige me by not talking so," she said.

Mrs. Westgate sat watching her for some moments as she moved slowly about the room and went and stood at the window. "I will write to him this afternoon," she said at last.

"Do as you please!" Bessie answered; and presently she turned round. "I am not afraid to say that I like Lord Lambeth. I like him very much."

"He is not clever," Mrs. Westgate declared.

"Well, there have been clever people whom I have disliked," said Bessie Alden; "so that I suppose I may like a stupid one. Besides, Lord Lambeth is not stupid."

"Not so stupid as he looks!" exclaimed her sister, smiling.

"If I were in love with Lord Lambeth, as you said just now, it would be bad policy on your part to abuse him."

"My dear child, don't give me lessons in policy!" cried Mrs. Westgate. "The policy I mean to follow is very deep."

The young girl began to walk about the room again; then she stopped before her sister. "I have never heard in the course of five minutes," she said, "so many hints and innuendoes. I wish you would tell me in plain English what you mean."

"I mean that you may be much annoyed."

"That is still only a hint," said Bessie.

Her sister looked at her, hesitating an instant. "It will be said of you that you have come after Lord Lambeth—that you followed him."

Bessie Alden threw back her pretty head like a startled hind, and a look flashed into her face that made Mrs. Westgate rise from her chair. "Who says such things as that?" she demanded.

"People here."

"I don't believe it," said Bessie.

"You have a very convenient faculty of doubt. But my policy will be, as I say, very deep. I shall leave you to find out this kind of thing for yourself."

Bessie fixed her eyes upon her sister, and Mrs. Westgate thought for a moment there were tears in them. "Do they talk that way here?" she asked.

"You will see. I shall leave you alone."

"Don't leave me alone," said Bessie Alden. "Take me away."

"No; I want to see what you make of it," her sister continued.

"I don't understand."

"You will understand after Lord Lambeth has come," said Mrs. Westgate, with a little laugh.

The two ladies had arranged that on this afternoon Willie Woodley should go with them to Hyde Park, where Bessie Alden expected to derive much entertainment from sitting on a little green chair, under the great trees, beside Rotten Row. The want of a suitable escort had hitherto rendered this pleasure inaccessible; but no escort, now, for such an expedition, could have been more suitable than their devoted young countryman, whose mission in life, it might almost be said, was to find chairs for ladies, and who appeared on the stroke of half-past five with a white camellia in his button-hole.

"I have written to Lord Lambeth, my dear," said Mrs. Westgate to her sister, on coming into the room where Bessie Alden, drawing on her long grey gloves, was entertaining their visitor.

Bessie said nothing, but Willie Woodley exclaimed that his lordship was in town; he had seen his name in the *Morning Post*.

"Do you read the *Morning Post?*" asked Mrs. Westgate.

"Oh yes; it's great fun," Willie Woodley affirmed.

"I want so to see it," said Bessie, "there is so much about it in Thackeray."

"I will send it to you every morning," said Willie Woodley.

He found them what Bessie Alden thought excellent places, under the great trees, beside the famous avenue whose humours had been made familiar to the young girl's childhood by the pictures in *Punch*. The day was bright and warm, and the crowd of riders and spectators and the great procession of carriages were proportionately dense and brilliant. The scene bore the stamp of the London Season at its height, and Bessie Alden found more entertainment in it than she was able to express to her companions. She sat silent, under her parasol, and her imagination, according to its wont, let itself loose into the great changing assemblage of striking and suggestive figures. They stirred up a host of old impressions and preconceptions, and she found herself fitting a history to this person and a theory to that, and making a place for them all in her little private museum of types. But if she said little, her sister on one side and Willie Woodley on the other expressed themselves in lively alternation.

"Look at that green dress with blue flounces," said Mrs. Westgate. "*Quelle toilette!*"

"That's the Marquis of Blackborough," said the young man —"the one in the white coat. I heard him speak the other night in the House of Lords; it was something about ramrods; he called them *wamwods*. He's an awful swell."

"Did you ever see anything like the way they are pinned back?" Mrs. Westgate resumed. "They never know where to stop."

"They do nothing but stop," said Willie Woodley. "It prevents them from walking. Here comes a great celebrity—Lady Beatrice Bellevue. She's awfully fast; see what little steps she takes."

"Well, my dear," Mrs. Westgate pursued, "I hope you are getting some ideas for your *couturière?*"

"I am getting plenty of ideas," said Bessie, "but I don't know that my *couturière* would appreciate them."

Willie Woodley presently perceived a friend on horseback, who drove up beside the barrier of the Row and beckoned to him. He went forward and the crowd of pedestrians closed about him, so that for some ten minutes he was hidden from sight. At last he reappeared, bringing a gentleman with him—a gentleman whom Bessie at first supposed to be his friend dismounted. But at a second glance she found herself looking at Lord Lambeth, who was shaking hands with her sister.

"I found him over there," said Willie Woodley, "and I told him you were here."

And then Lord Lambeth, touching his hat a little, shook hands with Bessie. "Fancy your being here!" he said. He was blushing and smiling; he looked very handsome, and he had a kind of splendour that he had not had in America. Bessie Alden's imagination, as we know, was just then in exercise; so that the tall young Englishman, as he stood there looking down at her, had the benefit of it. "He is handsomer and more splendid than anything I have ever seen," she said to herself. And then she remembered that he was a Marquis, and she thought he looked like a Marquis.

"Really, you know," he cried, "you ought to have let a man know you were here!"

"I wrote to you an hour ago," said Mrs. Westgate.

"Doesn't all the world know it?" asked Bessie, smiling.

"I assure you I didn't know it!" cried Lord Lambeth. "Upon my honour I hadn't heard of it. Ask Woodley now; had I, Woodley?"

"Well, I think you are rather a humbug," said Willie Woodley.

"You don't believe that—do you, Miss Alden?" asked his lordship. "You don't believe I'm a humbug, eh?"

"No," said Bessie, "I don't."

"You are too tall to stand up, Lord Lambeth," Mrs. Westgate observed. "You are only tolerable when you sit down. Be so good as to get a chair."

He found a chair and placed it sidewise, close to the two ladies. "If I hadn't met Woodley I should never have found you," he went on. "Should I, Woodley?"

"Well, I guess not," said the young American.

"Not even with my letter?" asked Mrs. Westgate.

"Ah, well, I haven't got your letter yet; I suppose I shall get it this evening. It was awfully kind of you to write."

"So I said to Bessie," observed Mrs. Westgate.

"Did she say so, Miss Alden?" Lord Lambeth inquired. "I daresay you have been here a month."

"We have been here three," said Mrs. Westgate.

"Have you been here three months?" the young man asked again of Bessie.

"It seems a long time," Bessie answered.

"I say, after that you had better not call me a humbug!" cried Lord Lambeth. "I have only been in town three weeks; but you must have been hiding away. I haven't seen you anywhere."

"Where should you have seen us—where should we have gone?" asked Mrs. Westgate.

"You should have gone to Hurlingham," said Willie Woodley.

"No, let Lord Lambeth tell us," Mrs. Westgate insisted.

"There are plenty of places to go to," said Lord Lambeth—"each one stupider than the other. I mean people's houses; they send you cards."

"No one has sent us cards," said Bessie.

"We are very quiet," her sister declared. "We are here as travellers."

"We have been to Madame Tussaud's," Bessie pursued.

"Oh, I say!" cried Lord Lambeth.

"We thought we should find your image there," said Mrs. Westgate—"yours and Mr. Beaumont's."

"In the Chamber of Horrors?" laughed the young man.

"It did duty very well for a party," said Mrs. Westgate. "All the women were *décolletées*, and many of the figures looked as if they could speak if they tried."

"Upon my word," Lord Lambeth rejoined, "you see people at London parties that look as if they couldn't speak if they tried."

"Do you think Mr. Woodley could find us Mr. Beaumont?" asked Mrs. Westgate.

Lord Lambeth stared and looked round him. "I daresay he could. Beaumont often comes here. Don't you think you could find him, Woodley? Make a dive into the crowd."

"Thank you; I have had enough diving," said Willie Woodley. "I will wait till Mr. Beaumont comes to the surface."

"I will bring him to see you," said Lord Lambeth; "where are you staying?"

"You will find the address in my letter—Jones's Hotel."

"Oh, one of those places just out of Piccadilly? Beastly hole, isn't it?" Lord Lambeth inquired.

"I believe it's the best hotel in London," said Mrs. Westgate.

"But they give you awful rubbish to eat, don't they?" his lordship went on.

"Yes," said Mrs. Westgate.

"I always feel so sorry for the people that come up to town and go to live in those places," continued the young man. "They eat nothing but poison."

"Oh, I say!" cried Willie Woodley.

"Well, how do you like London, Miss Alden?" Lord Lambeth asked, unperturbed by this ejaculation.

"I think it's grand," said Bessie Alden.

"My sister likes it, in spite of the 'poison'!" Mrs. Westgate exclaimed.

"I hope you are going to stay a long time."

"As long as I can," said Bessie.

"And where is Mr. Westgate?" asked Lord Lambeth of this gentleman's wife.

"He's where he always is—in that tiresome New York."

"He must be tremendously clever," said the young man.

"I suppose he is," said Mrs. Westgate.

Lord Lambeth sat for nearly an hour with his American friends; but it is not our purpose to relate their conversation in full. He addressed a great many remarks to Bessie Alden, and finally turned towards her altogether, while Willie Woodley entertained Mrs. Westgate. Bessie herself said very little; she was on her guard, thinking of what her sister had said to her at lunch. Little by little, however, she interested herself in Lord Lambeth again, as she had done at Newport; only it seemed to her that here he might become more interesting. He would be an unconscious part of the antiquity, the impressiveness, the picturesqueness of England; and poor Bessie Alden, like many a Yankee maiden, was terribly at the mercy of picturesqueness.

"I have often wished I were at Newport again," said the young man. "Those days I spent at your sister's were awfully jolly."

"We enjoyed them very much; I hope your father is better."

"Oh dear, yes. When I got to England, he was out grouse-shooting. It was what you call in America a gigantic fraud. My mother had got nervous. My three weeks at Newport seemed like a happy dream."

"America certainly is very different from England," said Bessie.

"I hope you like England better, eh?" Lord Lambeth rejoined, almost persuasively.

"No Englishman can ask that seriously of a person of another country."

Her companion looked at her for a moment. "You mean it's a matter of course?"

"If I were English," said Bessie, "it would certainly seem to me a matter of course that every one should be a good patriot."

"Oh dear, yes; patriotism is everything," said Lord Lambeth, not quite following, but very contented. "Now, what are you going to do here?"

"On Thursday I am going to the Tower."

"The Tower?"

"The Tower of London. Did you never hear of it?"

"Oh yes, I have been there," said Lord Lambeth. "I was taken there by my governess, when I was six years old. It's a rum idea, your going there."

"Do give me a few more rum ideas," said Bessie. "I want to see everything of that sort. I am going to Hampton Court, and to Windsor, and to the Dulwich Gallery."

Lord Lambeth seemed greatly amused. "I wonder you don't go to the Rosherville Gardens."

"Are they interesting?" asked Bessie.

"Oh, wonderful!"

"Are they very old? That's all I care for," said Bessie.

"They are temendously old; they are all falling to ruins."

"I think there is nothing so charming as an old ruinous garden," said the young girl. "We must certainly go there."

Lord Lambeth broke out into merriment. "I say, Woodley," he cried, "here's Miss Alden wants to go to the Rosherville Gardens!"

Willie Woodley looked a little blank; he was caught in the

fact of ignorance of an apparently conspicuous feature of London life. But in a moment he turned it off. "Very well," he said, "I'll write for a permit."

Lord Lambeth's exhilaration increased. "'Gad, I believe you Americans would go anywhere!" he cried.

"We wish to go to Parliament," said Bessie. "That's one of the first things."

"Oh, it would bore you to death!" cried the young man.

"We wish to hear you speak."

"I never speak—except to young ladies," said Lord Lambeth, smiling.

Bessie Alden looked at him awhile; smiling, too, in the shadow of her parasol. "You are very strange," she murmured. "I don't think I approve of you."

"Ah, now, don't be severe, Miss Alden!" said Lord Lambeth, smiling still more. "Please don't be severe. I want you to like me—awfully."

"To like you awfully? You must not laugh at me, then, when I make mistakes. I consider it my right—as a free-born American—to make as many mistakes as I choose."

"Upon my word, I didn't laugh at you," said Lord Lambeth.

"And not only that," Bessie went on; "but I hold that all my mistakes shall be set down to my credit. You must think the better of me for them."

"I can't think better of you than I do," the young man declared.

Bessie Alden looked at him a moment again. "You certainly speak very well to young ladies. But why don't you address the House?—isn't that what they call it?"

"Because I have nothing to say," said Lord Lambeth.

"Haven't you a great position?" asked Bessie Alden.

He looked a moment at the back of his glove. "I'll set that down," he said, "as one of your mistakes—to your credit." And, as if he disliked talking about his position, he changed the subject. "I wish you would let me go with you to the Tower, and to Hampton Court, and to all those other places."

"We shall be most happy," said Bessie.

"And of course I shall be delighted to show you the Houses of Parliament—some day that suits you. There are a lot of things I want to do for you. I want you to have a good time. And I should like very much to present some of my friends to you, if it wouldn't bore you. Then it would be awfully kind of you to come down to Branches."

"We are much obliged to you, Lord Lambeth," said Bessie. "What is Branches?"

"It's a house in the country. I think you might like it."

Willie Woodley and Mrs. Westgate, at this moment, were sitting in silence, and the young man's ear caught these last words of Lord Lambeth's. "He's inviting Miss Bessie to one of his castles," he murmured to his companion.

Mrs. Westgate, foreseeing what she mentally called "complications," immediately got up; and the two ladies, taking leave of Lord Lambeth, returned, under Mr. Woodley's conduct, to Jones's Hotel.

V

LORD Lambeth came to see them on the morrow, bringing Percy Beaumont with him—the latter having instantly declared his intention of neglecting none of the usual offices of civility. This declaration, however, when his kinsman informed him of the advent of their American friends, had been preceded by another remark.

"Here they are, then, and you are in for it."

"What am I in for?" demanded Lord Lambeth.

"I will let your mother give it a name. With all respect to whom," added Percy Beaumont, "I must decline on this occasion to do any more police duty. Her Grace must look after you herself."

"I will give her a chance," said her Grace's son, a trifle grimly. "I shall make her go and see them."

"She won't do it, my boy."

"We'll see if she doesn't," said Lord Lambeth.

But if Percy Beaumont took a sombre view of the arrival of the two ladies at Jones's Hotel, he was sufficiently a man of the world to offer them a smiling countenance. He fell into animated conversation—conversation, at least, that was animated on her side—with Mrs. Westgate, while his companion made himself agreeable to the younger lady. Mrs. Westgate began confessing and protesting, declaring and expounding.

"I must say London is a great deal brighter and prettier just now than it was when I was here last—in the month of November. There is evidently a great deal going on, and you seem to have a good many flowers. I have no doubt it is very charming for all you people, and that you amuse yourselves immensely. It is very good of you to let Bessie and me come and sit and look at you. I suppose you will think I am very satirical, but I must confess that that's the feeling I have in London."

"I am afraid I don't quite understand to what feeling you allude," said Percy Beaumont.

"The feeling that it's all very well for you English people. Everything is beautifully arranged for you."

"It seems to me it is very well for some Americans, sometimes," rejoined Beaumont.

"For some of them, yes—if they like to be patronised. But I must say I don't like to be patronised. I may be very eccentric and undisciplined and unreasonable; but I confess I never was fond of patronage. I like to associate with people on the same terms as I do in my own country; that's a peculiar taste that I have. But here people seem to expect something else—Heaven knows what! I am afraid you will think I am very ungrateful, for I certainly have received a great deal of attention. The last time I was here, a lady sent me a message that I was at liberty to come and see her."

"Dear me, I hope you didn't go," observed Percy Beaumont.

"You are deliciously *naïf*, I must say that for you!" Mrs. Westgate exclaimed. "It must be a great advantage to you here in London. I suppose that if I myself had a little more *naïveté*, I should enjoy it more. I should be content to sit on a chair in the Park, and see the people pass, and be told that this is the Duchess of Suffolk, and that is the Lord Chamberlain, and that I must be thankful for the privilege of beholding them. I daresay it is very wicked and critical of me to ask for anything else. But I was always critical, and I freely confess to the sin of being fastidious. I am told there is some remarkably superior second-rate society provided here for strangers. *Merci!* I don't want any superior second-rate society. I want the society that I have been accustomed to."

"I hope you don't call Lambeth and me second-rate," Beaumont interposed.

"Oh, I am accustomed to you!" said Mrs. Westgate. "Do you know that you English sometimes make the most wonderful speeches? The first time I came to London, I went out to dine—as I told you, I have received a great deal of attention. After dinner, in the drawing-room, I had some conversation with an old lady; I assure you I had. I forget what we talked about; but she presently said, in allusion to something we were discussing, 'Oh, you know, the aristocracy do so-and-so; but in one's own class of life it is very different.' In one's own class of life! What is a poor unprotected American woman to do in a country where she is liable to have that sort of thing said to her?"

"You seem to get hold of some very queer old ladies; I compliment you on your acquaintance!" Percy Beaumont exclaimed. "If you are trying to bring me to admit that London is an odious place, you'll not succeed. I'm extremely fond of it, and I think it the jolliest place in the world."

"*Pour vous autres.* I never said the contrary," Mrs. Westgate retorted. I make use of this expression because both interlocutors had begun to raise their voices. Percy Beaumont naturally did not like to hear his country abused, and Mrs. Westgate, no less naturally, did not like a stubborn debater.

"Hallo!" said Lord Lambeth; "what are they up to now?"

And he came away from the window, where he had been standing with Bessie Alden.

"I quite agree with a very clever countrywoman of mine," Mrs. Westgate continued, with charming ardour, though with imperfect relevancy. She smiled at the two gentlemen for a moment with terrible brightness, as if to toss at their feet—upon their native heath—the gauntlet of defiance. "For me, there are only two social positions worth speaking of—that of an American lady and that of the Emperor of Russia."

"And what do you do with the American gentlemen?" asked Lord Lambeth.

"She leaves them in America!" said Percy Beaumont.

On the departure of their visitors, Bessie Alden told her sister that Lord Lambeth would come the next day, to go with them to the Tower, and that he had kindly offered to bring his "trap," and drive them thither. Mrs. Westgate listened in silence to this communication, and for some time afterwards she said nothing. But at last, "If you had not requested me the other day not to mention it," she began, "there is something I should venture to ask you." Bessie frowned a little; her dark blue eyes were more dark than blue. But her sister went on. "As it is, I will take the risk. You are not in love with Lord Lambeth: I believe it, perfectly. Very good. But is there, by chance, any danger of your becoming so? It's a very simple question; don't take offence. I have a particular reason," said Mrs. Westgate, "for wanting to know."

Bessie Alden for some moments said nothing; she only looked displeased. "No; there is no danger," she answered at last, curtly.

"Then I should like to frighten them," declared Mrs. Westgate, clasping her jewelled hands.

"To frighten whom?"

"All these people; Lord Lambeth's family and friends."

"How should you frighten them?" asked the young girl.

"It wouldn't be I—it would be you. It would frighten them to think that you should absorb his lordship's young affections."

Bessie Alden, with her clear eyes still overshadowed by her dark brows, continued to interrogate. "Why should that frighten them?"

Mrs. Westgate poised her answer with a smile before delivering it. "Because they think you are not good enough. You are a charming girl, beautiful and amiable, intelligent and clever, and as *bien-élevée* as it is possible to be; but you are not a fit match for Lord Lambeth."

Bessie Alden was immensely disgusted. "Where do you get such extraordinary ideas?" she asked. "You have said some such strange things lately. My dear Kitty, where do you collect them?"

Kitty was evidently enamoured of her idea. "Yes, it would put them on pins and needles, and it wouldn't hurt you. Mr. Beaumont is already most uneasy; I could soon see that."

The young girl meditated a moment. "Do you mean that they spy upon him—that they interfere with him?"

"I don't know what power they have to interfere, but I know that a British mamma may worry her son's life out."

It has been intimated that, as regards certain disagreeable things, Bessie Alden had a fund of scepticism. She abstained on the present occasion from expressing disbelief, for she wished not to irritate her sister. But she said to herself that Kitty had been misinformed—that this was a traveller's tale. Though she was a girl of a lively imagination, there could in the nature of things be, to her sense, no reality in the idea of her belonging to a vulgar category. What she said aloud was—"I must say that in that case I am very sorry for Lord Lambeth."

Mrs. Westgate, more and more exhilarated by her scheme, was smiling at her again. "If I could only believe it was safe!" she exclaimed. "When you begin to pity him, I, on my side, am afraid."

"Afraid of what?"

"Of your pitying him too much."

Bessie Alden turned away impatiently; but at the end of a minute she turned back. "What if I should pity him too much?" she asked.

Mrs. Westgate hereupon turned away, but after a moment's reflection she also faced her sister again. "It would come, after all, to the same thing," she said.

Lord Lambeth came the next day with his trap, and the two ladies, attended by Willie Woodley, placed themselves under his guidance and were conveyed eastward, through some of the duskier portions of the metropolis, to the great turreted donjon which overlooks the London shipping. They all descended from their vehicle and entered the famous enclosure; and they secured the services of a venerable beefeater, who, though there were many other claimants for legendary information, made a fine exclusive party of them and marched them through courts and corridors, through armouries and prisons. He delivered his usual peripatetic discourse, and they stopped and stared, and peeped and stooped, according to the official admonitions. Bessie Alden asked the old man in the crimson doublet a great many questions; she thought it a most fascinating place. Lord Lambeth was in high good-humour; he was constantly laughing; he enjoyed what he would have called the lark. Willie Woodley kept looking at the ceilings and tapping the walls with the knuckle of a pearl-grey glove; and Mrs. Westgate, asking at frequent intervals to be allowed to sit down and wait till they came back, was as frequently informed that they would never come back. To a great many of Bessie's questions—chiefly on collateral points of English history—the ancient warder was naturally unable to reply; whereupon she always appealed to Lord Lambeth. But his lordship was very ignorant. He declared that he knew nothing about that sort of thing, and he seemed greatly diverted at being treated as an authority.

"You can't expect every one to know as much as you," he said.

"I should expect you to know a great deal more," declared Bessie Alden.

"Women always know more than men about names and dates, and that sort of thing," Lord Lambeth rejoined. "There was Lady Jane Grey we have just been hearing about, who went in for Latin and Greek and all the learning of her age."

"*You* have no right to be ignorant, at all events," said Bessie.

"Why haven't I as good a right as any one else?"

"Because you have lived in the midst of all these things."

"What things do you mean? Axes and blocks and thumb-screws?"

"All these historical things. You belong to an historical family."

"Bessie is really too historical," said Mrs. Westgate, catching a word of this dialogue.

"Yes, you are too historical," said Lord Lambeth, laughing, but thankful for a formula. "Upon my honour, you are too historical!"

He went with the ladies a couple of days later to Hampton Court, Willie Woodley being also of the party. The afternoon was charming, the famous horse-chestnuts were in blossom, and Lord Lambeth, who quite entered into the spirit of the cockney excursionist, declared that it was a jolly old place. Bessie Alden was in ecstasies; she went about murmuring and exclaiming.

"It's too lovely," said the young girl, "it's too enchanting; it's too exactly what it ought to be!"

At Hampton Court the little flocks of visitors are not provided with an official bellwether, but are left to browse at discretion upon the local antiquities. It happened in this manner that, in default of another informant, Bessie Alden, who on doubtful questions was able to suggest a great many alternatives, found herself again applying for intellectual assistance to Lord Lambeth. But he again assured her that he was utterly helpless in such matters—that his education had been sadly neglected.

"And I am sorry it makes you unhappy," he added in a moment.

"You are very disappointing, Lord Lambeth," she said.

"Ah, now, don't say that!" he cried. "That's the worst thing you could possibly say."

"No," she rejoined; "it is not so bad as to say that I had expected nothing of you."

"I don't know. Give me a notion of the sort of thing you expected."

"Well," said Bessie Alden, "that you would be more what I should like to be—what I should try to be—in your place."

"Ah, my place!" exclaimed Lord Lambeth; "you are always talking about my place."

The young girl looked at him; he thought she coloured a little; and for a moment she made no rejoinder.

"Does it strike you that I am always talking about your place?" she asked.

"I am sure you do it a great honour," he said, fearing he had been uncivil.

"I have often thought about it," she went on after a moment. "I have often thought about your being an hereditary legislator. An hereditary legislator ought to know a great many things."

"Not if he doesn't legislate."

"But you will legislate; it's absurd your saying you won't. You are very much looked up to here—I am assured of that."

"I don't know that I ever noticed it."

"It is because you are used to it, then. You ought to fill the place."

"How do you mean, to fill it?" asked Lord Lambeth.

"You ought to be very clever and brilliant, and to know almost everything."

Lord Lambeth looked at her a moment. "Shall I tell you something?" he asked. "A young man in my position, as you call it—"

"I didn't invent the term," interposed Bessie Alden. "I have seen it in a great many books."

"Hang it, you are always at your books! A fellow in my position, then, does very well, whatever he does. That's about what I mean to say."

"Well, if your own people are content with you," said Bessie Alden, laughing, "it is not for me to complain. But I shall always think that, properly, you should have a great mind—a great character."

"Ah, that's very theoretic!" Lord Lambeth declared. "Depend upon it, that's a Yankee prejudice."

"Happy the country," said Bessie Alden, "where even people's prejudices are so elevated!"

"Well, after all," observed Lord Lambeth, "I don't know that I am such a fool as you are trying to make me out."

"I said nothing so rude as that; but I must repeat that you are disappointing."

"My dear Miss Alden," exclaimed the young man, "I am the best fellow in the world!"

"Ah, if it were not for that!" said Bessie Alden, with a smile.

Mrs. Westgate had a good many more friends in London than she pretended, and before long she had renewed acquaintance with most of them. Their hospitality was extreme, so that, one thing leading to another, she began, as the phrase is, to go out. Bessie Alden, in this way, saw something of what she found it a great satisfaction to call to herself English society. She went to balls and danced, she went to dinners and talked, she went to concerts and listened (at concerts Bessie always listened), she went to exhibitions and wondered. Her enjoyment was keen and her curiosity insatiable, and, grateful in general for all her opportunities, she especially prized the privilege of meeting certain celebrated persons—authors and artists, philosophers and statesmen—of whose renown she had been a humble and distant beholder, and who now, as a part of the habitual furniture of London drawing-rooms, struck her as stars fallen from the firmament and become palpable—revealing also, sometimes, on contact, qualities not to have been predicted of bodies sidereal. Bessie, who knew so many of her contemporaries by reputation, had a good many personal disappointments; but, on the other hand, she had innumerable satisfactions and enthusiasms, and she communicated the emotions of either class to a dear friend, of her own sex, in Boston, with whom she was in voluminous correspondence. Some of her reflections, indeed, she attempted to impart to Lord Lambeth, who came almost every day to Jones's Hotel, and whom Mrs. Westgate admitted to be really devoted. Captain Littledale, it appeared, had gone to India; and of several others of Mrs. Westgate's ex-pensioners—gentlemen who, as she said, had made, in New York, a club-house of her drawing-room— no tidings were to be obtained; but Lord Lambeth was certainly attentive enough to make up for the accidental absences, the short memories, all the other irregularities, of every one else. He drove them in the Park, he took them to visit private collections of pictures, and having a house of his own, invited them to dinner. Mrs. Westgate, following the fashion of many of her compatriots, caused herself and her sister to be presented at the English Court by her diplomatic representative—for it was in this manner that she alluded to the American Minister to England, inquiring what on earth he was put there for, if not to make the proper arrangements for one's going to a Drawing Room.

Lord Lambeth declared that he hated Drawing Rooms, but he participated in the ceremony on the day on which the two ladies at Jones's Hotel repaired to Buckingham Palace in a remarkable coach which his lordship had sent to fetch them. He had on a gorgeous uniform, and Bessie Alden was particularly struck with his appearance—especially when on her asking him, rather foolishly as she felt, if he were a loyal subject, he replied that he was a loyal subject to *her*. This declaration was emphasised by his dancing with her at a royal ball to which the two ladies afterwards went, and was not impaired by the fact that she thought he danced very ill. He seemed to her wonderfully kind; she asked herself, with growing vivacity, why he should be so kind. It was his disposition—that seemed the natural answer. She had told her sister that she liked him very much, and now that she liked him more she wondered why. She liked him for his disposition; to this question as well that seemed the natural answer. When once the impressions of London life began to crowd thickly upon her she completely forgot her sister's warning about the cynicism of public opinion. It had given her great pain at the moment; but there was no particular reason why she should remember it; it corresponded too little with any sensible reality; and it was disagreeable to Bessie to remember disagreeable things. So she was not haunted with the sense of a vulgar imputation. She was not in love with Lord Lambeth—she assured herself of that. It will immediately be observed that when such assurances become necessary the state of a young lady's affections is already ambiguous; and indeed Bessie Alden made no attempt to dissimulate—to herself, of course—a certain tenderness that she felt for the young nobleman. She said to herself that she liked the type to which he belonged—the simple, candid, manly, healthy English temperament. She spoke to herself of him as women speak of young men they like—alluded to his bravery (which she had never in the least seen tested), to his honesty and gentlemanliness; and was not silent upon the subject of his good looks. She was perfectly conscious, moreover, that she liked to think of his more adventitious merits—that her imagination was excited and gratified by the sight of a handsome young man endowed with such large opportunities—opportunities she hardly knew for what, but, as she supposed, for doing great things—for setting an example, for exerting an influence, for conferring happiness, for encouraging the arts. She had a kind of ideal of conduct for a young man who should find himself in this magnificent position, and she tried to adapt it to Lord Lambeth's deportment, as you might attempt to fit a silhouette in cut paper upon a shadow projected upon a wall. But Bessie Alden's silhouette refused to coincide with his lordship's image; and this want of harmony sometimes vexed her more than she thought reasonable. When he was absent it was of course less striking—then he seemed to her a sufficiently graceful combination of high responsibilities and amiable qualities. But when he sat there within sight, laughing and talking with his customary good humour and simplicity, she measured it more accurately, and she felt acutely that if Lord Lambeth's position was heroic, there was but little of the hero in the young man himself. Then her imagination wandered away from him—very far away; for it was an incontestable fact that at such moments he seemed distinctly dull. I am afraid that while Bessie's imagination was thus invidiously roaming, she cannot have been herself a very lively companion; but it may well have been that these occasional fits of indifference seemed to Lord Lambeth a part of the young girl's personal charm. It had been a part of this charm from the first that he felt that she judged him and measured him more freely and irresponsibly—more at her ease and her leisure, as it were—than several young ladies with whom he had been on the whole about as intimate. To feel this, and yet to feel that she also liked him, was very agreeable to Lord Lambeth. He fancied he had compassed that gratification so desirable to young men of title and fortune—being liked for himself. It is true that a cynical counsellor might have whispered to him, "Liked for yourself? Yes; but not so very much!" He had, at any rate, the constant hope of being liked more.

It may seem, perhaps, a trifle singular—but it is nevertheless true—that Bessie Alden, when he struck her as dull, devoted some time, on grounds of conscience, to trying to like him more. I say on grounds of conscience, because she felt that he had been extremely "nice" to her sister, and because she reflected that it was no more than fair that she should think as well of him as he thought of her. This effort was possibly sometimes not so successful as it might have been, for the result of it was occasionally a vague irritation, which expressed itself in hostile criticism of several British institutions. Bessie Alden went to some entertainments at which she met Lord Lambeth; but she went to others at which his lordship was neither actually nor potentially present; and it was chiefly on these latter occasions that she encountered those literary and artistic celebrities of whom mention has been made. After a while she reduced the matter to a principle. If Lord Lambeth should appear anywhere, it was a symbol that there would be no poets and philosophers; and in consequence—for it was almost a strict consequence—she used to enumerate to the young man these objects of her admiration.

"You seem to be awfully fond of that sort of people," said Lord Lambeth one day, as if the idea had just occurred to him.

"They are the people in England I am most curious to see," Bessie Alden replied.

"I suppose that's because you have read so much," said Lord Lambeth, gallantly.

"I have not read so much. It is because we think so much of them at home."

"Oh, I see!" observed the young nobleman. "In Boston."

"Not only in Boston; everywhere," said Bessie. "We hold them in great honour; they go to the best dinner-parties."

"I dare say you are right. I can't say I know many of them."

"It's a pity you don't," Bessie Alden declared. "It would do you good."

"I dare say it would," said Lord Lambeth, very humbly. "But I must say I don't like the looks of some of them."

"Neither do I—of some of them. But there are all kinds, and many of them are charming."

"I have talked with two or three of them," the young man went on, "and I thought they had a kind of fawning manner."

"Why should they fawn?" Bessie Alden demanded.

"I'm sure I don't know. Why, indeed?"

"Perhaps you only thought so," said Bessie.

"Well, of course," rejoined her companion, "that's a kind of thing that can't be proved."

"In America they don't fawn," said Bessie.

"Ah! well, then, they must be better company."

Bessie was silent a moment. "That is one of the things I don't like about England," she said; "your keeping the distinguished people apart."

"How do you mean, apart?"

"Why, letting them come only to certain places. You never see them."

Lord Lambeth looked at her a moment. "What people do you mean?"

"The eminent people—the authors and artists—the clever people."

"Oh, there are other eminent people besides those!" said Lord Lambeth.

"Well, you certainly keep them apart," repeated the young girl.

"And there are other clever people," added Lord Lambeth, simply.

Bessie Alden looked at him, and she gave a light laugh. "Not many," she said.

On another occasion—just after a dinner-party—she told him that there was something else in England she did not like.

"Oh, I say!" he cried; "haven't you abused us enough?"

"I have never abused you at all," said Bessie; "but I don't like your *precedence*."

"It isn't my precedence!" Lord Lambeth declared, laughing.

"Yes, it is yours—just exactly yours; and I think it's odious," said Bessie.

"I never saw such a young lady for discussing things! Has some one had the impudence to go before you?" asked his lordship.

"It is not the going before me that I object to," said Bessie; "it is their thinking that they have a right to do it—a right that I should recognise."

"I never saw such a young lady as you are for not 'recognising.' I have no doubt the thing is beastly, but it saves a lot of trouble."

"It makes a lot of trouble. It's horrid!" said Bessie.

"But how would you have the first people go?" asked Lord Lambeth. "They can't go last."

"Whom do you mean by the first people?"

"Ah, if you mean to question first principles!" said Lord Lambeth.

"If those are your first principles, no wonder some of your arrangements are horrid," observed Bessie Alden, with a very pretty ferocity. "I am a young girl, so of course I go last; but imagine what Kitty must feel on being informed that she is not at liberty to budge until certain other ladies have passed out!"

"Oh, I say, she is not 'informed'!" cried Lord Lambeth. "No one would do such a thing as that."

"She is made to feel it," the young girl insisted—"as if they were afraid she would make a rush for the door. No, you have a lovely country," said Bessie Alden, "but your precedence is horrid."

"I certainly shouldn't think your sister would like it," rejoined Lord Lambeth, with even exaggerated gravity. But Bessie Alden could induce him to enter no formal protest against this repulsive custom, which he seemed to think an extreme convenience.

VI

PERCY Beaumont all this time had been a very much less frequent visitor at Jones's Hotel than his noble kinsman; he had in fact called but twice upon the two American ladies. Lord Lambeth, who often saw him, reproached him with his neglect, and declared that although Mrs. Westgate had said nothing about it, he was sure that she was secretly wounded by it. "She suffers too much to speak," said Lord Lambeth.

"That's all gammon," said Percy Beaumont; "there's a limit to what people can suffer!" And, though sending no apologies to Jones's Hotel, he undertook in a manner to explain his absence. "You are always there," he said; "and that's reason enough for my not going."

"I don't see why. There is enough for both of us."

"I don't care to be a witness of your—your reckless passion," said Percy Beaumont.

Lord Lambeth looked at him with a cold eye, and for a moment said nothing. "It's not so obvious as you might suppose," he rejoined, dryly, "considering what a demonstrative beggar I am."

"I don't want to know anything about it—nothing whatever," said Beaumont. "Your mother asks me every time she sees me whether I believe you are really lost—and Lady Pimlico does the same. I prefer to be able to answer that I know nothing about it—that I never go there. I stay away for consistency's sake. As I said the other day, they must look after you themselves."

"You are devilish considerate," said Lord Lambeth. "They never question me."

"They are afraid of you. They are afraid of irritating you and making you worse. So they go to work very cautiously, and, somewhere or other, they get their information. They know a great deal about you. They know that you have been with those ladies to the dome of St. Paul's and—where was the other place?—to the Thames Tunnel."

"If all their knowledge is as accurate as that, it must be very valuable," said Lord Lambeth.

"Well, at any rate, they know that you have been visiting the 'sights of the metropolis.' They think—very naturally, as it seems to me—that when you take to visiting the sights of the metropolis with a little American girl, there is serious cause for alarm." Lord Lambeth responded to this intimation by scornful laughter, and his companion continued, after a pause: "I said just now I didn't want to know anything about the affair; but I will confess that I am curious to learn whether you propose to marry Miss Bessie Alden."

On this point Lord Lambeth gave his interlocutor no immediate satisfaction; he was musing, with a frown. "By Jove," he said, "they go rather too far. They *shall* find me dangerous—I promise them."

Percy Beaumont began to laugh. "You don't redeem your promises. You said the other day you would make your mother call."

Lord Lambeth continued to meditate. "I asked her to call," he said, simply.

"And she declined?"

"Yes, but she shall do it yet."

"Upon my word," said Percy Beaumont, "if she gets much more frightened I believe she will." Lord Lambeth looked at him, and he went on. "She will go to the girl herself."

"How do you mean, she will go to her?"

"She will beg her off, or she will bribe her. She will take strong measures."

Lord Lambeth turned away in silence, and his companion watched him take twenty steps and then slowly return. "I have invited Mrs. Westgate and Miss Alden to Branches," he said, "and this evening I shall name a day."

"And shall you invite your mother and your sisters to meet them?"

"Explicitly!"

"That will set the Duchess off," said Percy Beaumont. "I suspect she will come."

"She may do as she pleases."

Beaumont looked at Lord Lambeth. "You do really propose to marry the little sister, then?"

"I like the way you talk about it!" cried the young man. "She won't gobble me down; don't be afraid."

"She won't leave you on your knees," said Percy Beaumont. "What *is* the inducement?"

"You talk about proposing—wait till I have proposed," Lord Lambeth went on.

"That's right, my dear fellow; think about it," said Percy Beaumont.

"She's a charming girl," pursued his lordship.

"Of course she's a charming girl. I don't know a girl more charming, intrinsically. But there are other charming girls nearer home."

"I like her spirit," observed Lord Lambeth, almost as if he were trying to torment his cousin.

"What's the peculiarity of her spirit?"

"She's not afraid, and she says things out, and she thinks herself as good as any one. She is the only girl I have ever seen that was not dying to marry me."

"How do you know that, if you haven't asked her?"

"I don't know how; but I know it."

"I am sure she asked me questions enough about your property and your titles," said Beaumont.

"She has asked me questions, too; no end of them," Lord Lambeth admitted. "But she asked for information, don't you know."

"Information? Ay, I'll warrant she wanted it. Depend upon it that she is dying to marry you just as much and just as little as all the rest of them."

"I shouldn't like her to refuse me—I shouldn't like that."

"If the thing would be so disagreeable, then, both to you and to her, in Heaven's name leave it alone," said Percy Beaumont.

Mrs. Westgate, on her side, had plenty to say to her sister about the rarity of Mr. Beaumont's visits and the non-appearance of the Duchess of Bayswater. She professed, however, to derive more satisfaction from this latter circumstance than she could have done from the most lavish attentions on the part of this great lady. "It is most marked," she said, "most marked. It is a delicious proof that we have made them miserable. The day we dined with Lord Lambeth I was really sorry for the poor fellow." It will have been gathered that the entertainment offered by Lord Lambeth to his American friends had not been graced by the presence of his anxious mother. He had invited several choice spirits to meet them; but the ladies of his immediate family were to Mrs. Westgate's sense—a sense, possibly, morbidly acute—conspicuous by their absence.

"I don't want to express myself in a manner that you dislike," said Bessie Alden; "but I don't know why you should have so many theories about Lord Lambeth's poor mother. You know a great many young men in New York without knowing their mothers."

Mrs. Westgate looked at her sister, and then turned away. "My dear Bessie, you are superb!" she said.

"One thing is certain," the young girl continued. "If I believed I were a cause of annoyance—however unwitting—to Lord Lambeth's family, I should insist——"

"Insist upon my leaving England," said Mrs. Westgate.

"No, not that. I want to go to the National Gallery again; I want to see Stratford-on-Avon and Canterbury Cathedral. But I should insist upon his coming to see us no more."

"That would be very modest and very pretty of you—but you wouldn't do it now."

"Why do you say 'now'?" asked Bessie Alden. "Have I ceased to be modest?"

"You care for him too much. A month ago, when you said you didn't, I believe it was quite true. But at present, my dear child," said Mrs. Westgate, "you wouldn't find it quite so simple a matter never to see Lord Lambeth again. I have seen it coming on."

"You are mistaken," said Bessie. "You don't understand."

"My dear child, don't be perverse," rejoined her sister.

"I know him better, certainly, if you mean that," said Bessie. "And I like him very much. But I don't like him enough to make trouble for him with his family. However, I don't believe in that."

"I like the way you say 'however!'" Mrs. Westgate exclaimed. "Come, you would not marry him?"

"Oh no," said the young girl.

Mrs. Westgate, for a moment, seemed vexed. "Why not, pray?" she demanded.

"Because I don't care to," said Bessie Alden.

The morning after Lord Lambeth had had, with Percy Beaumont, that exchange of ideas which has just been narrated, the ladies at Jones's Hotel received from his lordship a written invitation to pay their projected visit to Branches Castle on the following Tuesday. "I think I have made up a very pleasant party," the young nobleman said. "Several people whom you know, and my mother and sisters, who have so long been regrettably prevented from making your acquaintance." Bessie Alden lost no time in calling her sister's attention to the injustice she had done the Duchess of Bayswater, whose hostility was now proved to be a vain illusion.

"Wait till you see if she comes," said Mrs. Westgate. "And if she is to meet us at her son's house the obligation was all the greater for her to call upon us."

Bessie had not to wait long, and it appeared that Lord Lambeth's mother now accepted Mrs. Westgate's view of her duties. On the morrow, early in the afternoon, two cards were brought to the apartment of the American ladies—one of them bearing the name of the Duchess of Bayswater and the other that of the Countess of Pimlico. Mrs. Westgate glanced at the clock. "It is not yet four," she said; "they have come early; they wish to see us. We will receive them." And she gave orders that her visitors should be admitted. A few moments later they were introduced, and there was a solemn exchange of amenities. The Duchess was a large lady, with a fine fresh colour; the Countess of Pimlico was very pretty and elegant.

The Duchess looked about her as she sat down—looked not especially at Mrs. Westgate. "I dare say my son has told you that I have been wanting to come and see you," she observed.

"You are very kind," said Mrs. Westgate, vaguely—her conscience not allowing her to assent to this proposition—and indeed not permitting her to enunciate her own with any appreciable emphasis.

"He says you were so kind to him in America," said the Duchess.

"We are very glad," Mrs. Westgate replied, "to have been able to make him a little more—a little less—a little more comfortable."

"I think he stayed at your house," remarked the Duchess of Bayswater, looking at Bessie Alden.

"A very short time," said Mrs. Westgate.

"Oh!" said the Duchess; and she continued to look at Bessie, who was engaged in conversation with her daughter.

"Do you like London?" Lady Pimlico had asked of Bessie, after looking at her a good deal—at her face and her hands, her dress and her hair.

"Very much indeed," said Bessie.

"Do you like this hotel?"

"It is very comfortable," said Bessie.

"Do you like stopping at hotels?" inquired Lady Pimlico, after a pause.

"I am very fond of travelling," Bessie answered, "and I suppose hotels are a necessary part of it. But they are not the part I am fondest of."

"Oh, I hate travelling!" said the Countess of Pimlico, and transferred her attention to Mrs. Westgate.

"My son tells me you are going to Branches," the Duchess presently resumed.

"Lord Lambeth has been so good as to ask us," said Mrs. Westgate, who perceived that her visitor had now begun to look at her, and who had her customary happy consciousness of a distinguished appearance. The only mitigation of her felicity on this point was that, having inspected her visitor's own costume, she said to herself, "She won't know how well I am dressed!"

"He has asked me to go, but I am not sure I shall be able," murmured the Duchess.

"He had offered us the p—— the prospect of meeting you," said Mrs. Westgate.

"I hate the country at this season," responded the Duchess.

Mrs. Westgate gave a little shrug. "I think it is pleasanter than London."

But the Duchess's eyes were absent again; she was looking very fixedly at Bessie. In a moment she slowly rose, walked to a chair that stood empty at the young girl's right hand, and silently seated herself. As she was a majestic, voluminous woman, this little transaction had, inevitably, an air of somewhat impressive intention. It diffused a certain awkwardness, which Lady Pimlico, as a sympathetic daughter, perhaps desired to rectify in turning to Mrs. Westgate.

"I dare say you go out a great deal," she observed.

"No, very little. We are strangers, and we didn't come here for society."

"I see," said Lady Pimlico. "It's rather nice in town just now."

"It's charming," said Mrs. Westgate. "But we only go to see a few people—whom we like."

"Of course one can't like every one," said Lady Pimlico.

"It depends upon one's society," Mrs. Westgate rejoined.

The Duchess, meanwhile, had addressed herself to Bessie. "My son tells me the young ladies in America are so clever."

"I am glad they made so good an impression on him," said Bessie, smiling.

The Duchess was not smiling; her large fresh face was very tranquil. "He is very susceptible," she said. "He thinks every one clever, and sometimes they are."

"Sometimes," Bessie assented, smiling still.

The Duchess looked at her a little and then went on— "Lambeth is very susceptible, but he is very volatile, too."

"Volatile?" asked Bessie.

"He is very inconstant. It won't do to depend on him."

"Ah!" said Bessie; "I don't recognise that description. We have depended on him greatly—my sister and I—and he has never disappointed us."

"He will disappoint you yet," said the Duchess.

Bessie gave a little laugh, as if she were amused at the Duchess's persistency. "I suppose it will depend on what we expect of him."

"The less you expect the better," Lord Lambeth's mother declared.

"Well," said Bessie, "we expect nothing unreasonable."

The Duchess, for a moment, was silent, though she appeared to have more to say. "Lambeth says he has seen so much of you," she presently began.

"He has been to see us very often—he has been very kind," said Bessie Alden.

"I dare say you are used to that. I am told there is a great deal of that in America."

"A great deal of kindness?" the young girl inquired, smiling.

"Is that what you call it? I know you have different expressions."

"We certainly don't always understand each other," said Mrs. Westgate, the termination of whose interview with Lady Pimlico allowed her to give her attention to their elder visitor.

"I am speaking of the young men calling so much upon the young ladies," the Duchess explained.

"But surely in England," said Mrs. Westgate, "the young ladies don't call upon the young men?"

"Some of them do—almost!" Lady Pimlico declared. "When the young men are a great *parti*."

"Bessie, you must make a note of that," said Mrs. Westgate. "My sister," she added, "is a model traveller. She writes down all the curious facts she hears, in a little book she keeps for the purpose."

The Duchess was a little flushed; she looked all about the room, while her daughter turned to Bessie. "My brother told us you were wonderfully clever," said Lady Pimlico.

"He should have said my sister," Bessie answered—"when she says such things as that."

"Shall you be long at Branches?" the Duchess asked, abruptly, of the young girl.

"Lord Lambeth has asked us for three days," said Bessie.

"I shall go," the Duchess declared, "and my daughter too."

"That will be charming!" Bessie rejoined.

"Delightful!" murmured Mrs. Westgate.

"I shall expect to see a deal of you," the Duchess continued. "When I go to Branches I monopolise my son's guests."

"They must be most happy," said Mrs. Westgate, very graciously.

"I want immensely to see it—to see the Castle," said Bessie

to the Duchess. "I have never seen one—in England at least; and you know we have none in America."

"Ah! you are fond of castles?" inquired her Grace.

"Immensely!" replied the young girl. "It has been the dream of my life to live in one."

The Duchess looked at her a moment, as if she hardly knew how to take this assurance, which, from her Grace's point of view, was either very artless or very audacious. "Well," she said, rising, "I will show you Branches myself." And upon this the two great ladies took their departure.

"What did they mean by it?" asked Mrs. Westgate, when they were gone.

"They meant to be polite," said Bessie, "because we are going to meet them."

"It is too late to be polite," Mrs. Westgate replied, almost grimly. "They meant to overawe us by their fine manners and their grandeur, and to make you *lâcher prise*."

"*Lâcher prise?* What strange things you say!" murmured Bessie Alden.

"They meant to snub us, so that we shouldn't dare to go to Branches," Mrs. Westgate continued.

"On the contrary," said Bessie, "the Duchess offered to show me the place herself."

"Yes, you may depend upon it she won't let you out of her sight. She will show you the place from morning till night."

"You have a theory for everything," said Bessie.

"And you apparently have none for anything."

"I saw no attempt to 'overawe' us," said the young girl. "Their manners were not fine."

"They were not even good!" Mrs. Westgate declared.

Bessie was silent awhile, but in a few moments she observed that she had a very good theory. "They came to look at me!" she said, as if this had been a very ingenious hypothesis. Mrs. Westgate did it justice; she greeted it with a smile and pronounced it most brilliant; while in reality she felt that the young girl's scepticism, or her charity, or, as she had sometimes called it, appropriately, her idealism, was proof against irony. Bessie, however, remained meditative all the rest of that day and well on into the morrow.

On the morrow, before lunch, Mrs. Westgate had occasion to go out for an hour, and left her sister writing a letter. When she came back she met Lord Lambeth at the door of the hotel, coming away. She thought he looked slightly embarrassed; he was certainly very grave. "I am sorry to have missed you. Won't you come back?" she asked.

"No," said the young man, "I can't. I have seen your sister. I can never come back." Then he looked at her a moment, and took her hand. "Good-bye, Mrs. Westgate," he said. "You have been very kind to me." And with what she thought a strange, sad look in his handsome young face, he turned away.

She went in and she found Bessie still writing her letter; that is, Mrs. Westgate perceived she was sitting at the table with the pen in her hand and not writing. "Lord Lambeth has been here," said the elder lady at last.

Then Bessie got up and showed her a pale, serious face. She bent this face upon her sister for some time, confessing silently and, a little, pleading. "I told him," she said at last, "that we could not go to Branches."

Mrs. Westgate displayed just a spark of irritation. "He might have waited," she said with a smile, "till one had seen the Castle." Later, an hour afterwards, she said, "Dear Bessie, I wish you might have accepted him."

"I couldn't," said Bessie, gently.

"He is a dear good fellow," said Mrs. Westgate.

"I couldn't," Bessie repeated.

"If it is only," her sister added, "because those women will think that they succeeded—that they paralysed us!"

Bessie Alden turned away; but presently she added, "They were interesting; I should have liked to see them again."

"So should I!" cried Mrs. Westgate, significantly.

"And I should have liked to see the Castle," said Bessie. "But now we must leave England," she added.

Her sister looked at her. "You will not wait to go to the National Gallery?"

"Not now."

"Nor to Canterbury Cathedral?"

Bessie reflected a moment. "We can stop there on our way to Paris," she said.

Lord Lambeth did not tell Percy Beaumont that the contingency he was not prepared at all to like had occurred; but Percy Beaumont, on hearing that the two ladies had left London, wondered with some intensity what had happened; wondered, that is, until the Duchess of Bayswater came, a little, to his assistance. The two ladies went to Paris, and Mrs. Westgate beguiled the journey to that city by repeating several times, "That's what I regret; they will think they petrified us." But Bessie Alden seemed to regret nothing.

1878

WASHINGTON SQUARE

I

DURING a portion of the first half of the present century, and more particularly during the latter part of it, there flourished and practised in the city of New York a physician who enjoyed perhaps an exceptional share of the consideration which, in the United States, has always been bestowed upon distinguished members of the medical profession. This profession in America has constantly been held in honour, and more successfully than elsewhere has put forward a claim to the epithet of "liberal." In a country in which, to play a social part, you must either earn your income or make believe that you earn it, the healing art has appeared in a high degree to combine two recognised sources of credit. It belongs to the realm of the practical, which in the United States is a great recommendation; and it is touched by the light of science—a merit appreciated in a community in which the love of knowledge has not always been accompanied by leisure and opportunity. It was an element in Dr. Sloper's reputation that his learning and his skill were very evenly balanced; he was what you might call a scholarly doctor, and yet there was nothing abstract in his remedies—he always ordered you to take something. Though he was felt to be extremely thorough, he was not uncomfortably theoretic, and if he sometimes explained matters rather more minutely than might seem of use to the patient, he never went so far (like some practitioners one has heard of) as to trust to the explanation alone, but always left behind him an inscrutable prescription.

There were some doctors that left the prescription without offering any explanation at all; and he did not belong to that class
either, which was after all the most vulgar. It will be seen that I
am describing a clever man; and this is really the reason why
Dr. Sloper had become a local celebrity. At the time at which
we are chiefly concerned with him, he was some fifty years of
age, and his popularity was at its height. He was very witty, and
he passed in the best society of New York for a man of the
world—which, indeed, he was, in a very sufficient degree. I
hasten to add, to anticipate possible misconception, that he was
not the least of a charlatan. He was a thoroughly honest man—
honest in a degree of which he had perhaps lacked the opportunity to give the complete measure; and, putting aside the great
good-nature of the circle in which he practised, which was
rather fond of boasting that it possessed the "brightest" doctor
in the country, he daily justified his claim to the talents attrib-
uted to him by the popular voice. He was an observer, even a
philosopher, and to be bright was so natural to him, and (as the
popular voice said) came so easily, that he never aimed at mere
effect, and had none of the little tricks and pretensions of
second-rate reputations. It must be confessed that fortune had
favoured him, and that he had found the path to prosperity very
soft to his tread. He had married at the age of twenty-seven, for
love, a very charming girl, Miss Catherine Harrington, of New
York, who, in addition to her charms, had brought him a solid
dowry. Mrs. Sloper was amiable, graceful, accomplished, elegant, and in 1820 she had been one of the pretty girls of the
small but promising capital which clustered about the Battery
and overlooked the Bay, and of which the uppermost boundary
was indicated by the grassy waysides of Canal Street. Even at
the age of twenty-seven Austin Sloper had made his mark sufficiently to mitigate the anomaly of his having been chosen
among a dozen suitors by a young woman of high fashion, who
had ten thousand dollars of income and the most charming
eyes in the island of Manhattan. These eyes, and some of their

accompaniments, were for about five years a source of extreme satisfaction to the young physician, who was both a devoted and a very happy husband. The fact of his having married a rich woman made no difference in the line he had traced for himself, and he cultivated his profession with as definite a purpose as if he still had no other resources than his fraction of the modest patrimony which on his father's death he had shared with his brothers and sisters. This purpose had not been preponderantly to make money—it had been rather to learn something and to do something. To learn something interesting, and to do something useful—this was, roughly speaking, the programme he had sketched, and of which the accident of his wife having an income appeared to him in no degree to modify the validity. He was fond of his practice, and of exercising a skill of which he was agreeably conscious, and it was so patent a truth that if he were not a doctor there was nothing else he could be, that a doctor he persisted in being, in the best possible conditions. Of course his easy domestic situation saved him a good deal of drudgery, and his wife's affiliation to the "best people" brought him a good many of those patients whose symptoms are, if not more interesting in themselves than those of the lower orders, at least more consistently displayed. He desired experience, and in the course of twenty years he got a great deal. It must be added that it came to him in some forms which, whatever might have been their intrinsic value, made it the reverse of welcome. His first child, a little boy of extraordinary promise, as the Doctor, who was not addicted to easy enthusiasms, firmly believed, died at three years of age, in spite of everything that the mother's tenderness and the father's science could invent to save him. Two years later Mrs. Sloper gave birth to a second infant—an infant of a sex which rendered the poor child, to the Doctor's sense, an inadequate substitute for his lamented first-born, of whom he had promised himself to make an admirable man. The little girl was a disappointment; but this was not the worst. A week after her birth the young mother, who, as the phrase is, had been doing well, suddenly betrayed alarming symptoms, and before another week had elapsed Austin Sloper was a widower.

For a man whose trade was to keep people alive, he had certainly done poorly in his own family; and a bright doctor who within three years loses his wife and his little boy should perhaps be prepared to see either his skill or his affection impugned. Our friend, however, escaped criticism: that is, he escaped all criticism but his own, which was much the most competent and most formidable. He walked under the weight of this very private censure for the rest of his days, and bore for ever the scars of a castigation to which the strongest hand he knew had treated him on the night that followed his wife's death. The world, which, as I have said, appreciated him, pitied him too much to be ironical; his misfortune made him more interesting, and even helped him to be the fashion. It was observed that even medical families cannot escape the more insidious forms of disease, and that, after all, Dr. Sloper had lost other patients beside the two I have mentioned; which constituted an honourable precedent. His little girl remained to him, and though she was not what he had desired, he proposed to himself to make the best of her. He had on hand a stock of unexpended authority, by which the child, in its early years, profited largely. She had been named, as a matter of course, after her poor mother, and even in her most diminutive babyhood the Doctor never called her anything but Catherine. She grew up a very robust and healthy child, and her father, as he looked at her, often said to himself that, such as she was, he at least need have no fear of losing her. I say "such as she was," because, to tell the truth—— But this is a truth of which I will defer the telling.

II

WHEN THE child was about ten years old, he invited his sister, Mrs. Penniman, to come and stay with him. The Miss

Slopers had been but two in number, and both of them had
married early in life. The younger, Mrs. Almond by name, was
the wife of a prosperous merchant, and the mother of a blooming family. She bloomed herself, indeed, and was a comely,
comfortable, reasonable woman, and a favourite with her clever
brother, who, in the matter of women, even when they were
nearly related to him, was a man of distinct preferences. He
preferred Mrs. Almond to his sister Lavinia, who had married a
poor clergyman, of a sickly constitution and a flowery style of
eloquence, and then, at the age of thirty-three, had been left a
widow, without children, without fortune—with nothing but
the memory of Mr. Penniman's flowers of speech, a certain
vague aroma of which hovered about her own conversation.
Nevertheless he had offered her a home under his own roof,
which Lavinia accepted with the alacrity of a woman who had
spent the ten years of her married life in the town of Pough-
keepsie. The Doctor had not proposed to Mrs. Penniman to
come and live with him indefinitely; he had suggested that she
should make an asylum of his house while she looked about for
unfurnished lodgings. It is uncertain whether Mrs. Penniman
ever instituted a search for unfurnished lodgings, but it is beyond dispute that she never found them. She settled herself
with her brother and never went away, and when Catherine
was twenty years old her Aunt Lavinia was still one of the most
striking features of her immediate *entourage*. Mrs. Penniman's
own account of the matter was that she had remained to take
charge of her niece's education. She had given this account, at
least, to every one but the Doctor, who never asked for explanations which he could entertain himself any day with invent-
ing. Mrs. Penniman, moreover, though she had a good deal of a
certain sort of artificial assurance, shrank, for indefinable reasons, from presenting herself to her brother as a fountain of in-
struction. She had not a high sense of humour, but she had
enough to prevent her from making this mistake; and her
brother, on his side, had enough to excuse her, in her situation,
for laying him under contribution during a considerable part of

a lifetime. He therefore assented tacitly to the proposition which Mrs. Penniman had tacitly laid down, that it was of importance that the poor motherless girl should have a brilliant woman near her. His assent could only be tacit, for he had never been dazzled by his sister's intellectual lustre. Save when he fell in love with Catherine Harrington, he had never been dazzled, indeed, by any feminine characteristics whatever; and though he was to a certain extent what is called a ladies' doctor, his private opinion of the more complicated sex was not exalted. He regarded its complications as more curious than edifying, and he had an idea of the beauty of *reason*, which was on the whole meagrely gratified by what he observed in his female patients. His wife had been a reasonable woman, but she was a bright exception; among several things that he was sure of, this was perhaps the principal. Such a conviction, of course, did little either to mitigate or to abbreviate his widowhood; and it set a limit to his recognition, at the best, of Catherine's possibilities and of Mrs. Penniman's ministrations. He, nevertheless, at the end of six months, accepted his sister's permanent presence as an accomplished fact, and as Catherine grew older perceived that there were in effect good reasons why she should have a companion of her own imperfect sex. He was extremely polite to Lavinia, scrupulously, formally polite; and she had never seen him in anger but once in her life, when he lost his temper in a theological discussion with her late husband. With her he never discussed theology, nor, indeed, discussed anything; he contented himself with making known, very distinctly, in the form of a lucid ultimatum, his wishes with regard to Catherine.

Once, when the girl was about twelve years old, he had said to her—

"Try and make a clever woman of her, Lavinia; I should like her to be a clever woman."

Mrs. Penniman, at this, looked thoughtful a moment. "My dear Austin," she then inquired, "do you think it is better to be clever than to be good?"

"Good for what?" asked the Doctor. "You are good for nothing unless you are clever."

From this assertion Mrs. Penniman saw no reason to dissent; she possibly reflected that her own great use in the world was owing to her aptitude for many things.

"Of course I wish Catherine to be good," the Doctor said next day; "but she won't be any the less virtuous for not being a fool. I am not afraid of her being wicked; she will never have the salt of malice in her character. She is as good as good bread, as the French say; but six years hence I don't want to have to compare her to good bread and butter."

"Are you afraid she will be insipid? My dear brother, it is I who supply the butter; so you needn't fear!" said Mrs. Penniman, who had taken in hand the child's accomplishments, overlooking her at the piano, where Catherine displayed a certain talent, and going with her to the dancing-class, where it must be confessed that she made but a modest figure.

Mrs. Penniman was a tall, thin, fair, rather faded woman, with a perfectly amiable disposition, a high standard of gentility, a taste for light literature, and a certain foolish indirectness and obliquity of character. She was romantic, she was sentimental, she had a passion for little secrets and mysteries—a very innocent passion, for her secrets had hitherto always been as unpractical as addled eggs. She was not absolutely veracious; but this defect was of no great consequence, for she had never had anything to conceal. She would have liked to have a lover, and to correspond with him under an assumed name in letters left at a shop; I am bound to say that her imagination never carried the intimacy farther than this. Mrs. Penniman had never had a lover, but her brother, who was very shrewd, understood her turn of mind. "When Catherine is about seventeen," he said to himself, "Lavinia will try and persuade her that some young man with a moustache is in love with her. It will be quite untrue; no young man, with a moustache or without, will ever be in love with Catherine. But Lavinia will take it up, and talk to her about it; perhaps, even, if her taste for clandestine operations doesn't prevail with her, she will talk to me about it. Catherine won't see it, and won't believe it, fortunately for her peace of mind; poor Catherine isn't romantic."

She was a healthy well-grown child, without a trace of her mother's beauty. She was not ugly; she had simply a plain, dull, gentle countenance. The most that had ever been said for her was that she had a "nice" face, and, though she was an heiress, no one had ever thought of regarding her as a belle. Her father's opinion of her moral purity was abundantly justified; she was excellently, imperturbably good; affectionate, docile, obedient, and much addicted to speaking the truth. In her younger years she was a good deal of a romp, and, though it is an awkward confession to make about one's heroine, I must add that she was something of a glutton. She never, that I know of, stole raisins out of the pantry; but she devoted her pocket-money to the purchase of cream-cakes. As regards this, however, a critical attitude would be inconsistent with a candid reference to the early annals of any biographer. Catherine was decidedly not clever; she was not quick with her book, nor, indeed, with anything else. She was not abnormally deficient, and she mustered learning enough to acquit herself respectably in conversation with her contemporaries, among whom it must be avowed, however, that she occupied a secondary place. It is well known that in New York it is possible for a young girl to occupy a primary one. Catherine, who was extremely modest, had no desire to shine, and on most social occasions, as they are called, you would have found her lurking in the background. She was extremely fond of her father, and very much afraid of him; she thought him the cleverest and handsomest and most celebrated of men. The poor girl found her account so completely in the exercise of her affections that the little tremor of fear that mixed itself with her filial passion gave the thing an extra relish rather than blunted its edge. Her deepest desire was to please him, and her conception of happiness was to know that she had succeeded in pleasing him. She had never succeeded beyond a certain point. Though on the whole he was very kind to her, she was perfectly aware of this, and to go beyond the point in question seemed to her really something to live for. What she could not know, of course, was that she disappointed him, though on three or four occasions the Doctor had been almost frank about it. She grew up peacefully and prosperously, but at the age of eighteen Mrs. Penniman had not made a clever woman of her. Dr. Sloper would have liked to be proud of his daughter; but there was nothing to be proud of in poor Catherine. There was nothing, of course, to be ashamed of; but this was not enough for the Doctor, who was a proud man and would have enjoyed being able to think of his daughter as an unusual girl. There would have been a fitness in her being pretty and graceful, intelligent and distinguished; for her mother had been the most charming woman of her little day, and as regards her father, of course he knew his own value. He had moments of irritation at having produced a commonplace child, and he even went so far at times as to take a certain satisfaction in the thought that his wife had not lived to find her out. He was naturally slow in making this discovery himself, and it was not till Catherine had become a young lady grown that he regarded the matter as settled. He gave her the benefit of a great many doubts; he was in no haste to conclude. Mrs. Penniman frequently assured him that his daughter had a delightful nature; but he knew how to interpret this assurance. It meant, to his sense, that Catherine was not wise enough to discover that her aunt was a goose—a limitation of mind that could not fail to be agreeable to Mrs. Penniman. Both she and her brother, however, exaggerated the young girl's limitations; for Catherine, though she was very fond of her aunt, and conscious of the gratitude she owed her, regarded her without a particle of that gentle dread which gave its stamp to her admiration of her father. To her mind there was nothing of the infinite about Mrs. Penniman; Catherine saw her all at once, as it were, and was not dazzled by the apparition; whereas her father's great faculties seemed, as they stretched away, to lose themselves in a sort of luminous vagueness, which indicated, not that they stopped, but that Catherine's own mind ceased to follow them.

It must not be supposed that Dr. Sloper visited his disappointment upon the poor girl, or ever let her suspect that she had played him a trick. On the contrary, for fear of being unjust to her, he did his duty with exemplary zeal, and recognised that she was a faithful and affectionate child. Besides, he was a philosopher; he smoked a good many cigars over his disappointment, and in the fulness of time he got used to it. He satisfied himself that he had expected nothing, though, indeed, with a certain oddity of reasoning. "I expect nothing," he said to himself, "so that if she gives me a surprise, it will be all clear again. If she doesn't, it will be no loss." This was about the time Catherine had reached her eighteenth year, so that it will be seen her father had not been precipitate. At this time she seemed not only incapable of giving surprises; it was almost a question whether she could have received one—she was so quiet and irresponsive. People who expressed themselves roughly called her stolid. But she was irresponsive because she was shy, uncomfortably, painfully shy. This was not always understood, and she sometimes produced an impression of insensibility. In reality she was the softest creature in the world.

III

AS A CHILD she had promised to be tall, but when she was sixteen she ceased to grow, and her stature, like most other points in her composition, was not unusual. She was strong, however, and properly made, and, fortunately, her health was excellent. It has been noted that the Doctor was a philosopher, but I would not have answered for his philosophy if the poor girl had proved a sickly and suffering person. Her appearance of health constituted her principal claim to beauty, and her clear, fresh complexion, in which white and red were very equally distributed, was, indeed, an excellent thing to see. Her

eye was small and quiet, her features were rather thick, her
tresses brown and smooth. A dull, plain girl she was called by
rigorous critics—a quiet, ladylike girl, by those of the more
imaginative sort; but by neither class was she very elaborately
discussed. When it had been duly impressed upon her that she
was a young lady—it was a good while before she could believe
it—she suddenly developed a lively taste for dress: a lively taste
is quite the expression to use. I feel as if I ought to write it
very small, her judgment in this matter was by no means infallible; it was liable to confusions and embarrassments. Her great
indulgence of it was really the desire of a rather inarticulate
nature to manifest itself; she sought to be eloquent in her garments, and to make up for her diffidence of speech by a fine
frankness of costume. But if she expressed herself in her clothes
it is certain that people were not to blame for not thinking her
a witty person. It must be added that though she had the expectation of a fortune—Dr. Sloper for a long time had been
making twenty thousand dollars a year by his profession and
laying aside the half of it—the amount of money at her disposal was not greater than the allowance made to many poorer
girls. In those days in New York there were still a few altar-fires
flickering in the temple of Republican simplicity, and Dr.
Sloper would have been glad to see his daughter present herself,
with a classic grace, as a priestess of this mild faith. It made him
fairly grimace, in private, to think that a child of his should be
both ugly and overdressed. For himself, he was fond of the
good things of life, and he made a considerable use of them;
but he had a dread of vulgarity and even a theory that it was in-
creasing in the society that surrounded him. Moreover, the
standard of luxury in the United States thirty years ago was carried by no means so high as at present, and Catherine's clever
father took the old-fashioned view of the education of young
persons. He had no particular theory on the subject; it had
scarcely as yet become a necessity of self-defence to have a collection of theories. It simply appeared to him proper and reasonable that a well-bred young woman should not carry half

her fortune on her back. Catherine's back was a broad one, and would have carried a good deal; but to the weight of the paternal displeasure she never ventured to expose it, and our heroine was twenty years old before she treated herself, for evening wear, to a red satin gown trimmed with gold fringe; though this was an article which, for many years, she had coveted in secret. It made her look, when she sported it, like a woman of thirty; but oddly enough, in spite of her taste for fine clothes, she had not a grain of coquetry, and her anxiety when she put them on was as to whether they, and not she, would look well. It is a point on which history has not been explicit, but the assumption is warrantable; it was in the royal raiment just mentioned that she presented herself at a little entertainment given by her aunt, Mrs. Almond. The girl was at this time in her twenty-first year, and Mrs. Almond's party was the beginning of something very important.

Some three or four years before this, Dr. Sloper had moved his household gods up town, as they say in New York. He had been living ever since his marriage in an edifice of red brick, with granite copings and an enormous fanlight over the door, standing in a street within five minutes' walk of the City Hall, which saw its best days (from the social point of view) about 1820. After this, the tide of fashion began to set steadily northward, as, indeed, in New York, thanks to the narrow channel in which it flows, it is obliged to do, and the great hum of traffic rolled farther to the right and left of Broadway. By the time the Doctor changed his residence, the murmur of trade had become a mighty uproar, which was music in the ears of all good citizens interested in the commercial development, as they delighted to call it, of their fortunate isle. Dr. Sloper's interest in this phenomenon was only indirect—though, seeing that, as the years went on, half his patients came to be over-worked men of business, it might have been more immediate—and when most of his neighbours' dwellings (also ornamented with granite copings and large fanlights) had been converted into offices, warehouses, and shipping agencies, and otherwise applied to the base uses of commerce, he determined to look out for a quieter home. The ideal of quiet and of genteel retirement, in 1835, was found in Washington Square, where the Doctor built himself a handsome, modern, wide-fronted house, with a big balcony before the drawing-room windows, and a flight of white marble steps ascending to a portal which was also faced with white marble. This structure, and many of its neighbours, which it exactly resembled, were supposed, forty years ago, to embody the last results of architectural science, and they remain to this day very solid and honourable dwellings. In front of them was the square, containing a considerable quantity of inexpensive vegetation, enclosed by a wooden paling, which increased its rural and accessible appearance; and round the corner was the more august precinct of the Fifth Avenue, taking its origin at this point with a spacious and confident air which already marked it for high destinies. I know not whether it is owing to the tenderness of early associations, but this portion of New York appears to many persons the most delectable. It has a kind of established repose which is not of frequent occurrence in other quarters of the long, shrill city; it has a riper, richer, more honourable look than any of the upper ramifications of the great longitudinal thoroughfare—the look of having had something of a social history. It was here, as you might have been informed on good authority, that you had come into a world which appeared to offer a variety of sources of interest; it was here that your grandmother lived, in venerable solitude, and dispensed a hospitality which commended itself alike to the infant imagination and the infant palate; it was here that you took your first walks abroad, following the nursery-maid with unequal step and sniffing up the strange odour of the ailantus-trees which at that time formed the principal umbrage of the square, and diffused an aroma that you were not yet critical enough to dislike as it deserved; it was here, finally, that your first school, kept by a broad-bosomed, broad-based old lady with a ferule, who was always having tea in a blue cup, with a saucer that didn't match, enlarged the circle both of your observations and your sensations. It was here, at any rate, that my heroine spent many years of her life; which is my excuse for this topographical parenthesis.

Mrs. Almond lived much farther up town, in an embryonic street with a high number—a region where the extension of the city began to assume a theoretic air, where poplars grew beside the pavement (when there was one), and mingled their shade with the steep roofs of desultory Dutch houses, and where pigs and chickens disported themselves in the gutter. These elements of rural picturesqueness have now wholly departed from New York street scenery; but they were to be found within the memory of middle-aged persons, in quarters which now would blush to be reminded of them. Catherine had a great many cousins, and with her Aunt Almond's children, who ended by being nine in number, she lived on terms of considerable intimacy. When she was younger, they had been rather afraid of her; she was believed, as the phrase is, to be highly educated, and a person who lived in the intimacy of their Aunt Penniman had something of reflected grandeur. Mrs. Penniman, among the little Almonds, was an object of more admiration than sympathy. Her manners were strange and formidable, and her mourning robes—she dressed in black for twenty years after her husband's death, and then suddenly appeared, one morning, with pink roses in her cap—were complicated in odd, unexpected places with buckles, bugles, and pins, which discouraged familiarity. She took children too hard, both for good and for evil, and had an oppressive air of expecting subtle things of them; so that going to see her was a good deal like being taken to church and made to sit in a front pew. It was discovered after a while, however, that Aunt Penniman was but an accident in Catherine's existence, and not a part of its essence, and that when the girl came to spend a Saturday with her cousins, she was available for "follow-my-master," and even for leap-frog. On this basis an understanding was easily arrived at, and for several years Catherine fraternised with her young kinsmen. I say young kinsmen, because seven of the little Almonds were boys, and Catherine had a preference for those games which are most conveniently played in trousers. By degrees, however, the little Almonds' trousers began to lengthen, and the wearers to disperse and settle themselves in life. The elder children were older than Catherine, and the boys were sent to college or placed in counting-rooms. Of the girls, one married very punctually, and the other as punctually became engaged. It was to celebrate this latter event that Mrs. Almond gave the little party I have mentioned. Her daughter was to marry a stout young stockbroker, a boy of twenty; it was thought a very good thing.

IV

MRS. PENNIMAN, with more buckles and bangles than ever, came of course to the entertainment, accompanied by her niece; the Doctor, too, had promised to look in later in the evening. There was to be a good deal of dancing, and before it had gone very far, Marian Almond came up to Catherine, in company with a tall young man. She introduced the young man as a person who had a great desire to make our heroine's acquaintance, and as a cousin of Arthur Townsend, her own intended.

Marian Almond was a pretty little person of seventeen, with a very small figure and a very big sash, to the elegance of whose manners matrimony had nothing to add. She already had all the airs of a hostess, receiving the company, shaking her fan, saying that with so many people to attend to she should have no time to dance. She made a long speech about Mr. Townsend's cousin, to whom she administered a tap with her fan before turning away to other cares. Catherine had not understood all that she said; her attention was given to enjoying Marian's ease of manner and flow of ideas, and to looking at the young man, who was remarkably handsome. She had succeeded, however, as she often failed to do when people were presented to her, in catching his name, which appeared to be the same as that of Marian's little stockbroker. Catherine was always agitated by an introduction; it seemed a difficult moment, and she wondered that some people—her new acquaintance at this moment, for instance—should mind it so little. She wondered what she ought to say, and what would be the consequences of her saying nothing. The consequences at present were very agreeable. Mr. Townsend, leaving her no time for embarrassment, began to talk with an easy smile, as if he had known her for a year.

"What a delightful party! What a charming house! What an interesting family! What a pretty girl your cousin is!"

These observations, in themselves of no great profundity, Mr. Townsend seemed to offer for what they were worth, and as a contribution to an acquaintance. He looked straight into Catherine's eyes. She answered nothing; she only listened, and looked at him; and he, as if he expected no particular reply, went on to say many other things in the same comfortable and natural manner. Catherine, though she felt tongue-tied, was conscious of no embarrassment; it seemed proper that he should talk, and that she should simply look at him. What made it natural was that he was so handsome, or rather, as she phrased it to herself, so beautiful. The music had been silent for a while, but it suddenly began again; and then he asked her, with a deeper, intenser smile, if she would do him the honour of dancing with him. Even to this inquiry she gave no audible assent; she simply let him put his arm round her waist—as she did so it occurred to her more vividly than it had ever done before, that this was a singular place for a gentleman's arm to be—and in a moment he was guiding her round the room in the harmonious rotation of the polka. When they paused she felt that she was red; and then, for some moments, she stopped looking at him. She fanned herself, and looked at the flowers that were painted on her fan. He asked her if she would begin again, and she hesitated to answer, still looking at the flowers.

"Does it make you dizzy?" he asked, in a tone of great kindness.

Then Catherine looked up at him; he was certainly beautiful, and not at all red. "Yes," she said; she hardly knew why, for dancing had never made her dizzy.

"Ah, well, in that case," said Mr. Townsend, "we will sit still and talk. I will find a good place to sit."

He found a good place—a charming place; a little sofa that seemed meant only for two persons. The rooms by this time were very full; the dancers increased in number, and people stood close in front of them, turning their backs, so that Catherine and her companion seemed secluded and unobserved. "*We* will talk," the young man had said; but he still did all the talking. Catherine leaned back in her place, with her eyes fixed upon him, smiling and thinking him very clever. He had features like young men in pictures; Catherine had never seen such features—so delicate, so chiselled and finished—among the young New Yorkers whom she passed in the streets and met at parties. He was tall and slim, but he looked extremely strong. Catherine thought he looked like a statue. But a statue would not talk like that, and, above all, would not have eyes of so rare a colour. He had never been at Mrs. Almond's before; he felt very much like a stranger; and it was very kind of Catherine to take pity on him. He was Arthur Townsend's cousin—not very near; several times removed—and Arthur had brought him to present him to the family. In fact, he was a great stranger in New York. It was his native place; but he had not been there for many years. He had been knocking about the world, and living in far-away lands; he had only come back a month or two before. New York was very pleasant, only he felt lonely.

"You see, people forget you," he said, smiling at Catherine with his delightful gaze, while he leaned forward obliquely, turning towards her, with his elbows on his knees.

It seemed to Catherine that no one who had once seen him would ever forget him; but though she made this reflection she kept it to herself, almost as you would keep something precious.

They sat there for some time. He was very amusing. He asked her about the people that were near them; he tried to guess who some of them were, and he made the most laughable mistakes. He criticised them very freely, in a positive, off-hand way. Catherine had never heard any one—especially any young man—talk just like that. It was the way a young man might talk in a novel; or better still, in a play, on the stage, close before the footlights, looking at the audience, and with every one looking at him, so that you wondered at his presence of mind. And yet Mr. Townsend was not like an actor; he seemed so sincere, so natural. This was very interesting; but in the midst of it, Marian Almond came pushing through the crowd, with a little ironical cry, when she found these young people still together, which made every one turn round, and cost Catherine a conscious blush. Marian broke up their talk, and told Mr. Townsend—whom she treated as if she were already married, and he had become her cousin—to run away to her mother, who had been wishing for the last half-hour to introduce him to Mr. Almond.

"We shall meet again!" he said to Catherine as he left her, and Catherine thought it a very original speech.

Her cousin took her by the arm, and made her walk about. "I needn't ask you what you think of Morris!" the young girl exclaimed.

"Is that his name?"

"I don't ask you what you think of his name, but what you think of himself," said Marian.

"Oh, nothing particular!" Catherine answered, dissembling for the first time in her life.

"I have half a mind to tell him that!" cried Marian. "It will do him good. He's so terribly conceited."

"Conceited?" said Catherine, staring.

"So Arthur says, and Arthur knows about him."

"Oh, don't tell him!" Catherine murmured imploringly.

"Don't tell him he's conceited? I have told him so a dozen times."

At this profession of audacity, Catherine looked down at her little companion in amazement. She supposed it was because Marian was going to be married that she took so much on herself; but she wondered too, whether, when she herself should become engaged, such exploits would be expected of her.

Half an hour later she saw her aunt Penniman sitting in the embrasure of a window, with her head a little on one side, and her gold eye-glass raised to her eyes, which were wandering about the room. In front of her was a gentleman, bending forward a little, with his back turned to Catherine. She knew his back immediately, though she had never seen it; for when he left her, at Marian's instigation, he had retreated in the best order, without turning round. Morris Townsend—the name had already become very familiar to her, as if some one had been repeating it in her ear for the last half hour—Morris Townsend was giving his impressions of the company to her aunt, as he had done to herself; he was saying clever things, and Mrs. Penniman was smiling, as if she approved of them. As soon as Catherine had perceived this she moved away; she would not have liked him to turn round and see her. But it gave her pleasure— the whole thing. That he should talk with Mrs. Penniman, with whom she lived and whom she saw and talked with every day—that seemed to keep him near her, and to make him even easier to contemplate than if she herself had been the object of his civilities; and that Aunt Lavinia should like him, should not be shocked or startled by what he said, this also appeared to the girl a personal gain; for Aunt Lavinia's standard was extremely high, planted as it was over the grave of her late husband, in which, as she had convinced every one, the very genius of conversation was buried. One of the Almond boys, as Catherine called them, invited our heroine to dance a quadrille, and for a quarter of an hour her feet at least were occupied. This time she was not dizzy; her head was very clear. Just when the dance was over, she found herself in the crowd face to face with her father. Dr. Sloper had usually a little smile, never a very big one, and with his little smile playing in his clear eyes and on his neatly-shaved lips, he looked at his daughter's crimson gown.

"Is it possible that this magnificent person is my child?" he said.

You would have surprised him if you had told him so; but it is a literal fact that he almost never addressed his daughter save in the ironical form. Whenever he addressed her he gave her pleasure; but she had to cut her pleasure out of the piece, as it were. There were portions left over, light remnants and snippets of irony, which she never knew what to do with, which seemed too delicate for her own use; and yet Catherine, lamenting the limitations of her understanding, felt that they were too valuable to waste, and had a belief that if they passed over her head they yet contributed to the general sum of human wisdom.

"I am not magnificent," she said, mildly, wishing that she had put on another dress.

"You are sumptuous, opulent, expensive," her father rejoined. "You look as if you had eighty thousand a year."

"Well, so long as I haven't——" said Catherine illogically. Her conception of her prospective wealth was as yet very indefinite.

"So long as you haven't you shouldn't look as if you had. Have you enjoyed your party?"

Catherine hesitated a moment; and then, looking away, "I am rather tired," she murmured. I have said that this entertainment was the beginning of something important for Catherine. For the second time in her life she made an indirect answer; and the beginning of a period of dissimulation is certainly a significant date. Catherine was not so easily tired as that.

Nevertheless, in the carriage, as they drove home, she was as quiet as if fatigue had been her portion. Dr. Sloper's manner of addressing his sister Lavinia had a good deal of resemblance to the tone he had adopted towards Catherine.

"Who was the young man that was making love to you?" he presently asked.

"Oh, my good brother!" murmured Mrs. Penniman, in deprecation.

"He seemed uncommonly tender. Whenever I looked at you, for half an hour, he had the most devoted air."

"The devotion was not to me," said Mrs. Penniman. "It was to Catherine; he talked to me of her."

Catherine had been listening with all her ears. "Oh, Aunt Penniman!" she exclaimed faintly.

"He is very handsome; he is very clever; he expressed himself with a great deal—a great deal of felicity," her aunt went on.

"He is in love with this regal creature, then?" the Doctor inquired humorously.

"Oh, father," cried the girl, still more faintly, devoutly thankful the carriage was dark.

"I don't know that; but he admired her dress."

Catherine did not say to herself in the dark, "My dress only?" Mrs. Penniman's announcement struck her by its richness, not by its meagreness.

"You see," said her father, "he thinks you have eighty thousand a year."

"I don't believe he thinks of that," said Mrs. Penniman; "he is too refined."

"He must be tremendously refined not to think of that!"

"Well, he is!" Catherine exclaimed, before she knew it.

"I thought you had gone to sleep," her father answered. "The hour has come!" he added to himself. "Lavinia is going to get up a romance for Catherine. It's a shame to play such tricks on the girl. What is the gentleman's name?" he went on, aloud.

"I didn't catch it, and I didn't like to ask him. He asked to be introduced to me," said Mrs. Penniman, with a certain grandeur; "but you know how indistinctly Jefferson speaks." Jefferson was Mr. Almond. "Catherine, dear, what was the gentleman's name?"

For a minute, if it had not been for the rumbling of the carriage, you might have heard a pin drop.

"I don't know, Aunt Lavinia," said Catherine, very softly. And, with all his irony, her father believed her.

V

HE LEARNED what he had asked some three or four days later, after Morris Townsend, with his cousin, had called in

Washington Square. Mrs. Penniman did not tell her brother, on the drive home, that she had intimated to this agreeable young man, whose name she did not know, that, with her niece, she should be very glad to see him; but she was greatly pleased, and even a little flattered, when, late on a Sunday afternoon, the two gentlemen made their appearance. His coming with Arthur Townsend made it more natural and easy; the latter young man was on the point of becoming connected with the family, and Mrs. Penniman had remarked to Catherine that, as he was going to marry Marian, it would be polite in him to call. These events came to pass late in the autumn, and Catherine and her aunt had been sitting together in the closing dusk, by the firelight, in the high back-parlour.

Arthur Townsend fell to Catherine's portion, while his companion placed himself on the sofa, beside Mrs. Penniman. Catherine had hitherto not been a harsh critic; she was easy to please—she liked to talk with young men. But Marian's betrothed, this evening, made her feel vaguely fastidious; he sat looking at the fire and rubbing his knees with his hands. As for Catherine, she scarcely even pretended to keep up the conversation; her attention had fixed itself on the other side of the room; she was listening to what went on between the other Mr. Townsend and her aunt. Every now and then he looked over at Catherine herself and smiled, as if to show that what he said was for her benefit too. Catherine would have liked to change her place, to go and sit near them, where she might see and hear him better. But she was afraid of seeming bold—of looking eager; and, besides, it would not have been polite to Marian's little suitor. She wondered why the other gentleman had picked out her aunt—how he came to have so much to say to Mrs. Penniman, to whom, usually, young men were not especially devoted. She was not at all jealous of Aunt Lavinia, but she was a little envious, and above all she wondered; for Morris Townsend was an object on which she found that her imagination could exercise itself indefinitely. His cousin had been describing a house that he had taken in view of his union with Marian, and the domestic conveniences he meant to introduce into it; how Marian wanted a larger one, and Mrs. Almond recommended a smaller one, and how he himself was convinced that he had got the neatest house in New York.

"It doesn't matter," he said; "it's only for three or four years. At the end of three or four years we'll move. That's the way to live in New York—to move every three or four years. Then you always get the last thing. It's because the city's growing so quick —you've got to keep up with it. It's going straight up town— that's where New York's going. If I wasn't afraid Marian would be lonely, I'd go up there—right up to the top—and wait for it. Only have to wait ten years—they'd all come up after you. But Marian says she wants some neighbours—she doesn't want to be a pioneer. She says that if she's got to be the first settler she had better go out to Minnesota. I guess we'll move up little by little; when we get tired of one street we'll go higher. So you see we'll always have a new house; it's a great advantage to have a new house; you get all the latest improvements. They invent everything all over again about every five years, and it's a great thing to keep up with the new things. I always try and keep up with the new things of every kind. Don't you think that's a good motto for a young couple—to keep 'going higher?' That's the name of that piece of poetry—what do they call it?—*Excelsior!*"

Catherine bestowed on her junior visitor only just enough attention to feel that this was not the way Mr. Morris Townsend had talked the other night, or that he was talking now to her fortunate aunt. But suddenly his aspiring kinsman became more interesting. He seemed to have become conscious that she was affected by his companion's presence, and he thought it proper to explain it.

"My cousin asked me to bring him, or I shouldn't have taken the liberty. He seemed to want very much to come; you know he's awfully sociable. I told him I wanted to ask you first, but he said Mrs. Penniman had invited him. He isn't particular what he says when he wants to come somewhere! But Mrs. Penniman seems to think it's all right."

"We are very glad to see him," said Catherine. And she wished to talk more about him; but she hardly knew what to say. "I never saw him before," she went on presently.

Arthur Townsend stared.

"Why, he told me he talked with you for over half an hour the other night."

"I mean before the other night. That was the first time."

"Oh, he has been away from New York—he has been all round the world. He doesn't know many people here, but he's very sociable, and he wants to know every one."

"Every one?" said Catherine.

"Well, I mean all the good ones. All the pretty young ladies—like Mrs. Penniman!" And Arthur Townsend gave a private laugh.

"My aunt likes him very much," said Catherine.

"Most people like him—he's so brilliant."

"He's more like a foreigner," Catherine suggested.

"Well, I never knew a foreigner!" said young Townsend, in a tone which seemed to indicate that his ignorance had been optional.

"Neither have I," Catherine confessed, with more humility. "They say they are generally brilliant," she added, vaguely.

"Well, the people of this city are clever enough for me. I know some of them that think they are too clever for me; but they ain't!"

"I suppose you can't be too clever," said Catherine, still with humility.

"I don't know. I know some people that call my cousin too clever."

Catherine listened to this statement with extreme interest, and a feeling that if Morris Townsend had a fault it would naturally be that one. But she did not commit herself, and in a moment she asked:—"Now that he has come back, will he stay here always?"

"Ah," said Arthur, "if he can get something to do."

"Something to do?"

"Some place or other; some business."

"Hasn't he got any?" said Catherine, who had never heard of a young man—of the upper class—in this situation.

"No; he's looking round. But he can't find anything."

"I am very sorry," Catherine permitted herself to observe.

"Oh, he doesn't mind," said young Townsend. "He takes it easy—he isn't in a hurry. He is very particular."

Catherine thought he naturally would be, and gave herself up for some moments to the contemplation of this idea, in several of its bearings.

"Won't his father take him into his business—his office?" she at last inquired.

"He hasn't got any father—he has only got a sister. Your sister can't help you much."

It seemed to Catherine that if she were his sister she would disprove this axiom. "Is she—is she pleasant?" she asked in a moment.

"I don't know—I believe she's very respectable," said young Townsend. And then he looked across to his cousin and began to laugh. "Look here, we are talking about you," he added.

Morris Townsend paused in his conversation with Mrs. Penniman, and stared, with a little smile. Then he got up, as if he were going.

"As far as you are concerned, I can't return the compliment," he said to Catherine's companion. "But as regards Miss Sloper, it's another affair."

Catherine thought this little speech wonderfully well turned; but she was embarrassed by it, and she also got up. Morris Townsend stood looking at her and smiling; he put out his hand for farewell. He was going, without having said anything to her; but even on these terms she was glad to have seen him.

"I will tell her what you have said—when you go!" said Mrs. Penniman, with an insinuating laugh.

Catherine blushed, for she felt almost as if they were making sport of her. What in the world could this beautiful young man have said? He looked at her still, in spite of her blush; but very kindly and respectfully.

"I have had no talk with you," he said, "and that was what I came for. But it will be a good reason for coming another time; a little pretext—if I am obliged to give one. I am not afraid of what your aunt will say when I go."

With this the two young men took their departure; after which Catherine, with her blush still lingering, directed a serious and interrogative eye to Mrs. Penniman. She was incapable of elaborate artifice, and she resorted to no jocular device—to no affectation of the belief that she had been maligned—to learn what she desired.

"What did you say you would tell me?" she asked.

Mrs. Penniman came up to her, smiling and nodding a little, looked at her all over, and gave a twist to the knot of ribbon in her neck. "It's a great secret, my dear child; but he is coming a-courting!"

Catherine was serious still. "Is that what he told you?"

"He didn't say so exactly. But he left me to guess it. I'm a good guesser."

"Do you mean a-courting me?"

"Not me, certainly, miss; though I must say he is a hundred times more polite to a person who has no longer extreme youth to recommend her than most of the young men. He is thinking of some one else." And Mrs. Penniman gave her niece a delicate little kiss. "You must be very gracious to him."

Catherine stared—she was bewildered. "I don't understand you," she said; "he doesn't know me."

"Oh yes, he does; more than you think. I have told him all about you."

"Oh, Aunt Penniman!" murmured Catherine, as if this had been a breach of trust. "He is a perfect stranger—we don't know him." There was infinite modesty in the poor girl's "we."

Aunt Penniman, however, took no account of it; she spoke

even with a touch of acrimony. "My dear Catherine, you know very well that you admire him!"

"Oh, Aunt Penniman!" Catherine could only murmur again. It might very well be that she admired him—though this did not seem to her a thing to talk about. But that this brilliant stranger—this sudden apparition, who had barely heard the sound of her voice—took that sort of interest in her that was expressed by the romantic phrase of which Mrs. Penniman had just made use: this could only be a figment of the restless brain of Aunt Lavinia, whom every one knew to be a woman of powerful imagination.

VI

MRS. PENNIMAN even took for granted at times that other people had as much imagination as herself; so that when, half an hour later, her brother came in, she addressed him quite on this principle.

"He has just been here, Austin; it's such a pity you missed him."

"Whom in the world have I missed?" asked the Doctor.

"Mr. Morris Townsend; he has made us such a delightful visit."

"And who in the world is Mr. Morris Townsend?"

"Aunt Penniman means the gentleman—the gentleman whose name I couldn't remember," said Catherine.

"The gentleman at Elizabeth's party who was so struck with Catherine," Mrs. Penniman added.

"Oh, his name is Morris Townsend, is it? And did he come here to propose to you?"

"Oh, father," murmured the girl for all answer, turning away to the window, where the dusk had deepened to darkness.

"I hope he won't do that without your permission," said Mrs. Penniman, very graciously.

"After all, my dear, he seems to have yours," her brother answered.

Lavinia simpered, as if this might not be quite enough, and Catherine, with her forehead touching the window-panes, listened to this exchange of epigrams as reservedly as if they had not each been a pin-prick in her own destiny.

"The next time he comes," the Doctor added, "you had better call me. He might like to see me."

Morris Townsend came again, some five days afterwards; but Dr. Sloper was not called, as he was absent from home at the time. Catherine was with her aunt when the young man's name was brought in, and Mrs. Penniman, effacing herself and protesting, made a great point of her niece's going into the drawing-room alone.

"This time it's for you—for you only," she said. "Before, when he talked to me, it was only preliminary—it was to gain my confidence. Literally, my dear, I should not have the *courage* to show myself to-day."

And this was perfectly true. Mrs. Penniman was not a brave woman, and Morris Townsend had struck her as a young man of great force of character, and of remarkable powers of satire; a keen, resolute, brilliant nature, with which one must exercise a great deal of tact. She said to herself that he was "imperious," and she liked the word and the idea. She was not the least jealous of her niece, and she had been perfectly happy with Mr. Penniman, but in the bottom of her heart she permitted herself the observation: "That's the sort of husband I should have had!" He was certainly much more imperious—she ended by calling it imperial—than Mr. Penniman.

So Catherine saw Mr. Townsend alone, and her aunt did not come in even at the end of the visit. The visit was a long one; he sat there—in the front parlour, in the biggest arm-chair—for more than an hour. He seemed more at home this time—more familiar; lounging a little in the chair, slapping a cushion that was near him with his stick, and looking round the room a good deal, and at the objects it contained, as well as at Catherine; whom, however, he also contemplated freely. There was a smile of respectful devotion in his handsome eyes which seemed to Catherine almost solemnly beautiful; it made her think of a young knight in a poem. His talk, however, was not particularly knightly; it was light and easy and friendly; it took a practical turn, and he asked a number of questions about herself—what were her tastes—if she liked this and that—what were her habits. He said to her, with his charming smile, "Tell me about yourself; give me a little sketch." Catherine had very little to tell, and she had no talent for sketching; but before he went she had confided to him that she had a secret passion for the theatre, which had been but scantily gratified, and a taste for operatic music—that of Bellini and Donizetti, in especial (it must be remembered in extenuation of this primitive young woman that she held these opinions in an age of general darkness)—which she rarely had an occasion to hear, except on the hand-organ. She confessed that she was not particularly fond of literature. Morris Townsend agreed with her that books were tiresome things; only, as he said, you had to read a good many before you found it out. He had been to places that people had written books about, and they were not a bit like the descriptions. To see for yourself—that was the great thing; he always tried to see for himself. He had seen all the principal actors—he had been to all the best theatres in London and Paris. But the actors were always like the authors—they always exaggerated. He liked everything to be natural. Suddenly he stopped, looking at Catherine with his smile.

"That's what I like you for; you are so natural! Excuse me," he added; "you see I am natural myself."

And before she had time to think whether she excused him or not—which afterwards, at leisure, she became conscious that she did—he began to talk about music, and to say that it was his greatest pleasure in life. He had heard all the great singers in Paris and London—Pasta and Rubini and Lablache—and when you had done that, you could say that you knew what singing was.

"I sing a little myself," he said; "some day I will show you. Not to-day, but some other time."

And then he got up to go; he had omitted, by accident, to say that he would sing to her if she would play to him. He thought of this after he got into the street; but he might have spared his compunction, for Catherine had not noticed the lapse. She was thinking only that "some other time" had a delightful sound; it seemed to spread itself over the future.

This was all the more reason, however, though she was ashamed and uncomfortable, why she should tell her father that Mr. Morris Townsend had called again. She announced the fact abruptly, almost violently, as soon as the Doctor came into the house; and having done so—it was her duty—she took measures to leave the room. But she could not leave it fast enough; her father stopped her just as she reached the door.

"Well, my dear, did he propose to you to-day?" the Doctor asked.

This was just what she had been afraid he would say; and yet she had no answer ready. Of course she would have liked to take it as a joke—as her father must have meant it; and yet she would have liked, also, in denying it, to be a little positive, a little sharp; so that he would perhaps not ask the question again. She didn't like it—it made her unhappy. But Catherine could never be sharp; and for a moment she only stood, with her hand on the door-knob, looking at her satiric parent, and giving a little laugh.

"Decidedly," said the Doctor to himself, "my daughter is not brilliant!"

But he had no sooner made this reflection than Catherine found something; she had decided on the whole to take the thing as a joke.

"Perhaps he will do it the next time!" she exclaimed, with a repetition of her laugh. And she quickly got out of the room.

The Doctor stood staring; he wondered whether his daughter were serious. Catherine went straight to her own room, and by the time she reached it she bethought herself that there was something else—something better—she might have said. She almost wished, now, that her father would ask his question again, so that she might reply:—"Oh yes, Mr. Morris Townsend proposed to me, and I refused him!"

The Doctor, however, began to put his questions elsewhere; it naturally having occurred to him that he ought to inform himself properly about this handsome young man who had formed the habit of running in and out of his house. He addressed himself to the younger of his sisters, Mrs. Almond—not going to her for the purpose; there was no such hurry as that—but having made a note of the matter for the first opportunity. The Doctor was never eager, never impatient nor nervous; but he made notes of everything, and he regularly consulted his notes. Among them the information he obtained from Mrs. Almond about Morris Townsend took its place.

"Lavinia has already been to ask me," she said. "Lavinia is most excited; I don't understand it. It's not, after all, Lavinia that the young man is supposed to have designs upon. She is very peculiar."

"Ah, my dear," the Doctor replied, "she has not lived with me these twelve years without my finding it out!"

"She has got such an artificial mind," said Mrs. Almond, who always enjoyed an opportunity to discuss Lavinia's peculiarities with her brother. "She didn't want me to tell you that she had asked me about Mr. Townsend; but I told her I would. She always wants to conceal everything."

"And yet at moments no one blurts things out with such crudity. She is like a revolving lighthouse; pitch darkness alternating with a dazzling brilliancy! But what did you tell her?" the Doctor asked.

"What I tell you; that I know very little of him."

"Lavinia must have been disappointed at that," said the Doctor; "she would prefer him to have been guilty of some romantic crime. However, we must make the best of people. They tell me our gentleman is the cousin of the little boy to whom you are about to entrust the future of your little girl."

"Arthur is not a little boy; he is a very old man; you and I will never be so old. He is a distant relation of Lavinia's *protégé*. The name is the same, but I am given to understand that there are Townsends and Townsends. So Arthur's mother tells me; she talked about 'branches'—younger branches, elder branches, inferior branches—as if it were a royal house. Arthur, it appears, is of the reigning line, but poor Lavinia's young man is not. Beyond this, Arthur's mother knows very little about him; she has only a vague story that he has been 'wild.' But I know his sister a little, and she is a very nice woman. Her name is Mrs. Montgomery; she is a widow, with a little property and five children. She lives in the Second Avenue."

"What does Mrs. Montgomery say about him?"

"That he has talents by which he might distinguish himself."

"Only he is lazy, eh?"

"She doesn't say so."

"That's family pride," said the Doctor. "What is his profession?"

"He hasn't got any; he is looking for something. I believe he was once in the Navy."

"Once? What is his age?"

"I suppose he is upwards of thirty. He must have gone into the Navy very young. I think Arthur told me that he inherited a small property—which was perhaps the cause of his leaving the Navy—and that he spent it all in a few years. He travelled all over the world, lived abroad, amused himself. I believe it was a kind of system, a theory he had. He has lately come back to America, with the intention, as he tells Arthur, of beginning life in earnest."

"Is he in earnest about Catherine, then?"

"I don't see why you should be incredulous," said Mrs. Almond. "It seems to me that you have never done Catherine justice. You must remember that she has the prospect of thirty thousand a year."

The Doctor looked at his sister a moment, and then, with

the slightest touch of bitterness:—"You at least appreciate her," he said.

Mrs. Almond blushed.

"I don't mean that is her only merit; I simply mean that it is a great one. A great many young men think so; and you appear to me never to have been properly aware of that. You have always had a little way of alluding to her as an unmarriageable girl."

"My allusions are as kind as yours, Elizabeth," said the Doctor, frankly. "How many suitors has Catherine had, with all her expectations—how much attention has she ever received? Catherine is not unmarriageable, but she is absolutely unattractive. What other reason is there for Lavinia being so charmed with the idea that there is a lover in the house? There has never been one before, and Lavinia, with her sensitive, sympathetic nature, is not used to the idea. It affects her imagination. I must do the young men of New York the justice to say that they strike me as very disinterested. They prefer pretty girls—lively girls—girls like your own. Catherine is neither pretty nor lively."

"Catherine does very well; she has a style of her own—which is more than my poor Marian has, who has no style at all," said Mrs. Almond. "The reason Catherine has received so little attention is that she seems to all the young men to be older than themselves. She is so large, and she dresses—so richly. They are rather afraid of her, I think; she looks as if she had been married already, and you know they don't like married women. And if our young men appear disinterested," the Doctor's wiser sister went on, "it is because they marry, as a general thing, so young, before twenty-five, at the age of innocence and sincerity, before the age of calculation. If they only waited a little, Catherine would fare better."

"As a calculation? Thank you very much," said the Doctor.

"Wait till some intelligent man of forty comes along, and he will be delighted with Catherine," Mrs. Almond continued.

"Mr. Townsend is not old enough, then; his motives may be pure."

"It is very possible that his motives are pure; I should be very sorry to take the contrary for granted. Lavinia is sure of it, and, as he is a very prepossessing youth, you might give him the benefit of the doubt."

Dr. Sloper reflected a moment.

"What are his present means of subsistence?"

"I have no idea. He lives, as I say, with his sister."

"A widow, with five children? Do you mean he lives *upon* her?"

Mrs. Almond got up, and with a certain impatience: "Had you not better ask Mrs. Montgomery herself?" she inquired.

"Perhaps I may come to that," said the Doctor. "Did you say the Second Avenue?" He made a note of the Second Avenue.

VII

HE WAS, however, by no means so much in earnest as this might seem to indicate; and, indeed, he was more than any-thing else amused with the whole situation. He was not in the least in a state of tension or of vigilance, with regard to Cath-erine's prospects; he was even on his guard against the ridicule that might attach itself to the spectacle of a house thrown into agitation by its daughter and heiress receiving attentions un-precedented in its annals. More than this, he went so far as to promise himself some entertainment from the little drama—if drama it was—of which Mrs. Penniman desired to represent the ingenious Mr. Townsend as the hero. He had no intention, as yet, of regulating the *dénouement*. He was perfectly willing, as Elizabeth had suggested, to give the young man the benefit of every doubt. There was no great danger in it; for Catherine, at the age of twenty-two, was after all a rather mature blossom, such as could be plucked from the stem only by a vigorous jerk. The fact that Morris Townsend was poor—was not of necessity against him; the Doctor had never made up his mind that his daughter should marry a rich man. The fortune she would inherit struck him as a very sufficient provision for two reasonable persons, and if a penniless swain who could give a good account of himself should enter the lists, he should be judged quite upon his personal merits. There were other things besides. The Doctor thought it very vulgar to be precipitate in accusing people of mercenary motives, inasmuch as his door had as yet not been in the least besieged by fortune-hunters; and, lastly, he was very curious to see whether Catherine might really be loved for her moral worth. He smiled as he reflected that poor Mr. Townsend had been only twice to the house, and he said to Mrs. Penniman that the next time he should come she must ask him to dinner.

He came very soon again, and Mrs. Penniman had of course great pleasure in executing this mission. Morris Townsend accepted her invitation with equal good grace, and the dinner took place a few days later. The Doctor had said to himself, justly enough, that they must not have the young man alone; this would partake too much of the nature of encouragement. So two or three other persons were invited; but Morris Townsend, though he was by no means the ostensible, was the real occasion of the feast. There is every reason to suppose that he desired to make a good impression; and if he fell short of this result, it was not for want of a good deal of intelligent effort. The Doctor talked to him very little during dinner; but he observed him attentively, and after the ladies had gone out he pushed him the wine and asked him several questions. Morris was not a young man who needed to be pressed, and he found quite enough encouragement in the superior quality of the claret. The Doctor's wine was admirable, and it may be communicated to the reader that while he sipped it Morris reflected that a cellar-full of good liquor—there was evidently a cellar-full here—would be a most attractive idiosyncrasy in a father-in-law. The Doctor was struck with his appreciative guest; he saw that he was not a commonplace young man. "He has ability," said Catherine's father, "decided ability; he has a very good head if he chooses to use it. And he is uncommonly well turned out; quite the sort of figure that pleases the ladies. But I don't think I like him." The Doctor, however, kept his reflections to himself, and talked to his visitors about foreign lands, concerning which Morris offered him more information than he was ready, as he mentally phrased it, to swallow. Dr. Sloper had travelled but little, and he took the liberty of not believing everything this anecdotical idler narrated. He prided himself on being something of a physiognomist, and while the young man, chatting with easy assurance, puffed his cigar and filled his glass again, the Doctor sat with his eyes quietly fixed on his bright, expressive face. "He has the assurance of the devil himself," said Morris's host; "I don't think I ever saw such assurance. And his powers of invention are most remarkable. He is very knowing; they were not so knowing as that in my time. And a good head, did I say? I should think so—after a bottle of Madeira, and a bottle and a half of claret!"

After dinner Morris Townsend went and stood before Catherine, who was standing before the fire in her red satin gown.

"He doesn't like me—he doesn't like me at all!" said the young man.

"Who doesn't like you?" asked Catherine.

"Your father; extraordinary man!"

"I don't see how you know," said Catherine, blushing.

"I feel; I am very quick to feel."

"Perhaps you are mistaken."

"Ah, well; you ask him and you will see."

"I would rather not ask him, if there is any danger of his saying what you think."

Morris looked at her with an air of mock melancholy.

"It wouldn't give you any pleasure to contradict him?"

"I never contradict him," said Catherine.

"Will you hear me abused without opening your lips in my defence?"

"My father won't abuse you. He doesn't know you enough."

Morris Townsend gave a loud laugh, and Catherine began to blush again.

"I shall never mention you," she said, to take refuge from her confusion.

"That is very well; but it is not quite what I should have liked you to say. I should have liked you to say: 'If my father doesn't think well of you, what does it matter?'"

"Ah, but it would matter; I couldn't say that!" the girl exclaimed.

He looked at her for a moment, smiling a little; and the Doctor, if he had been watching him just then, would have seen a gleam of fine impatience in the sociable softness of his eye. But there was no impatience in his rejoinder—none, at least, save what was expressed in a little appealing sigh. "Ah, well, then, I must not give up the hope of bringing him round!"

He expressed it more frankly to Mrs. Penniman, later in the evening. But before that he sang two or three songs at Catherine's timid request; not that he flattered himself that this would help to bring her father round. He had a sweet, light tenor voice, and when he had finished, every one made some exclamation—every one, that is, save Catherine, who remained intensely silent. Mrs. Penniman declared that his manner of singing was "most artistic," and Dr. Sloper said it was "very taking—very taking indeed;" speaking loudly and distinctly, but with a certain dryness.

"He doesn't like me—he doesn't like me at all," said Morris Townsend, addressing the aunt in the same manner as he had done the niece. "He thinks I'm all wrong."

Unlike her niece, Mrs. Penniman asked for no explanation. She only smiled very sweetly, as if she understood everything; and, unlike Catherine too, she made no attempt to contradict him. "Pray, what does it matter?" she murmured softly.

"Ah, you say the right thing!" said Morris, greatly to the gratification of Mrs. Penniman, who prided herself on always saying the right thing.

The Doctor, the next time he saw his sister Elizabeth, let her know that he had made the acquaintance of Lavinia's *protégé*.

"Physically," he said, "he's uncommonly well set up. As an

anatomist, it is really a pleasure to me to see such a beautiful structure; although, if people were all like him, I suppose there would be very little need for doctors."

"Don't you see anything in people but their bones?" Mrs. Almond rejoined. "What do you think of him as a father?"

"As a father? Thank Heaven I am not his father!"

"No; but you are Catherine's. Lavinia tells me she is in love."

"She must get over it. He is not a gentleman."

"Ah, take care! Remember that he is a branch of the Townsends."

"He is not what I call a gentleman. He has not the soul of one. He is extremely insinuating; but it's a vulgar nature. I saw through it in a minute. He is altogether too familiar—I hate familiarity. He is a plausible coxcomb."

"Ah, well," said Mrs. Almond; "if you make up your mind so easily, it's a great advantage."

"I don't make up my mind easily. What I tell you is the result of thirty years of observation; and in order to be able to form that judgment in a single evening, I have had to spend a lifetime in study."

"Very possibly you are right. But the thing is for Catherine to see it."

"I will present her with a pair of spectacles!" said the Doctor.

VIII

IF IT WERE true that she was in love, she was certainly very quiet about it; but the Doctor was of course prepared to admit that her quietness might mean volumes. She had told Morris Townsend that she would not mention him to her father, and she saw no reason to retract this vow of discretion. It was no more than decently civil, of course, that after having dined in Washington Square, Morris should call there again; and it was no more than natural that, having been kindly received on this occasion, he should continue to present himself. He had had plenty of leisure on his hands; and thirty years ago, in New York, a young man of leisure had reason to be thankful for aids to self-oblivion. Catherine said nothing to her father about these visits, though they had rapidly become the most important, the most absorbing thing in her life. The girl was very happy. She knew not as yet what would come of it; but the present had suddenly grown rich and solemn. If she had been told she was in love, she would have been a good deal surprised; for she had an idea that love was an eager and exacting passion, and her own heart was filled in these days with the impulse of self-effacement and sacrifice. Whenever Morris Townsend had left the house, her imagination projected itself, with all its strength, into the idea of his soon coming back; but if she had been told at such a moment that he would not return for a year, or even that he would never return, she would not have complained nor rebelled, but would have humbly accepted the decree, and sought for consolation in thinking over the times she had already seen him, the words he had spoken, the sound of his voice, of his tread, the expression of his face. Love demands certain things as a right; but Catherine had no sense of her rights; she had only a consciousness of immense and unexpected favours. Her very gratitude for these things had hushed itself; for it seemed to her that there would be something of impudence in making a festival of her secret. Her father suspected Morris Townsend's visits, and noted her reserve. She seemed to beg pardon for it; she looked at him constantly in silence, as if she meant to say that she said nothing because she was afraid of irritating him. But the poor girl's dumb eloquence irritated him more than anything else would have done, and he caught himself murmuring more than once that it was a grievous pity his only child was a simpleton. His murmurs, however, were inaudible; and for a while he said nothing to any one. He would have liked to know exactly how often young Townsend came; but he had determined to ask no questions of the girl herself— to say nothing more to her that would show that he watched her. The Doctor had a great idea of being largely just: he wished to leave his daughter her liberty, and interfere only when the danger should be proved. It was not in his manner to obtain information by indirect methods, and it never even occurred to him to question the servants. As for Lavinia, he hated to talk to her about the matter; she annoyed him with her mock romanticism. But he had to come to this. Mrs. Penniman's convictions as regards the relations of her niece and the clever young visitor who saved appearances by coming ostensibly for both the ladies—Mrs. Penniman's convictions had passed into a riper and richer phase. There was to be no crudity in Mrs. Penniman's treatment of the situation; she had become as uncommunicative as Catherine herself. She was tasting of the sweets of concealment; she had taken up the line of mystery. "She would be enchanted to be able to prove to herself that she is persecuted," said the Doctor; and when at last he questioned her, he was sure she would contrive to extract from his words a pretext for this belief.

"Be so good as to let me know what is going on in the house," he said to her, in a tone which, under the circumstances, he himself deemed genial.

"Going on, Austin?" Mrs. Penniman exclaimed. "Why, I am sure I don't know! I believe that last night the old gray cat had kittens?"

"At her age?" said the Doctor. "The idea is startling—almost shocking. Be so good as to see that they are all drowned. But what else has happened?"

"Ah, the dear little kittens!" cried Mrs. Penniman. "I wouldn't have them drowned for the world!"

Her brother puffed his cigar a few moments in silence. "Your sympathy with kittens, Lavinia," he presently resumed, "arises from a feline element in your own character."

"Cats are very graceful, and very clean," said Mrs. Penniman, smiling.

"And very stealthy. You are the embodiment both of grace and of neatness; but you are wanting in frankness."

"You certainly are not, dear brother."

"I don't pretend to be graceful, though I try to be neat. Why haven't you let me know that Mr. Morris Townsend is coming to the house four times a week?"

Mrs. Penniman lifted her eyebrows. "Four times a week?"

"Five times, if you prefer it. I am away all day, and I see nothing. But when such things happen, you should let me know."

Mrs. Penniman, with her eyebrows still raised, reflected intently. "Dear Austin," she said at last, "I am incapable of betraying a confidence. I would rather suffer anything."

"Never fear; you shall not suffer. To whose confidence is it you allude? Has Catherine made you take a vow of eternal secrecy?"

"By no means. Catherine has not told me as much as she might. She has not been very trustful."

"It is the young man, then, who has made you his confidant? Allow me to say that it is extremely indiscreet of you to form secret alliances with young men. You don't know where they may lead you."

"I don't know what you mean by an alliance," said Mrs. Penniman. "I take a great interest in Mr. Townsend; I won't conceal that. But that's all."

"Under the circumstances, that is quite enough. What is the source of your interest in Mr. Townsend?"

"Why," said Mrs. Penniman, musing, and then breaking into her smile, "that he is so interesting!"

The Doctor felt that he had need of his patience. "And what makes him interesting?—his good looks?"

"His misfortunes, Austin."

"Ah, he has had misfortunes? That, of course, is always interesting. Are you at liberty to mention a few of Mr. Townsend's?"

"I don't know that he would like it," said Mrs. Penniman. "He has told me a great deal about himself—he has told me, in fact, his whole history. But I don't think I ought to repeat those things. He would tell them to you, I am sure, if he thought you would listen to him kindly. With kindness you may do anything with him."

The Doctor gave a laugh. "I shall request him very kindly, then, to leave Catherine alone."

"Ah!" said Mrs. Penniman, shaking her forefinger at her brother, with her little finger turned out, "Catherine has probably said something to him kinder than that!"

"Said that she loved him? Do you mean that?"

Mrs. Penniman fixed her eyes on the floor. "As I tell you, Austin, she doesn't confide in me."

"You have an opinion, I suppose, all the same. It is that I ask you for; though I don't conceal from you that I shall not regard it as conclusive."

Mrs. Penniman's gaze continued to rest on the carpet; but at last she lifted it, and then her brother thought it very expressive. "I think Catherine is very happy; that is all I can say."

"Townsend is trying to marry her—is that what you mean?"

"He is greatly interested in her."

"He finds her such an attractive girl?"

"Catherine has a lovely nature, Austin," said Mrs. Penniman, "and Mr. Townsend has had the intelligence to discover that."

"With a little help from you, I suppose. My dear Lavinia," cried the Doctor, "you are an admirable aunt!"

"So Mr. Townsend says," observed Lavinia, smiling.

"Do you think he is sincere?" asked her brother.

"In saying that?"

"No; that's of course. But in his admiration for Catherine?"

"Deeply sincere. He has said to me the most appreciative, the most charming things about her. He would say them to you, if he were sure you would listen to him—gently."

"I doubt whether I can undertake it. He appears to require a great deal of gentleness."

"He is a sympathetic, sensitive nature," said Mrs. Penniman.

Her brother puffed his cigar again in silence. "These delicate qualities have survived his vicissitudes, eh? All this while you haven't told me about his misfortunes."

"It is a long story," said Mrs. Penniman, "and I regard it as a sacred trust. But I suppose there is no objection to my saying that he has been wild—he frankly confesses that. But he has paid for it."

"That's what has impoverished him, eh?"

"I don't mean simply in money. He is very much alone in the world."

"Do you mean that he has behaved so badly that his friends have given him up?"

"He has had false friends, who have deceived and betrayed him."

"He seems to have some good ones too. He has a devoted sister, and half a dozen nephews and nieces."

Mrs. Penniman was silent a minute. "The nephews and nieces are children, and the sister is not a very attractive person."

"I hope he doesn't abuse her to you," said the Doctor; "for I am told he lives upon her."

"Lives upon her?"

"Lives with her, and does nothing for himself; it is about the same thing."

"He is looking for a position—most earnestly," said Mrs. Penniman. "He hopes every day to find one."

"Precisely. He is looking for it here—over there in the front parlour. The position of husband of a weak-minded woman with a large fortune would suit him to perfection!"

Mrs. Penniman was truly amiable, but she now gave signs of temper. She rose with much animation, and stood for a moment looking at her brother. "My dear Austin," she remarked, "if you regard Catherine as a weak-minded woman, you are particularly mistaken!" And with this she moved majestically away.

IX

IT WAS a regular custom with the family in Washington Square to go and spend Sunday evening at Mrs. Almond's. On the Sunday after the conversation I have just narrated, this custom was not intermitted; and on this occasion, towards the middle of the evening, Dr. Sloper found reason to withdraw to the library, with his brother-in-law, to talk over a matter of business. He was absent some twenty minutes, and when he came back into the circle, which was enlivened by the presence of several friends of the family, he saw that Morris Townsend had come in and had lost as little time as possible in seating himself on a small sofa, beside Catherine. In the large room, where several different groups had been formed, and the hum of voices and of laughter was loud, these two young persons might confabulate, as the Doctor phrased it to himself, without attracting attention. He saw in a moment, however, that his daughter was painfully conscious of his own observation. She sat motionless, with her eyes bent down, staring at her open fan, deeply flushed, shrinking together as if to minimise the indiscretion of which she confessed herself guilty.

The Doctor almost pitied her. Poor Catherine was not defiant; she had no genius for bravado; and as she felt that her father viewed her companion's attentions with an unsympathising eye, there was nothing but discomfort for her in the accident of seeming to challenge him. The Doctor felt, indeed, so sorry for her that he turned away, to spare her the sense of being watched; and he was so intelligent a man that, in his thoughts, he rendered a sort of poetic justice to her situation.

"It must be deucedly pleasant for a plain, inanimate girl like that to have a beautiful young fellow come and sit down beside her and whisper to her that he is her slave—if that is what this one whispers. No wonder she likes it, and that she thinks me a cruel tyrant; which of course she does, though she is afraid— she hasn't the animation necessary—to admit it to herself. Poor old Catherine!" mused the Doctor; "I verily believe she is capable of defending me when Townsend abuses me!"

And the force of this reflection, for the moment, was such in making him feel the natural opposition between his point of view and that of an infatuated child, that he said to himself that he was perhaps after all taking things too hard and crying out before he was hurt. He must not condemn Morris Townsend unheard. He had a great aversion to taking things too hard; he thought that half the discomfort and many of the disappointments of life come from it; and for an instant he asked himself whether, possibly, he did not appear ridiculous to this intelligent young man, whose private perception of incongruities he suspected of being keen. At the end of a quarter of an hour Catherine had got rid of him, and Townsend was now standing before the fireplace in conversation with Mrs. Almond.

"We will try him again," said the Doctor. And he crossed the room and joined his sister and her companion, making her a sign that she should leave the young man to him. She presently did so, while Morris looked at him, smiling, without a sign of evasiveness in his affable eye.

"He's amazingly conceited!" thought the Doctor; and then he said aloud: "I am told you are looking out for a position."

"Oh, a position is more than I should presume to call it," Morris Townsend answered. "That sounds so fine. I should like some quiet work—something to turn an honest penny."

"What sort of thing should you prefer?"

"Do you mean what am I fit for? Very little, I am afraid. I have nothing but my good right arm, as they say in the melodramas."

"You are too modest," said the Doctor. "In addition to your good right arm, you have your subtle brain. I know nothing of you but what I see; but I see by your physiognomy that you are extremely intelligent."

"Ah," Townsend murmured, "I don't know what to answer when you say that! You advise me, then, not to despair?"

And he looked at his interlocutor as if the question might have a double meaning. The Doctor caught the look and weighed it a moment before he replied. "I should be very sorry to admit that a robust and well-disposed young man need ever despair. If he doesn't succeed in one thing, he can try another. Only, I should add, he should choose his line with discretion."

"Ah, yes, with discretion," Morris Townsend repeated, sympathetically. "Well, I have been indiscreet, formerly; but I think I have got over it. I am very steady now." And he stood a moment, looking down at his remarkably neat shoes. Then at last, "Were you kindly intending to propose something for my advantage?" he inquired, looking up and smiling.

"Damn his impudence!" the Doctor exclaimed, privately. But in a moment he reflected that he himself had, after all, touched first upon this delicate point, and that his words might have been construed as an offer of assistance. "I have no particular proposal to make," he presently said; "but it occurred to me to let you know that I have you in my mind. Sometimes one hears of opportunities. For instance—should you object to leaving New York—to going to a distance?"

"I am afraid I shouldn't be able to manage that. I must seek my fortune here or nowhere. You see," added Morris Townsend, "I have ties—I have responsibilities here. I have a sister, a widow, from whom I have been separated for a long time, and to whom I am almost everything. I shouldn't like to say to her that I must leave her. She rather depends upon me, you see."

"Ah, that's very proper; family feeling is very proper," said Dr. Sloper. "I often think there is not enough of it in our city. I think I have heard of your sister."

"It is possible, but I rather doubt it; she lives so very quietly."

"As quietly, you mean," the Doctor went on, with a short laugh, "as a lady may do who has several young children."

"Ah, my little nephews and nieces—that's the very point! I am helping to bring them up," said Morris Townsend. "I am a kind of amateur tutor; I give them lessons."

"That's very proper, as I say; but it is hardly a career."

"It won't make my fortune!" the young man confessed.

"You must not be too much bent on a fortune," said the Doctor. "But I assure you I will keep you in mind; I won't lose sight of you!"

"If my situation becomes desperate I shall perhaps take the

liberty of reminding you!" Morris rejoined, raising his voice a little, with a brighter smile, as his interlocutor turned away.

Before he left the house the Doctor had a few words with Mrs. Almond.

"I should like to see his sister," he said. "What do you call her? Mrs. Montgomery. I should like to have a little talk with her."

"I will try and manage it," Mrs. Almond responded. "I will take the first opportunity of inviting her, and you shall come and meet her. Unless, indeed," Mrs. Almond added, "she first takes it into her head to be sick and to send for you."

"Ah no, not that; she must have trouble enough without that. But it would have its advantages, for then I should see the children. I should like very much to see the children."

"You are very thorough. Do you want to catechise them about their uncle?"

"Precisely. Their uncle tells me he has charge of their education, that he saves their mother the expense of school-bills. I should like to ask them a few questions in the commoner branches."

"He certainly has not the cut of a schoolmaster!" Mrs. Almond said to herself a short time afterwards, as she saw Morris Townsend in a corner bending over her niece, who was seated.

And there was, indeed, nothing in the young man's discourse at this moment that savoured of the pedagogue.

"Will you meet me somewhere to-morrow or next day?" he said, in a low tone, to Catherine.

"Meet you?" she asked, lifting her frightened eyes.

"I have something particular to say to you—very particular."

"Can't you come to the house? Can't you say it there?"

Townsend shook his head gloomily. "I can't enter your doors again!"

"Oh, Mr. Townsend!" murmured Catherine. She trembled as she wondered what had happened, whether her father had forbidden it.

"I can't in self-respect," said the young man. "Your father has insulted me."

"Insulted you?"

"He has taunted me with my poverty."

"Oh, you are mistaken—you misunderstood him!" Catherine spoke with energy, getting up from her chair.

"Perhaps I am too proud—too sensitive. But would you have me otherwise?" he asked, tenderly.

"Where my father is concerned, you must not be sure. He is full of goodness," said Catherine.

"He laughed at me for having no position! I took it quietly; but only because he belongs to you."

"I don't know," said Catherine; "I don't know what he thinks. I am sure he means to be kind. You must not be too proud."

"I will be proud only of you," Morris answered. "Will you meet me in the Square in the afternoon?"

A great blush on Catherine's part had been the answer to the declaration I have just quoted. She turned away, heedless of his question.

"Will you meet me?" he repeated. "It is very quiet there; no one need see us—toward dusk?"

"It is you who are unkind, it is you who laugh, when you say such things as that."

"My dear girl!" the young man murmured.

"You know how little there is in me to be proud of. I am ugly and stupid."

Morris greeted this remark with an ardent murmur, in which she recognised nothing articulate but an assurance that she was his own dearest.

But she went on. "I am not even—I am not even——" And she paused a moment.

"You are not what?"

"I am not even brave."

"Ah, then, if you are afraid, what shall we do?"

She hesitated awhile; then at last—"You must come to the house," she said; "I am not afraid of that."

"I would rather it were in the Square," the young man urged. "You know how empty it is, often. No one will see us."

"I don't care who sees us! But leave me now."

He left her resignedly; he had got what he wanted. Fortunately he was ignorant that half an hour later, going home with her father and feeling him near, the poor girl, in spite of her sudden declaration of courage, began to tremble again. Her father said nothing; but she had an idea his eyes were fixed upon her in the darkness. Mrs. Penniman also was silent; Morris Townsend had told her that her niece preferred, unromantically, an interview in a chintz-covered parlour to a sentimental tryst beside a fountain sheeted with dead leaves, and she was lost in wonderment at the oddity—almost the perversity—of the choice.

X

CATHERINE received the young man the next day on the ground she had chosen—amid the chaste upholstery of a New York drawing-room furnished in the fashion of fifty years ago. Morris had swallowed his pride and made the effort necessary to cross the threshold of her too derisive parent—an act of magnanimity which could not fail to render him doubly interesting.

"We must settle something—we must take a line," he declared, passing his hand through his hair and giving a glance at the long narrow mirror which adorned the space between the two windows, and which had at its base a little gilded bracket covered by a thin slab of white marble, supporting in its turn a backgammon board folded together in the shape of two volumes, two shining folios inscribed in letters of greenish gilt, *History of England.* If Morris had been pleased to describe the master of the house as a heartless scoffer, it is because he thought him too much on his guard, and this was the easiest way to express his own dissatisfaction—a dissatisfaction which he had made a point of concealing from the Doctor. It will probably seem to the reader, however, that the Doctor's vigilance was by no means excessive, and that these two young people had an open field. Their intimacy was now considerable, and it may appear that for a shrinking and retiring person our heroine had been liberal of her favours. The young man, within a few days, had made her listen to things for which she had not supposed that she was prepared; having a lively foreboding of difficulties, he proceeded to gain as much ground as possible in the present. He remembered that fortune favours the brave, and even if he had forgotten it, Mrs. Penniman would have remembered it for him. Mrs. Penniman delighted of all things in a drama, and she flattered herself that a drama would now be enacted. Combining as she did the zeal of the prompter with the impatience of the spectator, she had long since done her utmost to pull up the curtain. She, too, expected to figure in the performance—to be the confidant, the Chorus, to speak the epilogue. It may even be said that there were times when she lost sight altogether of the modest heroine of the play, in the contemplation of certain great passages which would naturally occur between the hero and herself.

What Morris had told Catherine at last was simply that he loved her, or rather adored her. Virtually, he had made known as much already—his visits had been a series of eloquent intimations of it. But now he had affirmed it in lover's vows, and, as a memorable sign of it, he had passed his arm round the girl's waist and taken a kiss. This happy certitude had come sooner than Catherine expected, and she had regarded it, very naturally, as a priceless treasure. It may even be doubted whether she had ever definitely expected to possess it; she had not been waiting for it, and she had never said to herself that at a given moment it must come. As I have tried to explain, she was not eager and exacting; she took what was given her from day to day; and if the delightful custom of her lover's visits, which yielded her a happiness in which confidence and timidity were strangely blended, had suddenly come to an end, she would not only not have spoken of herself as one of the forsaken, but she would not have thought of herself as one of the disappointed. After Morris had kissed her, the last time he was with her, as a ripe assurance of his devotion, she begged him to go away, to leave her alone, to let her think. Morris went away, taking another kiss first. But Catherine's meditations had lacked a certain coherence. She felt his kisses on her lips and on her cheeks for a long time afterwards; the sensation was rather an obstacle than an aid to reflection. She would have liked to see her situation all clearly before her, to make up her mind what she should do if, as she feared, her father should tell her that he disapproved of Morris Townsend. But all that she could see with any vividness was that it was terribly strange that anyone should disapprove of him; that there must in that case be some mistake, some mystery, which in a little while would be set at rest. She put off deciding and choosing; before the vision of a conflict with her father she dropped her eyes and sat motionless, holding her breath and waiting. It made her heart beat, it was intensely painful. When Morris kissed her and said these things—that also made her heart beat; but this was worse, and it frightened her. Nevertheless, to-day, when the young man spoke of settling something, taking a line, she felt that it was the truth, and she answered very simply and without hesitating.

"We must do our duty," she said; "we must speak to my father. I will do it to-night; you must do it to-morrow."

"It is very good of you to do it first," Morris answered. "The young man—the happy lover—generally does that. But just as you please!"

It pleased Catherine to think that she should be brave for his sake, and in her satisfaction she even gave a little smile. "Women have more tact," she said; "they ought to do it first. They are more conciliating; they can persuade better."

"You will need all your powers of persuasion. But, after all," Morris added, "you are irresistible."

"Please don't speak that way—and promise me this. To-morrow, when you talk with father, you will be very gentle and respectful."

"As much so as possible," Morris promised. "It won't be much use, but I shall try. I certainly would rather have you easily than have to fight for you."

"Don't talk about fighting; we shall not fight."

"Ah, we must be prepared," Morris rejoined; "you especially, because for you it must come hardest. Do you know the first thing your father will say to you?"

"No, Morris; please tell me."

"He will tell you I am mercenary."

"Mercenary?"

"It's a big word; but it means a low thing. It means that I am after your money."

"Oh!" murmured Catherine, softly.

The exclamation was so deprecating and touching that Morris indulged in another little demonstration of affection. "But he will be sure to say it," he added.

"It will be easy to be prepared for that," Catherine said. "I shall simply say that he is mistaken—that other men may be that way, but that you are not."

"You must make a great point of that, for it will be his own great point."

Catherine looked at her lover a minute, and then she said, "I shall persuade him. But I am glad we shall be rich," she added.

Morris turned away, looking into the crown of his hat. "No, it's a misfortune," he said at last. "It is from that our difficulty will come."

"Well, if it is the worst misfortune, we are not so unhappy. Many people would not think it so bad. I will persuade him, and after that we shall be very glad we have money."

Morris Townsend listened to this robust logic in silence. "I will leave my defence to you; it's a charge that a man has to stoop to defend himself from."

Catherine on her side was silent for a while; she was looking at him while he looked, with a good deal of fixedness, out of the window. "Morris," she said, abruptly, "are you very sure you love me?"

He turned round, and in a moment he was bending over her. "My own dearest, can you doubt it?"

"I have only known it five days," she said; "but now it seems to me as if I could never do without it."

"You will never be called upon to try!" And he gave a little tender, reassuring laugh. Then, in a moment, he added, "There is something you must tell me, too." She had closed her eyes after the last word she uttered, and kept them closed; and at this she nodded her head, without opening them. "You must tell me," he went on, "that if your father is dead against me, if he absolutely forbids our marriage, you will still be faithful."

Catherine opened her eyes, gazing at him, and she could give no better promise than what he read there.

"You will cleave to me?" said Morris. "You know you are your own mistress—you are of age."

"Ah, Morris!" she murmured, for all answer. Or rather not for all; for she put her hand into his own. He kept it awhile, and presently he kissed her again. This is all that need be recorded of their conversation; but Mrs. Penniman, if she had been present, would probably have admitted that it was as well it had not taken place beside the fountain in Washington Square.

XI

CATHERINE listened for her father when he came in that evening, and she heard him go to his study. She sat quiet, though her heart was beating fast, for nearly half an hour; then she went and knocked at his door—a ceremony without which she never crossed the threshold of this apartment. On entering it now she found him in his chair beside the fire, entertaining himself with a cigar and the evening paper.

"I have something to say to you," she began very gently; and she sat down in the first place that offered.

"I shall be very happy to hear it, my dear," said her father. He waited—waited, looking at her, while she stared, in a long silence, at the fire. He was curious and impatient, for he was sure she was going to speak of Morris Townsend; but he let her take her own time, for he was determined to be very mild.

"I am engaged to be married!" Catherine announced at last, still staring at the fire.

The Doctor was startled; the accomplished fact was more than he had expected. But he betrayed no surprise. "You do right to tell me," he simply said. "And who is the happy mortal whom you have honoured with your choice?"

"Mr. Morris Townsend." And as she pronounced her lover's name, Catherine looked at him. What she saw was her father's still gray eye and his clear-cut, definite smile. She contemplated these objects for a moment, and then she looked back at the fire; it was much warmer.

"When was this arrangement made?" the Doctor asked.

"This afternoon—two hours ago."

"Was Mr. Townsend here?"

"Yes, father; in the front parlour." She was very glad that she was not obliged to tell him that the ceremony of their betrothal had taken place out there under the bare ailantus-trees.

"Is it serious?" said the Doctor.

"Very serious, father."

Her father was silent a moment. "Mr. Townsend ought to have told me."

"He means to tell you to-morrow."

"After I know all about it from you? He ought to have told me before. Does he think I didn't care—because I left you so much liberty?"

"Oh, no," said Catherine; "he knew you would care. And we have been so much obliged to you for—for the liberty."

The Doctor gave a short laugh. "You might have made a better use of it, Catherine."

"Please don't say that, father," the girl urged, softly, fixing her dull and gentle eyes upon him.

He puffed his cigar awhile, meditatively. "You have gone very fast," he said at last.

"Yes," Catherine answered simply; "I think we have."

Her father glanced at her an instant, removing his eyes from the fire. "I don't wonder Mr. Townsend likes you. You are so simple and so good."

"I don't know why it is—but he *does* like me. I am sure of that."

"And are you very fond of Mr. Townsend?"

"I like him very much, of course—or I shouldn't consent to marry him."

"But you have known him a very short time, my dear."

"Oh," said Catherine, with some eagerness, "it doesn't take long to like a person—when once you begin."

"You must have begun very quickly. Was it the first time you saw him—that night at your aunt's party?"

"I don't know, father," the girl answered. "I can't tell you about that."

"Of course; that's your own affair. You will have observed that I have acted on that principle. I have not interfered, I have left you your liberty, I have remembered that you are no longer a little girl—that you have arrived at years of discretion."

"I feel very old—and very wise," said Catherine, smiling faintly.

"I am afraid that before long you will feel older and wiser yet. I don't like your engagement."

"Ah!" Catherine exclaimed, softly, getting up from her chair.

"No, my dear. I am sorry to give you pain; but I don't like it. You should have consulted me before you settled it. I have been too easy with you, and I feel as if you had taken advantage of my indulgence. Most decidedly, you should have spoken to me first."

Catherine hesitated a moment, and then—"It was because I was afraid you wouldn't like it!" she confessed.

"Ah, there it is! You had a bad conscience."

"No, I have not a bad conscience, father!" the girl cried out, with considerable energy. "Please don't accuse me of anything so dreadful." These words, in fact, represented to her imagination something very terrible indeed, something base and cruel, which she associated with malefactors and prisoners. "It was because I was afraid—afraid——" she went on.

"If you were afraid, it was because you had been foolish!"

"I was afraid you didn't like Mr. Townsend."

"You were quite right. I don't like him."

"Dear father, you don't know him," said Catherine, in a voice so timidly argumentative that it might have touched him.

"Very true; I don't know him intimately. But I know him enough. I have my impression of him. You don't know him either."

She stood before the fire, with her hands lightly clasped in front of her; and her father, leaning back in his chair and looking up at her, made this remark with a placidity that might have been irritating.

I doubt, however, whether Catherine was irritated, though she broke into a vehement protest. "I don't know him?" she cried. "Why, I know him—better than I have ever known any one!"

"You know a part of him—what he has chosen to show you. But you don't know the rest."

"The rest? What is the rest?"

"Whatever it may be. There is sure to be plenty of it."

"I know what you mean," said Catherine, remembering how Morris had forewarned her. "You mean that he is mercenary."

Her father looked up at her still, with his cold, quiet, reasonable eye. "If I meant it, my dear, I should say it! But there is an error I wish particularly to avoid—that of rendering Mr. Townsend more interesting to you by saying hard things about him."

"I won't think them hard, if they are true," said Catherine.

"If you don't, you will be a remarkably sensible young woman!"

"They will be your reasons, at any rate, and you will want me to hear your reasons."

The Doctor smiled a little. "Very true. You have a perfect right to ask for them." And he puffed his cigar a few moments. "Very well, then, without accusing Mr. Townsend of being in love only with your fortune—and with the fortune that you justly expect—I will say that there is every reason to suppose that these good things have entered into his calculation more largely than a tender solicitude for your happiness strictly requires. There is, of course, nothing impossible in an intelligent young man entertaining a disinterested affection for you. You are an honest, amiable girl, and an intelligent young man might easily find it out. But the principal thing that we know about this young man—who is, indeed, very intelligent—leads us to suppose that, however much he may value your personal merits, he values your money more. The principal thing we know about him is that he has led a life of dissipation, and has spent a fortune of his own in doing so. That is enough for me, my dear. I wish you to marry a young man with other antecedents—a young man who could give positive guarantees. If Morris Townsend has spent his own fortune in amusing himself, there is every reason to believe that he would spend yours."

The Doctor delivered himself of these remarks slowly, deliberately, with occasional pauses and prolongations of accent, which made no great allowance for poor Catherine's suspense as to his conclusion. She sat down at last, with her head bent and her eyes still fixed upon him; and strangely enough—I hardly know how to tell it—even while she felt that what he said went so terribly against her, she admired his neatness and nobleness of expression. There was something hopeless and oppressive in having to argue with her father; but she too, on her side, must try to be clear. He was so quiet; he was not at all angry; and she, too, must be quiet. But her very effort to be quiet made her tremble.

"That is not the principal thing we know about him," she said; and there was a touch of her tremor in her voice. "There are other things—many other things. He has very high abilities —he wants so much to do something. He is kind, and generous, and true," said poor Catherine, who had not suspected hitherto the resources of her eloquence. "And his fortune—his fortune that he spent—was very small!"

"All the more reason he shouldn't have spent it," cried the Doctor, getting up with a laugh. Then as Catherine, who had also risen to her feet again, stood there in her rather angular earnestness, wishing so much and expressing so little, he drew her towards him and kissed her. "You won't think me cruel?" he said, holding her a moment.

This question was not reassuring; it seemed to Catherine, on the contrary, to suggest possibilities which made her feel sick. But she answered coherently enough—"No, dear father; because if you knew how I feel—and you must know, you know everything—you would be so kind, so gentle."

"Yes, I think I know how you feel," the Doctor said. "I will be very kind—be sure of that. And I will see Mr. Townsend to-morrow. Meanwhile, and for the present, be so good as to mention to no one that you are engaged."

XII

ON THE morrow, in the afternoon, he stayed at home, awaiting Mr. Townsend's call—a proceeding by which it appeared to him (justly perhaps, for he was a very busy man) that he paid Catherine's suitor great honour, and gave both these young people so much the less to complain of. Morris presented himself with a countenance sufficiently serene—he appeared to have forgotten the "insult" for which he had solicited Catherine's sympathy two evenings before, and Dr. Sloper lost no time in letting him know that he had been prepared for his visit.

"Catherine told me yesterday what has been going on between you," he said. "You must allow me to say that it would have been becoming of you to give me notice of your intentions before they had gone so far."

"I should have done so," Morris answered, "if you had not had so much the appearance of leaving your daughter at liberty. She seems to me quite her own mistress."

"Literally, she is. But she has not emancipated herself morally quite so far, I trust, as to choose a husband without consulting me. I have left her at liberty, but I have not been in the least indifferent. The truth is that your little affair has come to a head with a rapidity that surprises me. It was only the other day that Catherine made your acquaintance."

"It was not long ago, certainly," said Morris, with great gravity. "I admit that we have not been slow to—to arrive at an understanding. But that was very natural, from the moment we were sure of ourselves—and of each other. My interest in Miss Sloper began the first time I saw her."

"Did it not by chance precede your first meeting?" the Doctor asked.

Morris looked at him an instant. "I certainly had already heard that she was a charming girl."

"A charming girl—that's what you think her?"

"Assuredly. Otherwise I should not be sitting here."

The Doctor meditated a moment. "My dear young man," he said at last, "you must be very susceptible. As Catherine's father, I have, I trust, a just and tender appreciation of her many good qualities; but I don't mind telling you that I have never thought of her as a charming girl, and never expected any one else to do so."

Morris Townsend received this statement with a smile that was not wholly devoid of deference. "I don't know what I might think of her if I were her father. I can't put myself in that place. I speak from my own point of view."

"You speak very well," said the Doctor; "but that is not all that is necessary. I told Catherine yesterday that I disapproved of her engagement."

"She let me know as much, and I was very sorry to hear it. I am greatly disappointed." And Morris sat in silence awhile, looking at the floor.

"Did you really expect I would say I was delighted, and throw my daughter into your arms?"

"Oh, no; I had an idea you didn't like me."

"What gave you the idea?"

"The fact that I am poor."

"That has a harsh sound," said the Doctor, "but it is about

the truth—speaking of you strictly as a son-in-law. Your absence of means, of a profession, of visible resources or prospects, places you in a category from which it would be imprudent for me to select a husband for my daughter, who is a weak young woman with a large fortune. In any other capacity I am perfectly prepared to like you. As a son-in-law, I abominate you!"

Morris Townsend listened respectfully. "I don't think Miss Sloper is a weak woman," he presently said.

"Of course you must defend her—it's the least you can do. But I have known my child twenty years, and you have known her six weeks. Even if she were not weak, however, you would still be a penniless man."

"Ah, yes; that is *my* weakness! And therefore, you mean, I am mercenary—I only want your daughter's money."

"I don't say that. I am not obliged to say it; and to say it, save under stress of compulsion, would be very bad taste. I say simply that you belong to the wrong category."

"But your daughter doesn't marry a category," Townsend urged, with his handsome smile. "She marries an individual—an individual whom she is so good as to say she loves."

"An individual who offers so little in return!"

"Is it possible to offer more than the most tender affection and a lifelong devotion?" the young man demanded.

"It depends how we take it. It is possible to offer a few other things besides, and not only is it possible, but it's usual. A lifelong devotion is measured after the fact; and meanwhile it is customary in these cases to give a few material securities. What are yours? A very handsome face and figure, and a very good manner. They are excellent as far as they go, but they don't go far enough."

"There is one thing you should add to them," said Morris; "the word of a gentleman!"

"The word of a gentleman that you will always love Catherine? You must be a very fine gentleman to be sure of that."

"The word of a gentleman that I am not mercenary; that my affection for Miss Sloper is as pure and disinterested a sentiment as was ever lodged in a human breast! I care no more for her fortune than for the ashes in that grate."

"I take note—I take note," said the Doctor. "But having done so, I turn to our category again. Even with that solemn vow on your lips, you take your place in it. There is nothing against you but an accident, if you will; but with my thirty years' medical practice, I have seen that accidents may have far-reaching consequences."

Morris smoothed his hat—it was already remarkably glossy —and continued to display a self-control which, as the Doctor was obliged to admit, was extremely creditable to him. But his disappointment was evidently keen.

"Is there nothing I can do to make you believe in me?"

"If there were I should be sorry to suggest it, for—don't you see?—I don't want to believe in you!" said the Doctor, smiling.

"I would go and dig in the fields."

"That would be foolish."

"I will take the first work that offers, to-morrow."

"Do so by all means—but for your own sake, not for mine."

"I see; you think I am an idler!" Morris exclaimed, a little too much in the tone of a man who has made a discovery. But he saw his error immediately and blushed.

"It doesn't matter what I think, when once I have told you I don't think of you as a son-in-law."

But Morris persisted. "You think I would squander her money."

The Doctor smiled. "It doesn't matter, as I say; but I plead guilty to that."

"That's because I spent my own, I suppose," said Morris. "I frankly confess that. I have been wild. I have been foolish. I will tell you every crazy thing I ever did, if you like. There were some great follies among the number—I have never concealed that. But I have sown my wild oats. Isn't there some proverb about a reformed rake? I was not a rake, but I assure you I have reformed. It is better to have amused oneself for a while and have done with it. Your daughter would never care for a milksop;

and I will take the liberty of saying that you would like one quite as little. Besides, between my money and hers there is a great difference. I spent my own; it was because it was my own that I spent it. And I made no debts; when it was gone I stopped. I don't owe a penny in the world."

"Allow me to inquire what you are living on now—though I admit," the Doctor added, "that the question, on my part, is inconsistent."

"I am living on the remnants of my property," said Morris Townsend.

"Thank you!" the Doctor gravely replied.

Yes, certainly, Morris's self-control was laudable. "Even admitting I attach an undue importance to Miss Sloper's fortune," he went on, "would not that be in itself an assurance that I should take good care of it?"

"That you should take too much care would be quite as bad as that you should take too little. Catherine might suffer as much by your economy as by your extravagance."

"I think you are very unjust!" The young man made this declaration decently, civilly, without violence.

"It is your privilege to think so, and I surrender my reputation to you! I certainly don't flatter myself I gratify you."

"Don't you care a little to gratify your daughter? Do you enjoy the idea of making her miserable?"

"I am perfectly resigned to her thinking me a tyrant for a twelvemonth."

"For a twelvemonth!" exclaimed Morris, with a laugh.

"For a lifetime, then! She may as well be miserable in that way as in the other."

Here at last Morris lost his temper. "Ah, you are not polite, sir!" he cried.

"You push me to it—you argue too much."

"I have a great deal at stake."

"Well, whatever it is," said the Doctor, "you have lost it!"

"Are you sure of that?" asked Morris; "are you sure your daughter will give me up?"

"I mean, of course, you have lost it as far as I am concerned. As for Catherine's giving you up—no, I am not sure of it. But as I shall strongly recommend it, as I have a great fund of respect and affection in my daughter's mind to draw upon, and as she has the sentiment of duty developed in a very high degree, I think it extremely possible."

Morris Townsend began to smooth his hat again. "I, too, have a fund of affection to draw upon!" he observed at last.

The Doctor at this point showed his own first symptoms of irritation. "Do you mean to defy me?"

"Call it what you please, sir! I mean not to give your daughter up."

The Doctor shook his head. "I haven't the least fear of your pining away your life. You are made to enjoy it."

Morris gave a laugh. "Your opposition to my marriage is all the more cruel, then! Do you intend to forbid your daughter to see me again?"

"She is past the age at which people are forbidden, and I am not a father in an old-fashioned novel. But I shall strongly urge her to break with you."

"I don't think she will," said Morris Townsend.

"Perhaps not. But I shall have done what I could."

"She has gone too far," Morris went on.

"To retreat? Then let her stop where she is."

"Too far to stop, I mean."

The Doctor looked at him a moment; Morris had his hand on the door. "There is a great deal of impertinence in your saying it."

"I will say no more, sir!" Morris answered; and, making his bow, he left the room.

XIII

IT MAY be thought the Doctor was too positive, and Mrs. Almond intimated as much. But as he said, he had his impression;

it seemed to him sufficient, and he had no wish to modify it. He had passed his life in estimating people (it was part of the medical trade), and in nineteen cases out of twenty he was right.

"Perhaps Mr. Townsend is the twentieth case," Mrs. Almond suggested.

"Perhaps he is, though he doesn't look to me at all like a twentieth case. But I will give him the benefit of the doubt, and, to make sure, I will go and talk with Mrs. Montgomery. She will almost certainly tell me I have done right; but it is just possible that she will prove to me that I have made the greatest mistake of my life. If she does, I will beg Mr. Townsend's pardon. You needn't invite her to meet me, as you kindly proposed; I will write her a frank letter, telling her how matters stand, and asking leave to come and see her."

"I am afraid the frankness will be chiefly on your side. The poor little woman will stand up for her brother, whatever he may be."

"Whatever he may be? I doubt that. People are not always so fond of their brothers."

"Ah," said Mrs. Almond, "when it's a question of thirty thousand a year coming into a family——"

"If she stands up for him on account of the money, she will be a humbug. If she is a humbug I shall see it. If I see it, I won't waste time with her."

"She is not a humbug—she is an exemplary woman. She will not wish to play her brother a trick simply because he is selfish."

"If she is worth talking to, she will sooner play him a trick than that he should play Catherine one. Has she seen Catherine, by the way—does she know her?"

"Not to my knowledge. Mr. Townsend can have had no particular interest in bringing them together."

"If she is an exemplary woman, no. But we shall see to what extent she answers your description."

"I shall be curious to hear her description of you!" said Mrs.

Almond, with a laugh. "And, meanwhile, how is Catherine taking it?"

"As she takes everything—as a matter of course."

"Doesn't she make a noise? Hasn't she made a scene?"

"She is not scenic."

"I thought a love-lorn maiden was always scenic."

"A fantastic widow is more so. Lavinia has made me a speech; she thinks me very arbitrary."

"She has a talent for being in the wrong," said Mrs. Almond. "But I am very sorry for Catherine, all the same."

"So am I. But she will get over it."

"You believe she will give him up?"

"I count upon it. She has such an admiration for her father."

"Oh, we know all about that! But it only makes me pity her the more. It makes her dilemma the more painful, and the effort of choosing between you and her lover almost impossible."

"If she can't choose, all the better."

"Yes, but he will stand there entreating her to choose, and Lavinia will pull on that side."

"I am glad she is not on my side; she is capable of ruining an excellent cause. The day Lavinia gets into your boat it capsizes. But she had better be careful," said the Doctor. "I will have no treason in my house!"

"I suspect she will be careful; for she is at bottom very much afraid of you."

"They are both afraid of me—harmless as I am!" the Doctor answered. "And it is on that that I build—on the salutary terror I inspire!"

XIV

HE WROTE his frank letter to Mrs. Montgomery, who punctually answered it, mentioning an hour at which he might present himself in the Second Avenue. She lived in a neat little house of red brick, which had been freshly painted, with the edges of the bricks very sharply marked out in white. It has now disappeared, with its companions, to make room for a row of structures more majestic. There were green shutters upon the windows, without slats, but pierced with little holes, arranged in groups; and before the house was a diminutive yard, ornamented with a bush of mysterious character, and surrounded by a low wooden paling, painted in the same green as the shutters. The place looked like a magnified baby-house, and might have been taken down from a shelf in a toy-shop. Dr. Sloper, when he went to call, said to himself, as he glanced at the objects I have enumerated, that Mrs. Montgomery was evidently a thrifty and self-respecting little person—the modest proportions of her dwelling seemed to indicate that she was of small stature—who took a virtuous satisfaction in keeping herself tidy, and had resolved that, since she might not be splendid, she would at least be immaculate. She received him in a little parlour, which was precisely the parlour he had expected: a small unspeckled bower, ornamented with a desultory foliage of tissue-paper, and with clusters of glass drops, amid which— to carry out the analogy—the temperature of the leafy season was maintained by means of a cast-iron stove, emitting a dry blue flame, and smelling strongly of varnish. The walls were embellished with engravings swathed in pink gauze, and the tables ornamented with volumes of extracts from the poets, usually bound in black cloth stamped with florid designs in jaundiced gilt. The Doctor had time to take cognisance of these details; for Mrs. Montgomery, whose conduct he pronounced under the circumstances inexcusable, kept him waiting some ten minutes before she appeared. At last, however, she rustled in, smoothing down a stiff poplin dress, with a little frightened flush in a gracefully rounded cheek.

She was a small, plump, fair woman, with a bright, clear eye, and an extraordinary air of neatness and briskness. But these qualities were evidently combined with an unaffected humility, and the Doctor gave her his esteem as soon as he had looked at her. A brave little person, with lively perceptions, and yet a disbelief in her own talent for social, as distinguished from practical, affairs—this was his rapid mental *résumé* of Mrs. Montgomery, who, as he saw, was flattered by what she regarded as the honour of his visit. Mrs. Montgomery, in her little red house in the Second Avenue, was a person for whom Dr. Sloper was one of the great men, one of the fine gentlemen of New York; and while she fixed her agitated eyes upon him, while she clasped her mittened hands together in her glossy poplin lap, she had the appearance of saying to herself that he quite answered her idea of what a distinguished guest would naturally be. She apologised for being late; but he interrupted her.

"It doesn't matter," he said; "for while I sat here I had time to think over what I wish to say to you, and to make up my mind how to begin."

"Oh, do begin!" murmured Mrs. Montgomery.

"It is not so easy," said the Doctor, smiling. "You will have gathered from my letter that I wish to ask you a few questions, and you may not find it very comfortable to answer them."

"Yes; I have thought what I should say. It is not very easy."

"But you must understand my situation—my state of mind. Your brother wishes to marry my daughter, and I wish to find out what sort of a young man he is. A good way to do so seemed to be to come and ask you; which I have proceeded to do."

Mrs. Montgomery evidently took the situation very seriously; she was in a state of extreme moral concentration. She kept her pretty eyes, which were illumined by a sort of brilliant modesty, attached to his own countenance, and evidently paid the most earnest attention to each of his words. Her expression indicated that she thought his idea of coming to see her a very superior conception, but that she was really afraid to have opinions on strange subjects.

"I am extremely glad to see you," she said, in a tone which seemed to admit, at the same time, that this had nothing to do with the question.

The Doctor took advantage of this admission. "I didn't come to see you for your pleasure; I came to make you say disagreeable things—and you can't like that. What sort of a gentleman is your brother?"

Mrs. Montgomery's illuminated gaze grew vague, and began to wander. She smiled a little, and for some time made no answer, so that the Doctor at last became impatient. And her answer, when it came, was not satisfactory. "It is difficult to talk about one's brother."

"Not when one is fond of him, and when one has plenty of good to say."

"Yes, even then, when a good deal depends on it," said Mrs. Montgomery.

"Nothing depends on it, for you."

"I mean for—for——" and she hesitated.

"For your brother himself. I see!"

"I mean for Miss Sloper," said Mrs. Montgomery.

The Doctor liked this; it had the accent of sincerity. "Exactly; that's the point. If my poor girl should marry your brother, everything—as regards her happiness—would depend on his being a good fellow. She is the best creature in the world, and she could never do him a grain of injury. He, on the other hand, if he should not be all that we desire, might make her very miserable. That is why I want you to throw some light upon his character, you know. Of course, you are not bound to do it. My daughter, whom you have never seen, is nothing to you; and I, possibly, am only an indiscreet and impertinent old man. It is perfectly open to you to tell me that my visit is in very bad taste and that I had better go about my business. But I don't think you will do this; because I think we shall interest you, my poor girl and I. I am sure that if you were to see Catherine, she would interest you very much. I don't mean because she is interesting in the usual sense of the word, but because you would feel sorry for her. She is so soft, so simple-minded, she would be such an easy victim! A bad husband would have remarkable facilities for making her miserable; for she would have neither the intelligence nor the resolution to get the better of him, and yet she would have an exaggerated power of suffering. I see," added the Doctor, with his most insinuating, his most professional laugh, "you are already interested!"

"I have been interested from the moment he told me he was engaged," said Mrs. Montgomery.

"Ah! he says that—he calls it an engagement?"

"Oh, he has told me you didn't like it."

"Did he tell you that I don't like *him*?"

"Yes, he told me that too. I said I couldn't help it!" added Mrs. Montgomery.

"Of course you can't. But what you can do is to tell me I am right—to give me an attestation, as it were." And the Doctor accompanied this remark with another professional smile.

Mrs. Montgomery, however, smiled not at all; it was obvious that she could not take the humorous view of his appeal. "That is a good deal to ask," she said at last.

"There can be no doubt of that; and I must, in conscience, remind you of the advantages a young man marrying my daughter would enjoy. She has an income of ten thousand dollars in her own right, left her by her mother; if she marries a husband I approve, she will come into almost twice as much more at my death."

Mrs. Montgomery listened in great earnestness to this splendid financial statement; she had never heard thousands of dollars so familiarly talked about. She flushed a little with excitement. "Your daughter will be immensely rich," she said softly.

"Precisely—that's the bother of it."

"And if Morris should marry her, he—he——" And she hesitated timidly.

"He would be master of all that money? By no means. He would be master of the ten thousand a year that she has from her mother; but I should leave every penny of my own fortune, earned in the laborious exercise of my profession, to public institutions."

Mrs. Montgomery dropped her eyes at this, and sat for some time gazing at the straw matting which covered her floor.

"I suppose it seems to you," said the Doctor, laughing, "that in so doing I should play your brother a very shabby trick."

"Not at all. That is too much money to get possession of so easily, by marrying. I don't think it would be right."

"It's right to get all one can. But in this case your brother wouldn't be able. If Catherine marries without my consent, she doesn't get a penny from my own pocket."

"Is that certain?" asked Mrs. Montgomery, looking up.

"As certain as that I sit here!"

"Even if she should pine away?"

"Even if she should pine to a shadow, which isn't probable."

"Does Morris know this?"

"I shall be most happy to inform him!" the Doctor exclaimed.

Mrs. Montgomery resumed her meditations, and her visitor, who was prepared to give time to the affair, asked himself whether, in spite of her little conscientious air, she was not playing into her brother's hands. At the same time he was half ashamed of the ordeal to which he had subjected her, and was touched by the gentleness with which she bore it. "If she were a humbug," he said, "she would get angry; unless she be very deep indeed. It is not probable that she is as deep as that."

"What makes you dislike Morris so much?" she presently asked, emerging from her reflections.

"I don't dislike him in the least as a friend, as a companion. He seems to me a charming fellow, and I should think he would be excellent company. I dislike him, exclusively, as a son-in-law. If the only office of a son-in-law were to dine at the paternal table, I should set a high value upon your brother. He dines capitally. But that is a small part of his function, which, in general, is to be a protector, and caretaker of my child, who is singularly ill-adapted to take care of herself. It is there that he doesn't satisfy me. I confess I have nothing but my impression to go by; but I am in the habit of trusting my impression. Of course you are at liberty to contradict it flat. He strikes me as selfish and shallow."

Mrs. Montgomery's eyes expanded a little, and the Doctor fancied he saw the light of admiration in them. "I wonder you have discovered he is selfish!" she exclaimed.

"Do you think he hides it so well?"

"Very well indeed," said Mrs. Montgomery. "And I think we are all rather selfish," she added quickly.

"I think so too; but I have seen people hide it better than he. You see I am helped by a habit I have of dividing people into classes, into types. I may easily be mistaken about your brother as an individual, but his type is written on his whole person."

"He is very good-looking," said Mrs. Montgomery.

The Doctor eyed her a moment. "You women are all the same! But the type to which your brother belongs was made to be the ruin of you, and you were made to be its handmaids and victims. The sign of the type in question is the determination—sometimes terrible in its quiet intensity—to accept nothing of life but its pleasures, and to secure these pleasures chiefly by the aid of your complaisant sex. Young men of this class never do anything for themselves that they can get other people to do for them, and it is the infatuation, the devotion, the superstition of others that keeps them going. These others in ninety-nine cases out of a hundred are women. What our young friends chiefly insist upon is that some one else shall suffer for them; and women do that sort of thing, as you must know, wonderfully well." The Doctor paused a moment, and then he added abruptly, "You have suffered immensely for your brother!"

This exclamation was abrupt, as I say, but it was also perfectly calculated. The Doctor had been rather disappointed at not finding his compact and comfortable little hostess surrounded in a more visible degree by the ravages of Morris Townsend's immorality; but he had said to himself that this was not because the young man had spared her, but because she had contrived to plaster up her wounds. They were aching there, behind the varnished stove, the festooned engravings, beneath her own neat little poplin bosom; and if he could only touch the tender spot, she would make a movement that would betray her. The words I have just quoted were an attempt to put his finger suddenly upon the place; and they had some of the success that he looked for. The tears sprang for a moment to Mrs. Montgomery's eyes, and she indulged in a proud little jerk of the head.

"I don't know how you have found that out!" she exclaimed.

"By a philosophic trick—by what they call induction. You know you have always your option of contradicting me. But kindly answer me a question. Don't you give your brother money? I think you ought to answer that."

"Yes, I have given him money," said Mrs. Montgomery.

"And you have not had much to give him?"

She was silent a moment. "If you ask me for a confession of poverty, that is easily made. I am very poor."

"One would never suppose it from your—your charming house," said the Doctor. "I learned from my sister that your income was moderate, and your family numerous."

"I have five children," Mrs. Montgomery observed; "but I am happy to say I can bring them up decently."

"Of course you can—accomplished and devoted as you are! But your brother has counted them over, I suppose?"

"Counted them over?"

"He knows there are five, I mean. He tells me it is he that brings them up."

Mrs. Montgomery stared a moment, and then quickly— "Oh yes; he teaches them——Spanish."

The Doctor laughed out. "That must take a great deal off your hands! Your brother also knows, of course, that you have very little money."

"I have often told him so!" Mrs. Montgomery exclaimed, more unreservedly than she had yet spoken. She was apparently taking some comfort in the Doctor's clairvoyance.

"Which means that you have often occasion to, and that he often sponges on you. Excuse the crudity of my language; I simply express a fact. I don't ask you how much of your money he has had, it is none of my business. I have ascertained what I suspected—what I wished." And the Doctor got up, gently smoothing his hat. "Your brother lives on you," he said as he stood there.

Mrs. Montgomery quickly rose from her chair, following her visitor's movements with a look of fascination. But then, with a certain inconsequence—"I have never complained of him!" she said.

"You needn't protest—you have not betrayed him. But I advise you not to give him any more money."

"Don't you see it is in my interest that he should marry a rich person?" she asked. "If, as you say, he lives on me, I can only wish to get rid of him, and to put obstacles in the way of his marrying is to increase my own difficulties."

"I wish very much you would come to me with your difficulties," said the Doctor. "Certainly, if I throw him back on your hands, the least I can do is to help you to bear the burden. If you will allow me to say so, then, I shall take the liberty of placing in your hands, for the present, a certain fund for your brother's support."

Mrs. Montgomery stared; she evidently thought he was jesting; but she presently saw that he was not, and the complication of her feelings became painful. "It seems to me that I ought to be very much offended with you," she murmured.

"Because I have offered you money? That's a superstition," said the Doctor. "You must let me come and see you again, and we will talk about these things. I suppose that some of your children are girls."

"I have two little girls," said Mrs. Montgomery.

"Well, when they grow up, and begin to think of taking husbands, you will see how anxious you will be about the moral character of these gentlemen. Then you will understand this visit of mine!"

"Ah, you are not to believe that Morris's moral character is bad!"

The Doctor looked at her a little, with folded arms. "There

is something I should greatly like—as a moral satisfaction. I should like to hear you say—'He is abominably selfish!'"

The words came out with the grave distinctness of his voice, and they seemed for an instant to create, to poor Mrs. Montgomery's troubled vision, a material image. She gazed at it an instant, and then she turned away. "You distress me, sir!" she exclaimed. "He is, after all, my brother, and his talents, his talents——" On these last words her voice quavered, and before he knew it she had burst into tears.

"His talents are first-rate!" said the Doctor. "We must find the proper field for them!" And he assured her most respectfully of his regret at having so greatly discomposed her. "It's all for my poor Catherine," he went on. "You must know her, and you will see."

Mrs. Montgomery brushed away her tears and blushed at having shed them. "I should like to know your daughter," she answered; and then, in an instant—"Don't let her marry him!"

Dr. Sloper went away with the words gently humming in his ears—"Don't let her marry him!" They gave him the moral satisfaction of which he had just spoken, and their value was the greater that they had evidently cost a pang to poor little Mrs. Montgomery's family pride.

XV

HE HAD been puzzled by the way that Catherine carried herself; her attitude at this sentimental crisis seemed to him unnaturally passive. She had not spoken to him again after that scene in the library, the day before his interview with Morris; and a week had elapsed without making any change in her manner. There was nothing in it that appealed for pity, and he was even a little disappointed at her not giving him an opportunity to make up for his harshness by some manifestation of liberality which should operate as a compensation. He thought a little of offering to take her for a tour in Europe; but he was determined to do this only in case she should seem mutely to reproach him. He had an idea that she would display a talent for mute reproaches, and he was surprised at not finding himself exposed to these silent batteries. She said nothing, either tacitly, or explicitly, and as she was never very talkative, there was now no especial eloquence in her reserve. And poor Catherine was not sulky—a style of behaviour for which she had too little histrionic talent; she was simply very patient. Of course she was thinking over her situation, and she was apparently doing so in a deliberate and unimpassioned manner, with a view of making the best of it.

"She will do as I have bidden her," said the Doctor, and he made the further reflection that his daughter was not a woman of a great spirit. I know not whether he had hoped for a little more resistance for the sake of a little more entertainment; but he said to himself, as he had said before, that though it might have its momentary alarms, paternity was, after all, not an exciting vocation.

Catherine meanwhile had made a discovery of a very different sort; it had become vivid to her that there was a great excitement in trying to be a good daughter. She had an entirely new feeling, which may be described as a state of expectant suspense about her own actions. She watched herself as she would have watched another person, and wondered what she would do. It was as if this other person, who was both herself and not herself, had suddenly sprung into being, inspiring her with a natural curiosity as to the performance of untested functions.

"I am glad I have such a good daughter," said her father, kissing her, after the lapse of several days.

"I am trying to be good," she answered, turning away, with a conscience not altogether clear.

"If there is anything you would like to say to me, you know you must not hesitate. You needn't feel obliged to be so quiet. I shouldn't care that Mr. Townsend should be a frequent topic of conversation, but whenever you have anything particular to say about him I shall be very glad to hear it."

"Thank you," said Catherine; "I have nothing particular at present."

He never asked her whether she had seen Morris again, because he was sure that if this had been the case she would tell him. She had in fact not seen him, she had only written him a long letter. The letter at least was long for her; and, it may be added, that it was long for Morris; it consisted of five pages, in a remarkably neat and handsome hand. Catherine's handwriting was beautiful, and she was even a little proud of it; she was extremely fond of copying, and possessed volumes of extracts which testified to this accomplishment; volumes which she had exhibited one day to her lover, when the bliss of feeling that she was important in his eyes was exceptionally keen. She told Morris in writing that her father had expressed the wish that she should not see him again, and that she begged he would not come to the house until she should have "made up her mind." Morris replied with a passionate epistle, in which he asked to what, in Heaven's name, she wished to make up her mind. Had not her mind been made up two weeks before, and could it be possible that she entertained the idea of throwing him off? Did she mean to break down at the very beginning of their ordeal, after all the promises of fidelity she had both given and extracted? And he gave an account of his own interview with her father—an account not identical at all points with that offered in these pages. "He was terribly violent," Morris wrote; "but you know my self-control. I have need of it all when I remember that I have it in my power to break in upon your cruel captivity." Catherine sent him in answer to this, a note of three lines. "I am in great trouble; do not doubt of my affection, but let me wait a little and think." The idea of a struggle with her father, of setting up her will against his own, was heavy on her soul, and it kept her formally submissive, as a great physical weight keeps us motionless. It never entered into her mind to throw her lover off; but from the first she tried to assure herself that there would be a peaceful way out of their difficulty. The assurance was vague, for it contained no element of positive conviction that her father would change his mind. She only had an idea that if she should be very good, the situation would in some mysterious manner improve. To be good, she must be patient, respectful, abstain from judging her father too harshly, and from committing any act of open defiance. He was perhaps right, after all, to think as he did; by which Catherine meant not in the least that his judgment of Morris's motives in seeking to marry her was perhaps a just one, but that it was probably natural and proper that conscientious parents should be suspicious and even unjust. There were probably people in the world as bad as her father supposed Morris to be, and if there were the slightest chance of Morris being one of these sinister persons, the Doctor was right in taking it into account. Of course he could not know what she knew, how the purest love and truth were seated in the young man's eyes; but Heaven, in its time, might appoint a way of bringing him to such knowledge. Catherine expected a good deal of Heaven, and referred to the skies the initiative, as the French say, in dealing with her dilemma. She could not imagine herself imparting any kind of knowledge to her father, there was something superior even in his injustice and absolute in his mistakes. But she could at least be good, and if she were only good enough, Heaven would invent some way of reconciling all things—the dignity of her father's errors and the sweetness of her own confidence, the strict performance of her filial duties and the enjoyment of Morris Townsend's affection. Poor Catherine would have been glad to regard Mrs. Penniman as an illuminating agent, a part which this lady herself indeed was but imperfectly prepared to play. Mrs. Penniman took too much satisfaction in the sentimental shadows of this little drama to have, for the moment, any great interest in dissipating them. She wished the plot to thicken, and the advice that she gave her niece tended, in her own imagination, to produce this result. It was rather incoherent counsel, and from one day to another it contradicted itself; but it was pervaded by an earnest desire that Catherine should do something striking.

"You must *act*, my dear; in your situation the great thing is to act," said Mrs. Penniman, who found her niece altogether beneath her opportunities. Mrs. Penniman's real hope was that the girl would make a secret marriage, at which she should officiate as brideswoman or duenna. She had a vision of this ceremony being performed in some subterranean chapel—subterranean chapels in New York were not frequent, but Mrs. Penniman's imagination was not chilled by trifles—and of the guilty couple—she liked to think of poor Catherine and her suitor as the guilty couple—being shuffled away in a fast-whirling vehicle to some obscure lodging in the suburbs, where she would pay them (in a thick veil) clandestine visits, where they would endure a period of romantic privation, and where ultimately, after she should have been their earthly providence, their intercessor, their advocate, and their medium of communication with the world, they should be reconciled to her brother in an artistic tableau, in which she herself should be somehow the central figure. She hesitated as yet to recommend this course to Catherine, but she attempted to draw an attractive picture of it to Morris Townsend. She was in daily communication with the young man, whom she kept informed by letters of the state of affairs in Washington Square. As he had been banished, as she said, from the house, she no longer saw him; but she ended by writing to him that she longed for an interview. This interview could take place only on neutral ground, and she bethought herself greatly before selecting a place of meeting. She had an inclination for Greenwood Cemetery, but she gave it up as too distant; she could not absent herself for so long, as she said, without exciting suspicion. Then she thought of the Battery, but that was rather cold and windy, besides one's being exposed to intrusion from the Irish emigrants who at this point alight, with large appetites, in the New World; and at last she fixed upon an oyster saloon in the Seventh Avenue, kept by a negro—an establishment of which she knew nothing save that she had noticed it in passing. She made an appointment with Morris Townsend to meet him there, and she went to the tryst at dusk, enveloped in an impenetrable veil. He kept her waiting for half-an-hour—he had almost the whole width of the city to traverse—but she liked to wait, it seemed to intensify the situation. She ordered a cup of tea, which proved excessively bad, and this gave her a sense that she was suffering in a romantic cause. When Morris at last arrived, they sat together for half-an-hour in the duskiest corner of a back shop; and it is hardly too much to say that this was the happiest half-hour that Mrs. Penniman had known for years. The situation was really thrilling, and it scarcely seemed to her a false note when her companion asked for an oyster-stew, and proceeded to consume it before her eyes. Morris, indeed, needed all the satisfaction that stewed oysters could give him, for it may be intimated to the reader that he regarded Mrs. Penniman in the light of a fifth wheel to his coach. He was in a state of irritation natural to a gentleman of fine parts who had been snubbed in a benevolent attempt to confer a distinction upon a young woman of inferior characteristics, and the insinuating sympathy of this somewhat desiccated matron appeared to offer him no practical relief. He thought her a humbug, and he judged of humbugs with a good deal of confidence. He had listened and made himself agreeable to her at first, in order to get a footing in Washington Square; and at present he needed all his self-command to be decently civil. It would have gratified him to tell her that she was a fantastic old woman, and that he should like to put her into an omnibus and send her home. We know, however, that Morris possessed the virtue of self-control, and he had moreover the constant habit of seeking to be agreeable; so that, although Mrs. Penniman's demeanour only exasperated his already unquiet nerves, he listened to her with a sombre deference in which she found much to admire.

XVI

THEY HAD of course immediately spoken of Catherine. "Did she send me a message, or—or anything?" Morris asked.

He appeared to think that she might have sent him a trinket or a lock of her hair.

Mrs. Penniman was slightly embarrassed, for she had not told her niece of her intended expedition. "Not exactly a message," she said; "I didn't ask her for one, because I was afraid to—to excite her."

"I am afraid she is not very excitable!" And Morris gave a smile of some bitterness.

"She is better than that. She is steadfast—she is true!"

"Do you think she will hold fast then?"

"To the death!"

"Oh, I hope it won't come to that," said Morris.

"We must be prepared for the worst, and that is what I wish to speak to you about."

"What do you call the worst?"

"Well," said Mrs. Penniman, "my brother's hard, intellectual nature."

"Oh, the devil!"

"He is impervious to pity," Mrs. Penniman added, by way of explanation.

"Do you mean that he won't come round?"

"He will never be vanquished by argument. I have studied him. He will be vanquished only by the accomplished fact."

"The accomplished fact?"

"He will come round afterwards," said Mrs. Penniman, with extreme significance. "He cares for nothing but facts; he must be met by facts!"

"Well," rejoined Morris, "it is a fact that I wish to marry his daughter. I met him with that the other day, but he was not at all vanquished."

Mrs. Penniman was silent a little, and her smile beneath the shadow of her capacious bonnet, on the edge of which her black veil was arranged curtain-wise, fixed itself upon Morris's face with a still more tender brilliancy. "Marry Catherine first, and meet him afterwards!" she exclaimed.

"Do you recommend that?" asked the young man, frowning heavily.

She was a little frightened, but she went on with considerable boldness. "That is the way I see it: a private marriage—a private marriage." She repeated the phrase because she liked it.

"Do you mean that I should carry Catherine off? What do they call it—elope with her?"

"It is not a crime when you are driven to it," said Mrs. Penniman. "My husband, as I have told you, was a distinguished clergyman; one of the most eloquent men of his day. He once married a young couple that had fled from the house of the young lady's father. He was so interested in their story. He had no hesitation, and everything came out beautifully. The father was afterwards reconciled, and thought everything of the young man. Mr. Penniman married them in the evening, about seven o'clock. The church was so dark, you could scarcely see; and Mr. Penniman was intensely agitated; he was so sympathetic. I don't believe he could have done it again."

"Unfortunately Catherine and I have not Mr. Penniman to marry us," said Morris.

"No, but you have me!" rejoined Mrs. Penniman, expressively. "I can't perform the ceremony, but I can help you. I can watch."

"The woman's an idiot," thought Morris; but he was obliged to say something different. It was not, however, materially more civil. "Was it in order to tell me this that you requested I would meet you here?"

Mrs. Penniman had been conscious of a certain vagueness in her errand, and of not being able to offer him any very tangible reward for his long walk. "I thought perhaps you would like to see one who is so near to Catherine," she observed with considerable majesty. "And also," she added, "that you would value an opportunity of sending her something."

Morris extended his empty hands with a melancholy smile. "I am greatly obliged to you, but I have nothing to send."

"Haven't you a *word*?" asked his companion, with her suggestive smile coming back.

Morris frowned again. "Tell her to hold fast," he said, rather curtly.

"That is a good word—a noble word. It will make her happy for many days. She is very touching, very brave," Mrs. Penniman went on, arranging her mantle and preparing to depart. While she was so engaged she had an inspiration. She found the phrase that she could boldly offer as a vindication of the step she had taken. "If you marry Catherine at all risks," she said, "you will give my brother a proof of your being what he pretends to doubt."

"What he pretends to doubt?"

"Don't you know what that is?" Mrs. Penniman asked, almost playfully.

"It does not concern me to know," said Morris, grandly.

"Of course it makes you angry."

"I despise it," Morris declared.

"Ah, you know what it is, then?" said Mrs. Penniman, shaking her finger at him. "He pretends that you like—you like the money."

Morris hesitated a moment; and then, as if he spoke advisedly—"I *do* like the money!"

"Ah, but not—but not as he means it. You don't like it more than Catherine?"

He leaned his elbows on the table and buried his head in his hands. "You torture me!" he murmured. And, indeed, this was almost the effect of the poor lady's too importunate interest in his situation.

But she insisted on making her point. "If you marry her in spite of him, he will take for granted that you expect nothing of him, and are prepared to do without it. And so he will see that you are disinterested."

Morris raised his head a little, following this argument. "And what shall I gain by that?"

"Why, that he will see that he has been wrong in thinking that you wished to get his money."

"And seeing that I wish he would go to the deuce with it, he will leave it to a hospital. Is that what you mean?" asked Morris.

"No, I don't mean that; though that would be very grand!" Mrs. Penniman quickly added. "I mean that having done you such an injustice, he will think it his duty, at the end, to make some amends."

Morris shook his head, though it must be confessed he was a little struck with this idea. "Do you think he is so sentimental?"

"He is not sentimental," said Mrs. Penniman; "but, to be perfectly fair to him, I think he has, in his own narrow way, a certain sense of duty."

There passed through Morris Townsend's mind a rapid wonder as to what he might, even under a remote contingency, be indebted to from the action of this principle in Dr. Sloper's breast, and the inquiry exhausted itself in his sense of the ludicrous. "Your brother has no duties to me," he said presently, "and I none to him."

"Ah, but he has duties to Catherine."

"Yes, but you see that on that principle Catherine has duties to him as well."

Mrs. Penniman got up, with a melancholy sigh, as if she thought him very unimaginative. "She has always performed them faithfully; and now do you think she has no duties to *you*?" Mrs. Penniman always, even in conversation, italicised her personal pronouns.

"It would sound harsh to say so! I am so grateful for her love," Morris added.

"I will tell her you said that! And now, remember that if you need me, I am there." And Mrs. Penniman, who could think of nothing more to say, nodded vaguely in the direction of Washington Square.

Morris looked some moments at the sanded floor of the shop; he seemed to be disposed to linger a moment. At last, looking up with a certain abruptness, "It is your belief that if she marries me he will cut her off?" he asked.

Mrs. Penniman stared a little, and smiled. "Why, I have explained to you what I think would happen—that in the end it would be the best thing to do."

"You mean that, whatever she does, in the long run she will get the money?"

"It doesn't depend upon her, but upon you. Venture to appear as disinterested as you are!" said Mrs. Penniman ingeniously. Morris dropped his eyes on the sanded floor again, pondering this; and she pursued. "Mr. Penniman and I had nothing, and we were very happy. Catherine, moreover, has her mother's fortune, which, at the time my sister-in-law married, was considered a very handsome one."

"Oh, don't speak of that!" said Morris; and, indeed, it was quite superfluous, for he had contemplated the fact in all its lights.

"Austin married a wife with money—why shouldn't you?"

"Ah! but your brother was a doctor," Morris objected.

"Well, all young men can't be doctors!"

"I should think it an extremely loathsome profession," said Morris, with an air of intellectual independence. Then, in a moment, he went on rather inconsequently, "Do you suppose there is a will already made in Catherine's favour?"

"I suppose so—even doctors must die; and perhaps a little in mine," Mrs. Penniman frankly added.

"And you believe he would certainly change it—as regards Catherine?"

"Yes; and then change it back again."

"Ah, but one can't depend on that!" said Morris.

"Do you want to *depend* on it?" Mrs. Penniman asked.

Morris blushed a little. "Well, I am certainly afraid of being the cause of an injury to Catherine."

"Ah! you must not be afraid. Be afraid of nothing, and everything will go well!"

And then Mrs. Penniman paid for her cup of tea, and Morris paid for his oyster stew, and they went out together into the dimly-lighted wilderness of the Seventh Avenue. The dusk had closed in completely, and the street lamps were separated by wide intervals of a pavement in which cavities and fissures played a disproportionate part. An omnibus, emblazoned with strange pictures, went tumbling over the dislocated cobble-stones.

"How will you go home?" Morris asked, following this vehicle with an interested eye. Mrs. Penniman had taken his arm.

She hesitated a moment. "I think this manner would be pleasant," she said; and she continued to let him feel the value of his support.

So he walked with her through the devious ways of the west side of the town, and through the bustle of gathering nightfall in populous streets, to the quiet precinct of Washington Square. They lingered a moment at the foot of Dr. Sloper's white marble steps, above which a spotless white door, adorned with a glittering silver plate, seemed to figure, for Morris, the closed portal of happiness; and then Mrs. Penniman's companion rested a melancholy eye upon a lighted window in the upper part of the house.

"That is my room—my dear little room!" Mrs. Penniman remarked.

Morris started. "Then I needn't come walking round the square to gaze at it."

"That's as you please. But Catherine's is behind; two noble windows on the second floor. I think you can see them from the other street."

"I don't want to see them, ma'am!" And Morris turned his back to the house.

"I will tell her you have been *here*, at any rate," said Mrs. Penniman, pointing to the spot where they stood; "and I will give her your message—that she is to hold fast!"

"Oh, yes! of course. You know I write her all that."

"It seems to say more when it is spoken! And remember, if you need me, that I am *there*;" and Mrs. Penniman glanced at the third floor.

On this they separated, and Morris, left to himself, stood looking at the house a moment; after which he turned away, and took a gloomy walk round the Square, on the opposite side, close to the wooden fence. Then he came back, and paused for a minute in front of Dr. Sloper's dwelling. His eyes travelled over it; they even rested on the ruddy windows of Mrs. Penniman's apartment. He thought it a devilish comfortable house.

XVII

MRS. PENNIMAN told Catherine that evening—the two ladies were sitting in the back parlour—that she had had an interview with Morris Townsend; and on receiving this news the girl started with a sense of pain. She felt angry for the moment; it was almost the first time she had ever felt angry. It seemed to her that her aunt was meddlesome; and from this came a vague apprehension that she would spoil something.

"I don't see why you should have seen him. I don't think it was right," Catherine said.

"I was so sorry for him—it seemed to me some one ought to see him."

"No one but I," said Catherine, who felt as if she were making the most presumptuous speech of her life, and yet at the same time had an instinct that she was right in doing so.

"But you wouldn't, my dear," Aunt Lavinia rejoined; "and I didn't know what might have become of him."

"I have not seen him, because my father has forbidden it," Catherine said, very simply.

There was a simplicity in this, indeed, which fairly vexed Mrs. Penniman. "If your father forbade you to go to sleep, I suppose you would keep awake!" she commented.

Catherine looked at her. "I don't understand you. You seem to be very strange."

"Well, my dear, you will understand me some day!" And

Mrs. Penniman, who was reading the evening paper, which she perused daily from the first line to the last, resumed her occupation. She wrapped herself in silence; she was determined Catherine should ask her for an account of her interview with Morris. But Catherine was silent for so long, that she almost lost patience; and she was on the point of remarking to her that she was very heartless, when the girl at last spoke.

"What did he say?" she asked.

"He said he is ready to marry you any day, in spite of everything."

Catherine made no answer to this, and Mrs. Penniman almost lost patience again; owing to which she at last volunteered the information that Morris looked very handsome, but terribly haggard.

"Did he seem sad?" asked her niece.

"He was dark under the eyes," said Mrs. Penniman. "So different from when I first saw him; though I am not sure that if I had seen him in this condition the first time, I should not have been even more struck with him. There is something brilliant in his very misery."

This was, to Catherine's sense, a vivid picture, and though she disapproved, she felt herself gazing at it. "Where did you see him?" she asked presently.

"In—in the Bowery; at a confectioner's," said Mrs. Penniman, who had a general idea that she ought to dissemble a little.

"Whereabouts is the place?" Catherine inquired, after another pause.

"Do you wish to go there, my dear?" said her aunt.

"Oh, no!" And Catherine got up from her seat and went to the fire, where she stood looking awhile at the glowing coals.

"Why are you so dry, Catherine?" Mrs. Penniman said at last.

"So dry?"

"So cold—so irresponsive."

The girl turned, very quickly. "Did *he* say that?"

Mrs. Penniman hesitated a moment. "I will tell you what he said. He said he feared only one thing—that you would be afraid."

"Afraid of what?"

"Afraid of your father."

Catherine turned back to the fire again, and then, after a pause, she said—"I *am* afraid of my father."

Mrs. Penniman got quickly up from her chair and approached her niece. "Do you mean to give him up, then?"

Catherine for some time never moved; she kept her eyes on the coals. At last she raised her head and looked at her aunt. "Why do you push me so?" she asked.

"I don't push you. When have I spoken to you before?"

"It seems to me that you have spoken to me several times."

"I am afraid it is necessary, then, Catherine," said Mrs. Penniman, with a good deal of solemnity. "I am afraid you don't feel the importance——" She paused a little; Catherine was looking at her. "The importance of not disappointing that gallant young heart!" And Mrs. Penniman went back to her chair, by the lamp, and, with a little jerk, picked up the evening paper again.

Catherine stood there before the fire, with her hands behind her, looking at her aunt, to whom it seemed that the girl had never had just this dark fixedness in her gaze. "I don't think you understand—or that you know me," she said.

"If I don't, it is not wonderful; you trust me so little."

Catherine made no attempt to deny this charge, and for some time more nothing was said. But Mrs. Penniman's imagination was restless, and the evening paper failed on this occasion to enchain it.

"If you succumb to the dread of your father's wrath," she said, "I don't know what will become of us."

"Did *he* tell you to say these things to me?"

"He told me to use my influence."

"You must be mistaken," said Catherine. "He trusts me."

"I hope he may never repent of it!" And Mrs. Penniman gave a little sharp slap to her newspaper. She knew not what to make of her niece, who had suddenly become stern and contradictious.

This tendency on Catherine's part was presently even more apparent. "You had much better not make any more appointments with Mr. Townsend," she said. "I don't think it is right."

Mrs. Penniman rose with considerable majesty. "My poor child, are you jealous of me?" she inquired.

"Oh, Aunt Lavinia!" murmured Catherine blushing.

"I don't think it is your place to teach me what is right."

On this point Catherine made no concession. "It can't be right to deceive."

"I certainly have not deceived *you*!"

"Yes; but I promised my father——"

"I have no doubt you promised your father. But I have promised him nothing!"

Catherine had to admit this, and she did so in silence. "I don't believe Mr. Townsend himself likes it," she said at last.

"Doesn't like meeting me?"

"Not in secret."

"It was not in secret; the place was full of people."

"But it was a secret place—away off in the Bowery."

Mrs. Penniman flinched a little. "Gentlemen enjoy such things," she remarked, presently. "I know what gentlemen like."

"My father wouldn't like it, if he knew."

"Pray, do you propose to inform him?" Mrs. Penniman inquired.

"No, Aunt Lavinia. But please don't do it again."

"If I do it again, you will inform him: is that what you mean? I do not share your dread of my brother; I have always known how to defend my own position. But I shall certainly never again take any step on your behalf; you are much too thankless. I knew you were not a spontaneous nature, but I believed you were firm, and I told your father that he would find you so. I am disappointed—but your father will not be!" And with this, Mrs. Penniman offered her niece a brief good-night, and withdrew to her own apartment.

XVIII

CATHERINE sat alone by the parlour fire—sat there for more than an hour, lost in her meditations. Her aunt seemed to her aggressive and foolish, and to see it so clearly—to judge Mrs. Penniman so positively—made her feel old and grave. She did not resent the imputation of weakness; it made no impression on her, for she had not the sense of weakness, and she was not hurt at not being appreciated. She had an immense respect for her father, and she felt that to displease him would be a misdemeanour analogous to an act of profanity in a great temple: but her purpose had slowly ripened, and she believed that her prayers had purified it of its violence. The evening advanced, and the lamp burned dim without her noticing it; her eyes were fixed upon her terrible plan. She knew her father was in his study—that he had been there all the evening; from time to time she expected to hear him move. She thought he would perhaps come, as he sometimes came, into the parlour. At last the clock struck eleven, and the house was wrapped in silence; the servants had gone to bed. Catherine got up and went slowly to the door of the library, where she waited a moment, motionless. Then she knocked, and then she waited again. Her father had answered her, but she had not the courage to turn the latch. What she had said to her aunt was true enough—she was afraid of him; and in saying that she had no sense of weakness she meant that she was not afraid of herself. She heard him move within, and he came and opened the door for her.

"What is the matter?" asked the Doctor. "You are standing there like a ghost."

She went into the room, but it was some time before she contrived to say what she had come to say. Her father, who was in his dressing-gown and slippers, had been busy at his writing-table, and after looking at her for some moments, and waiting for her to speak, he went and seated himself at his papers again. His back was turned to her—she began to hear the scratching of his pen. She remained near the door, with her heart thumping beneath her bodice; and she was very glad that his back was turned, for it seemed to her that she could more easily address herself to this portion of his person than to his face. At last she began, watching it while she spoke.

"You told me that if I should have anything more to say about Mr. Townsend you would be glad to listen to it."

"Exactly, my dear," said the Doctor, not turning round, but stopping his pen.

Catherine wished it would go on, but she herself continued. "I thought I would tell you that I have not seen him again, but that I should like to do so."

"To bid him good-bye?" asked the Doctor.

The girl hesitated a moment. "He is not going away."

The Doctor wheeled slowly round in his chair, with a smile that seemed to accuse her of an epigram; but extremes meet, and Catherine had not intended one. "It is not to bid him good-bye, then?" her father said.

"No, father, not that; at least, not for ever. I have not seen him again, but I should like to see him," Catherine repeated.

The Doctor slowly rubbed his under lip with the feather of his quill.

"Have you written to him?"

"Yes, four times."

"You have not dismissed him, then. Once would have done that."

"No," said Catherine; "I have asked him—asked him to wait."

Her father sat looking at her, and she was afraid he was going to break out into wrath; his eyes were so fine and cold.

"You are a dear, faithful child," he said at last. "Come here to your father." And he got up, holding out his hands toward her.

The words were a surprise, and they gave her an exquisite joy. She went to him, and he put his arm round her tenderly, soothingly; and then he kissed her. After this he said—

"Do you wish to make me very happy?"

"I should like to—but I am afraid I can't," Catherine answered.

"You can if you will. It all depends on your will."

"Is it to give him up?" said Catherine.

"Yes, it is to give him up."

And he held her still, with the same tenderness, looking into her face and resting his eyes on her averted eyes. There was a long silence; she wished he would release her.

"You are happier than I, father," she said, at last.

"I have no doubt you are unhappy just now. But it is better to be unhappy for three months and get over it, than for many years and never get over it."

"Yes, if that were so," said Catherine.

"It would be so; I am sure of that." She answered nothing, and he went on. "Have you no faith in my wisdom, in my tenderness, in my solicitude for your future?"

"Oh, father!" murmured the girl.

"Don't you suppose that I know something of men: their vices, their follies, their falsities?"

She detached herself, and turned upon him. "He is not vicious—he is not false!"

Her father kept looking at her with his sharp, pure eye. "You make nothing of my judgment, then?"

"I can't believe that!"

"I don't ask you to believe it, but to take it on trust."

Catherine was far from saying to herself that this was an ingenious sophism; but she met the appeal none the less squarely. "What has he done—what do you know?"

"He has never done anything—he is a selfish idler."

"Oh, father, don't abuse him!" she exclaimed, pleadingly.

"I don't mean to abuse him; it would be a great mistake. You may do as you choose," he added, turning away.

"I may see him again?"

"Just as you choose."

"Will you forgive me?"

"By no means."

"It will only be for once."

"I don't know what you mean by once. You must either give him up or continue the acquaintance."

"I wish to explain—to tell him to wait."

"To wait for what?"

"Till you know him better—till you consent."

"Don't tell him any such nonsense as that. I know him well enough, and I shall never consent."

"But we can wait a long time," said poor Catherine, in a tone which was meant to express the humblest conciliation, but which had upon her father's nerves the effect of an iteration not characterised by tact.

The Doctor answered, however, quietly enough: "Of course you can wait till I die, if you like."

Catherine gave a cry of natural horror.

"Your engagement will have one delightful effect upon you; it will make you extremely impatient for that event."

Catherine stood staring, and the Doctor enjoyed the point he had made. It came to Catherine with the force—or rather with the vague impressiveness—of a logical axiom which it was not in her province to controvert; and yet, though it was a scientific truth, she felt wholly unable to accept it.

"I would rather not marry, if that were true," she said.

"Give me a proof of it, then; for it is beyond a question that by engaging yourself to Morris Townsend you simply wait for my death."

She turned away, feeling sick and faint; and the Doctor went on. "And if you wait for it with impatience, judge, if you please, what *his* eagerness will be!"

Catherine turned it over—her father's words had such an authority for her that her very thoughts were capable of obeying him. There was a dreadful ugliness in it, which seemed to glare at her through the interposing medium of her own feebler reason. Suddenly, however, she had an inspiration—she almost knew it to be an inspiration.

"If I don't marry before your death, I will not after," she said.

To her father, it must be admitted, this seemed only another epigram; and as obstinacy, in unaccomplished minds, does not usually select such a mode of expression, he was the more surprised at this wanton play of a fixed idea.

"Do you mean that for an impertinence?" he inquired; an inquiry of which, as he made it, he quite perceived the grossness.

"An impertinence? Oh, father, what terrible things you say!"

"If you don't wait for my death, you might as well marry immediately; there is nothing else to wait for."

For some time Catherine made no answer; but finally she said—

"I think Morris—little by little—might persuade you."

"I shall never let him speak to me again. I dislike him too much."

Catherine gave a long, low sigh; she tried to stifle it, for she had made up her mind that it was wrong to make a parade of her trouble, and to endeavour to act upon her father by the meretricious aid of emotion. Indeed, she even thought it wrong—in the sense of being inconsiderate—to attempt to act upon his feelings at all; her part was to effect some gentle, gradual change in his intellectual perception of poor Morris's character. But the means of effecting such a change were at present shrouded in mystery, and she felt miserably helpless and hopeless. She had exhausted all arguments, all replies. Her father might have pitied her, and in fact he did so; but he was sure he was right.

"There is one thing you can tell Mr. Townsend, when you see him again," he said: "that if you marry without my consent, I don't leave you a farthing of money. That will interest him more than anything else you can tell him."

"That would be very right," Catherine answered. "I ought not in that case to have a farthing of your money."

"My dear child," the Doctor observed, laughing, "your simplicity is touching. Make that remark, in that tone, and with that expression of countenance, to Mr. Townsend, and take a note of his answer. It won't be polite—it will express irritation; and I shall be glad of that, as it will put me in the right; unless, indeed—which is perfectly possible—you should like him the better for being rude to you."

"He will never be rude to me," said Catherine, gently.

"Tell him what I say, all the same."

She looked at her father, and her quiet eyes filled with tears.

"I think I will see him, then," she murmured, in her timid voice.

"Exactly as you choose!" And he went to the door and opened it for her to go out. The movement gave her a terrible sense of his turning her off.

"It will be only once, for the present," she added, lingering a moment.

"Exactly as you choose," he repeated, standing there with his hand on the door. "I have told you what I think. If you see him, you will be an ungrateful, cruel child; you will have given your old father the greatest pain of his life."

This was more than the poor girl could bear; her tears overflowed, and she moved towards her grimly consistent parent with a pitiful cry. Her hands were raised in supplication, but he sternly evaded this appeal. Instead of letting her sob out her misery on his shoulder, he simply took her by the arm and directed her course across the threshold, closing the door gently but firmly behind her. After he had done so, he remained listening. For a long time there was no sound; he knew that she was standing outside. He was sorry for her, as I have said; but he was so sure he was right. At last he heard her move away, and then her footstep creaked faintly upon the stairs.

The Doctor took several turns round his study, with his hands in his pockets, and a thin sparkle, possibly of irritation, but partly also of something like humour, in his eye. "By Jove," he said to himself, "I believe she will stick—I believe she will stick!" And this idea of Catherine "sticking" appeared to have a comical side, and to offer a prospect of entertainment. He determined, as he said to himself, to see it out.

XIX

IT WAS for reasons connected with this determination that on the morrow he sought a few words of private conversation with Mrs. Penniman. He sent for her to the library, and he there informed her that he hoped very much that, as regarded this affair of Catherine's, she would mind her *p*'s and *q*'s.

"I don't know what you mean by such an expression," said his sister. "You speak as if I were learning the alphabet."

"The alphabet of common sense is something you will never learn," the Doctor permitted himself to respond.

"Have you called me here to insult me?" Mrs. Penniman inquired.

"Not at all. Simply to advise you. You have taken up young Townsend; that's your own affair. I have nothing to do with your sentiments, your fancies, your affections, your delusions; but what I request of you is that you will keep these things to yourself. I have explained my views to Catherine; she understands them perfectly, and anything that she does further in the way of encouraging Mr. Townsend's attentions will be in deliberate opposition to my wishes. Anything that you should do in the way of giving her aid and comfort will be—permit me the expression—distinctly treasonable. You know high treason is a capital offense; take care how you incur the penalty."

Mrs. Penniman threw back her head, with a certain expansion of the eye which she occasionally practised. "It seems to me that you talk like a great autocrat."

"I talk like my daughter's father."

"Not like your sister's brother!" cried Lavinia.

"My dear Lavinia," said the Doctor, "I sometimes wonder whether I am your brother. We are so extremely different. In spite of differences, however, we can, at a pinch, understand each other; and that is the essential thing just now. Walk straight with regard to Mr. Townsend; that's all I ask. It is highly probable you have been corresponding with him for the last three weeks—perhaps even seeing him. I don't ask you— you needn't tell me." He had a moral conviction that she would contrive to tell a fib about the matter, which it would disgust him to listen to. "Whatever you have done, stop doing it. That's all I wish."

"Don't you wish also by chance to murder your child?" Mrs. Penniman inquired.

"On the contrary, I wish to make her live and be happy."

"You will kill her; she passed a dreadful night."

"She won't die of one dreadful night, nor of a dozen. Remember that I am a distinguished physician."

Mrs. Penniman hesitated a moment. Then she risked her retort. "Your being a distinguished physician has not prevented you from already losing *two members* of your family!"

She had risked it, but her brother gave her such a terribly incisive look—a look so like a surgeon's lancet—that she was frightened at her courage. And he answered her in words that corresponded to the look: "It may not prevent me, either, from losing the society of still another."

Mrs. Penniman took herself off, with whatever air of depreciated merit was at her command, and repaired to Catherine's room, where the poor girl was closeted. She knew all about her dreadful night, for the two had met again, the evening before, after Catherine left her father. Mrs. Penniman was on the landing of the second floor when her niece came upstairs. It was not remarkable that a person of so much subtlety should have discovered that Catherine had been shut up with the Doctor. It was still less remarkable that she should have felt an extreme curiosity to learn the result of this interview, and that this sentiment, combined with her great amiability and generosity, should have prompted her to regret the sharp words lately exchanged between her niece and herself. As the unhappy girl came into sight, in the dusky corridor, she made a lively demonstration of sympathy. Catherine's bursting heart was equally oblivious. She only knew that her aunt was taking her into her arms. Mrs. Penniman drew her into Catherine's own room, and the two women sat there together, far into the small hours; the younger one with her head on the other's lap, sobbing and sobbing at first in a soundless, stifled manner, and then at last perfectly still. It gratified Mrs. Penniman to be able to feel conscientiously that this scene virtually removed the interdict which Catherine had placed upon her further communion with Morris Townsend. She was not gratified, however, when, in coming back to her niece's room before breakfast, she found that Catherine had risen and was preparing herself for this meal.

"You should not go to breakfast," she said; "you are not well enough, after your fearful night."

"Yes, I am very well, and I am only afraid of being late."

"I can't understand you!" Mrs. Penniman cried. "You should stay in bed for three days."

"Oh, I could never do that!" said Catherine, to whom this idea presented no attractions.

Mrs. Penniman was in despair, and she noted, with extreme annoyance, that the trace of the night's tears had completely vanished from Catherine's eyes. She had a most impracticable *physique*. "What effect do you expect to have upon your father," her aunt demanded, "if you come plumping down, without a vestige of any sort of feeling, as if nothing in the world had happened?"

"He would not like me to lie in bed," said Catherine, simply.

"All the more reason for your doing it. How else do you expect to move him?"

Catherine thought a little. "I don't know how; but not in that way. I wish to be just as usual." And she finished dressing, and, according to her aunt's expression, went plumping down into the paternal presence. She was really too modest for consistent pathos.

And yet it was perfectly true that she had had a dreadful night. Even after Mrs. Penniman left her she had had no sleep. She lay staring at the uncomforting gloom, with her eyes and ears filled with the movement with which her father had turned her out of his room, and of the words in which he had told her that she was a heartless daughter. Her heart was breaking. She had heart enough for that. At moments it seemed to her that she believed him, and that to do what she was doing, a girl must indeed be bad. She *was* bad; but she couldn't help it. She would try to appear good, even if her heart were perverted; and from time to time she had a fancy that she might accomplish something by ingenious concessions to form, though she should persist in caring for Morris. Catherine's ingenuities were indefinite, and we are not called upon to expose their hollowness. The best of them perhaps showed itself in that freshness of aspect which was so discouraging to Mrs. Penniman, who was amazed at the absence of haggardness in a young woman who for a whole night had lain quivering beneath a father's curse. Poor Catherine was conscious of her freshness; it gave her a feeling about the future which rather added to the weight upon her mind. It seemed a proof that she was strong and solid and dense, and would live to a great age—longer than might be generally convenient; and this idea was depressing, for it appeared to saddle her with a pretension the more, just when the cultivation of any pretension was inconsistent with her doing right. She wrote that day to Morris Townsend, requesting him to come and see her on the morrow; using very few words, and explaining nothing. She would explain everything face to face.

XX

ON THE morrow, in the afternoon, she heard his voice at the door, and his step in the hall. She received him in the big, bright front parlour, and she instructed the servant that if any one should call she was particularly engaged. She was not afraid of her father's coming in, for at that hour he was always driving about town. When Morris stood there before her, the first thing that she was conscious of was that he was even more beautiful to look at than fond recollection had painted him; the next was that he had pressed her in his arms. When she was free again it appeared to her that she had now indeed thrown herself into the gulf of defiance, and even, for an instant, that she had been married to him.

He told her that she had been very cruel, and had made him very unhappy; and Catherine felt acutely the difficulty of her destiny, which forced her to give pain in such opposite quarters. But she wished that, instead of reproaches, however tender, he would give her help; he was certainly wise enough, and clever enough, to invent some issue from their troubles. She expressed this belief, and Morris received the assurance as if he thought it natural; but he interrogated, at first—as was natural too—rather than committed himself to marking out a course.

"You should not have made me wait so long," he said. "I don't know how I have been living; every hour seemed like years. You should have decided sooner."

"Decided?" Catherine asked.

"Decided whether you would keep me or give me up."

"Oh, Morris," she cried, with a long tender murmur, "I never thought of giving you up!"

"What, then, were you waiting for?" The young man was ardently logical.

"I thought my father might—might——" and she hesitated.

"Might see how unhappy you were?"

"Oh, no! But that he might look at it differently."

"And now you have sent for me to tell me that at last he does so. Is that it?"

This hypothetical optimism gave the poor girl a pang. "No, Morris," she said solemnly, "he looks at it still in the same way."

"Then why have you sent for me?"

"Because I wanted to see you!" cried Catherine, piteously.

"That's an excellent reason, surely. But did you want to look at me only? Have you nothing to tell me?"

His beautiful persuasive eyes were fixed upon her face, and she wondered what answer would be noble enough to make to such a gaze as that. For a moment her own eyes took it in, and then—"I *did* want to look at you!" she said, gently. But after this speech, most inconsistently, she hid her face.

Morris watched her for a moment, attentively. "Will you marry me to-morrow?" he asked suddenly.

"To-morrow?"

"Next week, then. Any time within a month."

"Isn't it better to wait?" said Catherine.

"To wait for what?"

She hardly knew for what; but this tremendous leap alarmed her. "Till we have thought about it a little more."

He shook his head, sadly and reproachfully. "I thought you had been thinking about it these three weeks. Do you want to turn it over in your mind for five years? You have given me more than time enough. My poor girl," he added in a moment, "you are not sincere!"

Catherine coloured from brow to chin, and her eyes filled with tears. "Oh, how can you say that?" she murmured.

"Why, you must take me or leave me," said Morris, very reasonably. "You can't please your father and me both; you must choose between us."

"I have chosen you!" she said, passionately.

"Then marry me next week."

She stood gazing at him. "Isn't there any other way?"

"None that I know of for arriving at the same result. If there is, I should be happy to hear of it."

Catherine could think of nothing of the kind, and Morris's luminosity seemed almost pitiless. The only thing she could think of was that her father might, after all, come round, and she articulated, with an awkward sense of her helplessness in doing so, a wish that this miracle might happen.

"Do you think it is in the least degree likely?" Morris asked.

"It would be, if he could only know you!"

"He can know me if he will. What is to prevent it?"

"His ideas, his reasons," said Catherine. "They are so—so terribly strong." She trembled with the recollection of them yet.

"Strong?" cried Morris. "I would rather you should think them weak."

"Oh, nothing about my father is weak!" said the girl.

Morris turned away, walking to the window, where he stood looking out. "You are terribly afraid of him!" he remarked at last.

She felt no impulse to deny it, because she had no shame in it; for if it was no honour to herself, at least it was an honour to him. "I suppose I must be," she said, simply.

"Then you don't love me—not as I love you. If you fear your father more than you love me, then your love is not what I hoped it was."

"Ah, my friend!" she said, going to him.

"Do *I* fear anything?" he demanded, turning round on her. "For your sake what am I not ready to face?"

"You are noble—you are brave!" she answered, stopping short at a distance that was almost respectful.

"Small good it does me, if you are so timid."

"I don't think that I am—*really*," said Catherine.

"I don't know what you mean by 'really.' It is really enough to make us miserable."

"I should be strong enough to wait—to wait a long time."

"And suppose after a long time your father should hate me worse than ever?"

"He wouldn't—he couldn't!"

"He would be touched by my fidelity? Is that what you mean? If he is so easily touched, then why should you be afraid of him?"

This was much to the point, and Catherine was struck by it. "I will try not to be," she said. And she stood there, submissively, the image, in advance, of a dutiful and responsible wife. This image could not fail to recommend itself to Morris Townsend, and he continued to give proof of the high estimation in which he held her. It could only have been at the prompting of such a sentiment that he presently mentioned to her that the course recommended by Mrs. Penniman was an immediate union, regardless of consequences.

"Yes, Aunt Penniman would like that," Catherine said, simply—and yet with a certain shrewdness. It must, however, have been in pure simplicity, and from motives quite untouched by sarcasm, that, a few moments after, she went on to say to Morris that her father had given her a message for him. It was quite on her conscience to deliver this message, and had the mission been ten times more painful she would have as scrupulously performed it. "He told me to tell you—to tell you very distinctly, and directly from himself, that if I marry without his consent, I shall not inherit a penny of his fortune. He made a great point of this. He seemed to think—he seemed to think——"

Morris flushed, as any young man of spirit might have flushed at an imputation of baseness.

"What did he seem to think?"

"That it would make a difference."

"It *will* make a difference—in many things. We shall be by many thousands of dollars the poorer; and that is a great difference. But it will make none in my affection."

"We shall not want the money," said Catherine; "for you know I have a good deal myself."

"Yes, my dear girl, I know you have something. And he can't touch that!"

"He would never," said Catherine. "My mother left it to me."

Morris was silent awhile. "He was very positive about this, was he?" he asked at last. "He thought such a message would annoy me terribly, and make me throw off the mask, eh?"

"I don't know what he thought," said Catherine, wearily.

"Please tell him that I care for his message as much as for that!" And Morris snapped his fingers sonorously.

"I don't think I could tell him that."

"Do you know you sometimes disappoint me?" said Morris.

"I should think I might. I disappoint every one—father and Aunt Penniman."

"Well, it doesn't matter with me, because I am fonder of you than they are."

"Yes, Morris," said the girl, with her imagination—what there was of it—swimming in this happy truth, which seemed, after all, invidious to no one.

"Is it your belief that he will stick to it—stick to it for ever, to this idea of disinheriting you?—that your goodness and patience will never wear out his cruelty?"

"The trouble is that if I marry you, he will think I am not good. He will think that a proof."

"Ah, then, he will never forgive you!"

This idea, sharply expressed by Morris's handsome lips, renewed for a moment, to the poor girl's temporarily pacified conscience, all its dreadful vividness. "Oh, you must love me very much!" she cried.

"There is no doubt of that, my dear!" her lover rejoined. "You don't like that word 'disinherited,'" he added in a moment.

"It isn't the money; it is that he should—that he should feel so."

"I suppose it seems to you a kind of curse," said Morris. "It must be very dismal. But don't you think," he went on presently, "that if you were to try to be very clever, and to set rightly about it, you might in the end conjure it away? Don't you think," he continued further, in a tone of sympathetic speculation, "that a really clever woman, in your place, might bring him round at last? Don't you think——"

Here, suddenly, Morris was interrupted; these ingenious inquiries had not reached Catherine's ears. The terrible word "disinheritance," with all its impressive moral reprobation, was still ringing there; seemed indeed to gather force as it lingered. The mortal chill of her situation struck more deeply into her child-like heart, and she was overwhelmed by a feeling of lone-liness and danger. But her refuge was there, close to her, and she put out her hands to grasp it. "Ah, Morris," she said, with a shudder, "I will marry you as soon as you please!" And she surrendered herself, leaning her head on his shoulder.

"My dear good girl!" he exclaimed, looking down at his prize. And then he looked up again, rather vaguely, with parted lips and lifted eyebrows.

XXI

DR. SLOPER very soon imparted his conviction to Mrs. Almond, in the same terms in which he had announced it to himself. "She's going to stick, by Jove! she's going to stick."

"Do you mean that she is going to marry him?" Mrs. Almond inquired.

"I don't know that; but she is not going to break down. She is going to drag out the engagement, in the hope of making me relent."

"And shall you not relent?"

"Shall a geometrical proposition relent? I am not so superficial."

"Doesn't geometry treat of surfaces?" asked Mrs. Almond, who, as we know, was clever, smiling.

"Yes; but it treats of them profoundly. Catherine and her young man are my surfaces; I have taken their measure."

"You speak as if it surprised you."

"It is immense; there will be a great deal to observe."

"You are shockingly cold-blooded!" said Mrs. Almond.

"I need to be, with all this hot blood about me. Young Townsend indeed is cool; I must allow him that merit."

"I can't judge him," Mrs. Almond answered; "but I am not at all surprised at Catherine."

"I confess I am a little; she must have been so deucedly divided and bothered."

"Say it amuses you outright! I don't see why it should be such a joke that your daughter adores you."

"It is the point where the adoration stops that I find it interesting to fix."

"It stops where the other sentiment begins."

"Not at all—that would be simple enough. The two things are extremely mixed up, and the mixture is extremely odd. It will produce some third element, and that's what I am waiting to see. I wait with suspense—with positive excitement; and that is a sort of emotion that I didn't suppose Catherine would ever provide for me. I am really very much obliged to her."

"She will cling," said Mrs. Almond; "she will certainly cling."

"Yes; as I say, she will stick."

"Cling is prettier. That's what those very simple natures always do, and nothing could be simpler than Catherine. She doesn't take many impressions; but when she takes one she keeps it. She is like a copper kettle that receives a dent; you may polish up the kettle, but you can't efface the mark."

"We must try and polish up Catherine," said the Doctor. "I will take her to Europe."

"She won't forget him in Europe."

"He will forget her, then."

Mrs. Almond looked grave. "Should you really like that?"

"Extremely!" said the Doctor.

Mrs. Penniman, meanwhile, lost little time in putting herself again in communication with Morris Townsend. She requested him to favour her with another interview, but she did not on this occasion select an oyster-saloon as the scene of their meeting. She proposed that he should join her at the door of a certain church, after service on Sunday afternoon, and she was careful not to appoint the place of worship which she usually visited, and where, as she said, the congregation would have spied upon her. She picked out a less elegant resort, and on issuing from its portal at the hour she had fixed she saw the young man standing apart. She offered him no recognition till she had crossed the street and he had followed her to some distance. Here, with a smile—"Excuse my apparent want of cordiality," she said. "You know what to believe about that. Prudence before everything." And on his asking her in what direction they should walk, "Where we shall be least observed," she murmured.

Morris was not in high good-humour, and his response to this speech was not particularly gallant. "I don't flatter myself we shall be much observed anywhere." Then he turned recklessly toward the centre of the town. "I hope you have come to tell me that he has knocked under," he went on.

"I am afraid I am not altogether a harbinger of good; and yet, too, I am to a certain extent a messenger of peace. I have been thinking a great deal, Mr. Townsend," said Mrs. Penniman.

"You think too much."

"I suppose I do; but I can't help it, my mind is so terribly active. When I give myself, I give myself. I pay the penalty in my headaches, my famous headaches—a perfect circlet of pain! But I carry it as a queen carries her crown. Would you believe that I have one now? I wouldn't, however, have missed our rendezvous for anything. I have something very important to tell you."

"Well, let's have it," said Morris.

"I was perhaps a little headlong the other day in advising you to marry immediately. I have been thinking it over, and now I see it just a little differently."

"You seem to have a great many different ways of seeing the same object."

"Their number is infinite!" said Mrs. Penniman, in a tone which seemed to suggest that this convenient faculty was one of her brightest attributes.

"I recommend you to take one way and stick to it," Morris replied.

"Ah! but it isn't easy to choose. My imagination is never quiet, never satisfied. It makes me a bad adviser, perhaps; but it makes me a capital friend!"

"A capital friend who gives bad advice!" said Morris.

"Not intentionally—and who hurries off, at every risk, to make the most humble excuses!"

"Well, what do you advise me now?"

"To be very patient; to watch and wait."

"And is that bad advice or good?"

"That is not for me to say," Mrs. Penniman rejoined, with some dignity. "I only pretend it's sincere."

"And will you come to me next week and recommend something different and equally sincere?"

"I may come to you next week and tell you that I am in the streets!"

"In the streets?"

"I have had a terrible scene with my brother, and he threatens, if anything happens, to turn me out of the house. You know I am a poor woman."

Morris had a speculative idea that she had a little property; but he naturally did not press this.

"I should be very sorry to see you suffer martyrdom for me," he said. "But you make your brother out a regular Turk."

Mrs. Penniman hesitated a little.

"I certainly do not regard Austin as a satisfactory Christian."

"And am I to wait till he is converted?"

"Wait, at any rate, till he is less violent. Bide your time, Mr. Townsend; remember the prize is great!"

Morris walked along some time in silence, tapping the railings and gateposts very sharply with his stick.

"You certainly are devilish inconsistent!" he broke out at last. "I have already got Catherine to consent to a private marriage."

Mrs. Penniman was indeed inconsistent, for at this news she gave a little jump of gratification.

"Oh! when and where?" she cried. And then she stopped short.

Morris was a little vague about this.

"That isn't fixed; but she consents. It's deuced awkward, now, to back out."

Mrs. Penniman, as I say, had stopped short; and she stood there with her eyes fixed brilliantly on her companion.

"Mr. Townsend," she proceeded, "shall I tell you something? Catherine loves you so much that you may do anything."

This declaration was slightly ambiguous, and Morris opened his eyes.

"I am happy to hear it! But what do you mean by 'anything'?"

"You may postpone—you may change about; she won't think the worse of you."

Morris stood there still, with his raised eyebrows; then he said simply and rather dryly—"Ah!" After this he remarked to Mrs. Penniman that if she walked so slowly she would attract notice, and he succeeded, after a fashion, in hurrying her back to the domicile of which her tenure had become so insecure.

XXII

HE HAD slightly misrepresented the matter in saying that Catherine had consented to take the great step. We left her just now declaring that she would burn her ships behind her; but Morris, after having elicited this declaration, had become conscious of good reasons for not taking it up. He avoided, gracefully enough, fixing a day, though he left her under the impression that he had his eye on one. Catherine may have had her difficulties; but those of her circumspect suitor are also worthy of consideration. The prize was certainly great; but it was only to be won by striking the happy mean between precipitancy and caution. It would be all very well to take one's jump and trust to Providence; Providence was more especially on the side of clever people, and clever people were known by an indisposition to risk their bones. The ultimate reward of a union with a young woman who was both unattractive and impoverished ought to be connected with immediate disadvantages by some very palpable chain. Between the fear of losing

Catherine and her possible fortune altogether, and the fear of taking her too soon and finding this possible fortune as void of actuality as a collection of emptied bottles, it was not comfortable for Morris Townsend to choose; a fact that should be remembered by readers disposed to judge harshly of a young man who may have struck them as making but an indifferently successful use of fine natural parts. He had not forgotten that in any event Catherine had her own ten thousand a year; he had devoted an abundance of meditation to this circumstance. But with his fine parts he rated himself high, and he had a perfectly definite appreciation of his value, which seemed to him inadequately represented by the sum I have mentioned. At the same time he reminded himself that this sum was considerable, that everything is relative, and that if a modest income is less desirable than a large one, the complete absence of revenue is nowhere accounted an advantage. These reflections gave him plenty of occupation, and made it necessary that he should trim his sail. Dr. Sloper's opposition was the unknown quantity in the problem he had to work out. The natural way to work it out was by marrying Catherine; but in mathematics there are many short cuts, and Morris was not without a hope that he should yet discover one. When Catherine took him at his word and consented to renounce the attempt to mollify her father, he drew back skilfully enough, as I have said, and kept the wedding-day still an open question. Her faith in his sincerity was so complete that she was incapable of suspecting that he was playing with her; her trouble just now was of another kind. The poor girl had an admirable sense of honour; and from the moment she had brought herself to the point of violating her father's wish, it seemed to her that she had no right to enjoy his protection. It was on her conscience that she ought to live under his roof only so long as she conformed to his wisdom. There was a great deal of glory in such a position, but poor Catherine felt that she had forfeited her claim to it. She had cast her lot with a young man against whom he had solemnly warned her, and broken the contract under which he provided her with a happy home. She could not give up the young man, so she must leave the home; and the sooner the object of her preference offered her another the sooner her situation would lose its awkward twist. This was close reasoning; but it was commingled with an infinite amount of merely instinctive penitence. Catherine's days, at this time, were dismal, and the weight of some of her hours was almost more than she could bear. Her father never looked at her, never spoke to her. He knew perfectly what he was about, and this was part of a plan. She looked at him as much as she dared (for she was afraid of seeming to offer herself to his observation), and she pitied him for the sorrow she had brought upon him. She held up her head and busied her hands, and went about her daily occupations; and when the state of things in Washington Square seemed intolerable, she closed her eyes and indulged herself with an intellectual vision of the man for whose sake she had broken a sacred law. Mrs. Penniman, of the three persons in Washington Square, had much the most of the manner that belongs to a great crisis. If Catherine was quiet, she was quietly quiet, as I may say, and her pathetic effects, which there was no one to notice, were entirely unstudied and unintended. If the Doctor was stiff and dry and absolutely indifferent to the presence of his companions, it was so lightly, neatly, easily done, that you would have had to know him well to discover that on the whole he rather enjoyed having to be so disagreeable. But Mrs. Penniman was elaborately reserved and significantly silent; there was a richer rustle in the very deliberate movements to which she confined herself, and when she occasionally spoke, in connection with some very trivial event, she had the air of meaning something deeper than what she said. Between Catherine and her father nothing had passed since the evening she went to speak to him in his study. She had something to say to him—it seemed to her she ought to say it; but she kept it back, for fear of irritating him. He also had something to say to her; but he was determined not to speak first. He was interested, as we know, in seeing how, if she were left to herself, she would "stick." At last she told him she had seen Morris Townsend again, and that their relations remained quite the same.

"I think we shall marry—before very long. And probably, meanwhile, I shall see him rather often; about once a week, not more."

The Doctor looked at her coldly from head to foot, as if she had been a stranger. It was the first time his eyes had rested on her for a week, which was fortunate, if that was to be their expression. "Why not three times a day?" he asked. "What prevents your meeting as often as you choose?"

She turned away a moment; there were tears in her eyes. Then she said, "It is better once a week."

"I don't see how it is better. It is as bad as it can be. If you flatter yourself that I care for little modifications of that sort, you are very much mistaken. It is as wrong of you to see him once a week as it would be to see him all day long. Not that it matters to me, however."

Catherine tried to follow these words, but they seemed to lead towards a vague horror from which she recoiled. "I think we shall marry pretty soon," she repeated at last.

Her father gave her his dreadful look again, as if she were some one else. "Why do you tell me that? It's no concern of mine."

"Oh, father!" she broke out, "don't you care, even if you do feel so?"

"Not a button. Once you marry, it's quite the same to me when or where or why you do it; and if you think to compound for your folly by hoisting your flag in this way, you may spare yourself the trouble."

With this he turned away. But the next day he spoke to her of his own accord, and his manner was somewhat changed. "Shall you be married within the next four or five months?" he asked.

"I don't know, father," said Catherine. "It is not very easy for us to make up our minds."

"Put it off, then, for six months, and in the meantime I will take you to Europe. I should like you very much to go."

It gave her such delight, after his words of the day before, to hear that he should "like" her to do something, and that he still had in his heart any of the tenderness of preference, that she gave a little exclamation of joy. But then she became conscious that Morris was not included in this proposal, and that—as regards really going—she would greatly prefer to remain at home with him. But she blushed, none the less, more comfortably than she had done of late. "It would be delightful to go to Europe," she remarked, with a sense that the idea was not original, and that her tone was not all it might be.

"Very well, then, we will go. Pack up your clothes."

"I had better tell Mr. Townsend," said Catherine.

Her father fixed his cold eyes upon her. "If you mean that you had better ask his leave, all that remains to me is to hope he will give it."

The girl was sharply touched by the pathetic ring of the words; it was the most calculated, the most dramatic little speech the Doctor had ever uttered. She felt that it was a great thing for her, under the circumstances, to have this fine opportunity of showing him her respect; and yet there was something else that she felt as well, and that she presently expressed. "I sometimes think that if I do what you dislike so much, I ought not to stay with you."

"To stay with me?"

"If I live with you, I ought to obey you."

"If that's your theory, it's certainly mine," said the Doctor, with a dry laugh.

"But if I don't obey you, I ought not to live with you—to enjoy your kindness and protection."

This striking argument gave the Doctor a sudden sense of having underestimated his daughter; it seemed even more than worthy of a young woman who had revealed the quality of unaggressive obstinacy. But it displeased him—displeased him deeply, and he signified as much. "That idea is in very bad taste," he said. "Did you get it from Mr. Townsend?"

"Oh no; it's my own!" said Catherine eagerly.

"Keep it to yourself, then," her father answered, more than ever determined she should go to Europe.

XXIII

IF MORRIS Townsend was not to be included in this journey, no more was Mrs. Penniman, who would have been thankful for an invitation, but who (to do her justice) bore her disappointment in a perfectly lady-like manner. "I should enjoy seeing the works of Raphael and the ruins—the ruins of the Pantheon," she said to Mrs. Almond; "but on the other hand, I shall not be sorry to be alone and at peace for the next few months in Washington Square. I want rest; I have been through so much in the last four months." Mrs. Almond thought it rather cruel that her brother should not take poor Lavinia abroad; but she easily understood that, if the purpose of his expedition was to make Catherine forget her lover, it was not in his interest to give his daughter this young man's best friend as a companion. "If Lavinia had not been so foolish, she might visit the ruins of the Pantheon," she said to herself; and she continued to regret her sister's folly, even though the latter assured her that she had often heard the relics in question most satisfactorily described by Mr. Penniman. Mrs. Penniman was perfectly aware that her brother's motive in undertaking a foreign tour was to lay a trap for Catherine's constancy; and she imparted this conviction very frankly to her niece.

"He thinks it will make you forget Morris," she said (she always called the young man "Morris" now); "out of sight, out of mind, you know. He thinks that all the things you will see over there will drive him out of your thoughts."

Catherine looked greatly alarmed. "If he thinks that, I ought to tell him beforehand."

Mrs. Penniman shook her head. "Tell him afterwards, my dear! After he has had all the trouble and the expense! That's the way to serve him." And she added, in a softer key, that it must be delightful to think of those who love us among the ruins of the Pantheon.

Her father's displeasure had cost the girl, as we know, a great deal of deep-welling sorrow—sorrow of the purest and most generous kind, without a touch of resentment or rancour; but for the first time, after he had dismissed with such contemptuous brevity her apology for being a charge upon him, there was a spark of anger in her grief. She had felt his contempt; it had scorched her; that speech about her bad taste made her ears burn for three days. During this period she was less considerate; she had an idea—a rather vague one, but it was agreeable to her sense of injury—that now she was absolved from penance, and might do what she chose. She chose to write to Morris Townsend to meet her in the Square and take her to walk about the town. If she were going to Europe out of respect to her father, she might at least give herself this satisfaction. She felt in every way at present more free and more resolute; there was a force that urged her. Now at last, completely and unreservedly, her passion possessed her.

Morris met her at last, and they took a long walk. She told him immediately what had happened—that her father wished to take her away. It would be for six months, to Europe; she would do absolutely what Morris should think best. She hoped inexpressibly that he would think it best she should stay at home. It was some time before he said what he thought: he asked, as they walked along, a great many questions. There was one that especially struck her; it seemed so incongruous.

"Should you like to see all those celebrated things over there?"

"Oh, no, Morris!" said Catherine, quite deprecatingly.

"Gracious Heaven, what a dull woman!" Morris exclaimed to himself.

"He thinks I will forget you," said Catherine; "that all these things will drive you out of my mind."

"Well, my dear, perhaps they will!"

"Please don't say that," Catherine answered gently, as they walked along. "Poor father will be disappointed."

Morris gave a little laugh. "Yes, I verily believe that your poor father will be disappointed! But you will have seen Europe," he added humorously. "What a take-in!"

"I don't care for seeing Europe," Catherine said.

"You ought to care, my dear. And it may mollify your father."

Catherine, conscious of her obstinacy, expected little of this, and could not rid herself of the idea that in going abroad and yet remaining firm, she should play her father a trick. "Don't you think it would be a kind of deception?" she asked.

"Doesn't he want to deceive you?" cried Morris. "It will serve him right! I really think you had better go."

"And not be married for so long?"

"Be married when you come back. You can buy your wedding-clothes in Paris." And then Morris, with great kindness of tone, explained his view of the matter. It would be a good thing that she should go; it would put them completely in the right. It would show they were reasonable and willing to wait. Once they were so sure of each other, they could afford to wait—what had they to fear? If there was a particle of chance that her father would be favourably affected by her going, that ought to settle it; for, after all, Morris was very unwilling to be the cause of her being disinherited. It was not for himself, it was for her and for her children. He was willing to wait for her; it would be hard, but he could do it. And over there, among beautiful scenes and noble monuments, perhaps the old gentleman would be softened; such things were supposed to exert a humanising influence. He might be touched by her gentleness, her patience, her willingness to make any sacrifice but *that* one; and if she should appeal to him some day, in some celebrated spot—in Italy, say, in the evening; in Venice, in a gondola, by moonlight—if she should be a little clever about it and touch the right chord, perhaps he would fold her in his arms and tell her that he forgave her. Catherine was immensely struck with this conception of the affair, which seemed eminently worthy of her lover's brilliant intellect; though she viewed it askance in so far as it depended upon her own powers of execution. The idea of being "clever" in a gondola by moonlight appeared to her to involve elements of which her grasp was not active. But it was settled between them that she should tell her father that she was ready to follow him obediently anywhere, making the mental reservation that she loved Morris Townsend more than ever.

She informed the Doctor she was ready to embark, and he made rapid arrangements for this event. Catherine had many farewells to make, but with only two of them are we actively concerned. Mrs. Penniman took a discriminating view of her niece's journey; it seemed to her very proper that Mr. Townsend's destined bride should wish to embellish her mind by a foreign tour.

"You leave him in good hands," she said, pressing her lips to Catherine's forehead. (She was very fond of kissing people's foreheads; it was an involuntary expression of sympathy with the intellectual part.) "I shall see him often; I shall feel like one of the vestals of old, tending the sacred flame."

"You behave beautifully about not going with us," Catherine answered, not presuming to examine this analogy.

"It is my pride that keeps me up," said Mrs. Penniman, tapping the body of her dress, which always gave forth a sort of metallic ring.

Catherine's parting with her lover was short, and few words were exchanged.

"Shall I find you just the same when I come back?" she asked; though the question was not the fruit of scepticism.

"The same—only more so!" said Morris, smiling.

It does not enter into our scheme to narrate in detail Dr. Sloper's proceedings in the Eastern hemisphere. He made the grand tour of Europe, travelled in considerable splendour, and (as was to have been expected in a man of his high cultivation) found so much in art and antiquity to interest him, that he remained abroad, not for six months, but for twelve. Mrs. Penniman, in Washington Square, accommodated herself to his absence. She enjoyed her uncontested dominion in the empty house, and flattered herself that she made it more attractive to their friends than when her brother was at home. To Morris Townsend, at least, it would have appeared that she made it singularly attractive. He was altogether her most frequent visitor, and Mrs. Penniman was very fond of asking him to tea. He had his chair—a very easy one—at the fireside in the back-parlour (when the great mahogany sliding-doors, with silver knobs and hinges, which divided this apartment from its more formal neighbour, were closed), and he used to smoke cigars in the Doctor's study, where he often spent an hour in turning over the curious collections of its absent proprietor. He thought Mrs. Penniman a goose, as we know; but he was no goose himself, and, as a young man of luxurious tastes and scanty resources, he found the house a perfect castle of indolence. It became for him a club with a single member. Mrs. Penniman saw much less of her sister than while the Doctor was at home; for Mrs. Almond had felt moved to tell her that she disapproved of her relations with Mr. Townsend. She had no business to be so friendly to a young man of whom their brother thought so meanly, and Mrs. Almond was surprised at her levity in foisting a most deplorable engagement upon Catherine.

"Deplorable?" cried Lavinia. "He will make her a lovely husband!"

"I don't believe in lovely husbands," said Mrs. Almond; "I only believe in good ones. If he marries her, and she comes into Austin's money, they may get on. He will be an idle, amiable, selfish, and doubtless tolerably good-natured fellow. But if she doesn't get the money and he finds himself tied to her, Heaven have mercy on her! He will have none. He will hate her for his disappointment, and take his revenge; he will be pitiless and cruel. Woe betide poor Catherine! I recommend you to talk a little with his sister; it's a pity Catherine can't marry *her*!"

Mrs. Penniman had no appetite whatever for conversation with Mrs. Montgomery, whose acquaintance she made no trouble to cultivate; and the effect of this alarming forecast of her niece's destiny was to make her think it indeed a thousand pities that Mr. Townsend's generous nature should be embittered. Bright enjoyment was his natural element, and how could he be comfortable if there should prove to be nothing to enjoy? It became a fixed idea with Mrs. Penniman that he should yet enjoy her brother's fortune, on which she had acuteness enough to perceive that her own claim was small.

"If he doesn't leave it to Catherine, it certainly won't be to leave it to me," she said.

XXIV

THE DOCTOR, during the first six months he was abroad, never spoke to his daughter of their little difference; partly on system, and partly because he had a great many other things to think about. It was idle to attempt to ascertain the state of her affections without direct inquiry, because, if she had not had an expressive manner among the familiar influences of home, she failed to gather animation from the mountains of Switzerland or the monuments of Italy. She was always her father's docile and reasonable associate—going through their sight-seeing in deferential silence, never complaining of fatigue, always ready to start at the hour he had appointed over-night, making no foolish criticisms and indulging in no refinements of appreciation. "She is about as intelligent as the bundle of shawls," the Doctor said; her main superiority being that while the bundle of shawls sometimes got lost, or tumbled out of the carriage, Catherine was always at her post, and had a firm and ample seat. But her father had expected this, and he was not constrained to set down her intellectual limitations as a tourist to sentimental depression; she had completely divested herself of the characteristics of a victim, and during the whole time that they were abroad she never uttered an audible sigh. He supposed she was in correspondence with Morris Townsend; but he held his peace about it, for he never saw the young man's letters, and Catherine's own missives were always given to the courier to post. She heard from her lover with considerable regularity, but his letters came enclosed in Mrs. Penniman's; so that whenever the Doctor handed her a packet addressed in his sister's hand, he was an involuntary instrument of the passion he condemned. Catherine made this reflection, and six months earlier she would have felt bound to give him warning; but now she deemed herself absolved. There was a sore spot in her heart that his own words had made when once she spoke to him as she thought honour prompted; she would try and please him as far as she could, but she would never speak that way again. She read her lover's letters in secret.

One day at the end of the summer, the two travellers found themselves in a lonely valley of the Alps. They were crossing one of the passes, and on the long ascent they had got out of the carriage and had wandered much in advance. After a while the Doctor descried a footpath which, leading through a transverse valley, would bring them out, as he justly supposed, at a much higher point of the ascent. They followed this devious way, and finally lost the path; the valley proved very wild and rough, and their walk became rather a scramble. They were good walkers, however, and they took their adventure easily; from time to time they stopped, that Catherine might rest; and then she sat upon a stone and looked about her at the hard-featured rocks and the glowing sky. It was late in the afternoon, in the last of August; night was coming on, and, as they had reached a great elevation, the air was cold and sharp. In the west there was a great suffusion of cold, red light, which made the sides of the little valley look only the more rugged and dusky. During one of their pauses, her father left her and wandered away to some high place, at a distance, to get a view. He was out of sight; she sat there alone, in the stillness, which was just touched by the vague murmur, somewhere, of a mountain brook. She thought of Morris Townsend, and the place was so desolate and lonely that he seemed very far away. Her father remained absent a long time; she began to wonder what had become of him. But at last he reappeared, coming towards her in the clear twilight, and she got up, to go on. He made no motion to proceed, however, but came close to her, as if he had something to say. He stopped in front of her and stood looking at her, with eyes that had kept the light of the flushing snow-summits on which they had just been fixed. Then, abruptly, in a low tone, he asked her an unexpected question—

"Have you given him up?"

The question was unexpected, but Catherine was only superficially unprepared.

"No, father!" she answered.

He looked at her again, for some moments, without speaking.

"Does he write to you?" he asked.

"Yes—about twice a month."

The Doctor looked up and down the valley, swinging his stick; then he said to her, in the same low tone—

"I am very angry."

She wondered what he meant—whether he wished to frighten her. If he did, the place was well chosen; this hard, melancholy dell, abandoned by the summer light, made her feel her loneliness. She looked around her, and her heart grew cold; for a moment her fear was great. But she could think of nothing to say, save to murmur gently, "I am sorry."

"You try my patience," her father went on, "and you ought to know what I am. I am not a very good man. Though I am very smooth externally, at bottom I am very passionate; and I assure you I can be very hard."

She could not think why he told her these things. Had he brought her there on purpose, and was it part of a plan? What was the plan? Catherine asked herself. Was it to startle her suddenly into a retraction—to take an advantage of her by dread? Dread of what? The place was ugly and lonely, but the place could do her no harm. There was a kind of still intensity about her father which made him dangerous, but Catherine hardly went so far as to say to herself that it might be part of his plan to fasten his hand—the neat, fine, supple hand of a distinguished physician—in her throat. Nevertheless, she receded a step. "I am sure you can be anything you please," she said. And it was her simple belief.

"I am very angry," he replied, more sharply.

"Why has it taken you so suddenly?"

"It has not taken me suddenly. I have been raging inwardly for the last six months. But just now this seemed a good place to flare out. It's so quiet, and we are alone."

"Yes, it's very quiet," said Catherine vaguely, looking about her. "Won't you come back to the carriage?"

"In a moment. Do you mean that in all this time you have not yielded an inch?"

"I would if I could, father; but I can't."

The Doctor looked round him too. "Should you like to be left in such a place as this, to starve?"

"What do you mean?" cried the girl.

"That will be your fate—that's how he will leave you."

He would not touch her, but he had touched Morris. The warmth came back to her heart. "That is not true, father," she broke out, "and you ought not to say it! It is not right, and it's not true!"

He shook his head slowly. "No, it's not right, because you won't believe it. But it *is* true. Come back to the carriage."

He turned away, and she followed him; he went faster, and was presently much in advance. But from time to time he stopped, without turning round, to let her keep up with him, and she made her way forward with difficulty, her heart beating with the excitement of having for the first time spoken to him in violence. By this time it had grown almost dark, and she ended by losing sight of him. But she kept her course, and after a little, the valley making a sudden turn, she gained the road, where the carriage stood waiting. In it sat her father, rigid and silent; in silence, too, she took her place beside him.

It seemed to her, later, in looking back upon all this, that for days afterwards not a word had been exchanged between them.

The scene had been a strange one, but it had not permanently affected her feeling towards her father, for it was natural, after all, that he should occasionally make a scene of some kind, and he had let her alone for six months. The strangest part of it was that he had said he was not a good man; Catherine wondered a great deal what he had meant by that. The statement failed to appeal to her credence, and it was not grateful to any resentment that she entertained. Even in the utmost bitterness that she might feel, it would give her no satisfaction to think him less complete. Such a saying as that was a part of his great subtlety —men so clever as he might say anything and mean anything. And as to his being hard, that surely, in a man, was a virtue.

He let her alone for six months more—six months during which she accommodated herself without a protest to the extension of their tour. But he spoke again at the end of this time; it was at the very last, the night before they embarked for New York, in the hotel at Liverpool. They had been dining together in a great dim, musty sitting-room; and then the cloth had been removed, and the Doctor walked slowly up and down. Catherine at last took her candle to go to bed, but her father motioned her to stay.

"What do you mean to do when you get home?" he asked, while she stood there with her candle in her hand.

"Do you mean about Mr. Townsend?"

"About Mr. Townsend."

"We shall probably marry."

The Doctor took several turns again while she waited. "Do you hear from him as much as ever?"

"Yes; twice a month," said Catherine, promptly.

"And does he always talk about marriage?"

"Oh, yes! That is, he talks about other things too, but he always says something about that."

"I am glad to hear he varies his subjects; his letters might otherwise be monotonous."

"He writes beautifully," said Catherine, who was very glad of a chance to say it.

"They always write beautifully. However, in a given case that doesn't diminish the merit. So, as soon as you arrive, you are going off with him?"

This seemed a rather gross way of putting it, and something that there was of dignity in Catherine resented it. "I cannot tell you till we arrive," she said.

"That's reasonable enough," her father answered. "That's all I ask of you—that you *do* tell me, that you give me definite notice. When a poor man is to lose his only child, he likes to have an inkling of it beforehand."

"Oh, father, you will not lose me!" Catherine said, spilling her candle-wax.

"Three days before will do," he went on, "if you are in a position to be positive then. He ought to be very thankful to me, do you know. I have done a mighty good thing for him in taking you abroad; your value is twice as great, with all the knowledge and taste that you have acquired. A year ago, you were perhaps a little limited—a little rustic; but now you have seen everything, and appreciated everything, and you will be a most entertaining companion. We have fattened the sheep for him before he kills it!" Catherine turned away, and stood staring at the blank door. "Go to bed," said her father; "and, as we don't go aboard till noon, you may sleep late. We shall probably have a most uncomfortable voyage."

XXV

THE VOYAGE was indeed uncomfortable, and Catherine, on arriving in New York, had not the compensation of "going off," in her father's phrase, with Morris Townsend. She saw him, however, the day after she landed; and, in the meantime, he formed a natural subject of conversation between our heroine and her Aunt Lavinia, with whom, the night she disembarked, the girl was closeted for a long time before either lady retired to rest.

"I have seen a great deal of him," said Mrs. Penniman. "He is not very easy to know. I suppose you think you know him; but you don't, my dear. You will some day; but it will only be after you have lived with him. I may almost say *I* have lived with him," Mrs. Penniman proceeded, while Catherine stared. "I think I know him now; I have had such remarkable opportunities. You will have the same—or rather, you will have better!" and Aunt Lavinia smiled. "Then you will see what I mean. It's a wonderful character, full of passion and energy, and just as true!"

Catherine listened with a mixture of interest and apprehension. Aunt Lavinia was intensely sympathetic, and Catherine, for the past year, while she wandered through foreign galleries and churches, and rolled over the smoothness of posting roads, nursing the thoughts that never passed her lips, had often longed for the company of some intelligent person of her own sex. To tell her story to some kind woman—at moments it seemed to her that this would give her comfort, and she had more than once been on the point of taking the landlady, or the nice young person from the dressmaker's, into her confidence. If a woman had been near her she would on certain occasions have treated such a companion to a fit of weeping; and she had an apprehension that, on her return, this would form her response to Aunt Lavinia's first embrace. In fact, however, the two ladies had met, in Washington Square, without tears, and when they found themselves alone together a certain dryness fell upon the girl's emotion. It came over her with a greater force that Mrs. Penniman had enjoyed a whole year of her lover's society, and it was not a pleasure to her to hear her aunt explain and interpret the young man, speaking of him as if her own knowledge of him were supreme. It was not that Catherine was jealous; but her sense of Mrs. Penniman's innocent falsity, which had lain dormant, began to haunt her again, and she was glad that she was safely at home. With this, however, it was a blessing to be able to talk of Morris, to sound his name, to be with a person who was not unjust to him.

"You have been very kind to him," said Catherine. "He has written me that, often. I shall never forget that, Aunt Lavinia."

"I have done what I could; it has been very little. To let him come and talk to me, and give him his cup of tea—that was all. Your Aunt Almond thought it was too much, and used to scold me terribly; but she promised me, at least, not to betray me."

"To betray you?"

"Not to tell your father. He used to sit in your father's study!" said Mrs. Penniman, with a little laugh.

Catherine was silent a moment. This idea was disagreeable to her, and she was reminded again, with pain, of her aunt's secretive habits. Morris, the reader may be informed, had had the tact not to tell her that he sat in her father's study. He had known her but for a few months, and her aunt had known her for fifteen years; and yet he would not have made the mistake of thinking that Catherine would see the joke of the thing. "I am sorry you made him go into father's room," she said, after a while.

"I didn't make him go; he went himself. He liked to look at the books, and all those things in the glass cases. He knows all about them; he knows all about everything."

Catherine was silent again; then, "I wish he had found some employment," she said.

"He has found some employment! It's beautiful news, and he told me to tell you as soon as you arrived. He has gone into partnership with a commission-merchant. It was all settled, quite suddenly, a week ago."

This seemed to Catherine indeed beautiful news; it had a fine prosperous air. "Oh, I'm so glad!" she said; and now, for a moment, she was disposed to throw herself on Aunt Lavinia's neck.

"It's much better than being under some one; and he has never been used to that," Mrs. Penniman went on. "He is just as good as his partner—they are perfectly equal! You see how right he was to wait. I should like to know what your father can say now! They have got an office in Duane Street, and little printed cards; he brought me one to show me. I have got it in my room, and you shall see it to-morrow. That's what he said to me the last time he was here—'You see how right I was to wait!' He has got other people under him, instead of being a subordinate. He could never be a subordinate; I have often told him I could never think of him in that way."

Catherine assented to this proposition, and was very happy to know that Morris was his own master; but she was deprived of the satisfaction of thinking that she might communicate this news in triumph to her father. Her father would care equally little whether Morris were established in business or transported for life. Her trunks had been brought into her room, and further reference to her lover was for a short time suspended, while she opened them and displayed to her aunt some of the spoils of foreign travel. These were rich and abundant; and Catherine had brought home a present to every one—to every one save Morris, to whom she had brought simply her undiverted heart. To Mrs. Penniman she had been lavishly generous, and Aunt Lavinia spent half an hour in unfolding and folding again, with little ejaculations of gratitude and taste. She marched about for some time in a splendid cashmere shawl, which Catherine had begged her to accept, settling it on her shoulders, and twisting down her head to see how low the point descended behind.

"I shall regard it only as a loan," she said. "I will leave it to you again when I die; or rather," she added, kissing her niece again, "I will leave it to your first-born little girl!" And draped in her shawl, she stood there smiling.

"You had better wait till she comes," said Catherine.

"I don't like the way you say that," Mrs. Penniman rejoined, in a moment. "Catherine, are you changed?"

"No; I am the same."

"You have not swerved a line?"

"I am exactly the same," Catherine repeated, wishing her aunt were a little less sympathetic.

"Well, I am glad!" and Mrs. Penniman surveyed her cashmere

in the glass. Then, "How is your father?" she asked in a moment, with her eyes on her niece. "Your letters were so meagre —I could never tell!"

"Father is very well."

"Ah, you know what I mean," said Mrs. Penniman, with a dignity to which the cashmere gave a richer effect. "Is he still implacable?"

"Oh, yes!"

"Quite unchanged?"

"He is, if possible, more firm."

Mrs. Penniman took off her great shawl, and slowly folded it up. "That is very bad. You had no success with your little project?"

"What little project?"

"Morris told me all about it. The idea of turning the tables on him, in Europe; of watching him, when he was agreeably impressed by some celebrated sight—he pretends to be so artistic, you know—and then just pleading with him and bringing him round."

"I never tried it. It was Morris's idea; but if he had been with us, in Europe, he would have seen that father was never impressed in that way. He *is* artistic—tremendously artistic; but the more celebrated places we visited, and the more he admired them, the less use it would have been to plead with him. They seemed only to make him more determined—more terrible," said poor Catherine. "I shall never bring him round, and I expect nothing now."

"Well, I must say," Mrs. Penniman answered, "I never supposed you were going to give it up."

"I have given it up. I don't care now."

"You have grown very brave," said Mrs. Penniman, with a short laugh. "I didn't advise you to sacrifice your property."

"Yes, I am braver than I was. You asked me if I had changed; I have changed in that way. Oh," the girl went on, "I have changed very much. And it isn't my property. If *he* doesn't care for it, why should I?"

Mrs. Penniman hesitated. "Perhaps he does care for it."

"He cares for it for my sake, because he doesn't want to injure me. But he will know—he knows already—how little he need be afraid about that. Besides," said Catherine, "I have got plenty of money of my own. We shall be very well off; and now hasn't he got his business? I am delighted about that business." She went on talking, showing a good deal of excitement as she proceeded. Her aunt had never seen her with just this manner, and Mrs. Penniman, observing her, set it down to foreign travel, which had made her more positive, more mature. She thought also that Catherine had improved in appearance; she looked rather handsome. Mrs. Penniman wondered whether Morris Townsend would be struck with that. While she was engaged in this speculation, Catherine broke out, with a certain sharpness, "Why are you so contradictory, Aunt Penniman? You seem to think one thing at one time, and another at another. A year ago, before I went away, you wished me not to mind about displeasing father; and now you seem to recommend me to take another line. You change about so."

This attack was unexpected, for Mrs. Penniman was not used, in any discussion, to seeing the war carried into her own country—possibly because the enemy generally had doubts of finding subsistence there. To her own consciousness, the flowery fields of her reason had rarely been ravaged by a hostile force. It was perhaps on this account that in defending them she was majestic rather than agile.

"I don't know what you accuse me of, save of being too deeply interested in your happiness. It is the first time I have been told I am capricious. That fault is not what I am usually reproached with."

"You were angry last year that I wouldn't marry immediately, and now you talk about my winning my father over. You told me it would serve him right if he should take me to Europe for nothing. Well, he has taken me for nothing, and you ought to be satisfied. Nothing is changed—nothing but my feeling about father. I don't mind nearly so much now. I have been as good as I could, but he doesn't care. Now I don't care either. I don't know whether I have grown bad; perhaps I have. But I don't care for that. I have come home to be married—that's all I know. That ought to please you, unless you have taken up some new idea; you are so strange. You may do as you please; but you must never speak to me again about pleading with father. I shall never plead with him for anything; that is all over. He has put me off. I am come home to be married."

This was a more authoritative speech than she had ever heard on her niece's lips, and Mrs. Penniman was proportionately startled. She was indeed a little awe-struck, and the force of the girl's emotion and resolution left her nothing to reply. She was easily frightened, and she always carried off her discomfiture by a concession; a concession which was often accompanied, as in the present case, by a little nervous laugh.

XXVI

IF SHE had disturbed her niece's temper—she began from this moment forward to talk a good deal about Catherine's temper, an article which up to that time had never been mentioned in connection with our heroine—Catherine had opportunity, on the morrow, to recover her serenity. Mrs. Penniman had given her a message from Morris Townsend, to the effect that he would come and welcome her home on the day after her arrival. He came in the afternoon; but, as may be imagined, he was not on this occasion made free of Dr. Sloper's study. He had been coming and going, for the past year, so comfortably and irresponsibly, that he had a certain sense of being wronged by finding himself reminded that he must now limit his horizon to the front-parlour, which was Catherine's particular province.

"I am very glad you have come back," he said; "it makes me very happy to see you again." And he looked at her, smiling, from head to foot; though it did not appear, afterwards, that he agreed with Mrs. Penniman (who, womanlike, went more into details) in thinking her embellished.

To Catherine he appeared resplendent; it was some time before she could believe again that this beautiful young man was her own exclusive property. They had a great deal of characteristic lovers' talk—a soft exchange of inquiries and assurances. In these matters Morris had an excellent grace, which flung a picturesque interest even over the account of his début in the commission-business—a subject as to which his companion earnestly questioned him. From time to time he got up from the sofa where they sat together, and walked about the room; after which he came back, smiling and passing his hand through his hair. He was unquiet, as was natural in a young man who has just been re-united to a long-absent mistress, and Catherine made the reflection that she had never seen him so excited. It gave her pleasure, somehow, to note this fact. He asked her questions about her travels, to some of which she was unable to reply, for she had forgotten the names of places and the order of her father's journey. But for the moment she was so happy, so lifted up by the belief that her troubles at last were over, that she forgot to be ashamed of her meagre answers. It seemed to her now that she could marry him without the remnant of a scruple or a single tremor save those that belonged to joy. Without waiting for him to ask, she told him that her father had come back in exactly the same state of mind—that he had not yielded an inch.

"We must not expect it now," she said, "and we must do without it."

Morris sat looking and smiling. "My poor dear girl!" he exclaimed.

"You mustn't pity me," said Catherine; "I don't mind it now—I am used to it."

Morris continued to smile, and then he got up and walked about again. "You had better let me try him!"

"Try to bring him over? You would only make him worse," Catherine answered, resolutely.

"You say that because I managed it so badly before. But I should manage it differently now. I am much wiser; I have had a year to think of it. I have more tact."

"Is that what you have been thinking of for a year?"

"Much of the time. You see, the idea sticks in my crop. I don't like to be beaten."

"How are you beaten if we marry?"

"Of course, I am not beaten on the main issue; but I am, don't you see, on all the rest of it—on the question of my reputation, of my relations with your father, of my relations with my own children, if we should have any."

"We shall have enough for our children—we shall have enough for everything. Don't you expect to succeed in business?"

"Brilliantly, and we shall certainly be very comfortable. But it isn't of the mere material comfort I speak; it is of the moral comfort," said Morris—"of the intellectual satisfaction!"

"I have great moral comfort now," Catherine declared, very simply.

"Of course you have. But with me it is different. I have staked my pride on proving to your father that he is wrong; and now that I am at the head of a flourishing business, I can deal with him as an equal. I have a capital plan—do let me go at him!"

He stood before her with his bright face, his jaunty air, his hands in his pockets; and she got up, with her eyes resting on his own. "Please don't, Morris; please don't," she said; and there was a certain mild, sad firmness in her tone which he heard for the first time. "We must ask no favours of him—we must ask nothing more. He won't relent, and nothing good will come of it. I know it now—I have a very good reason."

"And pray; what is your reason?"

She hesitated to bring it out, but at last it came. "He is not very fond of me!"

"Oh, bother!" cried Morris, angrily.

"I wouldn't say such a thing without being sure. I saw it, I felt it, in England, just before he came away. He talked to me one night—the last night; and then it came over me. You can tell when a person feels that way. I wouldn't accuse him if he hadn't made me feel that way. I don't accuse him; I just tell you that that's how it is. He can't help it; we can't govern our affections. Do I govern mine? mightn't he say that to me? It's because he is so fond of my mother, whom we lost so long ago. She was beautiful, and very, very brilliant; he is always thinking of her. I am not at all like her; Aunt Penniman has told me that. Of course it isn't my fault; but neither is it his fault. All I mean is, it's true; and it's a stronger reason for his never being reconciled than simply his dislike for you."

"'Simply?'" cried Morris, with a laugh, "I am much obliged for that!"

"I don't mind about his disliking you now; I mind everything less. I feel differently; I feel separated from my father."

"Upon my word," said Morris, "you are a queer family!"

"Don't say that—don't say anything unkind," the girl entreated. "You must be very kind to me now, because, Morris—because," and she hesitated a moment—"because I have done a great deal for you."

"Oh, I know that, my dear!"

She had spoken up to this moment without vehemence or outward sign of emotion, gently, reasoningly, only trying to explain. But her emotion had been ineffectually smothered, and it betrayed itself at last in the trembling of her voice. "It is a great thing to be separated like that from your father, when you have worshipped him before. It has made me very unhappy; or it would have made me so if I didn't love you. You can tell when a person speaks to you as if—as if——"

"As if what?"

"As if they despised you!" said Catherine, passionately. "He spoke that way the night before we sailed. It wasn't much, but it was enough, and I thought of it on the voyage, all the time. Then I made up my mind. I will never ask him for anything again, or expect anything from him. It would not be natural now. We must be very happy together, and we must not seem to depend upon his forgiveness. And Morris, Morris, you must never despise me!"

This was an easy promise to make, and Morris made it with fine effect. But for the moment he undertook nothing more onerous.

XXVII

THE DOCTOR, of course, on his return, had a good deal of talk with his sisters. He was at no great pains to narrate his travels or to communicate his impressions of distant lands to Mrs. Penniman, upon whom he contented himself with bestowing a memento of his enviable experience, in the shape of a velvet gown. But he conversed with her at some length about matters nearer home, and lost no time in assuring her that he was still an inflexible father.

"I have no doubt you have seen a great deal of Mr. Townsend, and done your best to console him for Catherine's absence," he said. "I don't ask you, and you needn't deny it. I wouldn't put the question to you for the world, and expose you to the inconvenience of having to—a—excogitate an answer. No one has betrayed you, and there has been no spy upon your proceedings. Elizabeth has told no tales, and has never mentioned you except to praise your good looks and good spirits. The thing is simply an inference of my own—an induction, as the philosophers say. It seems to me likely that you would have offered an asylum to an interesting sufferer. Mr. Townsend has been a good deal in the house; there is something in the house that tells me so. We doctors, you know, end by acquiring fine perceptions, and it is impressed upon my sensorium that he has sat in these chairs, in a very easy attitude, and warmed himself at that fire. I don't grudge him the comfort of it; it is the only one he will ever enjoy at my expense. It seems likely, indeed, that I shall be able to economise at his own. I don't know what you may have said to him, or what you may say hereafter; but I should like you to know that if you have encouraged him to believe that he will gain anything by hanging on, or that I have budged a hair's breadth from the position I took up a year ago, you have played him a trick for which he may exact reparation. I'm not sure that he may not bring a suit against you. Of course you have done it conscientiously; you have made yourself believe that I can be tired out. This is the most baseless hallucination that ever visited the brain of a genial optimist. I am not in the least tired; I am as fresh as when I started; I am good for fifty years yet. Catherine appears not to have budged an inch either; she is equally fresh; so we are about where we were before. This, however, you know as well as I. What I wish is simply to give you notice of my own state of mind! Take it to heart, dear Lavinia. Beware of the just resentment of a deluded fortune-hunter!"

"I can't say I expected it," said Mrs. Penniman. "And I had a sort of foolish hope that you would come home without that odious ironical tone with which you treat the most sacred subjects."

"Don't undervalue irony, it is often of great use. It is not, however, always necessary, and I will show you how gracefully I can lay it aside. I should like to know whether you think Morris Townsend will hang on."

"I will answer you with your own weapons," said Mrs. Penniman. "You had better wait and see!"

"Do you call such a speech as that one of my own weapons? I never said anything so rough."

"He will hang on long enough to make you very uncomfortable, then."

"My dear Lavinia," exclaimed the Doctor, "do you call that irony? I call it pugilism."

Mrs. Penniman, however, in spite of her pugilism, was a good deal frightened, and she took counsel of her fears. Her brother meanwhile took counsel, with many reservations, of Mrs. Almond, to whom he was no less generous than to Lavinia, and a good deal more communicative.

"I suppose she has had him there all the while," he said. "I must look into the state of my wine! You needn't mind telling me now; I have already said all I mean to say to her on the subject."

"I believe he was in the house a good deal," Mrs. Almond answered. "But you must admit that your leaving Lavinia quite alone was a great change for her, and that it was natural she should want some society."

"I do admit that, and that is why I shall make no row about the wine; I shall set it down as compensation to Lavinia. She is capable of telling me that she drank it all herself. Think of the inconceivable bad taste, in the circumstances, of that fellow making free with the house—or coming there at all! If that doesn't describe him, he is indescribable."

"His plan is to get what he can. Lavinia will have supported him for a year," said Mrs. Almond. "It's so much gained."

"She will have to support him for the rest of his life, then!" cried the Doctor. "But without wine, as they say at the *tables d'hôte*."

"Catherine tells me he has set up a business, and is making a great deal of money."

The Doctor stared. "She has not told me that—and Lavinia didn't deign. Ah!" he cried, "Catherine has given me up. Not that it matters, for all that the business amounts to."

"She has not given up Mr. Townsend," said Mrs. Almond. "I saw that in the first half-minute. She has come home exactly the same."

"Exactly the same; not a grain more intelligent. She didn't notice a stick or a stone all the while we were away—not a picture nor a view, not a statue nor a cathedral."

"How could she notice? She had other things to think of; they are never for an instant out of her mind. She touches me very much."

"She would touch me if she didn't irritate me. That's the effect she has upon me now. I have tried everything upon her; I really have been quite merciless. But it is of no use whatever;

she is absolutely *glued*. I have passed, in consequence, into the exasperated stage. At first I had a good deal of a certain genial curiosity about it; I wanted to see if she really would stick. But, good Lord, one's curiosity is satisfied! I see she is capable of it, and now she can let go."

"She will never let go," said Mrs. Almond.

"Take care, or you will exasperate me too. If she doesn't let go, she will be shaken off—sent tumbling into the dust! That's a nice position for my daughter. She can't see that if you are going to be pushed you had better jump. And then she will complain of her bruises."

"She will never complain," said Mrs. Almond.

"That I shall object to even more. But the deuce will be that I can't prevent anything."

"If she is to have a fall," said Mrs. Almond, with a gentle laugh, "we must spread as many carpets as we can." And she carried out this idea by showing a great deal of motherly kindness to the girl.

Mrs. Penniman immediately wrote to Morris Townsend. The intimacy between these two was by this time consummate, but I must content myself with noting but a few of its features. Mrs. Penniman's own share in it was a singular sentiment, which might have been misinterpreted, but which in itself was not discreditable to the poor lady. It was a romantic interest in this attractive and unfortunate young man, and yet it was not such an interest as Catherine might have been jealous of. Mrs. Penniman had not a particle of jealousy of her niece. For herself, she felt as if she were Morris's mother or sister—a mother or sister of an emotional temperament—and she had an absorbing desire to make him comfortable and happy. She had striven to do so during the year that her brother left her an open field, and her efforts had been attended with the success that has been pointed out. She had never had a child of her own, and Catherine, whom she had done her best to invest with the importance that would naturally belong to a youthful Penniman, had only partly rewarded her zeal. Catherine, as an object of affection and solicitude, had never had that picturesque charm which (as it seemed to her) would have been a natural attribute of her own progeny. Even the maternal passion in Mrs. Penniman would have been romantic and factitious, and Catherine was not constituted to inspire a romantic passion. Mrs. Penniman was as fond of her as ever, but she had grown to feel that with Catherine she lacked opportunity. Sentimentally speaking, therefore, she had (though she had not disinherited her niece) adopted Morris Townsend, who gave her opportunity in abundance. She would have been very happy to have a handsome and tyrannical son, and would have taken an extreme interest in his love affairs. This was the light in which she had come to regard Morris, who had conciliated her at first, and made his impression by his delicate and calculated deference—a sort of exhibition to which Mrs. Penniman was particularly sensitive. He had largely abated his deference afterwards, for he economised his resources, but the impression was made, and the young man's very brutality came to have a sort of filial value. If Mrs. Penniman had had a son, she would probably have been afraid of him, and at this stage of our narrative she was certainly afraid of Morris Townsend. This was one of the results of his domestication in Washington Square. He took his ease with her—as, for that matter, he would certainly have done with his own mother.

XXVIII

THE LETTER was a word of warning; it informed him that the Doctor had come home more impracticable than ever. She might have reflected that Catherine would supply him with all the information he needed on this point; but we know that Mrs. Penniman's reflections were rarely just; and, moreover, she felt that it was not for her to depend on what Catherine might do. She was to do her duty, quite irrespective of Catherine. I have said that her young friend took his ease with her, and it is an illustration of the fact that he made no answer to her letter. He took note of it, amply; but he lighted his cigar with it, and he waited, in tranquil confidence that he should receive another. "His state of mind really freezes my blood," Mrs. Penniman had written, alluding to her brother; and it would have seemed that upon this statement she could hardly improve. Nevertheless, she wrote again, expressing herself with the aid of a different figure. "His hatred of you burns with a lurid flame—the flame that never dies," she wrote. "But it doesn't light up the darkness of your future. If my affection could do so, all the years of your life would be an eternal sunshine. I can extract nothing from C.; she is so terribly secretive, like her father. She seems to expect to be married very soon, and has evidently made preparations in Europe—quantities of clothing, ten pairs of shoes, etc. My dear friend, you cannot set up in married life simply with a few pairs of shoes, can you? Tell me what you think of this. I am intensely anxious to see you; I have so much to say. I miss you dreadfully; the house seems so empty without you. What is the news down town? Is the business extending? That dear little business—I think it's so brave of you! Couldn't I come to your office?—just for three minutes? I might pass for a customer—is that what you call them? I might come in to buy something—some shares or some railroad things. *Tell me what you think of this plan.* I would carry a little reticule, like a woman of the people."

In spite of the suggestion about the reticule, Morris appeared to think poorly of the plan, for he gave Mrs. Penniman no encouragement whatever to visit his office, which he had already represented to her as a place peculiarly and unnaturally difficult to find. But as she persisted in desiring an interview—up to the last, after months of intimate colloquy, she called these meetings "interviews"—he agreed that they should take a walk together, and was even kind enough to leave his office for this purpose, during the hours at which business might have been supposed to be liveliest. It was no surprise to him, when they met at a street-corner, in a region of empty lots and undeveloped pavements (Mrs. Penniman being attired as much as possible like a "woman of the people"), to find that, in spite of her urgency, what she chiefly had to convey to him was the assurance of her sympathy. Of such assurances, however, he had already a voluminous collection, and it would not have been worth his while to forsake a fruitful avocation merely to hear Mrs. Penniman say, for the thousandth time, that she had made his cause her own. Morris had something of his own to say. It was not an easy thing to bring out, and while he turned it over the difficulty made him acrimonious.

"Oh yes, I know perfectly that he combines the properties of a lump of ice and a red-hot coal," he observed. "Catherine has made it thoroughly clear, and you have told me so till I am sick of it. You needn't tell me again; I am perfectly satisfied. He will never give us a penny; I regard that as mathematically proved."

Mrs. Penniman at this point had an inspiration.

"Couldn't you bring a lawsuit against him?" She wondered that this simple expedient had never occurred to her before.

"I will bring a lawsuit against *you*," said Morris, "if you ask me any more such aggravating questions. A man should know when he is beaten," he added, in a moment. "I must give her up!"

Mrs. Penniman received this declaration in silence, though it made her heart beat a little. It found her by no means unprepared, for she had accustomed herself to the thought that, if Morris should decidedly not be able to get her brother's money, it would not do for him to marry Catherine without it. "It would not do" was a vague way of putting the thing; but Mrs. Penniman's natural affection completed the idea, which, though it had not as yet been so crudely expressed between them as in the form that Morris had just given it, had nevertheless been implied so often, in certain easy intervals of talk, as he sat stretching his legs in the Doctor's well-stuffed arm-chairs, that she had grown first to regard it with an emotion which she flattered herself was philosophic, and then to have a secret tenderness for it. The fact that she kept her tenderness secret proves, of course, that she was ashamed of it; but she managed to blink her shame by reminding herself that she was, after all, the official protector of her niece's marriage. Her logic would scarcely have passed muster with the Doctor. In the first place, Morris *must* get the money, and she would help him to it. In the second, it was plain it would never come to him, and it would be a grievous pity he should marry without it—a young man who might so easily find something better. After her brother had delivered himself, on his return from Europe, of that incisive little address that has been quoted, Morris's cause seemed so hopeless that Mrs. Penniman fixed her attention exclusively upon the latter branch of her argument. If Morris had been her son, she would certainly have sacrificed Catherine to a superior conception of his future; and to be ready to do so as the case stood was therefore even a finer degree of devotion. Nevertheless, it checked her breath a little to have the sacrificial knife, as it were, suddenly thrust into her hand.

Morris walked along a moment, and then he repeated, harshly—

"I must give her up!"

"I think I understand you," said Mrs. Penniman, gently.

"I certainly say it distinctly enough—brutally and vulgarly enough."

He was ashamed of himself, and his shame was uncomfortable; and as he was extremely intolerant of discomfort, he felt vicious and cruel. He wanted to abuse somebody, and he began, cautiously—for he was always cautious—with himself.

"Couldn't you take her down a little?" he asked.

"Take her down?"

"Prepare her—try and ease me off."

Mrs. Penniman stopped, looking at him very solemnly.

"My poor Morris, do you know how much she loves you?"

"No, I don't. I don't want to know. I have always tried to keep from knowing. It would be too painful."

"She will suffer much," said Mrs. Penniman.

"You must console her. If you are as good a friend to me as you pretend to be, you will manage it."

Mrs. Penniman shook her head, sadly.

"You talk of my 'pretending' to like you; but I can't pretend to hate you. I can only tell her I think very highly of you; and how will that console her for losing you?"

"The Doctor will help you. He will be delighted at the thing being broken off, and, as he is a knowing fellow, he will invent something to comfort her."

"He will invent a new torture!" cried Mrs. Penniman. "Heaven deliver her from her father's comfort. It will consist of his crowing over her and saying, 'I always told you so!'"

Morris coloured a most uncomfortable red.

"If you don't console her any better than you console me, you certainly won't be of much use! It's a damned disagreeable necessity; I feel it extremely, and you ought to make it easy for me."

"I will be your friend for life!" Mrs. Penniman declared.

"Be my friend *now*!" And Morris walked on.

She went with him; she was almost trembling.

"Should you like me to tell her?" she asked.

"You mustn't tell her, but you can—you can——" And he hesitated, trying to think what Mrs. Penniman could do. "You can explain to her why it is. It's because I can't bring myself to step in between her and her father—to give him the pretext he grasps at so eagerly (it's a hideous sight) for depriving her of her rights."

Mrs. Penniman felt with remarkable promptitude the charm of this formula.

"That's so like you," she said; "it's so finely felt."

Morris gave his stick an angry swing.

"Oh, botheration!" he exclaimed perversely.

Mrs. Penniman, however, was not discouraged.

"It may turn out better than you think. Catherine is, after all, so very peculiar." And she thought she might take it upon herself to assure him that, whatever happened, the girl would be very quiet—she wouldn't make a noise. They extended their walk, and, while they proceeded, Mrs. Penniman took upon herself other things besides, and ended by having assumed a considerable burden; Morris being ready enough, as may be imagined, to put everything off upon her. But he was not for a single instant the dupe of her blundering alacrity; he knew that of what she promised she was competent to perform but an insignificant fraction, and the more she professed her willingness to serve him, the greater fool he thought her.

"What will you do if you don't marry her?" she ventured to inquire in the course of this conversation.

"Something brilliant," said Morris. "Shouldn't you like me to do something brilliant?"

The idea gave Mrs. Penniman exceeding pleasure.

"I shall feel sadly taken in if you don't."

"I shall have to, to make up for this. This isn't at all brilliant, you know."

Mrs. Penniman mused a little, as if there might be some way of making out that it was; but she had to give up the attempt, and, to carry off the awkwardness of failure, she risked a new inquiry.

"Do you mean—do you mean another marriage?"

Morris greeted this question with a reflection which was hardly the less impudent from being inaudible. "Surely, women are more crude than men!" And then he answered audibly—

"Never in the world!"

Mrs. Penniman felt disappointed and snubbed, and she relieved herself in a little vaguely sarcastic cry. He was certainly perverse.

"I give her up not for another woman, but for a wider career!" Morris announced.

This was very grand; but still Mrs. Penniman, who felt that she had exposed herself, was faintly rancorous.

"Do you mean never to come to see her again?" she asked, with some sharpness.

"Oh no, I shall come again; but what is the use of dragging it out? I have been four times since she came back, and it's terribly awkward work. I can't keep it up indefinitely; she oughtn't to expect that, you know. A woman should never keep a man dangling!" he added, finely.

"Ah, but you must have your last parting!" urged his companion, in whose imagination the idea of last partings occupied a place inferior in dignity only to that of first meetings.

XXIX

HE CAME again, without managing the last parting; and again and again, without finding that Mrs. Penniman had as yet done much to pave the path of retreat with flowers. It was devilish awkward, as he said, and he felt a lively animosity for Catherine's aunt, who, as he had now quite formed the habit of saying to himself, had dragged him into the mess and was bound in common charity to get him out of it. Mrs. Penniman, to tell the truth, had, in the seclusion of her own apartment—and, I may add, amid the suggestiveness of Catherine's, which wore in those days the appearance of that of a young lady laying out her *trousseau*—Mrs. Penniman had measured her responsibilities, and taken fright at their magnitude. The task of preparing Catherine and easing off Morris presented difficulties which increased in the execution, and even led the impulsive Lavinia to ask herself whether the modification of the young man's original project had been conceived in a happy spirit. A brilliant future, a wider career, a conscience exempt from the reproach of interference between a young lady and her natural rights—these excellent things might be too troublesomely purchased. From Catherine herself Mrs. Penniman received no assistance whatever; the poor girl was apparently without suspicion of her danger. She looked at her lover with eyes of undiminished trust, and though she had less confidence in her aunt than in a young man with whom she had exchanged so many tender vows, she gave her no handle for explaining or confessing. Mrs. Penniman, faltering and wavering, declared Catherine was very stupid, put off the great scene, as she would have called it, from day to day, and wandered about very uncomfortably, primed, to repletion, with her apology, but unable to bring it to the light. Morris's own scenes were very small ones just now; but even these were beyond his strength. He made his visits as brief as possible, and, while he sat with his mistress, found terribly little to talk about. She was waiting for him, in vulgar parlance, to name the day; and so long as he was unprepared to be explicit on this point, it seemed a mockery to pretend to talk about matters more abstract. She had no airs and no arts; she never attempted to disguise her expectancy. She was waiting on his good pleasure, and would wait modestly and patiently; his hanging back at this supreme time might appear strange, but of course he must have a good reason for it. Catherine would have made a wife of the gentle old-fashioned pattern—regarding reasons as favours and windfalls, but no more expecting one every day than she would have expected a bouquet of camellias. During the period of her engagement, however, a young lady even of the most slender pretensions counts upon more bouquets than at other times; and there was a want of perfume in the air at this moment which at last excited the girl's alarm.

"Are you sick?" she asked of Morris. "You seem so restless, and you look pale."

"I am not at all well," said Morris; and it occurred to him that, if he could only make her pity him enough, he might get off.

"I am afraid you are overworked; you oughtn't to work so much."

"I must do that." And then he added, with a sort of calculated brutality, "I don't want to owe you everything!"

"Ah, how can you say that?"

"I am too proud," said Morris.

"Yes—you are too proud!"

"Well, you must take me as I am," he went on; "you can never change me."

"I don't want to change you," she said, gently. "I will take you as you are!" And she stood looking at him.

"You know people talk tremendously about a man's marrying a rich girl," Morris remarked. "It's excessively disagreeable."

"But I am not rich!" said Catherine.

"You are rich enough to make me talked about!"

"Of course you are talked about. It's an honour!"

"It's an honour I could easily dispense with."

She was on the point of asking him whether it were not a compensation for this annoyance that the poor girl who had the misfortune to bring it upon him, loved him so dearly and believed in him so truly; but she hesitated, thinking that this would perhaps seem an exacting speech, and while she hesitated, he suddenly left her.

The next time he came, however, she brought it out, and she told him again that he was too proud. He repeated that he couldn't change, and this time she felt the impulse to say that with a little effort he might change.

Sometimes he thought that if he could only make a quarrel with her it might help him; but the question was how to quarrel with a young woman who had such treasures of concession. "I suppose you think the effort is all on your side!" he was reduced to exclaiming. "Don't you believe that I have my own effort to make?"

"It's all yours now," she said. "My effort is finished and done with!"

"Well, mine is not."

"We must bear things together," said Catherine. "That's what we ought to do."

Morris attempted a natural smile. "There are some things which we can't very well bear together—for instance, separation."

"Why do you speak of separation?"

"Ah! you don't like it; I knew you wouldn't!"

"Where are you going, Morris?" she suddenly asked.

He fixed his eye on her for a moment, and for a part of that moment she was afraid of it. "Will you promise not to make a scene?"

"A scene!—do I make scenes?"

"All women do!" said Morris, with the tone of large experience.

"I don't. Where are you going?"

"If I should say I was going away on business, should you think it very strange?"

She wondered a moment, gazing at him. "Yes—no. Not if you will take me with you."

"Take you with me—on business?"

"What is your business? Your business is to be with me."

"I don't earn my living with you," said Morris. "Or rather," he cried with a sudden inspiration, "that's just what I do—or what the world says I do!"

This ought perhaps to have been a great stroke, but it miscarried. "Where are you going?" Catherine simply repeated.

"To New Orleans. About buying some cotton."

"I am perfectly willing to go to New Orleans," Catherine said.

"Do you suppose I would take you to a nest of yellow fever?" cried Morris. "Do you suppose I would expose you at such a time as this?"

"If there is yellow fever, why should you go? Morris, you must not go!"

"It is to make six thousand dollars," said Morris. "Do you grudge me that satisfaction?"

"We have no need of six thousand dollars. You think too much about money!"

"You can afford to say that! This is a great chance; we heard of it last night." And he explained to her in what the chance consisted; and told her a long story, going over more than once several of the details, about the remarkable stroke of business which he and his partner had planned between them.

But Catherine's imagination, for reasons best known to herself, absolutely refused to be fired. "If you can go to New Orleans, I can go," she said. "Why shouldn't you catch yellow fever quite as easily as I? I am every bit as strong as you, and not in the least afraid of any fever. When we were in Europe, we were in very unhealthy places; my father used to make me take some pills. I never caught anything, and I never was nervous.

What will be the use of six thousand dollars if you die of a fever? When persons are going to be married, they oughtn't to think so much about business. You shouldn't think about cotton, you should think about me. You can go to New Orleans some other time—there will always be plenty of cotton. It isn't the moment to choose—we have waited too long already." She spoke more forcibly and volubly than he had ever heard her, and she held his arm in her two hands.

"You said you wouldn't make a scene!" cried Morris. "I call this a scene."

"It's you that are making it! I have never asked you anything before. We have waited too long already." And it was a comfort to her to think that she had hitherto asked so little; it seemed to make her right to insist the greater now.

Morris bethought himself a little. "Very well, then; we won't talk about it any more. I will transact my business by letter." And he began to smooth his hat, as if to take leave.

"You won't go?" And she stood looking up at him.

He could not give up his idea of provoking a quarrel; it was so much the simplest way! He bent his eyes on her upturned face, with the darkest frown he could achieve. "You are not discreet. You mustn't bully me!"

But, as usual, she conceded everything. "No, I am not discreet; I know I am too pressing. But isn't it natural? It is only for a moment."

"In a moment you may do a great deal of harm. Try and be calmer the next time I come."

"When will you come?"

"Do you want to make conditions?" Morris asked. "I will come next Saturday."

"Come to-morrow," Catherine begged; "I want you to come to-morrow. I will be very quiet," she added; and her agitation had by this time become so great that the assurance was not becoming. A sudden fear had come over her; it was like the solid conjunction of a dozen disembodied doubts, and her imagination, at a single bound, had traversed an enormous distance. All her being, for the moment, centred in the wish to keep him in the room.

Morris bent his head and kissed her forehead. "When you are quiet, you are perfection," he said; "but when you are violent, you are not in character."

It was Catherine's wish that there should be no violence about her save the beating of her heart, which she could not help; and she went on, as gently as possible, "Will you promise to come to-morrow?"

"I said Saturday!" Morris answered, smiling. He tried a frown at one moment, a smile at another; he was at his wit's end.

"Yes, Saturday too," she answered, trying to smile. "But to-morrow first." He was going to the door, and she went with him quickly. She leaned her shoulder against it; it seemed to her that she would do anything to keep him.

"If I am prevented from coming to-morrow, you will say I have deceived you!" he said.

"How can you be prevented? You can come if you will."

"I am a busy man—I am not a dangler!" cried Morris, sternly.

His voice was so hard and unnatural that, with a helpless look at him, she turned away; and then he quickly laid his hand on the door-knob. He felt as if he were absolutely running away from her. But in an instant she was close to him again, and murmuring in a tone none the less penetrating for being low, "Morris, you are going to leave me."

"Yes, for a little while."

"For how long?"

"Till you are reasonable again."

"I shall never be reasonable in that way!" And she tried to keep him longer; it was almost a struggle. "Think of what I have done!" she broke out. "Morris, I have given up everything!"

"You shall have everything back!"

"You wouldn't say that if you didn't mean something. What is it?—what has happened?—what have I done?—what has changed you?"

"I will write to you—that is better," Morris stammered.

"Ah, you won't come back!" she cried, bursting into tears.

"Dear Catherine," he said, "don't believe that! I promise you that you shall see me again!" And he managed to get away and to close the door behind him.

XXX

IT WAS almost her last outbreak of passive grief; at least, she never indulged in another that the world knew anything about. But this one was long and terrible; she flung herself on the sofa and gave herself up to her misery. She hardly knew what had happened; ostensibly she had only had a difference with her lover, as other girls had had before, and the thing was not only not a rupture, but she was under no obligation to regard it even as a menace. Nevertheless, she felt a wound, even if he had not dealt it; it seemed to her that a mask had suddenly fallen from his face. He had wished to get away from her; he had been angry and cruel, and said strange things, with strange looks. She was smothered and stunned; she buried her head in the cushions, sobbing and talking to herself. But at last she raised herself, with the fear that either her father or Mrs. Penniman would come in; and then she sat there, staring before her, while the room grew darker. She said to herself that perhaps he would come back to tell her he had not meant what he said; and she listened for his ring at the door, trying to believe that this was probable. A long time passed, but Morris remained absent; the shadows gathered; the evening settled down on the meagre elegance of the light, clear-coloured room; the fire went out. When it had grown dark, Catherine went to the window and looked out; she stood there for half an hour, on the mere chance that he would come up the steps. At last she turned away, for she saw her father come in. He had seen her at the window looking out, and he stopped a moment at the bottom of the white steps, and gravely, with an air of exaggerated courtesy, lifted his hat to her. The gesture was so incongruous to the condition she was in, this stately tribute of respect to a poor girl despised and forsaken was so out of place, that the thing gave her a kind of horror, and she hurried away to her room. It seemed to her that she had given Morris up.

She had to show herself half an hour later, and she was sustained at table by the immensity of her desire that her father should not perceive that anything had happened. This was a great help to her afterwards, and it served her (though never as much as she supposed) from the first. On this occasion Dr. Sloper was rather talkative. He told a great many stories about a wonderful poodle that he had seen at the house of an old lady whom he visited professionally. Catherine not only tried to appear to listen to the anecdotes of the poodle, but she endeavoured to interest herself in them, so as not to think of her scene with Morris. That perhaps was an hallucination; he was mistaken, she was jealous; people didn't change like that from one day to another. Then she knew that she had had doubts before—strange suspicions, that were at once vague and acute—and that he had been different ever since her return from Europe: whereupon she tried again to listen to her father, who told a story so remarkably well. Afterwards she went straight to her own room; it was beyond her strength to undertake to spend the evening with her aunt. All the evening, alone, she questioned herself. Her trouble was terrible; but was it a thing of her imagination, engendered by an extravagant sensibility, or did it represent a clear-cut reality, and had the worst that was possible actually come to pass? Mrs. Penniman, with a degree of tact that was as unusual as it was commendable, took the line of leaving her alone. The truth is, that her suspicions having been aroused, she indulged a desire, natural to a timid person, that the explosion should be localised. So long as the air still vibrated she kept out of the way.

She passed and repassed Catherine's door several times in the course of the evening, as if she expected to hear a plaintive moan behind it. But the room remained perfectly still; and accordingly, the last thing before retiring to her own couch, she applied for admittance. Catherine was sitting up, and had a book that she pretended to be reading. She had no wish to go to bed, for she had no expectation of sleeping. After Mrs. Penniman had left her she sat up half the night, and she offered her visitor no inducement to remain. Her aunt came stealing in very gently, and approached her with great solemnity.

"I am afraid you are in trouble, my dear. Can I do anything to help you?"

"I am not in any trouble whatever, and do not need any help," said Catherine, fibbing roundly, and proving thereby that not only our faults, but our most involuntary misfortunes, tend to corrupt our morals.

"Has nothing happened to you?"

"Nothing whatever."

"Are you very sure, dear?"

"Perfectly sure."

"And can I really do nothing for you?"

"Nothing, aunt, but kindly leave me alone," said Catherine.

Mrs. Penniman, though she had been afraid of too warm a welcome before, was now disappointed at so cold a one; and in relating afterwards, as she did to many persons, and with considerable variations of detail, the history of the termination of her niece's engagement, she was usually careful to mention that the young lady, on a certain occasion, had "hustled" her out of the room. It was characteristic of Mrs. Penniman that she related this fact, not in the least out of malignity to Catherine, whom she very sufficiently pitied, but simply from a natural disposition to embellish any subject that she touched.

Catherine, as I have said, sat up half the night, as if she still expected to hear Morris Townsend ring at the door. On the morrow this expectation was less unreasonable; but it was not gratified by the reappearance of the young man. Neither had he written; there was not a word of explanation or reassurance. Fortunately for Catherine she could take refuge from her excitement, which had now become intense, in her determination that her father should see nothing of it. How well she deceived her father we shall have occasion to learn; but her innocent arts were of little avail before a person of the rare perspicacity of Mrs. Penniman. This lady easily saw that she was agitated, and if there was any agitation going forward, Mrs. Penniman was not a person to forfeit her natural share in it. She returned to the charge the next evening, and requested her niece to lean upon her—to unburden her heart. Perhaps she should be able to explain certain things that now seemed dark, and that she knew more about than Catherine supposed. If Catherine had been frigid the night before, to-day she was haughty.

"You are completely mistaken, and I have not the least idea what you mean. I don't know what you are trying to fasten on me, and I have never had less need of any one's explanations in my life."

In this way the girl delivered herself, and from hour to hour kept her aunt at bay. From hour to hour Mrs. Penniman's curiosity grew. She would have given her little finger to know what Morris had said and done, what tone he had taken, what pretext he had found. She wrote to him, naturally, to request an interview; but she received, as naturally, no answer to her petition. Morris was not in a writing mood; for Catherine had addressed him two short notes which met with no acknowledgment. These notes were so brief that I may give them entire. "Won't you give me some sign that you didn't mean to be so cruel as you seemed on Tuesday?"—that was the first; the other was a little longer. "If I was unreasonable or suspicious, on Tuesday—if I annoyed you or troubled you in any way—I beg your forgiveness, and I promise never again to be so foolish. I am punished enough, and I don't understand. Dear Morris, you are killing me!" These notes were despatched on the Friday and Saturday; but Saturday and Sunday passed without bringing the poor girl the satisfaction she desired. Her punishment accumulated; she continued to bear it, however, with a good deal of superficial fortitude. On Saturday morning, the Doctor, who had been watching in silence, spoke to his sister Lavinia.

"The thing has happened—the scoundrel has backed out!"

"Never!" cried Mrs. Penniman, who had bethought herself what she should say to Catherine, but was not provided with a line of defence against her brother, so that indignant negation was the only weapon in her hands.

"He has begged for a reprieve, then, if you like that better!"

"It seems to make you very happy that your daughter's affections have been trifled with."

"It does," said the Doctor; "for I had foretold it! It's a great pleasure to be in the right."

"Your pleasures make one shudder!" his sister exclaimed.

Catherine went rigidly through her usual occupations; that is, up to the point of going with her aunt to church on Sunday morning. She generally went to afternoon service as well; but on this occasion her courage faltered, and she begged of Mrs. Penniman to go without her.

"I am sure you have a secret," said Mrs. Penniman, with great significance, looking at her rather grimly.

"If I have, I shall keep it!" Catherine answered, turning away.

Mrs. Penniman started for church; but before she had arrived, she stopped and turned back, and before twenty minutes had elapsed she re-entered the house, looked into the empty parlours, and then went upstairs and knocked at Catherine's door. She got no answer; Catherine was not in her room, and Mrs. Penniman presently ascertained that she was not in the house. "She has gone to him, she has fled!" Lavinia cried, clasping her hands with admiration and envy. But she soon perceived that Catherine had taken nothing with her—all her personal property in her room was intact—and then she jumped at the hypothesis that the girl had gone forth, not in tenderness, but in resentment. "She has followed him to his own door—she has burst upon him in his own apartment!" It was in these terms that Mrs. Penniman depicted to herself her niece's errand, which, viewed in this light, gratified her sense of the picturesque only a shade less strongly than the idea of a clandestine marriage. To visit one's lover, with tears and re-proaches, at his own residence, was an image so agreeable to Mrs. Penniman's mind that she felt a sort of aesthetic disap-pointment at its lacking, in this case, the harmonious accompa-niments of darkness and storm. A quiet Sunday afternoon appeared an inadequate setting for it; and, indeed, Mrs. Penni-man was quite out of humour with the conditions of the time, which passed very slowly as she sat in the front parlour in her bonnet and her cashmere shawl, awaiting Catherine's return.

This event at last took place. She saw her—at the window—mount the steps, and she went to await her in the hall, where she pounced upon her as soon as she had entered the house, and drew her into the parlour, closing the door with solemnity. Catherine was flushed, and her eye was bright. Mrs. Penniman hardly knew what to think.

"May I venture to ask where you have been?" she demanded.

"I have been to take a walk," said Catherine. "I thought you had gone to church."

"I did go to church; but the service was shorter than usual. And pray where did you walk?"

"I don't know!" said Catherine.

"Your ignorance is most extraordinary! Dear Catherine, you can trust me."

"What am I to trust you with?"

"With your secret—your sorrow."

"I have no sorrow!" said Catherine fiercely.

"My poor child," Mrs. Penniman insisted, "you can't deceive me. I know everything. I have been requested to—a—to con-verse with you."

"I don't want to converse!"

"It will relieve you. Don't you know Shakespeare's lines?—'the grief that does not speak!' My dear girl, it is better as it is."

"What is better?" Catherine asked.

She was really too perverse. A certain amount of perversity was to be allowed for in a young lady whose lover had thrown her over; but not such an amount as would prove inconvenient to his apologists. "That you should be reasonable," said Mrs. Penniman, with some sternness. "That you should take counsel of worldly prudence, and submit to practical considerations. That you should agree to—a—separate."

Catherine had been ice up to this moment, but at this word she flamed up. "Separate? What do you know about our separating?"

Mrs. Penniman shook her head with a sadness in which there was almost a sense of injury. "Your pride is my pride, and your susceptibilities are mine. I see your side perfectly, but I also"—and she smiled with melancholy suggestiveness—"I also see the situation as a whole!"

This suggestiveness was lost upon Catherine, who repeated her violent inquiry. "Why do you talk about separation; what do you know about it?"

"We must study resignation," said Mrs. Penniman, hesitating, but sententious at a venture.

"Resignation to what?"

"To a change of—of our plans."

"My plans have not changed!" said Catherine, with a little laugh.

"Ah, but Mr. Townsend's have," her aunt answered very gently.

"What do you mean?"

There was an imperious brevity in the tone of this inquiry, against which Mrs. Penniman felt bound to protest; the information with which she had undertaken to supply her niece was after all a favour. She had tried sharpness, and she had tried sternness; but neither would do; she was shocked at the girl's obstinacy. "Ah, well," she said, "if he hasn't told you!..." and she turned away.

Catherine watched her a moment in silence; then she hurried after her, stopping her before she reached the door. "Told me what? What do you mean? What are you hinting at and threatening me with?"

"Isn't it broken off?" asked Mrs. Penniman.

"My engagement? Not in the least!"

"I beg your pardon in that case. I have spoken too soon!"

"Too soon! Soon or late," Catherine broke out, "you speak foolishly and cruelly!"

"What has happened between you, then?" asked her aunt, struck by the sincerity of this cry. "For something certainly has happened."

"Nothing has happened but that I love him more and more!"

Mrs. Penniman was silent an instant. "I suppose that's the reason you went to see him this afternoon."

Catherine flushed as if she had been struck. "Yes, I did go to see him! But that's my own business."

"Very well, then; we won't talk about it." And Mrs. Penniman moved towards the door again. But she was stopped by a sudden imploring cry from the girl.

"Aunt Lavinia, *where* has he gone?"

"Ah, you admit then that he has gone away? Didn't they know at his house?"

"They said he had left town. I asked no more questions; I was ashamed," said Catherine, simply enough.

"You needn't have taken so compromising a step if you had had a little more confidence in me," Mrs. Penniman observed, with a good deal of grandeur.

"Is it to New Orleans?" Catherine went on, irrelevantly.

It was the first time Mrs. Penniman had heard of New Orleans in this connection; but she was averse to letting Catherine know that she was in the dark. She attempted to strike an illumination from the instructions she had received from Morris. "My dear Catherine," she said, "when a separation has been agreed upon, the farther he goes away the better."

"Agreed upon? Has he agreed upon it with you?" A consummate sense of her aunt's meddlesome folly had come over her during the last five minutes, and she was sickened at the thought that Mrs. Penniman had been let loose, as it were, upon her happiness.

"He certainly has sometimes advised with me," said Mrs. Penniman.

"Is it you, then, that have changed him and made him so unnatural?" Catherine cried. "Is it you that have worked on him and taken him from me? He doesn't belong to you, and I don't see how you have anything to do with what is between us! Is it you that have made this plot and told him to leave me? How could you be so wicked, so cruel? What have I ever done to you; why can't you leave me alone? I was afraid you would spoil everything; for you *do* spoil everything you touch! I was afraid of you all the time we were abroad; I had no rest when I thought that you were always talking to him." Catherine went on with growing vehemence, pouring out in her bitterness and in the clairvoyance of her passion (which suddenly, jumping all processes, made her judge her aunt finally and without appeal), the uneasiness which had lain for so many months upon her heart.

Mrs. Penniman was scared and bewildered; she saw no prospect of introducing her little account of the purity of Morris's motives. "You are a most ungrateful girl!" she cried. "Do you scold me for talking with him? I am sure we never talked of anything but you!"

"Yes; and that was the way you worried him; you made him tired of my very name! I wish you had never spoken of me to him; I never asked your help!"

"I am sure if it hadn't been for me he would never have come to the house, and you would never have known what he thought of you," Mrs. Penniman rejoined, with a good deal of justice.

"I wish he never had come to the house, and that I never had known it! That's better than this," said poor Catherine.

"You are a very ungrateful girl," Aunt Lavinia repeated.

Catherine's outbreak of anger and the sense of wrong gave her, while they lasted, the satisfaction that comes from all assertion of force; they hurried her along, and there is always a sort of pleasure in cleaving the air. But at the bottom she hated to be violent, and she was conscious of no aptitude for organised resentment. She calmed herself with a great effort, but with great rapidity, and walked about the room a few moments, trying to say to herself that her aunt had meant everything for the best. She did not succeed in saying it with much conviction, but after a little she was able to speak quietly enough.

"I am not ungrateful, but I am very unhappy. It's hard to be grateful for that," she said. "Will you please tell me where he is?"

"I haven't the least idea; I am not in secret correspondence with him!" And Mrs. Penniman wished indeed that she were, so that she might let him know how Catherine abused her, after all she had done.

"Was it a plan of his, then, to break off——?" By this time Catherine had become completely quiet.

Mrs. Penniman began again to have a glimpse of her chance for explaining. "He shrank—he shrank," she said. "He lacked courage, but it was the courage to injure you! He couldn't bear to bring down on you your father's curse."

Catherine listened to this with her eyes fixed upon her aunt, and continued to gaze at her for some time afterwards. "Did he tell you to say that?"

"He told me to say many things—all so delicate, so discriminating. And he told me to tell you he hoped you wouldn't despise him."

"I don't," said Catherine. And then she added: "And will he stay away for ever?"

"Oh, for ever is a long time. Your father, perhaps, won't live for ever."

"Perhaps not."

"I am sure you appreciate—you understand—even though your heart bleeds," said Mrs. Penniman. "You doubtless think him too scrupulous. So do I, but I respect his scruples. What he asks of you is that you should do the same."

Catherine was still gazing at her aunt, but she spoke at last, as if she had not heard or not understood her. "It has been a regular plan, then. He has broken it off deliberately; he has given me up."

"For the present, dear Catherine. He has put it off only."

"He has left me alone," Catherine went on.

"Haven't you *me*?" asked Mrs. Penniman, with much expression.

Catherine shook her head slowly. "I don't believe it!" and she left the room.

XXXI

THOUGH she had forced herself to be calm, she preferred practising this virtue in private, and she forbore to show herself at tea—a repast which, on Sundays, at six o'clock, took the place of dinner. Dr. Sloper and his sister sat face to face, but Mrs. Penniman never met her brother's eye. Late in the evening she went with him, but without Catherine, to their sister Almond's, where, between the two ladies, Catherine's unhappy situation was discussed with a frankness that was conditioned by a good deal of mysterious reticence on Mrs. Penniman's part.

"I am delighted he is not to marry her," said Mrs. Almond, "but he ought to be horsewhipped all the same."

Mrs. Penniman, who was shocked at her sister's coarseness, replied that he had been actuated by the noblest of motives—the desire not to impoverish Catherine.

"I am very happy that Catherine is not to be impoverished—but I hope he may never have a penny too much! And what does the poor girl say to *you*?" Mrs. Almond asked.

"She says I have a genius for consolation," said Mrs. Penniman.

This was the account of the matter that she gave to her sister, and it was perhaps with the consciousness of genius that, on her return that evening to Washington Square, she again presented herself for admittance at Catherine's door. Catherine came and opened it; she was apparently very quiet.

"I only want to give you a little word of advice," she said. "If your father asks you, say that everything is going on."

Catherine stood there, with her hand on the knob looking at her aunt, but not asking her to come in. "Do you think he will ask me?"

"I am sure he will. He asked me just now, on our way home from your Aunt Elizabeth's. I explained the whole thing to your Aunt Elizabeth. I said to your father I know nothing about it."

"Do you think he will ask me, when he sees—when he sees——?" But here Catherine stopped.

"The more he sees, the more disagreeable he will be," said her aunt.

"He shall see as little as possible!" Catherine declared.

"Tell him you are to be married."

"So I am," said Catherine, softly; and she closed the door upon her aunt.

She could not have said this two days later—for instance, on Tuesday, when she at last received a letter from Morris Townsend. It was an epistle of considerable length, measuring five large square pages, and written at Philadelphia. It was an explanatory document, and it explained a great many things, chief among which were the considerations that had led the writer to take advantage of an urgent "professional" absence to try and banish from his mind the image of one whose path he had crossed only to scatter it with ruins. He ventured to expect but partial success in this attempt, but he could promise her that, whatever his failure, he would never again interpose between her generous heart and her brilliant prospects and filial duties. He closed with an intimation that his professional pursuits might compel him to travel for some months, and with the hope that when they should each have accommodated themselves to what was sternly involved in their respective positions—even should this result not be reached for years—they should meet as friends, as fellow-sufferers, as innocent but philosophic victims of a great social law. That her life should be peaceful and happy was the dearest wish of him who ventured still to subscribe himself her most obedient servant. The letter was beautifully written, and Catherine, who kept it for many years after this, was able, when her sense of the bitterness of its meaning and the hollowness of its tone had grown less acute, to admire its grace of expression. At present, for a long time after she received it, all she had to help her was the determination, daily more rigid, to make no appeal to the compassion of her father.

He suffered a week to elapse, and then one day, in the morning, at an hour at which she rarely saw him, he strolled into the back-parlour. He had watched his time, and he found her alone. She was sitting with some work, and he came and stood in front of her. He was going out, he had on his hat and was drawing on his gloves.

"It doesn't seem to me that you are treating me just now with all the consideration I deserve," he said in a moment.

"I don't know what I have done," Catherine answered, with her eyes on her work.

"You have apparently quite banished from your mind the request I made you at Liverpool, before we sailed; the request that you would notify me in advance before leaving my house."

"I have not left your house!" said Catherine.

"But you intend to leave it, and by what you gave me to understand, your departure must be impending. In fact, though you are still here in body, you are already absent in spirit. Your mind has taken up its residence with your prospective husband, and you might quite as well be lodged under the conjugal roof, for all the benefit we get from your society."

"I will try and be more cheerful!" said Catherine.

"You certainly ought to be cheerful, you ask a great deal if you are not. To the pleasure of marrying a brilliant young man, you add that of having your own way; you strike me as a very lucky young lady!"

Catherine got up; she was suffocating. But she folded her work, deliberately and correctly, bending her burning face upon it. Her father stood where he had planted himself; she hoped he would go, but he smoothed and buttoned his gloves, and then he rested his hands upon his hips.

"It would be a convenience to me to know when I may expect to have an empty house," he went on. "When you go, your aunt marches."

She looked at him at last, with a long silent gaze, which, in spite of her pride and her resolution, uttered part of the appeal she had tried not to make. Her father's cold gray eye sounded her own, and he insisted on his point.

"Is it to-morrow? Is it next week, or the week after?"

"I shall not go away!" said Catherine.

The Doctor raised his eyebrows. "Has he backed out?"

"I have broken off my engagement."

"Broken it off?"

"I have asked him to leave New York, and he has gone away for a long time."

The Doctor was both puzzled and disappointed, but he solved his perplexity by saying to himself that his daughter simply misrepresented—justifiably, if one would, but nevertheless, misrepresented—the facts; and he eased off his disappointment, which was that of a man losing a chance for a little triumph that he had rather counted on, by a few words that he uttered aloud.

"How does he take his dismissal?"

"I don't know!" said Catherine, less ingeniously than she had hitherto spoken.

"You mean you don't care? You are rather cruel, after encouraging him and playing with him for so long!"

The Doctor had his revenge after all.

XXXII

OUR STORY has hitherto moved with very short steps, but as it approaches its termination it must take a long stride. As time went on, it might have appeared to the Doctor that his daughter's account of her rupture with Morris Townsend, mere bravado as he had deemed it, was in some degree justified by the sequel. Morris remained as rigidly and unremittingly absent as if he had died of a broken heart, and Catherine had apparently buried the memory of this fruitless episode as deep as if it had terminated by her own choice. We know that she had been deeply and incurably wounded, but the Doctor had no means of knowing it. He was certainly curious about it, and would have given a good deal to discover the exact truth; but it was his punishment that he never knew—his punishment, I mean, for the abuse of sarcasm in his relations with his daughter. There was a good deal of effective sarcasm in her keeping him in the dark, and the rest of the world conspired with her, in this sense, to be sarcastic. Mrs. Penniman told him nothing, partly because he never questioned her—he made too light of Mrs. Penniman for that—and partly because she flattered herself that a tormenting reserve, and a serene profession of ignorance, would avenge her for his theory that she had meddled in the matter. He went two or three times to see Mrs. Montgomery, but Mrs. Montgomery had nothing to impart. She simply knew that her brother's engagement was broken off, and now that Miss Sloper was out of danger, she preferred not to bear witness in any way against Morris. She had done so before— however unwillingly—because she was sorry for Miss Sloper; but she was not sorry for Miss Sloper now—not at all sorry. Morris had told her nothing about his relations with Miss Sloper at the time, and he had told her nothing since. He was always away, and he very seldom wrote to her; she believed he had gone to California. Mrs. Almond had, in her sister's phrase, "taken up" Catherine violently since the recent catastrophe; but though the girl was very grateful to her for her kindness, she revealed no secrets, and the good lady could give the Doctor no satisfaction. Even, however, had she been able to narrate to him the private history of his daughter's unhappy love-affair, it would have given her a certain comfort to leave him in ignorance; for Mrs. Almond was at this time not altogether in sympathy with her brother. She had guessed for herself that Catherine had been cruelly jilted—she knew nothing from Mrs. Penniman, for Mrs. Penniman had not ventured to lay the famous explanation of Morris's motives before Mrs. Almond, though she had thought it good enough for Catherine—and she pronounced her brother too consistently indifferent to what the poor creature must have suffered and must still be suffering. Dr. Sloper had his theory, and he rarely altered his theories. The marriage would have been an abominable one, and the girl had had a blessed escape. She was not to be pitied for that, and to pretend to condole with her would have been to make concessions to the idea that she had ever had a right to think of Morris.

"I put my foot on this idea from the first, and I keep it there now," said the Doctor. "I don't see anything cruel in that; one can't keep it there too long." To this Mrs. Almond more than once replied that if Catherine had got rid of her incongruous lover, she deserved the credit of it, and that to bring herself to her father's enlightened view of the matter must have cost her an effort that he was bound to appreciate.

"I am by no means sure she has got rid of him," the Doctor said. "There is not the smallest probability that, after having been as obstinate as a mule for two years, she suddenly became amenable to reason. It is infinitely more probable that he got rid of her."

"All the more reason you should be gentle with her."

"I *am* gentle with her. But I can't do the pathetic; I can't pump up tears, to look graceful, over the most fortunate thing that ever happened to her."

"You have no sympathy," said Mrs. Almond; "that was never your strong point. You have only to look at her to see that, right or wrong, and whether the rupture came from herself or from him, her poor little heart is grievously bruised."

"Handling bruises—and even dropping tears on them— doesn't make them any better! My business is to see she gets no more knocks, and that I shall carefully attend to. But I don't at all recognise your description of Catherine. She doesn't strike me in the least as a young woman going about in search of a moral poultice. In fact, she seems to me much better than while the fellow was hanging about. She is perfectly comfortable and blooming; she eats and sleeps, takes her usual exercise, and overloads herself, as usual, with finery. She is always knitting some purse or embroidering some handkerchief, and it seems to me she turns these articles out about as fast as ever. She hasn't much to say; but when had she anything to say? She had her little dance, and now she is sitting down to rest. I suspect that, on the whole, she enjoys it."

"She enjoys it as people enjoy getting rid of a leg that has been crushed. The state of mind after amputation is doubtless one of comparative repose."

"If your leg is a metaphor for young Townsend, I can assure you he has never been crushed. Crushed? Not he! He is alive and perfectly intact, and that's why I am not satisfied."

"Should you have liked to kill him?" asked Mrs. Almond.

"Yes, very much. I think it is quite possible that it is all a blind."

"A blind?"

"An arrangement between them. *Il fait le mort*, as they say in France; but he is looking out of the corner of his eye. You can depend upon it he has not burned his ships; he has kept one to come back in. When I am dead, he will set sail again, and then she will marry him."

"It is interesting to know that you accuse your only daughter of being the vilest of hypocrites," said Mrs. Almond.

"I don't see what difference her being my only daughter makes. It is better to accuse one than a dozen. But I don't accuse any one. There is not the smallest hypocrisy about Catherine, and I deny that she even pretends to be miserable."

The Doctor's idea that the thing was a "blind" had its intermissions and revivals; but it may be said on the whole to have increased as he grew older; together with his impression of Catherine's blooming and comfortable condition. Naturally, if he had not found grounds for viewing her as a lovelorn maiden during the year or two that followed her great trouble, he found none at a time when she had completely recovered her self-possession. He was obliged to recognise the fact that if the two young people were waiting for him to get out of the way, they were at least waiting very patiently. He had heard from time to time that Morris was in New York; but he never remained there long, and, to the best of the Doctor's belief, had no communication with Catherine. He was sure they never met, and he had reason to suspect that Morris never wrote to her. After the letter that has been mentioned, she heard from him twice again, at considerable intervals; but on none of these occasions did she write herself. On the other hand, as the Doctor observed, she averted herself rigidly from the idea of marrying other people. Her opportunities for doing so were not numerous, but they occurred often enough to test her disposition. She refused a widower, a man with a genial temperament, a handsome fortune, and three little girls (he had heard that she was very fond of children, and he pointed to his own with some confidence); and she turned a deaf ear to the solicitations of a clever young lawyer, who, with the prospect of a great practice, and the reputation of a most agreeable man, had had the shrewdness, when he came to look about him for a wife, to believe that she would suit him better than several younger and prettier girls. Mr. Macalister, the widower, had desired to make a marriage of reason, and had chosen Catherine for what he supposed to be her latent matronly qualities; but John Ludlow, who was a year the girl's junior, and spoken of always as a young man who might have his "pick," was seriously in love with her. Catherine, however, would never look at him; she made it plain to him that she thought he came to see her too often. He afterwards consoled himself, and married a very different person, little Miss Sturtevant, whose attractions were obvious to the dullest comprehension. Catherine, at the time of these events, had left her thirtieth year well behind her, and had quite taken her place as an old maid. Her father would have preferred she should marry, and he once told her that he hoped she would not be too fastidious. "I should like to see you an honest man's wife before I die," he said. This was after John Ludlow had been compelled to give it up, though the Doctor had advised him to persevere. The Doctor exercised no further pressure, and had the credit of not "worrying" at all over his daughter's singleness. In fact he worried rather more than appeared, and there were considerable periods during which he felt sure that Morris Townsend was hidden behind some door. "If he is not, why doesn't she marry?" he asked himself. "Limited as her intelligence may be, she must understand perfectly well that she is made to do the usual thing." Catherine, however, became an admirable old maid. She formed habits, regulated her days upon a system of her own, interested herself in charitable institutions, asylums, hospitals, and aid-societies; and went generally, with an even and noiseless step, about the rigid business of her life. This life had, however, a secret history as well as a public one—if I may talk of the public history of a mature and diffident spinster for whom publicity had always a combination of terrors. From her own point of view the great facts of her career were that Morris Townsend had trifled with her affection, and that her father had broken its spring. Nothing could ever alter these facts; they were always there, like her name, her age, her plain face. Nothing could ever undo the wrong or cure the pain that Morris had inflicted on her, and nothing could ever make her feel towards her father as she felt in her younger years. There was something dead in her life, and her duty was to try and fill the void. Catherine recognised this duty to the utmost; she had a great disapproval of brooding and moping. She had of course no faculty for quenching memory in dissipation; but she mingled freely in the usual gaieties of the town, and she became at last an inevitable figure at all respectable entertainments. She was greatly liked, and as time went on she grew to be a sort of kindly maiden-aunt to the younger portion of society. Young girls were apt to confide to her their love-affairs (which they never did to Mrs. Penniman), and young men to be fond of her without knowing why. She developed a few harmless eccentricities; her habits, once formed, were rather stiffly maintained; her opinions, on all moral and social matters, were extremely conservative; and before she was forty she was regarded as an old-fashioned person, and an authority on customs that had passed away. Mrs. Penniman, in comparison, was quite a girlish figure; she grew younger as she advanced in life. She lost none of her relish for beauty and mystery, but she had little opportunity to exercise it. With Catherine's later wooers she failed to establish relations as intimate as those which had given her so many interesting hours in the society of Morris Townsend. These gentlemen had an indefinable mistrust of her good offices, and they never talked to her about Catherine's charms. Her ringlets, her buckles and bangles glistened more brightly with each succeeding year, and she remained quite the same officious and imaginative Mrs. Penniman, and the odd mixture of impetuosity and circumspection, that we have hitherto known. As regards one point, however, her circumspection prevailed, and she must be given due credit for it. For upwards of seventeen years she never mentioned Morris Townsend's name to her niece. Catherine was grateful to her, but this consistent silence, so little in accord with her aunt's character, gave her a certain alarm, and she could never wholly rid herself of a suspicion that Mrs. Penniman sometimes had news of him.

XXXIII

LITTLE by little Dr. Sloper had retired from his profession; he visited only those patients in whose symptoms he recognised a certain originality. He went again to Europe, and remained two years; Catherine went with him, and on this occasion Mrs. Penniman was of the party. Europe apparently had few surprises for Mrs. Penniman, who frequently remarked, in the most romantic sites—"You know I am very familiar with all this." It should be added that such remarks were usually not addressed to her brother, or yet to her niece, but to fellow-tourists who happened to be at hand, or even to the cicerone or the goat-herd in the foreground.

One day, after his return from Europe, the Doctor said something to his daughter that made her start—it seemed to come from so far out of the past.

"I should like you to promise me something before I die."

"Why do you talk about your dying?" she asked.

"Because I am sixty-eight years old."

"I hope you will live a long time," said Catherine.

"I hope I shall! But some day I shall take a bad cold, and then it will not matter much what any one hopes. That will be the manner of my exit, and when it takes place, remember I told you so. Promise me not to marry Morris Townsend after I am gone."

This was what made Catherine start, as I have said; but her start was a silent one, and for some moments she said nothing. "Why do you speak of him?" she asked at last.

"You challenge everything I say. I speak of him because he's a topic, like any other. He's to be seen, like any one else, and he is still looking for a wife—having had one and got rid of her, I don't know by what means. He has lately been in New York, and at your cousin Marian's house; your Aunt Elizabeth saw him there."

"They neither of them told me," said Catherine.

"That's their merit; it's not yours. He has grown fat and bald, and he has not made his fortune. But I can't trust those facts alone to steel your heart against him, and that's why I ask you to promise."

"Fat and bald;" these words presented a strange image to Catherine's mind, out of which the memory of the most beautiful young man in the world had never faded. "I don't think you understand," she said. "I very seldom think of Mr. Townsend."

"It will be very easy for you to go on, then. Promise me, after my death, to do the same."

Again, for some moments, Catherine was silent; her father's request deeply amazed her; it opened an old wound and made it ache afresh. "I don't think I can promise that," she answered.

"It would be a great satisfaction," said her father.

"You don't understand. I can't promise that."

The Doctor was silent a minute. "I ask you for a particular reason. I am altering my will."

This reason failed to strike Catherine; and indeed she scarcely understood it. All her feelings were merged in the sense that he was trying to treat her as he had treated her years before. She had suffered from it then; and now all her experience, all her acquired tranquillity and rigidity, protested. She had been so humble in her youth that she could now afford to have a little pride, and there was something in this request, and in her father's thinking himself so free to make it, that seemed an injury to her dignity. Poor Catherine's dignity was not aggressive; it never sat in state; but if you pushed far enough you could find it. Her father had pushed very far.

"I can't promise," she simply repeated.

"You are very obstinate," said the Doctor.

"I don't think you understand."

"Please explain, then."

"I can't explain," said Catherine. "And I can't promise."

"Upon my word," her father explained, "I had no idea how obstinate you are!"

She knew herself that she was obstinate, and it gave her a certain joy. She was now a middle-aged woman.

About a year after this, the accident that the Doctor had spoken of occurred; he took a violent cold. Driving out to Bloomingdale one April day to see a patient of unsound mind, who was confined in a private asylum for the insane, and whose family greatly desired a medical opinion from an eminent source, he was caught in a spring shower, and being in a buggy, without a hood, he found himself soaked to the skin. He came home with an ominous chill, and on the morrow he was seriously ill. "It is congestion of the lungs," he said to Catherine; "I shall need very good nursing. It will make no difference, for I shall not recover; but I wish everything to be done, to the smallest detail, as if I should. I hate an ill-conducted sick-room; and you will be so good as to nurse me on the hypothesis that I shall get well." He told her which of his fellow-physicians to send for, and gave her a multitude of minute directions; it was quite on the optimistic hypothesis that she nursed him. But he had never been wrong in his life, and he was not wrong now. He was touching his seventieth year, and though he had a very well-tempered constitution, his hold upon life had lost its firmness. He died after three weeks' illness, during which Mrs. Penniman, as well as his daughter, had been assiduous at his bedside.

On his will being opened after a decent interval, it was found to consist of two portions. The first of these dated from ten years back, and consisted of a series of dispositions by which he left the great mass of his property to his daughter, with becoming legacies to his two sisters. The second was a codicil, of recent origin, maintaining the annuities to Mrs. Penniman and Mrs. Almond, but reducing Catherine's share to a fifth of what he had first bequeathed her. "She is amply provided for from her mother's side," the document ran, "never having spent more than a fraction of her income from this source; so that her fortune is already more than sufficient to attract those unscrupulous adventurers whom she has given me reason to believe that she persists in regarding as an interesting class." The large remainder of his property, therefore, Dr. Sloper had divided into seven unequal parts, which he left, as endowments, to as many different hospitals and schools of medicine, in various cities of the Union.

To Mrs. Penniman it seemed monstrous that a man should play such tricks with other people's money; for after his death, of course, as she said, it was other people's. "Of course you will dispute the will," she remarked, fatuously, to Catherine.

"Oh no," Catherine answered, "I like it very much. Only I wish it had been expressed a little differently!"

XXXIV

IT WAS her habit to remain in town very late in the summer; she preferred the house in Washington Square to any other habitation whatever, and it was under protest that she used to go to the seaside for the month of August. At the sea she spent her month at an hotel. The year that her father died she intermitted this custom altogether, not thinking it consistent with deep mourning; and the year after that she put off her departure till so late that the middle of August found her still in the heated solitude of Washington Square. Mrs. Penniman, who was fond of a change, was usually eager for a visit to the country; but this year she appeared quite content with such rural impressions as she could gather, at the parlour window, from the ailantus-trees behind the wooden paling. The peculiar fragrance of this vegetation used to diffuse itself in the evening air, and Mrs. Penniman, on the warm nights of July, often sat at the open window and inhaled it. This was a happy moment for Mrs. Penniman; after the death of her brother she felt more free to obey her impulses. A vague oppression had disappeared from her life, and she enjoyed a sense of freedom of which she had not been conscious since the memorable time, so long ago, when the Doctor went abroad with Catherine and left her at home to entertain Morris Townsend. The year that had elapsed since her brother's death reminded her of that happy time, because, although Catherine, in growing older, had become a person to be reckoned with, yet her society was a very different thing, as Mrs. Penniman said, from that of a tank of cold water. The elder lady hardly knew what use to make of this larger margin of her life; she sat and looked at it very much as she had often sat, with her poised needle in her hand, before her tapestry-frame. She had a confident hope, however, that her rich impulses, her talent for embroidery, would still find their application, and this confidence was justified before many months had elapsed.

Catherine continued to live in her father's house in spite of its being represented to her that a maiden lady of quiet habits might find a more convenient abode in one of the smaller dwellings, with brown stone fronts, which had at this time begun to adorn the transverse thoroughfares in the upper part of the town. She liked the earlier structure—it had begun by this time to be called an "old" house—and proposed to herself to end her days in it. If it was too large for a pair of unpretending gentlewomen, this was better than the opposite fault; for Catherine had no desire to find herself in closer quarters with her aunt. She expected to spend the rest of her life in Washington Square, and to enjoy Mrs. Penniman's society for the whole of this period; as she had a conviction that, long as she might live, her aunt would live at least as long, and always retain her brilliancy and activity. Mrs. Penniman suggested to her the idea of a rich vitality.

On one of those warm evenings in July of which mention has been made, the two ladies sat together at an open window, looking out on the quiet Square. It was too hot for lighted lamps, for reading, or for work; it might have appeared too hot even for conversation, Mrs. Penniman having long been speechless. She sat forward in the window, half on the balcony, humming a little song. Catherine was within the room, in a low rocking-chair, dressed in white, and slowly using a large palmetto fan. It was in this way, at this season, that the aunt and niece, after they had had tea, habitually spent their evenings.

"Catherine," said Mrs. Penniman at last, "I am going to say something that will surprise you."

"Pray do," Catherine answered; "I like surprises. And it is so quiet now."

"Well, then, I have seen Morris Townsend."

If Catherine was surprised, she checked the expression of it; she gave neither a start nor an exclamation. She remained, indeed, for some moments intensely still, and this may very well have been a symptom of emotion. "I hope he was well," she said at last.

"I don't know; he is a great deal changed. He would like very much to see you."

"I would rather not see him," said Catherine, quickly.

"I was afraid you would say that. But you don't seem surprised!"

"I am—very much."

"I met him at Marian's," said Mrs. Penniman. "He goes to Marian's, and they are so afraid you will meet him there. It's my belief that that's why he goes. He wants so much to see you." Catherine made no response to this, and Mrs. Penniman went on. "I didn't know him at first; he is so remarkably changed. But he knew me in a minute. He says I am not in the least changed. You know how polite he always was. He was coming away when I came, and we walked a little distance together. He is still very handsome, only, of course, he looks older, and he is not so—so animated as he used to be. There was a touch of sadness about him; but there was a touch of sadness about him before—especially when he went away. I am afraid he has not been very successful—that he has never got thoroughly established. I don't suppose he is sufficiently plodding, and that, after all, is what succeeds in this world." Mrs. Penniman had not mentioned Morris Townsend's name to her niece for upwards of the fifth of a century; but now that she had broken the spell, she seemed to wish to make up for lost time, as if there had been a sort of exhilaration in hearing herself talk of him. She proceeded, however, with considerable caution, pausing occasionally to let Catherine give some sign. Catherine gave no other sign than to stop the rocking of her chair and the swaying of her fan; she sat motionless and silent. "It was on Tuesday last," said Mrs. Penniman, "and I have been hesitating ever since about telling you. I didn't know how you might like it. At last I thought that it was so long ago that you would probably not have any particular feeling. I saw him again, after meeting him at Marian's. I met him in the street, and he went a few steps with me. The first thing he said was about you; he asked ever so many questions. Marian didn't want me to speak to you; she didn't want you to know that they receive him. I told him I was sure that after all these years you couldn't have any feeling about that; you couldn't grudge him the hospitality of his own cousin's house. I said you would be bitter indeed if you did that. Marian has the most extraordinary ideas about what happened between you; she seems to think he behaved in some very unusual manner. I took the liberty of reminding her of the real facts, and placing the story in its true light. *He* has no bitterness, Catherine, I can assure you; and he might be excused for it, for things have not gone well with him. He has been all over the world, and tried to establish himself everywhere; but his evil star was against him. It is most interesting to hear him talk of his evil star. Everything failed; everything but his—you know, you remember—his proud, high spirit. I believe he married some lady somewhere in Europe. You know they marry in such a peculiar matter-of-course way in Europe; a marriage of reason they call it. She died soon afterwards; as he said to me, she only flitted across his life. He has not been in New York for ten years; he came back a few days ago. The first thing he did was to ask me about you. He had heard you had never married; he seemed very much interested about that. He said you had been the real romance of his life."

Catherine had suffered her companion to proceed from point to point, and pause to pause, without interrupting her; she fixed her eyes on the ground and listened. But the last phrase I have quoted was followed by a pause of peculiar significance, and then, at last, Catherine spoke. It will be observed that before doing so she had received a good deal of information about Morris Townsend. "Please say no more; please don't follow up that subject."

"Doesn't it interest you?" asked Mrs. Penniman, with a certain timorous archness.

"It pains me," said Catherine.

"I was afraid you would say that. But don't you think you could get used to it? He wants so much to see you."

"Please don't, Aunt Lavinia," said Catherine, getting up from her seat. She moved quickly away, and went to the other window, which stood open to the balcony; and here, in the embrasure, concealed from her aunt by the white curtains, she remained a long time, looking out into the warm darkness. She had had a great shock; it was as if the gulf of the past had suddenly opened, and a spectral figure had risen out of it. There were some things she believed she had got over, some feelings that she had thought of as dead; but apparently there was a certain vitality in them still. Mrs. Penniman had made them stir themselves. It was but a momentary agitation, Catherine said to herself; it would presently pass away. She was trembling, and her heart was beating so that she could feel it; but this also would subside. Then, suddenly, while she waited for a return of her calmness, she burst into tears. But her tears flowed very silently, so that Mrs. Penniman had no observation of them. It was perhaps, however, because Mrs. Penniman suspected them that she said no more that evening about Morris Townsend.

XXXV

HER REFRESHED attention to this gentleman had not those limits of which Catherine desired, for herself, to be conscious; it lasted long enough to enable her to wait another week before speaking of him again. It was under the same circumstances that she once more attacked the subject. She had been sitting with her niece in the evening; only on this occasion, as the night was not so warm, the lamp had been lighted, and Catherine had placed herself near it with a morsel of fancy-work. Mrs. Penniman went and sat alone for half an hour on the balcony; then she came in, moving vaguely about the room. At last she sank into a seat near Catherine, with clasped hands, and a little look of excitement.

"Shall you be angry if I speak to you again about *him*?" she asked.

Catherine looked up at her quietly. "Who is *he*?"

"He whom you once loved."

"I shall not be angry, but I shall not like it."

"He sent you a message," said Mrs. Penniman. "I promised him to deliver it, and I must keep my promise."

In all these years Catherine had had time to forget how little she had to thank her aunt for in the season of her misery; she had long ago forgiven Mrs. Penniman for taking too much upon herself. But for a moment this attitude of interposition and disinterestedness, this carrying of messages and redeeming of promises, brought back the sense that her companion was a dangerous woman. She had said she would not be angry; but for an instant she felt sore. "I don't care what you do with your promise!" she answered.

Mrs. Penniman, however, with her high conception of the sanctity of pledges, carried her point. "I have gone too far to re-treat," she said, though precisely what this meant she was not at pains to explain. "Mr. Townsend wishes most particularly to see you, Catherine; he believes that if you knew how much, and why, he wishes it, you would consent to do so."

"There can be no reason," said Catherine; "no good reason."

"His happiness depends upon it. Is not that a good reason?" asked Mrs. Penniman, impressively.

"Not for me. My happiness does not."

"I think you will be happier after you have seen him. He is going away again—going to resume his wanderings. It is a very lonely, restless, joyless life. Before he goes he wishes to speak to you; it is a fixed idea with him—he is always thinking of it. He has something very important to say to you. He believes that you never understood him—that you never judged him rightly, and the belief has always weighed upon him terribly. He wishes to justify himself; he believes that in a very few words he could do so. He wishes to meet you as a friend."

Catherine listened to this wonderful speech, without paus-ing in her work; she had now had several days to accustom her-self to think of Morris Townsend again as an actuality. When it was over she said simply, "Please say to Mr. Townsend that I wish he would leave me alone."

She had hardly spoken when a sharp, firm ring at the door vibrated through the summer night. Catherine looked up at the clock; it marked a quarter-past nine—a very late hour for visitors, especially in the empty condition of the town. Mrs.

Penniman at the same moment gave a little start, and then Catherine's eyes turned quickly to her aunt. They met Mrs. Penniman's and sounded them for a moment, sharply. Mrs. Penniman was blushing; her look was a conscious one; it seemed to confess something. Catherine guessed its meaning, and rose quickly from her chair.

"Aunt Penniman," she said, in a tone that scared her companion, "have you taken *the liberty*...?"

"My dearest Catherine," stammered Mrs. Penniman, "just wait till you see him!"

Catherine had frightened her aunt, but she was also frightened herself; she was on the point of rushing to give orders to the servant, who was passing to the door, to admit no one; but the fear of meeting her visitor checked her.

"Mr. Morris Townsend."

This was what she heard, vaguely but recognisably articulated by the domestic, while she hesitated. She had her back turned to the door of the parlour, and for some moments she kept it turned, feeling that he had come in. He had not spoken, however, and at last she faced about. Then she saw a gentleman standing in the middle of the room, from which her aunt had discreetly retired.

She would never have known him. He was forty-five years old, and his figure was not that of the straight, slim young man she remembered. But it was a very fine person, and a fair and lustrous beard, spreading itself upon a well-presented chest, contributed to its effect. After a moment Catherine recognised the upper half of the face, which, though her visitor's clustering locks had grown thin, was still remarkably handsome. He stood in a deeply deferential attitude, with his eyes on her face. "I have ventured—I have ventured," he said; and then he paused, looking about him, as if he expected her to ask him to sit down. It was the old voice; but it had not the old charm. Catherine, for a minute, was conscious of a distinct determination not to invite him to take a seat. Why had he come? It was wrong for him to come. Morris was embarrassed, but Catherine gave him no help. It was not that she was glad of his embarrassment; on the contrary, it excited all her own liabilities of this kind, and gave her great pain. But how could she welcome him when she felt so vividly that he ought not to have come? "I wanted so much—I was determined," Morris went on. But he stopped again; it was not easy. Catherine still said nothing, and he may well have recalled with apprehension her ancient faculty of silence. She continued to look at him, however, and as she did so she made the strangest observation. It seemed to be he, and yet not he; it was the man who had been everything, and yet this person was nothing. How long ago it was—how old she had grown—how much she had lived! She had lived on something that was connected with *him*, and she had consumed it in doing so. This person did not look unhappy. He was fair and well-preserved, perfectly dressed, mature and complete. As Catherine looked at him, the story of his life defined itself in his eyes: he had made himself comfortable, and he had never been caught. But even while her perception opened itself to this, she had no desire to catch him; his presence was painful to her, and she only wished he would go.

"Will you not sit down?" he asked.

"I think we had better not," said Catherine.

"I offend you by coming?" He was very grave; he spoke in a tone of the richest respect.

"I don't think you ought to have come."

"Did not Mrs. Penniman tell you—did she not give you my message?"

"She told me something, but I did not understand."

"I wish you would let *me* tell you—let me speak for myself."

"I don't think it is necessary," said Catherine.

"Not for you, perhaps, but for me. It would be a great satisfaction—and I have not many." He seemed to be coming nearer; Catherine turned away. "Can we not be friends again?" he said.

"We are not enemies," said Catherine. "I have none but friendly feelings to you."

"Ah, I wonder whether you know the happiness it gives me to hear you say that!" Catherine uttered no intimation that she measured the influence of her words; and he presently went on, "You have not changed—the years have passed happily for you."

"They have passed very quietly," said Catherine.

"They have left no marks; you are admirably young." This time he succeeded in coming nearer—he was close to her; she saw his glossy perfumed beard, and his eyes above it looking strange and hard. It was very different from his old—from his young—face. If she had first seen him this way she would not have liked him. It seemed to her that he was smiling, or trying to smile. "Catherine," he said, lowering his voice, "I have never ceased to think of you."

"Please don't say those things," she answered.

"Do you hate me?"

"Oh no," said Catherine.

Something in her tone discouraged him, but in a moment he recovered himself. "Have you still some kindness for me, then?"

"I don't know why you have come here to ask me such things!" Catherine exclaimed.

"Because for many years it has been the desire of my life that we should be friends again."

"That is impossible."

"Why so? Not if you will allow it."

"I will not allow it!" said Catherine.

He looked at her again in silence. "I see; my presence troubles you and pains you. I will go away; but you must give me leave to come again."

"Please don't come again," she said.

"Never?—never?"

She made a great effort; she wished to say something that would make it impossible he should ever again cross her threshold. "It is wrong of you. There is no propriety in it—no reason for it."

"Ah, dearest lady, you do me injustice!" cried Morris Townsend. "We have only waited, and now we are free."

"You treated me badly," said Catherine.

"Not if you think of it rightly. You had your quiet life with your father—which was just what I could not make up my mind to rob you of."

"Yes; I had that."

Morris felt it to be a considerable damage to his cause that he could not add that she had had something more besides; for it is needless to say that he had learnt the contents of Dr. Sloper's will. He was nevertheless not at a loss. "There are worse fates than that!" he exclaimed with expression; and he might have been supposed to refer to his own unprotected situation. Then he added, with a deeper tenderness, "Catherine, have you never forgiven me?"

"I forgave you years ago, but it is useless for us to attempt to be friends."

"Not if we forget the past. We have still a future, thank God!"

"I can't forget—I don't forget," said Catherine. "You treated me too badly. I felt it very much; I felt it for years." And then she went on, with her wish to show him that he must not come to her this way. "I can't begin again—I can't take it up. Everything is dead and buried. It was too serious; it made a great change in my life. I never expected to see you here."

"Ah, you are angry!" cried Morris, who wished immensely that he could extort some flash of passion from her mildness. In that case he might hope.

"No, I am not angry. Anger does not last, that way, for years. But there are other things. Impressions last, when they have been strong.—But I can't talk."

Morris stood stroking his beard, with a clouded eye. "Why have you never married?" he asked abruptly. "You have had opportunities."

"I didn't wish to marry."

"Yes, you are rich, you are free; you had nothing to gain."

"I had nothing to gain," said Catherine.

Morris looked vaguely round him, and gave a deep sigh. "Well, I was in hopes that we might still have been friends."

"I meant to tell you, by my aunt, in answer to your message—if you had waited for an answer—that it was unnecessary for you to come in that hope."

"Good-bye, then," said Morris. "Excuse my indiscretion."

He bowed, and she turned away—standing there, averted, with her eyes on the ground, for some moments after she had heard him close the door of the room.

In the hall he found Mrs. Penniman, fluttered and eager; she appeared to have been hovering there under the irreconcilable promptings of her curiosity and her dignity.

"That was a precious plan of yours!" said Morris, clapping on his hat.

"Is she so hard?" asked Mrs. Penniman.

"She doesn't care a button for me—with her confounded little dry manner."

"Was it very dry?" pursued Mrs. Penniman, with solicitude.

Morris took no notice of her question; he stood musing an instant, with his hat on. "But why the deuce, then, would she never marry?"

"Yes—why indeed?" sighed Mrs. Penniman. And then, as if from a sense of the inadequacy of this explanation, "But you will not despair—you will come back?"

"Come back? Damnation!" And Morris Townsend strode out of the house, leaving Mrs. Penniman staring.

Catherine, meanwhile, in the parlour, picking up her morsel of fancy-work, had seated herself with it again—for life, as it were.

1881

THE IMPRESSIONS OF A COUSIN

I

NEW YORK, *April* 3, 1873.—There are moments when I feel that she has asked too much of me—especially since our arrival in this country. These three months have not done much toward making me happy here. I don't know what the difference is—or rather I do; and I say this only because it's less trouble. It is no trouble, however, to say that I like New York less than Rome: that, after all, *is* the difference. And then there's nothing to sketch! For ten years I have been sketching, and I really believe I do it very well. But how can I sketch Fifty-third Street? There are times when I even say to myself, How can I even inhabit Fifty-third Street? When I turn into it from the Fifth Avenue the vista seems too hideous: the narrow, impersonal houses, with the dry, hard tone of their brown-stone, a surface as uninteresting as that of sandpaper; their steep, stiff stoops, giving you such a climb to the door; their lumpish balustrades, porticoes, and cornices, turned out by the hundred and adorned with heavy excrescences—such an eruption of ornament and such a poverty of effect! I suppose my superior tone would seem very pretentious if anybody were to read this shameless record of personal emotion; and I should be asked why an expensive up-town residence is not as good as a slimy Italian palazzo. My answer, of course, is that I can sketch the palazzo and can do nothing with the up-town residence. I can live in it, of course, and be very grateful for the shelter; but that doesn't count. Putting aside that odious fashion of popping into the "parlours" as soon as you cross the threshold—no interval, no approach—these places are wonderfully comfortable. This one of Eunice's is perfectly arranged; and we have so much space that she has given me a sitting-room of my own—an immense luxury. Her kindness, her affection, are the most charming, delicate, natural thing I ever conceived. I don't know what can have put it into her head to like me so much; I suppose I should say into her heart, only I don't like to write about Eunice's heart—that tender, shrinking, shade-loving, and above all fresh and youthful, organ. There is a certain self-complacency, perhaps, in my assuming that her generosity is mere affection; for her conscience is so inordinately developed that she attaches the idea of duty to everything—even to her relations to a poor, plain, unloved and unlovable third-cousin. Whether she is fond of me or not, she thinks it right to be fond of me; and the effort of her life is to do what is right. In matters of duty, in short, she is a real little artist; and her masterpiece (in that way) is coming back here to live. She can't like it; her tastes are not here. If she did like it, I am sure she would never have invented such a phrase as the one of which she delivered herself the other day— "I think one's life has more dignity in one's own country." That's a phrase made up after the fact. No one ever gave up living in Europe because there is a want of dignity in it. Poor Eunice talks of "one's own country" as if she kept the United States in the back-parlour. I have yet to perceive the dignity of living in Fifty-third Street. This, I suppose, is very treasonable; but a woman isn't obliged to be patriotic. I believe I should be a good patriot if I could sketch my native town. But I can't make a picture of the brown-stone stoops in the Fifth Avenue, or the platform of the elevated railway in the Sixth. Eunice has suggested to me that I might find some subjects in the Park, and I have been there to look for them. But somehow the blistered *sentiers* of asphalt, the rock-work caverns, the huge iron bridges spanning little muddy lakes, the whole crowded, cockneyfied place, making up so many faces to look pretty, don't appeal to me—haven't, from beginning to end, a discoverable "bit."

Besides, it's too cold to sit on a campstool under this clean-swept sky, whose depths of blue air do very well, doubtless, for the floor of heaven, but are quite too far away for the ceiling of earth. The sky over here seems part of the world at large; in Europe it's part of the particular place. In summer, I dare say, it will be better; and it will go hard with me if I don't find somewhere some leafy lane, some cottage roof, something in some degree mossy or mellow. Nature here, of course, is very fine, though I am afraid only in large pieces; and with my little yard-measure (it used to serve for the Roman Campagna!) I don't know what I shall be able to do. I must try to rise to the occasion.

The Hudson is beautiful; I remember that well enough; and Eunice tells me that when we are in *villeggiatura* we shall be close to the loveliest part of it. Her cottage, or villa, or whatever they call it (Mrs. Ermine, by the way, always speaks of it as a "country-seat"), is more or less opposite to West Point, where it makes one of its grandest sweeps. Unfortunately, it has been let these three years that she has been abroad, and will not be vacant till the first of June. Mr. Caliph, her trustee, took upon himself to do that; very impertinently, I think, for certainly if I had Eunice's fortune I shouldn't let my houses—I mean, of course, those that are so personal. Least of all should I let my "country-seat." It's bad enough for people to appropriate one's sofas and tables, without appropriating one's flowers and trees and even one's views. There is nothing so personal as one's horizon,—the horizon that one commands, whatever it is, from one's window. Nobody else has just that one. Mr. Caliph, by the way, is apparently a person of the incalculable, irresponsible sort. It would have been natural to suppose that having the greater part of my cousin's property in his care, he would be in New York to receive her at the end of a long absence and a boisterous voyage. Common civility would have suggested that, especially as he was an old friend, or rather a young friend, of both her parents. It was an odd thing to make him sole trustee; but that was Cousin Letitia's doing: "she thought it would be so much easier for Eunice to see only one person." I believe she had found that effort the limit of her own energy; but she might have known that Eunice would have given her best attention, every day, to twenty men of business, if such a duty had been presented to her. I don't think poor Cousin Letitia knew very much; Eunice speaks of her much less than she speaks of her father, whose death would have been the greater sorrow if she dared to admit to herself that she preferred one of her parents to the other. The number of things that the poor girl doesn't dare to admit to herself! One of them, I am sure, is that Mr. Caliph is acting improperly in spending three months in Washington, just at the moment when it would be most convenient to her to see him. He has pressing business there, it seems (he is a good deal of a politician—not that I know what people do in Washington), and he writes to Eunice every week or two that he will "finish it up" in ten days more, and then will be completely at her service; but he never finishes it up—never arrives. She has not seen him for three years; he certainly, I think, ought to have come out to her in Europe. She doesn't know that, and I haven't cared to suggest it, for she wishes (very naturally) to think him a pearl of trustees. Fortunately he sends her all the money she needs; and the other day he sent her his brother, a rather agitated (though not in the least agitating) youth, who presented himself about lunch-time—Mr. Caliph having (as he explained) told him that this was the best hour to call. What does Mr. Caliph know about it, by the way? It's little enough he has tried! Mr. Adrian Frank had of course nothing to say about business; he only came to be agreeable, and to tell us that he had just seen his brother in Washington—as if that were any comfort! They are brothers only in the sense that they are children of the same mother; Mrs. Caliph having accepted consolations in her widowhood and produced this blushing boy, who is ten years younger than the accomplished Caliph. (I say accomplished Caliph for the phrase. I haven't the least idea of his accomplishments. Somehow, a man with that name ought to have a good many.) Mr. Frank, the second husband, is dead as well as herself, and the young man has a very good fortune. He is shy and simple, colours immensely and becomes alarmed at his own silences; but is tall and straight and clear-eyed, and is, I imagine, a very estimable youth. Eunice says that he is as different as possible from his step-brother; so that perhaps, though she doesn't mean it in that way, his step-brother is not estimable. I shall judge of that for myself, if he ever gives me a chance.

Young Frank, at any rate, is a gentleman, and in spite of his blushes has seen a great deal of the world. Perhaps that is what he is blushing for: there are so many things we humans have no reason to be proud of. He stayed to lunch, and talked a little about the far East—Babylon, Palmyra, Ispahan, and that sort of thing—from which he is lately returned. He also is a sketcher, though evidently he doesn't show. He asked to see my things, however; and I produced a few old water-colours, of other days and other climes, which I have luckily brought to America—produced them with my usual calm assurance. It was clear he thought me very clever; so I suspect that in not showing he himself is rather wise. When I said there was nothing here to sketch, that rectangular towns won't do, etc., he asked me why I didn't try people. What people? the people in the Fifth Avenue? They are even less pictorial than their houses. I don't perceive that those in the Sixth are any better, or those in the Fourth and Third, or in the Seventh and Eighth. Good heavens! what a nomenclature! The city of New York is like a tall sum in addition, and the streets are like columns of figures. What a place for me to live, who hate arithmetic! I have tried Mrs. Ermine, but that is only because she asked me to: Mrs. Ermine asks for whatever she wants. I don't think she cares for it much, for though it's bad, it's not bad enough to please her. I thought she would be rather easy to do, as her countenance is made up largely of negatives—no colour, no form, no intelligence; I should simply have to leave a sort of brilliant blank. I found, however, there was difficulty in representing an expression which consisted so completely of the absence of that

article. With her large, fair, featureless face, unillumined by a
ray of meaning, she makes the most incoherent, the most unexpected, remarks. She asked Eunice, the other day, whether she
should not bring a few gentlemen to see her—she seemed to
know so few, to be so lonely. Then when Eunice thanked her,
and said she needn't take that trouble: she was not lonely, and
in any case did not desire her solitude to be peopled in that
manner—Mrs. Ermine declared blandly that it was all right,
but that she supposed this was the great advantage of being an
orphan, that you might have gentlemen brought to see you. "I
don't like being an orphan, even for that," said Eunice; who indeed does not like it at all, though she will be twenty-one next
month, and has had several years to get used to it. Mrs. Ermine
is very vulgar, yet she thinks she has high distinction. I am very
glad our cousinship is not on the same side. Except that she is
an idiot and a bore, however, I think there is no harm in her.
Her time is spent in contemplating the surface of things—and
for that I don't blame her, for I myself am very fond of the surface. But she doesn't see what she looks at, and in short is very
tiresome. That is one of the things poor Eunice won't admit to
herself—that Lizzie Ermine will end by boring us to death.
Now that both her daughters are married, she has her time
quite on her hands; for the sons-in-law, I am sure, can't encourage her visits. She may, however, contrive to be with them as
well as here, for, as a poor young husband once said to me, a
belle-mère, after marriage, is as inevitable as stickiness after eat-
ing honey. A fool can do plenty of harm without deep intentions. After all, intentions fail; and what you know an accident
by is that it doesn't. Mrs. Ermine doesn't like me; she thinks she
ought to be in my shoes—that when Eunice lost her old governess, who had remained with her as "companion," she ought,
instead of picking me up in Rome, to have come home and
thrown herself upon some form of kinship more cushiony. She
is jealous of me, and vexed that I don't give her more opportunities; for I know that she has made up her mind that I ought
to be a Bohemian: in that case she could persuade Eunice that I

am a very unfit sort of person. I am single, not young, not
pretty, not well off, and not very desirous to please; I carry a
palette on my thumb, and very often have stains on my
apron—though except for those stains I pretend to be immacu-
lately neat. What right have I *not* to be a Bohemian, and not to
teach Eunice to make cigarettes? I am convinced Mrs. Ermine
is disappointed that I don't smoke. Perhaps, after all, she is
right, and that I am too much a creature of habits, of rules. A
few people have been good enough to call me an artist; but I
am not. I am only, in a small way, a worker. I walk too straight;
it's ten years since any one asked me to dance! I wish I could
oblige you, Mrs. Ermine, by dipping into Bohemia once in a
while. But one can't have the defects of the qualities one doesn't
possess. I am not an artist, I am too much of a critic. I suppose
a she-critic is a kind of monster; women should only be criticised. That's why I keep it all to myself—myself being this little
book. I grew tired of myself some months ago, and locked myself up in a desk. It was a kind of punishment, but it was also a
great rest, to stop judging, to stop caring, for a while. Now that
I have come out, I suppose I ought to take a vow not to be ill-
natured.

As I read over what I have written here, I wonder whether it
was worth while to have reopened my journal. Still, why not
have the benefit of being thought disagreeable—the luxury of
recorded observation? If one is poor, plain, proud—and in this
very private place I may add, clever—there are certain necessary revenges!

April 10.—Adrian Frank has been here again, and we rather
like him. (That will do for the first note of a more genial tone.)
His eyes are very blue, and his teeth very white—two things
that always please me. He became rather more communicative,
and almost promised to show me his sketches—in spite of the
fact that he is evidently as much as ever struck with my own
ability. Perhaps he has discovered that I am trying to be genial!
He wishes to take us to drive—that is, to take Eunice; for of
course I shall go only for propriety. She doesn't go with young

men alone; that element was not included in her education. She said to me yesterday, "The only man I shall drive alone with will be the one I marry." She talks so little about marrying that this made an impression on me. That subject is supposed to be a girl's inevitable topic; but no young women could occupy themselves with it less than she and I do. I think I may say that we never mention it at all. I suppose that if a man were to read this he would be greatly surprised and not particularly edified. As there is no danger of any man's reading it, I may add that I always take tacitly for granted that Eunice will marry. She doesn't in the least pretend that she won't; and if I am not mistaken she is capable of the sort of affection that is expected of a good wife. The longer I live with her the more I see that she is a dear girl. Now that I know her better, I perceive that she is perfectly natural. I used to think that she tried too much—that she watched herself, perhaps, with a little secret admiration. But that was because I couldn't conceive of a girl's motives being so simple. She only wants not to suffer—she is immensely afraid of that. Therefore, she wishes to be universally tender— to mitigate the general sum of suffering, in the hope that she herself may come off easily. Poor thing! she doesn't know that we can diminish the amount of suffering for others only by taking to ourselves a part of their share. The amount of that commodity in the world is always the same; it is only the distribution that varies. We all try to dodge our portion, and some of us succeed. I find the best way is not to think about it, and to make little water-colours. Eunice thinks that the best way is to be very generous, to condemn no one unheard.

A great many things happen that I don't mention here; incidents of social life, I believe they call them. People come to see us, and sometimes they invite us to dinner. We go to certain concerts, many of which are very good. We take a walk every day; and I read to Eunice, and she plays to me. Mrs. Ermine makes her appearance several times a week, and gives us the news of the town—a great deal more of it than we have any use for. She thinks we live in a hole; and she has more than once

expressed her conviction that I can do nothing socially for
Eunice. As to that, she is perfectly right; I am aware of my social insignificance. But I am equally aware that my cousin has
no need of being pushed. I know little of the people and things
of this place; but I know enough to see that, whatever they are,
the best of them are at her service. Mrs Ermine thinks it a great
pity that Eunice should have come too late in the season to "go
out" with her; for after this there are few entertainments at
which my protecting presence is not sufficient. Besides, Eunice
isn't eager; I often wonder at her indifference. She never thinks
of the dances she has missed, nor asks about those at which she
still may figure. She isn't sad, and it doesn't amount to melancholy; but she certainly is rather detached. She likes to read, to
talk with me, to make music, and to dine out when she sup-
poses there will be "real conversation." She is extremely fond of
real conversation; and we flatter ourselves that a good deal of it
takes place between us. We talk about life and religion and art
and George Eliot; all that, I hope, is sufficiently real. Eunice
understands everything, and has a great many opinions; she is
quite the modern young woman, though she hasn't modern
manners. But all this doesn't explain to me why, as Mrs. Ermine
says, she should wish to be so dreadfully quiet. That lady's suspicion to the contrary notwithstanding, it is not I who make
her so. I would go with her to a party every night if she should
wish it, and send out cards to proclaim that we "receive." But
her ambitions are not those of the usual girl; or, at any rate, if
she is waiting for what the usual girl waits for, she is waiting
very patiently. As I say, I can't quite make out the secret of her
patience. However, it is not necessary I should; it was no part of
the bargain on which I came to her that we were to conceal
nothing from each other. I conceal a great deal from Eunice; at
least I hope I do: for instance, how fearfully I am bored. I think
I am as patient as she; but then I have certain things to help
me—my age, my resignation, my ability, and, I suppose I may
add, my conceit. Mrs. Ermine doesn't bring the young men, but
she talks about them, and calls them Harry and Freddy. She

wants Eunice to marry, though I don't see what she is to gain by it. It is apparently a disinterested love of matrimony—or rather, I should say, a love of weddings. She lives in a world of "engagements," and announces a new one every time she comes in. I never heard of so much marrying in all my life before. Mrs. Ermine is dying to be able to tell people that Eunice is engaged; that distinction should not be wanting to a cousin of hers. Whoever marries her, by the way, will come into a very good fortune. Almost for the first time, three days ago, she told me about her affairs.

She knows less about them than she believes—I could see that; but she knows the great matter; which is, that in the course of her twenty-first year, by the terms of her mother's will she becomes mistress of her property, of which for the last seven years Mr. Caliph has been sole trustee. On that day Mr. Caliph is to make over to her three hundred thousand dollars, which he has been nursing and keeping safe. So much on every occasion seems to be expected of this wonderful man! I call him so because I think it was wonderful of him to have been appointed sole depositary of the property of an orphan by a very anxious, scrupulous, affectionate mother, whose one desire, when she made her will, was to prepare for her child a fruitful majority, and whose acquaintance with him had not been of many years, though her esteem for him was great. He had been a friend—a very good friend—of her husband, who, as he neared his end, asked him to look after his widow. Eunice's father didn't however make him trustee of his little estate; he put that into other hands, and Eunice has a very good account of it. It amounts, unfortunately, but to some fifty thousand dollars. Her mother's proceedings with regard to Mr. Caliph were very feminine—so I may express myself in the privacy of these pages. But I believe all women are very feminine in their relations with Mr. Caliph. "Haroun-al-Raschid" I call him to Eunice; and I suppose he expects to find us in a state of Oriental prostration. She says, however, that he is not the least of a Turk, and that nothing could be kinder or more considerate than he was three years ago, before she went to Europe. He was constantly with her at that time, for many months; and his attentions have evidently made a great impression on her. That sort of thing naturally would, on a girl of seventeen; and I have told her she must be prepared to think him much less brilliant a personage to-day. I don't know what he will think of some of her plans of expenditure,—laying out an Italian garden at the house on the river, founding a cot at the children's hospital, erecting a music room in the rear of this house. Next winter Eunice proposes to receive; but she wishes to have an original-ity, in the shape of really good music. She will evidently be rather extravagant, at least at first. Mr. Caliph of course will have no more authority; still, he may advise her as a friend.

April 23.—This afternoon, while Eunice was out, Mr. Frank made his appearance, having had the civility, as I afterwards learned, to ask for me, in spite of the absence of the *padronina*. I told him she was at Mrs. Ermine's, and that Mrs. Ermine was her cousin.

"Then I can say what I should not be able to say if she were here," he said, smiling that singular smile which has the effect of showing his teeth and drawing the lids of his eyes together. If he were a young countryman, one would call it a grin. It is not exactly a grin, but it is very simple.

"And what may that be?" I asked, with encouragement.

He hesitated a little, while I admired his teeth, which I am sure he has no wish to exhibit; and I expected something won-derful. "Considering that she is fair, she is really very pretty," he said at last.

I was rather disappointed, and I went so far as to say to him that he might have made that remark in her presence.

This time his blue eyes remained wide open: "So you really think so?"

"'Considering that she's fair,' that part of it, perhaps, might have been omitted; but the rest surely would have pleased her."

"Do you really think so?"

"Well, 'really very pretty' is, perhaps, not quite right; it seems to imply a kind of surprise. You might have omitted the 'really.'"

"You want me to omit everything," he said, laughing, as if he thought me wonderfully amusing.

"The gist of the thing would remain, 'You are very pretty'; that would have been unexpected and agreeable."

"I think you are laughing at me!" cried poor Mr. Frank, without bitterness. "I have no right to say that till I know she likes me."

"She does like you; I see no harm in telling you so." He seemed to me so modest, so natural, that I felt as free to say this to him as I would have been to a good child: more, indeed, than to a good child, for a child to whom one would say that would be rather a prig, and Adrian Frank is not a prig. I could see this by the way he answered; it was rather odd.

"It will please my brother to know that!"

"Does he take such an interest in the impressions you make?"

"Oh yes; he wants me to appear well." This was said with the most touching innocence; it was a complete confession of inferiority. It was, perhaps, the tone that made it so; at any rate, Adrian Frank has renounced the hope of ever appearing as well as his brother. I wonder if a man must be really inferior, to be in such a state of mind as that. He must at all events be very fond of his brother, and even, I think, have sacrificed himself a good deal. This young man asked me ever so many questions about my cousin; frankly, simply; as if, when one wanted to know, it was perfectly natural to ask. So it is, I suppose; but why should he want to know? Some of his questions were certainly idle. What can it matter to him whether she has one little dog or three, or whether she is an admirer of the music of the future? "Does she go out much, or does she like a quiet evening at home?" "Does she like living in Europe, and what part of Europe does she prefer?" "Has she many relatives in New York, and does she see a great deal of them?" On all these points I was obliged to give Mr. Frank a certain satisfaction; and after that, I thought I had a right to ask why he wanted to know. He was evidently surprised at being challenged, blushed a good deal, and made me feel for a moment as if I had asked a vulgar question. I saw he had no particular reason; he only wanted to be civil, and that is the way best known to him of expressing an interest. He was confused; but he was not so confused that he took his departure. He sat half an hour longer, and let me make up to him by talking very agreeably for the shock I had administered. I may mention here—for I like to see it in black and white—that I *can* talk very agreeably. He listened with the most flattering attention, showing me his blue eyes and his white teeth in alternation, and laughing largely, as if I had a command of the comical. I am not conscious of that. At last, after I had paused a little, he said to me, apropos of nothing: "Do you think the realistic school are—a—to be admired?" Then I saw that he had already forgotten my earlier check— such was the effect of my geniality—and that he would ask me as many questions about myself as I would let him. I answered him freely, but I answered him as I chose. There are certain things about myself I never shall tell, and the simplest way not to tell is to say the contrary. If people are indiscreet, they must take the consequences. I declared that I held the realistic school in horror; that I found New York the most interesting, the most sympathetic of cities; and that I thought the American girl the finest result of civilisation. I am sure I convinced him that I am a most remarkable woman. He went away before Eunice returned. He is a charming creature—a kind of Yankee Donatello. If I could only be his Miriam, the situation would be almost complete, for Eunice is an excellent Hilda.

April 26.—Mrs. Ermine was in great force to-day; she described all the fine things Eunice can do when she gets her money into her own hands. A set of Mechlin lace, a *rivière* of diamonds which she saw the other day at Tiffany's, a set of Russian sables that she knows of somewhere else, a little English phaeton with a pair of ponies and a tiger, a family of pugs to waddle about in the drawing-room—all these luxuries

Mrs. Ermine declares indispensable. "I should like to know that you have them—it would do me real good," she said to Eunice. "I like to see people with handsome things. It would give me more pleasure to know you have that set of Mechlin than to have it myself. I can't help that—it's the way I am made. If other people have handsome things I see them more; and then I do want the good of others—I don't care if you think me vain for saying so. I shan't be happy till I see you in an English phaeton. The groom oughtn't to be more than three feet six. I think you ought to show for what you are."

"How do you mean, for what I am?" Eunice asked.

"Well, for a charming girl, with a very handsome fortune."

"I shall never show any more than I do now."

"I will tell you what you do—you show Miss Condit." And Mrs. Ermine presented me her large, foolish face. "If you don't look out, she'll do you up in Morris papers, and then all the Mechlin lace in the world won't matter!"

"I don't follow you at all—I never follow you," I said, wishing I could have sketched her just as she sat there. She was quite grotesque.

"I would rather go without you," she repeated.

"I think that after I come into my property I shall do just as I do now," said Eunice. "After all, where will the difference be? I have to-day everything I shall ever have. It's more than enough."

"You won't have to ask Mr. Caliph for everything."

"I ask him for nothing now."

"Well, my dear," said Mrs. Ermine, "you don't deserve to be rich."

"I am not rich," Eunice remarked.

"Ah, well, if you want a million!"

"I don't want anything," said Eunice.

That's not exactly true. She does want something, but I don't know what it is.

May 2.—Mr. Caliph is really very delightful. He made his appearance to-day and carried everything before him. When I say he carried everything, I mean he carried me; for Eunice had not my prejudices to get over. When I said to her after he had gone, "Your trustee is a very clever man," she only smiled a little, and turned away in silence. I suppose she was amused with the air of importance with which I announced this discovery. Eunice had made it several years ago, and could not be excited about it. I had an idea that some allusion would be made to the way he has neglected her—some apology at least for his long absence. But he did something better than this. He made no definite apology; he only expressed, in his manner, his look, his voice, a tenderness, a charming benevolence, which included and exceeded all apologies. He looks rather tired and preoccupied; he evidently has a great many irons of his own in the fire, and has been thinking these last weeks of larger questions than the susceptibilities of a little girl in New York who happened several years ago to have an exuberant mother. He is thoroughly genial, and is the best talker I have seen since my return. A totally different type from the young Adrian. He is not in the least handsome—is, indeed, rather ugly; but with a fine, expressive, pictorial ugliness. He is forty years old, large and stout, may even be pronounced fat; and there is something about him that I don't know how to describe except by calling it a certain richness. I have seen Italians who have it, but this is the first American. He talks with his eyes, as well as with his lips, and his features are wonderfully mobile. His smile is quick and delightful; his hands are well-shaped, but distinctly fat; he has a pale complexion and a magnificent brown beard—the beard of Haroun-al-Raschid. I suppose I must write it very small; but I have an intimate conviction that he is a Jew, or of Jewish origin. I see that in his plump, white face, of which the tone would please a painter, and which suggests fatigue, but is nevertheless all alive; in his remarkable eye, which is full of old expressions—expressions which linger there from the past, even when they are not active to-day; in his profile, in his anointed beard, in the very rings on his large pointed fingers. There is not a touch of all this in his step-brother; so I suppose the

Jewish blood is inherited from his father. I don't think he looks like a gentleman; he is something apart from all that. If he is not a gentleman, he is not in the least a bourgeois—neither is he of the Bohemian type. In short, as I say, he is a Jew; and Jews of the upper class have a style of their own. He is very clever, and I think genuinely kind. Nothing could be more charming than his way of talking to Eunice—a certain paternal interest mingled with an air of respectful gallantry (he gives her good advice, and at the same time pays her compliments); the whole thing being not in the least overdone. I think he found her changed—"more of a person," as Mrs. Ermine says; I even think he was a little surprised. She seems slightly afraid of him, which rather surprised me—she was, from her own account, so familiar with him of old. He is decidedly florid, and was very polite to me; that was a part of the floridity. He asked if we had seen his step-brother; begged us to be kind to him and to let him come and see us often. He doesn't know many people in New York, and at that age it is everything (I quote Mr. Caliph) for a young fellow to be at his ease with one or two charming women. "Adrian takes a great deal of knowing; is horribly shy; but is most intelligent, and has one of the sweetest natures! I'm very fond of him—he's all I've got. Unfortunately the poor boy is cursed with a competence. In this country there is nothing for such a young fellow to do; he hates business, and has absolutely no talent for it. I shall send him back here the next time I see him." Eunice made no answer to this, and, in fact, had little answer to make to most of Mr. Caliph's remarks, only sitting looking at the floor with a smile. I thought it proper therefore to reply that we had found Mr. Frank very pleasant, and hoped he would soon come again. Then I mentioned that the other day I had had a long visit from him alone; we had talked for an hour, and become excellent friends. Mr. Caliph, as I said this, was leaning forward with his elbow on his knee and his hand uplifted, grasping his thick beard. The other hand, with the elbow out, rested on the other knee; his head was turned toward me, askance. He looked at me a moment with his deep bright eye—the eye of a much older man than he; he might have been posing for a water-colour. If I had painted him, it would have been in a high-peaked cap, and an amber-coloured robe, with a wide girdle of pink silk wound many times round his waist, stuck full of knives with jewelled handles. Our eyes met, and we sat there exchanging a glance. I don't know whether he's vain, but I think he must see I appreciate him; I am sure he understands everything.

"I like you when you say that," he remarked at the end of a minute.

"I am glad to hear you like me!" This sounds horrid and pert as I relate it.

"I don't like every one," said Mr. Caliph.

"Neither do Eunice and I; do we, Eunice?"

"I am afraid we only try to," she answered, smiling her most beautiful smile.

"Try to? Heaven forbid! I protest against that," I cried. I said to Mr. Caliph that Eunice was too good.

"She comes honestly by that. Your mother was an angel, my child," he said to her.

Cousin Letitia was not an angel, but I have mentioned that Mr. Caliph is florid. "You used to be very good to her," Eunice murmured, raising her eyes to him.

He had got up; he was standing there. He bent his head, smiling like an Italian. "You must be the same, my child."

"What can I do?" Eunice asked.

"You can believe in me—you can trust me."

"I do, Mr. Caliph. Try me and see!"

This was unexpectedly gushing, and I instinctively turned away. Behind my back, I don't know what he did to her—I think it possible he kissed her. When you call a girl "my child," I suppose you may kiss her; but that may be only my bold imagination. When I turned round he had taken up his hat and stick, to say nothing of buttoning a very tightly-fitting coat round a very spacious person, and was ready to offer me his hand in farewell.

"I am so glad you are with her. I am so glad she has a companion so accomplished—so capable."

"So capable of what?" I said, laughing; for the speech was absurd, as he knows nothing about my accomplishments.

There is nothing solemn about Mr. Caliph; but he gave me a look which made it appear to me that my levity was in bad taste. Yes, humiliating as it is to write it here, I found myself rebuked by a Jew with fat hands! "Capable of advising her well!" he said softly.

"Ah, don't talk about advice," Eunice exclaimed. "Advice always gives an idea of trouble, and I am very much afraid of trouble."

"You ought to get married," he said, with his smile coming back to him.

Eunice coloured and turned away, and I observed—to say something—that this was just what Mrs. Ermine said.

"Mrs. Ermine? ah, I hear she's a charming woman!" And shortly after that he went away.

That was almost the only weak thing he said—the only thing for mere form, for of course no one can really think her charming; least of all a clever man like that. I don't like Americans to resemble Italians, or Italians to resemble Americans; but putting that aside, Mr. Caliph is very prepossessing. He is wonderfully good company; he will spoil us for other people. He made no allusion to business, and no appointment with Eunice for talking over certain matters that are pending; but I thought of this only half an hour after he had gone. I said nothing to Eunice about it, for she would have noticed the omission herself, and that was enough. The only other point in Mr. Caliph that was open to criticism is his asking Eunice to believe in him—to trust him. Why shouldn't she, pray? If that speech was curious—and, strange to say, it almost appeared so—it was incredibly naïf. But this quality is insupposable of Mr. Caliph; who ever heard of a naïf Jew? After he had gone I was on the point of saying to Eunice, "By the way, why did you never mention that he is a Hebrew? That's an important detail." But an impulse that I am not able to define stopped me, and now I am glad I didn't speak. I don't believe Eunice ever made the discovery, and I don't think she would like it if she did make it. That I should have done so on the instant only proves that I am in the habit of studying the human profile!

May 9.—Mrs. Ermine must have discovered that Mr. Caliph has heard she is charming, for she is perpetually coming in here with the hope of meeting him. She appears to think that he comes every day; for when she misses him, which she has done three times (that is, she arrives just after he goes), she says that if she doesn't catch him on the morrow she will go and call upon him. She is capable of that, I think; and it makes no difference that he is the busiest of men and she the idlest of women. He has been here four times since his first call, and has the air of wishing to make up for the neglect that preceded it. His manner to Eunice is perfect; he continues to call her "my child," but in a superficial, impersonal way, as a Catholic priest might do it. He tells us stories of Washington, describes the people there, and makes us wonder whether we should care for K Street and 14 ½ Street. As yet, to the best of my knowledge, not a word about Eunice's affairs; he behaves as if he had simply forgotten them. It was, after all, not out of place the other day to ask her to "believe in him"; the faith wouldn't come as a matter of course. On the other hand he is so pleasant that one would believe in him just to oblige him. He has a great deal of trust-business, and a great deal of law-business of every kind. So at least he says; we really know very little about him but what he tells us. When I say "we," of course I speak mainly for myself, as I am perpetually forgetting that he is not so new to Eunice as he is to me. She knows what she knows, but I only know what I see. I have been wondering a good deal what is thought of Mr. Caliph "down-town," as they say here, but without much result, for naturally I can't go down-town and see. The appearance of the thing prevents my asking questions about him; it would be very compromising to Eunice, and make people think that she complains of him—which is so far from being the case. She likes him just as he is, and is apparently quite satisfied. I gather, moreover, that he is thought very brilliant, though a little peculiar, and that he has made a great deal of money. He has a way of his own of doing things, and carries imagination and humour, and a sense of the beautiful, into Wall Street and the Stock Exchange. Mrs. Ermine announced the other day that he is "considered the most fascinating man in New York"; but that is the romantic up-town view of him, and not what I want. His brother has gone out of town for a few days, but he continues to recommend the young Adrian to our hospitality. There is something really touching in his relation to that rather limited young man.

May 11.—Mrs. Ermine is in high spirits; she has met Mr. Caliph—I don't know where—and she quite confirms the up-town view. She thinks him the most fascinating man she has ever seen, and she wonders that we should have said so little about him. He is so handsome, so high-bred; his manners are so perfect; he's a regular old dear. I think, of course ill-naturedly, several degrees less well of him since I have heard Mrs. Ermine's impressions. He is not handsome, he is not high-bred, and his manners are not perfect. They are original, and they are expressive; and if one likes him there is an interest in looking for what he will do and say. But if one should happen to dislike him, one would detest his manners and think them familiar and vulgar. As for breeding, he has about him, indeed, the marks of antiquity of race; yet I don't think Mrs. Ermine would have liked me to say, "Oh yes, all Jews have blood!" Besides, I couldn't before Eunice. Perhaps I consider Eunice too much; perhaps I am betrayed by my old habit of trying to see through millstones; perhaps I interpret things too richly—just as (I know) when I try to paint an old wall I attempt to put in too much "character"; character being in old walls, after all, a finite quantity. At any rate she seems to me rather nervous about Mr. Caliph: that appeared after a little when Mrs. Ermine came back to the subject. She had a great deal to say about the oddity of her never having seen him before, of old, "for after all," as she remarked, "we move in the same society—he moves in the very best." She used to hear Eunice talk about her trustee, but she supposed a trustee must be some horrid old man with a lot of papers in his hand, sitting all day in an office. She never supposed he was a prince in disguise. "We've got a trustee somewhere, only I never see him; my husband does all the business. No wonder he keeps him out of the way if he resembles Mr. Caliph." And then suddenly she said to Eunice, "My dear, why don't you marry him? I should think you would want to." Mrs. Ermine doesn't look through millstones; she contents herself with giving them a poke with her parasol. Eunice coloured, and said she hadn't been asked; she was evidently not pleased with Mrs. Ermine's joke, which was of course as flat as you like. Then she added in a moment—"I should be very sorry to marry Mr. Caliph, even if he were to ask me. I like him, but I don't like him enough for that."

"I should think he would be quite in your style—he's so literary. They say he writes," Mrs. Ermine went on.

"Well, I don't write," Eunice answered, laughing.

"You could if you would try. I'm sure you could make a lovely book." Mrs. Ermine's amiability is immense.

"It's safe for you to say that—you never read."

"I have no time," said Mrs. Ermine, "but I like literary conversation. It saves time, when it comes in that way. Mr. Caliph has ever so much."

"He keeps it for you. With us he is very frivolous," I ventured to observe.

"Well, what you call frivolous! I believe you think the prayer-book frivolous."

"Mr. Caliph will never marry any one," Eunice said, after a moment. "That I am very sure of."

Mrs. Ermine stared; there never is so little expression in her face as when she is surprised. But she soon recovered herself. "Don't you believe that! He will take some quiet little woman, after you have all given him up."

Eunice was sitting at the piano, but had wheeled round on

the stool when her cousin came in. She turned back to it and struck a few vague chords, as if she were feeling for something. "Please don't speak that way; I don't like it," she said, as she went on playing.

"I will speak any way you like!" Mrs. Ermine cried, with her vacant laugh.

"I think it very low." For Eunice this was severe. "Girls are not always thinking about marriage. They are not always thinking of people like Mr. Caliph—that way."

"They must have changed then, since my time! Wasn't it so in yours, Miss Condit?" She's so stupid that I don't think she meant to make a point.

"I had no 'time,' Mrs. Ermine. I was born an old maid."

"Well, the old maids are the worst. I don't see why it's low to talk about marriage. It's thought very respectable to marry. You have only to look round you."

"I don't want to look round me; it's not always so beautiful, what you see," Eunice said, with a small laugh and a good deal of perversity, for a young woman so reasonable.

"I guess you read too much," said Mrs. Ermine, getting up and setting her bonnet-ribbons at the mirror.

"I should think he would hate them!" Eunice exclaimed, striking her chords.

"Hate who?" her cousin asked.

"Oh, all the silly girls."

"Who is 'he,' pray?" This ingenious inquiry was mine.

"Oh, the Grand Turk!" said Eunice, with her voice covered by the sound of her piano. Her piano is a great resource.

May 12.—This afternoon, while we were having our tea, the Grand Turk was ushered in, carrying the most wonderful bouquet of Boston roses that seraglio ever produced. (That image, by the way, is rather mixed; but as I write for myself alone, it may stand.) At the end of ten minutes he asked Eunice if he might see her alone—"on a little matter of business." I instantly rose to leave them, but Eunice said that she would rather talk with him in the library; so she led him off to that apartment. I remained in the drawing-room, saying to myself that I had at last discovered the *fin mot* of Mr. Caliph's peculiarities, which is so very simple that I am a great goose not to have perceived it before. He is a man with a system; and his system is simply to keep business and entertainment perfectly distinct. There may be pleasure for him in his figures, but there are no figures in his pleasure—which has hitherto been to call upon Eunice as a man of the world. Today he was to be the trustee; I could see it in spite of his bouquet, as soon as he came in. The Boston roses didn't contradict that, for the excellent reason that as soon as he had shaken hands with Eunice, who looked at the flowers and not at him, he presented them to Catherine Condit. Eunice then looked at this lady; and as I took the roses I met her eyes, which had a charming light of pleasure. It would be base in me, even in this strictly private record, to suggest that she might possibly have been displeased; but if I cannot say that the expression of her face was lovely without appearing in some degree to point to an ignoble alternative, it is the fault of human nature. Why Mr. Caliph should suddenly think it necessary to offer flowers to Catherine Condit—that is a line of inquiry by itself. As I said some time back, it's a part of his floridity. Besides, any presentation of flowers seems sudden; I don't know why, but it's always rather a *coup de théâtre.* I am writing late at night; they stand on my table, and their fragrance is in the air. I don't say it for the flowers, but no one has ever treated poor Miss Condit with such consistent consideration as Mr. Caliph. Perhaps she is morbid: this is probably the Diary of a Morbid Woman; but in such a matter as that she admires consistency. That little glance of Eunice comes back to me as I write; she is a pure, enchanting soul. Mrs. Ermine came in while she was in the library with Mr. Caliph, and immediately noticed the Boston roses, which effaced all the other flowers in the room.

"Were they sent from her seat?" she asked. Then, before I could answer, "I am going to have some people to dinner today; they would look very well in the middle."

"If you wish me to offer them to you, I really can't; I prize them too much."

"Oh, are they yours? Of course you prize them! I don't suppose you have many."

"These are the first I have ever received—from Mr. Caliph."

"From Mr. Caliph? Did he give them to *you*?" Mrs. Ermine's intonations are not delicate. That "*you*" should be in enormous capitals.

"With his own hand—a quarter of an hour ago." This sounds triumphant, as I write it; but it was no great sensation to triumph over Mrs. Ermine.

She laid down the bouquet, looking almost thoughtful. "He *does* want to marry Eunice," she declared in a moment. This is the region in which, after a flight of fancy, she usually alights. I am sick of the irrepressible verb; just at that moment, however, it was unexpected, and I answered that I didn't understand.

"That's why he gives you flowers," she explained. But the explanation made the matter darker still, and Mrs. Ermine went on: "Isn't there some French proverb about paying one's court to the mother in order to gain the daughter? Eunice is the daughter, and you are the mother."

"And you are the grandmother, I suppose! Do you mean that he wishes me to intercede?"

"I can't imagine why else!" and smiling, with her wide lips, she stared at the flowers.

"At that rate you too will get your bouquet," I said.

"Oh, I have no influence! You ought to do something in return—to offer to paint his portrait."

"I don't offer that, you know; people ask me. Besides, you have spoiled me for common models!"

It strikes me, as I write this, that we had gone rather far—farther than it seemed at the time. We might have gone farther yet, however, if at this moment Eunice had not come back with Mr. Caliph, who appeared to have settled his little matter of business briskly enough. He remained the man of business to the end, and, to Mrs. Ermine's evident disappointment, declined to sit down again. He was in a hurry; he had an engagement.

"Are you going up or down? I have a carriage at the door," she broke in.

"At Fifty-third Street one is usually going down"; and he gave his peculiar smile, which always seems so much beyond the scope of the words it accompanies. "If you will give me a lift I shall be very grateful."

He went off with her, she being much divided between the prospect of driving with him and her loss of the chance to find out what he had been saying to Eunice. She probably believed he had been proposing to her, and I hope he mystified her well in the carriage.

He had not been proposing to Eunice; he had given her a cheque, and made her sign some papers. The cheque was for a thousand dollars, but I have no knowledge of the papers. When I took up my abode with her I made up my mind that the only way to preserve an appearance of disinterestedness was to know nothing whatever of the details of her pecuniary affairs. She has a very good little head of her own, and if she shouldn't understand them herself it would be quite out of my power to help her. I don't know why I should care about *appearing* disinterested, when I have in quite sufficient measure the consciousness of being so; but in point of fact I do, and I value that purity as much as any other. Besides, Mr. Caliph is her supreme adviser, and of course makes everything clear to her. At least I hope he does. I couldn't help saying as much as this to Eunice.

"My dear child, I suppose you understand what you sign. Mr. Caliph ought to be—what shall I call it?—crystalline."

She looked at me with the smile that had come into her face when she saw him give me the flowers. "Oh yes, I think so. If I didn't, it's my own fault. He explains everything so beautifully that it's a pleasure to listen. I always read what I sign."

"Je l'espère bien!" I said, laughing.

She looked a little grave. "The closing up a trust is very complicated."

"Yours is not closed yet? It strikes me as very slow."

"Everything can't be done at once. Besides, he has asked for a little delay. Part of my affairs, indeed, are now in my own hands; otherwise I shouldn't have to sign."

"Is that a usual request—for delay?"

"Oh yes, perfectly. Besides, I don't want everything in my own control. That is, I want it some day, because I think I ought to accept the responsibilities, as I accept all the pleasures; but I am not in a hurry. This way is so comfortable, and Mr. Caliph takes so much trouble for me."

"I suppose he has a handsome commission," I said, rather crudely.

"He has no commission at all; he would never take one."

"In your place, I would much rather he should take one."

"I have asked him to, but he won't!" Eunice said, looking now extremely grave.

Her gravity indeed was so great that it made me smile. "He is wonderfully generous!"

"He is indeed."

"And is it to be indefinitely delayed—the termination of his trust?"

"Oh no; only a few months, 'till he gets things into shape,' as he says."

"He has had several years for that, hasn't he?"

Eunice turned away; evidently our talk was painful to her. But there was something that vaguely alarmed me in her taking, or at least accepting, the sentimental view of Mr. Caliph's services. "I don't think you are kind, Catherine; you seem to suspect him," she remarked, after a little.

"Suspect him of what?"

"Of not wishing to give up the property."

"My dear Eunice, you put things into terrible words! Seriously, I should never think of suspecting him of anything so silly. What could his wishes count for? Is not the thing regulated by law—by the terms of your mother's will? The trust expires of itself at a certain period, doesn't it? Mr. Caliph, surely, has only to act accordingly."

"It is just what he is doing. But there are more papers necessary, and they will not be ready for a few weeks more."

"Don't have too many papers; they are as bad as too few. And take advice of some one else—say of your cousin Ermine, who is so much more sensible than his wife."

"I want no advice," said Eunice, in a tone which showed me that I had said enough. And presently she went on, "I thought you liked Mr. Caliph."

"So I do, immensely. He gives beautiful flowers."

"Ah, you are horrid!" she murmured.

"Of course I am horrid. That's my business—to be horrid." And I took the liberty of being so again, half an hour later, when she remarked that she must take good care of the cheque Mr. Caliph had brought her, as it would be a good while before she should have another. "Why should it be longer than usual?" I asked. "Is he going to keep your income for himself?"

"I am not to have any till the end of the year—any from the trust, at least. Mr. Caliph has been converting some old houses into shops, so that they will bring more rent. But the alterations have to be paid for—and he takes part of my income to do it."

"And pray what are you to live on meanwhile?"

"I have enough without that; and I have savings."

"It strikes me as a cool proceeding, all the same."

"He wrote to me about it before we came home, and I thought that way was best."

"I don't think he ought to have asked you," I said. "As your trustee, he acts in his discretion."

"You are hard to please," Eunice answered.

That is perfectly true; but I rejoined that I couldn't make out whether he consulted her too much or too little. And I don't know that my failure to make it out in the least matters!

May 13.—Mrs. Ermine turned up to-day at an earlier hour than usual, and I saw as soon as she got into the room that she had something to announce. This time it was not an engage-ment. "He sent me a bouquet—Boston roses—quite as many as yours! They arrived this morning, before I had finished breakfast." This speech was addressed to me, and Mrs. Ermine looked almost brilliant. Eunice scarcely followed her.

"She is talking about Mr. Caliph," I explained.

Eunice stared a moment; then her face melted into a deep little smile. "He seems to give flowers to every one but to me." I could see that this reflection gave her remarkable pleasure.

"Well, when he gives them, he's thinking of you," said Mrs. Ermine. "He wants to get us on his side."

"On his side?"

"Oh yes; some day he will have need of us!" And Mrs. Ermine tried to look sprightly and insinuating. But she is too utterly *fade*, and I think it is not worth while to talk any more to Eunice just now about her trustee. So, to anticipate Mrs. Ermine, I said to her quickly, but very quietly—

"He sent you flowers simply because you had taken him into your carriage last night. It was an acknowledgment of your great kindness."

She hesitated a moment. "Possibly. We had a charming drive—ever so far down-town." Then, turning to Eunice, she exclaimed, "My dear, you don't know that man till you have had a drive with him!" When does one know Mrs. Ermine? Every day she is a surprise!

May 19.—Adrian Frank has come back to New York, and has been three times at this house—once to dinner, and twice at tea-time. After his brother's strong expression of the hope that we should take an interest in him, Eunice appears to have thought that the least she could do was to ask him to dine. She appears never to have offered this privilege to Mr. Caliph, by the way; I think her view of his cleverness is such that she imag-ines she knows no one sufficiently brilliant to be invited to meet him. She thought Mrs. Ermine good enough to meet Mr. Frank, and she had also young Woodley—Willie Woodley, as they call him—and Mr. Latrobe. It was not very amusing. Mrs.

Ermine made love to Mr. Woodley, who took it serenely; and the dark Latrobe talked to me about the Seventh Regiment—an impossible subject. Mr. Frank made an occasional remark to Eunice, next whom he was placed; but he seemed constrained and frightened, as if he knew that his step-brother had recommended him highly and felt it was impossible to come up to the mark. He is really very modest; it is impossible not to like him. Every now and then he looked at me, with his clear blue eye conscious and expanded, as if to beg me to help him on with Eunice; and then, when I threw in a word, to give their conversation a push, he looked at her in the same way, as if to express the hope that she would not abandon him. There was no danger of this, she only wished to be agreeable to him; but she was nervous and preoccupied, as she always is when she has people to dinner—she is so afraid they may be bored—and I think that half the time she didn't understand what he said. She told me afterwards that she liked him more even than she liked him at first; that he has, in her opinion, better manners, in spite of his shyness, than any of the young men; and that he must have a nice nature to have such a charming face;—all this she told me, and she added that, notwithstanding all this, there is something in Mr. Adrian Frank that makes her uncomfortable. It is perhaps rather heartless, but after this, when he called two days ago, I went out of the room and left them alone together. The truth is, there is something in this tall, fair, vague, inconsequent youth, who would look like a Prussian lieutenant if Prussian lieutenants ever hesitated, and who is such a singular mixture of confusion and candour—there is something about him that is not altogether to my own taste, and that is why I took the liberty of leaving him. Oddly enough, I don't in the least know what it is; I usually know why I dislike people. I don't dislike the blushing Adrian, however—that is, after all, the oddest part. No, the oddest part of it is that I think I have a feeling of pity for him; that is probably why (if it were not my duty sometimes to remain) I should always depart when he comes. I don't like to see the people I pity; to be pitied by me is

too low a depth. Why I should lavish my compassion on Mr.
Frank of course passes my comprehension. He is young, intelligent, in perfect health, master of a handsome fortune, and
favourite brother of Haroun-al-Raschid. Such are the consequences of being a woman of imagination. When, at dinner, I
asked Eunice if he had been as interesting as usual, she said she
would leave it to me to judge; he had talked altogether about
Miss Condit! He thinks her very attractive! Poor fellow, when it
is necessary he doesn't hesitate, though I can't imagine why it
should be necessary. I think that *au fond* he bores Eunice a little; like many girls of the delicate, sensitive kind, she likes
older, more confident men.

May 24.—He has just made me a remarkable communication! This morning I went into the Park in quest of a "bit," with
some colours and brushes in a small box, and that wonderfully
compressible campstool which I can carry in my pocket. I wandered vaguely enough, for half an hour, through the carefully-
arranged scenery, the idea of which appears to be to represent
the earth's surface *en raccourci*, and at last discovered a small
clump of birches which, with their white stems and their little
raw green bristles, were not altogether uninspiring. The place
was quiet—there were no nurse-maids nor bicycles; so I took
up a position and enjoyed an hour's successful work. At last I
heard some one say behind me, "I think I ought to tell you I'm
looking!" It was Adrian Frank, who had recognised me at a distance, and, without my hearing him, had walked across the
grass to where I sat. This time I couldn't leave him, for I hadn't
finished my sketch. He sat down near me, on an artistically-
preserved rock, and we ended by having a good deal of talk—in
which, however, I did the listening, for I can't express myself in
two ways at once. What I listened to was this—that Mr. Caliph
wishes his step-brother to "make up" to Eunice, and that the
candid Adrian wishes to know what I think of his chances.

"Are you in love with her?" I asked.

"Oh dear, no! If I were in love with her I should go straight
in, without—without this sort of thing."

"You mean without asking people's opinion?"

"Well, yes. Without even asking yours."

I told him that he needn't say "even" mine; for mine would not be worth much. His announcement rather startled me at first, but after I had thought of it a little, I found in it a good deal to admire. I have seen so many "arranged" marriages that have been happy, and so many "sympathetic" unions that have been wretched, that the political element doesn't altogether shock me. Of course I can't imagine Eunice making a political marriage, and I said to Mr. Frank, very promptly, that she might consent if she could be induced to love him, but would never be governed in her choice by his advantages. I said "advantages" in order to be polite; the singular number would have served all the purpose. His only advantage is his fortune; for he has neither looks, talents, nor position that would dazzle a girl who is herself clever and rich. This, then, is what Mr. Caliph has had in his head all this while—this is what has made him so anxious that we should like his step-brother. I have an idea that I ought to be rather scandalised, but I feel my pulse and find that I am almost pleased. I don't mean at the idea of her marrying poor Mr. Frank; I mean at such an indication that Mr. Caliph takes an interest in her. I don't know whether it is one of the regular duties of a trustee to provide the trustful with a husband; perhaps in that case his merit may be less. I suppose he has said to himself that if she marries his step-brother she won't marry a worse man. Of course it is possible that he may not have thought of Eunice at all, and may simply have wished the guileless Adrian to do a good thing without regard to Eunice's point of view. I am afraid that even this idea doesn't shock me. Trying to make people marry is, under any circumstances, an unscrupulous game; but the offence is minimised when it is a question of an honest man marrying an angel. Eunice is the angel, and the young Adrian has all the air of being honest. It would, naturally, not be the union of her secret dreams, for the hero of those pure visions would have to be clever and distinguished. Mr. Frank is neither of these things, but I believe he is perfectly good. Of course he is weak—to come and take a wife simply because his brother has told him to—or is he doing it simply for form, believing that she will never have him, that he consequently doesn't expose himself, and that he will therefore have on easy terms, since he seems to value it, the credit of having obeyed Mr. Caliph? Why he should value it is a matter between themselves, which I am not obliged to know. I don't think I care at all for the relations of men between themselves. Their relations with women are bad enough, but when there is no woman to save it a little—*merci*! I shouldn't think that the young Adrian would care to subject himself to a simple refusal, for it is not gratifying to receive the cold shoulder, even from a woman you don't want to marry. After all, he may want to marry her; there are all sorts of reasons in things. I told him I wouldn't undertake to do anything, and the more I think of it the less I am willing. It would be a weight off my mind to see her comfortably settled in life, beyond the possibility of marrying some highly varnished brute—a fate in certain circumstances quite open to her. She is perfectly capable—with her folded angel's wings—of bestowing herself upon the baker, upon the fish-monger, if she were to take a fancy to him. The clever man of her dreams might beat her or get tired of her; but I am sure that Mr. Frank, if he should pronounce his marriage-vows, would keep them to the letter. From that to pushing her into his arms, however, is a long way. I went so far as to tell him that he had my good wishes; but I made him understand that I can give him no help. He sat for some time poking a hole in the earth with his stick and watching the operation. Then he said, with his wide, exaggerated smile—the one thing in his face that recalls his brother, though it is so different—"I think I should like to try." I felt rather sorry for him, and made him talk of something else; and we separated without his alluding to Eunice, though at the last he looked at me for a moment intently, with something on his lips, which was probably a return to his idea. I stopped him; I told him I always required solitude for my finishing-touches. He thinks me *brusque* and queer, but he went away. I don't know what he means to do; I am curious to see whether he will begin his siege. It can scarcely be said, as yet, to have begun—Eunice, at any rate, is all unconscious.

June 6.—Her unconsciousness is being rapidly dispelled; Mr. Frank has been here every day since I last wrote. He is a singular youth, and I don't make him out; I think there is more in him than I supposed at first. He doesn't bore us, and he has become, to a certain extent, one of the family. I like him very much, and he excites my curiosity. I don't quite see where he expects to come out. I mentioned some time back that Eunice had told me he made her uncomfortable; and now, if that continues, she appears to have resigned herself. He has asked her repeatedly to drive with him, and twice she has consented; he has a very pretty pair of horses, and a vehicle that holds but two persons. I told him I could give him no positive help, but I do leave them together. Of course Eunice has noticed this—it is the only intimation I have given her that I am aware of his intentions. I have constantly expected her to say something, but she has said nothing, and it is possible that Mr. Frank is making an impression. He makes love very reasonably; evidently his idea is to be intensely gradual. Of course it isn't gradual to come every day; but he does very little on any one occasion. That, at least, is my impression; for when I talk of his making love I don't mean that I see it. When the three of us are together he talks to me quite as much as to her, and there is no difference in his manner from one of us to the other. His shyness is wearing off, and he blushes so much less that I have discovered his natural hue. It has several shades less of crimson than I supposed. I have taken care that he should not see me alone, for I don't wish him to talk to me of what he is doing—I wish to have nothing to say about it. He has looked at me several times in the same way in which he looked just before we parted, that day he found me sketching in the Park; that is, as if he wished to have some special understanding with me. But I don't want a special understanding, and I pretend not to see his looks. I don't exactly see why Eunice doesn't speak to me, and why she expresses no surprise at Mr. Frank's sudden devotion. Perhaps Mr. Caliph has notified her, and she is prepared for everything—prepared even to accept the young Adrian. I have an idea he will be rather taken in if she does. Perhaps the day will come soon when I shall think it well to say: "Take care, take care; you *may* succeed!" He improves on acquaintance; he knows a great many things, and he is a gentleman to his finger-tips. We talk very often about Rome; he has made out every inscription for himself, and has got them all written down in a little book. He brought it the other afternoon and read some of them out to us, and it was more amusing than it may sound. I listen to such things because I can listen to anything about Rome; and Eunice listens possibly because Mr. Caliph has told her to. She appears ready to do anything he tells her; he has been sending her some more papers to sign. He has not been here since the day he gave me the flowers; he went back to Washington shortly after that. She has received several letters from him, accompanying documents that look very legal. She has said nothing to me about them, and since I uttered those words of warning which I noted here at the time, I have asked no questions and offered no criticism. Sometimes I wonder whether I myself had not better speak to Mr. Ermine; it is only the fear of being idiotic and meddlesome that restrains me. It seems to me so odd there should be no one else; Mr. Caliph appears to have everything in his own hands. We are to go down to our "seat," as Mrs. Ermine says, next week. That brilliant woman has left town herself, like many other people, and is staying with one of her daughters. Then she is going to the other, and then she is coming to Eunice, at Cornerville.

II

JUNE 8.—Late this afternoon—about an hour before dinner —Mr. Frank arrived with what Mrs. Ermine calls his equipage, and asked her to take a short drive with him. At first she declined—said it was too hot, too late, she was too tired; but he seemed very much in earnest and begged her to think better of it. She consented at last, and when she had left the room to arrange herself, he turned to me with a little grin of elation. I saw he was going to say something about his prospects, and I determined, this time, to give him a chance. Besides, I was curious to know how he believed himself to be getting on. To my surprise, he disappointed my curiosity; he only said, with his timid brightness, "I am always so glad when I carry my point."

"Your point? Oh yes. I think I know what you mean."

"It's what I told you that day." He seemed slightly surprised that I should be in doubt as to whether he had really presented himself as a lover.

"Do you mean to ask her to marry you?"

He stared a little, looking graver. "Do you mean to-day?"

"Well, yes, to-day, for instance; you have urged her so to drive."

"I don't think I will do it to-day; it's too soon."

His gravity was natural enough, I suppose; but it had suddenly become so intense that the effect was comical, and I could not help laughing. "Very good; whenever you please."

"Don't you think it's too soon?" he asked.

"Ah, I know nothing about it."

"I have seen her alone only four or five times."

"You must go on as you think best," I said.

"It's hard to tell. My position is very difficult." And then he began to smile again. He is certainly very odd.

It is my fault, I suppose, that I am too impatient of what I don't understand; and I don't understand this odd mixture of calculation and passion, or the singular alternation of Mr. Frank's confessions and reserves. "I can't enter into your position," I said; "I can't advise you or help you in any way." Even to myself my voice sounded a little hard as I spoke, and he was evidently discomposed by it.

He blushed as usual, and fell to putting on his gloves. "I

think a great deal of your opinion, and for several days I have wanted to ask you."

"Yes, I have seen that."

"How have you seen it?"

"By the way you have looked at me."

He hesitated a moment. "Yes, I have looked at you—I know that. There is a great deal in your face to see."

This remark, under the circumstances, struck me as absurd; I began to laugh again. "You speak of it as if it were a collection of curiosities." He looked away now, he wouldn't meet my eye, and I saw that I had made him feel thoroughly uncomfortable. To lead the conversation back into the commonplace, I asked him where he intended to drive.

"It doesn't matter much where we go—it's so pretty everywhere now." He was evidently not thinking of his drive, and suddenly he broke out, "I want to know whether you think she likes me."

"I haven't the least idea. She hasn't told me."

"Do you think she knows that I mean to propose to her?"

"You ought to be able to judge of that better than I."

"I am afraid of taking too much for granted; also of taking her by surprise."

"So that—in her agitation—she might accept you? Is that what you are afraid of?"

"I don't know what makes you say that. I wish her to accept me."

"Are you very sure?"

"Perfectly sure. Why not? She is a charming creature."

"So much the better, then; perhaps she will."

"You don't believe it," he exclaimed, as if it were very clever of him to have discovered that.

"You think too much of what I believe. That has nothing to do with the matter."

"No, I suppose not," said Mr. Frank, apparently wishing very much to agree with me.

"You had better find out as soon as possible from Eunice herself," I added.

"I haven't expected to know—for some time."

"Do you mean for a year or two? She will be ready to tell you before that."

"Oh no—not a year or two; but a few weeks."

"You know you come to the house every day. You ought to explain to her."

"Perhaps I had better not come so often."

"Perhaps not!"

"I like it very much," he said, smiling.

I looked at him a moment; I don't know what he has got in his eyes. "Don't change! You are such a good young man that I don't know what we should do without you." And I left him to wait alone for Eunice.

From my window, above, I saw them leave the door; they make a fair, bright young couple as they sit together. They had not been gone a quarter of an hour when Mr. Caliph's name was brought up to me. He had asked for me—me alone; he begged that I would do him the favour to see him for ten minutes. I don't know why this announcement should have made me nervous; but it did. My heart beat at the prospect of entering into direct relations with Mr. Caliph. He is very clever, much thought of, and talked of; and yet I had vaguely suspected him—of I don't know what! I became conscious of that, and felt the responsibility of it; though I didn't foresee, and indeed don't think I foresee yet, any danger of a collision between us. It is to be noted, moreover, that even a woman who is both plain and conceited must feel a certain agitation at entering the presence of Haroun-al-Raschid. I had begun to dress for dinner, and I kept him waiting till I had taken my usual time to finish. I always take some such revenge as that upon men who make me nervous. He is the sort of man who feels immediately whether a woman is well-dressed or not; but I don't think this reflection really had much to do with my putting on the freshest of my three little French gowns.

He sat there, watch in hand; at least he slipped it into his pocket as I came into the room. He was not pleased at having had to wait, and when I apologised, hypocritically, for having kept him, he answered, with a certain dryness, that he had come to transact an important piece of business in a very short space of time. I wondered what his business could be, and whether he had come to confess to me that he had spent Eunice's money for his own purposes. Did he wish me to use my influence with her not to make a scandal? He didn't look like a man who has come to ask a favour of that kind; but I am sure that if he ever does ask it he will not look at all as he might be expected to look. He was clad in white garments, from head to foot, in recognition of the hot weather, and he had half a dozen roses in his button-hole. This time his flowers were for himself. His white clothes made him look as big as Henry VIII; but don't tell me he is not a Jew! He's a Jew of the artistic, not of the commercial type; and as I stood there I thought him a very strange person to have as one's trustee. It seemed to me that he would carry such an office into transcendental regions, out of all common jurisdictions; and it was a comfort to me to remember that I have no property to be taken care of. Mr. Caliph kept a pocket-handkerchief, with an enormous monogram, in his large tapering hand, and every other moment he touched his face with it. He evidently suffers from the heat. With all that, *il est bien beau.* His business was not what had at first occurred to me; but I don't know that it was much less strange.

"I knew I should find you alone, because Adrian told me this morning that he meant to come and ask our young friend to drive. I was glad of that; I have been wishing to see you alone, and I didn't know how to manage it."

"You see it's very simple. Didn't you send your brother?" I asked. In another place, to another person, this might have sounded impertinent; but evidently, addressed to Mr. Caliph, things have a special measure, and this I instinctively felt. He will take a great deal, and he will give a great deal.

He looked at me a moment, as if he were trying to measure what I would take. "I see you are going to be a very satisfactory person to talk with," he answered. "That's exactly what I counted on. I want you to help me."

"I thought there was some reason why Mr. Frank should urge Eunice so to go," I went on; refreshed a little, I admit, by these words of commendation. "At first she was unwilling."

"Is she usually unwilling—and does he usually have to be urgent?" he asked, like a man pleased to come straight to the point.

"What does it matter, so long as she consents in the end?" I responded, with a smile that made him smile. There is a singular stimulus, even a sort of excitement, in talking with him; he makes one wish to venture. And this not as women usually venture, because they have a sense of impunity, but, on the contrary, because one has a prevision of penalties—those penalties which give a kind of dignity to sarcasm. He must be a dangerous man to irritate.

"Do you think she will consent, in the end?" he inquired; and though I had now foreseen what he was coming to, I felt that, even with various precautions, which he had plainly decided not to take, there would still have been a certain crudity in it when, a moment later, he put his errand into words. "I want my little brother to marry her, and I want you to help me bring it about." Then he told me that he knew his brother had already spoken to me, but that he believed I had not promised him much countenance. He wished me to think well of the plan; it would be a delightful marriage.

"Delightful for your brother, yes. That's what strikes me most."

"Delightful for him, certainly; but also very pleasant for Eunice, as things go here. Adrian is the best fellow in the world; he's a gentleman; he hasn't a vice or a fault; he is very well educated; and he has twenty thousand a year. A lovely property."

"Not in trust?" I said, looking into Mr. Caliph's extraordinary eyes.

"Oh no; he has full control of it. But he is wonderfully careful."

"He doesn't trouble you with it?"

"Oh, dear, no; why should he? Thank God, I haven't got that on my back. His property comes to him from his father, who had nothing to do with me; didn't even like me, I think. He has capital advisers—presidents of banks, overseers of hospitals, and all that sort of thing. They have put him in the way of some excellent investments."

As I write this, I am surprised at my audacity; but, somehow, it didn't seem so great at the time, and he gave absolutely no sign of seeing more in what I said than appeared. He evidently desires the marriage immensely, and he was thinking only of putting it before me so that I too should think well of it; for evidently, like his brother, he has the most exaggerated opinion of my influence with Eunice. On Mr. Frank's part this doesn't surprise me so much; but I confess it seems to me odd that a man of Mr. Caliph's acuteness should make the mistake of taking me for one of those persons who covet influence and like to pull the wires of other people's actions. I have a horror of influence, and should never have consented to come and live with Eunice if I had not seen that she is at bottom much stronger than I, who am not at all strong, in spite of my grand airs. Mr. Caliph, I suppose, cannot conceive of a woman in my dependent position being indifferent to opportunities for working in the dark; but he ought to leave those vulgar imputations to Mrs. Ermine. He ought, with his intelligence, to see one as one is; or do I possibly exaggerate that intelligence? "Do you know I feel as if you were asking me to take part in a conspiracy?" I made that announcement with as little delay as possible.

He stared a moment, and then he said that he didn't in the least repudiate that view of his proposal. He admitted that he was a conspirator—in an excellent cause. All match-making was conspiracy. It was impossible that as a superior woman I should enter into his ideas, and he was sure that I had seen too much of the world to say anything so *banal* as that the young people were not in love with each other. That was only a basis for marriage when better things were lacking. It was decent, it was fitting, that Eunice should be settled in life; his conscience would not be at rest about her until he should see that well arranged. He was not in the least afraid of that word "arrangement"; a marriage was an eminently practical matter, and it could not be too much arranged. He confessed that he took the European view. He thought that a young girl's elders ought to see that she marries in a way in which certain definite proprieties are observed. He was sure of his brother; he knew how faultless Adrian was. He talked for some time, and said a great deal that I had said to myself the other day, after Mr. Frank spoke to me; said, in particular, very much what I had thought, about the beauty of arrangements—that there are far too few among Americans who marry, that we are the people in the world who divorce and separate most, that there would be much less of this sort of thing if young people were helped to choose; if marriages were, as one might say, presented to them. I listened to Mr. Caliph with my best attention, thinking it was odd that, on his lips, certain things which I had phrased to myself in very much the same way should sound so differently. They ought to have sounded better, uttered as they were with the energy, the authority, the lucidity, of a man accustomed to making arguments; but somehow they didn't. I am afraid I am very perverse. I answered—I hardly remember what; but there was a taint of that perversity in it. As he rejoined, I felt that he was growing urgent—very urgent; he has an immense desire that something may be done. I remember saying at last, "What I don't understand is why your brother should wish to marry my cousin. He has told me he is not in love with her. Has your presentation of the idea, as you call it—has that been enough? Is he acting simply at your request?"

I saw that his reply was not perfectly ready, and for a moment those strange eyes of his emitted a ray that I had not seen before. They seemed to say, "Are you really taking liberties with me? Be on your guard; I may be dangerous." But he always smiles. Yes, I think he is dangerous, though I don't know exactly what he could do to me. I believe he would smile at the hangman, if he were condemned to meet him. He is very angry with his brother for having admitted to me that the sentiment he entertains for Eunice is not a passion; as if it would have been possible for him, under my eyes, to pretend that he is in love! I don't think I am afraid of Mr. Caliph; I don't desire to take liberties with him (as his eyes seemed to call it) or with any one; but, decidedly, I am not afraid of him. If it came to protecting Eunice, for instance; to demanding justice—But what extravagances am I writing? He answered, in a moment, with a good deal of dignity, and even a good deal of reason, that his brother has the greatest admiration for my cousin, that he agrees fully and cordially with everything he (Mr. Caliph) has said to him about its being an excellent match, that he wants very much to marry, and wants to marry as a gentleman should. If he is not in love with Eunice, moreover, he is not in love with any one else.

"I hope not!" I said, with a laugh; whereupon Mr. Caliph got up, looking, for him, rather grave.

"I can't imagine why you should suppose that Adrian is not acting freely. I don't know what you imagine my means of coercion to be."

"I don't imagine anything. I think I only wish he had thought of it himself."

"He would never think of anything that is for his good. He is not in the least interested."

"Well, I don't know that it matters, because I don't think Eunice will see it—as we see it."

"Thank you for saying 'we.' Is she in love with some one else?"

"Not that I know of; but she may expect to be, some day. And better than that, she may expect—very justly—some one to be in love with her."

"Oh, in love with her! How you women talk! You all of you want the moon. If she is not content to be thought of as Adrian thinks of her, she is a very silly girl. What will she have more than tenderness? That boy is all tenderness."

"Perhaps he is too tender," I suggested. "I think he is afraid to ask her."

"Yes, I know he is nervous—at the idea of a refusal. But I should like her to refuse him once."

"It is not of that he is afraid—it is of her accepting him."

Mr. Caliph smiled, as if he thought this very ingenious. "You don't understand him. I'm so sorry! I had an idea that—with your knowledge of human nature, your powers of observation—you would have perceived how he is made. In fact, I rather counted on that." He said this with a little tone of injury which might have made me feel terribly inadequate if it had not been accompanied with a glance that seemed to say that, after all, he was generous and he forgave me. "Adrian's is one of those natures that are inflamed by not succeeding. He doesn't give up; he thrives on opposition. If she refuses him three or four times he will adore her!"

"She is sure then to be adored—though I am not sure it will make a difference with her. I haven't yet seen a sign that she cares for him."

"Why then does she go out to drive with him?" There was nothing brutal in the elation with which Mr. Caliph made this point; still, he looked a little as if he pitied me for exposing myself to a refutation so prompt.

"That proves nothing, I think. I would go to drive with Mr. Frank, if he should ask me, and I should be very much surprised if it were regarded as an intimation that I am ready to marry him."

Mr. Caliph had his hands resting on his thighs, and in this position, bending forward a little, with his smile he said, "Ah, but he doesn't want to marry *you*!"

That was a little brutal, I think; but I should have appeared ridiculous if I had attempted to resent it. I simply answered that I had as yet seen no sign even that Eunice is conscious of

Mr. Frank's intentions. I think she is, but I don't think so from anything she has said or done. Mr. Caliph maintains that she is capable of going for six months without betraying herself, all the while quietly considering and making up her mind. It is possible he is right—he has known her longer than I. He is far from wishing to wait for six months, however; and the part I must play is to bring matters to a crisis. I told him that I didn't see why he did not speak to her directly—why he should operate in this roundabout way. Why shouldn't he say to her all that he had said to me—tell her that she would make him very happy by marrying his little brother? He answered that this is impossible, that the nearness of relationship would make it unbecoming; it would look like a kind of nepotism. The thing must appear to come to pass of itself—and I, somehow, must be the author of that appearance! I was too much a woman of the world, too acquainted with life, not to see the force of all this. He had a great deal to say about my being a woman of the world; in one sense it is not all complimentary; one would think me some battered old dowager who had married off fifteen daughters. I feel that I am far from all that when Mr. Caliph leaves me so mystified. He has some other reason for wishing these nuptials than love of the two young people, but I am unable to put my hand on it. Like the children at hide-and-seek, however, I think I "burn." I don't like him, I mistrust him; but he is a very charming man. His geniality, his richness, his magnetism, I suppose I should say, are extraordinary; he fascinates me, in spite of my suspicions. The truth is, that in his way he is an artist, and in my little way I am also one; and the artist in me recognises the artist in him, and cannot quite resist the temptation to foregather. What is more than this, the artist in him has recognised the artist in me—it is very good of him—and would like to establish a certain freemasonry. "Let us take together the artistic view of life"; that is simply the meaning of his talking so much about my being a woman of the world. That is all very well; but it seems to me there would be a certain baseness in our being artists together at the expense of poor little Eunice. I should like to know some of Mr. Caliph's secrets, but I don't wish to give him any of mine in return for them. Yet I gave him something before he departed; I hardly know what, and hardly know how he extracted it from me. It was a sort of promise that I would after all speak to Eunice,— "as I should like to have you, you know." He remained there for a quarter of an hour after he got up to go; walking about the room with his hands on his hips; talking, arguing, laughing, holding me with his eyes, his admirable face—as natural, as dramatic, and at the same time as diplomatic, as an Italian. I am pretty sure he was trying to produce a certain effect, to entangle, to magnetise me. Strange to say, Mr. Caliph compromises himself, but he doesn't compromise his brother. He has a private reason, but his brother has nothing to do with his privacies. That was my last word to him.

"The moment I feel sure that I may do something for your brother's happiness—your brother's alone—by pleading his cause with Eunice—that moment I will speak to her. But I can do nothing for yours."

In answer to this, Mr. Caliph said something very unexpected. "I wish I had known you five years ago!"

There are many meanings to that; perhaps he would have liked to put me out of the way. But I could take only the polite meaning. "Our acquaintance could never have begun too soon."

"Yes, I should have liked to know you," he went on, "in spite of the fact that you are not kind, that you are not just. Have I asked you to do anything for my happiness? My happiness is nothing. I have nothing to do with happiness. I don't deserve it. It is only for my little brother—and for your charming cousin."

I was obliged to admit that he was right; that he had asked nothing for himself. "But I don't want to do anything for you even by accident!" I said—laughing, of course.

This time he was grave. He stood looking at me a moment, then put out his hand. "Yes, I wish I had known you!"

There was something so expressive in his voice, so handsome in his face, so tender and respectful in his manner, as he said this, that for an instant I was really moved, and I was on the point of saying with feeling, "I wish indeed you had!" But that instinct of which I have already spoken checked me—the sense that somehow, as things stand, there can be no *rapprochement* between Mr. Caliph and me that will not involve a certain sacrifice of Eunice. So I only replied, "You seem to me strange, Mr. Caliph. I must tell you that I don't understand you."

He kept my hand, still looking at me, and went on as if he had not heard me. "I am not happy—I am not wise nor good." Then suddenly, in quite a different tone, "For God's sake, let her marry my brother!"

There was a quick passion in these words which made me say, "If it is so pressing as that, you certainly ought to speak to her. Perhaps she'll do it to oblige you!"

We had walked into the hall together, and the last I saw of him he stood in the open doorway, looking back at me with his smile. "Hang the nepotism! I *will* speak to her!"

Cornerville, July 6.—A whole month has passed since I have made an entry; but I have a good excuse for this dreadful gap. Since we have been in the country I have found subjects enough and to spare, and I have been painting so hard that my hand, of an evening, has been glad to rest. This place is very lovely, and the Hudson is as beautiful as the Rhine. There are the words, in black and white, over my signature; I can't do more than that. I have said it a dozen times, in answer to as many challenges, and now I record the opinion with all the solemnity I can give it. May it serve for the rest of the summer! This is an excellent old house, of the style that was thought impressive, in this country, forty years ago. It is painted a cheerful slate-colour, save for a multitude of pilasters and facings which are picked out in the cleanest and freshest white. It has a kind of clumsy gable or apex, on top; a sort of roofed terrace, below, from which you may descend to a lawn dotted with delightful old trees; and between the two, in the second story, a deep verandah, let into the body of the building, and ornamented with white balustrades, considerably carved, and big blue stone jars. Add to this a multitude of green shutters and striped awnings, and a mass of Virginia creepers and wisterias, and fling over it the lavish light of the American summer, and you have a notion of some of the conditions of our *villeggiatura*. The great condition, of course, is the splendid river, lying beneath our rounded headland in vast silvery stretches and growing almost vague on the opposite shore. It is a country of views; you are always peeping down an avenue, or ascending a mound, or going round a corner, to look at one. They are rather too shining, too high-pitched, for my little purposes; all nature seems glazed with light and varnished with freshness. But I manage to scrape something off. Mrs. Ermine is here, as brilliant as her setting; and so, strange to say, is Adrian Frank. Strange, for this reason, that the night before we left town I went into Eunice's room and asked her whether she knew, or rather whether she suspected, what was going on. A sudden impulse came to me; it seemed to me unnatural that in such a situation I should keep anything from her. I don't want to interfere, but I think I want even less to carry too far my aversion to interference, and without pretending to advise Eunice, it was revealed to me that she ought to know that Mr. Caliph had come to see me on purpose to induce me to work upon her. It was not till after he was gone that it occurred to me he had sent his brother in advance, on purpose to get Eunice out of the way, and that this was the reason the young Adrian would take no refusal. He was really in excellent training. It was a very hot night. Eunice was alone in her room, without a lamp; the windows were wide open, and the dusk was clarified by the light of the street. She sat there, among things vaguely visible, in a white wrapper, with her fair hair on her shoulders, and I could see her eyes move toward me when I asked her whether she knew that Mr. Frank wished to marry her. I could see her smile, too, as she answered that she knew he thought he did, but also knew he didn't.

"Of course I have only his word for it," I said.

"Has he told you?"

"Oh yes, and his brother, too."

"His brother?" And Eunice slowly got up.

"It's an idea of Mr. Caliph's as well. Indeed Mr. Caliph may have been the first. He came here to-day, while you were out, to tell me how much he should like to see it come to pass. He has set his heart upon it, and he wished me to engage to do all in my power to bring it about. Of course I can't do anything, can I?"

She had sunk into her chair again as I went on; she sat there looking before her, in the dark. Before she answered me she gathered up her thick hair with her hands, twisted it together, and holding it in place on top of her head, with one hand, tried to fasten a comb into it with the other. I passed behind her to help her; I could see she was agitated. "Oh no, you can't do anything," she said, after a moment, with a laugh that was not like her usual laughter. "I know all about it; they have told me, of course." Her tone was forced, and I could see that she had not really known all about it—had not known that Mr. Caliph is pushing his brother. I went to the window and looked out a little into the hot, empty street, where the gas lamps showed me, up and down, the hundred high stoops, exactly alike, and as ugly as a bad dream. While I stood there a thought suddenly dropped into my mind, which has lain ever since where it fell. But I don't wish to move it, even to write it here. I stayed with Eunice for ten minutes; I told her everything that Mr. Caliph had said to me. She listened in perfect silence—I could see that she was glad to listen. When I related that he didn't wish to speak to her himself on behalf of his brother, because that would seem indelicate, she broke in, with a certain eagerness, "Yes, that is very natural!"

"And now you can marry Mr. Frank without my help!" I said, when I had done.

She shook her head sadly, though she was smiling again. "It's too late for your help. He has asked me to marry him, and I have told him he can hope for it—never!"

I was surprised to hear he had spoken, and she said nothing about the time or place. It must have been that afternoon, during their drive. I said that I was rather sorry for our poor young friend, he was such a very nice fellow. She agreed that he was remarkably nice, but added that this was not a sufficient reason for her marrying him; and when I said that he would try again, that I had Mr. Caliph's assurance that he would not be easy to get rid of, and that a refusal would only make him persist, she answered that he might try as often as he liked; he was so little disagreeable to her that she would take even that from him. And now, to give him a chance to try again, she has asked him down here to stay, thinking apparently that Mrs. Ermine's presence puts us *en règle* with the proprieties. I should add that she assured me there was no real danger of his trying again; he had told her he meant to, but he had said it only for form. Why should he, since he was not in love with her? It was all an idea of his brother's, and she was much obliged to Mr. Caliph, who took his duties much too seriously and was not in the least bound to provide her with a husband. Mr. Frank and she had agreed to remain friends, as if nothing had happened; and I think she then said something about her intending to ask him to this place. A few days after we got here, at all events, she told me that she had written to him, proposing his coming; whereupon I intimated that I thought it a singular overture to make to a rejected lover whom one didn't wish to encourage. He would take it as encouragement, or at all events Mr. Caliph would. She answered that she didn't care what Mr. Caliph thinks, and that she knew Mr. Frank better than I, and knew therefore that he had absolutely no hope. But she had a particular reason for wishing him to be here. That sounded mysterious, and she couldn't tell me more; but in a month or two I would guess her reason. As she said this she looked at me with a brighter smile than she has had for weeks; for I protest that she is troubled—Eunice is greatly troubled. Nearly a month has elapsed, and I haven't guessed that reason. Here is Adrian Frank, at any rate, as I say; and I can't make out whether he persists or renounces. His manner to Eunice is just the same; he is always polite and always shy, never inattentive and never unmistakable. He has not said a word more to me about his suit. Apart from this he is very sympathetic, and we sit about sketching together in the most fraternal manner. He made to me a day or two since a very pretty remark; viz., that he would rather copy a sketch of mine than try, himself, to do the place from nature. This perhaps does not look so *galant* as I repeat it here; but with the tone and glance with which he said it, it really almost touched me. I was glad, by the way, to hear from Eunice the night before we left town that she doesn't care what Mr. Caliph thinks; only, I should be gladder still if I believed it. I don't, unfortunately; among other reasons because it doesn't at all agree with that idea which descended upon me with a single jump—from heaven knows where—while I looked out of her window at the stoops. I observe with pleasure, however, that he doesn't send her any more papers to sign. These days pass softly, quickly, but with a curious, an unnatural, stillness. It is as if there were something in the air—a sort of listening hush. That sounds very fantastic, and I suppose such remarks are only to be justified by my having the artistic temperament—that is, if I have it! If I haven't, there is no excuse; unless it be that Eunice is distinctly uneasy, and that it takes the form of a voluntary, exaggerated calm, of which I feel the contact, the tension. She is as quiet as a mouse and yet as restless as a flame. She is neither well nor happy; she doesn't sleep. It is true that I asked Mr. Frank the other day what impression she made on him, and he replied, with a little start, and a smile of alacrity, "Oh, delightful, as usual!"—so that I saw he didn't know what he was talking about. He is tremendously sunburnt, and as red as a tomato. I wish he would look a little less at my daubs and a little more at the woman he wishes to marry. In summer I always suffice to myself, and I am so much interested in my work that if I hope, devoutly, as I do, that nothing is going to happen to Eunice, it is probably quite as much from selfish motives as from others. If anything were to happen to her I should be immensely interrupted. Mrs. Ermine is bored, *par exemple*! She is dying to have a garden-party, at which she can drag a long train over the lawn; but day follows day and this entertainment does not take place. Eunice has promised it, however, for another week, and I believe means to send out invitations immediately. Mrs. Ermine has offered to write them all; she has, after all, *du bon*. But the fatuity of her misunderstandings of everything that surrounds her passes belief. She sees nothing that really occurs, and gazes complacently into the void. Her theory is always that Mr. Caliph is in love with Eunice,—she opened up to me on the subject only yesterday, because with no one else to talk to but the young Adrian, who dodges her, she doesn't in the least mind that she hates me, and that I think her a goose— that Mr. Caliph is in love with Eunice, but that Eunice, who is queer enough for anything, doesn't like him, so that he has sent down his step-brother to tell stories about the good things he has done, and to win over her mind to a more favourable view. Mrs. Ermine believes in these good things, and appears to think such action on Mr. Caliph's part both politic and dramatic. She has not the smallest suspicion of the real little drama that has been going on under her nose. I wish I had that absence of vision; it would be a great rest. Heaven knows I see more than I want—for instance when I see that my poor little cousin is pinched with pain, and yet that I can't relieve her, can't even advise her. I couldn't do the former even if I would, and she wouldn't let me do the latter even if I could. It seems too pitiful, too incredible, that there should be no one to turn to. Surely, if I go up to town for a day next week, as seems probable, I may call upon William Ermine. Whether I *may* or not, I will.

July 11.—She has been getting letters, and they have made her worse. Last night I spoke to her—I asked her to come into my room. I told her that I saw she was in distress; that it was terrible to me to see it; that I was sure that she has some miserable secret. Who was making her suffer this way? No one had the right—not even Mr. Caliph, if Mr. Caliph it was, to whom she appeared to have conceded every right. She broke down completely, burst into tears, confessed that she is troubled about money. Mr. Caliph has again requested a delay as to his handing in his accounts, and has told her that she will have no income for another year. She thinks it strange; she is afraid that everything isn't right. She is not afraid of being poor; she holds that it's vile to concern one's self so much about money. But there is something that breaks her heart in thinking that Mr. Caliph should be in fault. She had always admired him, she had always believed in him, she had always—— What it was, in the third place, that she had always done I didn't learn, for at this point she buried her head still deeper in my lap and sobbed for half an hour. Her grief was melting. I was never more troubled, and this in spite of the fact that I was furious at her strange air of acceptance of a probable calamity. She is afraid that everything isn't right, forsooth! I should think it was not, and should think it hadn't been for heaven knows how long. This is what has been in the air; this is what was hanging over us. But Eunice is simply amazing. She declines to see a lawyer; declines to hold Mr. Caliph accountable; declines to complain, to inquire, to investigate in any way. I am sick, I am terribly perplexed—I don't know what to do. Her tears dried up in an instant as soon as I made the very obvious remark that the beautiful, the mysterious, the captivating Caliph is no better than a common swindler; and she gave me a look which might have frozen me if, when I am angry, I were freezable. She took it *de bien haut*; she intimated to me that if I should ever speak in that way again of Mr. Caliph we must part company for ever. She was distressed; she admitted that she felt injured. I had seen for myself how far that went. But she didn't pretend to judge him. He had been in trouble,—he had told her that; and his trouble was worse than hers, inasmuch as his honour was at stake, and it had to be saved.

"It's charming to hear you speak of his honour," I cried, quite regardless of the threat she had just uttered. "Where was his honour when he violated the most sacred of trusts? Where was his honour when he went off with your fortune? Those are questions, my dear, that the courts will make him answer. He shall make up to you every penny that he has stolen, or my name is not Catherine Condit!"

Eunice gave me another look, which seemed meant to let me know that I had suddenly become in her eyes the most indecent of women; and then she swept out of the room. I immediately sat down and wrote to Mr. Ermine, in order to have my note ready to send up to town at the earliest hour the next morning. I told him that Eunice was in dreadful trouble about her money-matters, and that I believed he would render her a great service, though she herself had no wish to ask it, by coming down to see her at his first convenience. I reflected, of course, as I wrote, that he could do her no good if she should refuse to see him; but I made up for this by saying to myself that I at least should see him, and that he would do me good. I added in my note that Eunice had been despoiled by those who had charge of her property; but I didn't mention Mr. Caliph's name. I was just closing my letter when Eunice came into my room again. I saw in a moment that she was different from anything she had ever been before—or at least had ever seemed. Her excitement, her passion, had gone down; even the traces of her tears had vanished. She was perfectly quiet, but all her softness had left her. She was as solemn and impersonal as the priestess of a cult. As soon as her eyes fell upon my letter she asked me to be so good as to inform her to whom I had been writing. I instantly satisfied her, telling her what I had written; and she asked me to give her the document. "I must let you know that I shall immediately burn it up," she added; and she went on to say that if I should send it to Mr. Ermine she herself would write to him by the same post that he was to heed nothing I had said. I tore up my letter, but I announced to Eunice that I would go up to town and see the person to whom I had addressed it. "That brings us precisely to what I came in to say," she answered; and she proceeded to demand of me a solemn vow that I would never speak to a living soul of what I had learned in regard to her affairs. They were her affairs exclusively, and no business of mine or of any other human being; and she had a perfect right to ask and to expect this promise. She has, indeed—more's the pity; but it was impossible to me to admit just then—indignant and excited as I was—that I recognised the right. I did so at last, however, and I made the promise. It seems strange to me to write it here; but I am pledged by a tremendous vow, taken in this "intimate" spot, in the small hours of the morning, never to lift a finger, never to speak a word, to redress any wrong that Eunice may have received at the hands of her treacherous trustee, to bring it to the knowledge of others, or to invoke justice, compensation or pity. How she extorted this concession from me is more than I can say: she did so by the force of her will, which, as I have already had occasion to note, is far stronger than mine; and by the vividness of her passion, which is none the less intense because it burns inward and makes her heart glow while her face remains as clear as an angel's. She seated herself with folded hands, and declared she wouldn't leave the room until I had satisfied her. She is in a state of extraordinary exaltation, and from her own point of view she was eloquent enough. She returned again and again to the fact that she did not judge Mr. Caliph; that what he may have done is between herself and him alone; and that if she had not been betrayed to speaking of it to me in the first shock of finding that certain allowances would have to be made for him, no one need ever have suspected it. She was now perfectly ready to make those allowances. She was unspeakably sorry for Mr. Caliph. He had been in urgent need of money, and he had used hers: pray, whose else would I have wished him to use? Her money had been an insupportable bore to him from the day it was thrust into his hands. To make him her trustee had been in the worst possible taste; he was not the sort of person to make a convenience of, and it had been odious to take advantage of his good nature. She had always been ashamed of owing him so much. He had been perfect in all his relations with her, though he must have hated her and her wretched little investments from the first. If she had lost money, it was not his fault; he had lost a great deal more for himself than he had lost for her. He was the kindest, the most delightful, the most interesting of men. Eunice brought out all this with pure defiance; she had never treated herself before to the luxury of saying it, and it was singular to think that she found her first pretext, her first boldness, in the fact that he had ruined her. All this looks almost grotesque as I write it here; but she imposed it upon me last night with all the authority of her passionate little person. I agreed, as I say, that the matter was none of my business; that is now definite enough. Two other things are equally so. One is that she is to be plucked like a chicken; the other is that she is in love with the precious Caliph, and has been so for years! I didn't dare to write that the other night, after the beautiful idea had suddenly flowered in my mind; but I don't care what I write now. I am so horribly tongue-tied that I must at least relieve myself here. Of course I wonder now that I never guessed her secret before; especially as I was perpetually hovering on the edge of it. It explains many things, and it is very terrible. In love with a pickpocket! *Merci!* I am glad fate hasn't played me that trick.

July 14.—I can't get over the idea that he is to go scot-free. I grind my teeth at it as I sit at work, and I find myself using the most livid, the most indignant colours. I have had another talk with Eunice, but I don't in the least know what she is to live on. She says she has always her father's property, and that this will be abundant; but that of course she cannot pretend to live as she has lived hitherto. She will have to go abroad again and economise; and she will probably have to sell this place—that is, if she can. "If she can," of course means if there is anything to sell; if it isn't devoured with mortgages. What I want to know is, whether Justice, in such a case as this, will not step in, notwithstanding the silence of the victim. If I could only give her a hint—the angel of the scales and sword—in spite of my detestable promise! I can't find out about Mr. Caliph's impunity, as it is impossible for me to allude to the matter to any one who would be able to tell me. Yes, the more I think of it the more reason I see to rejoice that fate hasn't played me that trick of making me fall in love with a common thief! Suffering keener than my poor little cousin's I cannot possibly imagine, or a power of self-sacrifice more awful. Fancy the situation, when the only thing one can do for the man one loves is to forgive him for stealing! What a delicate attention, what a touching proof of tenderness! This Eunice can do; she has waited all these years to do something. I hope she is pleased with her opportunity. And yet when I say she has forgiven him for stealing, I lose myself in the mystery of her exquisite spirit. Who knows what it is she has forgiven—does she even know herself? She consents to being injured, despoiled, and finds in consenting a kind of rapture. But I notice that she has said no more about Mr. Caliph's honour. That substantive she condemns herself never to hear again without a quiver, for she has condoned something too ignoble. What I further want to know is, what conceivable tone he has taken—whether he has made a clean breast of it, and thrown himself upon her mercy; or whether he has sought refuge in bravado, in prevarication? Not indeed that it matters, save for the spectacle of the thing, which I find rich. I should also like much to know whether everything has gone, whether something may yet be saved. It is safe to say that she doesn't know the worst, and that if he has admitted the case is bad, we may take for granted that it leaves nothing to be desired. Let him alone to do the thing handsomely! I have a right to be violent, for there was a moment when he made me like him, and I feel as if he had cheated me too. Her being in love with him makes it perfect; for of course it was in that that he saw his opportunity to fleece her. I don't pretend to say how he discovered it, for she has watched herself as a culprit watches a judge; but from the moment he guessed it he must have seen that he could do what he liked. It is true that this doesn't agree very well with his plan that she should marry his step-brother; but I prefer to believe it, because it makes him more horrible. And apropos of Adrian Frank, it is very well I like *him* so much (that comes out rather plump, by the way), inasmuch as if I didn't it would be quite open to me to believe that he is in league with Caliph. There has been nothing to prove that he has not said to his step-brother, "Very good; you take all you can get, and I will marry her, and being her husband, hush it up,"—nothing but the expression of his blue eyes. That is very little, when we think that expressions and eyes are a specialty of the family, and haven't prevented Mr. Caliph from being a robber. It is those eyes of his that poor Eunice is in love with, and it is for their sake that she forgives him. But the young Adrian's are totally different, and not nearly so fine, which I think a great point in his favour. Mr. Caliph's are southern eyes, and the young Adrian's are eyes of the north. Moreover, though he is so amiable and obliging, I don't think he is amiable enough to *endosser* his brother's victims to that extent, even to save his brother's honour. He needn't care so much about that honour, since Mr. Caliph's name is not his name. And then, poor fellow, he is too stupid; he is almost as stupid as Mrs. Ermine. The two have sat together directing cards for Eunice's garden-party as placidly as if no one had a sorrow in life. Mrs. Ermine proposed this pastime to Mr. Frank; and as he has nothing in the world to do, it is as good an employment for him as another. But it exasperates me to see him sitting at the big table in the library, opposite to Mrs. E., while they solemnly pile one envelope on top of another. They have already a heap as high as their heads; they must have invited a thousand people. I can't imagine who they all are. It is an extraordinary time for Eunice to be giving a party—the day after she discovers that she is penniless; but of course it isn't Eunice, it's Mrs. Ermine. I said to her yesterday that if she was to change her mode of life—simple enough already, poor thing—she had better begin at once; and that her garden-party under Mrs. Ermine's direction would cost her a thousand dollars. She answered that she must go on, since it had already been talked about; she wished no one to know anything—to suspect anything. This would be her last extravagance, her farewell to society. If such resources were open to us poor heretics, I should suppose she meant to go into a convent. She exasperates me too—every one exasperates me. It is some satisfaction, however, to feel that my exasperation clears up my mind. It is Caliph who is "sold," after all. He would not have invented this alliance for his brother if he had known—if he had faintly suspected—that Eunice was in love with him, inasmuch as in this case he had assured impunity. Fancy his not knowing it—the idiot!

July 10.—They are still directing cards, and Mrs. Ermine has taken the whole thing on her shoulders. She has invited people that Eunice has never heard of—a pretty rabble she will have made of it! She has ordered a band of music from New York, and a new dress for the occasion—something in the last degree *champêtre*. Eunice is perfectly indifferent to what she does; I have discovered that she is thinking only of one thing. Mr. Caliph is coming, and the bliss of that idea fills her mind. The more people the better; she will not have the air of making petty economies to afflict him with the sight of what he has reduced her to!

"This is the way Eunice ought to live," Mrs. Ermine said to me this afternoon, rubbing her hands, after the last invitation had departed. When I say the last, I mean the last till she had remembered another that was highly important, and had floated back into the library to scribble it off. She writes a regular invitation-hand—a vague, sloping, silly hand, that looks as if it had done nothing all its days but write, "Mr. and Mrs. Ermine request the pleasure"; or, "Mr. and Mrs. Ermine are delighted to accept." She told me that she knew Eunice far better than Eunice knew herself, and that her line in life was evidently to "receive." No one better than she would stand in a doorway and put out her hand with a smile; no one would be a more gracious and affable hostess, or make a more generous use of an ample fortune. She is really very trying, Mrs. Ermine, with her ample fortune; she is like a clock striking impossible hours. I think she must have engaged a special train for her guests—a train to pick up people up and down the river. Adrian Frank went to town to-day; he comes back on the 23d, and the festival takes place the next day. The festival,—Heaven help us! Eunice is evidently going to be ill; it's as much as I can do to keep from adding that it serves her right! It's a great relief to me that Mr. Frank has gone; this has ceased to be a place for him. It is ever so long since he has said anything to me about his "prospects." They are charming, his prospects!

July 26.—The garden-party has taken place, and a great deal more besides. I have been too agitated, too fatigued and bewildered, to write anything here; but I can't sleep to-night—I'm too nervous—and it is better to sit and scribble than to toss about. I may as well say at once that the party was very pretty —Mrs. Ermine may have that credit. The day was lovely; the lawn was in capital order; the music was good, and the *buffet* apparently inexhaustible. There was an immense number of people; some of them had come even from Albany—many of them strangers to Eunice, and protégés only of Mrs. Ermine; but they dispersed themselves on the grounds, and I have not heard as yet that they stole the spoons or plucked up the plants. Mrs. Ermine, who was exceedingly *champêtre*—white muslin and corn-flowers—told me that Eunice was "receiving adorably," was in her native element. She evidently inspired great curiosity; that was why every one had come. I don't mean because every one suspects her situation, but because as yet, since her return, she has been little seen and known, and is supposed to be a distinguished figure—clever, beautiful, rich, and a *parti*. I think she satisfied every one; she was voted most interesting, and except that she was deadly pale, she was prettier than any one else. Adrian Frank did not come back on the 23d, and did not arrive for the festival. So much I note without as yet understanding it. His absence from the garden-party, after all his exertions under the orders of Mrs. Ermine, is in need of an explanation. Mr. Caliph could give none, for Mr. Caliph was there. He professed surprise at not finding his brother; said he had not seen him in town, that he had no idea what had become of him. This is probably perfectly false. I am bound to believe that everything he says and does is false; and I have no doubt that they met in New York, and that Adrian told him his reason—whatever it was—for not coming back. I don't know how to relate what took place between Mr. Caliph and me; we had an extraordinary scene—a scene that gave my nerves the shaking from which they have not recovered. He is truly a most amazing personage. He is altogether beyond me; I don't pretend to fathom him. To say that he has no moral sense is nothing. I have seen other people who have had no moral sense; but I have seen no one with that impudence, that cynicism, that remorseless cruelty. We had a tremendous encounter; I thank heaven that strength was given me! When I found myself face to face with him, and it came over me that, blooming there in his diabolical assurance, it was he—he with his smiles, his bows, his gorgeous *bontonnière*, the wonderful air he has of being anointed and gilded—he that had ruined my poor Eunice, who grew whiter than ever as he approached: when I felt all this my blood began to tingle, and if I were only a handsome woman I might believe that my eyes shone like those of an avenging angel. He was as fresh as a day in June, enormous, and more than ever like Haroun-al-Raschid. I asked him to take a walk with me; and just for an instant, before accepting, he looked at me, as the French say, in the white of the eyes. But he pretended to be delighted, and we strolled away together to the path that leads down to the river. It was difficult to get away from the people—they were all over the place; but I made him go so far that at the end of ten minutes we were virtually alone together. It was delicious to see how he hated it. It was then that I asked him what had become of his step-brother, and that he professed, as I have said, the utmost ignorance of Adrian's whereabouts. I hated him; it was odious to me to be so close to him; yet I could have endured this for hours in order to make him feel that I despised him. To make him feel it without saying it—there was an inspiration in that idea; but it is very possible that it made me look more like a demon than like the angel I just mentioned. I told him in a moment, abruptly, that his step-brother would do well to remain away altogether in future; it was a farce his pretending to make my cousin reconsider her answer.

"Why, then, did she ask him to come down here?" He launched this inquiry with confidence.

"Because she thought it would be pleasant to have a man in the house; and Mr. Frank is such a harmless, discreet, accommodating one."

"Why, then, do you object to his coming back?"

He had made me contradict myself a little, and of course he enjoyed that. I was confused—confused by my agitation; and I made the matter worse. I was furious that Eunice had made me promise not to speak, and my anger blinded me, as great anger always does, save in organisations so fine as Mr. Caliph's.

"Because Eunice is in no condition to have company. She is very ill; you can see for yourself."

"Very ill? with a garden-party and a band of music! Why, then, did she invite us all?"

"Because she is a little crazy, I think."

"You are very consistent!" he cried, with a laugh. "I know people who think every one crazy but themselves. I have had occasion to talk business with her several times of late, and I find her mind as clear as a bell."

"I wonder if you will allow me to say that you talk business too much? Let me give you a word of advice: wind up her affairs at once without any more procrastination, and place them in her own hands. She is very nervous; she knows this ought to have been done already. I recommend you strongly to make an end of the matter."

I had no idea I could be so insolent, even in conversation with a swindler. I confess I didn't do it so well as I might, for my voice trembled perceptibly in the midst of my efforts to be calm. He had picked up two or three stones and was tossing them into the river, making them skim the surface for a long distance. He held one poised a moment, turning his eye askance on me; then he let it fly, and it danced for a hundred yards. I wondered whether in what I had just said I broke my vow to Eunice; and it seemed to me that I didn't, inasmuch as I appeared to assume that no irreparable wrong had been done her.

"Do you wish yourself to get control of her property?" Mr. Caliph inquired, after he had made his stone skim. It was magnificently said, far better than anything I could do; and I think I answered it—though it made my heart beat fast—almost with a smile of applause.

"Aren't you afraid?" I asked in a moment, very gently.

"Afraid of what—of you?"

"Afraid of justice—of Eunice's friends?"

"That means you, of course. Yes, I am very much afraid. When was a man not, in the presence of a clever woman?"

"I am clever; but I am not clever enough. If I were, you should have no doubt of it."

He folded his arms as he stood there before me, looking at me in that way I have mentioned more than once—like a genial Mephistopheles. "I must repeat what I have already told you, that I wish I had known you ten years ago!"

"How you must hate me to say that!" I exclaimed. "That's some comfort, just a little—your hating me."

"I can't tell you how it makes me feel to see you so indiscreet," he went on, as if he had not heard me. "Ah, my dear lady, don't meddle—a woman like you! Think of the bad taste of it."

"It's bad if you like; but yours is far worse."

"Mine! What do you know about mine? What do you know about me? See how superficial it makes you." He paused a moment, smiling almost compassionately; and then he said, with an abrupt change of tone and manner, as if our conversation wearied him and he wished to sum up and return to the house, "See that she marries Adrian; that's all you have to do!"

"That's a beautiful idea of yours! You know you don't believe in it yourself!" These words broke from me as he turned away, and we ascended the hill together.

"It's the only thing I believe in," he answered, very gravely.

"What a pity for you that your brother doesn't! For he doesn't—I persist in that!" I said this because it seemed to me just then to be the thing I could think of that would exasperate him most. The event proved I was right.

He stopped short in the path—gave me a very bad look. "Do you want him for yourself? Have *you* been making love to him?"

"Ah, Mr. Caliph, for a man who talks about taste!" I answered.

"Taste be damned!" cried Mr. Caliph, as we went on again.

"That's quite my idea!" He broke into an unexpected laugh, as if I had said something very amusing, and we proceeded in silence to the top of the hill. Then I suddenly said to him, as we emerged upon the lawn, "Aren't you really a little afraid?"

He stopped again, looking toward the house and at the brilliant groups with which the lawn was covered. We had lost the music, but we began to hear it again. "Afraid? of course I am! I'm immensely afraid. It comes over me in such a scene as this. But I don't see what good it does you to know."

"It makes me rather happy." That was a fib; for it didn't, somehow, when he looked and talked in that way. He has an absolutely bottomless power of mockery; and really, absurd as it appears, for that instant I had a feeling that it was quite magnanimous of him not to let me know what he thought of my idiotic attempt to frighten him. He feels strong and safe somehow, somewhere; but I can't discover why he should, inasmuch as he certainly doesn't know Eunice's secret, and it is only her state of mind that gives him impunity. He believes her to be merely credulous; convinced by his specious arguments that everything will be right in a few months; a little nervous, possibly—to justify my account of her—but for the present, at least, completely at his mercy. The present, of course, is only what now concerns him; for the future he has invented Adrian Frank. How he clings to this invention was proved by the last words he said to me before we separated on the lawn; they almost indicate that he has a conscience, and this is so extraordinary—

"She must marry Adrian! She must marry Adrian!"

With this he turned away and went to talk to various people whom he knew. He talked to every one; diffused his genial influence all over the place, and contributed greatly to the brilliancy of the occasion. I hadn't therefore the comfort of feeling that Mrs. Ermine was more of a waterspout than usual, when she said to me afterwards that Mr. Caliph was a man to adore, and that the party would have been quite "ordinary" without him. "I mean in comparison, you know." And then she said to me suddenly, with her blank impertinence: "Why don't you set your cap at him? I should think you would!"

"Is it possible you have not observed my frantic efforts to captivate him?" I answered. "Didn't you notice how I drew him away and made him walk with me by the river? It's too soon to say, but I really think I am gaining ground." For so mild a pleasure it really pays to mystify Mrs. Ermine! I kept away from Eunice till almost every one had gone. I knew that she would look at me in a certain way, and I didn't wish to meet her eyes. I have a bad conscience, for turn it as I would I *had* broken my vow. Mr. Caliph went away without my meeting him again; but I saw that half an hour before he left he strolled to a distance with Eunice. I instantly guessed what his business was; he had made up his mind to present to her directly, and in person, the question of her marrying his step-brother. What a happy inspiration, and what a well-selected occasion! When she came back I saw that she had been crying, though I imagine no one else did. I know the signs of her tears, even when she has checked them as quickly as she must have done to-day. Whatever it was that had passed between them, it diverted her from looking at me, when we were alone together, in that way I was afraid of. Mrs. Ermine is prolific; there is no end to the images that succeed each other in her mind. Late in the evening, after the last carriage had rolled away, we went up the staircase together, and at the top she detained me a moment.

"I have been thinking it over, and I am afraid that there is no chance for you. I have reason to believe that he proposed to-day to Eunice!"

August 19.—Eunice is very ill, as I was sure she would be, after the effort of her horrible festival. She kept going for three days more; then she broke down completely, and for a week now she has been in bed. I have had no time to write, for I have been constantly with her, in alternation with Mrs. Ermine. Mrs. Ermine was about to leave us after the garden-party, but when Eunice gave up she announced that she would stay and take care of her. Eunice tells me that she is a good nurse, except that she talks too much, and of course she gives me a chance to rest. Eunice's condition is strange; she has no fever, but her life seems to have ebbed away. She lies with her eyes shut, perfectly conscious, answering when she is spoken to, but immersed in absolute rest. It is as if she had had some terrible strain or fatigue, and wished to steep herself in oblivion. I am not anxious about her—am much less frightened than Mrs. Ermine or the doctor, for whom she is apparently dying of weakness. I tell the doctor I understand her condition—I have seen her so before. It will last probably a month, and then she will slowly pull herself together. The poor man accepts this theory for want of a better, and evidently depends upon me to see her through, as he says. Mrs. Ermine wishes to send for one of the great men from New York, but I have opposed this idea, and shall continue to oppose it. There is (to my mind) a kind of cruelty in exhibiting the poor girl to more people than are absolutely necessary. The dullest of them would see that she is in love. The seat of her illness is in her mind, in her soul, and no rude hands must touch her there. She herself has protested—she has murmured a prayer that she may be forced to see no one else. "I only want to be left alone—to be left alone." So we leave her alone—that is, we simply watch and wait. She will recover—people don't die of these things; she will live to suffer—to suffer always. I am tired to-night, but Mrs. Ermine is with her, and I shall not be wanted till morning; therefore, before I lie down, I will repair in these remarkable pages a serious omission. I scarcely know why I should have written all this, except that the history of things interests me, and I find that it is even a greater pleasure to write it than to read it. If what I have committed to this little book hitherto has not been profitless, I must make a note of an incident which I think more curious than any of the scenes I have described.

Adrian Frank reappeared the day after the garden-party— late in the afternoon, while I sat in the verandah and watched the sunset and Eunice strolled down to the river with Mrs. Ermine. I had heard no sound of wheels, and there was no evidence of a vehicle or of luggage. He had not come through the house, but walked round it from the front, having apparently been told by one of the servants that we were in the grounds. On seeing me he stopped, hesitated a moment, then came up to the steps, shook hands in silence, seated himself near me and looked at me through the dusk. This was all tolerably mysterious, and it was even more so after he had explained a little. I told him that he was a day after the fair, that he had been considerably missed, and even that he was slightly wanting in respect to Eunice. Since he had absented himself from her party it was not quite delicate to assume that she was ready to receive him at his own time. I don't know what made me so truculent—as if there were any danger of his having really not considered us, or his lacking a good reason. It was simply, I think, that my talk with Mr. Caliph the evening before had made me so much bad blood and left me in a savage mood. Mr. Frank answered that he had not stayed away by accident—he had stayed away on purpose; he had been for several days at Saratoga, and on returning to Cornerville had taken quarters at the inn in the village. He had no intention of presuming further on Eunice's hospitality, and had walked over from the hotel simply to bid us good-evening and give an account of himself.

"My dear Mr. Frank, your account is not clear!" I said, laughing. "What in the world were you doing at Saratoga?" I must add that his humility had completely disarmed me; I was ashamed of the brutality with which I had received him, and convinced afresh that he was the best fellow in the world.

"What was I doing at Saratoga? I was trying hard to forget you!"

This was Mr. Frank's rejoinder; and I give it exactly as he uttered it; or rather, not exactly, inasmuch as I cannot give the tone—the quick, startling tremor of his voice. But those are the words with which he answered my superficially-intended question. I saw in a moment that he meant a great deal by them—I became aware that we were suddenly in deep waters; that *he* was at least, and that he was trying to draw me into the stream. My surprise was immense, complete; I had absolutely not suspected what he went on to say to me. He said many things—but I needn't write them here. It is not in detail that I see the propriety of narrating this incident; I suppose a woman may be trusted to remember the form of such assurances. Let me simply say that the poor dear young man has an idea that he wants to marry me. For a moment,—just a moment—I thought he was jesting; then I saw, in the twilight, that he was pale with seriousness. He is perfectly sincere. It is strange, but it is real, and, moreover, it is his own affair. For myself, when I have said I was amazed, I have said everything; *en tête-à-tête* with myself I needn't blush and protest. I was not in the least annoyed or alarmed; I was filled with kindness and consideration, and I was extremely interested. He talked to me for a quarter of an hour; it seemed a very long time. I asked him to go away; not to wait till Eunice and Mrs. Ermine should come back. Of course I refused him, by the way.

It was the last thing I was expecting at this time of day, and it gave me a great deal to think of. I lay awake that night; I found I was more agitated than I supposed, and all sorts of visions came and went in my head. I shall not marry the young Adrian: I am bound to say that vision was not one of them; but as I thought over what he had said to me it became more clear, more conceivable. I began now to be a little surprised at my surprise. It appears that I have had the honour to please him from the first; when he began to come to see us it was not for Eunice, it was for me. He made a general confession on this subject. He was afraid of me; he thought me proud, sarcastic, cold, a hundred horrid things; it didn't seem to him possible that we should ever be on a footing of familiarity which would enable him to propose to me. He regarded me, in short, as un-attainable, out of the question, and made up his mind to ad-mire me for ever in silence. (In plain English, I suppose he thought I was too old, and he has simply got used to the differ-ence in our years.) But he wished to be near me, to see me, and hear me (I am really writing more details than seem worth while); so that when his step-brother recommended him to try and marry Eunice he jumped at the opportunity to make good his place. This situation reconciled everything. He could oblige his brother, he could pay a high compliment to my cousin, and he could see me every day or two. He was convinced from the first that he was in no danger; he was morally sure that Eunice would never smile upon his suit. He didn't know why, and he doesn't know why yet; it was only an instinct. That suit was avowedly perfunctory; still the young Adrian has been a great comedian. He assured me that if he had proved to be wrong, and Eunice had suddenly accepted him, he would have gone with her to the altar and made her an excellent husband; for he would have acquired in this manner the certainty of seeing for the rest of his life a great deal of me! To think of one's possess-ing, all unexpected, this miraculous influence! When he came down here, after Eunice had refused him, it was simply for the pleasure of living in the house with me; from that moment there was no comedy—everything was clear and comfortable betwixt him and Eunice. I asked him if he meant by this that she knew of the sentiments he entertained for her companion, and he answered that he had never breathed a word on this subject, and flattered himself that he had kept the thing dark. He had no reason to believe that she guessed his motives, and I may add that I have none either; they are altogether too extraordinary! As I have said, it was simply time, and the privilege of seeing more of me, that had dispelled his hesitation. I didn't reason with him; and though, once I was fairly enlightened, I gave him the most respectful attention, I didn't appear to consider his request too seriously. But I *did* touch upon the fact that I am five or six years older than he: I suppose I needn't mention that it was not in a spirit of coquetry. His rejoinder was very gallant; but it belongs to the class of details. He is really in love—heaven forgive him! but I shall not marry him. How strange are the passions of men!

I saw Mr. Frank the next day; I had given him leave to come back at noon. He joined me in the grounds, where as usual I had set up my easel. I left it to his discretion to call first at the house and explain both his absence and his presence to Eunice and Mrs. Ermine—the latter especially—ignorant as yet of his visit the night before, of which I had not spoken to them. He sat down beside me on a garden-chair and watched me as I went on with my work. For half an hour very few words passed between us; I felt that he was happy to sit there, to be near me, to see me—strange as it seems! and for myself there was a certain sweetness in knowing it, though it was the sweetness of charity, not of elation or triumph. He must have seen I was only pretending to paint—if he followed my brush, which I suppose he didn't. My mind was full of a determination I had arrived at after many waverings in the hours of the night. It had come to me toward morning as a kind of inspiration. I could never marry him, but was there not some way in which I could utilise his devotion? At the present moment, only forty-eight hours later, it seems strange, unreal, almost grotesque; but for ten minutes I thought I saw the light. As we sat there under the great trees, in the stillness of the noon, I suddenly turned and said to him—

"I thank you for everything you have told me; it gives me very nearly all the pleasure you could wish. I believe in you; I accept every assurance of your devotion. I think that devotion is capable of going very far; and I am going to put it to a tremendous test, one of the greatest, probably, to which a man was ever subjected."

He stared, leaning forward, with his hands on his knees. "Any test—any test——" he murmured.

"Don't give up Eunice, then; make another trial; I wish her to marry you!"

My words may have sounded like an atrocious joke, but they represented for me a great deal of hope and cheer. They brought a deep blush into Adrian Frank's face; he winced a little, as if he had been struck by a hand whose blow he could not return, and the tears suddenly started to his eyes. "Oh, Miss Condit!" he exclaimed.

What I saw before me was bright and definite; his distress seemed to me no obstacle, and I went on with a serenity of which I longed to make him perceive the underlying support. "Of course what I say seems to you like a deliberate insult; but nothing would induce me to give you pain if it were possible to spare you. But it isn't possible, my dear friend; it isn't possible. There is pain for you in the best thing I can say to you; there are situations in life in which we can only accept our pain. I can never marry you; I shall never marry any one. I am an old maid, and how can an old maid have a husband? I will be your friend, your sister, your brother, your mother, but I will never be your wife. I should like immensely to be your brother, for I don't like the brother you have got, and I think you deserve a better one. I believe, as I tell you, in everything you have said to me—in your affection, your tenderness, your honesty, the full consideration you have given to the whole matter. I am happier and richer for knowing it all; and I can assure you that it gives something to life which life didn't have before. We shall be good friends, dear friends, always, whatever happens. But I can't be your wife—I want you for some one else. You will say I have changed—that I ought to have spoken in this way three months ago. But I haven't changed—it is circumstances that have changed. I see reasons for your marrying my cousin that I didn't see then. I can't say that she will listen to you now, any more than she did then; I don't speak of her; I speak only of you and of myself. I wish you to make another attempt; and I wish you to make it, this time, with my full confidence and support. Moreover, I attach a condition to it—a condition I will tell you presently. Do you think me slightly demented, malignantly perverse, atrociously cruel? If you could see the bottom of my heart you would find something there which, I think, would almost give you joy. To ask you to do something you don't want to do as a substitute for something you desire, and to attach to the hard achievement a condition which will require a good deal of thinking of and will certainly make it harder—you may well believe I have some extraordinary reason for taking such a line as this. For remember, to begin with, that I can never marry you."

"Never—never—never?"

"Never, never, never."

"And what is your extraordinary reason?"

"Simply that I wish Eunice to have your protection, your kindness, your fortune."

"My fortune?"

"She has lost her own. She will be poor."

"Pray, how has she lost it?" the poor fellow asked, beginning to frown, and more and more bewildered.

"I can't tell you that, and you must never ask. But the fact is certain. The greater part of her property has gone; she has known it for some little time."

"For some little time? Why, she never showed any change."

"You never saw it, that was all! You were thinking of me," and I believe I accompanied this remark with a smile—a smile which was most inconsiderate, for it could only mystify him more.

I think at first he scarcely believed me. "What a singular time to choose to give a large party!" he exclaimed, looking at me with eyes quite unlike his old—or rather his young—ones; eyes that, instead of overlooking half the things before them (which was their former habit), tried to see a great deal more in my face, in my words, than was visible on the surface. I don't know what poor Adrian Frank saw—I shall never know all that he saw.

"I agree with you that it was a very singular time," I said. "You don't understand me—you can't—I don't expect you to"; I went on. "That is what I mean by devotion, and that is the kind of appeal I make to you: to take me on trust, to act in the dark, to do something simply because I wish it."

He looked at me as if he would fathom the depths of my soul, and my soul had never seemed to myself so deep. "To marry your cousin—that's all?" he said, with a strange little laugh.

"Oh no, it's not all: to be very kind to her as well."

"To give her plenty of money, above all?"

"You make me feel very ridiculous; but I should not make this request of you if you had not a fortune."

"She can have my money without marrying me."

"That's absurd. How could she take your money?"

"How, then, can she take me?"

"That's exactly what I wish to see. I told you with my own lips, weeks ago, that she would only marry a man she should love; and I may seem to contradict myself in taking up now a supposition so different. But, as I tell you, everything has changed."

"You think her capable, in other words, of marrying for money."

"For money? Is your money all there is of you? Is there a better fellow than you—is there a more perfect gentleman?"

He turned away his face at this, leaned it in his hands and groaned. I pitied him, but I wonder now that I shouldn't have pitied him more; that my pity should not have checked me. But I was too full of my idea. "It's like a fate," he murmured; "first my brother, and then you. I can't understand."

"Yes, I know your brother wants it—wants it now more than ever. But I don't care what your brother wants; and my idea is entirely independent of his. I have not the least conviction that you will succeed at first any better than you have done already. But it may be only a question of time, if you will wait and watch, and let me help you. You know you asked me to help you before, and then I wouldn't. But I repeat it again and again, at present everything is changed. Let me wait with you, let me watch with you. If you succeed, you will be very dear to me; if you fail, you will be still more so. You see it's an act of devotion, if there ever was one. I am quite aware that I ask of you something unprecedented and extraordinary. Oh, it may easily be too much for you. I can only put it before you—that's all; and as I say, I can help you. You will both be my children—I shall be near you always. If you can't marry me, perhaps you will make up your mind that this is the next best thing. You know you said that last night, yourself."

He had begun to listen to me a little, as if he were being persuaded. "Of course, I should let her know that I love you."

"She is capable of saying that you can't love me more than she does."

"I don't believe she is capable of saying any such folly. But we shall see."

"Yes; but not to-day, not to-morrow. Not at all for the present. You must wait a great many months."

"I will wait as long as you please."

"And you mustn't say a word to me of the kind you said last night."

"Is that your condition?"

"Oh no; my condition is a very different matter, and very difficult. It will probably spoil everything."

"Please, then, let me hear it at once."

"It is very hard for me to mention it; you must give me time." I turned back to my little easel and began to daub again; but I think my hand trembled, for my heart was beating fast. There was a silence of many moments; I couldn't make up my mind to speak.

"How in the world has she lost her money?" Mr. Frank

asked, abruptly, as if the question had just come into his mind. "Hasn't my brother the charge of her affairs?"

"Mr. Caliph is her trustee. I can't tell you how the losses have occurred."

He got up quickly. "Do you mean that they have occurred through *him*?"

I looked up at him, and there was something in his face which made me leave my work and rise also. "I will tell you my condition now," I said. "It is that you should ask no questions—not one!" This was not what I had had in my mind; but I had not courage for more, and this had to serve.

He had turned very pale, and I laid my hand on his arm, while he looked at me as if he wished to wrest my secret out of my eyes. My secret, I call it, by courtesy; God knows I had come terribly near telling it. God will forgive me, but Eunice probably will not. Had I broken my vow, or had I kept it? I asked myself this, and the answer, so far as I read it in Mr. Frank's eyes, was not reassuring. I dreaded his next question; but when it came it was not what I had expected. Something violent took place in his own mind—something I couldn't follow.

"If I do what you ask me, what will be my reward?"

"You will make me very happy."

"And what shall I make your cousin?—God help us!"

"Less wretched than she is to-day."

"Is she 'wretched'?" he asked, frowning as he did before—a most distressing change in his mild mask.

"Ah, when I think that I have to tell you that—that you have never noticed it—I despair!" I exclaimed, with a laugh.

I had laid my hand on his arm, and he placed his right hand upon it, holding it there. He kept it a moment in his grasp, and then he said, "Don't despair!"

"Promise me to wait," I answered. "Everything is in your waiting."

"I promise you!" After which he asked me to kiss him, and I did so, on the lips. It was as if he were starting on a journey—leaving me for a long time.

"Will you come when I send for you?" I asked.

"I adore you!" he said; and he turned quickly away, to leave the place without going near the house. I watched him, and in a moment he was gone. He has not reappeared; and when I found, at lunch, that neither Eunice nor Mrs. Ermine alluded to his visit, I determined to keep the matter to myself. I said nothing about it, and up to the moment Eunice was taken ill— the next evening—he was not mentioned between us. I believe Mrs. Ermine more than once gave herself up to wonder as to his whereabouts, and declared that he had not the perfect manners of his step-brother, who was a religious observer of the *convenances*; but I think I managed to listen without confusion. Nevertheless, I had a bad conscience, and I have it still. It throbs a good deal as I sit there with Eunice in her darkened room. I *have* given her away; I *have* broken my vow. But what I wrote above is not true; she *will* forgive me! I sat at my easel for an hour after Mr. Frank left me, and then suddenly I found that I had cured myself of my folly by giving it out. It was the result of a sudden passion of desire to do something for Eunice. Passion is blind, and when I opened my eyes I saw ten thousand difficulties; that is, I saw one, which contained all the rest. That evening I wrote to Mr. Frank, to his New York address, to tell him that I had had a fit of madness, and that it had passed away; but that I was sorry to say it was not any more possible for me to marry him. I have had no answer to this letter; but what answer can he make to that last declaration? He will continue to adore me. How strange are the passions of men!

New York, November 20.—I have been silent for three months, for good reasons. Eunice was ill for many weeks, but there was never a moment when I was really alarmed about her; I knew she would recover. In the last days of October she was strong enough to be brought up to town, where she had business to transact, and now she is almost herself again. I say almost, advisedly; for she will never be herself,—her old, sweet, trustful self, so far as I am concerned. She has simply not forgiven me! Strange things have happened—things that I don't dare to consider too closely, lest I should not forgive myself. Eunice is in complete possession of her property! Mr. Caliph has made over to her everything—everything that had passed away; everything of which, three months ago, he could give no account whatever. He was with her in the country for a long day before we came up to town (during which I took care not to meet her), and after our return he was in and out of this house repeatedly. I once asked Eunice what he had to say to her, and she answered that he was "explaining." A day or two later she told me that he had given a complete account of her affairs; everything was in order; she had been wrong in what she told me before. Beyond this little statement, however, she did no further penance for the impression she had given of Mr. Caliph's earlier conduct. She doesn't yet know what to think; she only feels that if she has recovered her property there has been some interference; and she traces, or at least imputes, such interference to me. If I have interfered, I have broken my vow; and for this, as I say, the gentle creature can't forgive me. If the passions of men are strange, the passions of women are stranger still! It was sweeter for her to suffer at Mr Caliph's hands than to receive her simple dues from them. She looks at me askance, and her coldness shows through a conscientious effort not to let me see the change in her feeling. Then she is puzzled and mystified; she can't tell what has happened, or how and why it has happened. She has waked up from her illness into a different world—a world in which Mr. Caliph's accounts were correct after all; in which, with the washing away of his stains, the colour has been quite washed out of his rich physiognomy. She vaguely feels that a sacrifice, a great effort of some kind, has been made for her, whereas her plan of life was to make the sacrifices and efforts herself. Yet she asks me no questions; the property is her right, after all, and I think there are certain things she is afraid to know. But I am more afraid than she, for it comes over me that a great sacrifice has indeed been made. I have not seen Adrian Frank since he parted from me under the trees three months ago. He has gone to Europe, and the day before he left I got a note from him. It contained only these words: "When you send for me I will come. I am waiting, as you told me." It is my belief that up to the moment I spoke of Eunice's loss of money and requested him to ask no questions, he had not definitely suspected his noble kinsman, but that my words kindled a train that lay all ready. He went away then to his shame, to the intolerable weight of it, and to heaven knows what sickening explanations with his step-brother! That gentleman has a still more brilliant bloom; he looks to my mind exactly as people look who have accepted a sacrifice; and he hasn't had another word to say about Eunice's marrying Mr. Adrian Frank. Mrs. Ermine sticks to her idea that Mr. Caliph and Eunice will make a match; but my belief is that Eunice is cured. Oh yes, she is cured! But I have done more than I meant to do, and I have not done it as I meant to do it; and I am very weary, and I shall write no more.

November 27.—Oh yes, Eunice is cured! And that is what she has not forgiven me. Mr. Caliph told her yesterday that Mr. Frank meant to spend the winter in Rome.

December 3.—I have decided to return to Europe, and have written about my apartment in Rome. I shall leave New York, if possible, on the 10th. Eunice tells me she can easily believe I shall be happier there.

December 7.—I *must* note something I had the satisfaction to-day to say to Mr. Caliph. He has not been here for three weeks, but this afternoon he came to call. He is no longer the trustee; he is only the visitor. I was alone in the library, into which he was ushered; and it was ten minutes before Eunice appeared. We had some talk, though my disgust for him is now unspeakable. At first it was of a very perfunctory kind; but suddenly he said, with more than his old impudence, "That was a most extraordinary interview of ours, at Cornerville!" I was surprised at his saying only this, for I expected him to take his revenge on me by some means or other for having put his brother on the scent of his misdeeds. I can only account for his silence on that subject by the supposition that Mr. Frank has been able to extract from him some pledge that I shall not be molested. He was, however, such an image of unrighteous success that the sight of him filled me with gall, and I tried to think of something which would make him smart.

"I don't know what you have done, nor how you have done it," I said; "but you took a very roundabout way to arrive at certain ends. There was a time when you might have married Eunice."

It was of course nothing new that we were frank with each other, and he only repeated, smiling, "Married Eunice?"

"She was very much in love with you last spring."

"Very much in love with me?"

"Oh, it's over now. Can't you imagine that? She's cured."

He broke into a laugh, but I felt I had startled him.

"You are the most delightful woman!" he cried.

"Think how much simpler it would have been—I mean originally, when things were right, if they ever were right. Don't you see my point? But now it's too late. She has seen you when you were not on show. I assure you she is cured!"

At this moment Eunice came in, and just afterwards I left the room. I am sure it was a revelation, and that I have given him a *mauvais quart d'heure*.

Rome, February 23.—When I came back to this dear place Adrian Frank was not here, and I learned that he had gone to Sicily. A week ago I wrote to him: "You said you would come if I should send for you. I should be glad if you would come now." Last evening he appeared, and I told him that I could no longer endure my suspense in regard to a certain subject. Would he kindly inform me what he had done in New York after he left me under the trees at Cornerville? Of what sacrifice had he been guilty; to what high generosity—terrible to me to think of—had he committed himself? He would tell me very little; but he is almost a poor man. He has just enough income to live in Italy.

May 9.—Mrs. Ermine has taken it into her head to write to me. I have heard from her three times; and in her last letter, received yesterday, she returns to her old refrain that Eunice and Mr. Caliph will soon be united. I don't know what may be going on; but can it be possible that I put it into his head? Truly, I have a felicitous touch!

May 15.—I told Adrian yesterday that I would marry him if ever Eunice should marry Mr. Caliph. It was the first time I had mentioned his step-brother's name to him since the explanation I had attempted to have with him after he came back to Rome; and he evidently didn't like it at all.

In the Tyrol, August.—I sent Mrs. Ermine a little water-colour in return for her last letter, for I can't write to her, and that is easier. She now writes me again, in order to get another water-colour. She speaks of course of Eunice and Mr. Caliph, and for the first time there appears a certain reality in what she says. She complains that Eunice is very slow in coming to the point, and relates that poor Mr. Caliph, who has taken her into his confidence, seems at times almost to despair. Nothing would suit him better of course than to appropriate two fortunes: two are so much better than one. But however much he may have explained, he can hardly have explained everything. Adrian Frank is in Scotland; in writing to him three days ago I had occasion to repeat that I will marry him on the day on which a certain other marriage takes place. In that way I am safe. I shall send another water-colour to Mrs. Ermine. Water-colours or no, Eunice doesn't write to me. It is clear that she hasn't forgiven me! She regards me as perjured; and of course I am. Perhaps she will marry him after all.

1908

THE JOLLY CORNER

I

"EVERY ONE asks me what I 'think' of everything," said Spencer Brydon; "and I make answer as I can—begging or dodging the question, putting them off with any nonsense. It wouldn't matter to any of them really," he went on, "for, even were it possible to meet in that stand-and-deliver way so silly a demand on so big a subject, my 'thoughts' would still be almost altogether about something that concerns only myself." He was talking to Miss Staverton, with whom for a couple of months now he had availed himself of every possible occasion to talk; this disposition and this resource, this comfort and support, as the situation in fact presented itself, having promptly enough taken the first place in the considerable array of rather unattenuated surprises attending his so strangely belated return to America. Everything was somehow a surprise; and that might be natural when one had so long and so consistently neglected everything, taken pains to give surprises so much margin for play. He had given them more than thirty years—thirty-three, to be exact; and they now seemed to him to have organised their performance quite on the scale of that licence. He had been twenty-three on leaving New York—he was fifty-six today: unless indeed he were to reckon as he had sometimes, since his repatriation, found himself feeling; in which case he would have lived longer than is often allotted to man. It would have taken a century, he repeatedly said to himself, and said also to Alice Staverton, it would have taken a longer absence and a more averted mind than those even of which he had been guilty, to pile up the differences, the newnesses, the queernesses, above all the bignesses, for the better or the worse, that at present assaulted his vision wherever he looked.

The great fact all the while however had been the incalculability; since he *had* supposed himself, from decade to decade, to be allowing, and in the most liberal and intelligent manner, for brilliancy of change. He actually saw that he had allowed for nothing; he missed what he would have been sure of finding, he found what he would never have imagined. Proportions and values were upside-down; the ugly things he had expected, the ugly things of his far-away youth, when he had too promptly waked up to a sense of the ugly—these uncanny phenomena placed him rather, as it happened, under the charm; whereas the "swagger" things, the modern, the monstrous, the famous things, those he had more particularly, like thousands of ingenuous enquirers every year, come over to see, were exactly his sources of dismay. They were as so many set traps for displeasure, above all for reaction, of which his restless tread was constantly pressing the spring. It was interesting, doubtless, the whole show, but it would have been too disconcerting hadn't a certain finer truth saved the situation. He had distinctly not, in this steadier light, come over *all* for the monstrosities; he had come, not only in the last analysis but quite on the face of the act, under an impulse with which they had nothing to do. He had come—putting the thing pompously—to look at his "property," which he had thus for a third of a century not been within four thousand miles of; or, expressing it less sordidly, he had yielded to the humour of seeing again his house on the jolly corner, as he usually, and quite fondly, described it—the one in which he had first seen the light, in which various members of his family had lived and had died, in which the holidays of his over-schooled boyhood had been passed and the few social flowers of his chilled adolescence gathered, and which, alienated then for so long a period, had, through the successive deaths of his two brothers and the termination of old arrange-

ments, come wholly into his hands. He was the owner of another, not quite so "good"—the jolly corner having been, from
far back, superlatively extended and consecrated; and the value
of the pair represented his main capital, with an income con-
sisting, in these later years, of their respective rents which
(thanks precisely to their original excellent type) had never
been depressingly low. He could live in "Europe," as he had
been in the habit of living, on the product of these flourishing
New York leases, and all the better since, that of the second
structure, the mere number in its long row, having within a
twelvemonth fallen in, renovation at a high advance had proved
beautifully possible.

These were items of property indeed, but he had found
himself since his arrival distinguishing more than ever between
them. The house within the street, two bristling blocks westward, was already in course of reconstruction as a tall mass of
flats; he had acceded, some time before, to overtures for this
conversion—in which, now that it was going forward, it had
been not the least of his astonishments to find himself able, on
the spot, and though without a previous ounce of such experience, to participate with a certain intelligence, almost with a
certain authority. He had lived his life with his back so turned
to such concerns and his face addressed to those of so different
an order that he scarce knew what to make of this lively stir, in
a compartment of his mind never yet penetrated, of a capacity
for business and a sense for construction. These virtues, so
common all round him now, had been dormant in his own
organism—where it might be said of them perhaps that they
had slept the sleep of the just. At present, in the splendid autumn weather—the autumn at least was a pure boon in the terrible place—he loafed about his "work" undeterred, secretly
agitated; not in the least "minding" that the whole proposition,
as they said, was vulgar and sordid, and ready to climb ladders,
to walk the plank, to handle materials and look wise about
them, to ask questions, in fine, and challenge explanations and
really "go into" figures.

It amused, it verily quite charmed him; and, by the same stroke, it amused, and even more, Alice Staverton, though perhaps charming her perceptibly less. She wasn't however going to be better off for it, as *he* was—and so astonishingly much: nothing was now likely, he knew, ever to make her better off than she found herself, in the afternoon of life, as the delicately frugal possessor and tenant of the small house in Irving Place to which she had subtly managed to cling through her almost unbroken New York career. If he knew the way to it now better than to any other address among the dreadful multiplied numberings which seemed to him to reduce the whole place to some vast ledger-page, overgrown, fantastic, of ruled and crisscrossed lines and figures—if he had formed, for his consolation, that habit, it was really not a little because of the charm of his having encountered and recognised, in the vast wilderness of the wholesale, breaking through the mere gross generalisation of wealth and force and success, a small still scene where items and shades, all delicate things, kept the sharpness of the notes of a high voice perfectly trained, and where economy hung about like the scent of a garden. His old friend lived with one maid and herself dusted her relics and trimmed her lamps and polished her silver; she stood off, in the awful modern crush, when she could, but she sallied forth and did battle when the challenge was really to "spirit," the spirit she after all confessed to, proudly and a little shyly, as to that of the better time, that of *their* common, their quite far-away and antediluvian social period and order. She made use of the street-cars when need be, the terrible things that people scrambled for as the panic-stricken at sea scramble for the boats; she affronted, inscrutably, under stress, all the public concussions and ordeals; and yet, with that slim mystifying grace of her appearance, which defied you to say if she were a fair young woman who looked older through trouble, or a fine smooth older one who looked young through successful indifference; with her precious reference, above all, to memories and histories into which he could enter, she was as exquisite for him as some pale

pressed flower (a rarity to begin with), and, failing other sweet-
nesses, she was a sufficient reward of his effort. They had communities of knowledge, "their" knowledge (this discriminating
possessive was always on her lips) of presences of the other age,
presences all over laid, in his case, by the experience of a man
and the freedom of a wanderer, overlaid by pleasure, by infi-
delity, by passages of life that were strange and dim to her, just
by "Europe" in short, but still unobscured, still exposed and
cherished, under that pious visitation of the spirit from which
she had never been diverted.

She had come with him one day to see how his "apartment-
house" was rising; he had helped her over gaps and explained to
her plans, and while they were there had happened to have, before her, a brief but lively discussion with the man in charge,
the representative of the building-firm that had undertaken his
work. He had found himself quite "standing-up" to this personage over a failure on the latter's part to observe some detail
of one of their noted conditions, and had so lucidly urged his
case that, besides ever so prettily flushing, at the time, for sympathy in his triumph, she had afterwards said to him (though
to a slightly greater effect of irony) that he had clearly for too
many years neglected a real gift. If he had but stayed at home
he would have anticipated the inventor of the sky-scraper. If he
had but stayed at home he would have discovered his genius in
time really to start some new variety of awful architectural hare
and run it till it burrowed in a gold-mine. He was to remember
these words, while the weeks elapsed, for the small silver ring
they had sounded over the queerest and deepest of his own
lately most disguised and most muffled vibrations.

It had begun to be present to him after the first fortnight, it
had broken out with the oddest abruptness, this particular
wanton wonderment: it met him there—and this was the image under which he himself judged the matter, or at least, not a
little, thrilled and flushed with it—very much as he might have
been met by some strange figure, some unexpected occupant,
at a turn of one of the dim passages of an empty house. The

quaint analogy quite hauntingly remained with him, when he didn't indeed rather improve it by a still intenser form: that of his opening a door behind which he would have made sure of finding nothing, a door into a room shuttered and void, and yet so coming, with a great suppressed start, on some quite erect confronting presence, something planted in the middle of the place and facing him through the dusk. After that visit to the house in construction he walked with his companion to see the other and always so much the better one, which in the eastward direction formed one of the corners, the "jolly" one precisely, of the street now so generally dishonoured and disfigured in its westward reaches, and of the comparatively conservative Avenue. The Avenue still had pretensions, as Miss Staverton said, to decency; the old people had mostly gone, the old names were unknown, and here and there an old association seemed to stray, all vaguely, like some very aged person, out too late, whom you might meet and feel the impulse to watch or follow, in kindness, for safe restoration to shelter.

They went in together, our friends; he admitted himself with his key, as he kept no one there, he explained, preferring, for his reasons, to leave the place empty, under a simple arrangement with a good woman living in the neighbourhood and who came for a daily hour to open windows and dust and sweep. Spencer Brydon had his reasons and was growingly aware of them; they seemed to him better each time he was there, though he didn't name them all to his companion, any more than he told her as yet how often, how quite absurdly often, he himself came. He only let her see for the present, while they walked through the great blank rooms, that absolute vacancy reigned and that, from top to bottom, there was nothing but Mrs. Muldoon's broomstick, in a corner, to tempt the burglar. Mrs. Muldoon was then on the premises, and she loquaciously attended the visitors, preceding them from room to room and pushing back shutters and throwing up sashes—all to show them, as she remarked, how little there was to see.

There was little indeed to see in the great gaunt shell where the main dispositions and the general apportionment of space, the style of an age of ampler allowances, had nevertheless for its master their honest pleading message, affecting him as some good old servant's, some lifelong retainer's appeal for a character, or even for a retiring-pension; yet it was also a remark of Mrs. Muldoon's that, glad as she was to oblige him by her noonday round, there was a request she greatly hoped he would never make of her. If he should wish her for any reason to come in after dark she would just tell him, if he "plased," that he must ask it of somebody else.

The fact that there was nothing to see didn't militate for the worthy woman against what one *might* see, and she put it frankly to Miss Staverton that no lady could be expected to like, could she? "craping up to thim top storeys in the ayvil hours." The gas and the electric light were off the house, and she fairly evoked a gruesome vision of her march through the great grey rooms—so many of them as there were too!—with her glimmering taper. Miss Staverton met her honest glare with a smile and the profession that she herself certainly would recoil from such an adventure. Spencer Brydon meanwhile held his peace—for the moment; the question of the "evil" hours in his old home had already become too grave for him. He had begun some time since to "crape," and he knew just why a packet of candles addressed to that pursuit had been stowed by his own hand, three weeks before, at the back of a drawer of the fine old sideboard that occupied, as a "fixture," the deep recess in the dining-room. Just now he laughed at his companions— quickly however changing the subject; for the reason that, in the first place, his laugh struck him even at that moment as starting the odd echo, the conscious human resonance (he scarce knew how to qualify it) that sounds made while he was there alone sent back to his ear or his fancy; and that, in the second, he imagined Alice Staverton for the instant on the point of asking him, with a divination, if he ever so prowled.

There were divinations, he was unprepared for, and he had at all events averted enquiry by the time Mrs. Muldoon had left them, passing on to other parts.

There was happily enough to say, on so consecrated a spot, that could be said freely and fairly; so that a whole train of declarations was precipitated by his friend's having herself broken out, after a yearning look round: "But I hope you don't mean they want you to pull *this* to pieces!" His answer came, promptly, with his re-awakened wrath: it was of course exactly what they wanted, and what they were "at" him for, daily, with the iteration of people who couldn't for their life understand a man's liability to decent feelings. He had found the place, just as it stood and beyond what he could express, an interest and a joy. There were values other than the beastly rent-values, and in short, in short—! But it was thus Miss Staverton took him up. "In short you're to make so good a thing of your sky-scraper that, living in luxury on *those* ill-gotten gains, you can afford for a while to be sentimental here!" Her smile had for him, with the words, the particular mild irony with which he found half her talk suffused; an irony without bitterness and that came, exactly, from her having so much imagination—not, like the cheap sarcasms with which one heard most people, about the world of "society," bid for the reputation of cleverness, from nobody's really having any. It was agreeable to him at this very moment to be sure that when he had answered, after a brief demur, "Well yes: so precisely, you may put it!" her imagination would still do him justice. He explained that even if never a dollar were to come to him from the other house he would nevertheless cherish this one; and he dwelt, further, while they lingered and wandered, on the fact of the stupefaction he was already exciting, the positive mystification he felt himself create.

He spoke of the value of all he read into it, into the mere sight of the walls, mere shapes of the rooms, mere sound of the floors, mere feel, in his hand, of the old silver-plated knobs of the several mahogany doors, which suggested the pressure of the palms of the dead; the seventy years of the past in fine that these things represented, the annals of nearly three generations, counting his grandfather's, the one that had ended there, and the impalpable ashes of his long-extinct youth, afloat in the very air like microscopic motes. She listened to everything; she was a woman who answered intimately but who utterly didn't chatter. She scattered abroad therefore no cloud of words; she could assent, she could agree, above all she could encourage, without doing that. Only at the last she went a little further than he had done himself. "And then how do you know? You may still, after all, want to live here." It rather indeed pulled him up, for it wasn't what he had been thinking, at least in her sense of the words. "You mean I may decide to stay on for the sake of it?"

"Well, *with* such a home—!" But, quite beautifully, she had too much tact to dot so monstrous an *i*, and it was precisely an illustration of the way she didn't rattle. How could any one—of any wit—insist on any one else's "wanting" to live in New York?

"Oh," he said, "I *might* have lived here (since I had my opportunity early in life); I might have put in here all these years. Then everything would have been different enough—and, I dare say, 'funny' enough. But that's another matter. And then the beauty of it—I mean of my perversity, of my refusal to agree to a 'deal'—is just in the total absence of a reason. Don't you see that if I had a reason about the matter at all it would *have* to be the other way, and would then be inevitably a reason of dollars? There are no reasons here *but* of dollars. Let us therefore have none whatever—not the ghost of one."

They were back in the hall then for departure, but from where they stood the vista was large, through an open door, into the great square main saloon, with its almost antique felicity of brave spaces between windows. Her eyes came back from that reach and met his own a moment. "Are you very sure the 'ghost' of one doesn't, much rather, serve—?"

He had a positive sense of turning pale. But it was as near as they were then to come. For he made answer, he believed, between a glare and a grin: "Oh ghosts—of course the place must swarm with them! I should be ashamed of it if it didn't. Poor Mrs. Muldoon's right, and it's why I haven't asked her to do more than look in."

Miss Staverton's gaze again lost itself, and things she didn't utter, it was clear, came and went in her mind. She might even for the minute, off there in the fine room, have imagined some element dimly gathering. Simplified like the death-mask of a handsome face, it perhaps produced for her just then an effect akin to the stir of an expression in the "set" commemorative plaster. Yet whatever her impression may have been she produced instead a vague platitude. "Well, if it were only furnished and lived in—!"

She appeared to imply that in case of its being still furnished he might have been a little less opposed to the idea of a return. But she passed straight into the vestibule, as if to leave her words behind her, and the next moment he had opened the house-door and was standing with her on the steps. He closed the door and, while he re-pocketed his key, looking up and down, they took in the comparatively harsh actuality of the Avenue, which reminded him of the assault of the outer light of the Desert on the traveller emerging from an Egyptian tomb. But he risked before they stepped into the street his gathered answer to her speech. "For me it *is* lived in. For me it *is* furnished." At which it was easy for her to sigh "Ah yes—!" all vaguely and discreetly; since his parents and his favourite sister, to say nothing of other kin, in numbers, had run their course and met their end there. That represented, within the walls, in-effaceable life.

It was a few days after this that, during an hour passed with her again, he had expressed his impatience of the too flattering curiosity—among the people he met—about his appreciation of New York. He had arrived at none at all that was socially producible, and as for that matter of his "thinking" (thinking the better or the worse of anything there) he was wholly taken up with one subject of thought. It was mere vain egoism, and it was moreover, if she liked, a morbid obsession. He found all things come back to the question of what he personally might have been, how he might have led his life and "turned out," if he had not so, at the outset, given it up. And confessing for the first time to the intensity within him of this absurd speculation—which but proved also, no doubt, the habit of too selfishly thinking—he affirmed the impotence there of any other source of interest, any other native appeal. "What would it have made of me, what would it have made of me? I keep for ever wondering, all idiotically; as if I could possibly know! I see what it has made of dozens of others, those I meet, and it positively aches within me, to the point of exasperation, that it would have made something of me as well. Only I can't make out *what*, and the worry of it, the small rage of curiosity never to be satisfied, brings back what I remember to have felt, once or twice, after judging best, for reasons, to burn some important letter unopened. I've been sorry, I've hated it—I've never known what was in the letter. You may of course say it's a trifle—!"

"I don't say it's a trifle," Miss Staverton gravely interrupted.

She was seated by her fire, and before her, on his feet and restless, he turned to and fro between this intensity of his idea and a fitful and unseeing inspection, through his single eye-glass, of the dear little old objects on her chimney-piece. Her interruption made him for an instant look at her harder. "I shouldn't care if you did!" he laughed, however; "and it's only a figure, at any rate, for the way I now feel. *Not* to have followed my perverse young course—and almost in the teeth of my father's curse, as I may say; not to have kept it up, so, 'over there,' from that day to this, without a doubt or a pang; not, above all, to have liked it, to have loved it, so much, loved it, no doubt, with such an abysmal conceit of my own preference: some variation from *that*, I say, must have produced some different effect for my life and for my 'form.' I should have stuck here—if it had been possible; and I was too young, at twenty-three, to judge, *pour deux sous*, whether it *were* possible. If I had waited I might have seen it was, and then I might have been, by staying here, something nearer to one of these types who have been hammered so hard and made so keen by their conditions. It isn't that I admire them so much—the question of any charm in them, or of any charm, beyond that of the rank money-passion, exerted by their conditions *for* them, has nothing to do with the matter: it's only a question of what fantastic, yet perfectly possible, development of my own nature I mayn't have missed. It comes over me that I had then a strange *alter ego* deep down somewhere within me, as the full-blown flower is in the small tight bud, and that I just took the course, I just transferred him to the climate, that blighted him for once and for ever."

"And you wonder about the flower," Miss Staverton said. "So do I, if you want to know; and so I've been wondering these several weeks. I believe in the flower," she continued, "I feel it would have been quite splendid, quite huge and monstrous."

"Monstrous above all!" her visitor echoed; "and I imagine, by the same stroke, quite hideous and offensive."

"You don't believe that," she returned; "if you did you wouldn't wonder. You'd know, and that would be enough for you. What you feel—and what I feel *for* you—is that you'd have had power."

"You'd have liked me that way?" he asked.

She barely hung fire. "How should I not have liked you?"

"I see. You'd have liked me, have preferred me, a billionaire!"

"How should I not have liked you?" she simply again asked.

He stood before her still—her question kept him motionless. He took it in, so much there was of it; and indeed his not otherwise meeting it testified to that. "I know at least what I am," he simply went on; "the other side of the medal's clear enough. I've not been edifying—I believe I'm thought in a hundred quarters to have been barely decent. I've followed strange paths and worshipped strange gods; it must have come to you again and again—in fact you've admitted to me as much —that I was leading, at any time these thirty years, a selfish frivolous scandalous life. And you see what it has made of me."

She just waited, smiling at him. "You see what it has made of *me*."

"Oh you're a person whom nothing can have altered. You were born to be what you are, anywhere, anyway: you've the perfection nothing else could have blighted. And don't you see how, without my exile, I shouldn't have been waiting till now—?" But he pulled up for the strange pang.

"The great thing to see," she presently said, "seems to me to be that it has spoiled nothing. It hasn't spoiled your being here at last. It hasn't spoiled this. It hasn't spoiled your speaking—" She also however faltered.

He wondered at everything her controlled emotion might mean. "Do you believe then—too dreadfully!—that I *am* as good as I might ever have been?"

"Oh no! Far from it!" With which she got up from her chair and was nearer to him. "But I don't care," she smiled.

"You mean I'm good enough?"

She considered a little. "Will you believe it if I say so? I mean will you let that settle your question for you?" And then as if making out in his face that he drew back from this, that he had some idea which, however absurd, he couldn't yet bargain away: "Oh you don't care either—but very differently: you don't care for anything but yourself."

Spencer Brydon recognised it—it was in fact what he had absolutely professed. Yet he importantly qualified. "*He* isn't myself. He's the just so totally other person. But I do want to see him," he added. "And I can. And I shall."

Their eyes met for a minute while he guessed from something in hers that she divined his strange sense. But neither of them otherwise expressed it, and her apparent understanding, with no protesting shock, no easy derision, touched him more deeply than anything yet, constituting for his stifled perversity, on the spot, an element that was like breathable air. What she said however was unexpected. "Well, *I've* seen him."

"You—?"

"I've seen him in a dream."

"Oh a 'dream'—!" It let him down.

"But twice over," she continued. "I saw him as I see you now."

"You've dreamed the same dream—?"

"Twice over," she repeated. "The very same."

This did somehow a little speak to him, as it also gratified him. "You dream about me at that rate?"

"Ah about *him*!" she smiled.

His eyes again sounded her. "Then you know all about him." And as she said nothing more: "What's the wretch like?"

She hesitated, and it was as if he were pressing her so hard that, resisting for reasons of her own, she had to turn away. "I'll tell you some other time!"

II

IT WAS after this that there was most of a virtue for him, most of a cultivated charm, most of a preposterous secret thrill, in the particular form of surrender to his obsession and of address to what he more and more believed to be his privilege. It was what in these weeks he was living for—since he really felt life to begin but after Mrs. Muldoon had retired from the scene and, visiting the ample house from attic to cellar, making sure he was alone, he knew himself in safe possession and, as he tacitly expressed it, let himself go. He sometimes came twice in the twenty-four hours; the moments he liked best were those of gathering dusk, of the short autumn twilight; this was the time of which, again and again, he found himself hoping most. Then he could, as seemed to him, most intimately wander and wait, linger and listen, feel his fine attention, never in his life before so fine, on the pulse of the great vague place: he preferred the lampless hour and only wished he might have prolonged each day the deep crepuscular spell. Later—rarely much before midnight, but then for a considerable vigil—he watched with his glimmering light; moving slowly, holding it high, playing it far, rejoicing above all, as much as he might, in open vistas, reaches of communication between rooms and by passages; the long straight chance or show, as he would have called it, for the revelation he pretended to invite. It was practice he found he could perfectly "work" without exciting remark; no one was in the least the wiser for it; even Alice Staverton, who was moreover a well of discretion, didn't quite fully imagine.

He let himself in and let himself out with the assurance of calm proprietorship; and accident so far favoured him that, if a fat Avenue "officer" had happened on occasion to see him entering at eleven-thirty, he had never yet, to the best of his belief, been noticed as emerging at two. He walked there on the crisp November nights, arrived regularly at the evening's end; it was as easy to do this after dining out as to take his way to a club or to his hotel. When he left his club, if he hadn't been dining out, it was ostensibly to go to his hotel; and when he left his hotel, if he had spent a part of the evening there, it was ostensibly to go to his club. Everything was easy in fine; everything conspired and promoted: there was truly even in the strain of his experience something that glossed over, something that salved and simplified, all the rest of consciousness. He circulated, talked, renewed, loosely and pleasantly, old relations—met indeed, so far as he could, new expectations and seemed to make out on the whole that in spite of the career, of such different contacts, which he had spoken of to Miss Staverton as ministering so little, for those who might have watched it, to edification, he was positively rather liked than not. He was a dim secondary social success—and all with people who had truly not an idea of him. It was all mere surface sound, this murmur of their welcome, this popping of their corks—just as his gestures of response were the extravagant shadows, emphatic in proportion as they meant little, of some game of *ombres chinoises*. He projected himself all day, in thought, straight over the bristling line of hard unconscious heads and into the other, the real, the waiting life; the life that, as soon as he had heard behind him the click of his great house-door, began for him, on the jolly corner, as beguilingly as the slow opening bars of some rich music follows the tap of the conductor's wand.

He always caught the first effect of the steel point of his stick on the old marble of the hall pavement, large black-and-white squares that he remembered as the admiration of his childhood and that had then made in him, as he now saw, for the growth of an early conception of style. This effect was the dim reverberating tinkle as of some far-off bell hung who should say where?—in the depths of the house, of the past, of that mystical other world that might have flourished for him had he not, for weal or woe, abandoned it. On this impression he did ever the same thing; he put his stick noiselessly away in a corner—feeling the place once more in the likeness of some great glass bowl, all precious concave crystal, set delicately humming by the play of a moist finger round its edge. The concave crystal held, as it were, this mystical other world, and the indescribably fine murmur of its rim was the sigh there, the scarce audible pathetic wail to his strained ear, of all the old baffled forsworn possibilities. What he did therefore by this appeal of his hushed presence was to wake them into such measure of ghostly life as they might still enjoy. They were shy, all but unappeasably shy, but they weren't really sinister; at least they weren't as he had hitherto felt them—before they had taken the Form he so yearned to make them take, the Form he at moments saw himself in the light of fairly hunting on tiptoe, the points of his evening-shoes, from room to room and from storey to storey.

That was the essence of his vision—which was all rank folly, if one would, while he was out of the house and otherwise occupied, but which took on the last verisimilitude as soon as he was placed and posted. He knew what he meant and what he wanted; it was as clear as the figure on a cheque presented in demand for cash. His *alter ego* "walked"—that was the note of his image of him, while his image of his motive for his own odd pastime was the desire to waylay him and meet him. He roamed, slowly, warily, but all restlessly, he himself did—Mrs.

Muldoon had been right, absolutely, with her figure of their "craping"; and the presence he watched for would roam restlessly too. But it would be as cautious and as shifty; the conviction of its probable, in fact its already quite sensible, quite audible evasion of pursuit grew for him from night to night, laying on him finally a rigour to which nothing in his life had been comparable. It had been the theory of many superficially-judging persons, he knew, that he was wasting that life in a surrender to sensations, but he had tasted of no pleasure so fine as his actual tension, had been introduced to no sport that demanded at once the patience and the nerve of this stalking of a creature more subtle, yet at bay perhaps more formidable, than any beast of the forest. The terms, the comparisons, the very practices of the chase positively came again into play; there were even moments when passages of his occasional experience as a sportsman, stirred memories, from his younger time, of moor and mountain and desert, revived for him—and to the increase of his keenness—by the tremendous force of analogy. He found himself at moments—once he had placed his single light on some mantel-shelf or in some recess—stepping back into shelter or shade, effacing himself behind a door or in an embrasure, as he had sought of old the vantage of rock and tree; he found himself holding his breath and living in the joy of the instant, the supreme suspense created by big game alone.

He wasn't afraid (though putting himself the question as he believed gentlemen on Bengal tiger-shoots or in close quarters with the great bear of the Rockies had been known to confess to having put it); and this indeed—since here at least he might be frank!—because of the impression, so intimate and so strange, that he himself produced as yet a dread, produced certainly a strain, beyond the liveliest he was likely to feel. They fell for him into categories, they fairly became familiar, the signs, for his own perception, of the alarm his presence and his vigilance created; though leaving him always to remark, portentously, on his probably having formed a relation, his probably enjoying a consciousness, unique in the experience of man.

People enough, first and last, had been in terror of apparitions, but who had ever before so turned the tables and become himself, in the apparitional world, an incalculable terror? He might have found this sublime had he quite dared to think of it; but he didn't too much insist, truly, on that side of his privilege. With habit and repetition he gained to an extraordinary degree the power to penetrate the dusk of distances and the darkness of corners, to resolve back into their innocence the treacheries of uncertain light, the evil-looking forms taken in the gloom by mere shadows, by accidents of the air, by shifting effects of perspective; putting down his dim luminary he could still wander on without it, pass into other rooms and, only knowing it was there behind him in case of need, see his way about, visually project for his purpose a comparative clearness. It made him feel, this acquired faculty, like some monstrous stealthy cat; he wondered if he would have glared at these moments with large shining yellow eyes, and what it mightn't verily be, for the poor hard-pressed *alter ego*, to be confronted with such a type.

He liked however the open shutters; he opened everywhere those Mrs. Muldoon had closed, closing them as carefully afterwards, so that she shouldn't notice: he liked—oh this he did like, and above all in the upper rooms!—the sense of the hard silver of the autumn stars through the window-panes, and scarcely less the flare of the street-lamps below, the white electric lustre which it would have taken curtains to keep out. This was human actual social; this was of the world he had lived in, and he was more at his ease certainly for the countenance, coldly general and impersonal, that all the while and in spite of his detachment it seemed to give him. He had support of course mostly in the rooms at the wide front and the prolonged side; it failed him considerably in the central shades and the parts at the back. But if he sometimes, on his rounds, was glad of his optical reach, so none the less often the rear of the house affected him as the very jungle of his prey. The place was there more subdivided; a large "extension" in particular, where small rooms for servants had been multiplied, abounded in nooks

and corners, in closets and passages, in the ramifications especially of an ample back staircase over which he leaned, many a
time, to look far down—not deterred from his gravity even
while aware that he might, for a spectator, have figured some
solemn simpleton playing at hide-and-seek. Outside in fact he
might himself make that ironic *rapprochement*; but within the
walls, and in spite of the clear windows, his consistency was
proof against the cynical light of New York.

It had belonged to that idea of the exasperated consciousness of his victim to become a real test for him; since he had
quite put it to himself from the first that, oh distinctly! he
could "cultivate" his whole perception. He had felt it as above
all open to cultivation—which indeed was but another name
for his manner of spending his time. He was bringing it on,
bringing it to perfection, by practice; in consequence of which
it had grown so fine that he was now aware of impressions, at-
testations of his general postulate, that couldn't have broken
upon him at once. This was the case more specifically with a
phenomenon at last quite frequent for him in the upper rooms,
the recognition—absolutely unmistakeable, and by a turn dat-
ing from a particular hour, his resumption of his campaign after a diplomatic drop, a calculated absence of three nights—of
his being definitely followed, tracked at a distance carefully
taken and to the express end that he should the less confidently,
less arrogantly, appear to himself merely to pursue. It worried,
it finally quite broke him up, for it proved, of all the conceivable impressions, the one least suited to his book. He was kept
in sight while remaining himself—as regards the essence of his
position—sightless, and his only recourse then was in abrupt
turns, rapid recoveries of ground. He wheeled about, retracing
his steps, as if he might so catch in his face at least the stirred
air of some other quick revolution. It was indeed true that his
fully dislocalised thought of these manœuvres recalled to him
Pantaloon, at the Christmas farce, buffeted and tricked from
behind by ubiquitous Harlequin; but it left intact the influence
of the conditions themselves each time he was re-exposed to

them, so that in fact this association, had he suffered it to become constant, would on a certain side have but ministered to his intenser gravity. He had made, as I have said, to create on the premises the baseless sense of a reprieve, his three absences; and the result of the third was to confirm the after-effect of the second.

On his return, that night—the night succeeding his last intermission—he stood in the hall and looked up the staircase with a certainty more intimate than any he had yet known. "He's *there*, at the top, and waiting—not, as in general, falling back for disappearance. He's holding his ground, and it's the first time—which is a proof, isn't it? that something has happened for him." So Brydon argued with his hand on the banister and his foot on the lowest stair; in which position he felt as never before the air chilled by his logic. He himself turned cold in it, for he seemed of a sudden to know what now was involved. "Harder pressed?—yes, he takes it in, with its thus making clear to him that I've come, as they say, 'to stay.' He finally doesn't like and can't bear it, in the sense, I mean, that his wrath, his menaced interest, now balances with his dread. I've hunted him till he has 'turned': that, up there, is what has happened—he's the fanged or the antlered animal brought at last to bay." There came to him, as I say—but determined by an influence beyond my notation!—the acuteness of this certainty; under which however the next moment he had broken into a sweat that he would as little have consented to attribute to fear as he would have dared immediately to act upon it for enterprise. It marked none the less a prodigious thrill, a thrill that represented sudden dismay, no doubt, but also represented, and with the self-same throb, the strangest, the most joyous, possibly the next minute almost the proudest, duplication of consciousness.

"He has been dodging, retreating, hiding, but now, worked up to anger, he'll fight!"—this intense impression made a single mouthful, as it were, of terror and applause. But what was wondrous was that the applause, for the felt fact, was so eager, since, if it was his other self he was running to earth, this ineffable identity was thus in the last resort not unworthy of him. It bristled there—somewhere near at hand, however unseen still —as the hunted thing, even as the trodden worm of the adage *must* at last bristle; and Brydon at this instant tasted probably of a sensation more complex than had ever before found itself consistent with sanity. It was as if it would have shamed him that a character so associated with his own should triumphantly succeed in just skulking, should to the end not risk the open, so that the drop of this danger was, on the spot, a great lift of the whole situation. Yet with another rare shift of the same subtlety he was already trying to measure by how much more he himself might now be in peril of fear; so rejoicing that he could, in another form, actively inspire that fear, and simultaneously quaking for the form in which he might passively know it.

The apprehension of knowing it must after a little have grown in him, and the strangest moment of his adventure perhaps, the most memorable or really most interesting, afterwards, of his crisis, was the lapse of certain instants of concentrated conscious *combat*, the sense of a need to hold on to something, even after the manner of a man slipping and slipping on some awful incline; the vivid impulse, above all, to move, to act, to charge, somehow and upon something—to show himself, in a word, that he wasn't afraid. The state of "holding-on" was thus the state to which he was momentarily reduced; if there had been anything, in the great vacancy, to seize, he would presently have been aware of having clutched it as he might under a shock at home have clutched the nearest chair-back. He had been surprised at any rate—of this he *was* aware—into something unprecedented since his original appropriation of the place; he had closed his eyes, held them tight, for a long minute, as with that instinct of dismay and that terror of vision. When he opened them the room, the other contiguous rooms, extraordinarily, seemed lighter—so light, almost, that at first he took the change for day. He stood firm, however that might be, just where he had paused; his resistance had helped him—it was as if there were something he had tided over. He knew after a little what this was—it had been in the imminent danger of flight. He had stiffened his will against going; without this he would have made for the stairs, and it seemed to him that, still with his eyes closed, he would have descended them, would have known how, straight and swiftly, to the bottom.

Well, as he had held out, here he was—still at the top, among the more intricate upper rooms and with the gauntlet of the others, of all the rest of the house, still to run when it should be his time to go. He would go at his time—only at his time: didn't he go every night very much at the same hour? He took out his watch—there was light for that: it was scarcely a quarter past one, and he had never withdrawn so soon. He reached his lodgings for the most part at two—with his walk of a quarter of an hour. He would wait for the last quarter—he wouldn't stir till then; and he kept his watch there with his eyes on it, reflecting while he held it that this deliberate wait, a wait with an effort, which he recognised, would serve perfectly for the attestation he desired to make. It would prove his courage —unless indeed the latter might most be proved by his budging at last from his place. What he mainly felt now was that, since he hadn't originally scuttled, he had his dignities—which had never in his life seemed so many—all to preserve and to carry aloft. This was before him in truth as a physical image, an image almost worthy of an age of greater romance. That remark indeed glimmered for him only to glow the next instant with a finer light; since what age of romance, after all, could have matched either the state of his mind or, "objectively," as they said, the wonder of his situation? The only difference would have been that, brandishing his dignities over his head as in a parchment scroll, he might then—that is in the heroic time—have proceeded downstairs with a drawn sword in his other grasp.

At present, really, the light he had set down on the mantel of the next room would have to figure his sword; which utensil, in the course of a minute, he had taken the requisite number of steps to possess himself of. The door between the rooms was open, and from the second another door opened to a third. These rooms, as he remembered, gave all three upon a common corridor as well, but there was a fourth, beyond them, without issue save through the preceding. To have moved, to have heard his step again, was appreciably a help; though even in recognising this he lingered once more a little by the chimney-piece on which his light had rested. When he next moved, just hesitating where to turn, he found himself considering a circumstance that, after his first and comparatively vague apprehension of it, produced in him the start that often attends some pang of recollection, the violent shock of having ceased happily to forget. He had come into sight of the door in which the brief chain of communication ended and which he now surveyed from the nearer threshold, the one not directly facing it. Placed at some distance to the left of this point, it would have admitted him to the last room of the four, the room without other approach or egress, had it not, to his intimate conviction, been closed *since* his former visitation, the matter probably of a quarter of an hour before. He stared with all his eyes at the wonder of the fact, arrested again where he stood and again holding his breath while he sounded its sense. Surely it had been *subsequently* closed—that is it had been on his previous passage indubitably open!

He took it full in the face that something had happened between—that he couldn't not have noticed before (by which he meant on his original tour of all the rooms that evening) that such a barrier had exceptionally presented itself. He had indeed since that moment undergone an agitation so extraordinary that it might have muddled for him any earlier view; and he tried to convince himself that he might perhaps then have gone into the room and, inadvertently, automatically, on coming out, have drawn the door after him. The difficulty was that this exactly was what he never did; it was against his whole policy, as he might have said, the essence of which was to keep vistas clear. He had them from the first, as he was well aware, quite on the brain: the strange apparition, at the far end of one of them, of his baffled "prey" (which had become by so sharp an irony so little the term now to apply!) was the form of success his imagination had most cherished, projecting into it always a refinement of beauty. He had known fifty times the start of perception that had afterwards dropped; had fifty times gasped to himself "There!" under some fond brief hallucination. The house, as the case stood, admirably lent itself; he might wonder at the taste, the native architecture of the particular time, which could rejoice so in the multiplication of doors—the opposite extreme to the modern, the actual almost complete proscription of them; but it had fairly contributed to provoke this obsession of the presence encountered telescopically, as he might say, focussed and studied in diminishing perspective and as by a rest for the elbow.

It was with these considerations that his present attention was charged—they perfectly availed to make what he saw portentous. He *couldn't*, by any lapse, have blocked that aperture; and if he hadn't, if it was unthinkable, why what else was clear but that there had been another agent? Another agent?—he had been catching, as he felt, a moment back, the very breath of him; but when had he been so close as in this simple, this logical, this completely personal act? It was so logical, that is, that one might have *taken* it for personal; yet for what did Brydon take it, he asked himself, while, softly panting, he felt his eyes almost leave their sockets. Ah this time at last they *were*, the two, the opposed projections of him, in presence; and this time, as much as one would, the question of danger loomed. With it rose, as not before, the question of courage—for what he knew the blank face of the door to say to him was "Show us how much you have!" It stared, it glared back at him with that challenge; it put to him the two alternatives: should he just push it open or not? Oh to have this consciousness was to *think*—and to think, Brydon knew, as he stood there, was, with the lapsing moments, not to have acted! Not to have acted—that was the misery and the pang—was even still not to act; was in fact *all* to feel the thing in another, in a new and terrible way. How long did he pause and how long did he debate? There was presently nothing to measure it; for his vibration had already changed—as just by the effect of its intensity. Shut up there, at bay, defiant, and with the prodigy of the thing palpably proveably *done*, thus giving notice like some stark signboard—under that accession of accent the situation itself had turned; and Brydon at last remarkably made up his mind on what it had turned to.

It had turned altogether to a different admonition; to a supreme hint, for him, of the value of Discretion! This slowly dawned, no doubt—for it could take its time; so perfectly, on his threshold, had he been stayed, so little as yet had he either advanced or retreated. It was the strangest of all things that now when, by his taking ten steps and applying his hand to a latch, or even his shoulder and his knee, if necessary, to a panel, all the hunger of his prime need might have been met, his high curiosity crowned, his unrest assuaged—it was amazing, but it was also exquisite and rare, that insistence should have, at a touch, quite dropped from him. Discretion—he jumped at that; and yet not, verily, at such a pitch, because it saved his nerves or his skin, but because, much more valuably, it saved the situation. When I say he "jumped" at it I feel the consonance of this term with the fact that—at the end indeed of I know not how long—he did move again, he crossed straight to the door. He wouldn't touch it—it seemed now that he might *if* he would: he would only just wait there a little, to show, to prove, that he wouldn't. He had thus another station, close to the thin partition by which revelation was denied him; but with his eyes bent and his hands held off in a mere intensity of stillness. He listened as if there had been something to hear, but this attitude, while it lasted, was his own communication. "If you won't then—good: I spare you and I give up. You affect me as by the appeal positively for pity: you convince me that for reasons rigid and sublime—what do I know?—we both of us should have suffered. I respect them then, and, though moved and privileged as, I believe, it has never been given to man, I retire, I renounce—never, on my honour, to try again. So rest for ever—and let *me*!"

That, for Brydon was the deep sense of this last demonstration—solemn, measured, directed, as he felt it to be. He brought it to a close, he turned away; and now verily he knew how deeply he had been stirred. He retraced his steps, taking up his candle, burnt, he observed, well-nigh to the socket, and marking again, lighten it as he would, the distinctness of his footfall; after which, in a moment, he knew himself at the other side of the house. He did here what he had not yet done at these hours—he opened half a casement, one of those in the front, and let in the air of the night; a thing he would have taken at any time previous for a sharp rupture of his spell. His spell was now, and it didn't matter—broken by his concession and his surrender, which made it idle henceforth that he should ever come back. The empty street—its other life so marked even by the great lamplit vacancy—was within call, within touch; he stayed there as to be in it again, high above it though he was still perched; he watched as for some comforting common fact, some vulgar human note, the passage of a scavenger or a thief, some night-bird however base. He would have blessed that sign of life; he would have welcomed positively the slow approach of his friend the policeman, whom he had hitherto only sought to avoid, and was not sure that if the patrol had come into sight he mightn't have felt the impulse to get into relation with it, to hail it, on some pretext, from his fourth floor.

The pretext that wouldn't have been too silly or too compromising, the explanation that would have saved his dignity and kept his name, in such a case, out of the papers, was not definite to him: he was so occupied with the thought of recording his Discretion—as an effect of the vow he had just uttered to his intimate adversary—that the importance of this loomed large and something had overtaken all ironically his sense of proportion. If there had been a ladder applied to the front of

the house, even one of the vertiginous perpendiculars em-
ployed by painters and roofers and sometimes left standing
overnight, he would have managed somehow, astride of the
window-sill, to compass by outstretched leg and arm that mode
of descent. If there had been some such uncanny thing as he
had found in his room at hotels, a workable fire-escape in the
form of notched cable or a canvas shoot, he would have availed
himself of it as a proof—well, of his present delicacy. He nursed
that sentiment, as the question stood, a little in vain, and
even—at the end of he scarce knew, once more, how long—
found it, as by the action on his mind of the failure of response
of the outer world, sinking back to vague anguish. It seemed to
him he had waited an age for some stir of the great grim hush;
the life of the town was itself under a spell—so unnaturally, up
and down the whole prospect of known and rather ugly objects, the blankness and the silence lasted. Had they ever, he
asked himself, the hard-faced houses, which had begun to look
livid in the dim dawn, had they ever spoken so little to any
need of his spirit? Great built voids, great crowded stillnesses
put on, often, in the heart of cities, for the small hours, a sort
of sinister mask, and it was of this large collective negation that
Brydon presently became conscious—all the more that the
break of day was, almost incredibly, now at hand, proving to
him what a night he had made of it.

   He looked again at his watch, saw what had become of his
time-values (he had taken hours for minutes—not, as in other
tense situations, minutes for hours) and the strange air of the
streets was but the weak, the sullen flush of a dawn in which
everything was still locked up. His choked appeal from his own
open window had been the sole note of life, and he could but
break off at last as for a worse despair. Yet while so deeply de-
moralised he was capable again of an impulse denoting—at
least by his present measure—extraordinary resolution; of retracing his steps to the spot where he had turned cold with the
extinction of his last pulse of doubt as to there being in the
place another presence than his own. This required an effort

strong enough to sicken him; but he had his reason, which over-mastered for the moment everything else. There was the whole of the rest of the house to traverse, and how should he screw himself to that if the door he had seen closed were at present open? He could hold to the idea that the closing had practically been for him an act of mercy, a chance offered him to descend, depart, get off the ground and never again profane it. This conception held together, it worked; but what it meant for him depended now clearly on the amount of forbearance his recent action, or rather his recent inaction, had engendered. The image of the "presence," whatever it was, waiting there for him to go—this image had not yet been so concrete for his nerves as when he stopped short of the point at which certainty would have come to him. For, with all his resolution, or more exactly with all his dread, he did stop short—he hung back from really seeing. The risk was too great and his fear too definite: it took at this moment an awful specific form.

He knew—yes, as he had never known anything—that, *should* he see the door open, it would all too abjectly be the end of him. It would mean that the agent of his shame—for his shame was the deep abjection—was once more at large and in general possession; and what glared him thus in the face was the act that this would determine for him. It would send him straight about to the window he had left open, and by that window, be long ladder and dangling rope as absent as they would, he saw himself uncontrollably insanely fatally take his way to the street. The hideous chance of this he at least could avert; but he could only avert it by recoiling in time from assurance. He had the whole house to deal with, this fact was still there; only he now knew that uncertainty alone could start him. He stole back from where he had checked himself—merely to do so was suddenly like safety—and, making blindly for the greater staircase, left gaping rooms and sounding passages behind. Here was the top of the stairs, with a fine large dim descent and three spacious landings to mark off. His instinct was all for mildness, but his feet were harsh on the floors, and, strangely, when he had in a couple of minutes become aware of this, it counted somehow for help. He couldn't have spoken, the tone of his voice would have scared him, and the common conceit or resource of "whistling in the dark" (whether literally or figuratively) have appeared basely vulgar; yet he liked none the less to hear himself go, and when he had reached his first landing—taking it all with no rush, but quite steadily—that stage of success drew from him a gasp of relief.

The house, withal, seemed immense, the scale of space again inordinate; the open rooms to no one of which his eyes deflected, gloomed in their shuttered state like mouths of caverns; only the high skylight that formed the crown of the deep well created for him a medium in which he could advance, but which might have been, for queerness of colour, some watery under-world. He tried to think of something noble, as that his property was really grand, a splendid possession; but this nobleness took the form too of the clear delight with which he was finally to sacrifice it. They might come in now, the builders, the destroyers—they might come as soon as they would. At the end of two flights he had dropped to another zone, and from the middle of the third, with only one more left, he recognised the influence of the lower windows, of half-drawn blinds, of the occasional gleam of street-lamps, of the glazed spaces of the vestibule. This was the bottom of the sea, which showed an illumination of its own and which he even saw paved—when at a given moment he drew up to sink a long look over the banisters—with the marble squares of his childhood. By that time indubitably he felt, as he might have said in a commoner cause, better; it had allowed him to stop and draw breath, and the ease increased with the sight of the old black-and-white slabs. But what he most felt was that now surely, with the element of impunity pulling him as by hard firm hands, the case was settled for what he might have seen above had he dared that last look. The closed door, blessedly remote now, was still closed—and he had only in short to reach that of the house.

He came down further, he crossed the passage forming the access to the last flight; and if here again he stopped an instant it was almost for the sharpness of the thrill of assured escape. It made him shut his eyes—which opened again to the straight slope of the remainder of the stairs. Here was impunity still, but impunity almost excessive; inasmuch as the side-lights and the high fan-tracery of the entrance were glimmering straight into the hall; an appearance produced, he the next instant saw, by the fact that the vestibule gaped wide, that the hinged halves of the inner door had been thrown far back. Out of that again the *question* sprang at him, making his eyes, as he felt, half-start from his head, as they had done, at the top of the house, before the sign of the other door. If he had left that one open, hadn't he left this one closed, and wasn't he now in *most* immediate presence of some inconceivable occult activity? It was as sharp, the question, as a knife in his side, but the answer hung fire still and seemed to lose itself in the vague darkness to which the thin admitted dawn, glimmering archwise over the whole outer door, made a semicircular margin, a cold silvery nimbus that seemed to play a little as he looked—to shift and expand and contract.

It was as if there had been something within it, protected by indistinctness and corresponding in extent with the opaque surface behind, the painted panels of the last barrier to his escape, of which the key was in his pocket. The indistinctness mocked him even while he stared, affected him as somehow shrouding or challenging certitude, so that after faltering an instant on his step he let himself go with the sense that here *was* at last something to meet, to touch, to take, to know—something all unnatural and dreadful, but to advance upon which was the condition for him either of liberation or of supreme defeat. The penumbra, dense and dark, was the virtual screen of a figure which stood in it as still as some image erect in a niche or as some black-vizored sentinel guarding a treasure. Brydon was to know afterwards, was to recall and make out, the particular thing he had believed during the rest of his descent. He saw, in its great grey glimmering margin, the central vagueness diminish, and he felt it to be taking the very form toward which, for so many days, the passion of his curiosity had yearned. It gloomed, it loomed, it was something, it was somebody, the prodigy of a personal presence.

Rigid and conscious, spectral yet human, a man of his own substance and stature waited there to measure himself with his power to dismay. This only could it be—this only till he recognised, with his advance, that what made the face dim was the pair of raised hands that covered it and in which, so far from being offered in defiance, it was buried as for dark deprecation. So Brydon, before him, took him in; with every fact of him now, in the higher light, hard and acute—his planted stillness, his vivid truth, his grizzled bent head and white masking hands, his queer actuality of evening-dress, of dangling double eye-glass, of gleaming silk lappet and white linen, of pearl button and gold watch-guard and polished shoe. No portrait by a great modern master could have presented him with more intensity, thrust him out of his frame with more art, as if there had been "treatment," of the consummate sort, in his every shade and salience. The revulsion, for our friend, had become, before he knew it, immense—this drop, in the act of apprehension, to the sense of his adversary's inscrutable manœuvre. That meaning at least, while he gaped, it offered him; for he could but gape at his other self in this other anguish, gape as a proof that *he*, standing there for the achieved, the enjoyed, the triumphant life, couldn't be faced in his triumph. Wasn't the proof in the splendid covering hands, strong and completely spread?—so spread and so intentional that, in spite of a special verity that surpassed every other, the fact that one of these hands had lost two fingers, which were reduced to stumps, as if accidentally shot away, the face was effectually guarded and saved.

"Saved," though, *would* it be?—Brydon breathed his wonder till the very impunity of his attitude and the very insistence of his eyes produced, as he felt, a sudden stir which showed the next instant as a deeper portent, while the head raised itself, the betrayal of a braver purpose. The hands, as he looked, began to move, to open; then, as if deciding in a flash, dropped from the face and left it uncovered and presented. Horror, with the sight, had leaped into Brydon's throat, gasping there in a sound he couldn't utter; for the bared identity was too hideous as *his*, and his glare was the passion of his protest. The face, *that* face, Spencer Brydon's?—he searched it still, but looking away from it in dismay and denial, falling straight from his height and sublimity. It was unknown, inconceivable, awful, disconnected from any possibility—! He had been "sold," he inwardly moaned, stalking such game as this: the presence before him was a presence, the horror within him a horror, but the waste of his nights had been only grotesque and the success of his adventure an irony. Such an identity fitted his at *no* point, made its alternative monstrous. A thousand times yes, as it came upon him nearer now—the face was the face of a stranger. It came upon him nearer now, quite as one of those expanding fantastic images projected by the magic lantern of childhood; for the stranger, whoever he might be, evil, odious, blatant, vulgar, had advanced as for aggression, and he knew himself give ground. Then harder pressed still, sick with the force of his shock, and falling back as under the hot breath and the roused passion of a life larger than his own, a rage of personality before which his own collapsed, he felt the whole vision turn to darkness and his very feet give way. His head went round; he was going; he had gone.

III

WHAT had next brought him back, clearly—though after how long?—was Mrs. Muldoon's voice, coming to him from quite near, from so near that he seemed presently to see her as kneeling on the ground before him while he lay looking up at her; himself not wholly on the ground, but half raised and up-held—conscious, yes, of tenderness of support and, more particularly, of a head pillowed in extraordinary softness and faintly refreshing fragrance. He considered, he wondered, his wit but half at his service; then another face intervened, bending more directly over him, and he finally knew that Alice Staverton had made her lap an ample and perfect cushion to him, and that she had to this end seated herself on the lowest degree of the staircase, the rest of his long person remaining stretched on his old black-and-white slabs. They were cold, these marble squares of his youth; but *he* somehow was not, in this rich return of consciousness—the most wonderful hour, little by little, that he had ever known, leaving him, as it did, so gratefully, so abysmally passive, and yet as with a treasure of intelligence waiting all round him for quiet appropriation; dissolved, he might call it, in the air of the place and producing the golden glow of a late autumn afternoon. He had come back, yes—come back from further away than any man but himself had ever travelled; but it was strange how with this sense what he had come back *to* seemed really the great thing, and as if his prodigious journey had been all for the sake of it. Slowly but surely his consciousness grew, his vision of his state thus completing itself: he had been miraculously *carried* back—lifted and carefully borne as from where he had been picked up, the uttermost end of an interminable grey passage. Even with this he was suffered to rest, and what had now brought him to knowledge was the break in the long mild motion.

It had brought him to knowledge, to knowledge—yes, this was the beauty of his state; which came to resemble more and more that of a man who has gone to sleep on some news of a great inheritance, and then, after dreaming it away, after profaning it with matters strange to it, has waked up again to serenity of certitude and has only to lie and watch it grow. This was the drift of his patience—that he had only to let it shine on him. He must moreover, with intermissions, still have been lifted and borne; since why and how else should he have known himself, later on, with the afternoon glow intenser, no longer at the foot of his stairs—situated as these now seemed at that dark other end of his tunnel—but on a deep window-bench of his high saloon, over which had been spread, couch-fashion, a mantle of soft stuff lined with grey fur that was familiar to his eyes and that one of his hands kept fondly feeling as for its pledge of truth. Mrs. Muldoon's face had gone, but the other, the second he had recognised, hung over him in a way that showed how he was still propped and pillowed. He took it all in, and the more he took it the more it seemed to suffice: he was as much at peace as if he had had food and drink. It was the two women who had found him, on Mrs. Muldoon's having plied, at her usual hour, her latch-key—and on her having above all arrived while Miss Staverton still lingered near the house. She had been turning away, all anxiety, from worrying the vain bell-handle—her calculation having been of the hour of the good woman's visit; but the latter, blessedly, had come up while she was still there, and they had entered together. He had then lain, beyond the vestibule, very much as he was lying now —quite, that is, as he appeared to have fallen, but all so wondrously without bruise or gash; only in a depth of stupor. What he most took in, however, at present, with the steadier clearance, was that Alice Staverton had for a long unspeakable moment not doubted he was dead.

"It must have been that I *was*." He made it out as she held him. "Yes—I can only have died. You brought me literally to life. Only," he wondered, his eyes rising to her, "only, in the name of all the benedictions, how?"

It took her but an instant to bend her face and kiss him, and something in the manner of it, and in the way her hands clasped and locked his head while he felt the cool charity and virtue of her lips, something in all this beatitude somehow answered everything. "And now I keep you," she said.

"Oh keep me, keep me!" he pleaded while her face still hung over him: in response to which it dropped again and stayed close, clingingly close. It was the seal of their situation—of which he tasted the impress for a long blissful moment in silence. But he came back. "Yet how did you know—?"

"I was uneasy. You were to have come, you remember—and you had sent no word."

"Yes, I remember—I was to have gone to you at one today." It caught on to their "old" life and relation—which were so near and so far. "I was still out there in my strange darkness—where was it, what was it? I must have stayed there so long." He could but wonder at the depth and the duration of his swoon.

"Since last night?" she asked with a shade of fear for her possible indiscretion.

"Since this morning—it must have been: the cold dim dawn of today. Where have I been," he vaguely wailed, "where have I been?" He felt her hold him close, and it was as if this helped him now to make in all security his mild moan. "What a long dark day!"

All in her tenderness she had waited a moment. "In the cold dim dawn?" she quavered.

But he had already gone on piecing together the parts of the whole prodigy. "As I didn't turn up you came straight—?"

She barely cast about. "I went first to your hotel—where they told me of your absence. You had dined out last evening and hadn't been back since. But they appeared to know you had been at your club."

"So you had the idea of *this*—?"

"Of what?" she asked in a moment.

"Well—of what has happened."

"I believed at least you'd have been here. I've known, all along," she said, "that you've been coming."

" 'Known' it—?"

"Well, I've believed it. I said nothing to you after that talk we had a month ago—but I felt sure. I knew you *would*," she declared.

"That I'd persist, you mean?"

"That you'd see him."

"Ah but I didn't!" cried Brydon with his long wail. "There's somebody—an awful beast; whom I brought, too horribly, to bay. But it's not me."

At this she bent over him again, and her eyes were in his eyes. "No—it's not you." And it was as if, while her face hovered, he might have made out in it, hadn't it been so near, some particular meaning blurred by a smile. "No, thank heaven," she repeated—"it's not you! Of course it wasn't to have been."

"Ah but it *was*," he gently insisted. And he stared before him now as he had been staring for so many weeks. "I was to have known myself."

"You couldn't!" she returned consolingly. And then reverting, and as if to account further for what she had herself done, "But it wasn't only *that*, that you hadn't been at home," she went on. "I waited till the hour at which we had found Mrs. Muldoon that day of my going with you; and she arrived, as I've told you, while, failing to bring any one to the door, I lingered in my despair on the steps. After a little, if she hadn't come, by such a mercy, I should have found means to hunt her up. But it wasn't," said Alice Staverton, as if once more with her fine intention—"it wasn't only that."

His eyes, as he lay, turned back to her. "What more then?"

She met it, the wonder she had stirred. "In the cold dim dawn, you say? Well, in the cold dim dawn of this morning I too saw you."

"Saw *me*—?"

"Saw *him*," said Alice Staverton. "It must have been at the same moment."

He lay an instant taking it in—as if he wished to be quite reasonable. "At the same moment?"

"Yes—in my dream again, the same one I've named to you. He came back to me. Then I knew it for a sign. He had come to you."

At this Brydon raised himself; he had to see her better. She helped him when she understood his movement, and he sat up, steadying himself beside her there on the window-bench and with his right hand grasping her left. "*He* didn't come to me."

"You came to yourself," she beautifully smiled.

"Ah I've come to myself now—thanks to you, dearest. But this brute, with his awful face—this brute's a black stranger. He's none of *me*, even as I *might* have been," Brydon sturdily declared.

But she kept the clearness that was like the breath of infallibility. "Isn't the whole point that you'd have been different?"

He almost scowled for it. "As different as *that*—?"

Her look again was more beautiful to him than the things of this world. "Haven't you exactly wanted to know *how* different? So this morning," she said, "you appeared to me."

"Like *him*?"

"A black stranger!"

"Then how did you know it was I?"

"Because, as I told you weeks ago, my mind, my imagination, had worked so over what you might, what you mightn't have been—to show you, you see, how I've thought of you. In the midst of that you came to me—that my wonder might be answered. So I knew," she went on; "and believed that, since the question held you too so fast, as you told me that day, you too would see for yourself. And when this morning I again saw I knew it would be because you had—and also then, from the first moment, because you somehow wanted me. *He* seemed to tell me of that. So why," she strangely smiled, "shouldn't I like him?"

It brought Spencer Brydon to his feet. "You 'like' that horror—?"

"I *could* have liked him. And to me," she said, "he was no horror. I had accepted him."

"'Accepted'—?" Brydon oddly sounded.

"Before, for the interest of his difference—yes. And as *I* didn't disown him, as *I* knew him—which you at last, confronted with him in his difference, so cruelly didn't, my dear—well, he must have been, you see, less dreadful to me. And it may have pleased him that I pitied him."

She was beside him on her feet, but still holding his hand—

still with her arm supporting him. But though it all brought for him thus a dim light, "You 'pitied' him?" he grudgingly, resentfully asked.

"He has been unhappy; he has been ravaged," she said.

"And haven't I been unhappy? Am not I—you've only to look at me!—ravaged?"

"Ah I don't say I like him *better*," she granted after a thought. "But he's grim, he's worn—and things have happened to him. He doesn't make shift, for sight, with your charming monocle."

"No"—it struck Brydon: "I couldn't have sported mine downtown. They'd have guyed me there."

"His great convex pince-nez—I saw it, I recognised the kind—is for his poor ruined sight. And his poor right hand—!"

"Ah!" Brydon winced—whether for his proved identity or for his lost fingers. Then, "He has a million a year," he lucidly added. "But he hasn't you."

"And he isn't—no, he isn't—*you*!" she murmured as he drew her to his breast.

1909

CRAPY CORNELIA

I

THREE times within a quarter of an hour—shifting the while his posture on his chair of contemplation—had he looked at his watch as for its final sharp hint that he should decide, that he should get up. His seat was one of a group fairly sequestered, unoccupied save for his own presence, and from where he lingered he looked off at a stretch of lawn freshened by recent April showers and on which sundry small children were at play. The trees, the shrubs, the plants, every stem and twig just ruffled as by the first touch of the light finger of the relenting year, struck him as standing still in the blest hope of more of the same caress; the quarter about him held its breath after the fashion of the child who waits with the rigour of an open mouth and shut eyes for the promised sensible effect of his having been good. So, in the windless, sun-warmed air of the beautiful afternoon, the Park of the winter's end had struck White-Mason as waiting; even New York, under such an impression, was "good," good enough—for *him*: its very sounds were faint, were almost sweet, as they reached him from so seemingly far beyond the wooded horizon that formed the remoter limit of his large shallow glade. The tones of the frolic infants ceased to be nondescript and harsh—were in fact almost as fresh and decent as the frilled and puckered and ribboned garb of the little girls, which had always a way, in those parts, of so portentously flaunting the daughters of the strange native—that is of the overwhelmingly alien—populace at him.

Not that these things in particular were his matter of meditation now; he had wanted, at the end of his walk, to sit apart a little and think—and had been doing that for twenty minutes, even though as yet to no break in the charm of procrastination. But he had looked without seeing and listened without hearing: all that had been positive for him was that he hadn't failed vaguely to feel. He had felt in the first place, and he continued to feel—yes, at forty-eight quite as much as at any point of the supposed reign of younger intensities—the great spirit of the air, the fine sense of the season, the supreme appeal of Nature, he might have said, to his time of life; quite as if she, easy, indulgent, indifferent, cynical Power, were offering him the last chance it would rest with his wit or his blood to embrace. Then with that he had been entertaining, to the point and with the prolonged consequence of accepted immobilization, the certitude that if he did call on Mrs. Worthingham and find her at home he couldn't in justice to himself not put to her the question that had lapsed the other time, the last time, through the irritating and persistent, even if accidental, presence of others. What friends she had—the people who so stupidly, so wantonly stuck! If they *should*, he and she, come to an understanding, that would presumably have to include certain members of her singularly ill-composed circle, in whom it was incredible to him that he should ever take an interest. This defeat, to do himself justice—he had bent rather predominantly on *that*, you see; ideal justice to *her*, with her possible conception of what it should consist of, being another and quite a different matter— he had had the fact of the Sunday afternoon to thank for; she didn't "keep" that day for him, since they hadn't, up to now, quite begun to cultivate the appointment or assignation founded on explicit sacrifices. He might at any rate look to find this pleasant practical Wednesday—should he indeed, at his actual rate, stay it before it ebbed—more liberally and intendingly given him.

The sound he at last most wittingly distinguished in his nook was the single deep note of half-past five borne to him from some high-perched public clock. He finally got up with the sense that the time from then on *ought* at least to be felt as sacred to him. At this juncture it was—while he stood there shaking his garments, settling his hat, his necktie, his shirt-cuffs, fixing the high polish of his fine shoes as if for some re-flection in it of his straight and spare and grizzled, his refined and trimmed and dressed, his altogether distinguished person, that of a gentleman abundantly settled, but of a bachelor markedly nervous—at this crisis it was, doubtless, that he at once most measured and least resented his predicament. If he should go he would almost to a certainty find her, and if he should find her he would almost to a certainty come to the point. He wouldn't put it off again—there was that high con-sideration for him of justice at least to himself. He had never yet denied himself anything so apparently fraught with possi-bilities as the idea of proposing to Mrs. Worthingham—never yet, in other words, denied himself anything he had so dis-tinctly wanted to do; and the results of that wisdom had re-mained for him precisely the precious parts of experience. Counting only the offers of his honourable hand, these had been on three remembered occasions at least the consequence of an impulse as sharp and a self-respect as reasoned; a self-respect that hadn't in the least suffered, moreover, from the failure of each appeal. He had been met in the three cases—the only ones he at all compared with his present case—by the frank confes-sion that he didn't somehow, charming as he was, cause himself to be superstitiously believed in; and the lapse of life, afterward, had cleared up many doubts.

It *wouldn't* have done, he eventually, he lucidly saw, each time he had been refused; and the candour of his nature was such that he could live to think of these very passages as a proof of how right he had been—right, that is, to have put himself forward always, by the happiest instinct, only in impossible conditions. He had the happy consciousness of having exposed the important question to the crucial test, and of having es-caped, by that persistent logic, a grave mistake. What better proof of his escape than the fact that he was now free to renew the all-interesting inquiry, and should be exactly, about to do so in different and better conditions? The conditions were better by as much more—as much more of his career and character, of his situation, his reputation he could even have called it, of his knowledge of life, of his somewhat extended means, of his possibly augmented charm, of his certainly improved mind and temper—as was involved in the actual impending settlement. Once he had got into motion, once he had crossed the Park and passed out of it, entering, with very little space to traverse, one of the short new streets that abutted on its east side, his step became that of a man young enough to find confidence, quite to find felicity, in the sense, in almost any sense, of action. He could still enjoy almost anything, absolutely an unpleasant thing, in default of a better, that might still remind him he wasn't so old. The standing newness of everything about him would, it was true, have weakened this cheer by too much presuming on it; Mrs. Worthingham's house, before which he stopped, had that gloss of new money, that glare of a piece fresh from the mint and ringing for the first time on any counter, which seems to claim for it, in any transaction, something more than the "face" value.

This could but be yet more the case for the impression of the observer introduced and committed. On our friend's part I mean, after his admission and while still in the hall, the sense of the general shining immediacy, of the still unhushed clamour of the shock, was perhaps stronger than he had ever known it. That broke out from every corner as the high pitch of interest, and with a candour that—no, certainly—he had never seen equalled; every particular expensive object shrieking at him in its artless pride that it had just "come home." He met the whole vision with something of the grimace produced on persons without goggles by the passage from a shelter to a blinding light; and if he had—by a perfectly possible chance—been "snap-shotted" on the spot, would have struck you as showing for his first tribute to the temple of Mrs. Worthingham's charm-

ing presence a scowl almost of anguish. He wasn't constitutionally, it may at once be explained for him, a goggled person; and
he was condemned, in New York, to this frequent violence of
transition—having to reckon with it whenever he went out, as
who should say, from himself. The high pitch of interest, to his
taste, was the pitch of history, the pitch of acquired and earned
suggestion, the pitch of association, in a word; so that he lived
by preference, incontestably, if not in a rich gloom, which would
have been beyond his means and spirits, at least amid objects
and images that confessed to the tone of time.

He had ever felt that an indispensable presence—with a
need of it moreover that interfered at no point with his gentle
habit, not to say his subtle art, of drawing out what was left
him of his youth, of thinly and thriftily spreading the rest of
that choicest jam-pot of the cupboard of consciousness over the
remainder of a slice of life still possibly thick enough to bear it;
or in other words of moving the melancholy limits, the significant signs, constantly a little further on, very much as property-
marks or staked boundaries are sometimes stealthily shifted at
night. He positively cherished in fact, as against the too invet-
erate gesture of distressfully guarding his eyeballs—so many
New York aspects seemed to keep him at it—an ideal of adjusted appreciation, of courageous curiosity, of fairly letting the
world about him, a world of constant breathless renewals and
merciless substitutions, make its flaring assault on its own inordinate terms. Newness *was* value in the piece—for the acquisi-
tor, or at least sometimes might be, even though the act of
"blowing" hard, the act marking a heated freshness of arrival, or
other form of irruption, could never minister to the peace of
those already and long on the field; and this if only because
maturer tone was after all most appreciable and most consoling
when one staggered back to it, wounded, bleeding, blinded,
from the riot of the raw—or, to put the whole experience more
prettily, no doubt, from excesses of light.

II

IF HE WENT in, however, with something of his more or less inevitable scowl, there were really, at the moment, two rather valid reasons for screened observation; the first of these being that the whole place seemed to reflect as never before the lustre of Mrs. Worthingham's own polished and prosperous little person—to smile, it struck him, with her smile, to twinkle not only with the gleam of her lovely teeth, but with that of all her rings and brooches and bangles and other gewgaws, to curl and spasmodically cluster as in emulation of her charming complicated yellow tresses, to surround the most animated of pink-and-white, of ruffled and ribboned, of frilled and festooned Dresden china shepherdesses with exactly the right system of rococo curves and convolutions and other flourishes, a perfect bower of painted and gilded and moulded conceits. The second ground of this immediate impression of scenic extravagance, almost as if the curtain rose for him to the first act of some small and expensively mounted comic opera, was that she hadn't, after all, awaited him in fond singleness, but had again just a trifle inconsiderately exposed him to the drawback of having to reckon, for whatever design he might amiably entertain, with the presence of a third and quite superfluous person, a small black insignificant but none the less oppressive stranger. It was odd how, on the instant, the little lady engaged with her did affect him as comparatively black—very much as if that had absolutely, in such a medium, to be the graceless appearance of any item not positively of some fresh shade of a light colour or of some pretty pretension to a charming twist. Any witness of their meeting, his hostess should surely have felt, would have been a false note in the whole rosy glow; but what note so false as that of the dingy little presence that she might actually, by a refinement of her perhaps always too visible study of effect, have provided as a positive contrast or foil? whose name and intervention, moreover, she appeared to be no more moved to mention and account for than she might have been to "present"

—whether as stretched at her feet or erect upon disciplined haunches—some shaggy old domesticated terrier or poodle.

Extraordinarily, after he had been in the room five minutes —a space of time during which his fellow-visitor had neither budged nor uttered a sound—he had made Mrs. Worthingham out as all at once perfectly pleased to see him, completely aware of what he had most in mind, and singularly serene in face of his sense of their impediment. It was as if for all the world she didn't take it for one, the immobility, to say nothing of the seeming equanimity, of their tactless companion; at whom meanwhile indeed our friend himself, after his first ruffled perception, no more adventured a look than if advised by his constitutional kindness that to notice her in any degree would perforce be ungraciously to glower. He talked after a fashion with the woman as to whose power to please and amuse and serve him, as to whose really quite organised and indicated fitness for lighting up his autumn afternoon of life his conviction had lately strained itself so clear; but he was all the while carrying on an intenser exchange with his own spirit and trying to read into the charming creature's behaviour, as he could only call it, some confirmation of his theory that she also had her inward flutter and anxiously counted on him. He found support, happily for the conviction just named, in the idea, at no moment as yet really repugnant to him, the idea bound up in fact with the finer essence of her appeal, that she had her own vision too of her quality and her price, and that the last appearance she would have liked to bristle with was that of being forewarned and eager.

He had, if he came to think of it, scarce definitely warned her, and he probably wouldn't have taken to her so consciously in the first instance without an appreciative sense that, as she was a little person of twenty superficial graces, so she was also a little person with her secret pride. She might just have planted her mangy lion—not to say her muzzled house-dog—there in his path as a symbol that she wasn't cheap and easy; which would be a thing he couldn't possibly wish his future wife to have shown herself in advance, even if to him alone. That she could make him put himself such questions was precisely part of the attaching play of her iridescent surface, the shimmering interfusion of her various aspects; that of her youth with her independence—her pecuniary perhaps in particular, that of her vivacity with her beauty, that of her facility above all with her odd novelty; the high modernity, as people appeared to have come to call it, that made her so much more "knowing" in some directions than even he, man of the world as he certainly was, could pretend to be, though all on a basis of the most unconscious and instinctive and luxurious assumption. She was "up" to everything, aware of everything—if one counted from a short enough time back (from week before last, say, and as if quantities of history had burst upon the world within the fortnight); she was likewise surprised at nothing, and in that direction one might reckon as far ahead as the rest of her lifetime, or at any rate as the rest of his, which was all that would concern him: it was as if the suitability of the future to her personal and rather pampered tastes was what she most took for granted, so that he could see her, for all her Dresden-china shoes and her flutter of wondrous befrilled contemporary skirts, skip by the side of the coming age as over the floor of a ball-room, keeping step with its monstrous stride and prepared for every figure of the dance.

Her outlook took form to him suddenly as a great square sunny window that hung in assured fashion over the immensity of life. There rose toward it as from a vast swarming *plaza* a high tide of motion and sound; yet it was at the same time as if even while he looked her light gemmed hand, flashing on him in addition to those other things the perfect polish of the prettiest pink finger-nails in the world, had touched a spring, the most ingenious of recent devices for instant ease, which dropped half across the scene a soft-coloured mechanical blind, a fluttered, fringed awning of charmingly toned silk, such as would make a bath of cool shade for the favoured friend leaning with her there—that is for the happy couple itself—on the balcony. The great view would be the prospect and privilege of the very state he coveted—since didn't he covet it?—the state of being so securely at her side; while the wash of privacy, as one might count it, the broad fine brush dipped into clear umber and passed, full and wet, straight across the strong scheme of colour, would represent the security itself, all the uplifted inner elegance, the condition, so ideal, of being shut out from nothing and yet of having, so gaily and breezily aloft, none of the burden or worry of anything. Thus, as I say, for our friend, the place itself, while his vivid impression lasted, portentously opened and spread, and what was before him took, to his vision, though indeed at so other a crisis, the form of the "glimmering square" of the poet; yet, for a still more remarkable fact, with an incongruous object usurping at a given instant the privilege of the frame and seeming, even as he looked, to block the view.

The incongruous object was a woman's head, crowned with a little sparsely feathered black hat, an ornament quite unlike those the women mostly noticed by White-Mason were now "wearing," and that grew and grew, that came nearer and nearer, while it met his eyes, after the manner of images in the kinematograph. It had presently loomed so large that he saw nothing else—not only among the things at a considerable distance, the things Mrs. Worthingham would eventually, yet unmistakably, introduce him to, but among those of this lady's various attributes and appurtenances as to which he had been in the very act of cultivating his consciousness. It was in the course of another minute the most extraordinary thing in the world: everything had altered, dropped, darkened, disappeared; his imagination had spread its wings only to feel them flop all grotesquely at its sides as he recognised in his hostess's quiet companion, the oppressive alien who hadn't indeed interfered with his fanciful flight, though she had prevented his immediate declaration and brought about the thud, not to say the felt violent shock, of his fall to earth, the perfectly plain identity of Cornelia Rasch. It was she who had remained there at attention; it was she their companion hadn't introduced; it was she he had forborne to face with his fear of incivility. He stared at her—everything else went.

"Why it has been *you* all this time?"

Miss Rasch fairly turned pale. "I was waiting to see if you'd know me."

"Ah, my dear Cornelia"—he came straight out with it—"rather!"

"Well, it isn't," she returned with a quick change to red now, "from having taken much time to look at me!"

She smiled, she even laughed, but he could see how she had felt his unconsciousness, poor thing; the acquaintance, quite the friend of his youth, as she had been, the associate of his childhood, of his early manhood, of his middle age in fact, up to a few years back, not more than ten at the most; the associate too of so many of his associates and of almost all of his relations, those of the other time, those who had mainly gone for ever; the person in short whose noted disappearance, though it might have seemed final, had been only of recent seasons. She was present again now, all unexpectedly—he had heard of her having at last, left alone after successive deaths and with scant resources, sought economic salvation in Europe, the promised land of American thrift—she was present as this almost ancient and this oddly unassertive little rotund figure whom one seemed no more obliged to address than if she had been a black satin ottoman "treated" with buttons and gimp; a class of object as to which the policy of blindness was imperative. He felt the need of some explanatory plea, and before he could think had uttered one at Mrs. Worthingham's expense. "Why, you see we weren't introduced——!"

"No—but I didn't suppose I should have to be named to you."

"Well, my dear woman, you haven't—do me that justice!" He could at least make this point. "I felt all the while—!" However, it would have taken him long to say what he had been feeling; and he was aware now of the pretty projected light of

Mrs. Worthingham's wonder. She looked as if, out for a walk with her, he had put her to the inconvenience of his stopping to speak to a strange woman in the street.

"I never supposed you knew her!"—it was to him his hostess excused herself.

This made Miss Rasch spring up, distinctly flushed, distinctly strange to behold, but not vulgarly nettled—Cornelia was incapable of that; only rather funnily bridling and laughing, only showing that this was all she had waited for, only saying just the right thing, the thing she could make so clearly a jest. "Of course if you *had* you'd have presented him."

Mrs. Worthingham looked while answering at White-Mason. "I didn't want you to go—which you see you do as soon as he speaks to you. But I never dreamed——!"

"That there was anything between us? Ah, there are no end of things!" He, on his side, though addressing the younger and prettier woman, looked at his fellow-guest; to whom he even continued: "When did you get back? May I come and see you the very first thing?"

Cornelia gasped and wriggled—she practically giggled; she had lost every atom of her little old, her little young, though always unaccountable prettiness, which used to peep so, on the bare chance of a shot, from behind indefensible features, that it almost made watching her a form of sport. He had heard vaguely of her, it came back to him (for there had been no letters; their later acquaintance, thank goodness, hadn't involved that) as experimenting, for economy, and then as settling, to the same rather dismal end, somewhere in England, at one of those intensely English places, St. Leonards, Cheltenham, Bognor, Dawlish—which, awfully, *was* it?—and she now affected him for all the world as some small squirming, exclaiming, genteelly conversing old maid of a type vaguely associated with the three-volume novels he used to feed on (besides his so often encountering it in "real life") during a far-away stay of his own at Brighton. Odder than any element of his ex-gossip's identity itself, however, was the fact that she somehow, with it all,

rejoiced his sight. Indeed the supreme oddity was that the manner of her reply to his request for leave to call should have
absolutely charmed his attention. She didn't look at him; she
only, from under her frumpy, crapy, curiously exotic hat, and
with her good little near-sighted insinuating glare, expressed to
Mrs. Worthingham, while she answered him, wonderful arch
things, the overdone things of a shy woman. "Yes, you may
call—but only when this dear lovely lady has done with you!"
The moment after which she had gone.

III

FORTY minutes later he was taking his way back from the
queer miscarriage of his adventure; taking it, with no conscious
positive felicity, through the very spaces that had witnessed
shortly before the considerable serenity of his assurance. He
had said to himself then, or had as good as said it, that, since he
might do perfectly as he liked, it couldn't fail for him that he
must soon retrace those steps, humming, to all intents, the first
bars of a wedding-march; so beautifully had it cleared up that
he was "going to like" letting Mrs. Worthingham accept him.
He was to have hummed no wedding-march, as it seemed to be
turning out—he had none, up to now, to hum; and yet, extraordinarily, it wasn't in the least because she had refused him.
Why then hadn't he liked as much as he had intended to like
it putting the pleasant act, the act of not refusing him, in her
power? Could it all have come from the awkward minute of his
failure to decide sharply, on Cornelia's departure, whether or
no he would attend her to the door? He hadn't decided at all—
what the deuce had been in him?—but had danced to and fro
in the room, thinking better of each impulse and then thinking
worse. He had hesitated like an ass erect on absurd hind legs
between two bundles of hay; the upshot of which must have
been his giving the falsest impression. In what way that was to
be for an instant considered had their common past committed

him to crapy Cornelia? He repudiated with a whack on the gravel any ghost of an obligation.

What he could get rid of with scanter success, unfortunately, was the peculiar sharpness of his sense that, though mystified by his visible flurry—and yet not mystified enough for a sympathetic question either—his hostess had been, on the whole, even more frankly diverted: which was precisely an example of that newest, freshest, finest freedom in her, the air and the candour of assuming, not "heartlessly," not viciously, not even very consciously, but with a bright pampered confidence which would probably end by affecting one's nerves as the most impertinent stroke in the world, that every blest thing coming up for her in any connection was somehow matter for her general recreation. There she was again with the innocent egotism, the gilded and overflowing anarchism, really, of her doubtless quite unwitting but none the less rabid modern note. Her grace of ease was perfect, but it was all grace of ease, not a single shred of it grace of uncertainty or of difficulty—which meant, when you came to see, that, for its happy working, not a grain of provision was left by it to mere manners. This was clearly going to be the music of the future—that if people were but rich enough and furnished enough and fed enough, exercised and sanitated and manicured and generally advised and advertised and made "knowing" enough, *avertis* enough, as the term appeared to be nowadays in Paris, all they had to do for civility was to take the amused ironic view of those who might be less initiated. In *his* time, when he was young or even when he was only but a little less middle-aged, the best manners had been the best kindness, and the best kindness had mostly been some art of not insisting on one's luxurious differences, of concealing rather, for common humanity, if not for common decency, a part at least of the intensity or the ferocity with which one might be "in the know."

Oh, the "know"—Mrs. Worthingham was in it, all instinctively, inevitably, and as a matter of course, up to her eyes; which didn't, however, the least little bit prevent her being as ignorant as a fish of everything that really and intimately and fundamentally concerned *him*, poor dear old White-Mason. She didn't, in the first place, so much as know who he was— by which he meant know who and what it was to *be* a White-Mason, even a poor and a dear and old one, "anyway." That indeed—he did her perfect justice—was of the very essence of the newness and freshness and beautiful, brave, social irresponsibility by which she had originally dazzled him: just exactly that circumstance of her having no instinct for any old quality or quantity or identity, a single historic or social value, as he might say, of the New York of his already almost legendary past; and that additional one of his, on his side, having, so far as this went, cultivated blankness, cultivated positive prudence, as to her own personal background—the vagueness, at the best, with which all honest gentlefolk, the New Yorkers of his approved stock and conservative generation, were content, as for the most part they were indubitably wise, to surround the origins and antecedents and queer unimaginable early influences of persons swimming into their ken from those parts of the country that quite necessarily and naturally figured to their view as "God-forsaken" and generally impossible.

The few scattered surviving representatives of a society once "good"—*rari nantes in gurgite vasto*—were liable, at the pass things had come to, to meet, and even amid old shades once sacred, or what was left of such, every form of social impossibility, and, more irresistibly still, to find these apparitions often carry themselves (often at least in the case of the women) with a wondrous wild gallantry, equally imperturbable and inimitable, the sort of thing that reached its maximum in Mrs. Worthingham. Beyond that who ever wanted to look up their annals, to reconstruct their steps and stages, to dot their i's in fine, or to "go behind" anything that was theirs? One wouldn't do that for the world—a rudimentary discretion forbade it; and yet this check from elementary undiscussable taste quite consorted with a due respect for them, or at any rate with a due respect for oneself in connection with them; as was just exemplified in what would be his own, what would be poor dear old White-Mason's, insurmountable aversion to having, on any pretext, the doubtless very queer spectre of the late Mr. Worthingham presented to him. No question had he asked, or would he ever ask, should his life—that is should the success of his courtship—even intimately depend on it, either about that obscure agent of his mistress's actual affluence or about the happy head-spring itself, and the apparently copious tributaries, of the golden stream.

From all which marked anomalies, at any rate, what was the moral to draw? He dropped into a Park chair again with that question, he lost himself in the wonder of why he had come away with his homage so very much unpaid. Yet it didn't seem at all, actually, as if he could say or conclude, as if he could do anything but keep on worrying—just in conformity with his being a person who, whether or no familiar with the need to make his conduct square with his conscience and his taste, was never wholly exempt from that of making his taste and his conscience square with his conduct. To this latter occupation he further abandoned himself, and it didn't release him from his second brooding session till the sweet spring sunset had begun to gather and he had more or less cleared up, in the deepening dusk, the effective relation between the various parts of his ridiculously agitating experience. There were vital facts he seemed thus to catch, to seize, with a nervous hand, and the twilight helping, by their vaguely whisked tails; unquiet truths that swarmed out after the fashion of creatures bold only at eventide, creatures that hovered and circled, that verily brushed his nose, in spite of their shyness. Yes, he had practically just sat on with his "mistress"—heaven save the mark!—as if *not* to come to the point; as if it had absolutely come up that there would be something rather vulgar and awful in doing so. The whole stretch of his stay after Cornelia's withdrawal had been consumed by his almost ostentatiously treating himself to the opportunity of which he was to make nothing. It was as if he had sat and watched himself—that came back to him: Shall

I now or sha'n't I? Will I now or won't I? "Say within the next three minutes, say by a quarter past six, or by twenty minutes past, at the furthest—always if nothing more comes up to prevent."

What had already come up to prevent was, in the strangest and drollest, or at least in the most preposterous, way in the world, that not Cornelia's presence, but her very absence, with its distraction of his thoughts, the thoughts that lumbered after her, had made the difference; and without his being the least able to tell why and how. He put it to himself after a fashion by the image that, this distraction once created, his working round to his hostess again, his reverting to the matter of his errand, began suddenly to represent a return from so far. That was simply all—or rather a little less than all; for something else had contributed. "I never dreamed you knew her," and "I never dreamed *you* did," were inevitably what had been exchanged between them—supplemented by Mrs. Worthingham's mere scrap of an explanation: "Oh yes—to the small extent you see. Two years ago in Switzerland when I was at a high place for an 'aftercure,' during twenty days of incessant rain, she was the only person in an hotel of roaring, gorging, smoking Germans with whom I couldn't have a word of talk. She and I were the only speakers of English, and were thrown together like castaways on a desert island and in a raging storm. She was ill besides, and she had no maid, and mine looked after her, and she was very grateful—writing to me later on and saying she should certainly come to see me if she ever returned to New York. She *has* returned, you see—and there she was, poor little creature!" Such was Mrs. Worthingham's tribute—to which even his asking her if Miss Rasch had ever happened to speak of him caused her practically to add nothing. Visibly she had never thought again of anyone Miss Rasch had spoken of or anything Miss Rasch had said; right as she was, naturally, about her being a little clever queer creature. This was perfectly true, and yet it was probably—by being *all* she could dream of about her—what had paralysed his proper gallantry. Its effect had been not in what it simply stated, but in what, under his secretly disintegrating criticism, it almost luridly symbolised.

He had quitted his seat in the Louis Quinze drawing-room without having, as he would have described it, done anything but give the lady of the scene a superior chance not to betray a defeated hope—not, that is, to fail of the famous "pride" mostly supposed to prop even the most infatuated women at such junctures; by which chance, to do her justice, she had thoroughly seemed to profit. But he finally rose from his later station with a feeling of better success. He had by a happy turn of his hand got hold of the most precious, the least obscure of the flitting, circling things that brushed his ears. What he wanted—as justifying for him a little further consideration— was there before him from the moment he could put it that Mrs. Worthingham had no data. He almost hugged that word —it suddenly came to mean so much to him. No data, he felt, for a conception of the sort of thing the New York of "his time" had been in his personal life—the New York so unexpectedly, so vividly and, as he might say, so perversely called back to all his senses by its identity with that of poor Cornelia's time: since even she had had a time, small show as it was likely to make now, and his time and hers had been the same. Cornelia figured to him while he walked away as, by contrast and opposition, a massive little bundle of data; his impatience to go to see her sharpened as he thought of this: so certainly should he find out that wherever he might touch her, with a gentle though firm pressure, he would, as the fond visitor of old houses taps and fingers a disfeatured, overpapered wall with the conviction of a wainscot-edge beneath, recognise some small extrusion of history.

IV

THERE would have been a wonder for us meanwhile in his continued use, as it were, of his happy formula—brought out to Cornelia Rasch within ten minutes, or perhaps only within twenty, of his having settled into the quite comfortable chair that, two days later, she indicated to him by her fireside. He had arrived at her address through the fortunate chance of his having noticed her card, as he went out, deposited, in the good old New York fashion, on one of the rococo tables of Mrs. Worthingham's hall. His eye had been caught by the pencilled indication that was to affect him, the next instant, as fairly placed there for his sake. This had really been his luck, for he shouldn't have liked to write to Mrs. Worthingham for guidance—*that* he felt, though too impatient just now to analyze the reluctance. There was nobody else he could have approached for a clue, and with this reflection he was already aware of how it testified to their rare little position, his and Cornelia's—position as conscious, ironic, pathetic survivors together of a dead and buried society—that there would have been, in all the town, under such stress, not a member of their old circle left to turn to. Mrs. Worthingham had practically, even if accidentally, helped him to knowledge; the last nail in the coffin of the poor dear extinct past had been planted for him by his having thus to reach his antique contemporary through perforation of the newest newness. The note of this particular recognition was in fact the more prescribed to him that the ground of Cornelia's return to a scene swept so bare of the associational charm was certainly inconspicuous. What had she then come back for?—he had asked himself that; with the effect of deciding that it probably would have been, a little, to "look after" her remnant of property. Perhaps she had come to save what little might still remain of that shrivelled interest; perhaps she had been, by those who took care of it for her, further swindled and despoiled, so that she wished to get at the facts. Perhaps on the other hand—it was a more cheerful chance—her investments, decently administered, were making larger returns, so that the rigorous thrift of Bognor could be finally relaxed.

He had little to learn about the attraction of Europe, and

rather expected that in the event of his union with Mrs. Worthingham he should find himself pleading for it with the competence of one more in the "know" about Paris and Rome, about Venice and Florence, than even she could be. He could have lived on in *his* New York, that is in the sentimental, the spiritual, the more or less romantic visitation of it; but had it been positive for him that he could live on in hers?—unless indeed the possibility of this had been just (like the famous *vertige de l'abîme*, like the solicitation of danger, or otherwise of the dreadful) the very hinge of his whole dream. However that might be, his curiosity was occupied rather with the conceivable hinge of poor Cornelia's: it was perhaps thinkable that even Mrs. Worthingham's New York, once it should have become possible again at all, might have put forth to this lone exile a plea that wouldn't be in the chords of Bognor. For himself, after all, too, the attraction had been much more of the Europe over which one might move at one's ease, and which therefore could but cost, and cost much, right and left, than of the Europe adapted to scrimping. He saw himself on the whole scrimping with more zest even in Mrs. Worthingham's New York than under the inspiration of Bognor. Apart from which it was yet again odd, not to say perceptibly pleasing to him, to note where the emphasis of his interest fell in this fumble of fancy over such felt oppositions as the new, the latest, the luridest power of money and the ancient reserves and moderations and mediocrities. These last struck him as showing by contrast the old brown surface and tone as of velvet rubbed and worn, shabby, and even a bit dingy, but all soft and subtle and still velvety—which meant still dignified; whereas the angular facts of current finance were as harsh and metallic and bewildering as some stacked "exhibit" of ugly patented inventions, things his mediæval mind forbade his taking in. He had for instance the sense of knowing the pleasant little old Rasch fortune— pleasant as far as it went; blurred memories and impressions of what it had been and what it hadn't, of how it had grown and how languished and how melted; they came back to him and put on such vividness that he could almost have figured himself testify for them before a bland and encouraging Board. The idea of taking the field in any manner on the subject of Mrs. Worthingham's resources would have affected him on the other hand as an odious ordeal, some glare of embarrassment and exposure in a circle of hard unhelpful attention, of converging, derisive, unsuggestive eyes.

In Cornelia's small and quite cynically modern flat—the house had a grotesque name, "The Gainsborough," but at least wasn't an awful boarding-house, as he had feared, and she could receive him quite honourably, which was so much to the good —he would have been ready to use at once to her the greatest freedom of friendly allusion: "Have you still your old 'family interest' in those two houses in Seventh Avenue?—one of which was next to a corner grocery, don't you know? and was occupied as to its lower part by a candy-shop where the proportion of the stock of suspectedly stale popcorn to that of rarer and stickier joys betrayed perhaps a modest capital on the part of your father's, your grandfather's, or whoever's tenant, but out of which I nevertheless remember once to have come as out of a bath of sweets, with my very garments, and even the separate hairs of my head, glued together. The other of the pair, a tobacconist's, further down, had before it a wonderful huge Indian who thrust out wooden cigars at an indifferent world—you could buy candy cigars too, at the pop-corn shop, and I greatly preferred them to the wooden; I remember well how I used to gape in fascination at the Indian and wonder if the last of the Mohicans was like him; besides admiring so the resources of a family whose 'property' was in such forms. I haven't been round there lately—we must go round together; but don't tell me the forms have utterly perished!" It was after *that* fashion he might easily have been moved, and with almost no transition, to break out to Cornelia—quite as if taking up some old talk, some old community of gossip, just where they had left it; even with the consciousness perhaps of overdoing a little, of putting at its maximum, for the present harmony, recovery, recapture (what should he call it?) the pitch and quantity of what the past had held for them.

He didn't in fact, no doubt, dart straight off to Seventh Avenue, there being too many other old things and much nearer and long subsequent; the point was only that for everything they spoke of after he had fairly begun to lean back and stretch his legs, and after she had let him, above all, light the first of a succession of cigarettes—for everything they spoke of he positively cultivated extravagance and excess, piling up the crackling twigs as on the very altar of memory; and that by the end of half an hour she had lent herself, all gallantly, to their game. It was the game of feeding the beautiful iridescent flame, ruddy and green and gold, blue and pink and amber and silver, with anything they could pick up, anything that would burn and flicker. Thick-strown with such gleanings the occasion seemed indeed, in spite of the truth that they perhaps wouldn't have proved, under cross-examination, to have rubbed shoulders in the other life so very hard. Casual contacts, qualified communities enough, there had doubtless been, but not particular "passages," nothing that counted, as he might think of it, for their "very own" together, for nobody's else at all. These shades of historic exactitude didn't signify; the more and the less that there had been made perfect terms—and just by his being there and by her rejoicing in it—with their present need to have *had* all their past could be made to appear to have given them. It was to this tune they proceeded, the least little bit as if they knowingly pretended—he giving her the example and setting her the pace of it, and she, poor dear, after a first inevitable shyness, an uncertainty of wonder, a breathlessness of courage, falling into step and going whatever length he would.

She showed herself ready for it, grasping gladly at the perception of what he must mean; and if she didn't immediately and completely fall in—not in the first half-hour, not even in the three or four others that his visit, even whenever he consulted his watch, still made nothing of—she yet understood enough as soon as she understood that, if their finer economy hadn't so beautifully served, he might have been conveying this, that, and the other incoherent and easy thing by the comparatively clumsy method of sound and statement. "No, I never made love to you; it would in fact have been absurd, and I don't care—though I almost know, in the sense of almost remembering!—who did and who didn't; but you were always about, and so was I, and, little as you may yourself care who *I* did it to, I dare say you remember (in the sense of having known of it!) any old appearances that told. But we can't afford at this time of day not to help each other to have had—well, everything there was, since there's no more of it now, nor any way of coming by it *except so*; and therefore let us make together, let us make over and recreate, our lost world; for which we have after all and at the worst such a lot of material. You were in particular my poor dear sisters' friend—they thought you the funniest little brown thing possible; so isn't that again to the good? You were mine only to the extent that you were so much in and out of the house—as how much, if we come to that, wasn't one in and out, south of Thirtieth Street and north of Washington Square, in those days, those spacious, sociable, Arcadian days, that we flattered ourselves we filled with the modern fever, but that were so different from any of these arrangements of pretended hourly Time that dash themselves forever to pieces as from the fiftieth floors of sky-scrapers."

This was the kind of thing that was in the air, whether he said it or not, and that could hang there even with such quite other things as more crudely came out; came in spite of its being perhaps calculated to strike us that these last would have been rather and most the unspoken and the indirect. They were Cornelia's contribution, and as soon as she had begun to talk of Mrs. Worthingham—*he* didn't begin it!—they had taken their place bravely in the centre of the circle. There they made, the while, their considerable little figure, but all within the ring formed by fifty other allusions, fitful but really intenser irruptions that hovered and wavered and came and went, joining hands at moments and whirling round as in chorus, only then again to dash at the slightly huddled centre with a free twitch or peck or push or other taken liberty, after the fashion of irregular frolic motions in a country dance or a Christmas game.

"You're so in love with her and want to marry her!"—she said it all sympathetically and yearningly, poor crapy Cornelia; as if it were to be quite taken for granted that she knew all about it. And then when he had asked how she knew—why she took so informed a tone about it; all on the wonder of her seeming so much more "in" it just at that hour than he himself quite felt he could figure for: "Ah, how but from the dear lovely thing herself? Don't you suppose *she* knows it?"

"Oh, she absolutely 'knows' it, does she?"—he fairly heard himself ask that; and with the oddest sense at once of sharply wanting the certitude and yet of seeing the question, of hearing himself say the words, through several thicknesses of some wrong medium. He came back to it from a distance; as he would have had to come back (this was again vivid to him) should he have got round again to his ripe intention three days before— after his now present but then absent friend, that is, had left him planted before his now absent but then present one for the purpose. "Do you mean she—at all confidently!—expects?" he went on, not much minding if it couldn't but sound foolish; the time being given it for him meanwhile by the sigh, the wondering gasp, all charged with the unutterable, that the tone of his appeal set in motion. He saw his companion look at him, but it might have been with the eyes of thirty years ago; when—very likely!—he had put her some such question about some girl long since dead. Dimly at first, then more distinctly, didn't it surge back on him for the very strangeness that there had been some such passage as this between them—yes, about Mary Cardew!—in the autumn of '68?

"Why, don't you realise your situation?" Miss Rasch struck him as quite beautifully wailing—above all to such an effect of deep interest, that is, on her own part and in him.

"My situation?"—he echoed, he considered; but reminded afresh, by the note of the detached, the far-projected in it, of what he had last remembered of his sentient state on his once taking ether at the dentist's.

"Yours and hers—the situation of her adoring you. I suppose you at least know it," Cornelia smiled.

Yes, it was like the other time and yet it wasn't. *She* was like—poor Cornelia was—everything that used to be; that somehow was most definite to him. Still he could quite reply "Do you call it—her adoring me—*my* situation?"

"Well, it's a part of yours, surely—if you're in love with her."

"Am I, ridiculous old person! in love with her?" White-Mason asked.

"I may be a ridiculous old person," Cornelia returned—"and, for that matter, of course I am! But she's young and lovely and rich and clever: so what could be more natural?"

"Oh, I was applying that opprobrious epithet—!" He didn't finish, though he meant he had applied it to himself. He had got up from his seat; he turned about and, taking in, as his eyes also roamed, several objects in the room, serene and sturdy, not a bit cheap-looking, little old New York objects of '68, he made, with an inner art, as if to recognise them—made so, that is, for himself; had quite the sense for the moment of asking them, of imploring them, to recognise *him*, to be for him things of his own past. Which they truly were, he could have the next instant cried out; for it meant that if three or four of them, small sallow carte-de-visite photographs, faithfully framed but spectrally faded, hadn't in every particular, frames and balloon skirts and false "property" balustrades of unimaginable terraces and all, the tone of time, the secret for warding and easing off the perpetual imminent ache of one's protective scowl, one would verily but have to let the scowl stiffen, or to take up seriously the question of blue goggles, during what might remain of life.

V

W'HAT HE actually took up from a little old Twelfth-Street table that piously preserved the plain mahogany circle, with never a curl nor a crook nor a hint of a brazen flourish, what he paused there a moment for commerce with, his back presented to crapy Cornelia, who sat taking that view of him, during this opportunity, very protrusively and frankly and fondly, was one of the wasted mementos just mentioned, over which he both uttered and suppressed a small comprehensive cry. He stood there another minute to look at it, and when he turned about still kept it in his hand, only holding it now a little behind him. "You *must* have come back to stay—with all your beautiful things. What else does it mean?"

"'Beautiful'?" his old friend commented with her brow all wrinkled and her lips thrust out in expressive dispraise. They might at that rate have been scarce more beautiful than she herself. "Oh, don't talk so—after Mrs. Worthingham's! *They're* wonderful, if you will: such things, such things! But one's own poor relics and odds and ends are one's own at least; and one *has*— yes—come back to them. They're all I have in the world to come back to. They were stored, and what I was paying—!" Miss Rasch wofully added.

He had possession of the small old picture; he hovered there; he put his eyes again to it intently; then again held it a little behind him as if it might have been snatched away or the very feel of it, pressed against him, was good to his palm. "Mrs. Worthingham's things? You think them beautiful?"

Cornelia did now, if ever, show an odd face. "Why, certainly prodigious, or whatever. Isn't that conceded?"

"No doubt every horror, at the pass we've come to, is conceded. That's just what I complain of."

"Do you *complain*?"—she drew it out as for surprise: she couldn't have imagined such a thing.

"To me her things are awful. They're the newest of the new."

"Ah, but the old forms!"

"Those are the most blatant. I mean the swaggering repro-
ductions."

"Oh but," she pleaded, "we can't all be *really* old."

"No, we can't, Cornelia. But *you* can—!" said White-Mason
with the frankest appreciation.

She looked up at him from where she sat as he could imagine her looking up at the curate at Bognor.

"Thank you, sir! If that's all you want——!"

"It *is*," he said, "all I want—or almost."

"Then no wonder such a creature as that," she lightly moralised, "won't suit you!"

He bent upon her, for all the weight of his question, his
smoothest stare. "You hold she certainly won't suit me?"

"Why, what can I tell about it? Haven't you by this time
found out?"

"No, but I think I'm finding." With which he began again
to explore.

Miss Rasch immensely wondered. "You mean you don't expect to come to an understanding with her?" And then as even
to this straight challenge he made at first no answer: "Do you
mean you give it up?"

He waited some instants more, but not meeting her eyes—
only looking again about the room. "What do you think of my
chance?"

"Oh," his companion cried, "what has what I think to do
with it? How can I think anything but that she must like you?"

"Yes—of course. But how much?"

"Then don't you really know?" Cornelia asked.

He kept up his walk, oddly preoccupied and still not looking at her. "Do you, my dear?"

She waited a little. "If you haven't really put it to her I don't
suppose she knows."

This at last arrested him again. "My dear Cornelia, she
doesn't know——!"

He had paused as for the desperate tone, or at least the large emphasis of it, so that she took him up. "The more reason then to help her to find it out."

"I mean," he explained, "that she doesn't know anything."

"Anything?"

"Anything else, I mean—even if she does know *that.*"

Cornelia considered of it. "But what else need she—in particular—know? Isn't that the principal thing?"

"Well"—and he resumed his circuit—"she doesn't know anything that *we* know. But nothing," he re-emphasised—"nothing whatever!"

"Well, can't she do without that?"

"Evidently she can—and evidently she does, beautifully. But the question is whether *I* can!"

He had paused once more with his point—but she glared, poor Cornelia, with her wonder. "Surely if you know for yourself——!"

"Ah, it doesn't seem enough for me to know for myself! One wants a woman," he argued—but still, in his prolonged tour, quite without his scowl—"to know *for* one, to know *with* one. That's what you do now," he candidly put to her.

It made her again gape. "Do you mean you want to marry *me?*"

He was so full of what he did mean, however, that he failed even to notice it. "She doesn't in the least know, for instance, how old I am."

"That's because you're so young!"

"Ah, there you are!"—and he turned off afresh and as if almost in disgust. It left her visibly perplexed—though even the perplexed Cornelia was still the exceedingly pointed; but he had come to her aid after another turn. "Remember, please, that I'm pretty well as old as you."

She had all her point at least, while she bridled and blinked, for this. "You're exactly a year and ten months older."

It checked him there for delight. "You remember my birthday?"

She twinkled indeed like some far-off light of home. "I remember every one's. It's a little way I've always had—and that I've never lost."

He looked at her accomplishment, across the room, as at some striking, some charming phenomenon. "Well, *that's* the sort of thing I want!" All the ripe candour of his eyes confirmed it.

What could she do therefore, she seemed to ask him, but repeat her question of a moment before?—which indeed, presently she made up her mind to. "Do you want to marry *me*?"

It had this time better success—if the term may be felt in any degree to apply. All his candour, or more of it at least, was in his slow, mild, kind, considering head-shake. "No, Cornelia —not to *marry* you."

His discrimination was a wonder; but since she was clearly treating him now as if everything about him was, so she could as exquisitely meet it. "Not at least," she convulsively smiled, "until you've honourably tried Mrs. Worthingham. Don't you really *mean* to?" she gallantly insisted.

He waited again a little; then he brought out: "I'll tell you presently." He came back, and as by still another mere glance over the room, to what seemed to him so much nearer. "That table *was* old Twelfth-Street?"

"Everything here was."

"Oh, the pure blessings! With you, ah, with you, I haven't to wear a green shade." And he had retained meanwhile his small photograph, which he again showed himself. "Didn't we talk of Mary Cardew?"

"Why, do you remember it?"—she marvelled to extravagance.

"You make me. You connect me with it. You connect it with *me*." He liked to display to her this excellent use she thus had, the service she rendered. "There are so many connections— there will *be* so many. I feel how, with you, they must all come up again for me: in fact you're bringing them out already, just while I look at you, as fast as ever you can. The fact that you knew every one—!" he went on; yet as if there were more in that too than he could quite trust himself about.

"Yes, I knew every one," said Cornelia Rasch; but this time with perfect simplicity. "I knew, I imagine, more than you do —or more than you did."

It kept him there, it made him wonder with his eyes on her. "Things about *them*—our people?"

"Our people. Ours only now."

Ah, such an interest as he felt in this—taking from her while, so far from scowling, he almost gaped, all it might mean! "Ours indeed—and it's awfully good they are; or that we're still here for them! Nobody else is—nobody but you: not a cat!"

"Well, I *am* a cat!" Cornelia grinned.

"Do you mean you can tell me things—?" It was too beautiful to believe.

"About what really *was*?" She artfully considered, holding him immensely now. "Well, unless they've come to you with time; unless you've learned—or found out."

"Oh," he reassuringly cried—reassuringly, it most seemed, for himself—"nothing has come to me with time, everything has gone from me. How can I find out now! What creature has an idea——?"

She threw up her hands with the shrug of old days—the sharp little shrug his sisters used to imitate and that she hadn't had to go to Europe for. The only thing was that he blessed her for bringing it back. "Ah, the ideas of people now——!"

"Yes, their ideas are certainly not about *us*." But he ruefully faced it. "We've none the less, however, to live with them."

"With their ideas—?" Cornelia questioned.

"With *them*—these modern wonders; such as they are!" Then he went on: "It must have been to help me you've come back."

She said nothing for an instant about that, only nodding instead at his photograph. "What has become of yours? I mean of *her*."

This time it made him turn pale. "You remember I *have* one?"

She kept her eyes on him. "In a 'pork-pie' hat, with her hair in a long net. That was so 'smart' then; especially with one's skirt looped up, over one's hooped magenta petticoat, in little festoons, and a row of very big onyx beads over one's braided velveteen sack—braided quite plain and very broad, don't you know?"

He smiled for her extraordinary possession of these things— she was as prompt as if she had had them before her. 'Oh, rather—'don't I know?' You wore brown velveteen, and, on those remarkably small hands, funny gauntlets—like mine."

"Oh, do *you* remember? But like yours?" she wondered.

"I mean like hers in my photograph." But he came back to the present picture. "This is better, however, for really showing her lovely head."

"Mary's head was a perfection!" Cornelia testified.

"Yes—it was better than her heart."

"Ah, don't say that!" she pleaded. "You weren't fair."

"Don't you think I was fair?" It interested him immensely— and the more that he indeed mightn't have been; which he seemed somehow almost to hope.

"She didn't think so—to the very end."

"She didn't?"—ah the right things Cornelia said to him! But before she could answer he was studying again closely the small faded face. "No, she doesn't, she doesn't. Oh, her charming sad eyes and the way they *say* that, across the years, straight into mine! But I don't know, I don't know!" White-Mason quite comfortably sighed.

His companion appeared to appreciate this effect. "That's just the way you used to flirt with her, poor thing. Wouldn't you like to have it?" she asked.

"This—for my very own?" He looked up delighted. "I really may?"

"Well, if you'll give me yours. We'll exchange."

"That's a charming idea. We'll exchange. But you must come and get it at my rooms—where you'll see my things."

For a little she made no answer—as if for some feeling. Then she said: "You asked me just now why I've come back."

He stared as for the connection; after which with a smile: "Not to do *that*——?"

She waited briefly again, but with a queer little look. "I can do those things now; and—yes!—that's in a manner why. I came," she then said, "because I knew of a sudden one day—knew as never before—that I was old."

"I see. I see." He quite understood—she had notes that so struck him. "And how did you like it?"

She hesitated—she decided. "Well, if I liked it, it was on the principle perhaps on which some people like high game!"

"High game—that's good!" he laughed. "Ah, my dear, we're 'high'!"

She shook her head. "No, not you—yet. I at any rate didn't want any more adventures," Cornelia said.

He showed their small relic again with assurance. "You wanted *us*. Then here we are. Oh, how we can talk!—with all those things you know! You *are* an invention. And you'll see there are things *I* know. I shall turn up here—well, daily."

She took it in, but only after a moment answered. "There was something you said just now you'd tell me. Don't you mean to try——?"

"Mrs. Worthingham?" He drew from within his coat his pocket-book and carefully found a place in it for Mary Cardew's carte-de-visite, folding it together with deliberation over which he put it back. Finally he spoke. "No—I've decided. I can't—I don't want to."

Cornelia marvelled—or looked as if she did. "Not for all she has?"

"Yes—I know all she has. But I also know all she hasn't. And, as I told you, she herself doesn't—hasn't a glimmer of a suspicion of it; and never will have."

Cornelia magnanimously thought. "No—but she knows other things."

He shook his head as at the portentous heap of them. "Too many—too many. And other indeed—*so* other. Do you know," he went on, "that it's as if *you*—by turning up for me—had brought that home to me?"

"'For you,'" she candidly considered. "But what—since you can't marry me!—can you do with me?"

Well, he seemed to have it all. "Everything. I can live with you—just this way." To illustrate which he dropped into the other chair by her fire; where, leaning back, he gazed at the flame. "I can't give you up. It's very curious. It has come over me as it did over you when you renounced Bognor. That's it—I know it at last, and I see one can like it. I'm 'high.' You needn't deny it. That's my taste. I'm old." And in spite of the considerable glow there of her little household altar he said it without the scowl.

1909

A ROUND OF VISITS

I

HE HAD been out but once since his arrival, Mark Monteith; that was the next day after—he had disembarked by night on the previous; then everything had come at once, as he would have said, everything had changed. He had got in on Tuesday; he had spent Wednesday for the most part down town, looking into the dismal subject of his anxiety—the anxiety that, under a sudden decision, had brought him across the unfriendly sea at mid-winter, and it was through information reaching him on Wednesday evening that he had measured his loss, measured above all his pain. These were two distinct things, he felt, and, though both bad, one much worse than the other. It wasn't till the next three days had pretty well ebbed, in fact, that he knew himself for so badly wounded. He had waked up on Thursday morning, so far as he had slept at all, with the sense, together, of a blinding New York blizzard and of a deep sore inward ache. The great white savage storm would have kept him at the best within doors, but his stricken state was by itself quite reason enough.

He so felt the blow indeed, so gasped, before what had happened to him, at the ugliness, the bitterness, and, beyond these things, the sinister strangeness, that, the matter of his dismay little by little detaching and projecting itself, settling there face to face with him as something he must now live with always, he might have been in charge of some horrid alien thing, some violent, scared, unhappy creature whom there was small joy, of a truth, in remaining with, but whose behaviour wouldn't perhaps bring him under notice, nor otherwise compromise him, so long as he should stay to watch it. A young jibbering ape of one of the more formidable sorts, or an ominous infant panther smuggled into the great gaudy hotel and whom it might yet be important he shouldn't advertise, couldn't have affected him as needing more domestic attention. The great gaudy hotel—The Pocahontas, but carried out largely on "Du Barry" lines—made all about him, beside, behind, below, above, in blocks and tiers and superpositions, a sufficient defensive hugeness; so that, between the massive labyrinth and the New York weather, life in a lighthouse during a gale would scarce have kept him more apart. Even when in the course of that worse Thursday it had occurred to him for vague relief that the odious certified facts couldn't be all his misery, and that, with his throat and a probable temperature, a brush of the epidemic, which was for ever brushing him, accounted for something, even then he couldn't resign himself to bed and broth and dimness, but only circled and prowled the more within his high cage, only watched the more from his tenth story the rage of the elements.

In the afternoon he had a doctor—the caravanserai, which supplied everything in quantities, had one for each group of so many rooms—just in order to be assured that he was *grippé* enough for anything. What his visitor, making light of his attack, perversely told him was that he was, much rather, "blue" enough, and from causes doubtless known to himself—which didn't come to the same thing; but he "gave him something," prescribed him warmth and quiet and broth and courage, and came back the next day to readminister this last dose. He then pronounced him better, and on Saturday pronounced him well —all the more that the storm had abated and the snow had been dealt with as New York, at a push, knew how to deal with things. Oh, how New York knew how to deal—to deal, that is, with other accumulations lying passive to its hand—was exactly what Mark now ached with his impression of; so that, still threshing about in this consciousness, he had on the Saturday come near to breaking out as to what was the matter with him. The Doctor brought in somehow the air of the hotel—which, cheerfully and conscientiously, by his simple philosophy, the good man wished to diffuse; breathing forth all the echoes of other woes and worries and pointing the honest moral that, especially with such a thermometer, there were enough of these to go round. Our sufferer, by that time, would have liked to tell some one; extracting, to the last acid strain of it, the full strength of his sorrow, taking it all in as he could only do by himself and with the conditions favourable at least to this, had been his natural first need. But now, he supposed, he *must* be better; there was something of his heart's heaviness he wanted so to give out.

He had rummaged forth on the Thursday night half a dozen old photographs stuck into a leather frame, a small show-case that formed part of his usual equipage of travel—he mostly set it up on a table when he stayed anywhere long enough; and in one of the neat gilt-edged squares of this convenient portable array, as familiar as his shaving-glass or the hair-brushes, of backs and monograms now so beautifully toned and wasted, long ago given him by his mother, Phil Bloodgood handsomely faced him. Not contemporaneous, and a little faded, but so saying what it said only the more dreadfully, the image seemed to sit there, at an immemorial window, like some long effective and only at last exposed "decoy" of fate. It was *because* he was so beautifully good-looking, because he was so charming and clever and frank—besides being one's third cousin, or whatever it was, one's early school-fellow and one's later college classmate —that one had abjectly trusted him. To live thus with his unremoved, undestroyed, engaging, treacherous face, had been, as our traveller desired, to live with all of the felt pang; had been to consume it in such a single hot, sore mouthful as would so far as possible dispose of it and leave but cold dregs. Thus, if the Doctor, casting about for pleasantness, had happened to notice him there, salient since he was, and possibly by the same stroke even to know him, as New York—and more or less to its cost now, mightn't one say?—so abundantly and agreeably had, the cup would have overflowed and Monteith, for all he could be sure of the contrary, would have relieved himself positively in tears.

"Oh, *he's* what's the matter with me—that, looking after some of my poor dividends, as he for the ten years of my absence had served me by doing, he has simply jockeyed me out of the whole little collection, such as it was, and taken the opportunity of my return, inevitably at last bewildered and uneasy, to 'sail,' ten days ago, for parts unknown and as yet unguessable. It isn't the beastly values themselves, however; that's only awkward and I can still live, though I don't quite know how I shall turn round; it's the horror of *his* having done it, and done it to *me*—without a mitigation or, so to speak, a warning or an excuse." That, at a hint or a jog, is what he would have brought out—only to feel afterward, no doubt, that he had wasted his impulse and profaned even a little his sincerity. The Doctor didn't in the event so much as glance at his cluster of portraits—which fact quite put before our friend the essentially more vivid range of imagery that a pair of eyes transferred from room to room and from one queer case to another, in such a place as that, would mainly be adjusted to. It wasn't for *him* to relieve himself touchingly, strikingly or whatever, to such a man: such a man might much more pertinently—save for professional discretion—have emptied out there his own bag of wonders; prodigies of observation, flowers of oddity, flowers of misery, flowers of the monstrous, gathered in current hotel practice. Countless possibilities, making doctors perfunctory, Mark felt, swarmed and seethed at their doors; it showed for an incalculable world, and at last, on Sunday, he decided to leave his room.

II

EVERYTHING, as he passed through the place, went on—all the offices of life, the whole bustle of the market, and withal, surprisingly, scarce less that of the nursery and the playground; the whole sprawl in especial of the great gregarious fireside: it was a complete social scene in itself, on which types might figure and passions rage and plots thicken and dramas develop, without reference to any other sphere, or perhaps even to anything at all outside. The signs of this met him at every turn as he threaded the labyrinth, passing from one extraordinary masquerade of expensive objects, one portentous "period" of decoration, one violent phase of publicity, to another: the heavy heat, the luxuriance, the extravagance, the quantity, the colour, gave the impression of some wondrous tropical forest, where vociferous, bright-eyed, and feathered creatures, of every variety of size and hue, were half smothered between undergrowths of velvet and tapestry and ramifications of marble and bronze. The fauna and the flora startled him alike, and among them his bruised spirit drew in and folded its wings. But he roamed and rested, exploring and in a manner enjoying the vast rankness— in the depth of which he suddenly encountered Mrs. Folliott, whom he had last seen, six months before, in London, and who had spoken to him then, precisely, of Phil Bloodgood, for several years previous her confidential American agent and factotum too, as she might say, but at that time so little in her good books, for the extraordinary things he seemed to be doing, that she was just hurrying home, she had made no scruple of mentioning, to take everything out of his hands.

Mark remembered how uneasy she had made him—how that very talk with her had wound him up to fear, as so acute and intent a little person she affected him; though he had affirmed with all emphasis and flourish his own confidence and defended, to iteration, his old friend. This passage had remained with him for a certain pleasant heat of intimacy, his partner, of the charming appearance, being what she was; he

liked to think how they had fraternised over their difference
and called each other idiots, or almost, without offence. It was
always a link to have scuffled, failing a real scratch, with such a
character; and he had at present the flutter of feeling that something of this would abide. *He* hadn't been hurrying home, at
the London time, in any case; he was doing nothing then, and
had continued to do it; he would want, before showing suspicion—that had been his attitude—to have more, after all, to go
upon. Mrs. Folliott also, and with a great actual profession of
it, remembered and rejoiced; and, also staying in the house as
she was, sat with him, under a spreading palm, in a wondrous
rococo salon, surrounded by the pinkest, that is the fleshiest,
imitation Boucher panels, and wanted to know if he *now* stood
up for his swindler. She would herself have tumbled on a cloud,
very passably, in a fleshy Boucher manner, hadn't she been
over-dressed for such an exercise; but she was quite realistically
aware of what had so naturally happened—she was prompt
about Bloodgood's "flight."

She had acted with energy, on getting back—she had saved
what she could; which hadn't, however, prevented her losing
all disgustedly some ten thousand dollars. She was lovely, lively,
friendly, interested, she connected Monteith perfectly with their
discussion that day during the water-party on the Thames; but,
sitting here with him half an hour, she talked only of her peculiar, her cruel sacrifice—since she should never get a penny
back. He had felt himself, on their meeting, quite yearningly
reach out to her—so decidedly, by the morning's end, and that
of his scattered sombre stations, had he been sated with mean-
ingless contacts, with the sense of people all about him intensely, though harmlessly, animated, yet at the same time rasp-
ingly indifferent. *They* would have, he and she at least, their
common pang—through which fact, somehow, he should feel
less stranded. It wasn't that he wanted to be pitied—he fairly
didn't pity himself; he winced, rather, and even to vicarious
anguish, as it rose again, for poor shamed Bloodgood's doom-
ridden figure. But he wanted, as with a desperate charity, to

give some easier turn to the mere ugliness of the main facts; to work off his obsession from them by mixing with it some other blame, some other pity, it scarce mattered what—if it might be some other experience; as an effect of which larger ventilation it would have, after a fashion and for a man of free sensibility, a diluted and less poisonous taste.

By the end of five minutes of Mrs. Folliott, however, he felt his dry lips seal themselves to a makeshift simper. She could *take* nothing—no better, no broader perception of anything than fitted her own small faculty; so that though she must have recalled or imagined that he had still, up to lately, had interests at stake, the rapid result of her egotistical little chatter was to make him wish he might rather have conversed with the French waiter dangling in the long vista that showed the oriental *café* as a climax, or with the policeman, outside, the top of whose helmet peeped above the ledge of a window. She bewailed her wretched money to excess—she who, he was sure, had quantities more; she pawed and tossed her bare bone, with her little extraordinarily gemmed and manicured hands, till it acted on his nerves; she rang all the changes on the story, the dire fatality, of her having wavered and muddled, thought of this and but done that, of her stupid failure to have pounced, when she had first meant to, in season. She abused the author of their wrongs—recognizing thus too Monteith's right to loathe him —for the desperado he assuredly had proved, but with a vulgarity of analysis and an incapacity for the higher criticism, as her listener felt it to be, which made him determine resentfully, almost grimly, that she shouldn't have the benefit of a grain of *his* vision or *his* version of what had befallen them, and of how, in particular, it had come; and should never dream thereby (though much would she suffer from that!) of how interesting he might have been. She had, in a finer sense, no manners, and to be concerned with her in any retrospect was—since their discourse was of losses—to feel the dignity of history incur the very gravest. It was true that such fantasies, or that any shade of inward irony, would be Greek to Mrs. Folliott.

It was also true, however, and not much more strange, when she had presently the comparatively happy thought of "Lunch with *us*, you poor dear!" and mentioned three or four of her "crowd"—a new crowd, rather, for her, all great Sunday lunchers there and immense fun, who would in a moment be turning up—that this seemed to him as easy as anything else; so that after a little, deeper in the jungle and while, under the temperature as of high noon, with the crowd complete and "ordering," he wiped the perspiration from his brow, he felt he was letting himself go. He did that certainly to the extent of leaving far behind any question of Mrs. Folliott's manners. They didn't matter there—nobody's did; and if she ceased to lament her ten thousand it was only because, among higher voices, she couldn't make herself heard. Poor Bloodgood didn't have a show, as they might have said, didn't get through at any point; the crowd was so new that—there either having been no hue and cry for him, or having been too many others, for other absconders, in the intervals—they had never so much as heard of him and would have no more of Mrs. Folliott's true inwardness, on that subject at least, than she had lately cared to have of Monteith's.

There was nothing like a crowd, this unfortunate knew, for making one feel lonely, and he felt so increasingly during the meal; but he got thus at least in a measure away from the terrible little lady; after which, and before the end of the hour, he wanted still more to get away from everyone else. He was in fact about to perform this manœuvre when he was checked by the jolly young woman he had been having on his left and who had more to say about the Hotels, up and down the town, than he had ever known a young woman to have to say on any subject at all; she expressed herself in hotel terms exclusively, the names of those establishments playing through her speech as the *leit-motif* might have recurrently flashed and romped through a piece of profane modern music. She wanted to present him to the pretty girl she had brought with her, and who had apparently signified to her that she must do so.

"I think you know my brother-in-law, Mr. Newton Winch,"

the pretty girl had immediately said; she moved her head and shoulders together, as by a common spring, the effect of a stiff neck or of something loosened in her back hair; but becoming, queerly enough, all the prettier for doing so. He had seen in the papers, her brother-in-law, Mr. Monteith's arrival—Mr. Mark P. Monteith, wasn't it?—and where he was, and she had been with him, three days before, at the time; whereupon he had said "Hullo, what can have brought old Mark back?" He seemed to have believed—Newton had seemed—that that shirker, as he called him, never *would* come; and she guessed that if she had known she was going to meet such a former friend ("Which he claims you are, sir," said the pretty girl) he would have asked her to find out what the trouble could be. But the real satisfaction would just be, she went on, if his former friend would himself go and see him and tell him; he had appeared of late so down.

"Oh, I remember him"—Mark didn't repudiate the friendship, placing him easily; only then he wasn't married and the pretty girl's sister must have come in later: which showed, his not knowing such things, how they had lost touch. The pretty girl was sorry to have to say in return to this that her sister wasn't living—had died two years after marrying; so that Newton was up there in Fiftieth Street alone; where (in explanation of his being "down") he had been shut up for days with bad *grippe*; though now on the mend, or she wouldn't have gone to him, not she, who had had it nineteen times and didn't want to have it again. But the horrid poison just seemed to have entered into poor Newton's soul.

"That's the way it *can* take you, don't you know?" And then as, with her single twist, she just charmingly hunched her eyes at our friend, "Don't you want to go to see him?"

Mark bethought himself: "Well, I'm going to see a lady——"

She took the words from his mouth. "Of course you're going to see a lady—every man in New York is. But Newton isn't a lady, unfortunately for him, to-day; and Sunday afternoon in this place, in this weather, alone——!"

"Yes, isn't it awful?"—he was quite drawn to her.

"Oh, *you've* got your lady!"

"Yes, I've got my lady, thank goodness!" The fervour of which was his sincere tribute to the note he had had on Friday morning from Mrs. Ash, the only thing that had a little tempered his gloom.

"Well then, feel for others. Fit him in. Tell him why!"

"Why I've come back? I'm glad I *have*—since it was to see *you*!" Monteith made brave enough answer, promising to do what he could. He liked the pretty girl, with her straight attack and her free awkwardness—also with her difference from the others through something of a sense and a distinction given her by so clearly having Newton on her mind. Yet it was odd to him, and it showed the lapse of the years, that Winch—as he had known him of old—could *be* to that degree on anyone's mind.

III

OUTSIDE in the intensity of the cold—it was a jump from the Tropics to the Pole—he felt afresh the force of what he had just been saying; that if it weren't for the fact of Mrs. Ash's good letter of welcome, despatched, characteristically, as soon as she had, like the faithful sufferer in Fiftieth Street, observed his name, in a newspaper, on one of the hotel-lists, he should verily, for want of a connection and an abutment, have scarce dared to face the void and the chill together, but have sneaked back into the jungle and there tried to lose himself. He made, as it was, the opposite effort, resolute to walk, though hovering now and then at vague crossways, radiations of roads to nothing, or taking cold counsel of the long but still sketchy vista, as it struck him, of the northward Avenue, bright and bleak, fresh and harsh, rich and evident somehow, a perspective like a page of florid modern platitudes. He didn't quite know what he had expected for his return—not certainly serenades and deputations; but without Mrs. Ash his mail would have quite lacked geniality, and it was as if Phil Bloodgood had gone off not only with so large a slice of his small *peculium*, but with all the broken bits of the past, the loose ends of old relationships, that he had supposed he might pick up again. Well, perhaps he should still pick up a few—by the sweat of his brow; no motion of their own at least, he by this time judged, would send them fluttering into his hand.

Which reflections but quickened his forecast of this charm of the old Paris inveteracy renewed—the so-prized custom of nine years before, when he still believed in results from his fond frequentation of the Beaux Arts; that of walking over the river to the Rue de Marignan, precisely, every Sunday without exception, and sitting at her fireside, and often all offensively, no doubt, outstaying every one. How he had used to want those hours then, and how again, after a little, at present, the Rue de Marignan might have been before him! He had gone to her there at that time with his troubles, such as they were, and they had always worked for her amusement—which had been her happy, her clever way of taking them: she couldn't have done anything better for them in that phase, poor innocent things compared with what they might have been, than be amused by them. Perhaps that was what she would still be—with those of his present hour; now too they might inspire her with the touch she best applied and was most instinctive mistress of: this didn't at all events strike him as what he should most resent. It wasn't as if Mrs. Folliott, to make up for boring him with her own plaint, for example, had had so much as a gleam of conscious diversion over his.

"I'm *so* delighted to see you, I've such immensities to tell you!"—it began with the highest animation twenty minutes later, the very moment he stood there, the sense of the Rue de Marignan in the charming room and in the things about all reconstituted, regrouped, wonderfully preserved, down to the very sitting-places in the same relations, and down to the faint sweet mustiness of generations of cigarettes; but everything else different, and even vaguely alien, and by a measure still other than that of their own stretched interval and of the dear delightful woman's just a little pathetic alteration of face. He had allowed for the nine years, and so, it was to be hoped, had she; but the last thing, otherwise, that would have been touched, he immediately felt, was the quality, the intensity, of her care to see him. She cared, oh so visibly and touchingly and almost radiantly—save for her being, yes, distinctly, a little *more* battered than from even a good nine years' worth; nothing could in fact have perched with so crowning an impatience on the heap of what she had to "tell" as that special shade of revived consciousness of having him in particular to tell it to. It wasn't perhaps much to matter how soon she brought out and caused to ring, as it were, on the little recognised marqueterie table between them (such an anciently envied treasure), the heaviest goldpiece of current history she was to pay him with for having just so felicitously come back: he knew already, without the telling, that intimate domestic tension must lately, within those walls, have reached a climax and that he could serve supremely—oh how he was going to serve!—as the most sympathetic of all pairs of ears.

The whole thing was upon him, in any case, with the minimum of delay: Bob had had it from her, definitely, the first of the week, and it was absolutely final now, that they must set up avowedly separate lives—without horrible "proceedings" of any sort, but with her own situation, her independence, secured to her once for all. She had been coming to it, taking her time, and she had gone through—well, so old a friend would guess enough what; but she was at the point, oh blessedly now, where she meant to stay, he'd see if she didn't; with which, in this wonderful way, he himself had arrived for the cream of it and she was just selfishly glad. Bob had gone to Washington— ostensibly on business, but really to recover breath; she had, speaking vulgarly, knocked the wind out of him and was allowing him time to turn round. Mrs. Folliott moreover, she was sure, would have gone—was certainly believed to have been

seen there five days ago; and of course his first necessity, for
public use, would be to patch up something with Mrs. Folliott.
Mark knew about Mrs. Folliott?—who was only, for that matter, one of a regular "bevy." Not that it signified, however, if he
didn't: she would tell him about *her* later.

He took occasion from the first fraction of a break not quite
to know what he knew about Mrs. Folliott—though perhaps
he could imagine a little; and it was probably at this minute
that, having definitely settled to a position, and precisely in his
very own tapestry *bergère*, the one with the delicious little spectral "subjects" on the back and seat, he partly exhaled, and yet
managed partly to keep to himself, the deep resigned sigh of a
general comprehension. He knew what he was "in" for, he heard
her go on—she said it again and again, seemed constantly to
be saying it while she smiled at him with her peculiar fine
charm, her positive gaiety of sensibility, scarce dimmed: "I'm
just selfishly glad, just selfishly glad!" Well, she was going to
have reason to be; she was going to put the whole case to him,
all her troubles and plans, and each act of the tragi-comedy of
her recent existence, as to the dearest and safest sympathiser in
all the world. There would be no chance for *his* case, though it
was so much for his case he had come; yet there took place
within him but a mild, dumb convulsion, the momentary
strain of his substituting, by the turn of a hand, one prospect of
interest for another.

Squaring himself in his old *bergère*, and with his lips, during
the effort, compressed to the same passive grimace that had an
hour or two before operated for the encouragement of Mrs.
Folliott—just as it was to clear the stage completely for the
present more prolonged performance—he shut straight down,
as he even in the act called it to himself, on any personal claim
for social consideration and rendered a perfect little agony of
justice to the grounds of his friend's vividness. For it was all the
justice that could be expected of him that, though, secretly, he
wasn't going to be interested in her being interesting, she was
yet going to be so, all the same, by the very force of her lovely

material (Bob Ash *was* such a pure pearl of a donkey!) and he was going to keep on knowing she was—yes, to the very end. When after the lapse of an hour he rose to go, the rich fact that she *had* been was there between them, and with an effect of the frankly, fearlessly, harmlessly intimate fireside passage for it that went beyond even the best memories of the pleasant past. He hadn't "amused" her, no, in quite the same way as in the Rue de Marignan time—it had then been he who for the most part took frequent turns, emphatic, explosive, elocutionary, over that wonderful waxed parquet while she laughed as for the young perversity of him from the depths of the second, the matching *bergère*. To-day she herself held and swept the floor, putting him merely to the trouble of his perpetual "Brava!" But that was all through the change of basis—the amusement, another name only for the thrilled absorption, having been inevitably for *him*; as how could it have failed to be with such a regular "treat" to his curiosity? With the tea-hour now other callers were turning up, and he got away on the plea of his wanting so to think it all over. He hoped again he hadn't too queer a grin with his assurance to her, as if she would quite know what he meant, that he had been thrilled to the core. But she returned, quite radiantly, that he had carried *her* completely away; and her sincerity was proved by the final frankness of their temporary parting. "My pleasure of you is selfish, horribly, I admit; so that if *that* doesn't suit you—!" Her faded beauty flushed again as she said it.

IV

IN THE street again, as he resumed his walk, he saw how perfectly it would *have* to suit him and how he probably for a long time wouldn't be suited otherwise. Between them and that time, however, what mightn't for him, poor devil, on his new basis, have happened? She wasn't at any rate within any calculable period going to care so much for anything as for the so quaintly droll terms in which her rearrangement with her husband—thanks to that gentleman's inimitable fatuity—would have to be made. This was what it was to own, exactly, her special grace—the brightest gaiety in the finest sensibility; *such* a display of which combination, Mark felt as he went (if he could but have done it still more justice) she must have regaled him with! That exquisite last flush of her fadedness could only remain with him; yet while he presently stopped at a street-corner in a district redeemed from desolation but by a passage just then of a choked trolley-car that howled, as he paused for it, beneath the weight of its human accretions, he seemed to know the inward "sinking" that has been determined in a hungry man by some extravagant sight of the preparation of somebody else's dinner. Florence Ash was dining, so to speak, off the feast of appreciation, appreciation of what she had to "tell" him, that he had left her seated at; and she was welcome, assuredly—welcome, welcome, welcome, he musingly, he wistfully, and yet at the same time a trifle mechanically, repeated, stayed as he was a moment longer by the suffering shriek of another public vehicle and a sudden odd automatic return of his mind to the pretty girl, the flower of Mrs. Folliott's crowd, who had spoken to him of Newton Winch. It was extraordinarily as if, on the instant, she reminded him, from across the town, that *she* had offered him dinner: it was really quite strangely, while he stood there, as if she had told him where he could go and get it. With which, none the less, it was apparently where he wouldn't find her—and what was there, after all, of nutritive in the image of Newton Winch? He made up his mind in a moment that it owed that property, which the pretty girl had somehow made imputable, to the fact of its simply being just then the one image of anything known to him that the terrible place had to offer. Nothing, he a minute later reflected, could have been so "rum" as that, sick and sore, of a bleak New York eventide, he should have had nowhere to turn if not to the said Fiftieth Street.

That was the direction he accordingly took, for when he

found the number given him by the same remarkable agent of fate also present to his memory he recognised the direct intervention of Providence and how it absolutely required a miracle to explain his so precipitately embracing this loosest of connections. The miracle indeed soon grew clearer: Providence had, on some obscure system, chosen this very ridiculous hour to save him from cultivation of the sin of selfishness, the obsession of egotism, and was breaking him to its will by constantly directing his attention to the claims of others. Who could say what at that critical moment mightn't have become of Mrs. Folliott (otherwise too then so sadly embroiled!) if she hadn't been enabled to air to him her grievance and her rage?—just as who could deny that it must have done Florence Ash a world of good to have put her thoughts about Bob in order by the aid of a person to whom the vision of Bob in the light of those thoughts (or in other words to whom *her* vision of Bob and nothing else) would mean so delightfully much? It was on the same general lines that poor Newton Winch, bereft, alone, ill, perhaps dying, and with the drawback of a not very sympathetic personality—as Mark remembered it at least—to contend against in almost any conceivable appeal to human furtherance, it was on these lines, very much, that the luckless case in Fiftieth Street was offered him as a source of salutary discipline. The moment for such a lesson might strike him as strange, in view of the quite special and independent opportunity for exercise that his spirit had during the last three days enjoyed there in his hotel bedroom; but evidently his languor of charity needed some admonition finer than any it might trust to chance for, and by the time he at last, Winch's residence recognised, was duly elevated to his level and had pressed the electric button at his door, he felt himself acting indeed as under stimulus of a sharp poke in the side.

V

WITHIN the apartment to which he had been admitted, moreover, the fine intelligence we have imputed to him was in the course of three minutes confirmed; since it took him no longer than that to say to himself, facing his old acquaintance, that he had never seen anyone so improved. The place, which had the semblance of a high studio light as well as a general air of other profusions and amplitudes, might have put him off a little by its several rather glaringly false accents, those of contemporary domestic "art" striking a little wild. The scene was smaller, but the rich confused complexion of the Pocahontas, showing through Du Barry paint and patches, might have set the example—which had been followed with the costliest candour—so that, clearly, Winch was in these days rich, as most people in New York seemed rich; as, in spite of Bob's depredations, Florence Ash was, as even Mrs. Folliott was in spite of Phil Bloodgood's, as even Phil Bloodgood himself must have been for reasons too obvious; as in fine every one had a secret for being, or for feeling, or for looking, every one at least but Mark Monteith.

These facts were as nothing, however, in presence of his quick and strong impression that his pale, nervous, smiling, clean-shaven host had undergone since their last meeting some extraordinary process of refinement. He had been ill, unmistakably, and the effects of a plunge into plain clean living, where any fineness had remained, were often startling, sometimes almost charming. But independently of this, and for a much longer time, some principle of intelligence, some art of life, would discernibly have worked in him. Remembered from college years and from those two or three luckless and faithless ones of the Law School as constitutionally common, as consistently and thereby doubtless even rather powerfully coarse, clever only for uncouth and questionable things, he yet presented himself now as if he had suddenly and mysteriously been educated. There was a charm in his wide, "drawn," convalescent smile, in the way his fine fingers—had he anything like fine fingers of old?—played, and just fidgeted, over the prompt and perhaps a trifle incoherent offer of cigars, cordials, ashtrays, over the question of his visitor's hat, stick, fur coat, general best accommodation and ease; and how the deuce, accordingly, had charm, for coming out so on top, Mark wondered, "squared" the other old elements? For the short interval so to have dealt with him what force had it turned on, what patented process, of the portentous New York order in which there were so many, had it skilfully applied? Were these the things New York did when you just gave her *all* her head, and that he himself then had perhaps too complacently missed? Strange almost to the point of putting him positively off at first—quite as an exhibition of the uncanny—this sense of Newton's having all the while neither missed nor muffed anything, and having, as with an eye to the *coup de théâtre* to come, lowered one's expectations, at the start, to that abject pitch. It might have been taken verily as an act of bad faith—really for such a rare stroke of subtlety as could scarce have been achieved by a straight or natural aim.

So much as this at least came and went in Monteith's agitated mind; the oddest intensity of apprehension, admiration, mystification, which the high north-light of the March afternoon and the quite splendidly vulgar appeal of fifty overdone decorative effects somehow fostered and sharpened. Everything had already gone, however, the next moment, for wasn't the man he had come so much too intelligently himself to patronise absolutely bowling him over with the extraordinary speech: "See here, you know—you must be ill, or have had a bad shock, or some beastly upset: are you very sure you ought to have come out?" Yes, he after an instant believed his ears; coarse common Newton Winch, whom he had called on because he could, as a gentleman, after all afford to, coarse common Newton Winch, who had had troubles and been epidemically poisoned, lamentably sick, who bore in his face and in the very tension, quite exactly the "charm," of his manner, the traces of his late ordeal,

and, for that matter, of scarce completed gallant emergence—
this astonishing ex-comrade was simply writing himself at a
stroke (into our friend's excited imagination at all events) the
most distinguished of men. Oh, *he* was going to he interesting,
if Florence Ash had been going to be; but Mark felt how, under
the law of a lively present difference, that would be as an effect
of one's having one's self thoroughly rallied. He knew within
the minute that the tears stood in his eyes; he stared through
them at his friend with a sharp "Why, how do you know? How
can you?" To which he added before Winch could speak: "I met
your charming sister-in-law a couple of hours since—at lunch-
eon, at the Pocahontas; and heard from her that you were badly
laid up and had spoken of me. So I came to minister to you."

The object of this design hovered there again, considerably
restless, shifting from foot to foot, changing his place, beginning and giving up motions, striking matches for a fresh ciga-
rette, offering them again, redundantly, to his guest and then
not lighting himself—but all the while with the smile of another creature than the creature known to Mark; all the while
with the history of something that had happened to him ever
so handsomely shining out. Mark was conscious within himself
from this time on of two quite distinct processes of notation—
that of his practically instant surrender to the consequences of
the act of perception in his host of which the two women
trained supposably in the art of pleasing had been altogether
incapable; and that of some other condition on Newton's part
that left his own poor power of divination nothing less than
shamed. This last was signally the case on the former's saying,
ever so responsively, almost radiantly, in answer to his account
of how he happened to come: "Oh then it's very interesting!"
That was the astonishing note, after what he had been through:
neither Mrs. Folliott nor Florence Ash had so much as hinted
or breathed to him that *he* might have incurred that praise. No
wonder therefore he was now taken—with this fresh party's instant suspicion and imputation of it; though it was indeed for
some minutes next as if each tried to see which could accuse

the other of the greater miracle of penetration. Mark was so struck, in a word, with the extraordinarily straight guess Winch had had there in reserve for him that, other quick impressions helping, there was nothing for him but to bring out, himself: "There must be, my dear man, something rather wonderful the matter with you!" The quite more intensely and more irresistibly drawn grin, the quite unmistakably deeper consciousness in the dark, wide eye, that accompanied the not quite immediate answer to which remark he was afterward to remember.

"How do you know that—or why do you think it?"

"Because there *must* be—for you to see! I shouldn't have expected it."

"Then you take me for a damned fool?" laughed wonderful Newton Winch.

VI

HE COULD say nothing that, whether as to the sense of it or as to the way of it, didn't so enrich Mark's vision of him that our friend, after a little, as this effect proceeded, caught himself in the act of almost too curiously gaping. Everything, from moment to moment, fed his curiosity; such a question, for instance, as whether the quite ordinary peepers of the Newton Winch of their earlier youth could have looked, under any provocation, either dark or wide; such a question, above all, as how *this* incalculable apparition came by the whole startling power of play of its extravagantly sensitive labial connections— exposed, so to its advantage (he now jumped at one explanation) by the removal of what had probably been one of the vulgarest of moustaches. With this, at the same time, the oddity of that particular consequence was vivid to him; the glare of his curiosity fairly lasting while he remembered how he had once noted the very opposite turn of the experiment for Phil Bloodgood. He would have said in advance that poor Winch couldn't have afforded to risk showing his "real" mouth; just as he would have said that in spite of the fine ornament that so considerably muffled it Phil could only have gained by showing his. But to have seen Phil shorn—as he once had done—was earnestly to pray that he might promptly again bristle; beneath Phil's moustache lurked nothing to "make up" for it in case of removal. While he thought of which things the line of grimace, as he could only have called it, the mobile, interesting, ironic line the great double curve of which connected, in the face before him, the strong nostril with the lower cheek, became the very key to his first idea of Newton's capture of refinement. He had shaved and was happily transfigured. Phil Bloodgood had shaved and been wellnigh lost; though why should he just now too precipitately drag the reminiscence in?

That question too, at the queer touch of association, played up for Mark even under so much proof that the state of his own soul was being with the lapse of every instant registered. Phil Bloodgood had brought about the state of his soul—there was accordingly that amount of connection; only it became further remarkable that from the moment his companion had sounded him, and sounded him, he knew, down to the last truth of things, his disposition, his necessity to talk, the desire that had in the morning broken the spell of his confinement, the impulse that had thrown him so defeatedly into Mrs. Folliott's arms and into Florence Ash's, these forces seemed to feel their impatience ebb and their discretion suddenly grow. His companion was talking again, but just then, incongruously, made his need to communicate lose itself. It was as if his personal case had already been touched by some tender hand— and that, after all, was the modest limit of its greed. "I know now why you came back—did Lottie mention how I had wondered? But sit down, sit down—only let me, nervous beast as I am, take it standing!—and believe me when I tell you that I've now ceased to wonder. My dear chap, I *have* it! It can't but have been for poor Phil Bloodgood. He sticks out of you, the brute —as how, with what he has done to you, shouldn't he? There was a man to see me yesterday—Tim Slater, whom I don't think you know, but who's 'on' everything within about two minutes of its happening (I never saw such a fellow!) and who confirmed my supposition, all my own, however, mind you, at first, that you're one of the sufferers. So how the devil can you *not* feel knocked? Why *should* you look as if you were having the time of your life? What a hog to have played it on *you*, on *you*, of all his friends!" So Newton Winch continued, and so the air between the two men might have been, for a momentary watcher—which is indeed what I can but invite the reader to become—that of a nervously displayed, but all considerate, as well as most acute, curiosity on the one side, and that on the other, after a little, of an eventually fascinated acceptance of so much free and in especial of so much right attention. "Do you *mind* my asking you? Because if you do I won't press; but as a man whose own responsibilities, some of 'em at least, don't differ much, I gather, from some of his, one would like to know how he was ever allowed to get to the point—! But I *do* plough you up?"

Mark sat back in his chair, moved but holding himself, his elbows squared on each arm, his hands a bit convulsively interlocked across him—very much in fact as he had appeared an hour ago in the old tapestry *bergère*; but as his rigour was all then that of the grinding effort to profess and to give, so it was considerably now for the fear of too hysterically gushing. Somehow too—since his wound was to that extent open—he winced at hearing the author of it branded. He hadn't so much minded the epithets Mrs. Folliott had applied, for they were to the appropriator of *her* securities. As the appropriator of his own he didn't so much want to brand him as—just more "amusingly" even, if one would!—to make out, perhaps, with intelligent help, how such a man, in such a relation, *could* come to tread such a path: which was exactly the interesting light that Winch's curiosity and sympathy were there to assist him to. He pleaded at any rate immediately his advertising no grievance. "I feel sore, I admit, and it's a horrid sort of thing to have had happen; but when you call him a brute and a hog I rather squirm, for brutes and hogs never live, I guess, in the sort of hell in which he now must be."

Newton Winch, before the fireplace, his hands deep in his pockets, where his guest could see his long fingers beat a tattoo on his thighs, Newton Winch dangled and swung himself, and threw back his head and laughed. "Well, I must say you take it amazingly!—all the more that to see you again this way is to feel that if, all along, there was a man whose delicacy and confidence and general attitude might have marked him for a particular consideration, you'd have been the man." And they were more directly face to face again; with Newton smiling and smiling *so* appreciatively; making our friend in fact almost ask himself when before a man had ever grinned from ear to ear to the effect of its so becoming him. What he replied, however, was that Newton described in those flattering terms a client temptingly fatuous; after which, and the exchange of another protest or two in the interest of justice and decency, and another plea or two in that of the still finer contention that even the basest misdeeds had always somewhere or other, could one get at it, their propitiatory side, our hero found himself on his feet again, under the influence of a sudden failure of everything but horror—a horror determined by some turn of their talk and indeed by the very fact of the freedom of it. It was as if a far-borne sound of the hue and cry, a vision of his old friend hunted and at bay, had suddenly broken in—this other friend's, this irresistibly intelligent other companion's, practically vivid projection of that making the worst ugliness real. "Oh, it's just making my wry face to somebody, and your letting me and caring and wanting to know: that," Mark said, "is what does me good; not any other hideous question. I mean I don't take any interest in *my* case—what one wonders about, you see, is what can be done for him. I mean, that is"—for he floundered a little, not knowing at last quite what he did mean, a great rush of mere memories, a great humming sound as of thick, thick echoes, rising now to an assault that he met with his face indeed contorted. If he didn't take care he should howl; so he more or less successfully took care—yet with his host vividly watching him while he shook the danger temporarily off. "I don't mind—though it's rather *that*; my having felt this morning, after three dismal dumb bad days, that one's friends perhaps would be thinking of one. All I'm conscious of now—I give you my word—is that I'd like to see him."

"You'd like to see him?"

"Oh, I don't say," Mark ruefully smiled, "that I should like him to see *me*——!"

Newton Winch, from where he stood—and they were together now, on the great hearth-rug that was a triumph of modern orientalism—put out one of the noted fine hands and, with an expressive headshake, laid it on his shoulder. "Don't wish him that, Monteith—don't wish him that!"

"Well, but"—and Mark raised his eyebrows still higher— "he'd see I bear up; pretty well!"

"God forbid he should see, my dear fellow!" Newton cried as for the pang of it.

Mark had for his idea, at any rate, the oddest sense of an exaltation that grew by this use of frankness. "I'd go to him. Hanged if I wouldn't—anywhere!"

His companion's hand still rested on him. "You'd go to him?"

Mark stood up to it—though trying to sink solemnity as pretentious. "I'd go like a shot." And then he added: "And it's probably what—when we've turned round—I *shall* do."

"When 'we' have turned round?"

"Well"—he was a trifle disconcerted at the tone—"I say that because you'll have helped me."

"Oh, I do nothing but want to help you!" Winch replied— which made it right again; especially as our friend still felt himself reassuringly and sustainingly grasped. But Winch went on: "You *would* go to him—in kindness?"

"Well—to understand."

"To understand how he could swindle you?"

"Well," Mark kept on, "to try and make out with him

how, after such things—!" But he stopped; he couldn't name them.

It was as if his companion knew. "Such things as you've done for him, of course—such services as you've rendered him."

"Ah, from far back. If I could tell you," our friend vainly wailed—"if I could tell you!"

Newton Winch patted his shoulder. "Tell me—tell me!"

"The sort of relation, I mean; ever so many things of a kind—!" Again, however, he pulled up; he felt the tremor of his voice.

"Tell me, tell me," Winch repeated with the same movement.

The tone in it now made their eyes meet again, and with this presentation of the altered face Mark measured as not before, for some reason, the extent of the recent ravage. "You must have been ill indeed."

"Pretty bad. But I'm better. And you do me good"—with which the light of convalescence came back.

"I don't awfully bore you?"

Winch shook his head. "You keep me up—and you see how no one else comes near me."

Mark's eyes made out that he *was* better—though it wasn't yet that nothing was the matter with him. If there was ever a man with whom there was still something the matter—! Yet one couldn't insist on that, and meanwhile he clearly did want company. "Then there we are. I myself had no one to go to."

"You save my life," Newton renewedly grinned.

VII

"WELL, IT'S your own fault," Mark replied to that, "if you make me take advantage of you." Winch had withdrawn his hand, which was back, violently shaking keys or money, in his trousers pocket; and in this position he had abruptly a pause, a sensible absence, that might have represented either some odd drop of attention, some turn-off to another thought, or just simply the sudden act of listening. His guest had indeed himself—under suggestion—the impression of a sound. "Mayn't you perhaps—if you hear something—have a call?"

Mark had said it so lightly, however, that he was the more struck with his host's appearing to turn just paler; and, with it, the latter now *was* listening. "You hear something?"

"I thought *you* did." Winch himself, on Mark's own pressure of the outside bell, had opened the door of the apartment—an indication then, it sufficiently appeared, that Sunday afternoons were servants', or attendants', or even trained nurses' holidays. It had also marked the stage of his convalescence, and to that extent—after his first flush of surprise—had but smoothed Monteith's way. At present he barely gave further attention; detaching himself as under some odd cross-impulse, he had quitted the spot and then taken, in the wide room, a restless turn—only, however, to revert in a moment to his friend's just-uttered deprecation of the danger of boring him. "If I make you take advantage of me—that is blessedly talk to me—it's exactly what I want to do. Talk to me—talk to me!" He positively waved it on; pulling up again, however, in his own talk, to say with a certain urgency: "Hadn't you better sit down?"

Mark, who stayed before the fire, couldn't but excuse himself. "Thanks—I'm very well so. I think of things and I fidget."

Winch stood a moment with his eyes on the ground. "Are you very sure?"

"Quite—I'm all right if you don't mind."

"Then as you like!" With which, shaking to extravagance again his long legs, Newton had swung off—only with a movement that, now his back was turned, affected his visitor as the most whimsical of all the forms of his rather unnatural manner. He was curiously different with his back turned, as Mark now for the first time saw it—dangling and somewhat wavering, as from an excess of uncertainty of gait; and this impression was so strange, it created in our friend, uneasily and on the spot, such a need of explanation, that his speech was stayed long enough to give Winch time to turn round again. The latter had indeed by this moment reached one of the limits of the place, the wide studio bay, where he paused, his back to the light and his face afresh presented, to let his just passingly depressed and quickened eyes take in as much as possible of the large floor, range over it with such brief freedom of search as the disposition of the furniture permitted. He was looking for something, though the betrayed reach of vision was but of an instant. Mark caught it, however, and with his own sensibility all in vibration, found himself feeling at once that it meant something and that what it meant was connected with his entertainer's slightly marked appeal to him, the appeal of a moment before, not to remain standing. Winch knew by this time quite easily enough that he was hanging fire; which meant that they were suddenly facing each other across the wide space with a new consciousness.

Everything had changed—changed extraordinarily with the mere turning of that gentleman's back, the treacherous aspect of which its owner couldn't surely have suspected. If the question was of the pitch of their sensibility, at all events, it wouldn't be Mark's that should vibrate to least purpose. Visibly it had come to his host that something had within the few instants remarkably happened, but there glimmered on him an induction that still made him keep his own manner. Newton himself might now resort to any manner he liked. His eyes had raked the floor to recover the position of something dropped or misplaced, and something, above all, awkward or compromising; and he had wanted his companion not to command this scene from the hearth-rug, the hearth-rug where he had been just before holding him, hypnotising him to blindness, *because* the object in question would there be most exposed to sight. Mark embraced this with a further drop—while the apprehension penetrated—of his power to go on, and with an immense desire at the same time that his eyes should seem only to look at his friend; who broke out now, for that matter, with a fresh appeal. "Aren't you going to take advantage of me, man—aren't you going to *take* it?"

Everything had changed, we have noted, and nothing could more have proved it than the fact that, by the same turn, sincerity of desire had dropped out of Winch's chords, while irritation, sharp and almost imperious, had come in. "That's because he sees I see something!" Mark said to himself; but he had no need to add that it shouldn't prevent his seeing more—for the simple reason that, in a miraculous fashion, this was exactly what he did do in glaring out the harder. It was beyond explanation, but the very act of blinking thus in an attempt at showy steadiness became one and the same thing with an optical excursion lasting the millionth of a minute and making him aware that the edge of a rug, at the point where an arm-chair, pushed a little out of position, overstraddled it, happened just not wholly to have covered in something small and queer, neat and bright, crooked and compact, in spite of the strong toe-tip surreptitiously applied to giving it the right lift. Our gentleman, from where he hovered, and while looking straight at the master of the scene, yet saw, as by the tiny flash of a reflection from fine metal, *under* the chair. What he recognised, or at least guessed at, as sinister, made him for a moment turn cold, and that chill was on him while Winch again addressed him— as differently as possible from any manner yet used. "I beg of you in God's name to talk to me—to *talk* to me!"

It had the ring of pure alarm and anguish, but was by this turn at least more human than the dazzling glitter of intelligence to which the poor man had up to now been treating him. "It's you, my good friend, who are in deep trouble," Mark was accordingly quick to reply, "and I ask your pardon for being so taken up with my own sorry business."

"Of course I'm in deep trouble"—with which Winch came nearer again; "but turning you on was exactly what I wanted."

Mark Monteith, at this, couldn't, for all his rising dismay, but laugh out; his sense of the ridiculous so swallowed up, for that brief convulsion, his sense of the sinister. Of such convenience in pain, it seemed, was the fact of another's pain, and of so much worth again disinterested sympathy! "Your interest was then——?"

"My interest was in your being interesting. For you *are*! And my nerves—!" said Newton Winch with a face from which the mystifying smile had vanished, yet in which distinction, as Mark so persistently appreciated it, still sat in the midst of ravage.

Mark wondered and wondered—he made strange things out. "Your nerves have needed company." He could lay his hand on him now, even as shortly before he had felt Winch's own pressure of possession and detention. "As good for you yourself, that—or still better," he went on—"than I and my grievance were to have found you. Talk to *me*, talk to *me*, Newton Winch!" he added with an immense inspiration of charity.

"That's a different matter—that others but too much can do! But I'll say this. If you want to go to Phil Bloodgood——!"

"Well?" said Mark as he stopped. He stopped, and Mark had now a hand on each of his shoulders and held him at arm's-length, held him with a fine idea that was not disconnected from the sight of the small neat weapon he had been fingering in the low luxurious morocco chair—it was of the finest orange colour—and then had laid beside him on the carpet; where, after he had admitted his visitor, his presence of mind coming back to it and suggesting that he couldn't pick it up without making it more conspicuous, he had thought, by some swing of the foot or other casual manœuvre, to dissimulate its visibility.

They were at close quarters now as not before and Winch perfectly passive, with eyes that somehow had no shadow of a secret left and with the betrayal to the sentient hands that grasped him of an intense, an extraordinary general tremor. To Mark's challenge he opposed afresh a brief silence, but the very quality of it, with his face speaking, was that of a gaping wound. "Well, you needn't take *that* trouble. You see I'm such another."

"Such another as Phil——?"

He didn't blink. "I don't know for sure, but I guess I'm worse."

"Do you mean you're guilty——?"

"I mean I shall be wanted. Only I've stayed to take it."

Mark threw back his head, but only tightened his hands. He inexpressibly understood, and nothing in life had ever been so strange and dreadful to him as his thus helping himself by a longer and straighter stretch, as it were, to the monstrous sense of his friend's "education." It had been, in its immeasurable action, the education of business, of which the fruits were all around them. Yet prodigious was the interest, for prodigious truly—it seemed to loom before Mark—must have been the system. "To 'take' it?" he echoed; and then, though faltering a little, "To take what?"

He had scarce spoken when a long sharp sound shrilled in from the outer door, seeming of so high and peremptory a pitch that with the start it gave him his grasp of his host's shoulders relaxed an instant, though to the effect of no movement in *them* but what came from just a sensibly intenser vibration of the whole man. "For *that*!" said Newton Winch.

"Then you've known——?"

"I've expected. You've helped me to wait." And then as Mark gave an ironic wail: "You've tided me over. My condition has *wanted* somebody or something. Therefore, to complete this service, will you be so good as to open the door?"

Deep in the eyes Mark looked him, and still to the detection of no glimmer of the earlier man in the depths. The earlier man had been what he invidiously remembered—yet would *he* had been the whole simpler story! Then he moved his own eyes straight to the chair under which the revolver lay and which was but a couple of yards away. He felt his companion take this consciousness in, and it determined in them another long, mute exchange. "What do you mean to do?"

"Nothing."

"On your honour?"

"*My* 'honour'?" his host returned with an accent that he felt even as it sounded he should never forget.

It brought to his own face a crimson flush—he dropped his guarding hands. Then as for a last look at him: "You're wonderful!"

"We *are* wonderful," said Newton Winch, while, simultaneously with the words, the pressed electric bell again and for a longer time pierced the warm cigaretted air.

Mark turned, threw up his arms, and it was only when he had passed through the vestibule and laid his hand on the door-knob that the horrible noise dropped. The next moment he was face to face with two visitors, a nondescript personage in a high hat and an astrakhan collar and cuffs, and a great belted constable, a splendid massive New York "officer" of the type he had had occasion to wonder at much again in the course of his walk, the type so by itself—his wide observation quite suggested—among those of the peacemakers of the earth. The pair stepped straight in—no word was said; but as he closed the door behind them Mark heard the infallible crack of a discharged pistol and, so nearly with it as to make all one violence, the sound of a great fall; things the effect of which was to lift him, as it were, with his company, across the threshold of the room in a shorter time than that taken by this record of the fact. But their rush availed little; Newton was stretched on his back before the fire; he had held the weapon horribly to his temple, and his upturned face was disfigured. The emissaries of the law, looking down at him, exhaled simultaneously a gruff imprecation, and then while the worthy in the high hat bent over the subject of their visit the one in the helmet raised a severe pair of eyes to Mark. "Don't you think, sir, you might have prevented it?"

Mark took a hundred things in, it seemed to him—things of the scene, of the moment, and of all the strange moments before; but one appearance more vividly even than the others stared out at him. "I really think I must practically have caused it."

1910

NOTE ON THE TEXT

The texts in this collection are based, with several exceptions, on the first widely available version of each story, that is, as it initially appeared in book form. In most instances, the stories were printed in magazines, with James supervising volume publication shortly after. Several of the stories here, however, particularly the earlier ones, were never revised or collected by the author, or, as with "A Most Extraordinary Case," republished many years later with substantial alterations. "The Story of a Masterpiece," *Galaxy*, Vols. 5 (January 1868) and 6 (February 1868); "A Most Extraordinary Case," *Atlantic Monthly*, Vol. 21 (April 1868); "Crawford's Consistency," *Scribner's Monthly*, Vol. 12 (August 1876); "An International Episode," *Cornhill Magazine*, Vols. 38 (December 1878) and 39 (January 1879), revised for inclusion in *Daisy Miller: A Study, An International Episode, Four Meetings* (Macmillan, 1879); "Washington Square," *Cornhill Magazine*, (June–November 1880), revised for book publication (Macmillan, 1881); "The Impressions of a Cousin," *Century Magazine*, Vols. 27 (November 1883) and 28 (December 1883); "The Jolly Corner," *English Review*, Vol. 1 (December 1908), included in the New York Edition, Vol. 17 (Macmillan, 1907–1909); "Crapy Cornelia," *Harper's Monthly Magazine*, Vol. 119 (October 1909) and "A Round of Visits," *The English Review*, Vols. 5 (April 1910) and 6 (May 1910), both published in *The Finer Grain* (Charles Scribner's Sons, 1910).

The publisher wishes to thank Adrian Dover for his help with the bibliographical details of James's works.

TITLES IN SERIES